Praise for *The Blade Itself*

"You'd never guess that *The Blade Itself* is Joe Abercrombie's debut novel. He writes like a natural. There are great characters, sparky dialogue, an action-packed plot, and from the very first words ('The End') and an opening scene that is literally a cliffhanger, you know you are in for a cheeky, vivid, exhilarating ride."

Starburst (Five Star review)

"Critics compare Abercrombie to Dickens, but come on—Dickens was never so entertaining. This intricate story just flows, carrying along barbarian fighters with real courage (and real injuries), spoiled nobles with redeeming potential, mages with disconcerting agendas . . . plus the most sympathetic torturer ever. The First Law trilogy: an adventure whose characters grow in tough, surprising, satisfying ways, in a gritty, exotic world that is sometimes awful, and always fascinates. Expect fast, funny dialog, and one hell of a rush."

John Meaney, author of *Paradox* and *Bone Song*

"*The Blade Itself* is an admirably hard, fast, and unpretentious read . . . packs a mean punch in the bloodthirsty mayhem and mystery departments . . . a highly readable fantasy that isn't going to scare off mainstream readers or newcomers to the genre. *The Blade Itself* may not reinvent the wheel, but it does serve up a whole banquet of violent action and intrigue."

SFX

"For once nobody has tried to make a comparison with George R. R. Martin; instead the publisher promises something more akin to Tad Williams. But this seems wrongheaded, almost a missed opportunity. . . . Like Martin he has an ear for constructing dialogue patterns, as well as the beginnings of an epic self-confidence; certainly, his prose is fluent and shows great promise. There are none of the peaks and lows that are often common to debut novels. . . . *The Blade Itself* is an incredibly accomplished first novel."

Emerald City

"Fans of character-driven epics who are willing to take their heroes with a grain of moral ambiguity should add this novel to their 'must read' list. . . . *The Blade Itself* is a smartly written, sophisticated debut with compelling characters, a complex plot, and style to burn."

Strange Horizons

"In addition to excellent characterizations and fascinating world-building, Abercrombie also writes the best fight scenes I have read in ages. I'm glad the whole package is good, but I could happily recommend *The Blade Itself* for the fight scenes alone."

SFSite

"Now this is a breath of fresh air! A story told with wit, dash, and a keen eye for character. . . . Finding a writer like Abercrombie amidst the clutter of second-raters who crowd the fantasy genre is like the sun breaking through dark clouds; he wakes you up and reminds you why you took up reading in the first place."

Infinity Plus

"A promising start to a new fantasy series by a new writer. . . . [B]etter than a run of the mill fantasy. . . . [A]fter the first fifty or so pages I was hooked. . . . [A] surprisingly good debut novel . . . if you like many of the recently published dark fantasy (Steven Erikson, George R. R. Martin, and K. J. Parker spring to mind), then this is worth a read."

SFFWorld

THE BLADE ITSELF

THE BLADE ITSELF
Joe Abercrombie

an imprint of Prometheus Books
Amherst, NY

Published 2007 by Pyr®, an imprint of Prometheus Books

Inquiries should be addressed to
Pyr
59 John Glenn Drive
Amherst, New York 14228–2119
VOICE: 716–691–0133, ext. 210
FAX: 716–691–0137
WWW.PYRSF.COM

14 13 12 11   16 15

Library of Congress Cataloging-in-Publication Data

Abercrombie, Joe.
    The blade itself / Joe Abercrombie.
        p. cm.
    Originally published: London : Gollancz, an imprint of the Orion Publishing Group, 2006.
    ISBN 978–1–59102–594–8 (pbk.)
    I. Title.

PR6101.B49B57 2006
823'.92—dc22

2007028499

Printed in the United States of America on acid-free paper

For the Four Readers

You know who you are

THE END

L ogen plunged through the trees, bare feet slipping and sliding on the wet earth, the slush, the wet pine needles, breath rasping in his chest, blood thumping in his head. He stumbled and sprawled onto his side, nearly cut his chest open with his own axe, lay there panting, peering through the shadowy forest.

The Dogman had been with him until a moment before, he was sure, but there wasn't any sign of him now. As for the others, there was no telling. Some leader, getting split up from his boys like that. He should've been trying to get back, but the Shanka were all around. He could feel them moving between the trees, his nose was full of the smell of them. Sounded as if there was some shouting somewhere on his left, fighting maybe. Logen crept slowly to his feet, trying to stay quiet. A twig snapped and he whipped round.

There was a spear coming at him. A cruel-looking spear, coming at him fast with a Shanka on the other end of it.

"Shit," said Logen. He threw himself to one side, slipped and fell on his face, rolled away thrashing through the brush, expecting the spear through his back at any moment. He scrambled up, breathing hard. He saw the bright point poking at him again, dodged out of the way, slithered behind a big tree trunk. He peered out and the Flathead hissed and stabbed at him. He showed himself on the other side, just for a moment, then ducked away, jumped round the tree and swung the axe down, roaring loud as he could. There was a loud crack as the blade buried itself deep in the Shanka's skull. Lucky that, but then Logen reckoned he was due a little luck.

The Flathead stood there, blinking at him. Then it started to sway from side to side, blood dribbling down its face. Then it dropped like a stone, dragging the axe from Logen's fingers, thrashing around on the ground at his feet. He tried to grab hold of his axe-handle but the Shanka still somehow had a grip on its spear and the point was flailing around in the air.

"Gah!" squawked Logen as the spear cut a nick in his arm. He felt a shadow fall across his face. Another Flathead. A damn big one. Already in the air, arms outstretched. No time to get the axe. No time to get out of the way. Logen's mouth opened, but there was no time to say anything. What do you say at a time like that?

They crashed to the wet ground together, rolled together through the dirt and the thorns and the broken branches, tearing and punching and growling at each other. A tree root hit Logen in the head, hard, and made his ears ring. He had a knife somewhere, but he couldn't remember where. They rolled on, and on, downhill, the world flipping and flipping around, Logen trying to shake the fuzz out of his head and throttle the big Flathead at the same time. There was no stopping.

It had seemed a clever notion to pitch camp near the gorge. No chance of anyone sneaking up behind. Now, as Logen slid over the edge of the cliff on his belly, the idea lost much of its appeal. His hands scrabbled at the wet earth. Only dirt and brown pine needles. His fingers clutched, clutched at nothing. He was beginning to fall. He let go a little whimper.

His hands closed around something. A tree root, sticking out from the earth at the very edge of the gorge. He swung in space, gasping, but his grip was firm.

"Hah!" he shouted. "Hah!" He was still alive. It would take more than a few Flatheads to put an end to Logen Ninefingers. He started to pull himself up onto the bank but couldn't manage it. There was some great weight around his legs. He peered down.

The gorge was deep. Very deep with sheer, rocky sides. Here and there a tree clung to a crack, growing out into the empty air and spreading its leaves into space. The river hissed away far below, fast and angry, foaming white water fringed by jagged black stone. That was all bad, for sure, but the real problem was closer to hand. The big Shanka was still with him, swinging gently back and forth with its dirty hands clamped tight around his left ankle.

"Shit," muttered Logen. It was quite a scrape he was in. He'd been in some bad ones alright, and lived to sing the songs, but it was hard to see how this could get much worse. That got him thinking about his life. It seemed a bitter, pointless sort of a life now. No one was any better off because of it. Full of violence and pain, with not much but disappointment and hardship in between. His hands were starting to tire now, his forearms were burning. The big Flathead didn't look like it was going to fall off any time soon. In fact, it had dragged itself up his leg a way. It paused, glaring up at him.

If Logen had been the one clinging to the Shanka's foot, he would most likely have thought, "My life depends on this leg I'm hanging from—best not take any chances." A man would rather save himself than kill his enemy. Trouble was that the Shanka didn't think that way, and Logen knew it. So it wasn't much of a surprise when it opened its big mouth and sank its teeth into his calf.

"Aaaargh!" Logen grunted, and squealed and kicked out as hard as he could with his bare heel, kicked a bloody gash in the Shanka's head, but it wouldn't stop biting, and the harder he kicked, the more his hands slipped on the greasy root above. There wasn't much root left to hold on to, now, and what there was looked like snapping off any moment. He tried to think past the pain in his hands, the pain in his arms, the Flathead's teeth in his leg. He was going to fall. The only choice was between falling on rocks or falling on water, and that was a choice that more or less made itself.

Once you've got a task to do, it's better to do it than to live with the fear of it. That's what Logen's father would have said. So he planted his free foot firmly on the rock face, took one last deep breath, and flung himself out into empty space with all the strength he had left. He felt the biting teeth let go of him, then the grasping hands, and for a moment he was free.

Then he began to fall. Fast. The sides of the gorge flashed past—grey rock, green moss, patches of white snow, all tumbling around him.

Logen turned over slowly in the air, limbs flailing pointlessly, too scared to scream. The rushing wind whipped at his eyes, tugged at his clothes, plucked the breath out of his mouth. He saw the big Shanka hit the rock face beside him. He saw it break and bounce and flop off, dead for sure. That was a pleasing sight, but Logen's satisfaction was short-lived.

The water came up to meet him. It hit him in the side like a charging bull, punched the air out of his lungs, knocked the sense out of his head, sucked him in and down into the cold darkness . . .

PART I

"The blade itself incites to deeds of violence"
                                        Homer

THE SURVIVORS

The lapping of water in his ears. That was the first thing. The lapping of water, the rustling of trees, the odd click and twitter of a bird.

Logen opened his eyes a crack. Light, blurry bright through leaves. This was death? Then why did it hurt so much? His whole left side was throbbing. He tried to take a proper breath, choked, coughed up water, spat out mud. He groaned, flopped over onto his hands and knees, dragged himself up out of the river, gasping through clenched teeth, rolled onto his back in the moss and slime and rotten sticks at the water's edge.

He lay there for a moment, staring up at the grey sky beyond the black branches, breath wheezing in his raw throat.

"I am still alive," he croaked to himself. Still alive, in spite of the best efforts of nature, Shanka, men and beasts. Soaking wet and flat on his back, he started to chuckle. Reedy, gurgling laughter. Say one thing for Logen Ninefingers, say he's a survivor.

A cold wind blew across the rotting river bank, and Logen's laughter slowly died. Alive he might be, but staying alive, that was another question. He sat up, wincing at the pain. He tottered to his feet, leaning against the nearest tree trunk. He scraped the dirt out of his nose, his eyes, his ears. He pulled up his wet shirt to take a look at the damage.

His side was covered in bruises from the fall. Blue and purple stains all up his ribs. Tender to the touch, and no mistake, but it didn't feel like anything was broken. His leg was a mess. Torn and bloody from the Shanka's teeth. It hurt bad, but his foot still moved well enough, and that was the main thing. He'd need his foot, if he was going to get out of this.

He still had his knife in the sheath at his belt, and he was mightily glad to see it. You could never have too many knives in Logen's experience, and this was a good one, but the outlook was still bleak. He was on his own, in woods crawling with Flatheads. He had no idea where he was, but he could follow the river. The rivers all flowed north, from the mountains to the cold sea. Follow the river southwards, against the current. Follow the river and climb up, into the High Places where the Shanka couldn't find him. That was his only chance.

It would be cold up there, this time of year. Deadly cold. He looked down at his bare feet. It was just his luck that the Shanka had come while he had his boots off, trimming his blisters. No coat either—he'd been sitting near the fire. Like this, he wouldn't last a day in the mountains. His hands and feet would turn black in the night, and he'd die bit by bit before he even reached the passes. If he didn't starve first.

"Shit," he muttered. He had to go back to the camp. He had to hope the Flatheads had moved on, hope they'd left something behind. Something he could use to survive. That was an awful lot of hoping, but he had no choice. He never had any choices.

It had started to rain by the time Logen found the place. Spitting drops that plastered his hair to his skull, kept his clothes wet through. He pressed himself against a mossy trunk and peered out towards the camp, heart pounding, fingers of his right hand curled painful tight around the slippery grip of his knife.

He saw the blackened circle where the fire had been, half-burned sticks and ash trampled round it. He saw the big log Threetrees and Dow had been sitting on when the Flatheads came. He saw odd bits of torn and broken gear scattered across the clearing. He counted three dead Shanka crumpled on the ground, one with an arrow poking out of its chest. Three dead ones, but no sign of any alive. That was lucky. Just lucky enough to survive, as always. Still, they might be back at any moment. He had to be quick.

Logen scuttled out from the trees, casting about on the ground. His boots were still there where he'd left them. He snatched them up and dragged them on to his freezing feet, hopping around, almost slipping in his haste. His coat was there too, wedged under the log, battered and scarred from ten years of weather and war, torn and stitched back together, missing half a sleeve. His pack was lying shapeless in the brush nearby, its contents strewn out down the slope. He crouched, breathless, throwing it all back inside. A length of rope, his old clay pipe, some strips of dried meat, needle and twine, a dented flask with some liquor still sloshing inside. All good. All useful.

There was a tattered blanket snagged on a branch, wet and half caked in grime. Logen pulled it up, and grinned. His old, battered cook pot was underneath. Lying on its side, kicked off the fire in the fight maybe. He grabbed hold of it with both hands. It felt safe, familiar, dented and black-ened from years of hard use. He'd had that pot a long time. It had followed him all through the wars, across the North and back again. They had all cooked in it together, out on the trail, all eaten out of it. Forley, Grim, the Dogman, all of them.

Logen looked over the campsite again. Three dead Shanka, but none of his people. Maybe they were still out there. Maybe if he took a risk, tried to look—

"No." He said it quietly, under his breath. He knew better than that. There had been a lot of Flatheads. An awful lot. He had no idea how long he'd lain on the river bank. Even if a couple of the boys had got away, the Shanka would be hunting them, hunting them down in the forests. They were nothing but corpses now, for sure, scattered across the high valleys. All Logen could do was make for the mountains, and try to save his own sorry life. You have to be realistic. Have to be, however much it hurts.

"It's just you and me now," said Logen as he stuffed the pot into his pack and threw it over his shoulder. He started to limp off, as fast as he could. Uphill, towards the river, towards the mountains.

Just the two of them. Him and the pot.

They were the only survivors.

QUESTIONS

Why do I do this? Inquisitor Glokta asked himself for the thousandth time as he limped down the corridor. The walls were rendered and whitewashed, though none too recently. There was a seedy feel to the place and a smell of damp. There were no windows, as the hallway was deep beneath the ground, and the lanterns cast slow flowing shadows into every corner.

Why would anyone want to do this? Glokta's walking made a steady rhythm on the grimy tiles of the floor. First the confident click of his right heel, then the tap of his cane, then the endless sliding of his left foot, with the familiar stabbing pains in the ankle, knee, arse and back. Click, tap, pain. That was the rhythm of his walking.

The dirty monotony of the corridor was broken from time to time by a heavy door, bound and studded with pitted iron. On one occasion, Glokta thought he heard a muffled cry of pain from behind one. *I wonder what poor fool is being questioned in there? What crime they are guilty, or innocent of? What secrets are being picked at, what lies cut through, what treasons laid bare?* He didn't wonder long though. He was interrupted by the steps.

If Glokta had been given the opportunity to torture any one man, anyone at all, he would surely have chosen the inventor of steps. When he was young and widely admired, before his misfortunes, he had never really noticed them. He had sprung down them two at a time and gone blithely on his way. No more. *They're everywhere. You really can't change floors without them. And down is worse than up, that's the thing people never realise. Going up, you usually don't fall that far.*

He knew this flight well. Sixteen steps, cut from smooth stone, a little worn toward the centre, slightly damp, like everything down here. There was no banister, nothing to cling to. *Sixteen enemies. A challenge indeed.* It had taken Glokta a long time to develop the least painful method of descending stairs. He went sideways like a crab. Cane first, then left foot, then right, with more than the usual agony as his left leg took his weight, joined by a persistent stabbing in the neck. *Why should it hurt in my neck when I go down stairs? Does my neck take my weight? Does it?* Yet the pain could not be denied.

Glokta paused four steps from the bottom. He had nearly beaten them. His hand was trembling on the handle of his cane, his left leg aching like fury. He tongued his gums where his front teeth used to be, took a deep breath and stepped forward. His ankle gave way with a horrifying wrench and he plunged into space, twisting, lurching, his mind a cauldron of horror and despair. He stumbled onto the next step like a drunkard, fingernails scratching at the smooth wall, giving a squeal of terror. *You stupid, stupid bastard!* His cane clattered to the floor, his clumsy feet wrestled with the stones and he found himself at the bottom, by some miracle still standing.

And here it is. That horrible, beautiful, stretched out moment between stubbing your toe and feeling the hurt. How long do I have before the pain comes? How bad will it be when it does? Gasping, slack-jawed at the foot of the steps, Glokta felt a tingling of anticipation. *Here it comes . . .*

The agony was unspeakable, a searing spasm up his left side from foot to jaw. He squeezed his watering eyes tight shut, clamped his right hand over his mouth so hard that the knuckles clicked. His remaining teeth grated against each other as he locked his jaws together, but a high-pitched, jagged moan still whistled from him. *Am I screaming or laughing? How do I tell the difference?* He breathed, in heaving gasps, through his nose, snot bubbling out onto his hand, his twisted body shaking with the effort of staying upright.

The spasm passed. Glokta moved his limbs cautiously, one by one, testing the damage. His leg was on fire, his foot numb, his neck clicked with every movement, sending vicious little stings down his spine. *Pretty good, considering.* He bent down with an effort and snatched up his cane between two fingers, drew himself up once more, wiped the snot and tears on the back of his hand. *Truly a thrill. Did I enjoy it? For most people stairs are a mundane affair. For me, an adventure!* He limped off down the corridor, giggling quietly to himself. He was still smiling ever so faintly when he reached his own door and shuffled inside.

A grubby white box with two doors facing each other. The ceiling was too low for comfort, the room too brightly lit by blazing lamps. Damp was creeping out of one corner and the plaster had erupted with flaking blisters, speckled with black mould. Someone had tried to scrub a long bloodstain from one wall, but hadn't tried nearly hard enough.

Practical Frost was standing on the other side of the room, big arms folded across his big chest. He nodded to Glokta, with all the emotion of a stone, and Glokta nodded back. Between them stood a scarred, stained wooden table, bolted to the floor and flanked by two chairs. A naked fat man sat in one of them, hands tied tightly behind him and with a brown canvas bag over his head. His quick, muffled breathing was the only sound. It was cold down here, but he was sweating. *As well he should be.*

Glokta limped over to the other chair, leaned his cane carefully against the edge of the table top and slowly, cautiously, painfully sat down. He stretched his neck to the left and right, then allowed his body to slump into a position approaching comfort. If Glokta had been given the opportunity to shake the hand of any one man, any one at all, he would surely have chosen the inventor of chairs. *He has made my life almost bearable.*

Frost stepped silently out of the corner and took hold of the loose top of the bag between meaty, pale finger and heavy, white thumb. Glokta nodded and the Practical ripped it off, leaving Salem Rews blinking in the harsh light.

A mean, piggy, ugly little face. You mean, ugly pig, Rews. You disgusting swine. You're ready to confess right now, I'll bet, ready to talk and talk without interruption, until we're all sick of it. There was a big dark bruise across his cheek and another on his jaw above his double chin. As his watering eyes adjusted to the brightness he recognised Glokta sitting opposite him, and his face suddenly filled with hope. *A sadly, sadly misplaced hope.*

"Glokta, you have to help me!" he squealed, leaning forward as far as his bonds would allow, words bubbling out in a desperate, mumbling mess. "I'm falsely accused, you know it, I'm innocent! You've come to help me, yes? You're my friend! You have influence here. We're friends, friends! You could say something for me! I'm an innocent man, falsely accused! I'm—"

Glokta held up his hand for silence. He stared at Rews' familiar face for a moment, as though he had never laid eyes on him before. Then he turned to Frost. "Am I supposed to know this man?"

The albino said nothing. The bottom part of his face was hidden by his Practical's mask, and the top half gave nothing away. He stared unblinking at the prisoner in the chair, pink eyes as dead as a corpse. He hadn't blinked once since Glokta came into the room. *How can he do that?*

"It's me, Rews!" hissed the fat man, the pitch of his voice rising steadily towards panic. "Salem Rews, you know me, Glokta! I was with you in the war, before . . . you know . . . we're friends! We—"

Glokta held up his hand again and sat back, tapping one of his few remaining teeth with a fingernail as though deep in thought. "Rews. The name is familiar. A merchant, a member of the Guild of Mercers. A rich man by all accounts. I remember now . . ." Glokta leaned forward, pausing for effect. "He was a traitor! He was taken by the Inquisition, his property confiscated. You see, he had conspired to avoid the King's taxes." Rews' mouth was hanging open. "The King's taxes!" screamed Glokta, smashing his hand down on the table. The fat man stared, wide eyed, and licked at a tooth. *Upper right side, second from the back.*

"But where are our manners?" asked Glokta of no one in particular. "We may or may not have known each other once, but I don't think you and my assistant have been properly introduced. Practical Frost, say hello to this fat man."

It was an open-handed blow, but powerful enough to knock Rews clean out of his seat. The chair rattled but was otherwise unaffected. *How is that done? To knock him to the ground but leave the chair standing?* Rews sprawled gurgling across the floor, face flattened on the tiles.

"He reminds me of a beached whale," said Glokta absently. The albino grabbed Rews under the arm and hauled him up, flung him back into the chair. Blood seeped from a cut on his cheek, but his piggy eyes were hard now. *Blows make most men soften up, but some men harden. I never would have taken this one for a tough man, but life is full of surprises.*

Rews spat blood onto the table top. "You've gone too far here, Glokta, oh yes! The Mercers are an honourable guild; we have influence! They won't put up with this! I'm a known man! Even now my wife will be petitioning the King to hear my case!"

"Ah, your wife." Glokta smiled sadly. "Your wife is a very beautiful woman. Beautiful, and young. I fear, perhaps, a little too young for you. I fear she took the opportunity to be rid of you. I fear she came forward with your books. All the books." Rews' face paled.

"We looked at those books," Glokta indicated an imaginary pile of papers on his left, "we looked at the books in the treasury," indicating another on his right. "Imagine our surprise when we could not make the numbers add up. And then there were the night-time visits by your employees to warehouses in the old quarter, the small unregistered boats, the payments to officials, the forged documentation. Must I go on?" asked Glokta, shaking his head in profound disapproval. The fat man swallowed and licked his lips.

Pen and ink were placed before the prisoner, and the paper of confession, filled out in detail in Frost's beautiful, careful script, awaiting only the signature. *I'll get him right here and now.*

"Confess, Rews," Glokta whispered softly, "and put a painless end to this regrettable business. Confess and name your accomplices. We already know who they are. It will be easier on all of us. I don't want to hurt you, believe me, it will give me no pleasure." *Nothing will.* "Confess. Confess, and you will be spared. Exile in Angland is not so bad as they would have you believe. There is still pleasure to be had from life there, and the satisfaction of a day of honest work, in the service of your King. Confess!" Rews stared at the floor, licking at his tooth. Glokta sat back and sighed.

"Or not," he said, "and I can come back with my instruments." Frost moved forward, his massive shadow falling across the fat man's face. "Body found floating by the docks," Glokta breathed, "bloated by seawater and horribly mutilated . . . far . . . far beyond recognition." *He's ready to talk. He's fat and ripe and ready to burst.* "Were the injuries inflicted before or after death?" he asked the ceiling breezily. "Was the mysterious deceased a man or a woman even?" Glokta shrugged. "Who can say?"

There was a sharp knock at the door. Rews' face jerked up, filled with hope again. *Not now, damn it!* Frost went to the door, opened it a crack. Something was said. The door shut, Frost leaned down to whisper in Glokta's ear.

"Ith Theverar," came the half-tongued mumble, by which Glokta understood that Severard was at the door.

Already? Glokta smiled and nodded, as if it was good news. Rews' face fell a little. *How could a man whose business has been concealment find it impossible to hide his emotions in this room?* But Glokta knew how. *It's hard to stay calm when you're terrified, helpless, alone, at the mercy of men with no mercy at all. Who could know that better than me?* He sighed, and using his most world-weary tone of voice asked, "Do you wish to confess?"

"No!" The defiance had returned to the prisoner's piggy eyes now. He stared back, silent and watchful, and sucked. *Surprising. Very surprising. But then we're just getting started.*

"Is that tooth bothering you, Rews?" There was nothing Glokta didn't know about teeth. His own mouth had been worked on by the very best. *Or the very worst, depending on how you look at it.* "It seems that I must leave you now, but while I'm away, I'll be thinking about that tooth. I'll be considering very carefully what to do with it." He took hold of his cane. "I want you to think about me, thinking about your tooth. And I also want you to think, very carefully, about signing your confession."

Glokta got awkwardly to his feet, shaking out his aching leg. "I think you may respond well to a straightforward beating however, so I'm going to leave you in the company of Practical Frost for half an hour." Rews' mouth became a silent circle of surprise. The albino picked up the chair, fat man and all, and turned it slowly around. "He's absolutely the best there is at this kind of thing." Frost took out a pair of battered leather gloves and began to pull them carefully onto his big white hands, one finger at a time. "You always did like to have the very best of everything, eh, Rews?" Glokta made for the door.

"Wait! Glokta!" wailed Rews over his shoulder. "Wait I—"

Practical Frost clamped a gloved hand over the fat man's mouth and held a finger to his mask. "Thhhhhhh," he said. The door clicked shut.

Severard was leaning against the wall in the corridor, one foot propped on the plaster behind him, whistling tunelessly beneath his mask and running a hand through his long, lanky hair. As Glokta came through the door he straightened up and gave a little bow, and it was plain by his eyes that he was smiling. *He's always smiling.*

"Superior Kalyne wants to see you," he said in his broad, common accent, "and I'm of the opinion that I never saw him angrier."

"Severard, you poor thing, you must be terrified. Do you have the box?"

"I do."

"And you took something out for Frost?"

"I did."

"And something for your wife too, I hope?"

"Oh yes," said Severard, his eyes smiling more than ever, "My wife will be well taken care of. If I ever get one."

"Good. I hasten to answer the call of the Superior. When I have been with him for five minutes, come in with the box."

"Just barge into his office?"

"Barge in and stab him in the face for all I care."

"I'd consider that done, Inquisitor."

Glokta nodded, turned away, then turned back. "Don't really stab him, eh, Severard?"

The Practical smiled with his eyes and sheathed his vicious-looking knife. Glokta rolled his eyes up to the ceiling, then limped off, his cane tapping on the tiles, his leg throbbing. Click, tap, pain. That was the rhythm of his walking.

The Superior's office was a large and richly appointed room high up in the House of Questions, a room in which everything was too big and too fancy. A huge, intricate window dominated one wood-panelled wall, offering a view over the well-tended gardens in the courtyard below. An equally huge and ornate desk stood in the centre of a richly coloured carpet from somewhere warm and exotic. The head of a fierce animal from somewhere cold and exotic was mounted above a magnificent stone fireplace with a tiny, mean fire close to burning out inside.

Superior Kalyne himself made his office look small and drab. A vast, florid man in his late fifties, he had over-compensated for his thinning hair with magnificent white side whiskers. He was considered a daunting presence even within the Inquisition, but Glokta was past scaring, and they both knew it.

There was a big, fancy chair behind the desk, but the Superior was pacing up and down while he screamed, his arms waving. Glokta was seated on something which, while doubtless expensive, had clearly been designed to make its occupant as uncomfortable as possible. *It doesn't bother me much, though. Uncomfortable is as good as I ever get.*

He amused himself with the thought of Kalyne's head mounted above the fireplace instead of that fierce animal's, while the Superior ranted at him. *He's every bit like his fireplace, the big dolt. Looks impressive, but there's not much going on underneath. I wonder how he'd respond to an interrogation? I'd start with those ridiculous side whiskers.* But Glokta's face was a mask of attention and respect.

"Well you've outdone yourself this time, Glokta, you mad cripple! When the Mercers find out about this they'll have you flayed!"

"I've tried flaying, it tickles." *Damn it, keep your mouth shut and smile. Where's that whistling fool Severard? I'll have him flayed when I get out of here.*

"Oh yes, that's good, that's very good, Glokta, look at me laugh! And evasion of the King's taxes?" The Superior glowered down, whiskers bristling. "The King's taxes?" he screamed, spraying Glokta with spit. "They're all at it! The Mercers, the Spicers, all of them! Every damn fool with a boat!"

"But this was so open, Superior. It was an insult to us. I felt we had to—"

"You felt?" Kalyne was red-faced and vibrating with rage. "You were explicitly told to keep away from the Mercers, away from the Spicers, away from all the big guilds!" He strode up and down with ever greater speed. *You'll wear your carpet out at this rate. The big guilds will have to buy you a new one.*

"You felt, did you? Well he'll have to go back! We'll have to release him and you'll have to feel your way to a grovelling apology! It's a damn disgrace! You've made me look ridiculous! Where is he now?"

"I left him in the company of Practical Frost."

"With that mumbling animal?" The Superior tore at his hair in desperation. "Well that's it then, isn't it? He'll be a ruin now! We can't send him back in that condition! You're finished here, Glokta! Finished! I'm going straight to the Arch Lector! Straight to the Arch Lector!"

The huge door was kicked open and Severard sauntered in carrying a wooden box. *And not a moment too soon.* The Superior stared, speechless, open-mouthed with wrath, as Severard dropped it on the desk with a thump and a jingle.

"What the hell is the meaning of . . ." Severard pulled open the lid, and Kalyne saw the money. *All that lovely money.* He stopped in mid-rant, mouth stuck forming the next sound. He looked surprised, then he looked puzzled, then he looked cautious. He pursed his lips and slowly sat down.

"Thank you, Practical Severard," said Glokta. "You may go." The Superior was stroking thoughtfully at his side whiskers as Severard strolled out, his face returning gradually to its usual shade of pink. "Confiscated from Rews. The property of the Crown now, of course. I thought that I should give it to you, as my direct superior, so that you could pass it on to the Treasury." *Or buy a bigger desk, you leech.*

Glokta leaned forward, hands on his knees. "You could say, perhaps, that Rews went too far, that questions had been asked, that an example had to be made. We can't be seen to do nothing, after all. It'll make the big guilds nervous, keep them in line." *It'll make them nervous and you can screw more out of them.* "Or you could always tell them that I'm a mad cripple, and blame me for it."

The Superior was starting to like it now, Glokta could tell. He was trying not to show it, but his whiskers were quivering at the sight of all that money. "Alright, Glokta. Alright. Very well." He reached out and carefully shut the lid of the box. "But if you ever think of doing something like this again . . . talk to me first, would you? I don't like surprises."

Glokta struggled to his feet, limped towards the door. "Oh, and one more thing!" He turned stiffly back. Kalyne was staring at him severely from beneath his big, fancy brows. "When I go to see the Mercers, I'll need to take Rews' confession."

Glokta smiled broadly, showing the yawning gap in his front teeth. "That shouldn't be a problem, Superior."

Kalyne had been right. There was no way that Rews could have gone back in this condition. His lips were split and bloody, his sides covered in darkening bruises, his head lolled sideways, face swollen almost past recognition. *In short, he looks like a man ready to confess.*

"I don't imagine you enjoyed the last half hour, Rews, I don't imagine you enjoyed it much at all. Perhaps it was the worst half hour of your life, I really couldn't say. I'm thinking about what we have for you here, though, and the sad fact is . . . that's about as good as it gets. That's the high life." Glokta leaned forward, his face just inches from the bloody pulp of Rews' nose. "Practical Frost's a little girl compared to me," he whispered. "He's a kitten. Once I get started with you, Rews, you'll be looking back on this with nostalgia. You'll be begging me to give you half an hour with the Practical. Do you understand?" Rews was silent, except for the air whistling through his broken nose.

"Show him the instruments," whispered Glokta.

Frost stepped forward and opened the polished case with a theatrical flourish. It was a masterful piece of craftsmanship. As the lid was pulled back, the many trays inside lifted and fanned out, displaying Glokta's tools in all their gruesome glory. There were blades of every size and shape, needles curved and straight, bottles of oil and acid, nails and screws, clamps and pliers, saws, hammers, chisels. Metal, wood and glass glittered in the bright lamplight, all polished to mirror brightness and honed to a murderous sharpness. A big purple swelling under Rews' left eye had closed it completely, but the other darted over the instruments: terrified, fascinated. The functions of some were horribly obvious, the functions of others were horribly obscure. *Which scare him more, I wonder?*

"We were talking about your tooth, I think," murmured Glokta. Rews' eye flicked up to look at him. "Or would you like to confess?" *I have him, here he comes. Confess, confess, confess, confess . . .*

There was a sharp knock at the door. *Damn it again!* Frost opened it a crack and there was a brief whispering. Rews licked at his bloated lip. The door shut, the albino leaned to whisper in Glokta's ear.

"Ith the Arth Ector." Glokta froze. *The money was not enough. While I was shuffling back from Kalyne's office, the old bastard was reporting me to the Arch Lector. Am I finished then?* He felt a guilty thrill at the thought. *Well, I'll see to this fat pig first.*

"Tell Severard I'm on my way." Glokta turned back to talk to his prisoner, but Frost put a big white hand on his shoulder.

"O. The Arth Ector," Frost pointed to the door, "he'th ere. Ow."

Here? Glokta could feel his eyelid twitching. *Why?* He pushed himself up using the edge of the table. *Will they find me in the canal tomorrow? Dead and bloated, far . . . far beyond recognition?* The only emotion that he felt at the idea was a flutter of mild relief. *No more stairs.*

The Arch Lector of His Majesty's Inquisition was standing outside in the corridor. The grimy walls looked almost brown behind him, so brilliantly spotless were his long white coat, his white gloves, his shock of white hair. He was past sixty, but showed none of the infirmity of age. Every tall, clean-shaven, fine-boned inch of him was immaculately turned out. *He looks like a man who has never once in his life been surprised by anything.*

They had met once before, six years earlier when Glokta joined the Inquisition, and he hardly seemed to have changed. Arch Lector Sult. One of the most powerful men in the Union. *One of the most powerful men in the world, come to that.* Behind him, almost like outsized shadows, loomed two enormous, silent, black-masked Practicals.

The Arch Lector gave a thin smile when he saw Glokta shuffle out of his door. It said a lot, that smile. *Mild scorn, mild pity, the very slightest touch of menace. Anything but amusement.* "Inquisitor Glokta," he said, holding out one white-gloved hand, palm down. A ring with a huge purple stone flashed on his finger.

"I serve and obey, your Eminence." Glokta could not help grimacing as he bent slowly forward to touch his lips to the ring. A difficult and painful manoeuvre, it seemed to take forever. When he finally hoisted himself back upright, Sult was gazing at him calmly with his cool blue eyes. A look that implied he already understood Glokta completely, and was unimpressed.

"Come with me." The Arch Lector turned and swept away down the corridor. Glokta limped along after him, the silent Practicals marching close behind. Sult moved with an effortless, languid confidence, coat tails flapping gracefully out behind him. *Bastard.* Soon they reached a door, much like his own. The Arch Lector unlocked it and went inside, the Practicals took up positions either side of the doorway, arms folded. *A private interview then. One which I, perhaps, will never leave.* Glokta stepped over the threshold.

A box of grubby white plaster too brightly lit and with a ceiling too low for comfort. It had a big crack instead of a damp patch, but was otherwise identical to his own room. It had the scarred table, the cheap chairs, it even had a poorly cleaned bloodstain. *I wonder if they're painted on, for the effect?* One of the Practicals suddenly pulled the door shut with a loud bang. Glokta was intended to jump, but he couldn't be bothered.

Arch Lector Sult lowered himself gracefully into one of the seats, drew a heavy sheaf of yellowing papers across the table towards him. He waved his hand at the other chair, the one that would be used by the prisoner. The implications were not lost on Glokta.

"I prefer to stand, your Eminence."

Sult smiled at him. He had lovely, pointy teeth, all shiny white. "No, you don't."

He has me there. Glokta lowered himself ungracefully into the prisoner's chair while the Arch Lector turned over the first page of his wedge of documents, frowned and shook his head gently as though horribly disappointed by what he saw. *The details of my illustrious career, perhaps?*

"I had a visit from Superior Kalyne not long ago. He was most upset." Sult's hard blue eyes came up from his papers. "Upset with you, Glokta. He was quite vocal on the subject. He told me that you are an uncontrollable menace, that you act without a thought for the consequences, that you are a mad cripple. He demanded that you be removed from his department." The Arch Lector smiled, a cold, nasty smile, the kind Glokta used on his prisoners. *But with more teeth.* "I think he had it in mind that you be removed . . . altogether." They stared at each other across the table.

Is this where I beg for mercy? Is this where I crawl on the ground and kiss your feet? Well, I don't care enough to beg and I'm far too stiff to crawl. Your Practicals will have to kill me sitting down. Cut my throat. Bash my head in. Whatever. As long as they get on with it.

But Sult was in no rush. The white-gloved hands moved neatly, precisely, the pages hissed and crackled. "We have few men like you in the Inquisition, Glokta. A nobleman, from an excellent family. A champion swordsman, a dashing cavalry officer. A man once groomed for the very top." Sult looked him up and down as though he could hardly believe it.

"That was before the war, Arch Lector."

"Obviously. There was much dismay at your capture, and little hope that you would be returned alive. As the war dragged on and the months passed, hope diminished to nothing, but when the treaty was signed, you were among those prisoners returned to the Union." He peered at Glokta through narrowed eyes. "Did you talk?"

Glokta couldn't help himself, he spluttered with shrill laughter. It echoed strangely in the cold room. Not a sound you often heard down here. "Did I talk? I talked until my throat was raw. I told them everything I could think of. I screamed every secret I'd ever heard. I babbled like a fool. When I ran out of things to tell them I made things up. I pissed myself and cried like a girl. Everyone does."

"But not everyone survives. Two years in the Emperor's prisons. No one else lasted half that long. The physicians were sure you would never leave your bed again, but a year later you made your application to the Inquisition." *We both know it. We were both there. What do you want from me, and why not get on with it? I suppose some men just love the sound of their own voices.*

"I was told that you were crippled, that you were broken, that you could never be mended, that you could never be trusted. But I was inclined to give you a chance. Some fool wins the Contest every year, and wars produce many promising soldiers, but your achievement in surviving those two years was unique. So you were sent to the North, and put in charge of one of our mines there. What did you make of Angland?"

A filthy sink of violence and corruption. A prison where we have made slaves of the innocent and guilty alike in the name of freedom. A stinking hole where we send those we hate and those we are ashamed of to die of hunger, and disease, and hard labour. "It was cold," said Glokta.

"And so were you. You made few friends in Angland. Precious few among the Inquisition, and none among the exiles." He plucked a tattered letter from among the papers and cast a critical eye over it. "Superior Goyle told me that you were a cold fish, had no blood in you at all. He thought you'd never amount to anything, that he could make no use of you." *Goyle. That bastard. That butcher. I'd rather have no blood than no brains.*

"But after three years, production was up. It was doubled in fact. So you were brought back to Adua, to work under Superior Kalyne. I thought perhaps you would learn discipline with him, but it seems I was wrong. You insist on going your own way." The Arch Lector frowned up at him. "To be frank, I think that Kalyne is afraid of you. I think they all are. They don't like your arrogance, they don't like your methods, they don't like your . . . special insight into our work."

"And what do you think, Arch Lector?"

"Honestly? I'm not sure I like your methods much either, and I doubt that your arrogance is entirely deserved. But I like your results. I like your results very much." He slapped the bundle of papers closed and rested one hand on top of it, leaning across the table towards Glokta. *As I might lean towards my prisoners when I ask them to confess.* "I have a task for you. A task that should make better use of your talents than chasing around after petty smugglers. A task that may allow you to redeem yourself in the eyes of the Inquisition." The Arch Lector paused for a long moment. "I want you to arrest Sepp dan Teufel."

Glokta frowned. *Teufel?* "The Master of the Mints, your Eminence?"

"The very same."

The Master of the Royal Mints. An important man from an important family. A very big fish, to be hooked in my little tank. A fish with powerful friends. It could be dangerous, arresting a man like that. It could be fatal. "May I ask why?"

"You may not. Let me worry about the whys. You concentrate on obtaining a confession."

"A confession to what, Arch Lector?"

"Why, to corruption and high treason! It seems our friend the Master of the Mints has been most indiscreet in some of his personal dealings. It seems he has been taking bribes, conspiring with the Guild of Mercers to defraud the King. As such, it would be very useful if a ranking Mercer were to name him, in some unfortunate connection."

It can hardly be a coincidence that I have a ranking Mercer in my interrogation room, even as we speak. Glokta shrugged. "Once people start talking, it's shocking the names that tumble out."

"Good." The Arch Lector waved his hand. "You may go, Inquisitor. I will come for Teufel's confession this time tomorrow. You had better have it."

Glokta breathed slowly as he laboured back along the corridor. *Breath in, breath out. Calm.* He had not expected to leave that room alive. *And now I find myself moving in powerful circles. A personal task for the Arch Lector, squeezing a confession to high treason from one of the Union's most trusted officials. The most powerful of circles, but for how long? Why me? Because of my results?*

Or because I won't be missed?

"I apologise for all the interruptions today, really I do, it's like a brothel in here with all the coming and going." Rews twisted his cracked and swollen lips into a sad smile. *Smiling at a time like this, he's a marvel. But all things must end.* "Let us be honest, Rews. No one is coming to help you. Not today, not tomorrow, not ever. You will confess. The only choices you have are when, and the state you'll be in when you do. There's really nothing to be gained by putting it off. Except pain. We've got lots of that for you."

It was hard to read the expression on Rews' bloody face, but his shoulders sagged. He dipped the pen in the ink with a trembling hand, wrote his name, slightly slanted, across the bottom of the paper of confession. *I win again. Does my leg hurt any less? Do I have my teeth back? Has it helped me to destroy this man, who I once called a friend? Then why do I do this?* The scratching of the nib on the paper was the only reply.

"Excellent," said Glokta. Practical Frost turned the document over. "And this is the list of your accomplices?" He let his eye scan lazily over the names. *A handful of junior Mercers, three ship's captains, an officer of the city watch, a pair of minor customs officials. A tedious recipe indeed. Let us see if we can add some spice.* Glokta turned it around and pushed it back across the table. "Add Sepp dan Teufel's name to the list, Rews."

The fat man looked confused. "The Master of the Mints?" he mumbled, through his thick lips.

"That's the one."

"But I never met the man."

"So?" snapped Glokta. "Do as I tell you." Rews paused, mouth a little open. "Write, you fat pig." Practical Frost cracked his knuckles.

Rews licked his lips. "Sepp . . . dan . . . Teufel," he mumbled to himself as he wrote.

"Excellent." Glokta carefully shut the lid on his horrible, beautiful instruments. "I'm glad for both our sakes that we won't be needing these today."

Frost snapped the manacles shut on the prisoner's wrists and dragged him to his feet, started to march him toward the door at the back of the room. "What now?" shouted Rews over his shoulder.

"Angland, Rews, Angland. Don't forget to pack something warm." The door cracked shut behind him. Glokta looked at the list of names in his hands. Sepp dan Teufel's sat at the bottom. *One name. On the face of it, just like the others. Teufel. Just one more name. But such a perilous one.*

Severard was waiting outside in the corridor, smiling as always. "Shall I put the fat man in the canal?"

"No, Severard. Put him in the next boat to Angland."

"You're in a merciful mood today, Inquisitor."

Glokta snorted. "Mercy would be the canal. That swine won't last six weeks in the North. Forget him. We have to arrest Sepp dan Teufel tonight."

Severard's eyebrows rose. "Not the Master of the Mints?"

"None other. On the express orders of his Eminence the Arch Lector. It seems he's been taking money from the Mercers."

"Oh, for shame."

"We'll leave as soon as it gets dark. Tell Frost to be ready."

The thin Practical nodded, his long hair swaying. Glokta turned and hobbled up the corridor, cane tapping on the grimy tiles, left leg burning.

Why do I do this? He asked himself again.

Why do I do this?

NO CHOICE AT ALL

Logen woke with a painful jolt. He was lying awkwardly, head twisted against something hard, knees drawn up towards his chest. He opened his eyes a bleary crack. It was dark, but there was a faint glow coming from somewhere. Light through snow.

Panic stabbed at him. He knew where he was now. He'd piled some snow in the entrance to the tiny cave, to try and keep in the warmth, such as it was. It must have snowed while he was sleeping, and sealed him in. If the fall had been a heavy one there could be a lot of snow out there. Drifts deeper than a man was tall. He might never get out. He could have climbed all the way up out of the high valleys just to die in a hole in the rock, too cramped for him to even stretch out his legs.

Logen twisted round in the narrow space as best he could, dug away at the snow with his numb hands, floundering at it, grappling with it, hacking through it, mouthing breathless curses to himself. Light spilled in suddenly, searing bright. He shoved the last of the snow out of the way and dragged himself through into the open air.

The sky was a brilliant blue, the sun was blazing overhead. He turned his face towards it, closed his stinging eyes and let the light wash over him. The air was painful cold in his throat. Cutting cold. His mouth was dry as dust, his tongue a piece of wood, badly carved. He scooped up snow and shoved it into his mouth. It melted, he swallowed. Cold, it made his head hurt.

There was a graveyard stink coming from somewhere. Not just his own damp and sour sweat smell, though that was bad enough. It was the blanket, starting to rot. He had two pieces of it wrapped round his hands like mittens, tied round his wrists with twine, another round his head, like a dirty, foul-smelling hood. His boots were stuffed tight with it. The rest was wrapped round and round his body, under his coat. It smelled bad, but it had saved his life last night, and that was a good trade to Logen's mind. It would stink a good deal more before he could afford to get rid of it.

He floundered to his feet and stared about. A narrow valley, steep sided and choked with snow. Three great peaks surrounded it, piles of dark grey stone and white snow against the blue sky. He knew them. Old friends, in fact. The only ones he had left. He was up in the High Places. The roof of the world. He was safe.

"Safe," he croaked to himself, but without much joy. Safe from food, certainly. Safe from warmth, without a doubt. Neither of those things would be troubling him up here. He'd escaped the Shanka, maybe, but this was a place for the dead, and if he stayed he'd be joining them.

He was brutal hungry as it was. His belly was a great, painful hole that called to him with piercing cries. He fumbled in his pack for the last strip of meat. An old, brown, greasy thing like a dry twig. That would hardly fill the gap, but it was all he had. He tore at it with his teeth, tough as old boot leather, and choked it down with some snow.

Logen shielded his eyes with his arm and looked northward down the valley, the way he'd come the day before. The ground dropped slowly away, snow and rock giving way to the pine-covered fells of the high valleys, trees giving way to a crinkled strip of grazing land, grassy hills giving way to the sea, a sparkling line on the far horizon. Home. The thought of it made Logen feel sick.

Home. That was where his family was. His father—wise and strong, a good man, a good leader to his people. His wife, his children. They were a good family. They deserved a better son, a better husband, a better father. His friends were there too. Old and new together. It would be good to see them all again, very good. To speak to his father in the long hall. To play with his children, to sit with his wife by the river. To talk of tactics with Threetrees. To hunt with the Dogman in the high valleys, crashing through the forest with a spear, laughing like a fool.

Logen felt a sudden painful longing. He nearly choked on the pain of it.

Trouble was, they were all dead. The hall was a ring of black splinters, the river a sewer. He'd never forget coming over the hill, seeing the burnt-out ruin in the valley below. Crawling through the ashes, fumbling for signs that someone got away, while the Dogman pulled at his shoulder and told him to give it up. Nothing but corpses, rotted past knowing. He was done looking for signs. They were all dead as the Shanka could make them, and that was dead for sure. He spat in the snow, brown spit from the dry meat. Dead and cold and rotted, or burned to ashes. Gone back to the mud.

Logen set his jaw and clenched his fists under the rotten shreds of blanket. He could go back to the ruins of the village by the sea, just one last time. He could charge down with a fighting roar in his throat, the way he had done at Carleon, when he'd lost a finger and won a reputation. He could put a few Shanka out of the world. Split them like he'd split Shama Heartless, shoulder to guts so his insides fell out. He could get vengeance for his father, his wife, his children, his friends. That would be a fitting end for the one they called the Bloody-Nine. To die killing. That might be a song worth the singing.

But at Carleon he'd been young and strong, and with his friends behind him. Now he was weak, and hungry, and alone as could be. He'd killed Shama Heartless with a long sword, sharp as anything. He looked down at his knife. It might be a good one, but he'd get precious little vengeance with it. And who'd sing the song anyway? The Shanka had poor singing voices and worse imaginations, if they even recognised the stinking beggar in the blanket after they'd shot him full of arrows. Perhaps the vengeance could wait, at least until he had a bigger blade to work with. You have to be realistic, after all.

South then, and become a wanderer. There was always work for a man with his skills. Hard work perhaps, and dark, but work all the same. There was an appeal in it, he had to admit. To have no one depending on him but himself, for his decisions to hold no importance, for no one's life or death to be in his hands. He had enemies in the south, that was a fact. But the Bloody-Nine had dealt with enemies before.

He spat again. Now that he had some spit he thought he might make the most of it. It was about all he did have—spit, an old pot, and some stinking bits of blanket. Dead in the north or alive in the south. That was what it came down to, and that was no choice at all.

You carry on. That's what he'd always done. That's the task that comes with surviving, whether you deserve to live or not. You remember the dead as best you can. You say some words for them. Then you carry on, and you hope for better.

Logen took in a long, cold breath, and blew it out. "Fare you well, my friends," he muttered. "Fare you well." Then he threw his pack over his shoulder, turned, and began to flounder through the deep snow. Downwards, southwards, out of the mountains.

It was raining, still. A soft rain that coated everything in cold dew, collected on the branches, on the leaves, on the needles, and dripped off in great fat drops that soaked through Logen's wet clothes and onto his wet skin.

He squatted, still and silent, in the damp brush, water running down his face, the bright blade of his knife glistening with wet. He felt the great motion of the forest and heard all its thousand sounds. The countless crawling of the insects, the blind scuttling of the moles, the timid rustling of the deer, the slow pulsing of the sap in the old tree trunks. Each thing alive in the forest was in search of its own kind of food, and he was the same. He let his mind settle on an animal close to him, moving cautiously through the woods to his right. Delicious. The forest grew silent but for the endless dripping of water from the branches. The world shrank down to Logen and his next meal.

When he reckoned it was close enough, he sprang forward and bore it down onto the wet ground. A young deer. It kicked and struggled but he was strong and quick, and he stabbed his knife into its neck and chopped the throat out. Hot blood surged from the wound, spilled out across Logen's hands, onto the wet earth.

He picked up the carcass and slung it over his shoulders. That would be good in a stew, maybe with some mushrooms. Very good. Then, once he'd eaten, he would ask the spirits for guidance. Their guidance was pretty useless, but the company would be welcome.

When he reached his camp it was close to sunset. It was a dwelling fit for a hero of Logen's stature—two big sticks holding a load of damp branches over a hollow in the dirt. Still, it was halfway dry in there, and the rain had stopped. He would have a fire tonight. It was a long time since he'd had a treat like that. A fire, and all his own.

Later, well fed and rested, Logen pressed a lump of chagga into his pipe. He'd found it growing a few days before at the base of a tree, big moist yellow discs of it. He'd broken off a good chunk for himself, but it hadn't dried out enough to smoke until today. Now he took a burning twig from the fire and stuck it in the bowl, puffing away hard until the fungus caught and began to burn, giving off its familiar earthy-sweet smell.

Logen coughed, blew out brown smoke and stared into the shifting flames. His mind went back to other times and other campfires. The Dogman was there, grinning, the light gleaming on his pointy teeth. Tul Duru was sitting opposite, big as a mountain, laughing like thunder. Forley the Weakest too, with those nervous eyes darting around, always a little scared. Rudd Threetrees was there, and Harding Grim, saying nothing. He never did say anything. That was why they called him Grim.

They were all there. Only they weren't. They were all dead, gone back to the mud. Logen tapped the pipe out into the fire and shoved it away. He had no taste for it now. His father had been right. You should never smoke alone.

He unscrewed the cap of the battered flask, took a mouthful, and blew it out in a spray of tiny drops. A gout of flame went up into the cold air. Logen wiped his lips, savouring the hot, bitter taste. Then he sat back against the knotted trunk of a pine, and waited.

It was a while before they came. Three of them. They came silently from the dancing shadows among the trees and made slowly for the fire, taking shape as they moved into the light.

"Ninefingers," said the first.

"Ninefingers," the second.

"Ninefingers," the third, voices like the thousand sounds of the forest.

"You're right welcome to my fire," said Logen. The spirits squatted and stared at him without expression. "Only three tonight?"

The one on the right spoke first. "Every year fewer of us wake from the winter. We are all that remain. A few more winters will pass, and we will sleep also. There will be none of us left to answer your call."

Logen nodded sadly. "Any news from the world?"

"We heard a man fell off a cliff but washed up alive, then crossed the High Places at the start of spring, wrapped in a rotten blanket, but we put no faith in such rumours."

"Very wise."

"Bethod has been making war," said the spirit in the centre.

Logen frowned. "Bethod is always making war. That's what he does."

"Yes. He has won so many fights now, with your help, he has given himself a golden hat."

"Shit on that bastard," said Logen, spitting into the fire, "what else?"

"North of the mountains, the Shanka run around and burn things."

"They love the fire," said the spirit in the centre.

"They do," said the one on the left, "even more than your kind, Ninefingers. They love and fear it." The spirit leaned forwards. "We heard there is a man seeking for you in the moors to the south."

"A powerful man," said the one in the centre.

"A Magus of the Old Time," the one on the left.

Logen frowned. He'd heard of these Magi. He met a sorcerer once, but he'd been easy to kill. No unnatural powers in particular, not that Logen had noticed. But a Magus was something else.

"We heard that the Magi are wise and strong," said the spirit in the centre, "and that such a one could take a man far and show him many things. But they are crafty too, and have their own purposes."

"What does he want?"

"Ask him." Spirits cared little for the business of men, they were always weak on the details. Still, this was better than the usual talk about trees.

"What will you do, Ninefingers?"

Logen considered a moment. "I will go south and find this Magus, and ask him what he wants from me."

The spirits nodded. They didn't show whether they thought it was a good idea or bad. They didn't care.

"Farewell then, Ninefingers," said the spirit on the right, "perhaps for the last time."

"I'll try to struggle on without you."

Logen's wit was wasted on them. They rose and moved away from the fire, fading gradually into the darkness. Soon they were gone, but Logen had to admit they had been more use than he dared to hope. They had given him a purpose.

He would head south in the morning, head south and find this Magus. Who knew? He might be a good talker. Had to be better than being shot full of arrows for nothing, at least. Logen looked into the flames, nodding slowly to himself.

He remembered other times and other campfires, when he had not been alone.

PLAYING WITH KNIVES

I t was a beautiful spring day in Adua, and the sun shone pleasantly through the branches of the aromatic cedar, casting a dappled shade on the players beneath. A pleasing breeze fluttered through the courtyard, so the cards were clutched tightly or weighted down with glasses or coins. Birds twittered from the trees, and the shears of a gardener clacked across from the far side of the lawn, making faint, agreeable echoes against the tall white buildings of the quadrangle. Whether or not the players found the large sum of money in the centre of the table pleasant depended, of course, on the cards they held.

Captain Jezal dan Luthar certainly liked it. He had discovered an uncanny talent for the game since he gained his commission in the King's Own, a talent which he had used to win large sums of money from his comrades. He didn't really need the money, of course, coming from such a wealthy family, but it had allowed him to maintain an illusion of thrift while spending like a sailor. Whenever Jezal went home, his father bored everyone on the subject of his good fiscal planning, and had rewarded him by buying his Captaincy just six months ago. His brothers had not been happy. Yes, the money was certainly useful, and there's nothing half so amusing as humiliating one's closest friends.

Jezal half sat, half lay back on his bench with one leg stretched out, and allowed his eyes to wander over the other players. Major West had rocked his chair so far onto its back legs that he looked in imminent danger of tipping over entirely. He was holding his glass up to the sun, admiring the way that the light filtered through the amber spirit inside. He had a faint, mysterious smile which seemed to say, "I am not a nobleman, and may be your social inferior, but I won a Contest and the King's favour on the battlefield and that makes me the better man, so you children will damn well do as I say." He was out of this hand though, and, in Jezal's opinion, far too cautious with his money anyway.

Lieutenant Kaspa was sitting forward, frowning and scratching his sandy beard, staring intently at his cards as though they were sums he didn't understand. He was a good-humoured young man but an oaf of a card player, and was always most appreciative when Jezal bought him drinks with his own money. Still, he could well afford to lose it: his father was one of the biggest landowners in the Union.

Jezal had often observed that the ever so slightly stupid will act more stupidly in clever company. Having lost the high ground already, they scramble eagerly for the position of likeable idiot, stay out of arguments they will only lose, and can hence be everyone's friend. Kaspa's look of baffled concentration seemed to say, "I am not clever, but honest and likeable, which is much more important. Cleverness is overrated. Oh, and I'm very, very rich, so everyone likes me regardless."

"I believe I'll stay with you," said Kaspa, and tossed a small stack of silver coins onto the table. They broke and flashed in the sun with a cheerful jingle. Jezal absently added up the total in his head. A new uniform perhaps? Kaspa always got a little quivery when he really held good cards, and he was not trembling now. To say that he was bluffing was to give him far too much credit; more likely he was simply bored with sitting out. Jezal had no doubt that he would fold up like a cheap tent on the next round of betting.

Lieutenant Jalenhorm scowled and tossed his cards onto the table. "I've had nothing but shit today!" he rumbled. He sat back in his chair and hunched his brawny shoulders with a frown that said, "I am big and manly, and have a quick temper, so I should be treated with respect by everyone." Respect was precisely what Jezal never gave him at the card table. A bad temper might be useful in a fight, but it's a liability where money is concerned. It was a shame his hand hadn't been a little better, or Jezal could've bullied him out of half his pay. Jalenhorm drained his glass and reached for the bottle.

That just left Brint, the youngest and poorest of the group. He licked his lips with an expression at once careful and slightly desperate, an expression which seemed to say, "I am not young or poor. I can afford to lose this money. I am every bit as important as the rest of you." He had a lot of money today; perhaps his allowance had just come in. Perhaps that was all he had to live on for the next couple of months. Jezal planned to take that money away from him and waste it all on women and drink. He had to stop himself giggling at the thought. He could giggle when he'd won the hand. Brint sat back and considered carefully. He might be some time making his decision, so Jezal took his pipe from the table.

He lit it at the lamp provided especially for that purpose and blew ragged smoke rings up into the branches of the cedar. He wasn't half as good at smoking as he was at cards, unfortunately, and most of the rings were no more than ugly puffs of yellow-brown vapour. If he was being completely honest, he didn't really enjoy smoking. It made him feel a bit sick, but it was very fashionable and very expensive, and Jezal would be damned if he would miss out on something fashionable just because he didn't like it. Besides, his father had bought him a beautiful ivory pipe the last time he was in the city, and it looked very well on him. His brothers had not been happy about that either, come to think of it.

"I'm in," said Brint.

Jezal swung his leg off the bench. "Then I raise you a hundred marks or so." He shoved his whole stack into the centre of the table. West sucked air through his teeth. A coin fell from the top of the pile, landed on its edge and rolled along the wood. It dropped to the flags beneath with the unmistakeable sound of falling money. The head of the gardener on the other side of the lawn snapped up instinctively, before he returned to his clipping of the grass.

Kaspa shoved his cards away as though they were burning his fingers and shook his head. "Damn it but I'm an oaf of a card player," he lamented, and leaned back against the rough brown trunk of the tree.

Jezal stared straight at Lieutenant Brint, a slight smile on his face, giving nothing away. "He's bluffing," rumbled Jalenhorm, "don't let him push you around, Brint."

"Don't do it, Lieutenant," said West, but Jezal knew he would. He had to look as if he could afford to lose. Brint didn't hesitate, he pushed all his own coins in with a careless flourish.

"That's a hundred, give or take." Brint was trying his hardest to sound masterful in front of the older officers, but his voice had a charming note of hysteria.

"Good enough," said Jezal, "we're all friends here. What do you have, Lieutenant?"

"I have earth." Brint's eyes had a slightly feverish look to them as he showed his cards to the group.

Jezal savoured the tense atmosphere. He frowned, shrugged, raised his eyebrows. He scratched his head thoughtfully. He watched Brint's expression change as he changed his own. Hope, despair, hope, despair. At length Jezal spread his cards out on the table. "Oh look. I have suns, again."

Brint's face was a picture. West gave a sigh and shook his head. Jalenhorm frowned. "I was sure he was bluffing," he said.

"How does he do it?" asked Kaspa, flicking a stray coin across the table.

Jezal shrugged. "It's all about the players, and nothing about the cards." He began to scoop up the heap of silver while Brint looked on, teeth gritted, face pale. The money jingled into the bag with a pleasant sound. Pleasant to Jezal, anyway. A coin dropped from the table and fell next to Brint's boot. "You couldn't fetch that for me could you Lieutenant?" asked Jezal, with a syrupy smile.

Brint stood up quickly, knocking into the table and making the coins and glasses jump and rattle. "I've things to do," he said in a thick voice, then shouldered roughly past Jezal, barging him against the trunk of the tree, and strode off toward the edge of the courtyard. He disappeared into the officers' quarters, head down.

"Did you see that?" Jezal was becoming ever more indignant with each passing moment. "Barging me like that, it's damn impolite! And me his superior officer as well! I've a good mind to put him on report!" A chorus of disapproving sounds greeted this mention of reports. "Well, he's a bad loser is all!"

Jalenhorm looked sternly out from beneath his brows. "You shouldn't bite him so hard. He isn't rich. He can't afford to lose."

"Well if he can't afford to lose he shouldn't play!" snapped Jezal, upset. "Who's the one told him I was bluffing? You should keep your big mouth shut!"

"He's new here," said West, "he just wants to fit in. Weren't you new once?"

"What are you, my father?" Jezal remembered being new with painful clarity, and the mention of it made him feel just a little ashamed.

Kaspa waved his hand. "I'll lend him some money, don't worry."

"He won't take it," said Jalenhorm.

"Well, that's his business." Kaspa closed his eyes and turned his face up to the sun. "Hot. Winter is truly over. Must be getting past midday."

"Shit!" shouted Jezal, starting up and gathering his things. The gardener paused in his trimming of the lawn and looked over at them. "Why didn't you say something, West?"

"What am I, your father?" asked the Major. Kaspa sniggered.

"Late again," said Jalenhorm, blowing out his cheeks. "The Lord Marshal will not be happy!"

Jezal snatched up his fencing steels and ran for the far side of the lawn. Major West ambled after him. "Come on!" shouted Jezal.

"I'm right behind you, Captain," he said. "Right behind you."

"Jab, jab, Jezal, jab, jab!" barked Lord Marshal Varuz, whacking him on the arm with his stick.

"Ow," yelped Jezal, and hefted the metal bar again.

"I want to see that right arm moving, Captain, darting like a snake! I want to be blinded by the speed of those hands!"

Jezal made a couple more clumsy lunges with the unwieldy lump of iron. It was utter torture. His fingers, his wrist, his forearm, his shoulder, were burning with the effort. He was soaked to the skin with sweat; it flew from his face in big drops. Marshal Varuz flicked his feeble efforts away. "Now, cut! Cut with the left!"

Jezal swung the big smith's hammer at the old man's head with all the strength in his left arm. He could barely lift the damn thing on a good day. Marshal Varuz stepped effortlessly aside and whacked him in the face with the stick.

"Yow!" wailed Jezal, as he stumbled back. He fumbled the hammer and it dropped on his foot. "Aaargh!" The iron bar clanged to the floor as he bent down to grab his screaming toes. He felt a stinging pain as Varuz whacked him across the arse, the sharp smack echoing across the courtyard, and he sprawled onto his face.

"That's pitiful!" shouted the old man. "You are embarrassing me in front of Major West!" The Major had rocked his chair back and was shaking with muffled laughter. Jezal stared at the Marshal's immaculately polished boots, seeing no pressing need to get up.

"Up, Captain Luthar!" shouted Varuz. "My time at least is valuable!"

"Alright! Alright!" Jezal clambered wearily to his feet and stood there swaying in the hot sun, panting for air, running with sweat.

Varuz stepped close to him and sniffed at his breath. "Have you been drinking today already?" he demanded, his grey moustaches bristling. "And last night too, no doubt!" Jezal had no reply. "Well damn you, then! We have work to do, Captain Luthar, and I cannot do it alone! Four months until the Contest, four months to make a master swordsman of you!"

Varuz waited for a reply, but Jezal could not think of one. He was only really doing this to make his father happy, but somehow he didn't think that was what the old soldier wanted to hear, and he could do without being hit again. "Bah!" Varuz barked in Jezal's face, and turned away, stick clenched tight behind him in both hands.

"Marshal Var—" Jezal began, but before he could finish the old soldier spun around and jabbed him right in the stomach.

"Gargh," said Jezal as he sank to his knees. Varuz stood over him.

"You are going to go on a little run for me, Captain."

"Aaaargh."

"You are going to run from here to the Tower of Chains. You are going to run up the tower to the parapet. We will know when you have arrived, as the Major and I will be enjoying a relaxing game of squares on the roof," he indicated the six-storey building behind him, "in plain view of the top of the tower. I will be able to see you with my eye-glass, so there will be no cheating this time!" and he whacked Jezal on the top of the head.

"Ow," said Jezal, rubbing his scalp.

"Having shown yourself on the roof, you will run back. You will run as fast as you can, and I know this to be true, because if you have not returned by the time we have finished our game, you will go again." Jezal winced.

"Major West is an excellent hand at squares, so it should take me half an hour to beat him. I suggest you begin at once."

Jezal lurched to his feet and jogged toward the archway at the far side of the courtyard, muttering curses.

"You'll need to go faster than that, Captain!" Varuz called after him. Jezal's legs were blocks of lead, but he urged them on.

"Knees up!" shouted Major West cheerily.

Jezal clattered down the passageway, past a smirking porter sitting by the door, and out onto into the broad avenue beyond. He jogged past the ivy-covered walls of the University, cursing the names of Varuz and West under his heaving breath, then by the near windowless mass of the House of Questions, its heavy front gate sealed tight. He passed a few colourless clerks hurrying this way and that, but the Agriont was quiet at this time of the afternoon, and Jezal saw nobody of interest until he passed into the park.

Three fashionable young ladies were sitting in the shade of a spreading willow by the lake, accompanied by an elderly chaperone. Jezal upped his pace immediately, and replaced his tortured expression with a nonchalant smile.

"Ladies," he said as he flashed past. He heard them giggling to one another behind him and silently congratulated himself, but slowed to half the speed as soon as he was out of sight.

"Varuz be damned," he said to himself, nearly walking as he turned onto the Kingsway, but had to speed up again straight away. Crown Prince Ladisla was not twenty strides off, holding forth to his enormous, brightly coloured retinue.

"Captain Luthar!" shouted his Highness, sunlight flashing off his outrageous golden buttons, "run for all you're worth! I have a thousand marks on you to win the Contest!"

Jezal had it on good authority that the Prince had backed Bremer dan Gorst to the tune of two thousand marks, but he still bowed as low as he possibly could while running. The prince's entourage of dandies cheered and shouted half-hearted encouragements at his receding back. "Bloody idiots," hissed Jezal under his breath, but he would have loved to be one of them.

He passed the huge stone effigies of six hundred years of High Kings on his right, the statues of their loyal retainers, slightly smaller, on his left. He nodded to the great Magus Bayaz just before he turned into the Square of

Marshals, but the wizard frowned back as disapprovingly as ever, the awe-inspiring effect only slightly diminished by a streak of white pigeon shit on his stony cheek.

With the Open Council in session the square was almost empty, and Jezal was able to amble over to the gate of the Halls Martial. A thick set sergeant nodded to him as he passed through, and Jezal wondered whether he might be from his own company—the common soldiers all looked the same, after all. He ignored the man and ran on between the towering white buildings.

"Perfect," muttered Jezal. Jalenhorm and Kaspa were sitting by the door to the Tower of Chains, smoking pipes and laughing. The bastards must have guessed that he'd be coming this way.

"For honour, and glory!" bellowed Kaspa, rattling his sword in its scabbard as Jezal ran by. "Don't keep the Lord Marshal waiting!" he shouted from behind, and Jezal heard the big man roaring with amusement.

"Bloody idiots," panted Jezal, shouldering open the heavy door, breath rasping as he started up the steep spiral staircase. It was one of the highest towers in the Agriont: there were two hundred and ninety-one steps in all. "Bloody steps," he cursed to himself. By the time he reached the hundredth his legs were burning and his chest was heaving. By the time he reached the two-hundredth he was a wreck. He walked the rest of the way, every footfall torture, and eventually burst out through a turret onto the roof and leaned on the parapet, blinking in the sudden brightness.

To the south the city was spread out below him, an endless carpet of white houses stretching all around the glittering bay. In the other direction, the view over the Agriont was even more impressive. A great confusion of magnificent buildings piled one upon the other, broken up by green lawns and great trees, circled by its wide moat and its towering wall, studded with a hundred lofty towers. The Kingsway sliced straight through the centre toward the Lords' Round, its bronze dome shining in the sunlight. The tall spires of the University stood behind, and beyond them loomed the grim immensity of the House of the Maker, rearing high over all like a dark mountain, casting its long shadow across the buildings below.

Jezal fancied that he saw the sun glint on Marshal Varuz's eye-glass in the distance. He cursed once again and made for the stairs.

Jezal was immensely relieved when he finally made it to the roof and saw that there were still a few white pieces on the board.

Marshal Varuz frowned up at him. "You are very lucky. The Major has put up an exceptionally determined defence." A smile broke West's features. "You must somehow have earned his respect, even if you have yet to win mine."

Jezal bent over with his hands on his knees, blowing hard and dripping sweat onto the floor. Varuz took the long case from the table, walked over to Jezal and flipped it open. "Show us your forms."

Jezal took the short steel in his left hand and the long in his right. They felt light as feathers after the heavy iron. Marshal Varuz backed away a step. "Begin."

He snapped into the first form, right arm extended, left close to the body. The blades swished and weaved through the air, glittering in the afternoon sun as Jezal moved from one familiar stance to the next with a practised smoothness. At length he was finished, and he let the steels drop to his sides.

Varuz nodded. "The Captain has fast hands, has he not?"

"Truly excellent," said Major West, smiling broadly. "A damn sight better than ever I was."

The Lord Marshal was less impressed. "Your knees are too far bent in the third form, and you must strive for more extension on the left arm in the fourth, but otherwise," he paused, "passable." Jezal breathed a sigh of relief. That was high praise indeed.

"Hah!" shouted the old man, striking him in the ribs with the end of the case. Jezal sank to the floor, hardly able to breathe. "Your reflexes need work, though, Captain. You should always be ready. Always. If you have steels in your hands. you damn well keep them up."

"Yes, sir," croaked Jezal.

"And your stamina is a disgrace, you are blowing like a carp. I have it on good authority that Bremer dan Gorst runs ten miles a day, and barely shows a sweat." Marshal Varuz leaned down over him. "From now on you will do the same. Oh yes. A circuit of the wall of the Agriont every morning at six, followed by an hour of sparring with Major West, who has been kind enough to agree to act as your partner. I am confident that he will point up all the little weaknesses in your technique."

Jezal winced and rubbed his aching ribs. "As for the carousing, I want an end to it. I am all for revelry in its proper place, but there will be time for celebration after the Contest, providing you have worked hard enough to win. Until then, clean living is what we need. Do you understand me, Captain Luthar?" He leaned down further, pronouncing every word with great care. "Clean. Living. Captain."

"Yes, Marshal Varuz," mumbled Jezal.

Six hours later he was drunker than shit. Laughing like a lunatic he plunged out into the street, head spinning. The cold air slapped him hard in the face, the mean little buildings weaved and swayed, the ill-lit road tipped like a sinking ship. Jezal wrestled manfully with the urge to vomit, took a swaggering step out into the street, turned to face the door. Smeary bright light and loud sounds of laughter and shouting washed out at him. A ragged shape flew from the tavern and struck him in the chest. Jezal grappled with it desperately, then fell. He hit the ground with a bone-jarring crash.

The world was dark for a moment, then he found himself squashed into the dirt with Kaspa on top of him. "Damn it!" he gurgled, tongue thick and clumsy in his mouth. He shoved the giggling Lieutenant away with his elbow, rolled over and lurched up, stumbling about as the street seesawed around him. Kaspa lay on his back in the dirt, choking with laughter, reeking of cheap booze and sour smoke. Jezal made a lame attempt to brush the dirt from his uniform. There was a big wet patch on his chest that smelled of beer. "Damn it!" he mumbled again. When had that happened?

He became aware of some shouting on the other side of the road. Two men grappling in a doorway. Jezal squinted hard, strained against the gloom. A big man had hold of some well-dressed fellow, and seemed to be tying his hands behind his back. Now he was forcing some kind of bag over his head. Jezal blinked in disbelief. It was far from a reputable area, but this seemed somewhat strong.

The door of the tavern banged open and West and Jalenhorm came out, deep in drunken conversation, something about someone's sister. Bright light cut across the street and illuminated the two struggling men starkly. The big one was dressed all in black, with a mask over the lower part of his face. He had white hair, white eyebrows, skin white as milk. Jezal stared at the white devil across the road, and he glared back with narrowed pink eyes.

"Help!" It was the fellow with the bag on his head, his voice shrill with fear. "Help, I am—" The white man dealt him a savage blow in the midriff and he folded up with a sigh.

"You there!" shouted West.

Jalenhorm was already rushing across the street.

"What?" said Kaspa, propped up on his elbows in the road.

Jezal's mind was full of mud, but his feet seemed to be following Jalenhorm, so he stumbled along with them, feeling very sick. West came behind him. The white ghost started up and turned to stand between them and his prisoner. Another man moved briskly out of the shadows, tall and thin, dressed all in black and masked, but with long greasy hair. He held up a gloved hand.

"Gentlemen," his whining commoner's voice was muffled by his mask, "gentlemen please, we're on the King's business!"

"The King conducts his business in the day-time," growled Jalenhorm.

The new arrival's mask twitched slightly as he smiled. "That's why he needs us for the night-time stuff, eh, friend?"

"Who is this man?" West was pointing at the fellow with the bag on his head.

The prisoner was struggling up again. "I am Sepp dan—oof!" The white monster silenced him with a heavy fist in the face, knocking him limp into the road.

Jalenhorm put a hand on the hilt of his sword, jaw clenching, and the white ghost loomed forward with a terrible speed. Close up he was even more massive, alien, and terrifying. Jalenhorm took an involuntary step back, stumbled on the rutted surface of the road and pitched onto his back with a crash. Jezal's head was thumping.

"Back!" bellowed West. His sword whipped out of its scabbard with a faint ringing.

"Thaaaaah!" hissed the monster, fists clenched like two big white rocks.

"Aargh," gurgled the man with the bag on his head.

Jezal's heart was in his mouth. He looked at the thin man. The thin man's eyes smiled back. How could anyone smile at a time like this? Jezal was surprised to see that he had a long, ugly knife in his hand. Where did that come from? He fumbled drunkenly for his sword.

"Major West!" came a voice from the shadows down the street. Jezal paused, uncertain, steel halfway out. Jalenhorm scrambled to his feet, the back of his uniform crusted with mud, pulled out his own sword. The pale monster stared at them unblinking, not retreating a finger's breadth.

"Major West!" came the voice again, accompanied now by a clicking, scraping sound. West's face had turned pale. A figure emerged from the shadows, limping badly, cane tapping on the dirt. His broad-brimmed hat obscured the upper part of his face, but his mouth was twisted into a strange smile. Jezal noticed with a sudden wave of nausea that his four front teeth were missing. He shuffled towards them, ignoring all the naked steel, and offered his free hand to West.

The Major slowly sheathed his sword, took the hand and shook it limply. "Colonel Glokta?" he asked in a husky voice.

"Your humble servant, though I'm no longer an army man. I'm with the King's Inquisition now." He reached up slowly and removed his hat. His face was deathly pale, deeply lined, close-cropped hair scattered with grey. His eyes stared out feverish bright from deep, dark rings, the left one noticeably narrower than the right, pink-rimmed and glistening wet. "And these are my assistants, Practicals Severard," the lanky one gave a mockery of a bow, "and Frost."

The white monster jerked the prisoner to his feet with one hand. "Hold on," said Jalenhorm, stepping forward, but the Inquisitor put a gentle hand on his arm.

"This man is a prisoner of His Majesty's Inquisition, Lieutenant Jalenhorm." The big man paused, surprised to be called by name. "I realise your motives are of the best, but he is a criminal, a traitor. I have a warrant for him, signed by Arch Lector Sult himself. He is most unworthy of your assistance, believe me."

Jalenhorm frowned and stared balefully at Practical Frost. The pale devil looked terrified. About as terrified as a stone. He hauled the prisoner over his shoulder without apparent effort and turned up the street. The one called Severard smiled with his eyes, sheathed his knife, bowed again and followed his companion, whistling tunelessly as he sauntered off.

The Inquisitor's left eyelid began to flutter and tears rolled down his pale cheek. He wiped it carefully on the back of his hand. "Please forgive me. Honestly. It's coming to something when a man can't control his own eyes, eh? Damn weeping jelly. Sometimes I think I should just have it out, and make do with a patch." Jezal's stomach roiled. "How long has it been, West? Seven years? Eight?"

A muscle was working on the side of the Major's head. "Nine."

"Imagine that. Nine years. Can you believe it? It seems like only yesterday. It was on the ridge, wasn't it, where we parted?"

"On the ridge, yes."

"Don't worry, West, I don't blame you in the least." Glokta slapped the Major warmly on the arm. "Not for that, anyway. You tried to talk me out of it, I remember. I had time enough to think about it in Gurkhul, after all. Lots of time to think. You were always a good friend to me. And now young Collem West, a Major in the King's Own, imagine that." Jezal had not the slightest idea what they were talking about. He wanted only to be sick, then go to bed.

Inquisitor Glokta turned toward him with a smile, displaying once again the hideous gap in his teeth. "And this must be Captain Luthar, for whom everyone has such high hopes in the coming Contest. Marshal Varuz is a hard master, is he not?" He waved his cane weakly at Jezal. "Jab, jab, eh, Captain? Jab, jab."

Jezal felt his bile rising. He coughed and looked down at his feet, willing the world to remain motionless. The Inquisitor looked around expectantly at each of them in turn. West looked pale. Jalenhorm mud-stained and sulky. Kaspa was still sitting in the road. None of them had anything to say.

Glokta cleared his throat. "Well, duty calls," he bowed stiffly, "but I hope to see you all again. Very soon." Jezal found himself hoping he never saw the man again.

"Perhaps we might fence again sometime?" muttered Major West.

Glokta gave a good natured laugh. "Oh, I would enjoy that, West, but I find that I'm ever so slightly crippled these days. If you're after a fight, I'm sure that Practical Frost could oblige you," he looked over at Jalenhorm, "but I must warn you, he doesn't fight like a gentleman. I wish you all a pleasant evening." He placed his hat back on his head then turned slowly and shuffled off down the dingy street.

The three officers watched him limp away in an interminable, awkward silence. Kaspa finally stumbled over. "What was all that about?" he asked.

"Nothing," said West through gritted teeth. "Best we forget it ever happened."

TEETH AND FINGERS

Time is short. We must work quickly. Glokta nodded to Severard, and he smiled and pulled the bag off Sepp dan Teufel's head.

The Master of the Mints was a strong, noble-looking man. His face was already starting to bruise. "What is the meaning of this?" he roared, all bluster and bravado. "Do you know who I am?"

Glokta snorted. "Of course we know who you are. Do you think we are in the habit of snatching people from the streets at random?"

"I am the Master of the Royal Mints!" yelled the prisoner, struggling at his bonds. Practical Frost looked on impassively, arms folded. The irons were already glowing orange in the brazier. "How dare you . . ."

"We cannot have these constant interruptions!" shouted Glokta. Frost kicked Teufel savagely in the shin and he yelped with pain. "How can our prisoner sign his paper of confession if his hands are tied? Please release him."

Teufel stared suspiciously around as the albino untied his wrists. Then he saw the cleaver. The polished blade shone mirror bright in the harsh lamp light. *Truly a thing of beauty. You'd like to have that, wouldn't you, Teufel? I bet you'd like to cut my head off with it.* Glokta almost hoped that he would, his right hand seemed to be reaching for it, but he used it to shove the paper of confession away instead.

"Ah," said Glokta, "the Master of the Mints is a right-handed gentleman."

"A right-handed gentleman," Severard hissed in the prisoner's ear.

Teufel was staring across the table through narrowed eyes. "I know you! Glokta, isn't it? The one who was captured in Gurkhul, the one they tortured.

Sand dan Glokta, am I right? Well, you're in over your head this time, I can tell you! Right in over your head! When High Justice Marovia hears about this . . ."

Glokta sprang to his feet, his chair screeching on the tiles. His left leg was agony, but he ignored it. "Look at this!" he hissed, then opened his mouth wide, giving the horrified prisoner a good look at his teeth. *Or what's left of them.* "You see that? You see? Where they cracked out the teeth above, they left them below, and where they took them out below, they left them above, all the way to the back. See?" Glokta pulled his cheeks back with his fingers so Teufel could get a better view. "They did it with a tiny chisel. A little bit each day. It took months." Glokta sat down stiffly, then smiled wide.

"What excellent work, eh? The irony of it! To leave you half your teeth, but not a one of 'em any use! I have soup most days." The Master of the Mints swallowed hard. Glokta could see a drop of sweat running down his neck. "And the teeth were just the beginning. I have to piss sitting down like a woman, you know. I'm thirty-five years old, and I need help getting out of bed." He leaned back again and stretched out his leg with a wince. "Every day is its own little hell for me. Every day. So tell me, can you seriously believe that anything you might say could scare me?"

Glokta studied his prisoner, taking his time. *No longer half so sure of himself.* "Confess," he whispered. "Then we can ship you off to Angland and still get some sleep tonight."

Teufel's face had turned almost as pale as Practical Frost's, but he said nothing. *The Arch Lector will be here soon. Already on his way, most likely. If there is no confession when he arrives . . . we'll all be off to Angland. At best.* Glokta took hold of his cane and got to his feet. "I like to think of myself as an artist, but artistry takes time and we have wasted half the evening searching for you in every brothel in the city. Thankfully, Practical Frost has a keen nose and an excellent sense of direction. He can sniff out a rat in a shithouse."

"A rat in a shithouse," echoed Severard, eyes glittering bright in the orange glow from the brazier.

"We are on a tight schedule so let me be blunt. You will confess to me within ten minutes."

Teufel snorted and folded his arms. "Never."

"Hold him." Frost seized the prisoner from behind and folded him in a vice-like grip, pinning his right arm to his side. Severard grabbed hold of his left wrist and spread his fingers out on the scarred table-top. Glokta curled his fist round the smooth grip of the cleaver, the blade scraping against the wood as he pulled it slowly towards him. He stared down at Teufel's hand. *What beautiful fingernails he has. How long and glossy. You cannot work down a mine with nails like that.* Glokta raised the cleaver high.

"Wait!" screamed the prisoner.

Bang! The heavy blade bit deep into the table top, neatly paring off Teufel's middle fingernail. He was breathing fast now, and there was a sheen of sweat on his forehead. *Now we'll see what kind of a man you really are.*

"I think you can see where this is going," said Glokta. "You know, they did it to a corporal who was captured with me, one cut a day. He was a tough man, very tough. They made it past his elbow before he died." Glokta lifted the cleaver again. "Confess."

"You couldn't . . ."

Bang! The cleaver took off the very tip of Teufel's middle finger. Blood bubbled out on to the table top. Severard's eyes were smiling in the lamp light. Teufel's jaw dropped. *But the pain will be a while coming.* "Confess!" bellowed Glokta.

Bang! The cleaver took off the top of Teufel's ring finger, and a little disc out of his middle finger which rolled a short way and dropped off onto the floor. Frost's face was carved from marble. "Confess!"

Bang! The tip of Teufel's index finger jumped in the air. His middle finger was down to the first joint. Glokta paused, wiping the sweat from his forehead on the back of his hand. His leg was throbbing with the exertion. Blood was dripping onto the tiles with a steady tap, tap, tap. Teufel was staring wide-eyed at his shortened fingers.

Severard shook his head. "That's excellent work, Inquisitor." He flicked one of the discs of flesh across the table. "The precision . . . I'm in awe."

"Aaaargh!" screamed the Master of the Mints. *Now it dawns on him.* Glokta raised the cleaver once again.

"I will confess!" shrieked Teufel, "I will confess!"

"Excellent," said Glokta brightly.

"Excellent," said Severard.

"Etherer," said Practical Frost.

THE WIDE AND
BARREN NORTH

The Magi are an ancient and mysterious order, learned in the secrets of the world, practised in the ways of magic, wise and powerful beyond the dreams of men. That was the rumour. Such a one should have ways of finding a man, even a man alone in the wide and barren North. If that was so, then he was taking his time about it.

Logen scratched at his tangled beard and wondered what was keeping the great one. Perhaps he was lost. He asked himself again if he should have stayed in the forests, where food at least was plentiful. But to the south the spirits had said, and if you went south from the hills you came to these withered moors. So here he had waited in the briars and the mud, in bad weather, and mostly gone hungry.

His boots were worn out anyway, so he had set his miserable camp not far from the road, the better to see this wizard coming. Since the wars, the North was full of dangerous scum—deserting warriors turned bandit, peasants fled from their burned-out land, leaderless and desperate men with nothing left to lose, and so on. Logen wasn't worried, though. No one had a reason to come to this arsehole of the world. No one but him and the Magus.

So he sat and waited, looked for food, didn't find any, sat and waited some more. At this time of year the moors were often soaked by sudden downpours, but he would have smoky, thorny little fires by night if he could, to keep his flagging spirits up and attract any passing wizards. It had been raining this evening, but it had stopped a while before and it was dry enough for a fire. Now he had his pot over it, cooking a stew with the last of the meat he had brought with him from the forest. He would have to move on in the morning, and look for food. The Magus could catch up with him later, if he still cared.

He was stirring his meagre meal, and wondering whether to go back north or move on south tomorrow, when he heard the sound of hooves on the road. One horse, moving slowly. He sat back on his coat and waited. There was a neigh, the jingle of a harness. A rider came over the rise. With the watery sun low on the horizon behind, Logen couldn't see him clearly, but he sat stiff and awkward in his saddle, like a man not used to the road. He urged his horse gently in the direction of the fire and reined in a few yards away.

"Good evening," he said.

He was not in the least what Logen had been expecting. A gaunt, pale, sickly looking young man with dark rings round his eyes, long hair plastered to his head by the drizzle and a nervous smile. He seemed more wet than wise, and certainly didn't look powerful beyond the dreams of men. He looked mostly hungry, cold, and ill. He looked something like Logen felt, in fact.

"Shouldn't you have a staff?"

The young man looked surprised. "I don't . . . that is to say . . . er . . . I'm not a Magus." He trailed off and licked his lips nervously.

"The spirits told me to expect a Magus, but they're often wrong."

"Oh . . . well, I'm an apprentice. But my Master, the great Bayaz," and he bowed his head reverently, "is none other than the First of the Magi, great in High Art and learned in deep wisdom. He sent me to find you," he looked suddenly doubtful, "and bring you . . . you are Logen Ninefingers?"

Logen held up his left hand and looked at the pale young man through the gap where his middle finger used to be. "Oh good." The apprentice breathed a sigh of relief, then suddenly stopped himself. "Oh, that is to say . . . er . . . sorry about the finger."

Logen laughed. It was the first time since he dragged himself out of the river. It wasn't very funny but he laughed loud. It felt good. The young man smiled and slipped painfully from the saddle. "I am Malacus Quai."

"Malacus what?"

"Quai," he said, making for the fire.

"What kind of a name is that?"

"I am from the Old Empire."

Logen had never heard of any such place. "An empire, eh?"

"Well, it was, once. The mightiest nation in the Circle of the World."
The young man squatted down stiffly by the fire. "But the glory of the past
is long faded. It's not much more than a huge battlefield now." Logen
nodded. He knew well enough what one of those looked like. "It's far away.
In the west of the world." The apprentice waved his hand vaguely.

Logen laughed again. "That's east."

Quai smiled sadly. "I am a seer, though not, it seems, a very good one.
Master Bayaz sent me to find you, but the stars have not been auspicious and
I became lost in the bad weather." He pushed his hair out of his eyes and
spread his hands. "I had a packhorse, with food and supplies, and another
horse for you, but I lost them in a storm. I fear I am no outdoorsman."

"Seems not."

Quai took a flask from his pocket and leaned across with it. Logen took
it from him, opened it, took a swig. The hot liquor ran down his throat,
warmed him to the roots of his hair. "Well, Malacus Quai, you lost your food
but you kept hold of what really mattered. It takes an effort to make me smile
these days. You're right welcome at my fire."

"Thank you." The apprentice paused and held his palms out to the
meagre flames. "I haven't eaten for two days." He shook his head, hair flapping back and forth. "It has been . . . a difficult time." He licked his lips and
looked at the pot.

Logen passed him the spoon. Malacus Quai stared at it with big round
eyes. "Have you eaten?"

Logen nodded. He hadn't, but the wretched apprentice looked famished
and there was barely enough for one. He took another swig from the flask.
That would do for him, for now. Quai attacked the stew with relish. When
it was done he scraped the pot out, licked the spoon, then licked the edge of
the pot for good measure. He sat back against a big rock. "I am forever in
your debt, Logen Ninefingers, you've saved my life. I hardly dared hope you'd
be so gracious a host."

"You're not quite what I expected either, being honest." Logen pulled at
the flask again, and licked his lips. "Who is this Bayaz?"

"The First of the Magi, great in High Art and learned in deep wisdom. I fear he will be most seriously displeased with me."

"He's to be feared, then?"

"Well," replied the apprentice weakly, "he does have a bit of a temper."

Logen took another swallow. The warmth was spreading through his body now, the first time he had felt warm in weeks. There was a pause. "What does he want from me, Quai?"

There was no reply. The soft sound of snoring came from across the fire. Logen smiled and, wrapping himself in his coat, lay down to sleep as well.

The apprentice woke with a sudden fit of coughing. It was early morning and the dingy world was thick with mist. It was probably better that way. There was nothing to see but miles of mud, rock, and miserable brown gorse. Everything was coated in cold dew, but Logen had managed to get a sad tongue of fire going. Quai's hair was plastered to his pallid face. He rolled onto his side and coughed phlegm onto the ground.

"Aaargh," he croaked. He coughed and spat again.

Logen secured the last of his meagre gear on the unhappy horse. "Morning," he said, looking up at the white sky, "though not a good one."

"I will die. I will die, and then I will not have to move."

"We've got no food, so if we stay here you will die. Then I can eat you and go back over the mountains."

The apprentice smiled weakly. "What do we do?"

What indeed? "Where do we find this Bayaz?"

"At the Great Northern Library."

Logen had never heard of it, but then he'd never been that interested in books. "Which is where?"

"It's south of here, about four days' ride, beside a great lake."

"Do you know the way?"

The apprentice tottered to his feet and stood, swaying slightly, breathing fast and shallow. He was ghostly pale and his face had a sheen of sweat. "I think so," he muttered, but he hardly looked certain.

Neither Quai nor his horse would make four days without food, even providing they didn't get lost. Food had to be the first thing. To follow the road through the woods to the south was the best option, despite the greater risk. They might get killed by bandits, but the forage would be better, and the hunger would likely kill them otherwise.

"You'd better ride," said Logen.

"I lost the horses, I should be the one to walk."

Logen put his hand on Quai's forehead. It was hot and clammy. "You've a fever. You'd better ride."

The apprentice didn't try to argue. He looked down at Logen's ragged boots. "Can you take my boots?"

Logen shook his head. "Too small." He knelt down over the smouldering remains of the fire and pursed his lips.

"What are you doing?"

"Fires have spirits. I will keep this one under my tongue, and we can use it to light another fire later." Quai looked too ill to be surprised. Logen sucked up the spirit, coughed on the smoke, shuddered at the bitter taste. "You ready to leave?"

The apprentice raised his arms in a hopeless gesture. "I am packed."

Malacus Quai loved to talk. He talked as they made their way south across the moors, as the sun climbed into the grimy skies, as they entered the woods toward evening time. His illness did nothing to stop his chatter, but Logen didn't mind. It was a long time since anyone had talked to him, and it helped to take his mind off his feet. He was starving and tired, but it was his feet that were the problem. His boots were tatters of old leather, his toes cut and battered, his calf was still burning from the Shanka's teeth. Every step was an ordeal. Once they had called him the most feared man in the North. Now he was afraid of the smallest sticks and stones in the road. There was a joke in there somewhere. He winced as his foot hit a pebble.

". . . so I spent seven years studying with Master Zacharus. He is great among the Magi, the fifth of Juvens' twelve apprentices, a great man." Everything connected with the Magi seemed to be great in Quai's eyes. "He felt I was ready to come to the Great Northern Library and study with Master Bayaz, to earn my staff. But things have not been easy for me here. Master Bayaz is most demanding and . . ."

The horse stopped and snorted, shied and took a hesitant step back. Logen sniffed the air and frowned. There were men nearby, and badly washed ones. He should have noticed it sooner but his attention had been on his feet. Quai looked down at him. "What is it?"

As if in answer a man stepped out from behind a tree perhaps ten strides ahead, another a little further down the road. They were scum, without a doubt. Dirty, bearded, dressed in ragged bits of mismatched fur and leather. Not, on the whole, unlike Logen. The skinny one on the left had a spear with a barbed head. The big one on the right had a heavy sword speckled with rust, and an old dented helmet with a spike on top. They moved forward, grinning. There was a sound behind and Logen looked over his shoulder, his heart sinking. A third man, with a big boil on his face, was making his way cautiously down the road toward them, a heavy wood axe in his hands.

Quai leaned down from his saddle, eyes wide with fear. "Are they bandits?"

"You're the fucking seer," hissed Logen through gritted teeth.

They stopped a stride or two in front. The one with the helmet seemed to be in charge. "Nice horse," he growled. "Would you lend it to us?" The one with the spear grinned as he took hold of the bridle.

Things had taken a turn for the worse alright. A moment ago that had hardly seemed possible, but fate had found a way. Logen doubted that Quai would be much use in a fight. That left him alone against three or more, and with only a knife. If he did nothing he and Malacus would end up robbed, and more than likely killed. You have to be realistic about these things.

He looked the three bandits over again. They didn't expect a fight, not from two unarmed men—the spear was sideways on, the sword pointed at the ground. He didn't know about the axe, so he'd have to trust to luck with that one. It's a sorry fact that the man who strikes first usually strikes last, so Logen turned to the one with the helmet and spat the spirit in his face.

It ignited in the air and pounced on him hungrily. His head burst into spitting flames, the sword clattered to the ground. He clawed desperately at his face and his arms caught fire as well. He reeled screaming away.

Quai's horse startled at the flames and reared up, snorting. The skinny man stumbled back with a gasp and Logen leaped at him, grabbed the shaft of the spear with one hand and butted him in the face. His nose crunched against Logen's forehead and he staggered away with blood streaming down his chin. Logen jerked him back with the spear, swung his right arm round in a wide arc and punched him in the neck. He went down with a gurgle and Logen tore the spear from his hands.

He felt movement behind him and dropped to the ground, rolling away to his left. The axe whistled through the air above his head and cut a long slash in the horse's side, spattering drops of blood across the ground and ripping the buckle on the saddle girth open. Boil-face tottered away, spinning around after his axe. Logen sprang at him but his ankle twisted on a stone and he tottered like a drunkard, yelping at the pain. An arrow hummed past his face from somewhere in the trees behind and was lost in the bushes on the other side of the road. The horse snorted and kicked, eyes rolling madly, then took off down the road at a crazy gallop. Malacus Quai wailed as the saddle slid off its back and he was flung into the bushes.

There was no time to think about him. Logen charged at the axe-man with a roar, aiming the spear at his heart. He brought his axe up in time to nudge the point away, but not far enough. The spear spitted him through the shoulder, spun him round. There was a sharp crack as the shaft snapped, Logen lost his balance and pitched forward, bearing Boil-face down into the road. The spear-point sticking out of his back cut a deep gash into Logen's scalp as he fell on top of him. Logen seized hold of the axe-man's matted hair with both hands, pulled his head back and mashed his face into a rock.

He lurched to his feet, head spinning, wiping blood out of his eyes just in time to see an arrow zip out of the trees and thud into a trunk a stride or two away. Logen hurtled at the archer. He saw him now, a boy no more than fourteen, reaching for another arrow. Logen pulled out his knife. The boy was nocking the arrow to his bow, but his eyes were wide with panic. He fumbled the string and drove the arrow through his hand, looking greatly surprised.

Logen was on him. The boy swung the bow at him but he ducked below it and jumped forward, driving the knife up with both hands. The blade caught the boy under the chin and lifted him into the air, then snapped off in his neck. He dropped on top of Logen, the jagged shard of the knife cutting a long gash in his arm. Blood splattered everywhere, from the cut on

Logen's head, from the cut on Logen's arm, from the gaping wound in the boy's throat.

He shoved the corpse away, staggered against a tree and gasped for breath. His heart was pounding, the blood roaring in his ears, his stomach turning over. "I am still alive," he whispered, "I am still alive." The cuts on his head and his arm were starting to throb. Two more scars. It could have been a lot worse. He scraped the blood from his eyes and limped back to the road.

Malacus Quai was standing, staring ashen-faced at the three corpses. Logen took him by the shoulders, looked him up and down. "You hurt?"

Quai only stared at the bodies. "Are they dead?"

The corpse of the big one with the helmet was still smoking, making a disgustingly appetising smell. He had a good pair of boots on, Logen noticed, a lot better than his own. The one with the boil had his neck turned too far around to be alive, that and he had the broken spear through him. Logen rolled the skinny one over with his foot. He still had a look of surprise on his bloody face, eyes staring up at the sky, mouth open.

"Must've crushed his windpipe," muttered Logen. His hands were covered in blood. He grabbed one with the other to stop them from trembling.

"What about the one in the trees?"

Logen nodded. "What happened to the horse?"

"Gone," muttered Quai hopelessly. "What do we do?"

"We see if they've got any food." Logen pointed to the smoking corpse. "And you help me get his boots off."

FENCING PRACTICE

"Press him, Jezal, press him! Don't be shy!"

Jezal was only too willing to oblige. He sprang forward, lunging with his right. West was already off balance and he stumbled back, all out of form, only just managing to parry with his short steel. They were using half-edged blades today, to add a little danger to the proceedings. You couldn't really stab a man with one, but you could give him a painful scratch or two, if you tried hard enough. Jezal intended to give the Major a scratch for yesterday's humiliation.

"That's it, give him hell! Jab, jab, Captain! Jab, jab!"

West made a clumsy cut, but Jezal saw it coming and swatted the steel aside, still pressing forward, jabbing for all he was worth. He slashed with the left, and again. West blocked desperately, staggered back against the wall. Jezal had him at last. He cackled with glee as he lunged forward again with the long steel, but his opponent had come suddenly and surprisingly alive. West slipped away, shoved the lunge aside with disappointing firmness. Jezal stumbled forward, off balance, gave a shocked gasp as the point of his sword found a gap between two stones and his steel was wrenched out of his numb hand, lodged there wobbling in the wall.

West darted forward, ducked inside Jezal's remaining blade and slammed into him with his shoulder. "Ooof," said Jezal as he staggered back and crashed to the floor, fumbling his short steel. It skittered across the stones and Lord Marshal Varuz caught it smartly under his foot. The blunted point of West's sword hovered over Jezal's throat.

"Damn it!" he cursed, as the grinning Major offered him his hand.

"Yes," murmured Varuz with a deep sigh, "damn it indeed. An even more detestable performance than yesterday's, if that's possible! You let Major West make a fool of you again!" Jezal slapped West's hand away with a scowl and got to his feet. "He never once lost control of that bout! You allowed yourself to be drawn in, and then disarmed! Disarmed! My grandson would not have made that mistake, and he is eight years old!" Varuz whacked at the floor with his stick. "Explain to me please, Captain Luthar, how you will win a fencing match from a prone position, and without your steels?"

Jezal sulked and rubbed the back of his head.

"No? In future, if you fall off a cliff carrying your steels, I want to see you smashed to bits at the bottom, gripping them tightly in your dead fingers, do you hear me?"

"Yes, Marshal Varuz," mumbled a sullen Jezal, wishing the old bastard would take a tumble off a cliff himself. Or perhaps the Tower of Chains. That would be adequate. Maybe Major West could join him.

"Over-confidence is a curse to the swordsman! You must treat every opponent as though he will be your last. As for your footwork," and Varuz curled his lip with disgust, "fine and fancy coming forward, but put you on the back foot and you quite wither away. The Major only had to tap you and you fell down like a fainting schoolgirl."

West grinned across at him. He was loving this. Absolutely loving it, damn him.

"They say Bremer dan Gorst has a back leg like a pillar of steel. A pillar of steel they say! It would be easier to knock down the House of the Maker than him." The Lord Marshal pointed over at the outline of the huge tower, looming up over the buildings of the courtyard. "The House of the Maker!" he shouted in disgust.

Jezal sniffed and kicked at the floor with his boot. For the hundredth time he entertained the notion of giving it up and never holding a steel again. But what would people say? His father was absurdly proud of him, always boasting about his skill to anyone who would listen. He had his heart set on seeing his son fight in the Square of Marshals before a screaming crowd. If Jezal threw it over now his father would be mortified, and he could say goodbye to his commission, goodbye to his allowance, goodbye to his ambitions. No doubt his brothers would love that.

"Balance is the key," Varuz was spouting. "Your strength rises up through the legs! From now on we will add an hour on the beam to your training. Every day." Jezal winced. "So: a run, exercises with the heavy bar, forms, an hour of sparring, forms again, an hour on the beam." The Lord Marshal nodded with satisfaction. "That will suffice, for now. I will see you at six o'clock tomorrow morning, ice cold sober." Varuz frowned. "Ice. Cold. Sober."

"I can't do this forever, you know," said Jezal as he hobbled stiffly back towards his quarters. "How much of this horrible shit should a man have to take?"

West grinned. "This is nothing. I've never seen the old bastard so soft on anyone. He must really like you. He wasn't half so friendly with me."

Jezal wasn't sure he believed it. "Worse than this?"

"I didn't have the grounding that you've had. He made me hold the heavy bar over my head all afternoon until it fell on me." The Major winced slightly, as though even the memory was painful. "He made me run up and down the Tower of Chains in full armour. He had me sparring four hours a day, every day."

"How did you put up with it?"

"I didn't have a choice. I'm not a nobleman. Fencing was the only way for me to get noticed. But it paid off in the end. How many commoners do you know with a commission in the King's Own?"

Jezal shrugged. "Come to think of it, very few." As a nobleman himself, he didn't think there should be any.

"But you're from a good family, and a Captain already. If you can win the Contest there's no telling how far you could go. Hoff—the Lord Chamberlain, Marovia—the High Justice, Varuz himself for that matter, they were all champions in their day. Champions with the right blood always go on to great things."

Jezal snorted. "Like your friend Sand dan Glokta?"

The name dropped between them like a stone. "Well . . . almost always."

"Major West!" came a rough voice from behind. A thickset sergeant with a scar down his cheek was hurrying over to them.

"Sergeant Forest, how are you?" asked West, clapping the soldier warmly on the back. He had a touch with peasants, but then Jezal had to keep reminding himself that West was little better than a peasant himself. He might be educated, and an officer, and so forth, but he still had more in common with the sergeant than he did with Jezal, once you thought about it.

The sergeant beamed. "Very well, thank you, sir." He nodded respectfully to Jezal. "Morning, Captain."

Jezal favoured him with a terse nod and turned away to look up the avenue. He could think of no possible reason why an officer would want to be familiar with the common soldiers. Furthermore, he was scarred and ugly. Jezal had no use whatever for ugly people.

"What can I do for you?" West was asking.

"Marshal Burr wishes to see you, sir, for an urgent briefing. All senior officers are ordered to attend."

West's face clouded. "I'll be there as soon as I can." The sergeant saluted and strode off.

"What's all that about?" asked Jezal carelessly, watching some clerk chase around after a paper he had dropped.

"Angland. This King of the Northmen, Bethod." West said the name with a scowl, as though it left a bitter taste. "They say he's defeated all his enemies in the North, and now he's spoiling for a fight with The Union."

"Well, if it's a fight he wants," said Jezal airily. Wars were a fine thing, in his opinion, an excellent opportunity for glory and advancement. The paper fluttered past his boot on the light breeze, closely followed by the puffing clerk. Jezal grinned at him as he hurried past, bent almost double in his clumsy efforts to try and grab it.

The Major snatched up the grubby document and handed it over. "Thank you, sir," said the clerk, his sweaty face quite pitiful with gratitude, "thank you so much!"

"Think nothing of it," murmured West, and the clerk gave a sycophantic little bow and hurried away. Jezal was disappointed. He had been rather enjoying the chase. "There could be war, but that's the least of my troubles right now." West breathed a heavy sigh. "My sister is in Adua."

"I didn't know you had a sister."

"Well I do, and she's here."

"So?" Jezal had little enthusiasm for hearing about the Major's sister. West might have pulled himself up, but the rest of his family were distinctly beneath Jezal's notice. He was interested in meeting poor, common girls he could take advantage of, and rich, noble ones he might think about marrying. Anything in between was of no importance.

"Well, my sister can be charming but she is also a little . . . unconventional. She can be something of a handful in the wrong mood. Truth be told, I'd prefer to take care of a pack of Northmen than her."

"Come now, West," said Jezal absently, hardly taking any notice of what he was saying, "I'm sure she can't be that difficult."

The Major brightened. "Well, I'm relieved to hear you say that. She's always been keen to see the Agriont for herself, and I've been saying for years that I'd give her a tour if she ever came here. We'd arranged it for today in fact." Jezal had a sinking feeling. "Now, with this meeting—"

"But I have so little time these days!" whinged Jezal.

"I promise I'll make it up to you. We'll meet you at my quarters in an hour."

"Hold on . . ." But West was already striding away.

Don't let her be too ugly, Jezal was thinking as he slowly approached the door to Major West's quarters and raised his unwilling fist to knock. Just don't let her be too ugly. And not too stupid either. Anything but an afternoon wasted on a stupid girl. His hand was halfway to the door when he became aware of raised voices on the other side. He stood guiltily in the corridor, his ear drawing closer and closer to the wood, hoping to hear something complimentary about himself.

". . . and what about your maid?" came Major West's muffled voice, sounding greatly annoyed.

"I had to leave her at the house, there was a lot to do. Nobody's been there in months." West's sister. Jezal's heart sank. A deep voice, she sounded like a fat one. Jezal couldn't afford to be seen walking about the Agriont with a fat girl on his arm. It could ruin his reputation.

"But you can't just wander about the city on your own!"

"I got here alright, didn't I? You're forgetting who we are, Collem. I can make do without a servant. To most of the people here I'm no better than a servant anyway. Besides, I'll have your friend Captain Luthar to look after me."

"That's even worse, as you damn well know!"

"Well I wasn't to know that you'd be busy. I would've thought you'd make the time to see your own sister." She didn't sound an idiot, which was something, but fat and now peevish too. "Aren't I safe with your friend?"

"He's a good enough sort, but is he safe with you?" Jezal wasn't sure what the Major meant by that little comment. "And walking about the Agriont alone, and with a man you hardly know? Don't play the fool, I know you better than that! What will people think?"

"Shit on what they think." Jezal jerked away from the door. He wasn't used to hearing ladies use that sort of language. Fat, peevish and coarse, damn it. This might be even worse than he'd feared. He looked up the corridor, considering making a run for it, already working out his excuse. Curse his bad luck, though, someone was coming up the stairs now. He couldn't leave without being seen. He would just have to knock and get it over with. He gritted his teeth and pounded resentfully at the door.

The voices stopped suddenly, and Jezal put on an unconvincing friendly grin. Let the torture begin. The door swung open.

For some reason, he had been expecting a kind of shorter, fatter version of Major West, in a dress. He had been greatly mistaken. She was perhaps slightly fuller of figure than was strictly fashionable, since skinny girls were all the rage, but you couldn't call her fat, not fat at all. She had dark hair, dark skin, a little darker than would generally be thought ideal. He knew that a lady should remain out of the sun whenever possible, but looking at her, he really couldn't remember why. Her eyes were very dark, almost black, and blue eyes were turning the heads this season, but hers shone in the dim light of the doorway in a rather bewitching manner.

She smiled at him. A strange sort of smile, higher on one side than the other. It gave him a slightly uneasy feeling, as though she knew something funny that he didn't. Still, excellent teeth, all white and shiny. Jezal's anger was swiftly vanishing. The longer he looked at her the more her looks grew on him, and the emptier his head became of cogent thought.

"Hello," she said.

His mouth opened slightly, as if by force of habit, but nothing came out. His mind was a blank page.

"And you must be Captain Luthar?"

"Er . . ."

"I'm Collem's sister, Ardee," she slapped her forehead, "I'm such an idiot though, Collem will have told you all about me. I know the two of you are great friends."

Jezal glanced awkwardly at the Major, who was frowning back at him and looking somewhat put out. It would hardly do to say he had been entirely unaware of her existence until that morning. He struggled to frame even a mildly amusing reply, but nothing came to mind.

Ardee took hold of him by the elbow and drew him into the room, talking all the while. "I know you're a great fencer, but I've been told your wit is even sharper than your sword. So much so in fact, that you only use your sword upon your friends, as your wit is far too deadly." She looked at him expectantly. Silence.

"Well," he mumbled, "I do fence a bit." Pathetic. Utterly awful.

"Is this the right man, or do I have the gardener here?" She looked him over with a strange expression, hard to read. Perhaps it was the same sort of look Jezal would have while examining a horse he was thinking of buying: cautious, searching, intent, and ever so slightly disdainful. "Even the gardeners have splendid uniforms, it seems."

Jezal was almost sure that had been some kind of insult, but he was too busy trying to think of something witty to pay it too much mind. He knew he would have to speak now or spend the entire day in embarrassed silence, so he opened his mouth and trusted to luck. "I'm sorry if I seem dumbfounded, but Major West is such an unattractive man. How could I have expected so beautiful a sister?"

West snorted with laughter. His sister raised an eyebrow, and counted the points off on her fingers. "Mildly offensive to my brother, which is good. Somewhat amusing, which is also good. Honest, which is refreshing, and wildly complimentary to me, which, of course, is excellent. A little late, but on the whole worth waiting for." She looked Jezal in the eye. "The afternoon might not be a total loss."

Jezal wasn't sure he liked that last comment, and he wasn't sure he liked the way she looked at him, but he was enjoying looking at her, so he was prepared to forgive a lot. The women of his acquaintance rarely said anything clever, especially the fine-looking ones. He supposed they were trained to smile and nod and listen while the men did the talking. On the whole he agreed with that way of doing things, but the cleverness sat well on West's sister, and she had more than caught his curiosity. Fat and peevish were off the menu, of that there could be no doubt. As for coarse, well, handsome people are never coarse, are they? Just . . . unconventional. He was beginning to think that the afternoon, as she had said, might not be a total loss.

West made for the door. "It seems I must leave you two to make fools of one another. Lord Marshal Burr is expecting me. Don't do anything I wouldn't, eh?" The comment seemed to be aimed at Jezal, but West was looking at his sister.

"That would seem to allow virtually everything," she said, catching Jezal's eye. He was amazed to feel himself blushing like a little girl, and he coughed and looked down at his shoes.

West rolled his eyes. "Mercy," he said, as the door clicked shut.

"Would you care for a drink?" Ardee asked, already pouring wine into a glass. Alone with a beautiful young woman. Hardly a new experience, Jezal told himself, and yet he seemed to be lacking his usual confidence.

"Yes, thank you, most kind." Yes, a drink, a drink, just the thing to steady the nerves. She held the glass out to him and poured another for herself. He wondered if a young lady should be drinking at this time of day, but it seemed pointless to say anything. She wasn't his sister, after all.

"Tell me, Captain, how do you know my brother?"

"Well, he's my commanding officer, and we fence together." His brain was beginning to function again. "But then . . . you know that already."

She grinned at him. "Of course, but my governess always maintained that young men should be allowed their share of the conversation."

Jezal gave an ungainly cough as he was swallowing and spilled some wine down his jacket. "Oh dear," he said.

"Here, take this a moment." She gave him her glass and he took it without thinking, but then found himself without a free hand. When she started dabbing at his chest with a white handkerchief he could hardly object, though it did seem rather forward. Being honest, he might have objected if she wasn't so damn fine-looking. He wondered if she realised what an excellent view she was giving him down the front of her dress, but of course not, how could she? She was simply new here, unused to courtly manners, the artless ways of a country girl and so forth . . . nice view though, there was no denying that.

"There, that's better," she said, though the dabbing had made no apparent difference. Not to his uniform anyway. She took the glasses from him, drained her own quickly with a practised flick of her head and shoved them on the table. "Shall we go?"

"Yes . . . of course. Oh," and he offered her his arm.

She led him out into the corridor and down the stairs, chatting freely. It was a flurry of conversational blows and, as Marshal Varuz had pointed out earlier, his defence was weak. He parried desperately as they made their way across the wide Square of Marshals, but he could barely get a word in. It seemed as though it was Ardee who had been living there for years and Jezal who was the bumpkin from the provinces.

"The Halls Martial are behind there?" She nodded over at the looming wall that separated the headquarters of the Union's armies from the rest of the Agriont.

"Indeed they are. That is where the Lord Marshals have their offices, and so forth. And there are barracks there, and armouries, and, er . . ." He trailed off. He could not think of much else to say, but Ardee came to his rescue.

"So my brother must be somewhere in there. He's quite the famous soldier, I suppose. First through the breach at Ulrioch, and so on."

"Well, yes, Major West is very well respected here . . ."

"He can be such a bore, though, can't he? He does so love to be mysterious and troubled." She put on a faint, faraway smile and rubbed her chin thoughtfully, just as her brother might have done. She had captured the man perfectly, and Jezal had to laugh, but he was starting to wonder if she should be walking quite so close beside him, holding his arm in quite so intimate a way. Not that he objected of course. Quite the reverse, but people were looking.

"Ardee—" he said.

"So this must be the Kingsway."

"Er, yes, Ardee—"

She was gazing up at the magnificent statue of Harod the Great, his stern eyes fixed on the middle distance. "Harod the Great?" she asked.

"Er, yes. In the dark ages, before there was a Union, he fought to bring the Three Kingdoms together. He was the first High King." You idiot, thought Jezal, she knows that already, everyone does. "Ardee, I think your brother would not—"

"And this is Bayaz, the First of the Magi?"

"Yes, he was Harod's most trusted adviser. Ardee—"

"Is it true they still keep a vacant seat for him in the Closed Council?"

Jezal was taken aback. "I'd heard that there's an empty chair there, but I didn't know that—"

"They all look so serious, don't they?"

"Er . . . I suppose those were serious times," he said, grinning lamely.

A Knight Herald thundered down the avenue on a huge, well-lathered horse, the sun glinting on the golden wings of his helmet. Secretaries scattered to let him pass, and Jezal tried to guide Ardee gently out of the way. To his great dismay she refused to be moved. The horse flashed past within a few inches of her, close enough for the wind to flick her hair in Jezal's face. She turned to him with a flush of excitement on her cheek, otherwise utterly undaunted by her brush with severe injury.

"A Knight Herald?" she asked, taking Jezal's arm once again and leading him off down the Kingsway.

"Yes," squeaked Jezal, desperately trying to bring his voice under control, "the Knights Herald are entrusted with a grave responsibility. They carry messages from the King to every part of the Union." His heart had stopped hammering. "Even across the Circle Sea to Angland, Dagoska, and Westport. They are entrusted to speak with the King's voice, and so forbidden from speaking except on the King's business."

"Fedor dan Haden was on the boat on our way over, he's a Knight Herald.
We talked for hours." Jezal attempted unsuccessfully to contain his surprise.
"We talked about Adua, about the Union, about his family. Your name was
mentioned, actually." Jezal failed to look nonchalant once again. "In connection with the coming Contest." Ardee leaned even closer to him. "Fedor was
of the opinion that Bremer dan Gorst will cut you to pieces."

Jezal gave a strangled cough, but he rallied well. "Unfortunately, that
opinion seems widely held."

"But not by you, I trust?"

"Er . . ."

She stopped and took him by the hand, staring earnestly into his eyes.
"I'm sure that you'll get the better of him, no matter what they say. My
brother speaks very highly of you, and he's stingy with his praise."

"Er . . ." mumbled Jezal. His fingers were tingling pleasantly. Her eyes
were big and dark, and he found himself greatly at a loss for words. She had
this way of biting on her lower lip that made his thoughts stray. A fine, full
lip. He wouldn't have minded having a little chew on it himself. "Well,
thank you." He gave a gormless grin.

"So this is the park," said Ardee, turning away from him to admire the
greenery. "It's even more beautiful than I'd imagined."

"Erm . . . yes."

"How wonderful, to be at the heart of things. I've spent so much of my
life on the edge. There must be many important decisions made here, many
important people." Ardee allowed her hand to trail through the fronds of a
willow tree by the road. "Collem's worried there might be war in the North.
He was worried for my safety. I think that's why he wanted me to come here.
I think he worries too much. What do you think, Captain Luthar?"

He had been in blissful ignorance of the political situation until a couple
of hours before, but that would never do as a reply. "Well," he said, straining
to remember the name, and then with relief, "this Bethod could do with a
rap on the knuckles."

"They say he has twenty thousand Northmen under his banner." She
leaned towards him. "Barbarians," she murmured. "Savages," she whispered.
"I heard he skins his captives alive."

Jezal thought this was hardly suitable conversation for a young lady. "Ardee . . ." he began.

"But I'm sure with men like you and my brother to protect us, we womenfolk have nothing to worry about." And she turned and made off up the path. Jezal had to hurry once again to catch up.

"And is that the House of the Maker?" Ardee nodded towards the grim outline of the huge tower.

"Why, yes it is."

"Does no one go inside?"

"No one. Not in my lifetime anyway. The bridge is kept behind lock and key." He frowned up at the tower. Seemed strange now, that he never thought about it. Living in the Agriont, it was always there. You just got used to it somehow. "The place is sealed, I believe."

"Sealed?" Ardee moved very close to him. Jezal glanced around nervously but nobody was looking. "Isn't it strange that nobody goes in there? Isn't it a mystery?" He could almost feel her breath on his neck, "I mean to say, why not just break the door down?"

Jezal was finding it horribly difficult to concentrate with her so close. He wondered for a moment, both frightening and exciting, whether she might be flirting with him? No, no, of course not! Just not used to the city was all. The artless ways of a country girl . . . but then she was *very* close. If only she were a little less attractive or a little less confident. If only she were a little less . . . West's sister.

He coughed and looked off down the path, hoping vainly for a distraction. There were a few people moving along it, but no one that he recognised, unless . . . Ardee's spell was suddenly broken, and Jezal felt his skin go cold. A hunched figure, overdressed on this sunny day, was limping toward them, leaning heavily on a cane. He was bent over and wincing with every step, the faster-moving travellers giving him a wide berth. Jezal tried to steer Ardee away before he saw them, but she resisted gracefully and made a direct line for the shambling Inquisitor.

His head snapped up as they approached and his eyes glinted with recognition. Jezal's heart sank. There was no avoiding him now.

"Why, Captain Luthar," said Glokta warmly, shuffling a little too close and shaking his hand, "what a pleasure! I'm surprised that Varuz has let you go so early in the day. He must be mellowing in his old age."

"The Lord Marshal is still most demanding," snapped Jezal.

"I hope my Practicals didn't inconvenience you the other night." The Inquisitor shook his head sadly. "They have no manners. No manners at all. But they are the very best at what they do! I swear, the King doesn't have two more valuable servants."

"I suppose we all serve the King in our own way." There was a little more hostility in Jezal's voice than he had intended.

If Glokta was offended he didn't show it. "Quite so. I don't believe I know your friend."

"No. This is—"

"Actually, we've met," said Ardee, much to Jezal's surprise, giving her hand to the Inquisitor. "Ardee West."

Glokta's eyebrows rose. "No!" He bent down stiffly to kiss the back of her hand. Jezal saw his mouth twist as he straightened up, but the toothless grin soon returned. "Collem West's sister! But you are so much changed."

"For the better, I hope," she laughed. Jezal felt horribly uncomfortable.

"Why—yes indeed," said Glokta.

"And you are changed also, Sand." Ardee looked suddenly very sad. "We were all so worried in my family. We hoped and hoped for your safe return." Jezal saw a spasm run over Glokta's face. "Then when we heard you were hurt . . . how are you?"

The Inquisitor glanced at Jezal, his eyes cold as a slow death. Jezal stared down at his boots, a lump of fear in his throat. He had no need to be scared of this cripple, did he? But somehow he wished he was still at fencing practice. Glokta stared at Ardee, his left eye twitching slightly, and she looked back at him undaunted, her eyes full of quiet concern.

"I am well. As well as can be expected." His expression had turned very strange. Jezal felt more uncomfortable than ever. "Thank you for asking. Truly. Nobody ever does."

There was an awkward silence. The Inquisitor stretched his neck sideways and there was a loud click. "Ah!" he said, "that's got it. It's been a pleasure to see you again, both of you, but duty calls." He treated them to another revolting smile then hobbled off, his left foot scraping in the gravel.

Ardee frowned at his twisted back as he limped slowly away. "It's so sad," she said under her breath.

"What?" mumbled Jezal. He was thinking about that big white bastard in the street, those narrow pink eyes. The prisoner with the bag on his head. We all serve the King in our own way. Quite so. He gave an involuntary shiver.

"He and my brother used to be quite close. He came to stay with us one summer. My family were so proud to have him it was embarrassing. He used to fence with my brother every day, and he always won. The way he moved, it was something to see. Sand dan Glokta. He was the brightest star in the sky." She flashed her knowing half-smile again. "And now I hear you are."

"Er . . ." said Jezal, not sure whether she was praising him or poking fun. He could not escape the feeling that he had been out-fenced twice that day, once by each sibling.

He rather fancied that the sister had given him the worse beating.

THE MORNING RITUAL

It was a bright summer's day, and the park was filled to capacity with colourful revellers. Colonel Glokta strode manfully toward some meeting of great importance, people bowing and scraping respectfully away to give him room. He ignored most, favoured the more important ones with his brilliant smile. The lucky few beamed back at him, delighted to be noticed.

"I suppose we all serve the King in our own way," whined Captain Luthar, reaching for his steel, but Glokta was far too quick for him. His blade flashed with lightning speed, catching the sneering idiot through the neck.

Blood splattered across Ardee West's face. She clapped her hands in delight, looking at Glokta with shining eyes.

Luthar seemed surprised to be killed. "Hah. Quite so," said Glokta with a smile. The Captain pitched over onto his face, blood pouring from his punctured throat. The crowd roared their appreciation and Glokta indulged them with a deep, graceful bow. The cheering was redoubled.

"Oh, Colonel, you shouldn't," murmured Ardee as Glokta licked the blood from her cheek.

"Shouldn't what?" he growled, tipping her back in his arms and kissing her fiercely. The crowd were in a frenzy. She gasped as he broke away, looking up at him adoringly with those big dark eyes of hers, lips slightly parted.

"The Arth Ector wanth you," she said with a comely smile.

"What?" The crowd had fallen silent, damn them, and his left side was turning numb.

Ardee touched him tenderly on the cheek. "The Arth Ector!" she shouted.

There was a heavy knock at the door. Glokta's eyes flicked open.

Where am I? Who am I?

Oh no.

Oh yes. He realised straight away he had been sleeping badly, his body was twisted round under the blankets, his face pushed into the pillow. His whole left side was dead.

The beating on the door came heavier than before. "The Arth Ector!" came Frost's tongueless bellow from the other side.

Pain shot through Glokta's neck as he tried to raise his head from the pillow. *Ah, there's nothing like the first spasm of the day to get the mind working.* "Alright!" he croaked, "give me a minute, damn it!"

The albino's heavy footsteps thudded away down the corridor. Glokta lay still for a moment, then cautiously moved his right arm, ever so slowly, breath rasping with the effort, and tried to twist himself onto his back. He clenched his fist as the needling started in his left leg. *If only the damn thing would stay numb.* But the pain was coming on fast now. He was also becoming aware of an unpleasant smell. *Damn it. I've shit myself again.*

"Barnam!" howled Glokta, then waited, panting, left side throbbing with a vengeance. *Where is the old idiot?* "Barnam!" he screamed at the top of his lungs.

"Are you alright, sir?" came the servant's voice from beyond the door.

Alright? Alright, you old fool? Just when do you think I was last alright? "No, damn it! I've soiled the bed!"

"I've boiled water for a bath, sir. Can you get up?"

Once before Frost had had to break the door down. *Maybe I should let it stand open all night, but then how could I sleep?* "I think I can manage," Glokta hissed, tongue pressed into his empty gums, arms trembling as he hauled himself out of the bed and onto the chair beside it.

His grotesque, toeless left leg twitched to itself, still beyond his control. He glared down at it with a burning hatred. *Fucking horrible thing. Revolting, useless lump of flesh. Why didn't they just cut you off? Why don't I still?* But he knew why not. With his leg still on he could at least pretend to be half a man. He punched his withered thigh, then immediately regretted it. *Stupid, stupid.* The pain crept up his back, a little more intense than before, and growing with every second. *Come now, come now, let's not fight.* He started to rub gently at the wasted flesh. *We are stuck with each other, so why torment me?*

"Can you get to the door, sir?" Glokta wrinkled his nose at the smell then took hold of his cane and slowly, agonisingly, pushed himself to his feet. He hobbled across the room, almost slipping halfway there but righting himself with a searing twinge. He turned the key in the lock, leaning against the wall for balance, and hauled the door open.

Barnam was standing on the other side, his arms outstretched, ready to catch him. *The ignominy of it. To think that I, Sand dan Glokta, the greatest swordsman the Union has ever seen, must be carried to my bath by an old man so that I can wash my own shit off. They must be laughing loud now, all those fools I beat, if they still remember me. I'd be laughing too, if it didn't hurt so much.* But he let the weight off his left leg and put his arm round Barnam's shoulders without complaint. *What's the use after all? Might as well make it easy for myself. As easy as it can be.*

Glokta took a deep breath. "Go gently, the leg hasn't woken up yet." They hopped and stumbled down the corridor, slightly too narrow for both of them together. The bathroom seemed a mile away. *Or more. I'd rather walk a hundred miles as I used to be, than to the bathroom as I am. But that's my bad luck isn't it? You can't go back. Not ever.*

The steam felt deliciously warm on Glokta's clammy skin. With Barnam holding him under the arms he slowly lifted his right leg and put it gingerly into the water. *Damn it, that's hot.* The old servant helped him get the other leg in, then, taking him under the armpits, lowered him like a child, until he was immersed up to his neck.

"Ahhh." Glokta cracked a toothless smile. "Hot as the Maker's forge, Barnam, just the way I like it." The heat was getting into the leg now, and the pain was subsiding. *Not gone. Never gone. But better. A lot better.* Glokta began to feel almost as if he could face another day. *You have to learn to love the small things in life, like a hot bath. You have to love the small things, when you've nothing else.*

Practical Frost was waiting for him downstairs in the tiny dining room, his bulk wedged into a low chair against the wall. Glokta sagged into the other chair and caught a whiff from the steaming porridge bowl, wooden spoon sticking up at an angle without even touching the side. His stomach rumbled and his mouth began watering fiercely. *All the symptoms, in fact, of extreme nausea.*

"Hurray!" shouted Glokta. "Porridge again!" He looked over at the motionless Practical. "Porridge and honey, better than money, everything's funny, with porridge and honey!"

The pink eyes did not blink.

"It's a rhyme for children. My mother used to sing it to me. Never actually got me to eat this slop though. But now," and he dug the spoon in, "I can't get enough of it."

Frost stared back at him.

"Healthy," said Glokta, forcing down a mouthful of sweet mush and spooning up another, "delicious," choking down some more, "and here's the real clincher," he gagged slightly on the next swallow, "no chewing required." He shoved the mostly full bowl away and tossed the spoon after it. "Mmmmm," he hummed. "A good breakfast makes for a good day, don't you find?"

It was like staring at a whitewashed wall, but without all the emotion.

"So the Arch Lector wants me again, does he?"

The albino nodded.

"And what might our illustrious leader desire with the likes of us, do you think?"

A shrug.

"Hmmm." Glokta licked bits of porridge out of his empty gums. "Does he seem in a good mood, do you know?"

Another shrug.

"Come, come, Practical Frost, don't tell me everything at once, I can't take it in."

Silence. Barnam entered the room and cleared away the bowl. "Do you want anything else, sir?"

"Absolutely. A big half-raw slab of meat and a nice crunchy apple." He looked over at Practical Frost. "I used to love apples when I was a child."

How many times have I made that joke? Frost looked back impassively, there was no laughter there. Glokta turned to Barnam, and the old man gave a tired smile.

"Oh well," sighed Glokta. "A man has to have hope doesn't he?"

"Of course sir," muttered the servant, heading for the door.

Does he?

The Arch Lector's office was on the top floor of the House of Questions, and it was a long way up. Worse still, the corridors were busy with people. Practicals, clerks, Inquisitors, crawling like ants through a crumbling dung-hill. Whenever he felt their eyes on him Glokta would limp along, smiling, head held high. Whenever he felt himself alone he would pause and gasp, sweat and curse, and rub and slap the tenuous life back into his leg.

Why does it have to be so high? he asked himself as he shuffled up the dim halls and winding stairs of the labyrinthine building. By the time he reached the ante-chamber he was exhausted and blowing hard, left hand sore on the handle of his cane.

The Arch Lector's secretary examined him suspiciously from behind a big dark desk that took up half the room. There were some chairs placed opposite for people to get nervous waiting in, and two huge Practicals flanked the great double doors to the office, so still and grim as to appear a part of the furniture.

"Do you have an appointment?" demanded the secretary in a shrill voice. *You know who I am, you self-important little shit.*

"Of course," snapped Glokta, "do you think I limped all the way up here to admire your desk?"

The secretary looked down his nose at him. He was a pale, handsome young man with a mop of yellow hair. *The puffed up fifth son of some minor nobleman with over-active loins, and he thinks he can patronise me?* "And your name is?" he asked with a sneer.

Glokta's patience was worn out by the climb. He smashed his cane down on the top of the desk and the secretary near jumped out of his chair. "What are you? A fucking idiot? How many crippled Inquisitors do you have here?"

"Er . . ." said the secretary, mouth working nervously.

"Er? Er? Is that a number? Speak up!"

"Well I—"

"I'm Glokta, you dolt! Inquisitor Glokta!"

"Yes, sir, I—"

"Get your fat arse out of that chair, fool! Don't keep me waiting!" The secretary sprang up, hurried to the doors, pushed one open and stood aside respectfully. "That's better," growled Glokta, shuffling after him. He looked up at the Practicals as he hobbled past. He was almost sure one of them had a slight smile on his face.

The room had hardly changed since he was last there, six years before. It was a cavernous, round space, domed ceiling carved with gargoyle faces, its one enormous window offering a spectacular view over the spires of the University, a great section of the outer wall of the Agriont, and the looming outline of the House of the Maker beyond.

The chamber was mostly lined with shelves and cabinets, stacked high with neatly ordered files and papers. A few dark portraits peered down from the sparse white walls, including a huge one of the current King of the Union as a young man, looking wise and stern. *No doubt painted before he became a senile joke. These days there's usually a bit less authority and a bit more stray drool about him.* There was a heavy round table in the centre of the room, its surface painted with a map of the Union in exquisite detail. Every city in which there was a department of the Inquisition was marked with a precious stone, and a tiny silver replica of Adua rose out of the table at its hub.

The Arch Lector was sitting in an ancient high chair at this table, deep in conversation with another man: a gaunt, balding, sour-faced old fellow in dark robes. Sult beamed up as Glokta shuffled towards them, the other man's expression hardly changed.

"Why, Inquisitor Glokta, delighted you could join us. Do you know Surveyor General Halleck?"

"I have not had the pleasure," said Glokta. *Not that it looks like much of a pleasure, though.* The old bureaucrat stood and shook Glokta's hand without enthusiasm.

"And this is one of my Inquisitors, Sand dan Glokta."

"Yes indeed," murmured Halleck. "You used to be in the army, I believe. I saw you fence once."

Glokta tapped his leg with his cane. "That can't have been any time recently."

"No." There was a silence.

"The Surveyor General is likely soon to receive a most significant promotion," said Sult. "To a chair on the Closed Council itself." *The Closed Council? Indeed? A most significant promotion.*

Halleck seemed less than delighted, however. "I will consider it done when it is his Majesty's pleasure to invite me," he snapped, "and not before."

Sult floated smoothly over this rocky ground. "I am sure the Council feels that you are the only candidate worth recommending, now that Sepp dan Teufel is no longer being considered." *Our old friend Teufel? No longer considered for what?*

Halleck frowned and shook his head. "Teufel. I worked with the man for ten years. I never liked him," *or anyone else, by the look of you,* "but I would never have thought him a traitor."

Sult shook his head sadly. "We all feel it keenly, but here is his confession in black and white." He held up the folded paper with a doleful frown. "I fear the roots of corruption can run very deep. Who would know that better than I, whose sorry task it is to weed the garden?"

"Indeed, indeed," muttered Halleck, nodding grimly. "You deserve all of our thanks for that. You also, Inquisitor."

"Oh no, not I," said Glokta humbly. The three men looked at each other in a sham of mutual respect.

Halleck pushed back his chair. "Well, taxes do not collect themselves. I must return to my work."

"Enjoy your last few days in the job," said Sult. "I give you my word that the King will send for you soon!"

Halleck allowed himself the thinnest of smiles, then nodded stiffly to them and stalked away. The secretary ushered him out and pulled the heavy door shut. There was silence. *But I'm damned if I'll be the one to break it.*

"I expect you're wondering what this was all about, eh, Glokta?"

"The thought had crossed my mind, your Eminence."

"I bet it had." Sult swept from his chair and strode across to the window, his white-gloved hands clasped behind his back. "The world changes, Glokta, the world changes. The old order crumbles. Loyalty, duty, pride, honour. Notions that have fallen far from fashion. What has replaced them?" He glanced over his shoulder for a moment, and his lip curled. "Greed. Merchants have become the new power in the land. Bankers, shopkeepers, salesmen. Little men, with little minds and little ambitions. Men whose only loyalty is to themselves, whose only duty is to their own purses, whose only pride is in swindling their betters, whose only honour is weighed out in silver coin." *No need to ask where you stand on the merchant class.*

Sult scowled out at the view, then turned back into the room. "Now it seems anyone's son can get an education, and a business, and become rich. The merchant guilds: the Mercers, the Spicers and their like, grow steadily in wealth and influence. Jumped-up, posturing commoners dictating to their natural betters. Their fat and greedy fingers, fumbling at the strings of power. It is almost too much to stand." He gave a shudder as he paced across the floor.

"I will speak honestly with you, Inquisitor." The Arch Lector waved his graceful hand as though his honesty were a priceless gift. "The Union has never seemed more powerful, has never controlled more land, but beneath the façade we are weak. It is hardly a secret that the King has become entirely unable to make his own decisions. Crown Prince Ladisla is a fop, surrounded by flatterers and fools, caring for nothing but gambling and clothes. Prince Raynault is far better fitted to rule, but he is the younger brother. The Closed Council, whose task it should be to steer this leaking vessel, is packed with frauds and schemers. Some may be loyal, some are definitely not, each intent on pulling the King his own way." *How frustrating, when I suppose they should all be pulling him in yours?*

"Meanwhile, the Union is beset with enemies, dangers outside our borders, and dangers within. Gurkhul has a new and vigorous Emperor, fitting his country for another war. The Northmen are up in arms as well, skulking on the borders of Angland. In the Open Council the noblemen clamour for ancient rights, while in the villages the peasants clamour for new ones." He gave a deep sigh. "Yes, the old order crumbles, and no one has the heart or the stomach to support it."

Sult paused, staring up at one of the portraits: a hefty, bald man dressed all in white. Glokta recognised him well enough. *Zoller, the greatest of all Arch Lectors. Tireless champion of the Inquisition, hero to the torturer, scourge of the disloyal.* He glared down balefully from the wall, as though even beyond death he could burn traitors with a glance.

"Zoller," growled Sult. "Things were different in his day, I can tell you. No whinging peasants then, no swindling merchants, no sulking noblemen. If men forgot their place they were reminded with hot iron, and any carping judge who dared to whine about it was never heard from again. The Inquisition was a noble institution, filled with the best and the brightest. To serve their King and to root out disloyalty were their only desires, and their only rewards." *Oh, things were grand in the old days.*

The Arch Lector slid back into his seat and leaned forward across the table. "Now we have become a place where third sons of impoverished noblemen can line their pockets with bribes, or where near-criminal scum can indulge a passion for torture. Our influence with the King has been steadily eroded, our budgets have been steadily cut. Once we were feared and respected, Glokta, but now . . ." *We're a miserable sham.* Sult frowned, "Well, less so. Intrigues and treasons abound, and I fear that the Inquisition is no longer equal to its task. Too many of the Superiors can no longer be trusted. They are no longer concerned with the interests of the King, or of the state, or of anybody's interests beyond their own." *The Superiors? Not to be trusted? I swoon with the shock.* Sult's frown grew still deeper. "And now Feekt is dead."

Glokta looked up. *Now that is news.* "The Lord Chancellor?"

"It will become public knowledge tomorrow morning. He died suddenly a few nights ago, while you were busy with your friend Rews. There are still some questions surrounding his death, but the man was nearly ninety. The surprise is that he lasted this long. The golden Chancellor they called him, the greatest politician of his day. Even now they are setting his likeness in stone, for a statue on the Kingsway." Sult snorted to himself. "The greatest gift that any of us can hope for."

The Arch Lector's eyes narrowed to blue slits. "If you have any childish notions that the Union is controlled by its King, or by those prating blue-blood fools on the Open Council, you can let them wilt now. The Closed Council is where the power lies. More than ever since the King's illness. Twelve men, in twelve big, uncomfortable chairs, myself among them. Twelve men with very different ideas, and for twenty years, war and peace, Feekt held us in balance. He played off the Inquisition against the judges, the bankers against the military. He was the axle on which the Kingdom turned, the foundation on which it rested, and his death has left a hole. All kinds of gaping holes, and people will be rushing to fill them. I have a feeling that whining ass Marovia, that bleeding heart of a High Justice, that self-appointed champion of the common man, will be first in the queue. It is a fluid, and a dangerous situation." The Arch Lector planted his fists firmly on the table before him. "We must ensure that the wrong people do not take advantage of it."

Glokta nodded. *I think I take your meaning, Arch Lector. We must ensure that it is we who take advantage, and no one else.*

"It need hardly be said that the post of Lord Chancellor is one of the most powerful in the realm. The gathering of taxes, the treasury, the King's mints, all come under his auspices. Money, Glokta, money. And money is power, I need hardly tell you. A new Chancellor will be appointed tomorrow. The foremost candidate was our erstwhile Master of the Mints, Sepp dan Teufel." *I see. Something tells me he will no longer be under consideration.*

Sult's lip curled. "Teufel was closely linked with the merchant guilds, and the Mercers in particular." His sneer became a scowl. "In addition to which he was an associate of High Justice Marovia. So, you see, he would hardly have made a suitable Lord Chancellor." *No indeed. Hardly suitable.* "Surveyor General Halleck is a far better choice, in my opinion."

Glokta looked towards the door. "Him? Lord Chancellor?"

Sult got up smiling and moved over to a cabinet against the wall. "There really is no one else. Everyone hates him, and he hates everyone, except me. Furthermore, he is a hard-nosed conservative, who despises the merchant class and everything they stand for." He opened the cabinet and took out two glasses and an ornate decanter. "If not exactly a friendly face on the Council, he will at least be a sympathetic one, and damned hostile toward everyone else. I can hardly think of a more suitable candidate."

Glokta nodded. "He seems honest." *But not so honest that I'd trust him to put me in the bath. Would you, your Eminence?*

"Yes," said Sult, "he will be very valuable to us." He poured out two glasses of rich red wine. "And just as a bonus, I was able to arrange for a sympathetic new Master of the Mints as well. I hear that the Mercers are absolutely biting their tongues off with fury. Marovia's none too happy either, the bastard." Sult chuckled to himself. "All good news, and we have you to thank." He held out one of the glasses.

Poison? A slow death twitching and puking on the Arch Lector's lovely mosaic floor? Or just pitching onto my face on his table? But there was really no option but to grasp the glass and take a hearty swig. The wine was unfamiliar but delicious. *Probably from somewhere very beautiful and far away. At least if I die up here I won't have to make it back down all those steps.* But the Arch Lector was drinking too, all smiles and good grace. *So I suppose I will last out the afternoon, after all.*

"Yes, we have made a good first step. These are dangerous times alright, and yet danger and opportunity often walk hand in hand." Glokta felt a strange sensation creeping up his back. *Is that fear, or ambition, or both?* "I need someone to help me put matters in order. Someone who does not fear the Superiors, or the merchants, or even the Closed Council. Someone who can be relied upon to act with subtlety, and discretion, and ruthlessness. Someone whose loyalty to the Union is beyond question, but who has no friends within the government." *Someone who's hated by everyone? Someone to take the fall if things turn sour? Someone who will have few mourners at their funeral?*

"I have need of an Inquisitor Exempt, Glokta. Someone to operate beyond the Superiors's control, but with my full authority. Someone answerable only to me." The Arch Lector raised an eyebrow, as though the thought had only just come to him. "It strikes me that you are exceptionally well suited to this task. What do you think?"

I think the holder of such a post would have a great many enemies and only one friend. Glokta peered up at the Arch Lector. *And that friend might not be so very reliable. I think the holder of such a post might not last long.* "Could I have some time to consider it?"

"No."

Danger and opportunity often walk hand in hand . . . "Then I accept."

"Excellent. I do believe this is the start of a long and productive relationship." Sult smiled at him over the rim of his glass. "You know, Glokta, of all the merchants grubbing away out there, it is the Mercers I find the most unpalatable. It was largely through their influence that Westport entered the Union, and it was because of Westport's money that we won the Gurkish war. The King rewarded them, of course, with priceless trading rights, but ever since then their arrogance has been insufferable. Anyone would have thought they fought the battles themselves, for the airs they have put on, and the liberties they have taken. The honourable Guild of Mercers," he sneered. "It occurs to me, now that your friend Rews has given us the means to hook them in so deeply, it would be a shame to let them wriggle free."

Glokta was much surprised, though he thought he hid it well. *To go further? Why? The Mercers wriggle free and they keep on paying, and that keeps all kinds of people happy. As things are, they're scared and soft—wondering who Rews named, who might be next in the chair. If we go further they may be hurt, or finished entirely. Then they'll stop paying, and a lot of people will be unhappy. Some of them in this very building.* "I can easily continue my investigations, your Eminence, if you would like me to." Glokta took another sip. It really was an excellent wine.

"We must be cautious. Cautious and very thorough. The Mercers's money flows like milk. They have many friends, even amongst the highest circles of the nobility. Brock, Heugen, Isher, and plenty more besides. Some of the very greatest men in the land. They've all been known to suck at that tit, one time or another, and babies will cry when their milk is snatched away." A cruel grin flickered across Sult's face. "But still, if children are to learn discipline, they must sometimes be made to weep . . . who did that worm Rews name in his confession?"

Glokta leaned forward painfully and slid Rews' paper of confession toward him, unfolded it and scanned the list of names from bottom to top.

"Sepp dan Teufel, we all know."

"Oh, we know and love him, Inquisitor," said Sult, beaming down, "but I feel we may safely cross him off the list. Who else?"

"Well, let's see," Glokta took a leisurely look back at the paper. "There's Harod Polst, a Mercer." *A nobody.*

Sult waved his hand impatiently. "He's nobody."

"Solimo Scandi, a Mercer from Westport." *Also nobody.*

"No, no, Glokta, we can do better than Solimo what's-his-name can't we? These little Mercers are of no real interest. Pull up the root, and the leaves die by themselves."

"Quite so, Arch Lector. We have Villem dan Robb, minor nobility, holds a junior customs post." Sult looked thoughtful, shook his head. "Then there's—"

"Wait! Villem dan Robb . . ." The Arch Lector snapped his fingers, "His brother Kiral is one of the Queen's gentlemen. He snubbed me at a social gathering." Sult smiled. "Yes, Villem dan Robb, bring him in."

And so we go deeper. "I serve and obey, your Eminence. Is there anyone's name in particular that need be mentioned?" Glokta set down his empty glass.

"No." The Arch Lector turned away and waved his hand again. "Any of 'em, all of 'em. I don't care."

FIRST OF THE MAGI

The lake stretched away, fringed by steep rocks and dripping greenery, surface pricked by the rain, flat and grey as far as the eye could see. Logen's eye couldn't see too far in this weather, it had to be said. The opposite shore could have been a hundred strides away, but the calm waters looked deep. Very deep.

Logen had long ago given up any attempt at staying dry, and the water ran through his hair and down his face, dripped from his nose, his fingers, his chin. Being wet, tired, and hungry had become a part of life. It often had been, come to think on it. He closed his eyes and felt the rain patter against his skin, heard the water lapping on the shingle. He knelt by the lake, pulled the stopper from his flask and pushed it under the surface, watched the bubbles break as it filled up.

Malacus Quai stumbled out of the bushes, breathing fast and shallow. He sank down to his knees, crawled against the roots of a tree, coughed out phlegm onto the pebbles. His coughing sounded bad now. It came right up from his guts and made his whole rib cage rattle. He was even paler than he had been when they first met, and a lot thinner. Logen was somewhat thinner too. These were lean times, all in all. He walked over to the haggard apprentice and squatted down.

"Just give me a moment." Quai closed his sunken eyes and tipped his head back. "Just a moment." His mouth hung open, the tendons in his scrawny neck standing out. He looked like a corpse already.

"Don't rest too long. You might never get up."

Logen held out the flask. Quai didn't even lift his arm to take it, so Logen put it against his lips and tipped it up a little. He took a wincing swallow, coughed, then his head dropped back against the tree like a stone.

"Do you know where we are?" asked Logen.

The apprentice blinked out at the water as though he'd only just noticed it. "This must be the north end of the lake . . . there should be a track." His voice had sunk to a whisper. "At the southern end there's a road with two stones." He gave a sudden violent cough, swallowed with difficulty. "Follow the road over the bridge and you're there," he croaked.

Logen looked off along the beach at the dripping trees. "How far is it?" No answer. He took hold of the sick man's bony shoulder and shook it. Quai's eyelids flickered open, he stared up blearily, trying to focus. "How far?"

"Forty miles."

Logen sucked his teeth. Quai wouldn't be walking forty miles. He'd be lucky to make forty strides on his own. He knew it well enough, you could see it in his eyes. He'd be dead soon, Logen reckoned, a few days at the most. He'd seen stronger men die of a fever.

Forty miles. Logen thought about it carefully, rubbing his chin with his thumb. Forty miles.

"Shit," he whispered.

He dragged the pack over and pulled it open. They had some food left, but not much. A few shreds of tough dried meat, a heel of mouldy black bread. He looked out over the lake, so peaceful. They wouldn't be running out of drinking water any time soon at least. He pulled his heavy cookpot out of his pack and set it down on the shingle. They'd been together a long time, but there was nothing left to cook. You can't become attached to things, not out here in the wild. He tossed the rope away into the bushes, then threw the lightened pack over his shoulder.

Quai's eyes had closed again, and he was scarcely breathing. Logen still remembered the first time he had to leave someone behind, remembered it like it was yesterday. Strange how the boy's name had gone but the face was with him still.

The Shanka had taken a piece out of his thigh. A big piece. He'd moaned all the way, he couldn't walk. The wound was going bad, he was dying anyway. They had to leave him. No one had blamed Logen for it. The boy had been too young, he should never have gone. Bad luck was all, could happen to anyone. He'd cried after them as they made their way down the hillside in a grim, silent group, heads down. Logen seemed to hear the cries even when they'd left him far behind. He could still hear them.

In the wars it had been different. Men dropped from the columns all the time on the long marches, in the cold months. First they fell to the back, then they fell behind, then they fell over. The cold, the sick, the wounded. Logen shivered and hunched his shoulders. At first he'd tried to help them. Then he became grateful he wasn't one of them. Then he stepped over the corpses and hardly noticed them. You learn to tell when someone isn't getting up again. He looked at Malacus Quai. One more death in the wild was nothing to remark upon. You have to be realistic, after all.

The apprentice started from his fitful sleep and tried to push himself up. His hands were shaking bad. He looked up at Logen, eyes glittering bright. "I can't get up," he croaked.

"I know. I'm surprised you made it this far." It didn't matter so much now. Logen knew the way. If he could find that track he might make twenty miles a day.

"If you leave me some of the food . . . perhaps . . . after you get to the library . . . someone . . ."

"No," said Logen, setting his jaw. "I need the food."

Quai made a strange sound, somewhere between a cough and a sob.

Logen leaned down and set his right shoulder in Quai's stomach, pushed his arm under his back. "I can't carry you forty miles without it," and he straightened up, hauling the apprentice over his shoulder. He set off down the shore, holding Quai in place by his jacket, his boots crunching into the wet shingle. The apprentice didn't even move, just hung there like a sack of wet rags, his limp arms knocking against the backs of Logen's legs.

When he'd made it thirty strides or so Logen turned around and looked back. The pot was sitting forlorn by the lake, already filling up with rain-water. They'd been through a lot together, him and that pot.

"Fare you well, old friend."

The pot did not reply.

Logen set his shivering burden gently down at the side of the road and stretched his aching back, scratched at the dirty bandage on his arm, took a drink of water from his flask. Water was the only thing to have passed his sore lips that day, and the hunger was gnawing at his guts. At least it had stopped raining. You have to learn to love the small things in life, like dry boots. You have to love the small things, when you've nothing else.

Logen spat in the dirt and rubbed the life back into his fingers. There was no missing the place, that was sure. The two stones towered over the road, ancient and pitted, patched with green moss at the base and grey lichen higher up. They were covered in faded carvings, lines of letters in a script Logen couldn't understand, didn't even recognise. There was a forbidding feel about them though, a sense more of warning than welcome.

"The First Law . . ."

"What?" said Logen, surprised. Quai had been in an unpleasant place between sleep and waking ever since they left the pot behind two days before. The pot could have made more meaningful sounds in that time. That morning Logen had woken to find him scarcely breathing. He'd been sure that he was dead, to begin with, but the man was still clinging weakly to life. He didn't give up easy, you had to give him that.

Logen knelt down and shoved the wet hair out of Quai's face. The apprentice suddenly grabbed his wrist and started forward.

"It's forbidden," he whispered, staring at Logen with wide eyes, "to touch the Other Side!"

"Eh?"

"To speak with devils," he croaked, grabbing hold of Logen's battered coat. "The creatures of the world below are made of lies! You mustn't do it!"

"I won't," muttered Logen, wondering if he'd ever know what the apprentice was talking about. "I won't. For what that's worth."

It wasn't worth much. Quai had already dropped back into his twitching half-sleep. Logen chewed at his lip. He hoped the apprentice would wake again, but he didn't think it likely. Still, perhaps this Bayaz would be able to do something, he was the First of the Magi after all, great in high wisdom and so on. So Logen hefted Quai up onto his shoulder again and trudged between the ancient stones.

The road climbed steep into the rocks above the lake, here built up, there cut deep into the stony ground. It was worn and pitted with age, pocked with weeds. It switched back on itself again and again, and soon Logen was panting and sweating, his legs burning with the effort. His pace began to slow.

The fact was, he was getting tired. Not just tired from the climb, or from the back-breaking slog he'd walked that day with a half-dead apprentice over his shoulder, or from the slog the day before, or even from the fight in the woods. He was tired of everything. Of the Shanka, of the wars, of his whole life.

"I can't walk for ever, Malacus, I can't fight for ever. How much of this horrible shit should a man have to take? I need to sit down a minute. In a proper fucking chair! Is that too much to ask? Is it?" In this frame of mind, cursing and grumbling at every step, and with Quai's head knocking against his arse, Logen came to the bridge.

It was as ancient as the road, coated with creepers, simple and slender, arching maybe twenty strides across a dizzying gorge. Far below a river surged over jagged rocks, filling the air with noise and shining spray. On the far side a high wall had been built between towering faces of mossy stone, made with such care it was difficult to say where the natural cliff ended and the man-made one began. A single ancient door was set into it, faced with beaten copper, turned streaky green by the wet and the years.

As Logen picked his way carefully across the slippery stone he found himself wondering, through force of habit, how you could storm this place. You couldn't. Not with a thousand picked men. There was only a narrow shelf of rock before the door, no room to set a ladder or swing a ram. The wall was ten strides high at least, and the gate had a dreadful solid look. And if the defenders were to bring down the bridge . . . Logen peered over the edge, and swallowed. It was a long way down.

He took a deep breath and thumped on the damp green copper with his fist. Four big, booming knocks. He'd beat on the gates of Carleon like that, after the battle, and its people had rushed to surrender. No one rushed to do anything now.

He waited. He knocked again. He waited. He became wetter and wetter in the mist from the river. He ground his teeth. He raised his arm to knock again. A narrow hatch snapped open, and a pair of rheumy eyes stared at him coldly from between thick bars.

"Who's this now?" snapped a gruff voice.

"Logen Ninefingers is my name. I've—"

"Never heard of you."

Hardly the welcome Logen had been hoping for. "I've come to see Bayaz." No reply. "The First of the—"

"Yes. He's here." But the door didn't open. "He isn't taking visitors. I told that to the last messenger."

"I'm no messenger, I have Malacus Quai with me."

"Malaca what?"

"Quai, the apprentice."

"Apprentice?"

"He's very ill," said Logen slowly. "He may die."

"Ill, you say? Die, was it?"

"Yes."

"And what was your name again—"

"Just open the fucking door!" Logen shook his fist pointlessly at the slot. "Please."

"We don't let just anyone in . . . holdup. Show me your hands."

"What?"

"Your hands." Logen held his hands up. The watery eyes moved slowly across his fingers. "There are nine. There's one missing, see?" He shoved the stump at the hatch.

"Nine, is it? You should have said."

Bolts clanked and the door creaked slowly open. An elderly man, bent under an old-fashioned suit of armour, was staring at him suspiciously from the other side. He was holding a long sword much too heavy for him. Its point wobbled around wildly as he strained to keep it upright.

Logen held up his hands. "I surrender."

The ancient gatekeeper was not amused. He grunted sourly as Logen stepped past him, then he wrestled the door shut and fumbled with the bolts, turned and trudged away without another word. Logen followed him up a narrow valley lined with strange houses, weathered and mossy, half dug into the steep rocks, merging with the mountainside.

A dour-faced woman was working at a spinning wheel on a doorstep, and she frowned at Logen as he walked past with the unconscious apprentice over his shoulder. Logen smiled back at her. She was no beauty, that was sure, but it had been a very long time. The woman ducked into her house and kicked the door shut, leaving the wheel spinning. Logen sighed. The old magic was still there.

The next house was a bakery with a squat, smoking chimney. The smell of baking bread made Logen's empty stomach rumble. Further on, a couple of dark-haired children were laughing and playing, running round a scrubby old tree. They reminded Logen of his own children. They didn't look anything like them, but he was in a morbid frame of mind.

He had to admit to being a little disappointed. He'd been expecting something cleverer-looking, and a lot more beards. These folk didn't seem so very wise. They looked just like any other peasants. Not unlike his own village had looked before the Shanka came. He wondered if he was in the right place. Then they rounded a bend in the road.

Three great, tapering towers were built into the mountainside ahead, joined at their bases but separating higher up, covered in dark ivy. They seemed far older even than the ancient bridge and road, as old as the mountain itself. A jumbled mess of other buildings crowded around their feet, straggling around the sides of a wide courtyard in which people were busy with everyday chores. A thin woman was churning some milk on a stoop. A stocky blacksmith was trying to shoe a restless mare. An old, bald butcher in a stained apron had finished chopping up some animal and was washing his bloody forearms in a trough.

And on a set of wide steps before the tallest of the three towers sat a magnificent old man. He was dressed all in white, with a long beard, a hook nose, and white hair spilling from under a white skull-cap. Logen was impressed, finally. The First of the Magi surely looked the part. As Logen shuffled towards him he started up from the steps and hurried over, white coat flapping behind him.

"Set him down here," he muttered, indicating a patch of grass by the well, and Logen knelt and dumped Quai on the ground, as gently as he could with his back aching so much. The old man bent over him, laid a gnarled hand on his forehead.

"I brought your apprentice back," muttered Logen pointlessly.

"Mine?"

"Aren't you Bayaz?"

The old man laughed. "Oh no, I am Wells, head servant here at the Library."

"I am Bayaz," came a voice from behind. The butcher was walking slowly toward them, wiping his hands on a cloth. He looked maybe sixty but heavily built, with a strong face, deeply lined, and a close-cropped grey beard around his mouth. He was entirely bald, and the afternoon sun shone brightly off his tanned pate. He was neither handsome nor majestic, but as he came closer there did seem to be something about him. An assurance, an air of command. A man used to giving orders, and to being obeyed.

The First of the Magi took Logen's left hand in both of his and pressed it warmly. Then he turned it over and examined the stump of his missing finger.

"Logen Ninefingers, then. The one they call the Bloody-Nine. I have heard stories about you, even shut up here in my library."

Logen winced. He could guess what sort of stories the old man might have heard. "That was a long time ago."

"Of course. We all have a past, eh? I make no judgements on hearsay." And Bayaz smiled. A broad, white, beaming smile. His face lit up with friendly creases, but a hardness lingered around his eyes, deep-set and glistening green. A stony hardness. Logen grinned back, but he reckoned already that he wouldn't want to make an enemy of this man.

"And you have brought our missing lamb back to the fold." Bayaz frowned down at Malacus Quai, motionless on the grass. "How is he?"

"I think he will live, sir," said Wells, "but we should get him out of the cold."

The First of the Magi snapped his fingers and a sharp crack echoed from the buildings. "Help him." The smith hurried forward and took Quai's feet, and together he and Wells carried the apprentice through the tall door into the library.

"Now, Master Ninefingers, I have called and you have answered, and that shows good manners. Manners might be out of fashion in the North, but I want you to know that I appreciate them. Courtesy should be answered with courtesy, I have always thought. But what's this now?" The old gatekeeper was hurrying back across the yard, greatly out of breath. "Two visitors in one day? Whatever next?"

"Master Bayaz!" wheezed the gatekeeper, "there's riders at the gate, well horsed and well armed! They say they've an urgent message from the King of the Northmen!"

Bethod. It had to be. The spirits had said he had given himself a golden hat, and who else would have dared to call himself King of the Northmen? Logen swallowed. He'd got away from their last meeting with his life and nothing else, and yet it was better than many had managed, far better.

"Well, master?" asked the gatekeeper, "shall I tell them to be off?"

"Who leads them?"

"A fancy lad with a sour face. Said he's this King's son or something."

"Was it Calder or Scale? They're both something sour."

"The younger one, I reckon."

Calder then, that was something. Either one was bad, but Scale was much the worse. Both together were an experience to be avoided. Bayaz seemed to consider a moment. "Prince Calder may enter, but his men must remain beyond the bridge."

"Yes sir, beyond the bridge." The gatekeeper wheezed away. He'd love that, would Calder. Logen was greatly tickled by the thought of the so-called Prince screaming uselessly through that little slot.

"The King of the Northmen now, can you imagine?" Bayaz stared absently off down the valley. "I knew Bethod when he was not so grand. And so did you, eh, Master Ninefingers?"

Logen frowned. He'd known Bethod when he was next to nothing, a little chieftain like so many others. Logen had come for help against the Shanka, and Bethod had given it, at a price. Back then, the price had seemed light, and well worth the paying. Just to fight. To kill a few men. Logen had always found killing easy, and Bethod had seemed a man well worth fighting for—bold, proud, ruthless, venomously ambitious. All qualities that Logen had admired, back then, all qualities he thought he had himself. But time had changed them both, and the price had risen.

"He used to be a better man," Bayaz was musing, "but crowns sit badly on some people. Do you know his sons?"

"Better than I'd like."

Bayaz nodded. "They're absolute shit, aren't they? And I fear now they will never improve. Imagine that pin-head Scale a king. Ugh!" The wizard shuddered. "It almost makes you want to wish his father a long life. Almost, but not quite."

The little girl that Logen had seen playing scurried over. She had a chain of yellow flowers in her hands, and she held it up to the old wizard. "I made this," she said. Logen could hear the rapid pounding of hooves coming up the road.

"For me? How perfectly charming." Bayaz took the flowers from her. "Excellent work, my dear. The Master Maker himself could not have done better."

The rider clattered out into the yard, pulled his horse up savagely and swung from the saddle. Calder. The years had been kinder to him than to Logen, that much was clear. He was dressed all in fine blacks trimmed with dark fur. A big red jewel flashed on his finger, the hilt of his sword was set with gold. He'd grown and filled out, half the size of his brother Scale, but a big man still. His pale, proud face was pretty much as Logen remembered though, thin lips twisted in a permanent sneer.

He threw his reins at the woman churning milk then strode briskly across the yard, glowering about him, his long hair flapping in the breeze. When he was about ten strides away he saw Logen. His jaw dropped. Calder took a shocked half step back and his hand twitched towards his sword. Then he smiled a cold little smile.

"So you've taken to keeping dogs have you, Bayaz? I'd watch this one. He's been known to bite his master's hand." His lip curled further. "I could put him down for you if you'd like."

Logen shrugged. Hard words are for fools and cowards. Calder might have been both, but Logen was neither. If you mean to kill, you're better getting right to it than talking about it. Talk only makes the other man ready, and that's the last thing you want. So Logen said nothing. Calder could take that for weakness if he pleased, and so much the better. Fights might find Logen depressingly often, but he was long, long past looking for them.

Bethod's second son turned his contempt on the First of the Magi. "My father will be displeased, Bayaz! That my men must wait outside the gate shows little respect!"

"But I have so little, Prince Calder," said the wizard calmly. "Please don't be downhearted, though. Your last messenger wasn't allowed over the bridge, so you see we're making progress."

Calder scowled. "Why have you not answered my father's summons?"

"There are so many demands on my time." Bayaz held up the chain of flowers. "These don't make themselves, you know."

The Prince was not amused. "My father," he boomed, "Bethod, King of the Northmen, commands you to attend upon him at Carleon!" He cleared his throat. "He will not . . ." He coughed.

"What?" demanded Bayaz. "Speak up, child!"

"He commands . . ." The Prince coughed again, spluttered, choked. He put a hand to his throat. The air seemed to have become very still.

"Commands, does he?" Bayaz frowned. "Bring great Juvens back from the land of the dead. He may command me. He alone, and no other." The frown grew deeper still, and Logen had to resist a strange desire to back away. "You may not. Nor may your father, whatever he calls himself."

Calder sank slowly to his knees, face twisted, eyes watering. Bayaz looked him up and down. "What solemn attire, did somebody die? Here," and he tossed the chain of flowers over the Prince's head. "A little colour may lighten your mood. Tell your father he must come himself. I do not waste my time on fools and younger sons. I am old-fashioned in this. I like to talk to the horse's head, not the horse's arse. Do you understand me, boy?" Calder was sagging sideways, eyes red and bulging. The First of the Magi waved his hand. "You may go."

The Prince heaved in a ragged breath, coughed and reeled to his feet, stumbled for his horse and hauled himself up into the saddle with a deal less grace than he had got down. He shot a murderous glance over his shoulder as he made for the gate, but it didn't have quite the same weight with his face red as a slapped arse. Logen realised he was grinning, wide. It was a long time since he'd enjoyed himself this much.

"I understand that you can speak to the spirits."

Logen was caught off guard. "Eh?"

"To speak to the spirits." Bayaz shook his head. "It is a rare gift in these times. How are they?"

"What, the spirits?"

"Yes."

"Dwindling."

"Soon they will all sleep, eh? The magic leaks out of the world. That is the set order of things. Over the years my knowledge has grown, and yet my power has diminished."

"Calder seemed impressed."

"Bah." Bayaz waved his hand. "A mere nothing. A little trick of air and flesh, easily done. No, believe me, the magic ebbs away. It is a fact. A natural law. Still, there are many ways to crack an egg, eh, my friend? If one tool fails then we must try another." Logen was no longer entirely sure what they were talking about, but he was too tired to ask.

"Yes, indeed," murmured the First of the Magi. "There are many ways to crack an egg. Speaking of which, you look hungry."

Logen's mouth flooded with spit at the very mention of food. "Yes," he mumbled. "Yes . . . I could eat."

"Of course." Bayaz clapped him warmly on the shoulder. "And then perhaps a bath? Not that we are offended of course, but I find that there is nothing more soothing than hot water after a long walk, and you, I suspect, have had a very long walk indeed. Come with me, Master Ninefingers, you're safe here."

Food. Bath. Safety. Logen had to stop himself from weeping as he followed the old man into the library.

THE GOOD MAN

I t was a hot, hot day outside, and the sun shone brightly through the many-paned windows, casting criss-cross patterns on the wooden floor of the audience chamber. It was mid-afternoon, and the room was soupy warm and stuffy as a kitchen.

Fortis dan Hoff, the Lord Chamberlain, was red-faced and sweaty in his fur-trimmed robes of state, and had been in an increasingly filthy mood all afternoon. Harlen Morrow, his Under-Secretary for Audiences, looked even more uncomfortable, but then he had his terror of Hoff to contend with, in addition to the heat. Both men seemed greatly distressed in their own ways, but at least they got to sit down.

Major West was sweating steadily into his embroidered dress uniform. He had been standing in the same position, hands behind his back, teeth gritted, for nearly two hours while Lord Hoff sulked and grumbled and bellowed his way through the applicants and anyone else in view. West fervently wished, and not for the first time that afternoon, that he was lying under a tree in the park, with a strong drink. Or perhaps under a glacier, entombed within the ice. Anywhere but here.

Standing guard on these horrible audiences was hardly one of West's more pleasant duties, but it could have been worse. You had to spare a thought for the eight soldiers stood around the walls: they were in full armour. West was waiting for one of them to pass out and crash to the floor with a sound like a cupboard full of saucepans, no doubt to the great disgust of the Lord Chamberlain, but so far they were all somehow staying upright.

"Why is this damned room always the wrong temperature?" Hoff was demanding to know, as if the heat was an insult directed solely at him. "It's too hot half the year, too cold the other half! There's no air in here, no air at all! Why don't these windows open? Why can't we have a bigger room?"

"Er . . ." mumbled the harassed Under-Secretary, pushing his spectacles up his sweaty nose, "requests for audiences have always been held here, my Lord Chamberlain." He paused under the fearsome gaze of his superior. "Er . . . it is . . . traditional?"

"I know that, you dolt!" thundered Hoff, face crimson with heat and fury. "Who asked for your damn fool of an opinion anyway?"

"Yes, that is to say, no," stuttered Morrow, "that is to say, quite so, my Lord."

Hoff shook his head with a mighty frown, staring around the room in search of something else to displease him. "How many more must we endure today?"

"Er . . . four more, your worship."

"Damn it!" thundered the Chamberlain, shifting in his huge chair and flapping his fur-trimmed collar to let some air in. "This is intolerable!" West found himself in silent agreement. Hoff snatched up a silver goblet from the table and took a great slurp of wine. He was a great one for drinking, indeed he had been drinking all afternoon. It had not improved his temper. "Who's the next fool?" he demanded.

"Er . . ." Morrow squinted at a large document through his spectacles, tracing across the crabby writing with an inky finger. "Goodman Heath is next, a farmer from—"

"A farmer? A farmer did you say? So we must sit in this ridiculous heat, listening to some damn commoner moan on about how the weather has affected his sheep?"

"Well, my Lord," muttered Morrow, "it does seem as though, er, Goodman Heath has, er, a legitimate grievance against his, er, landlord, and—"

"Damn it all! I am sick to my stomach of other people's grievances!" The Lord Chamberlain took another swallow of wine. "Show the idiot in!"

The doors were opened and Goodman Heath was allowed into their presence. To underline the balance of power within the room, the Lord Chamberlain's table was raised up on a high dais, so that even standing the poor man had to look up at them. An honest face, but very gaunt. He held a battered hat before him in trembling hands. West shrugged his shoulders in discomfort as a drop of sweat ran down his back.

"You are Goodman Heath, correct?"

"Yes, my Lord," mumbled the peasant in a broad accent, "from—"

Hoff cut him off with consummate rudeness. "And you come before us seeking an audience with his August Majesty, the High King of the Union?"

Goodman Heath licked his lips. West wondered how far he had come to be made a fool of. A very long way, most likely. "My family have been put off our land. The landlord said we had not been paying the rent but—"

The Lord Chamberlain waved a hand. "Plainly this is a matter for the Commission for Land and Agriculture. His August Majesty the King is concerned with the welfare of all his subjects, no matter how mean," West almost winced at this slight, "but he cannot be expected to give personal attention to every trifling thing. His time is valuable, and so is mine. Good day." And that was it. Two of the soldiers pulled the double doors open for Goodman Heath to leave.

The peasant's face had gone very pale, his knuckles wringing at the brim of his hat. "Good my Lord," he stammered, "I've already been to the Commission . . ."

Hoff looked up sharply, making the farmer stammer to a halt. "Good day, I said!"

The peasant's shoulders slumped. He took a last look around the room. Morrow was examining something on the far wall with great interest and refused to meet his eye. The Lord Chamberlain stared back at him angrily, infuriated by this unforgivable waste of his time. West felt sick to be a part of it. Heath turned and shuffled away, head bowed. The doors swung shut.

Hoff bashed his fist on the table. "Did you see that?" He stared round fiercely at the sweating assembly. "The sheer gall of the man! Did you see that, Major West?"

"Yes, my Lord Chamberlain, I saw it all," said West stiffly. "It was a disgrace."

Fortunately, Hoff did not take his whole meaning. "A disgrace, Major West, you are quite right! Why the hell is it that all the promising young men go into the army? I want to know who is responsible for letting these beggars in here!" He glared at the Under-Secretary, who swallowed and stared at his documents. "What's next?"

"Er," mumbled Morrow, "Coster dan Kault, Magister of the Guild of Mercers."

"I know who he is, damn it!" snapped Hoff, wiping a fresh sheen of sweat from his face. "If it isn't the damn peasants it's the damn merchants!" he roared at the soldiers by the door, his voice easily loud enough to be heard in the corridor outside. "Show the grubbing old swindler in, then!"

Magister Kault could hardly have presented a more different appearance from the previous supplicant. He was a big, plump man, with a face as soft as his eyes were hard. His purple vesture of office was embroidered with yards of golden thread, so ostentatious that the Emperor of Gurkhul himself might have been embarrassed to wear it. He was accompanied by a pair of senior Mercers, their own attire scarcely less magnificent. West wondered if Goodman Heath could earn enough in ten years to pay for one of those gowns. He decided not, even if he hadn't been thrown off his land.

"My Lord Chamberlain," intoned Kault with an elaborate bow. Hoff acknowledged the head of the Guild of Mercers as faintly as humanly possible, with a raised eyebrow and an almost imperceptible twist of the lip. Kault waited for a greeting which he felt more befitting of his station, but none was forthcoming. He noisily cleared his throat. "I have come to seek an audience with his August Majesty . . ."

The Lord Chamberlain snorted. "The purpose of this session is to decide who is worthy of his Majesty's attention. If you aren't seeking an audience with him you have blundered into the wrong room." It was already clear that this interview would be every bit as unsuccessful as the last. There was a kind of horrible justice to it, West supposed. The great and the small were treated exactly alike.

Magister Kault's eyes narrowed slightly, but he continued. "The honourable Guild of Mercers, of whom I am the humble representative . . ." Hoff slurped wine noisily and Kault was obliged to pause for a moment. ". . . have been the victims of a most malicious and mischievous attack—"

"Fill this up, would you?" yelled the Lord Chamberlain, waving his empty goblet at Morrow. The Under-Secretary slipped eagerly from his chair and seized the decanter. Kault was forced to wait, teeth gritted, while the wine gurgled out.

"Continue!" blustered Hoff, waving his hand, "we don't have all day!"

"A most malicious and under-handed attack—"

The Lord Chamberlain squinted down. "An attack you say? A common assault is a matter for the City Watch!"

Magister Kault grimaced. He and his two companions were already starting to sweat. "Not an attack of that variety, my Lord Chamberlain, but an insidious and underhanded assault, designed to discredit the shining reputation of our Guild, and to damage our business interests in the Free Cities of Styria, and across the Union. An attack perpetrated by certain deceitful elements of his Majesty's Inquisition, and—"

"I have heard enough!" The Lord Chamberlain jerked up his big hand for silence. "If this is a matter of trade, then it should be handled by His Majesty's Commission for Trade and Commerce." Hoff spoke slowly and precisely, in the manner of a schoolmaster addressing his most disappointing pupil. "If this is a matter of law, then it should be handled by the department of High Justice Marovia. If it is a matter of the internal workings of his Majesty's Inquisition, then you must arrange an appointment with Arch Lector Sult. In any case, it is hardly a matter for the attention of his August Majesty."

The head of the Mercer's Guild opened his mouth but the Lord Chamberlain spoke over him, voice louder than ever. "Your King employs a Commission, selects a High Justice, and appoints an Arch Lector, so that he need not deal with every trifling issue himself! Incidentally, that is also why he grants licences to certain merchant guilds, and not to line the pockets . . ." and his lip twisted into an unpleasant sneer ". . . of the trading class! Good day." And the doors were opened.

Kault's face had turned pale with anger at that last comment. "You may depend upon it, Lord Chamberlain," he said coldly, "that we will seek redress elsewhere, and with the very greatest of persistence."

Hoff glared back at him for a very long while. "Seek it wherever you like," he growled, "and with as much persistence as you please. But not here. Good

. . . day!" If you could have stabbed someone in the face with the phrase "good day," the head of the Guild of Mercers would have lain dead on the floor.

Kault blinked a couple of times, then turned angrily and strode out with as much dignity as he could muster. His two lackeys followed close on his heels, their fabulous gowns flapping behind them. The doors were pushed shut.

Hoff smashed the table once again with his fist. "An outrage!" he spluttered. "Those arrogant swine! Do they seriously think they can flout the King's law and still seek the King's help when things turn sour?"

"Well, no," said Morrow, "of course . . ."

The Lord Chamberlain ignored his Under-Secretary and turned to West with a sneering smile. "Still, I fancy I could see the vultures circling around them, despite the low ceiling, eh, Major West?"

"Indeed, my Lord Chamberlain," mumbled West, thoroughly uncomfortable and wishing this torture would end. Then he could get back to his sister. His heart sank. She was even more of a handful than he remembered. She was clever alright, but he worried that she might be too clever for her own good. If only she would just marry some honest man and be happy. His position here was precarious enough, without her making a spectacle of herself.

"Vultures, vultures," Hoff was murmuring to himself. "Nasty-looking birds, but they have their uses. What's next?"

The sweating Under-Secretary looked even more uncomfortable than before as he fumbled for the right words. "We have a party of . . . diplomats?"

The Lord Chamberlain paused, goblet halfway to his mouth. "Diplomats? From whom?"

"Er . . . from this so-called King of the Northmen, Bethod."

Hoff burst out laughing. "Diplomats?" he cackled, mopping his face on his sleeve. "Savages, you mean!"

The Under-Secretary chuckled unconvincingly. "Ah yes, my Lord, ha, ha! Savages, of course!"

"But dangerous, eh, Morrow?" snapped the Lord Chamberlain, his good humour evaporating instantly. The Under-Secretary's cackling gurgled to a halt. "Very dangerous. We must be careful. Show them in!"

There were four of them. The two smallest were great big, fierce-looking men, scarred and bearded, clad in heavy battered armour. They had been disarmed at the gate of the Agriont, of course, but there was still a sense of danger about them, and West had the feeling they would have given up a lot of big, well-worn weapons. These were the sort of men who were crowded on the borders of Angland, hungry for war, not far from West's home.

With them came an older man, also in pitted armour, and with long hair and a great white beard. There was a livid scar across his face and through his eye, which was blind white. He had a broad smile on his lips though, and his pleasant demeanour was greatly at odds with that of his two dour companions, and with the fourth man, who came behind.

He had to stoop to get under the lintel, which was a good seven feet above the floor. He was swathed and hooded in a rough brown cloak, features invisible. As he straightened up, towering over everyone else, the room began to seem absurdly cramped. His sheer bulk was intimidating, but there was something more, something that seemed to come off him in sickly waves. The soldiers around the walls felt it, and they shifted uncomfortably. The Under-Secretary for Audiences felt it, sweating and twitching and fussing with his documents. Major West certainly felt it. His skin had gone cold despite the heat, and he could feel every hair on his body standing up under his damp uniform.

Only Hoff seemed unaffected. He looked the four Northmen up and down with a deep frown on his face, no more impressed with the hooded giant than he had been with Goodman Heath. "So you are messengers from Bethod." He rolled the words around in his mouth, then spat them out, "The King of the Northmen."

"We are," said the smiling old man, bowing with great reverence. "I am White-Eye Hansul." His voice was rich, round and pleasant, without any accent, not at all what West had been expecting.

"And you are Bethod's emissary?" asked Hoff casually, taking another swallow of wine from his goblet. For the first time ever West was pleased the Lord Chamberlain was in the room with him, but then he glanced up at the hooded man and the feeling of unease returned.

"Oh no," said White-Eye, "I am here merely as translator. This is the emissary of the King of the Northmen," and his good eye flicked nervously up to the dark figure in the cloak, as though even he was afraid. "Fenris." He stretched out the "s" on the end of the name so that it hissed in the air. "Fenris the Feared."

An apt name indeed. Major West thought back to songs he had heard in his childhood, stories of bloodthirsty giants in the mountains of the distant north. The room was silent for a moment.

"Humph," said the Lord Chamberlain, unmoved. "And you seek an audience with his August Majesty, the High King of the Union?"

"We do indeed, my Lord Chamberlain," said the old warrior. "Our master, Bethod, greatly regrets the hostility between our two nations. He wishes only to be on the best of terms with his southern neighbours. We bring an offer of peace from my King to yours, and a gift to show our good faith. Nothing more."

"Well, well," said Hoff, sitting back in his high chair with a broad smile. "A gracious request, graciously made. You may see the King in Open Council tomorrow, and present your offer, and your gift, before the foremost peers of the realm."

White-Eye bowed respectfully. "You are most kind, my Lord Chamberlain." He turned for the door, followed by the two dour warriors. The cloaked figure lingered for a moment, then he too slowly turned and stooped through the doorway. It wasn't until the doors were shut that West could breathe easily again. He shook his head and shrugged his sweaty shoulders. Songs about giants indeed. A great big man in a cloak was all. But looking again, that doorway really was very high . . .

"There, you see, Master Morrow?" Hoff looked intensely pleased with himself. "Hardly the savages you led me to expect! I feel we are close to a resolution of our northern problems, don't you?"

The Under-Secretary did not look in the least convinced. "Er . . . yes, my Lord, of course."

"Yes indeed. A lot of fuss over nothing. A lot of pessimistic, defeatist nonsense from our jumpy citizens up north, eh? War? Bah!" Hoff whacked his hand on the table again, making wine slop out of his goblet and spatter on the wood. "These Northmen wouldn't dare! Why, next thing you know they'll be petitioning us for membership of the Union! You see if I'm not right, eh, Major West?"

"Er . . ."

"Good! Excellent! We've got something done today at least! One more and we can get out of this damn furnace! Who do we have, Morrow?"

The Under-Secretary frowned and pushed his glasses up his nose. "Er . . . we have one Yoru Sulfur," he wrestled with the unfamiliar name.

"We have a who?"

"Er . . . Sulfir, or Sulfor, or something."

"Never heard of him," grunted the Lord Chamberlain, "what manner of a man is he? Some kind of a southerner? Not another peasant, please!"

The Under-Secretary examined his notes, and swallowed. "An emissary?"

"Yes, yes, but from whom?"

Morrow was positively cringing, like a child expecting a slap. "From the Great Order of Magi!" he blurted out.

There was a moment of stunned silence. West's eyebrows went up and his jaw came open, and he guessed that the same was happening, unseen, behind the visors of the soldiers. He winced instinctively as he anticipated the response of the Lord Chamberlain, but Hoff surprised them all by bursting into peals of laughter. "Excellent! At last some entertainment. It's been years since we had a Magus here! Show in the wizard! We mustn't keep him waiting!"

Yoru Sulfur was something of a disappointment. He had simple, travel-stained clothes, was scarcely better dressed than Goodman Heath had been, in fact. His staff was not shod with gold, had no lump of shining crystal on the end. His eye did not flash with a mysterious fire. He looked a fairly ordinary sort of a man in his middle thirties, slightly tired, as though after a long journey, but otherwise well at his ease before the Lord Chamberlain.

"A good day to you, gentlemen," he said, leaning on his staff. West was having some difficulty working out where he was from. Not the Union, because his skin was too dark, and not Gurkhul or the far south, because his skin was too light. Not from the North or from Styria. Further then, but where? Now that West looked at him more closely he noticed that his eyes were different colours: one blue, one green.

"And a good day to you, sir," said Hoff, smiling as though he really meant it. "My door is forever open to the Great Order of Magi. Tell me, do I have the pleasure of addressing great Bayaz himself?"

Sulfur looked puzzled. "No, was I wrongly announced? I am Yoru Sulfur. Master Bayaz is a bald gentleman." He pushed a hand through his own head of curly brown hair. "There is a statue of him outside in the avenue. But I did have the honour to study under him for several years. He is a most powerful and knowledgeable master."

"Of course! Of course he is! And how may we be of service?"

Yoru Sulfur cleared his throat, as though to tell a story. "On the death of King Harod the Great, Bayaz, the First of the Magi, left the Union. But he swore an oath to return."

"Yes, yes, that's true," chuckled Hoff. "Very true, every schoolchild knows it."

"And he pronounced that, when he returned, his coming would be heralded by another."

"True, also."

"Well," said Sulfur, smiling broadly, "here I am."

The Lord Chamberlain roared with laughter. "Here you are!" he shouted, thumping the table. Harlen Morrow allowed himself a little chuckle, but shut up immediately as Hoff's smile began to fade.

"During my tenure as Lord Chamberlain, I have had three members of the Great Order of Magi apply to me for audiences with the King. Two were most clearly insane, and one was an exceptionally courageous swindler." He leaned forward, placing his elbows on the table and steepling his fingers before him. "Tell me, Master Sulfur, which kind of Magus are you?"

"I am neither of those."

"I see. Then you will have documents."

"Of course." Sulfur reached into his coat and brought out a small letter, closed with a white seal, a single strange symbol stamped into it. He placed it carelessly on the table before the Lord Chamberlain.

Hoff frowned. He picked up the document and turned it over in his hands. He examined the seal carefully, then he dabbed his face with his sleeve, broke the wax, unfolded the thick paper and began to read.

Yoru Sulfur showed no sign of nerves. He didn't appear troubled by the heat. He strolled around the room, he nodded to the armoured soldiers, he didn't seem upset by their lack of response. He turned suddenly to West. "It's terribly hot in here, isn't it? It's a wonder these poor fellows don't pass out, and crash to the floor with a sound like a cupboard full of saucepans." West blinked. He had been thinking the very same thing.

The Lord Chamberlain put the letter down carefully on the table, no longer in the least amused. "It occurs to me that the Open Council would be the wrong place to discuss this matter."

"I agree. I was hoping for a private audience with Lord Chancellor Feekt."

"I am afraid that will not be possible." Hoff licked his lips. "Lord Feekt is dead."

Sulfur frowned. "That is most unfortunate."

"Indeed, indeed. We all feel his loss most keenly. Perhaps I and certain other members of the Closed Council can assist you."

Sulfur bowed his head. "I am guided by you, my Lord Chamberlain."

"I will try to arrange something for later this evening. Until then we will find you some lodgings within the Agriont . . . suitable for your station." He signalled to the guards, and the doors were opened.

"Thank you so much, Lord Hoff. Master Morrow. Major West." Sulfur nodded to them graciously, each in turn, and then turned and left. The doors were closed once more, leaving West wondering how the man had known his name.

Hoff turned to his Under-Secretary for Audiences. "Go immediately to Arch Lector Sult, and tell him we must meet at once. Then fetch High Justice Marovia, and Lord Marshal Varuz. Tell them it is a matter of the very highest importance, and not a word of this to anyone beyond those three." He shook his finger in Morrow's sweaty face. "Not a word!"

The Under-Secretary stared back, spectacles askew. "Now!" roared Hoff. Morrow leapt to his feet, stumbled on the hem of his gown, then hurried out through a side door. West swallowed, his mouth very dry.

Hoff stared long and hard at each man in the room. "As for the rest of you, not a word to anyone about any of this, or the consequences for all of you will be most severe! Now out, everyone out!" The soldiers clanked from the room immediately. West needed no further encouragement and he hurried after them, leaving the brooding Lord Chamberlain alone in his high chair.

West's thoughts were dark and confused as he pulled the door shut behind him. Fragments of old stories of the Magi, fears about war in the North, images of a hooded giant, towering up near the ceiling. There had been some strange and some sinister visitors to the Agriont that day, and he felt quite weighed down by worries. He tried to shrug them off, told himself it was all foolishness, but then all he could think of was his sister, cavorting about the Agriont like a fool.

He groaned to himself. She was probably with Luthar right now. Why the hell had he introduced the two of them? For some reason he had been expecting the same awkward, sickly, sharp-tongued girl he remembered from years ago. He had got quite a shock when this woman had turned up at his quarters. He had barely recognised her. Undoubtedly a woman, and a fine-looking one too. Meanwhile, Luthar was arrogant and rich and handsome and had all the self-restraint of a six-year old. He knew they had seen each other since, and more than once. Just as friends, of course. Ardee had no other friends here. Just friends.

"Shit!" he cursed. It was like putting a cat by the cream and trusting it not to stick its tongue in. Why the hell hadn't he thought it through? It was a damn disaster in the making! But what could he do about it now? He stared off miserably down the hallway.

There's nothing like seeing another's misery to make you forget your own, and Goodman Heath was a sorry sight indeed. He was sitting alone on a long bench, face deathly pale, staring off into space. He must have been sitting there all this time, while the Mercers and the Northmen and the Magus came and went, waiting for nothing but with nowhere left to go. West glanced up and down the hallway. There was no one else nearby. Heath was oblivious to him, mouth open, eyes glassy, battered hat forgotten on his knees.

West couldn't simply leave the man like this, he didn't have it in him.

"Goodman Heath," he said as he approached, and the peasant looked up at him, surprised. He fumbled for his hat and made to rise, muttering apologies.

"No, please, don't get up." West sat down on the bench. He stared at his feet, unable to look the man in the eye. There was an awkward silence. "I have a friend who sits on the Commission for Land and Agriculture. There might be something he can do for you . . ." He trailed off, embarrassed, squinting up the corridor.

The farmer gave a sad smile. "I'd be right grateful for anything you could do."

"Yes, yes, of course, I'll do what I can." It would do no good whatsoever, and they both knew it. West grimaced and bit his lip. "You'd better take this," and he pressed his purse into the peasant's limp, calloused fingers. Heath looked at him, mouth slightly open. West gave a quick, awkward smile then got to his feet. He was very keen to be off.

"Sir!" called Goodman Heath after him, but West was already hurrying down the corridor, and he didn't look back.

ON THE LIST

W*hy do I do this?*

The outline of Villem dan Robb's townhouse was cut out in black against the clear night sky. It was an unremarkable building, a two-story dwelling with a low wall and a gate in front, just like a hundred others in this street. *Our old friend Rews used to live in a palatial great villa near the market. Robb really should have asked him for some more ambitious bribes. Still. Lucky for us he didn't.* Elsewhere in the city the fashionable avenues would be brightly lit and busy with drunken revellers right through until dawn. But this secluded side street was far from the bright lights and the prying eyes.

We can work undisturbed.

Round the side of the building, on the upper floor, a lamp was burning in a narrow window. *Good. Our friend is at home. But still awake—we must tread gently.* He turned to Practical Frost and pointed down the side of the house. The albino nodded and slipped away silently across the street.

Glokta waited for him to reach the wall and disappear into the shadows beside the building, then he turned to Severard and pointed at the front door. The eyes of the lanky Practical smiled at him for a moment, then he scuttled quickly away, staying low, rolled over the low wall and dropped without a sound onto the other side.

Perfect so far, but now I must move. Glokta wondered why he had come. Frost and Severard were more than capable of dealing with Robb by themselves, and he would only slow them down. *I might even fall on my arse and alert the idiot to our presence. So why did I come?* But Glokta knew why. The feeling of excitement was already building in his throat. It felt almost like being alive.

He had muffled the end of his cane with a bit of rag, so he was able to limp to the wall, ever so delicately, without making too much noise. By that time Severard had swung the gate open, holding the hinge with one gloved hand so that it didn't make a noise. *Nice and neat. That little wall might as well be a hundred feet high for all my chances of getting over it.*

Severard was kneeling on the step against the front door, picking the lock. His ear was close to the wood, his eyes squinting with concentration, gloved hands moving deftly. Glokta's heart was beating fast, his skin prickly with tension. *Ah, the thrill of the hunt.*

There was a soft click, then another. Severard slipped his glittering picks into a pocket, then reached out and slowly, carefully turned the doorknob. The door swung silently open. *What a useful fellow he is. Without him and Frost I am just a cripple. They are my hands, my arms, my legs. But I am their brains.* Severard slipped inside and Glokta followed him, wincing with pain every time he put his weight on his left leg.

The hallway was dark, but there was a shaft of light spilling down the stairs from above and the banisters cast strange, distorted shadows on the wooden floor. Glokta pointed up the steps, and Severard nodded and began to tiptoe toward them, keeping his feet close to the wall. It seemed to take him an age to get there.

The third step made a quiet creaking sound as he put his weight on it. Glokta winced, Severard froze in place. They waited, still as statues. There was no sound from upstairs. Glokta began to breathe again. Severard moved ever so slowly upwards, step by gentle step. As he got towards the top he peered cautiously round the corner, back pressed against the wall, then he took the last step and disappeared from view without a sound.

Practical Frost emerged from the shadows at the far end of the corridor. Glokta raised an eyebrow at him but he shook his head. *Nobody downstairs.* He turned to the front door and started to close it, ever so gently. Only when it was shut did he slowly, slowly release the doorknob, so the latch slid silently into place.

"You'll want to see this."

Glokta gave a start at the sudden sound, turning round quickly and causing a jolt of pain to shoot through his back. Severard was standing, hands on hips, at the head of the stairs. He turned and made off towards the light, and Frost bounded up the steps after him, no longer making any pretence at stealth.

Why can no one ever stay on the ground floor? Always upstairs. At least he didn't have to try to be quiet as he struggled up the steps after his Practicals, right foot creaking, left foot scraping on the boards. Bright lamplight was flooding out into the upstairs corridor from an open door at the far end, and Glokta limped toward it. He paused as he crossed the threshold, catching his breath after the climb.

Oh dear me, what a mess. A big bookcase had been torn away from the wall, and books were scattered, open and closed, all about the floor. A glass of wine had been knocked over on the desk, making sodden red rags of the crumpled papers strewn across it. The bed was in disarray, the covers pulled half off, the pillows and the mattress slashed and spilling feathers. A wardrobe had its doors open, one of them dangling half off. A few tattered garments were hanging inside, but most were lying torn in a heap below.

A handsome young man lay on his back under the window, staring up, pale-faced and open mouthed at the ceiling. It would have been an understatement to say that his throat had been cut. It had been hacked so savagely that his head was only just still attached. There was blood splattered everywhere, on the torn clothes, on the slashed mattress, all over the body itself. There were a couple of smeared, bloody palm-prints on the wall, a great pool of blood across a good part of the floor, still wet. *He was killed tonight. Perhaps only a few hours ago. Perhaps only a few minutes.*

"I don't think he'll be answering our questions," said Severard.

"No." Glokta's eyes drifted over the wreckage. "I think he might be dead. But how did it happen?"

Frost fixed him with a pink eye and raised a white eyebrow. "Poithon?"

Severard spluttered with shrill laughter under his mask. Even Glokta allowed himself a chuckle. "Clearly. But how did our poison get in?"

"Open wi'ow," mumbled Frost, pointing at the floor.

Glokta limped into the room, careful not to let his feet or his cane touch the sticky mess of blood and feathers. "So, our poison saw the lamp burning, just as we did. He entered via the downstairs window. He climbed silently up the stairs." Glokta turned the corpse's hands over with the tip of his cane. *A few specks of blood from the neck, but no damage to the knuckles or the fingers. He did not struggle. He was taken by surprise.* He craned forward and peered at the gaping wound.

"A single, powerful cut. Probably with a knife."

"And Villem dan Robb has sprung a most serious leak," said Severard.

"And we are short one informant," mused Glokta. There had been no blood in the corridor. *Our man took pains not to get his feet wet while searching the room, however messy it may look. He was not angry or afraid. It was just a job.*

"The killer was a professional," murmured Glokta, "he came here with murder in mind. Then perhaps he made this little effort to give the appearance of a burglary, who can say? Either way, the Arch Lector won't be satisfied with a corpse." He looked up at his two Practicals. "Who's next on the list?"

This time there had been a struggle, without a doubt. *If a one-sided one.* Solimo Scandi was sprawled on his side, facing the wall, as though embarrassed by the state of his slashed and tattered nightshirt. There were deep cuts in his forearms. *Where he struggled vainly to ward off the blade.* He had crawled across the floor, leaving a bloody trail across the highly polished wood. *Where he struggled vainly to get away.* He had failed. The four gaping knife wounds in his back had been the end of him.

Glokta felt his face twitching as he looked down at the bloody corpse. *One body might just be a coincidence. Two make a conspiracy.* His eyelid fluttered. *Whoever did this knew we were coming, and when, and precisely who for. They are one step ahead of us. More than likely, our list of accomplices has already become a list of corpses.* There was a creaking sound behind Glokta and his head whipped round, sending shooting pains down his stiff neck. Nothing but the open window swinging in the breeze. *Calm, now. Calm, and think it out.*

"It would seem the honourable Guild of Mercers have been doing a little housekeeping."

"How could they know?" muttered Severard.

How indeed? "They must have seen Rews' list, or been told who was on it." *And that means . . .* Glokta licked at his empty gums. "Someone inside the Inquisition has been talking."

For once, Severard's eyes were not smiling. "If they know who's on the list, they know who wrote it. They know who we are."

Three more names on the list, perhaps? Down at the bottom? Glokta grinned. *How very exciting.* "You scared?"

"I'm not happy, I'll tell you that." He nodded down at the corpse. "A knife in the back isn't part of my plan."

"Nor mine, Severard, believe me." *No indeed. If I die, I'll never know who betrayed us.*

And I want to know.

A bright, cloudless spring day, and the park was busy with fops and idlers of every variety. Glokta sat very still on his bench, in the merciful shade of a spreading tree, and stared out at the shimmering greenery, the sparkling water, the happy, the drunken, the colourful revellers. There were people wedged together on the benches around the lake, pairs and groups scattered around the grass, drinking and talking and basking in the sun. There seemed no space for any more.

But no one came and sat next to Glokta. Occasionally somebody would hurry up, hardly able to believe their luck in finding such a spot, then they would see him sitting there. Their faces would fall and they would swerve away, or walk right past as though they had never meant to sit. *I drive them away as surely as the plague, but perhaps that's just as well. I don't need their company.*

He watched a group of young soldiers rowing a boat on the lake. One of them stood up, wobbling around, holding forth with a bottle in his hand. The boat rocked alarmingly, and his companions shouted at him to get down. Vague gales of good-natured laughter came wafting through the air, delayed a little by the distance. *Children. How young they look. How innocent. And such was I, not long ago. It seems a thousand years, though. Longer. It seems a different world.*

"Glokta."

He looked up, shading his eyes with his hand. It was Arch Lector Sult, arrived at last, a tall dark shape against the blue sky. Glokta thought he looked a little more tired, more lined, more drawn than usual as he stared coldly down.

"This had better be interesting." Sult flicked out the tails of his long white coat and lowered himself gracefully onto the bench. "The commoners are up in arms again near Keln. Some idiot of a landowner hangs a few peasants and now we have a mess to deal with! How hard can it be to manage a field full of dirt and a couple of farmers? You don't have to treat them well, just as long as you don't hang them!" His mouth was a straight, hard line as he glared out across the lawns. "This had better be damned interesting."

Then I'll try not to disappoint you. "Villem dan Robb is dead." As though to add emphasis to Glokta's statement, the drunken soldier slipped and toppled over the side of the boat, splashing into the water. His friend's screams of laughter reached Glokta a moment later. "He was murdered."

"Huh. It happens. Pick up the next man on the list." Sult got to his feet, frowning. "I didn't think you'd need my approval for every little thing. That's why I picked you for this job. Just get on with it!" he snapped as he turned away.

There's no need to rush, Arch Lector. That's the trouble with good legs, you tend to run around too much. If you have trouble moving, on the other hand, you don't move until you damn well know it's time. "The next man on the list also suffered a mishap."

Sult turned back, one eyebrow slightly raised. "He did?"

"They all did."

The Arch Lector pursed his lips, sat back down on the bench. "All of them?"

"All of them."

"Hmm," mused Sult. "That is interesting. The Mercers are cleaning up, are they? I hardly expected such ruthlessness. Times have changed, alright, times have certainly . . ." He trailed off, slowly starting to frown. "You think someone gave them Rews' list, don't you? You think one of ours has been talking. That's why you asked me to come here, isn't it?"

Did you think I was just avoiding the stairs? "Each one of them killed? Each and every name on our list? The very night we go to arrest them? I am not a great believer in coincidences." *Are you Arch Lector?*

He was evidently not. His face had turned very grim. "Who saw the confession?"

"Me, and my two Practicals, of course."

"You have absolute confidence in them?"

"Absolute." There was a pause. The boat was drifting, rudderless, as the soldiers scrambled about, oars sticking up in the air, the man in the water splashing and laughing, spraying water over his friends.

"The confession was in my office for some time," murmured the Arch Lector. "Some members of my staff could have seen it. Could have."

"You have absolute confidence in them, your Eminence?"

Sult stared at Glokta for a long, icy moment. "They wouldn't dare. They know me better than that."

"That leaves Superior Kalyne," said Glokta quietly.

The Arch Lector's lips hardly moved as he spoke. "You must tread carefully, Inquisitor, very carefully. The ground is not at all safe where you are walking. Fools do not become Superiors of the Inquisition, despite appearances. Kalyne has many friends, both within the House of Questions and outside it. Powerful friends. Any accusation against him must be backed up by the very strongest of proof." Sult stopped suddenly, waiting for a small group of ladies to pass out of earshot. "The very strongest of proof," he hissed, once they had moved away. "You must find me this assassin."

Easier said than done. "Of course, your Eminence, but my investigation has reached something of a dead end."

"Not quite. We still have one card left to play. Rews himself."

Rews? "But, Arch Lector, he will be in Angland by now." *Sweating down a mine or some such. If he has even lasted this long.*

"No. He is here in the Agriont, under lock and key. I thought it best to hold on to him." Glokta did his utmost to contain his surprise. *Clever. Very clever. Fools do not become Arch Lectors either, it seems.* "Rews will be your bait. I will have my secretary carry a message to Kalyne, letting him know that I have relented. That I am prepared to let the Mercers continue to operate, but under tighter control. That as a gesture of goodwill I have let Rews go. If Kalyne is the source of our leak, I daresay he will let the Mercers know that Rews is free. I daresay they will send this assassin to punish him for his loose tongue. I daresay you could take him while he is trying. If the killer doesn't come, well, we might have to look for our traitor elsewhere, and we have lost nothing."

"An excellent plan, your Eminence."

Sult stared at him coldly. "Of course. You will need somewhere to operate, somewhere far from the House of Questions. I will make the funds available, have Rews delivered to your Practicals, and let you know when Kalyne has the information. Find me this assassin, Glokta, and squeeze him. Squeeze him until the pips squeak." The boat lurched wildly as the soldiers tried to haul their wet companion in, then it suddenly turned right over, dumping them all into the water.

"I want names," hissed Sult, glowering at the splashing soldiers, "I want names, and evidence, and documents, and people who will stand up in Open Council and point fingers." He stood up smoothly from the bench. "Keep me informed." He strode off towards the House of Questions, feet crunching on the gravel of the path, and Glokta watched him go. *An excellent plan. I'm glad you're on my side, Arch Lector. You are on my side, aren't you?*

The soldiers had succeeded in hauling the upended boat onto the bank and were standing, dripping wet, shouting at one another, no longer so good-humoured. One of the oars was still floating, abandoned in the water, drifting gradually towards the point where the stream flowed from the lake. Soon it would pass under the bridge and be carried out, beneath the great walls of the Agriont and into the moat. Glokta watched it turning slowly round in the water. *A mistake. One should attend to the details. It is easy to forget the little things, but without the oar, the boat is useless.*

He let his gaze wander across some of the other faces in the park. His eye alighted on a handsome pair sitting on a bench by the lake. The young man was speaking quietly to the girl, a sad and earnest expression on his face. She got up quickly, moving away from him with her hands over her face. *Ah, the pain of the jilted lover. The loss, the anger, the shame. It seems as though you'll never recover. What poet was it who wrote there's no pain worse than the pain of a broken heart? Sentimental shit. He should have spent more time in the Emperor's prisons.* He smiled, opening his mouth and licking the empty gums where his front teeth used to be. *Broken hearts heal with time, but broken teeth never do.*

Glokta looked at the young man. He had an expression of slight amuse-ment on his face as he watched the weeping girl walk away. *The young bastard! I wonder if he's broken as many hearts as I did, in my youth? It hardly seems possible now. It takes me half an hour just to pluck up the courage to stand. The only women I've made cry lately have been the wives of those I've had exiled to Angland—*

"Sand."

Glokta turned around. "Lord Marshal Varuz, what an honour."

"Oh no, no," said the old soldier, sitting down on the bench with the swift, precise movements of the fencing master. "You look well," he said, but without really looking. *I look crippled, you mean.* "How are you, my old friend?" *I'm crippled, you old pompous old ass. And friend, is it? All those years since I came back, and you have never sought me out, not once. Is that a friendship?*

"Well enough, thank you, Lord Marshal."

Varuz shifted uncomfortably on the bench. "My latest student, Captain Luthar . . . perhaps you know him?"

"We are acquainted."

"You should see his forms." Varuz shook his head sadly. "He has the talent, alright, though he will never be in your class, Sand." *I don't know. I hope some day he'll be just as crippled as I am.* "But he has plenty of talent, enough to win. Only he's wasting it. Throwing it away." *Oh, the tragedy of it. I am so upset I could be sick. Had I eaten anything this morning.*

"He is lazy, Sand, and stubborn. He lacks courage. He lacks dedication. His heart is just not in it, and time is running out. I was wondering, if you have the time of course," Varuz looked Glokta in the eye for just an instant, "whether you might be able to speak to him for me."

I can hardly wait! Lecturing that whining ass would be the realisation of all my dreams. You arrogant old dolt, how dare you? You built your reputation on my successes, then when I needed your help you cut me off. And now you come to me, and seek my help, and call me friend?

"Of course, Marshal Varuz, I would be glad to speak to him. Anything for an old friend."

"Excellent, excellent! I'm sure you'll make all the difference! I train him every morning, in that courtyard near the House of the Maker, where I used to train you . . ." The old Marshal trailed off awkwardly.

"I will come as soon as my duties permit."

"Of course, your duties . . ." Varuz was already getting up, evidently keen to be on his way. Glokta held out his hand, making the old soldier pause for a moment. *You needn't worry, Lord Marshal, I am not contagious.* Varuz gave it a limp shake, as though worried it might snap off, then he mumbled his excuses and strode away, head held high. The dripping soldiers bowed and saluted as he walked past, somewhat embarrassed.

Glokta stretched out his leg, wondering whether to get up. *And go where? The world will not end if I sit here a moment longer. There is no rush. No rush.*

AN OFFER AND A GIFT

"**A**nd, forward!" bellowed Marshal Varuz.

Jezal lurched at him, toes curling round the edges of the beam, trying desperately to keep his balance, making a clumsy lunge or two just to give the impression of his heart being in it. Four hours of training a day were taking their toll on him, and he felt beyond mere exhaustion.

Varuz frowned and flicked Jezal's blunted steel aside, moving effortlessly along the beam as though it was a garden path. "And back!"

Jezal stumbled back on his heels, left arm waving stupidly around him in an attempt to keep his balance. Everything above his knees was aching terribly from the effort. Below the knees it was much, much worse. Varuz was over sixty, but he showed no signs of fatigue. He wasn't even sweating as he danced forward down the beam, swishing his steels around. Jezal himself was gasping for air as he parried desperately with his left hand, badly off balance, his right foot fishing in space for the safety of the beam behind him.

"And, forward!" Jezal's calves were in agony as he stumbled to change his direction and shove a blow at the infuriating old man, but Varuz did not move back. Instead he ducked under the despairing cut and used the back of his arm to sweep Jezal's feet away.

Jezal let out a howl as the courtyard turned over around him. His leg smacked painfully against the edge of the beam, then he sprawled on his face on the grass, chin thumping into the turf and making his teeth rattle. He rolled a short distance then lay there on his back, gasping like a fish snatched suddenly from the water, leg throbbing where it had collided with the beam on his way down. He would have yet another ugly bruise in the morning.

"Awful, Jezal, awful!" cried the old soldier as he sprang nimbly down onto the lawn. "You teeter about the beam as though it were a tightrope!" Jezal rolled over, cursing, and started to climb stiffly to his feet. "It is a solid piece of oak, wide enough to get lost in!" The Lord Marshal illustrated his point by whacking at the beam with his short steel, making splinters fly.

"I thought you said forward," moaned Jezal.

Varuz's eyebrows went up sharply. "Do you seriously suppose, Captain Luthar, that Bremer dan Gorst gives his opponents reliable information as to his intentions?"

"Bremer dan Gorst will be trying to beat me, you old shit! You are supposed to be helping me to beat him!" That was what Jezal thought, but he knew better than to say it. He just shook his head dumbly.

"No! No indeed he does not! He makes every effort to deceive and confuse his opponents, as all great swordsmen must!" The Lord Marshal paced up and down, shaking his head. Jezal considered again whether to give it all up. He was sick of falling into bed exhausted each night, at a time when he should have been just starting to get drunk. He was sick of waking up every morning, bruised and aching, to face another four interminable hours of running, beam, bar, forms. He was sick of being knocked on his arse by Major West. Most of all he was sick of being bullied by this old fool.

". . . A depressing display, Captain, very depressing. I do believe you are actually getting worse . . ."

Jezal would never win the Contest. No one expected him to, himself least of all. So why not give it up, and go back to his cards and late nights? Wasn't that all he really wanted from life? But then what would mark him out from a thousand other noble younger sons? He had decided long ago that he wanted to be something special. A Lord Marshal himself perhaps, and then Lord Chamberlain. Something big and important anyway. He wanted a big chair on the Closed Council, and to make big decisions. He wanted people to fawn and smile around him and hang on his every word. He wanted people to whisper, "There goes Lord Luthar!" as he swept past. Could he be happy being forever a richer, cleverer, better-looking version of Lieutenant Brint? Ugh! It was not to be thought of.

". . . We have a terribly long way to go, and not enough time to get there, not unless you change your attitude. Your sparring is lamentable, your stamina is still weak, and as for your balance, the less said about that the better . . ."

And what would everyone else think if he gave up? What would his father do? What would his brothers say? What about the other officers? He would look a coward. And then there was Ardee West. She seemed to have been much on his mind during the past couple of days. Would she lean so close to him if he didn't fence? Would she talk to him in such soft tones? Would she laugh at his jokes? Would she look up at him with those big, dark eyes, so he could almost feel her breath on his face—

"Are you listening, boy?" thundered Varuz. Jezal felt a bit of his breath on his face alright, and a deal of spit too.

"Yes, sir! Sparring lamentable, stamina weak!" Jezal swallowed nervously. "Less said about balance the better."

"That's right! I am beginning to think, though I can hardly believe it after the trouble you have put me to, that your heart really isn't in this." He glared into Jezal's eyes. "What do you think, Major?"

There was no reply. West was slumped in his chair, arms folded, frowning grimly and staring into space.

"Major West?" snapped the Lord Marshal.

He looked up suddenly, as though he had only just become aware of their presence. "I'm sorry, sir, I had become distracted."

"So I see." Varuz sucked his teeth. "It seems that nobody has been concentrating this morning." It was a great relief that some of the old man's anger had been deflected elsewhere, but Jezal's happiness was not long-lived.

"Very well," snapped the old Marshal, "if that's the way you want it. Starting tomorrow we will begin each session with a swim in the moat. A mile or two should do it." Jezal squeezed his teeth together to keep from screaming. "Cold water has a wonderful way of sharpening the senses. And perhaps we need to start a little earlier, to catch you in your most receptive frame of mind. That means we begin at five. In the meantime, Captain Luthar, I suggest that you consider whether you are here in order to win the Contest, or simply for the pleasure of my company." And he turned on his heel and stalked off.

Jezal waited until Varuz had left the courtyard before losing his temper, but once he was sure the old man was out of earshot he flung his steels against the wall in a fury.

"Damn it!" he shouted as the swords rattled to the ground. "Shit!" He looked around for something to kick that wouldn't hurt too much. His eye lighted on the leg of the beam, but he misjudged the kick badly and had to stifle the urge to grab his bruised foot and hop around like an idiot. "Shit, shit!" he raged.

West was disappointingly unimpressed. He got up, frowning, and made to follow Marshal Varuz.

"Where are you off to?" asked Jezal.

"Away," said West, over his shoulder, "I've seen enough."

"What does that mean?"

West stopped and turned to face him. "Amazing though it may seem, there are bigger problems in the world than this."

Jezal stood there open-mouthed as West stalked from the courtyard. "Just who do you think you are?" he shouted after him, once he was sure he was gone. "Shit, shit!" He considered giving the beam another kick, but thought better of it.

Jezal was in a foul mood on his way back to his quarters, so he stayed away from the busier parts of the Agriont, sticking to the quieter lanes and gardens to the side of the Kingsway. He glowered down at his feet as he walked, to further discourage any social encounter. But luck was not on his side.

"Jezal!" It was Kaspa, out for a stroll with a yellow-haired girl in expensive clothes. They had a severe-looking middle-aged woman with them, no doubt the girl's governess or some such. They had stopped to admire some piece of minor sculpture in a little-visited yard.

"Jezal!" Kaspa shouted again, waving his hat above his head. There was no avoiding them. He plastered an unconvincing smile onto his face and stalked over. The pale girl smiled at him as he approached, but if he was meant to be charmed he didn't feel it.

"Been fencing again, Luthar?" asked Kaspa pointlessly. Jezal was sweating and holding a pair of fencing steels. It was well known that he fenced every morning. You didn't need a fine mind to make the connection, which was fortunate, because Kaspa certainly didn't have one.

"Yes. How did you guess?" Jezal hadn't meant to kill the conversation quite so dead, but he passed it off with a false chuckle, and the smiles of the ladies soon returned.

"Hah, hah," laughed Kaspa, ever willing to be the butt of a joke. "Jezal, may I introduce my cousin, the Lady Ariss dan Kaspa? This is my superior officer, Captain Luthar." So this was the famous cousin. One of the Union's richest heiresses and from an excellent family. Kaspa was always babbling about what a beauty she was, but to Jezal she seemed a pale, skinny, sickly looking thing. She smiled weakly and offered out her limp, white hand.

He brushed it with the most perfunctory of kisses. "Charmed," he muttered, without relish. "I must apologise for my appearance, I've just been fencing."

"Yes," she squeaked, in a high, piping voice, once she was sure he had finished speaking. "I have heard you are a great fencer." There was a pause while she groped for something to say, then her eyes lit up. "Tell me Captain, is fencing really very dangerous?"

What insipid drivel. "Oh no, my lady, we only use blunted steels in the circle." He could have said more, but he was damned if he was going to make all the effort. He gave a thin smile. So did she. The conversation hovered over the abyss.

Jezal was about to make his excuses, the subject of fencing evidently exhausted, but Ariss cut him off by blundering on to another topic. "And tell me, Captain, is there really likely to be a war in the North?" Her voice had almost entirely faded away by the end of the sentence, but the chaperone stared on approvingly, no doubt delighted by the conversational skills of her charge.

Spare us. "Well it seems to me . . ." Jezal began. The pale, blue eyes of Lady Ariss stared back at him expectantly. Blue eyes are absolute crap, he reflected. He wondered which subject she was more ignorant of: fencing or politics? "What do you think?"

The chaperone's brow furrowed slightly. Lady Ariss looked somewhat taken aback, blushing slightly as she groped for words. "Well, er . . . that is to say . . . I'm sure that everything will . . . turn out well?"

Thank the fates! thought Jezal, we are saved! He had to get out of here. "Of course, everything will turn out well." He forced out one more smile. "It has been a real pleasure to make your acquaintance, but I'm afraid I'm on duty shortly, so I must leave you." He bowed with frosty formality. "Lieutenant Kaspa, Lady Ariss."

Kaspa clapped him on the arm, as friendly as ever. His ignorant waif of a cousin smiled uncertainly. The governess frowned at him as he passed, but Jezal took no notice.

He arrived at the Lords' Round just as the council members were returning from their lunchtime recess. He acknowledged the guards in the vestibule with a terse nod, then strode through the enormous doorway and down the central isle. A straggling column of the greatest peers of the realm were hard on his heels, and the echoing space was full of shuffling footsteps, grumblings and whisperings, as Jezal made his way around the curved wall to his place behind the high table.

"Jezal, how was fencing?" It was Jalenhorm, here early for once, and seizing on the opportunity to talk before the Lord Chamberlain arrived.

"I've had better mornings. Yourself?"

"Oh, I've been having a fine time. I met that cousin of Kaspa's, you know," he searched for the name.

Jezal sighed. "Lady Ariss."

"Yes, that's it! Have you seen her?"

"I was lucky enough to run into them just now."

"Phew!" exclaimed Jalenhorm, pursing his lips. "Isn't she stunning?"

"Hmm." Jezal looked away, bored, and watched the robed and fur-trimmed worthies file slowly to their places. At least he watched a sample of their least favourite sons and paid representatives. Very few of the magnates turned up in person for Open Council these days, not unless they had something significant to complain about. A lot of them didn't even bother to send someone in their place.

"I swear, one of the finest-looking girls I ever saw. I know Kaspa's always raving about her, but he didn't do her justice."

"Hmm." The councillors began to spread out, each man towards his own seat. The Lords' Round was designed like a theatre, the Union's leading noblemen sitting where the audience would be, on a great half-circle of banked benches with an aisle down the centre.

As in the theatre, some seats were better than others. The least important sat high up at the back, and the occupants' significance increased as you came forward. The front row was reserved for the heads of the very greatest families, or whoever they sent in their stead. Representatives from the south, from Dagoska and Westport, were on the left, nearest to Jezal. On the far right were those from the north and west, from Angland and Starikland. The bulk of the seating, in between, was for the old nobility of Midderland, the heart of the Union. The Union proper, as they would have seen it. As Jezal saw it too, for that matter.

"What poise, what grace," Jalenhorm was rhapsodising, "that wonderful fair hair, that milky-white skin, those fantastic blue eyes."

"And all of that money."

"Well yes, that too," smiled the big man. "Kaspa says his uncle is even richer than his father. Imagine that! And he has just the one child. She will inherit every mark of it. Every mark!" Jalenhorm could scarcely contain his excitement. "It's a lucky man that can bag her! What was her name again?"

"Ariss," said Jezal sourly. The Lords, or their proxies, had all shuffled and grumbled their way to their seats. It was a poor attendance: the benches were less than half full. That was about as full as it ever got. If the Lords' Round really had been a theatre, its owners would have been desperately in search of a new play.

"Ariss. Ariss." Jalenhorm smacked his lips as though the name left a sweet taste, "It's a lucky man that gets her."

"Yes indeed. A lucky man." Providing he prefers cash to conversation, that is. Jezal thought he might have preferred to marry the governess. At least she had seemed to have a bit of backbone.

The Lord Chamberlain had entered the hall now, and was making his way towards the dais on which the high table stood, just about where the stage would have been, had the Round been a theatre. He was followed by a gaggle of black-gowned secretaries and clerks, each man more or less encumbered with heavy books and sheaves of official-looking papers. With his crimson robes of state flapping behind him, Lord Hoff looked like nothing so much as a rare and stately gliding bird, pursued by a flock of troublesome crows.

"Here comes old vinegar," whispered Jalenhorm, as he sidled off to find his place on the other side of the table. Jezal put his hands behind his back and struck the usual pose, feet a little spread, chin high in the air. He swept an eye over the soldiers, regularly spaced around the curved wall, but each man was motionless and perfectly presented in full armour, as always. He took a deep breath and prepared himself for several hours of the most extreme tedium.

The Lord Chamberlain threw himself into his tall chair and called for wine. The secretaries took their places around him, leaving a space in the centre for the King, who was absent as usual. Documents were rustled, great ledgers were heaved open, pens were sharpened and rattled in ink wells. The Announcer walked to the end of the table and struck his staff of office on the floor for order. The whispering of the noblemen and their proxies, and that of the few attendees in the public gallery over their heads, gradually died down, leaving the vast chamber silent.

The Announcer puffed out his chest. "I call this meeting," he said, in slow and sonorous tones, as though he were giving the eulogy at a funeral, "of the Open Council of the Union . . ." he gave an unnecessarily long and significant pause. The Lord Chamberlain's eyes flicked angrily towards him, but the Announcer was not to be robbed of his moment of glory. He made everyone wait an instant longer before finishing, ". . . to order!"

"Thank you," said Hoff sourly. "I believe we were about to hear from the Lord Governor of Dagoska before we were interrupted by luncheon." The scratching nibs of quills accompanied his voice, as two clerks recorded his every word. The faint echoes of the pens merged with the echoes of his words in the great space above.

An elderly man struggled to his feet in the front row close to Jezal, some papers clasped before him in shaky hands.

"The Open Council," droned the Announcer, as ponderously as he dared, "recognises Rush dan Thuel, accepted proxy of Sand dan Vurms, the Lord Governor of Dagoska!"

"Thank you, sir." Thuel's cracking, wispy voice was absurdly small in the vast space. It barely carried as far as Jezal, and he was no more than ten strides away. "My Lords—" he began.

"Speak up!" called someone from the back. There was a ripple of laughter. The old man cleared his throat and tried again.

"My Lords, I come before you with an urgent message from the Lord Governor of Dagoska." His voice had already faded to its original, barely audible level, each word accompanied by the persistent scratching of quills. Whispers began to emanate from the public gallery above, making it still harder to hear him. "The threat posed to that great city by the Emperor of Gurkhul increases with every passing day."

Vague sounds of disapproval began to float up from the far side of the room, where the representatives from Angland were seated, but the bulk of the councillors simply looked bored. "Attacks on shipping, harassment of traders, and demonstrations beyond our walls, have compelled the Lord Governor to send me—"

"Lucky us!" somebody shouted. There was another wave of laughter, slightly louder this time.

"The city is built on but a narrow peninsula," persisted the old man, straining to make himself heard over the increasing background noise, "attached to a land controlled entirely by our bitter enemies the Gurkish, and separated from Midderland by wide leagues of salt water! Our defences are not all they might be! The Lord Governor is sorely in need of more funds . . ."

The mention of funds brought instant uproar from the assembly. Thuel's mouth was still moving, but there was no chance of hearing him now. The Lord Chamberlain frowned and took a swallow from his goblet. The clerk furthest from Jezal had laid down his quill and was rubbing his eyes with his inky thumb and forefinger. The clerk closest had just finished writing a line. Jezal craned forward to see. It said simply:

Some shouting here.

The Announcer thumped his staff on the tiles with a look of great self-satisfaction. The hubbub eventually died down but Thuel had now been taken with a coughing fit. He tried to speak but was unable, and eventually he waved his hand and sat down, very red in the face, while his neighbour thumped him on the back.

"If I may, Lord Chamberlain?" shouted a fashionable young man in the front row on the other side of the hall, leaping to his feet. The scratching of the quills began once again. "It seems to me—"

"The Open Council," cut in the Announcer, "recognises Hersel dan Meed, third son and accepted proxy of Fedor dan Meed, the Lord Governor of Angland!"

"It seems to me," continued the handsome young man, only slightly annoyed by this interruption, "that our friends in the south are forever expecting a full-scale attack by the Emperor!" Dissenting voices were now raised on the other side of the room. "An attack which never materialises! Did we not defeat the Gurkish only a few short years ago, or does my memory deceive me?" The booing increased in volume. "This scaremongering represents an unacceptable drain on the Union's resources!" He was shouting to be heard. "In Angland we have many miles of border and too few soldiers, while the threat from Bethod and his Northmen is very real! If anyone is in need of funds . . ."

The shouting was instantly redoubled. Cries of "Hear, hear!" "Nonsense!" "True!" and "Lies!" could be vaguely made out over the hubbub. Several of the representatives were on their feet, shouting. Some vigorously nodded their agreement, some violently shook their heads in dissent. Others yawned and stared around. Jezal could see one fellow, near to the back in the centre, who was almost certainly asleep, and in imminent danger of slumping into his neighbour's lap.

He allowed his eyes to wander up, over the faces ranged around the rail of the public gallery. He felt a strange tugging in his chest. Ardee West was up there, looking straight down at him. As their eyes met she smiled and waved. He was smiling himself, with his arm halfway up to wave, when he remembered where he was. He pushed his arm behind his back and looked around nervously, but was relieved to find that no one important had noticed his mistake. The smile would not quite leave his face though.

"My Lords!" roared the Lord Chamberlain, smashing his empty goblet down on the high table. He had the loudest voice Jezal had ever heard. Even Marshal Varuz could have learned a thing or two about shouting from Hoff. The sleeping man near the back started up, sniffing and blinking. The noise died away almost immediately. Those representatives left standing looked around guiltily, like naughty children called to account, and gradually sat down. The whispers from the public gallery went still. Order was restored.

"My Lords! I can assure you, the King has no more serious concern than the safety of his subjects, no matter where they are! The Union does not permit aggression against its people or property!" Hoff punctuated each comment by smashing his fist down in front of him. "From the Emperor of Gurkhul, from these savages in the North, or from anyone else!" He struck the table so hard on this last comment that ink splashed from a well and ran all over one of the clerks' carefully prepared documents. Calls of agreement and support greeted the Lord Chamberlain's patriotic display.

"As for the specific circumstance of Dagoska!" Thuel looked up hopefully, chest still shaking with suppressed coughs. "Is that city not possessed of some of the most powerful and extensive defences in the world? Did it not resist a siege by the Gurkish, less than a decade ago, for over a year? What has become of the walls, sir, the walls?" The great room fell quiet as everyone strained to hear the reply.

"Lord Chamberlain," wheezed Thuel, his voice nearly drowned out as one of the clerks turned the crackling page of his huge book and began scratching on the next, "the defences have fallen into poor repair, and we lack the soldiers to keep them properly manned. The Emperor is not ignorant of this," he whispered, all but inaudible, "I beg of you . . ." He dissolved into another fit of coughing, and dropped into his seat, accompanied by some light jeering from the Angland delegation.

Hoff frowned even more deeply. "It was my understanding that the defences of the city were to be maintained by monies raised locally, and by trade levies upon the Honourable Guild of Spicers, who have operated in Dagoska under an exclusive and highly profitable licence these past seven years. If resources cannot be found even to maintain the walls," and he swept the assembly with a dark eye, "perhaps it is time that this licence was put out to tender." There was a volley of angry mutterings around the public gallery.

"In any case, the Crown can spare no extra monies at present!" Jeers of dissatisfaction came from the Dagoska side of the room, hoots of agreement from the Angland side.

"As for the specific circumstance of Angland!" thundered the Lord

Chamberlain, turning toward Meed. "I believe we may shortly hear some good news, for you to take back to your father the Lord Governor." A cloud of excited whisperings rose up into the gilded dome above. The handsome young man looked pleasantly surprised, as well he might. It was rare indeed that anyone took good news away from the Open Council, or news of any kind for that matter.

Thuel had got control of his lungs once more, and he opened his mouth to speak, but he was interrupted by a great beating on the huge door behind the high table. The Lords looked up: surprised, expectant. The Lord Chamberlain smiled, in the manner of a magician who has just pulled off an exceptionally difficult trick. He signalled to the guards, the heavy iron bolts were drawn back, and the great, inlaid doors creaked slowly open.

Eight Knights of the Body, encased in glittering armour, faceless behind high, polished helmets, resplendent in purple cloaks marked on the back with a golden sun, stomped in unison down the steps and took their places to either side of the high table. They were closely followed by four trumpeters, who stepped smartly forward, raised their shining instruments to their lips and blew an ear-splitting fanfare. Jezal gritted his rattling teeth and narrowed his eyes, but eventually the ringing echoes faded. The Lord Chamberlain turned angrily toward the Announcer, who was staring at the new arrivals with his mouth open.

"Well?" hissed Hoff.

The Announcer jumped to life. "Ah . . . yes of course! My Lords and Ladies, I have the great honour to present . . ." he paused and took a huge breath, ". . . his Imperial Highness, the King of Angland, of Starikland, and of Midderland, the Protector of Westport and of Dagoska, his August Majesty, Guslav the Fifth, High King of the Union!" There was a great rustling noise as every man and woman in the hall shifted from their seats and down onto one knee.

The royal palanquin processed slowly through the doors, carried on the shoulders of six more faceless knights. The King was sitting in a gilded chair on top, propped up on rich cushions and swaying gently from side to side. He was staring about him with the startled expression of a man who went to sleep drunk, and has woken up in an unfamiliar room.

He looked awful. Enormously fat, lolling like a great hill swathed in fur and red silk, head squashed into his shoulders by the weight of the great, sparkling crown. His eyes were glassy and bulging, with huge dark bags hanging beneath, and the pink point of his tongue kept flicking nervously over his pale lips. He had great low jowls and a roll of fat around his neck, in fact his whole face gave the appearance of having slightly melted and started to run down off his skull. Such was the High King of the Union, but Jezal bowed his head a little lower as the palanquin approached, just the same.

"Oh," muttered his August Majesty, as though he had forgotten something, "please rise." The rustling noise filled the hall again as everybody rose and returned to their seats. The King turned toward Hoff, brow deeply furrowed, and Jezal heard him say, "Why am I here?"

"The Northmen, your Majesty."

"Oh yes!" The King's eyes lit up. He paused. "What about them?"

"Er . . ." but the Lord Chamberlain was saved from replying by the opening of the doors on the opposite side of the hall, the ones through which Jezal had first entered. Two strange men strode through and advanced down the aisle.

One was a grizzled old warrior with a scar and a blind eye, carrying a flat wooden box. The other was cloaked and hooded, every feature hidden, and so big that he made the whole hall seem out of proportion. The benches, the tables, even the guards, all suddenly looked like small versions designed for the use of children. As he passed, a couple of the representatives closest to the aisle cringed and shuffled away. Jezal frowned to himself. This hooded giant did not have the look of good news, whatever Lord Hoff might say. Angry and suspicious mutterings filled the echoing dome as the two Northmen took their places on the tiled floor before the high table.

"Your Majesty," said the Announcer, bowing so ridiculously low that he had to support himself with his staff, "the Open Council recognises Fenris the Feared, the envoy of Bethod, King of the Northmen, and his translator, White-Eye Hansul!"

The King was staring off happily towards one of the great windows in the curved wall, utterly oblivious, perhaps admiring the way the light shone through the beautiful stained glass, but he looked suddenly round, jowls vibrating, as the old half-blind warrior addressed him.

"Your Majesty. I bring brotherly greetings from my master, Bethod, King of the Northmen." The Round had fallen very still, and the clerks' scratching nibs seemed absurdly loud. The old warrior nodded at the great hooded shape beside him with an awkward smile. "Fenris the Feared brings an offer from Bethod to yourself. From King to King. From the North to the Union. An offer, and a gift." And he raised the wooden box.

The Lord Chamberlain gave a self-satisfied smirk. "Speak your offer first."

"It is an offer of peace. An endless peace between our two great nations." White-Eye bowed again. His manners were impeccable, Jezal had to admit. Not what one would expect from savages of the cold and distant North. His goodly speech would almost have been enough to put the room at ease, had it not been for the hooded man beside him, looming like a dark shadow.

The King's face twitched into a weak smile at this mention of peace however. "Good," he muttered. "Excellent. Peace. Capital. Peace is good."

"He asks but one small thing in return," said White-Eye.

The Lord Chamberlain's face had turned suddenly dour, but it was too late. "He has but to name it," said the King, smiling indulgently.

The hooded man stepped forward. "Angland," he hissed.

There was a moment of stillness, then the hall exploded with noise. There was a gale of disbelieving laughter from the public gallery. Meed was on his feet, red-faced and screaming. Thuel tottered up from his bench, then fell back coughing. Angry bellows were joined by hoots of derision. The King was staring about him with all the dignity of a startled rabbit.

Jezal's eyes were fixed on the hooded man. He saw a great hand slip out from his sleeve and reach for the clasp on his cloak. He blinked in surprise. Was the hand blue? Or was it just a trick of the light through the stained glass? The cloak dropped to the floor.

Jezal swallowed, his heart thumping loud in his ears. It was like staring at a terrible wound: the more he was revolted, the less he could look away. The laughter died, the shouting died, the great space became terribly still once more.

Fenris the Feared seemed larger yet without his cloak, towering over his cringing translator. Without any doubt, he was the biggest man that Jezal had ever seen, if man he was. His face was in constant, twisted, sneering motion. His bulging eyes twitched and blinked as they stared crazily round at the assembly. His thin lips smiled and grimaced and frowned by turns, never still. But all this seemed ordinary, by comparison with his strangest feature.

His whole left side, from head to toe, was covered in writing.

Crabby runes were scrawled across the left half of his shaven head, across his eyelid, his lips, his scalp, his ear. His huge left arm was tattooed blue with tiny writing, from bulging shoulder to the tips of his long fingers. Even his bare left foot was covered in strange letters. An enormous, inhuman, painted monster stood at the very heart of the Union's government. Jezal's jaw hung open.

Around the high table there were fourteen Knights of the Body, each man a hard-trained fighter of good blood. There were perhaps forty guardsmen of Jezal's own company around the walls, each one a seasoned veteran. They outnumbered these two Northmen more than twenty to one, and were well armed with the best steel the King's armouries could provide. Fenris the Feared carried no weapon. For all his size and strangeness, he should have been no threat to them.

But Jezal did not feel safe. He felt alone, weak, helpless, and terribly afraid. His skin was tingling, his mouth was dry. He felt a sudden urge to run, and hide, and never come out again.

And this strange effect was not limited to him, or even to those around the high table. Angry laughs turned to shocked gurgles as the painted monster turned slowly around in the centre of the circular floor, flickering eyes running over the crowd. Meed shrank back onto his bench, anger all leached out of him. A couple of worthies on the front row actually scrambled over the backs of their benches and into the row behind. Others looked away, or covered their faces with their hands. One of the soldiers dropped his spear, and it clattered loudly to the floor.

Fenris the Feared turned slowly to the high table, raising his great tattooed fist, opening his chasm of a mouth, a hideous spasm running over his face. "Angland!" he screamed, louder and more terrible by far than the Lord Chamberlain had ever been. The echoes of his voice bounced off the domed ceiling high above, resounded from the curved walls, filling the great space with piercing sound.

One of the Knights of the Body stumbled back and slipped, his armoured leg clanking against the edge of the high table.

The King shrank back and covered his face with his hand, one terrified eye staring out from between his fingers, crown teetering on his head.

The quill of one of the clerks dropped from his nerveless fingers. The hand of the other moved across the paper by habit while his mouth fell open, scrawling a messy word diagonally through the neat lines of script above.

Angland.

The Lord Chamberlain's face had turned waxy pale. He reached slowly for his goblet, raised it to his lips. It was empty. He placed it carefully back down on the table, but his hand was trembling, and the base rattled on the wood. He paused for a moment, breathing heavily through his nose. "Plainly, this offer is not acceptable."

"That is unfortunate," said White-Eye Hansul, "but there is still the gift." Every eye turned towards him. "In the North we have a tradition. On occasion, when there is bad blood between two clans, when there is the threat of war, champions come forward from each side, to fight for all their people, so that the issue might be decided . . . with only one death."

He slowly opened the lid of the wooden box. There was a long knife inside, blade polished mirror-bright. "His Greatness, Bethod, sends the Feared not only as his envoy, but as his champion. He will fight for Angland, if any here will face him, and spare you a war you will not win." He held the box up to the painted monster. "This is my master's gift to you, and there could be none richer . . . your lives."

Fenris's right hand darted out and snatched the knife from the box. He raised it high, blade flashing in the coloured light from the great windows. The knights should have jumped forward. Jezal should have drawn his sword. All should have rushed to the defence of the King, but nobody moved. Every mouth was agape, every eye fastened on that glinting tooth of steel.

The blade flashed down. Its point drove easily through skin and flesh until it was buried right to the hilt. The point emerged, dripping blood, from the underside of Fenris's own tattooed left arm. His face twitched, but no more than usual. The blade moved grotesquely as he stretched out his fingers, raised his left arm high for all to see. The drops of blood made a steady patter on the floor of the Lords' Round.

"Who will fight me?" he screamed, great cords of sinew bulging from his neck. His voice was almost painful to the ear.

Utter silence. The Announcer, who was closest to the Feared, and already on his knees, swooned and collapsed on his face.

Fenris turned his goggling eyes on the biggest knight before the table, a full head shorter than he was. "You?" he hissed. The unfortunate man's foot scraped on the floor as he backed away, no doubt wishing he had been born a dwarf.

A puddle of dark blood had spread across the floor beneath Fenris's elbow. "You?" he snarled at Fedor dan Meed. The young man turned slightly grey, teeth rattling together, no doubt wishing he was someone else's son.

Those blinking eyes swept across the ashen faces on the high table. Jezal's throat constricted as Fenris's eyes met his. "You?"

"Well I would, but I'm terribly busy this afternoon. Perhaps tomorrow?" The voice hardly sounded like his own. He certainly hadn't meant to say any such thing. But who else's could it be? The words floated confidently, breezily up towards the gilded dome above.

There was scattered laughter, a shout of "Bravo!" from somewhere at the back, but the eyes of the Feared did not leave Jezal's for an instant. He waited for the sounds to die, then his mouth twisted into a hideous leer.

"Tomorrow then," he whispered. Jezal's guts gave a sudden painful shift. The seriousness of the situation pressed itself upon him like a ton of rocks. Him? Fight that?

"No." It was the Lord Chamberlain. He was still pale, but his voice had regained much of its vigour. Jezal took heart, and fought manfully for control of his bowels. "No!" barked Hoff again. "There will be no duel here! There is no issue to decide! Angland is a part of the Union, by ancient law!"

White-Eye Hansul chuckled softly. "Ancient law? Angland is part of the North. Two hundred years ago there were Northmen there, living free. You wanted iron, so you crossed the sea, and slaughtered them and stole their land! It must be, then, that most ancient of laws: that the strong take what they wish from the weak?" His eyes narrowed. "We have that law also!"

Fenris the Feared ripped the knife from his arm. A few last drops of blood spattered onto the tiles, but that was all. There was no wound on the tattooed flesh. No mark at all. The knife clattered onto the tiles and lay there in the pool of blood at his feet. Fenris swept the assembly with his bulging, blinking, crazy eyes one last time, then he turned and strode across the floor and up the aisle, Lords and proxies scrambling away down their benches as he approached.

White-Eye Hansul bowed low. "Perhaps the time will come when you wish that you had accepted our offer, or our gift. You will hear from us," he said quietly, then he held up three fingers to the Lord Chamberlain. "When it is time, we will send three signs."

"Send three hundred if you wish," barked Hoff, "but this pantomime is over!"

White-Eye Hansul nodded pleasantly. "You will hear from us." And he turned and followed Fenris the Feared out of the Lords' Round. The great doors clapped shut. The quill of the nearest clerk scratched weakly against the paper.

You will hear from us.

Fedor dan Meed turned towards the Lord Chamberlain, jaw locked tight, handsome features contorted with fury. "And this is the good news you would have me convey to my father?" he screamed. The Open Council erupted. Bellowing, shouting, abuse directed toward anyone and everyone, chaos of the worst kind.

Hoff jumped up, chair toppling over behind him, mouthing angry words, but even he was drowned out by the uproar. Meed turned his back on him and stormed out. Other delegates from the Angland side of the room rose grimly and followed the son of their Lord Governor. Hoff stared after them, livid with anger, mouth working silently.

Jezal watched the King slowly take his hand from his face and lean down toward his Lord Chamberlain. "When are the Northmen getting here?" he whispered.

THE KING OF
THE NORTHMEN

L ogen breathed in deep, enjoying the unfamiliar feel of the cool breeze on his fresh-shaved jaw, and took in the view.

It was the beginning of a clear day. The dawn mist was almost gone, and from the balcony outside Logen's room, high up on the side of one of the towers of the library, you could see for miles. The great valley was spread out before him, split into stark layers. On top was the grey and puffy white of the cloudy sky. Then there was the ragged line of black crags that ringed the lake, and the dim brown suggestion of others beyond. Next came the dark green of the wooded slopes, then the thin, curving line of grey shingle on the beach. All was repeated in the still mirror of the lake below—another, shadowy world, upside down beneath his own.

Logen looked down at his hands, fingers spread out on the weathered stone of the parapet. There was no dirt, no dried blood under his cracked fingernails. They looked pale, soft, pinkish, strange. Even the scabs and scrapes on his knuckles were mostly healed. It was so long since Logen had been clean that he'd forgotten what it felt like. His new clothes were coarse against his skin, robbed of its usual covering of dirt and grease and dry sweat.

Looking out at the still lake, clean and well fed, he felt a different man. For a moment he wondered how this new Logen might turn out, but the bare stone of the parapet stared back at him where his missing finger used to be. That could never heal. He was Ninefingers still, the Bloody-Nine, and always would be. Unless he lost any more fingers. He did smell better though, that had to be admitted.

"Did you sleep well, Master Ninefingers?" Wells was in the doorway, peering out onto the balcony.

"Like a baby." Logen didn't have the heart to tell the old servant that he'd slept outside. The first night he'd tried the bed, rolling and wriggling, unable to come to terms with the strange comfort of a mattress and the unfamiliar warmth of blankets. Next he'd tried the floor. That had been an improvement. But the air had still seemed close, flat, stale. The ceiling had hung over him, seeming to creep ever lower, threatening to crush him with the weight of stone above. It was only when he'd lain down on the hard flags of the balcony, with his old coat spread over him and just the clouds and the stars above, that sleep had come. Some habits are hard to break.

"You have a visitor," said Wells.

"Me?"

Malacus Quai's head appeared around the door frame. His eyes were a little less sunken, the bags underneath them a little less dark. There was some colour to his skin, and some flesh on his bones. He no longer looked like a corpse, just gaunt and sick, as he had done when Logen first met him. He guessed that was about as healthy as Quai ever looked.

"Hah!" laughed Logen. "You survived!"

The apprentice gave a series of tired nods as he shambled across the room. He was swathed in a thick blanket which trailed on the floor and made it difficult for him to walk properly. He shuffled out of the door to the balcony and stood there, sniffing and blinking in the chill morning air.

Logen was more pleased to see him than he'd expected. He clapped him on the back like an old friend, perhaps a little too warmly. The apprentice stumbled, blanket tangled round his feet, and would have fallen if Logen hadn't put out an arm to steady him.

"Still not quite in fighting shape," muttered Quai, with a weak grin.

"You look a deal better than when I last saw you."

"So do you. You lost the beard I see, and the smell too. A few less scars and you'd look almost civilised."

Logen held his hands up. "Anything but that."

Wells ducked through the doorway into the bright morning light. He had a roll of cloth and a knife in his hand. "Could I see your arm, Master Ninefingers?"

Logen had almost forgotten about the cut. There was no new blood on the bandage, and when he unwound it there was a long, red-brown scab underneath, running almost all the way from wrist to elbow, surrounded by fresh pink skin. It hardly hurt any more, just itched. It crossed two other, older scars. One, a jagged grey effort near his wrist, he thought he might have got in the duel with Threetrees, all those years ago. Logen grimaced as he remembered the battering they'd given each other. The second scar, fainter, higher up, he wasn't sure about. Could've come from anywhere.

Wells bent down and tested the flesh round the wound while Quai peered cautiously over his shoulder. "It's mending well. You're a fast healer."

"Lots of practice."

Wells looked up at Logen's face, where the cut on his forehead had already faded to one more pink line. "I can see. Would it be foolish to advise you to avoid sharp objects in the future?"

Logen laughed. "Believe it or not, I always did my best to avoid them in the past. But they seem to seek me out, despite my efforts."

"Well," said the old servant, cutting off a fresh length of cloth and winding it carefully round Logen's forearm, "I hope this is the last bandage you ever need."

"So do I," said Logen, flexing his fingers. "So do I." But he didn't think it would be.

"Breakfast will be ready soon." And Wells left the two of them alone on the balcony.

They stood there in silence for a moment, then the wind blew up cold from the valley. Quai shivered and pulled his blanket tight around him. "Out there . . . by the lake. You could have left me. I would have left me."

Logen frowned. Time was he'd have done it and never given it a second thought, but things change. "I've left a lot of people, in my time. Reckon I'm sick of that feeling."

The apprentice pursed his lips and looked out at the valley, the woods, the distant mountains. "I never saw a man killed before."

"You're lucky."

"You've seen a lot of death, then?"

Logen winced. In his youth, he would have loved to answer that very question. He could have bragged, and boasted, and listed the actions he'd been in, the Named Men he'd killed. He couldn't say now when the pride had dried up. It had happened slowly. As the wars became bloodier, as the causes became excuses, as the friends went back to the mud, one by one. Logen rubbed at his ear, felt the big notch that Tul Duru's sword had made, long ago. He could have stayed silent. But for some reason, he felt the need to be honest.

"I've fought in three campaigns," he began. "In seven pitched battles. In countless raids and skirmishes and desperate defences, and bloody actions of every kind. I've fought in the driving snow, the blasting wind, the middle of the night. I've been fighting all my life, one enemy or another, one friend or another. I've known little else. I've seen men killed for a word, for a look, for nothing at all. A woman tried to stab me once for killing her husband, and I threw her down a well. And that's far from the worst of it. Life used to be cheap as dirt to me. Cheaper."

"I've fought ten single combats and I won them all, but I fought on the wrong side and for all the wrong reasons. I've been ruthless, and brutal, and a coward. I've stabbed men in the back, burned them, drowned them, crushed them with rocks, killed them asleep, unarmed, or running away. I've run away myself more than once. I've pissed myself with fear. I've begged for my life. I've been wounded, often, and badly, and screamed and cried like a baby whose mother took her tit away. I've no doubt the world would be a better place if I'd been killed years ago, but I haven't been, and I don't know why."

He looked down at his hands, pink and clean on the stone. "There are few men with more blood on their hands than me. None, that I know of. The Bloody-Nine they call me, my enemies, and there's a lot of 'em. Always more enemies, and fewer friends. Blood gets you nothing but more blood. It follows me now, always, like my shadow, and like my shadow I can never be free of it. I should never be free of it. I've earned it. I've deserved it. I've sought it out. Such is my punishment."

And that was all. Logen breathed a deep, ragged sigh and stared out at the lake. He couldn't bring himself to look at the man beside him, didn't want to see the expression on his face. Who wants to learn he's keeping company with the Bloody-Nine? A man who's wrought more death than the plague, and with less regret. They could never be friends now, not with all those corpses between them.

Then he felt Quai's hand clap him on the shoulder. "Well, there it is," he said, grinning from ear to ear, "but you saved me, and I'm right grateful for it!"

"I've saved a man this year, and only killed four. I'm born again." And they both laughed for a while, and it felt good.

"So, Malacus, I see you are back with us."

They turned, Quai stumbling on his blanket and looking a touch sick. The First of the Magi was standing in the doorway, dressed in a long white shirt with sleeves rolled up to the elbow. He still looked more like a butcher than a wizard to Logen.

"Master Bayaz . . . er . . . I was just coming to see you," stuttered Quai.

"Indeed? How fortunate for us both then, that I have come to you." The Magus stepped out onto the balcony. "It occurs to me that a man who is well enough to talk, and laugh, and venture out of doors, is doubtless well enough to read, and study, and expand his tiny mind. What would you say to that?"

"Doubtless . . ."

"Doubtless, yes! Tell me, how are your studies progressing?"

The wretched apprentice looked utterly confused. "They have been somewhat . . . interrupted?"

"You made no progress with Juvens's *Principles of Art* while you were lost in the hills in bad weather?"

"Er . . . no progress . . . no."

"And your knowledge of the histories. Did that develop far, while Master Ninefingers was carrying you back to the library?"

"Er . . . I must confess . . . it didn't."

"Your exercises and meditations though, surely you have been practising those, while unconscious this past week?"

"Well, er . . . no, the unconsciousness was . . . er . . ."

"So, tell me, would you say that you are ahead of the game, so to speak? Or have your studies fallen behind?"

Quai stared down at the floor. "They were behind when I left."

"Then perhaps then you could tell me where you plan to spend the day?"

The apprentice looked up hopefully. "At my desk?"

"Excellent!" Bayaz smiled wide. "I was about to suggest it, but you have anticipated me! Your keenness to learn does you much credit!" Quai nodded furiously and hurried towards the door, the hem of his blanket trailing on the flags.

"Bethod is coming," murmured Bayaz. "He will be here today." Logen's smile vanished, his throat felt suddenly tight. He remembered their last meeting well enough. Stretched out on his face on the floor of Bethod's hall at Carleon, beaten and broken and well chained up, dribbling blood into the straw and hoping the end wouldn't be too long coming. Then, no reason given, they'd let him go. Flung him out the gates with the Dogman, Threetrees, the Weakest and the rest, and told him never to come back. Never. The first time Bethod ever showed a grain of mercy, and the last, Logen didn't doubt.

"Today?" he asked, trying to keep his voice even.

"Yes, and soon. The King of the Northmen. Hah! The arrogance of him!" Bayaz glanced sidelong at Logen. "He is coming to ask me for a favour, and I would like you to be there."

"He won't like that."

"Exactly."

The wind felt colder than before. If Logen never saw Bethod again it would be far too soon. But some things have to be done. It's better to do them, than to live with the fear of them. That's what Logen's father would have said. So he took a deep breath and squared his shoulders. "I'll be there."

"Excellent. Then there is but one thing missing."

"What?"

Bayaz smirked. "You need a weapon."

It was dry in the cellars beneath the library. Dry and dark and very, very confusing. They'd gone up and down steps, around corners, past doors, taking here or there a turning to the left or right. The place was a warren. Logen hoped he didn't lose sight of the wizard's flickering torch, or he could easily be stuck beneath the library for ever.

"Dry down here, nice and dry," Bayaz was saying to himself, voice echoing down the passageway and merging with their flapping footfalls. "There's nothing worse than damp for books." He pulled up suddenly next to a heavy door. "Or for weapons." He gave the door a gentle shove and it swung silently open.

"Look at that! Hasn't been opened for years, but the hinges still move smooth as butter! That's craftsmanship for you! Why does no one care about craftsmanship anymore?" Bayaz stepped over the threshold without waiting for an answer, and Logen followed close behind.

The wizard's torch lit up a long, low hall with walls of rough stone blocks, the far end lost in shadows. The room was lined with racks and shelves, the floor littered with boxes and stands, everything heaped and bursting with a mad array of arms and armour. Blades and spikes and polished surfaces of wood and metal caught the flickering torchlight as Bayaz paced slowly across the stone floor, weaving between the weapons and casting around.

"Quite a collection," muttered Logen, as he followed the Magus through the clutter.

"A load of old junk mostly, but there should be a few things worth the finding." Bayaz took a helmet from a suit of ancient, gilded plate armour and looked it over with a frown. "What do you make of that?"

"I've never been much for armour."

"No, you don't strike me as the type. All very well on horseback, I dare say, but it's a pain in the arse when you've a journey to make on foot." He tossed the helmet back onto its stand, then stood there staring at the armour, lost in thought. "Once you've got it on, how do you piss?"

Logen frowned. "Er . . ." he said, but Bayaz was already moving off down the room, and taking the light with him.

"You must have used a few weapons in your time, Master Ninefingers. What's your preference for?"

"I've never really had one," said Logen, ducking under a rusty halberd leaning out from a rack. "A champion never knows what he might be called on to fight with."

"Of course, of course." Bayaz took up a long spear with a vicious barbed head, and wafted it around a bit. Logen stepped back cautiously. "Deadly enough. You could keep a man at bay with one of these. But a man with a spear needs a lot of friends, and they all need spears as well." Bayaz shoved it back on the rack and moved on.

"This looks fearsome." The Magus took hold of the gnarled shaft of a huge double-bladed axe. "Shit!" he said as he lifted it up, veins bulging out of his neck. "It's heavy enough!" He set it down with a thump, making the rack wobble. "You could kill a man with that! You could cut him clean in half! If he was standing still."

"This is better," said Logen. It was a simple, solid-looking sword, in a scabbard of weathered brown leather.

"Oh, yes indeed. Much, much better. That blade is the work of Kanedias, the Master Maker himself." Bayaz handed his torch to Logen and took the long sword from the rack.

"Has it ever occurred to you, Master Ninefingers, that a sword is different from other weapons? Axes and maces and so forth are lethal enough, but they hang on the belt like dumb brutes." He ran an eye over the hilt, plain cold metal scored with faint grooves for a good grip, glinting in the torchlight. "But a sword . . . a sword has a voice."

"Eh?"

"Sheathed it has little to say, to be sure, but you need only put your hand on the hilt and it begins to whisper in your enemy's ear." He wrapped his fingers tightly round the grip. "A gentle warning. A word of caution. Do you hear it?"

Logen nodded slowly. "Now," murmured Bayaz, "compare it to the sword half drawn." A foot length of metal hissed out of the sheath, a single silver letter shining near the hilt. The blade itself was dull, but its edge had a cold and frosty glint. "It speaks louder, does it not? It hisses a dire threat. It makes a deadly promise. Do you hear it?"

Logen nodded again, his eye fastened on that glittering edge. "Now compare it to the sword full drawn." Bayaz whipped the long blade from its sheath with a faint ringing sound, brought it up so that the point hovered inches from Logen's face. "It shouts now, does it not? It screams defiance! It bellows a challenge! Do you hear it?"

"Mmm," said Logen, leaning back and staring slightly cross-eyed at the shining point of the sword.

Bayaz let it drop and slid it gently back into its scabbard, something to Logen's relief. "Yes, a sword has a voice. Axes and maces and so forth are lethal enough, but a sword is a subtle weapon, and suited to a subtle man. You I think, Master Ninefingers, are subtler than you appear." Logen frowned as Bayaz held the sword out to him. He had been accused of many things in his life, but never subtlety. "Consider it a gift. My thanks for your good manners."

Logen thought about it a moment. He hadn't owned a proper weapon since before he crossed the mountains, and he wasn't keen to take one up again. But Bethod was coming, and soon. Better to have it, and not want it, than to want it, and not have it. Far, far better. You have to be realistic about these things.

"Thank you," said Logen, taking the sword from Bayaz and handing him back the torch. "I think."

A small fire crackled in the grate, and the room was warm, and homely, and comfortable.

But Logen didn't feel comfortable. He stood by the window, staring down into the courtyard below, nervous and twitchy and scared, like he used to be before a fight. Bethod was coming. He was somewhere out there. On the road through the woods, or passing between the stones, or across the bridge, or through the gate.

The First of the Magi didn't seem tense. He sat comfortably in his chair, his feet up on the table next to a long wooden pipe, leafing through a small white-bound book with a faint smile on his face. No one had ever looked calmer, and that only made Logen feel worse.

"Is it good?" asked Logen.

"Is what good?"

"The book."

"Oh yes. It is the best of books. It is Juvens's *Principles of Art*, the very cornerstone of my order." Bayaz waved his free hand at the shelves which covered two walls, and the hundreds of other identical books lined neatly upon them. "It's all the same. One book."

"One?" Logen's eyes scanned across the thick, white spines. "That's a pretty damn long book. Have you read it all?"

Bayaz chuckled. "Oh yes, many times. Every one of my order must read it, and eventually make their own copy." He turned the book around, so that

Logen could see. The pages were thickly covered with lines of neat, but unintelligible symbols. "I wrote these, long ago. You should read it too."

"I'm really not much of a reader."

"No?" asked Bayaz. "Shame." He flicked over the page and carried on.

"What about that one?" There was another book, sat alone on its side on the very top of one of the shelves, a large, black book, scarred and battered-looking. "That written by this Juvens as well?"

Bayaz frowned up at it. "No. His brother wrote that." He got up from his chair, stretched up and pulled it down. "This is a different kind of knowledge." He dragged open his desk drawer, slid the black book inside and slammed it shut. "Best left alone," he muttered, sitting back down and opening up the *Principles of Art* again.

Logen took a deep breath, put his left hand on the hilt of the sword, felt the cold metal pressing into his palm. The feel of it was anything but reassuring. He let go and turned back to the window, frowning down into the courtyard. He felt his breath catch in his throat.

"Bethod. He's here."

"Good, good," muttered Bayaz absently. "Who does he have with him?"

Logen peered at the three figures in the courtyard. "Scale," he said with a scowl. "And a woman. I don't recognise her. They're dismounting." Logen licked his dry lips. "They're coming in."

"Yes, yes," murmured Bayaz, "that is how one gets to a meeting. Try to calm yourself, my friend. Breathe."

Logen leaned back against the whitewashed plaster, arms folded, and took a deep breath. It didn't help. The hard knot of worry in his chest only pressed harder. He could hear heavy footsteps in the corridor outside. The doorknob turned.

Scale was the first into the room. Bethod's eldest son had always been burly, even as a boy, but since Logen last saw him he'd grown monstrous. His rock of a head seemed almost an afterthought on top of all that brawn, his skull a good deal narrower than his neck. He had a great block of jaw, a flat stub of a nose, and furious, bulging, arrogant little eyes. His thin mouth was twisted in a constant sneer, much like his younger brother Calder's, but there was less guile here and a lot more violence. He had a heavy broadsword on his hip, and his meaty hand was never far from it as he glowered at Logen, oozing malice from every pore.

The woman came next. She was very tall, slender and pale, almost ill-looking. Her slanting eyes were as narrow and cold as Scale's were bulging and wrathful, and were surrounded with a quantity of dark paint, which made them look narrower and colder still. There were golden rings on her long fingers, golden bracelets on her thin arms, golden chains around her white neck. She swept the room with her frosty blue eyes, each thing she noticed seeming to lift her to new heights of disgust and contempt. First the furniture, then the books, particularly Logen, and Bayaz most of all.

The self-styled King of the Northmen came last, and more magnificent than ever, robed in rich, coloured cloth and rare white furs. He wore a heavy golden chain across his shoulders, a golden circlet round his head, set with a single diamond, big as a bird's egg. His smiling face was more deeply lined than Logen remembered, his hair and beard touched with grey, but he was no less tall, no less vigorous, no less handsome, and he'd gained much of authority and wisdom—of majesty even. He looked every inch a great man, a wise man, a just man. He looked every inch a King. But Logen knew better.

"Bethod!" said Bayaz, warmly, snapping his book shut. "My old friend! You can hardly imagine what a joy it is to see you again." He swung his feet off the table, and gestured at the golden chain, the flashing diamond. "And to see you so hugely advanced in the world! I remember the time was you were happy to visit me alone. But I suppose great men must be attended on, and I see you have brought some . . . other people. Your charming son I know, of course. I see that you've been eating well at least, eh, Scale?"

"*Prince* Scale," rumbled Bethod's monstrous son, his eyes popping out even more.

"Hmm," said Bayaz, with an eyebrow raised. "I have not had the pleasure of meeting your other companion before."

"I am Caurib." Logen blinked. The woman's voice was the most beautiful thing he'd ever heard. Calming, soothing, intoxicating. "I am a sorceress," she sang, tossing her head with a scornful smile. "A sorceress, from the utmost north." Logen stood frozen, his mouth half open. His hatred seeped away. They were all friends here. More than friends. He couldn't take his eyes from her, didn't want to. The others in the room had faded. It was as if she was speaking only to him, and the fondest wish of his heart was that she should never stop—

But Bayaz only laughed. "A real sorceress, and you have the golden voice! How wonderful! It's a long time since I heard that one, but it will not serve you here." Logen shook his head clear and his hatred rushed back in, hot and reassuring. "Tell me, does one have to study, to become a sorceress? Or is it simply a question of jewellery, and a deal of paint about the face?" Caurib's eyes narrowed to deadly blue slits, but the First of the Magi didn't give her time to speak. "And from the *utmost* north, imagine that!" He shivered slightly. "It must be cold up there, this time of year. Rough on the nipples, eh? Have you come to us for the warm weather, or is there something else?"

"I go where my King commands," she hissed, pointed chin lifting a little higher.

"Your King?" asked Bayaz, staring about the room as though there must be someone else there, hiding in the corner.

"My father is King of the Northmen now!" snarled Scale. He sneered at Logen. "You should kneel to him, Bloody-Nine!" He sneered at Bayaz. "And so should you, old man!"

The First of the Magi spread his hands in apology. "Oh I'm afraid I don't kneel to anyone. Too old for it. Stiffness in the joints, you see."

Scale's boot thumped heavy on the floor as he began to move forward, a curse half out of his mouth, but his father placed a gentle hand on his arm. "Come now, my son, there is no need for kneeling here." His voice was cold and even as freshly fallen snow. "It is not fitting that we bicker. Are our interests not the same? Peace? Peace in the North? I have come only to ask for your wisdom, Bayaz, as I did in days past. Is it so wrong, to seek the help of an old friend?" No one had ever sounded more genuine, more reasonable, more trustworthy. But Logen knew better.

"But do we not have peace in the North already?" Bayaz leaned back in his chair, hands clasped before him. "Are the feuds not all ended? Were you not the victor? Do you not have everything you wanted, and more? King of the Northmen, eh? What help could I possibly offer you?"

"I only share my counsel with friends, Bayaz, and you have been no friend to me of late. You turn away my messengers, my son even. You play host to my sworn enemies." He frowned towards Logen, and his lip curled. "Do you know what manner of thing this is? The Bloody-Nine? An animal! A coward! An oath-breaker! Is that the kind of company that you prefer?"

Bethod smiled a friendly smile as he turned back to Bayaz, but there was no missing the threat in his words. "I fear the time has come for you to decide whether you are with me, or against me. There can be no middle ground in this. Either you are a part of my future, or a relic of the past. Yours is the choice, my friend." Logen had seen Bethod give such choices before. Some men had yielded. The rest had gone back to the mud.

But Bayaz, it seemed, was not to be rushed. "Which shall it be?" He reached forward slowly and took his pipe from the table. "The future, or the past?" He strolled over to the fire and squatted down, back turned to his three guests, took a stick from the grate, set it to the bowl, and puffed slowly away. It seemed to take an age for him to get the damn thing lit. "With, or against?" he mused as he returned to his chair.

"Well?" demanded Bethod.

Bayaz stared up at the ceiling and blew out a thin stream of yellow smoke. Caurib looked the old Magus up and down with icy contempt, Scale twitched with impatience, Bethod waited, eyes a little narrowed. Finally, Bayaz gave a heavy sigh. "Very well. I am with you."

Bethod smiled wide, and Logen felt a lurch of terrible disappointment. He had hoped for better from the First of the Magi. Damn foolish, how he never learned to stop hoping.

"Good," murmured the King of the Northmen. "I knew you would see my way of thinking, in the end." He slowly licked his lips, like a hungry man watching good food brought in. "I mean to invade Angland."

Bayaz raised an eyebrow, then he started to chuckle, then he thumped the table with his fist. "Oh that's good, that's very good! You find peace does not suit your kingdom, eh, Bethod? The clans are not used to being friends, are they? They hate each other and they hate you, am I right?"

"Well," smiled Bethod, "they are somewhat restive."

"I bet they are! But send them to war with the Union, then they will be a nation, eh? United against the common enemy, to be sure. And if you win?

You'll be the man who did the impossible! The man who drove the damn southerners out of the North! You'll be loved, or at any rate, more feared than ever. If you lose, well, at least you keep the clans busy a while, and sap their strength in the process. I remember now why I used to like you! An excellent plan!"

Bethod looked smug. "Of course. And we will not lose. The Union is soft, arrogant, unprepared. With your help—"

"My help?" interrupted Bayaz. "You presume too much."

"But you—"

"Oh, that." The Magus shrugged. "I am a liar."

Bayaz lifted his pipe to his mouth. There was a moment of stunned silence. Then Bethod's eyes narrowed. Caurib's widened. Scale's heavy brow crinkled with confusion. Logen's smile slowly returned.

"A liar?" hissed the sorceress. "And more besides, say I!" Her voice still had the singing note about it, but it was a different song now—hard, shrill, murderous sharp. "You old worm! Hiding here behind your walls, and your servants, and your books! Your time is long past, fool! You are nothing but words and dust!" The First of the Magi calmly pursed his lips and blew out smoke. "Words and dust, old worm! Well, we shall see. We will come to your library!" The wizard set his pipe carefully down on the table, a little smoke still curling up out of the bowl. "We will come back to your library, and put your walls to the hammer, your servants to the sword, and your books to the fire! To the—"

"Silence." Bayaz was frowning now, deeper even than he had at Calder, days before in the yard outside. Again Logen felt the desire to step away, but stronger by far. He found himself glancing around the room for a place to hide. Caurib's lips still moved, but only a meaningless croak came out.

"Break my walls, would you?" murmured Bayaz. His grey brows drew inwards, deep, hard grooves cutting into the bridge of his nose.

"Kill my servants, will you?" asked Bayaz. The room had turned very chill, despite the logs on the fire.

"Burn my books, say you?" thundered Bayaz. "You say too much, witch!" Caurib's knees buckled. Her white hand clawed at the door-frame, chains and bangles jingling together as she slumped against the wall.

"Words and dust, am I?" Bayaz thrust up four fingers. "Four gifts you had of me, Bethod—the sun in winter, a storm in summer, and two things you could never have known, but for my Art. What have you given me in return, eh? This lake and this valley, which were mine already, and but one other thing." Bethod's eyes flicked across to Logen, then back. "You owe me still, yet you send messengers to me, you make demands, you presume to *command* me? That is not my idea of manners."

Scale had caught up now, and his eyes were near popping out of his head. "Manners? What does a King need with manners? A King takes what he wants!" And he took a heavy step towards the table.

Now Scale was big enough and cruel enough, to be sure. Most likely you could never find a better man for kicking someone once he was down. But Logen wasn't down, not yet, and he was good and sick of listening to this bloated fool. He stepped forward to block Scale's path, resting his hand on the hilt of his sword. "Far enough."

The Prince looked Logen over with his bulging eyes, held up his meaty fist, squeezing his great fingers so the knuckles turned white. "Don't tempt me Ninefingers, you broken cur! Your day's long past! I could crush you like an egg!"

"You can try it, but I've no mind to let you. You know my work. One step more and I'll set to work on you, you fucking swollen pig."

"Scale!" snapped Bethod. "There is nothing for us here, that much is plain. We are leaving." The hulking prince locked his great lump of a jaw, his huge hands clenching and unclenching by his sides, glowering at Logen with the most bestial hatred imaginable. Then he sneered, and slowly backed away.

Bayaz leaned forward. "You said you would bring peace to the North, Bethod, and what have you done? You have piled war on war! The land is bled white with your pride and your brutality! King of the Northmen? Hah! You're not worth the helping! And to think, I had such high hopes for you!"

Bethod only frowned, his eyes as cold as the diamond on his forehead. "You have made an enemy of me, Bayaz, and I am a bad enemy to have. The very worst. You will yet regret this day's work." He turned his scorn on Logen. "As for you, Ninefingers, you will have no more mercy from me!

Every man in the North will be your enemy now! You will be hated, and hunted, and cursed, wherever you go! I will see to it!"

Logen shrugged. There was nothing new there. Bayaz stood up from his chair. "You've said your piece, now take your witch and get you gone!"

Caurib stumbled from the room first, still gasping for air. Scale gave Logen one last scowl, then he turned and lumbered away. The so-called King of the Northmen was the last to leave, nodding slowly and sweeping the room with a deadly glare. As their footsteps faded down the corridor Logen took a deep breath, steadied himself, and let his hand drop from the hilt of the sword.

"So," said Bayaz brightly, "that went well."

A ROAD BETWEEN
TWO DENTISTS

Past midnight, and it was dark in the Middleway. Dark and it smelled bad. It always smelled bad down by the docks: old salt water, rotten fish, tar and sweat and horse shit. In a few hours time this street would be thronging with noise and activity. Tradesmen shouting, labourers cursing under their loads, merchants hurrying to and fro, a hundred carts and wagons rumbling over the dirty cobbles. There would be an endless tide of people, thronging off the ships and thronging on, people from every part of the world, words shouted in every language under the sun. But at night it was still. Still and silent. *Silent as the grave, and even worse smelling.*

"It's down here," said Severard, strolling towards the shadowy mouth of a narrow alley, wedged in between two looming warehouses.

"Did he give you much trouble?" asked Glokta as he shuffled painfully after.

"Not too much." The Practical adjusted his mask, letting some air in behind. *Must get very clammy under there, all that breath and sweat. No wonder Practicals tend to have bad tempers.* "He gave Rews's mattress some trouble, stabbed it all to bits. Then Frost knocked him on the head. Funny thing. When that boy knocks a man on the head, the trouble all goes out of him."

"What about Rews?"

"Still alive." The light from Severard's lamp passed over a pile of putrid rubbish. Glokta heard rats squeaking in the darkness as they scurried away.

"You know all the best neighbourhoods, don't you Severard?"

"That's what you pay me for, Inquisitor." His dirty black boot squelched, heedless, into the stinking mush. Glokta limped gingerly around it, holding the hem of his coat up in his free hand. "I grew up 'round here," continued the Practical. "Folk don't ask questions."

"Except for us." *We always have questions.*

"Course." Severard gave a muffled giggle. "We're the Inquisition." His lamp picked out a dented iron gate, the high wall above topped with rusty spikes. "This is it." *Indeed, and what an auspicious-looking address it is.* The gate evidently didn't see much use, its brown hinges squealed in protest as the Practical unlocked it and heaved it open. Glokta stepped awkwardly over a puddle that had built up in a rut in the ground, cursing as his coat trailed in the foul water.

The hinges screamed again as Severard wrestled the heavy gate shut, forehead creasing with the effort, then he lifted the hood on his lantern, lighting up a wide ornamental courtyard, choked with rubble and weeds and broken wood.

"And here we are," said Severard.

It must once have been a magnificent building, in its way. *How much would all those windows have cost? How much all that decorative stonework? Visitors must have been awed by its owner's wealth, if not his good taste.* But no more. The windows were blinded with rotting boards, the swirls of masonry were choked with moss and caked with bird droppings. The thin layer of green marble on the pillars was cracked and flaking, exposing the rotten plaster underneath. All was crumbled, broken and decayed. Fallen lumps of the façade were strewn everywhere, casting long shadows on the high walls of the yard. Half the head of a broken cherub stared mournfully up at Glokta as he limped past.

He had been expecting some dingy warehouse, some dank cellar near the water. "What is this place?" he asked, staring up at the rotting palace.

"Some merchant built it, years ago." Severard kicked a lump of broken sculpture out of his way and it clattered off into the darkness. "A rich man, very rich. Wanted to live near his warehouses and his wharves, keep one eye on business." He strolled up the cracked and mossy steps to the huge, flaking front door. "He thought the idea might catch on, but how could it? Who'd want to live round here if they didn't have to? Then he lost all his money, as merchants do. His creditors have had trouble finding a buyer."

Glokta stared at a broken fountain, leaning at an angle and half-filled with stagnant water. "Hardly surprising."

Severard's lamp barely lit the cavernous space of the entrance hall. Two enormous, curved, slumping staircases loomed out of the gloom opposite them. A wide balcony ran around the walls at first floor level, but a great section of it had collapsed and crashed through the damp floorboards below, so that one of the stairways ended, amputated, hanging in the empty air. The damp floor was strewn with lumps of broken plaster, fallen roofing slates, shattered timbers and a spattering of grey bird droppings. The night sky peered in through several yawning holes in the roof. Glokta could hear the vague sound of pigeons cooing in amongst the shadowy rafters, and somewhere the slow dripping of water.

What a place. Glokta stifled a smile. *It reminds me of myself, in a way. We both were magnificent once, and we both have our best days far behind us.*

"It's big enough, wouldn't you say?" asked Severard, picking his way in amongst the rubble towards a yawning doorway under the broken staircase, his lamp casting strange, slanting shadows as he moved.

"Oh, I'd have thought so, unless we get more than a thousand prisoners at once." Glokta shuffled after him, leaning heavily on his cane, worried about his footing on the slimy floor. *I'll slip and fall right on my arse, right here in all this bird shit. That would be perfect.*

The arch opened into a crumbling hall, rotten plaster falling away in sheets, showing the damp bricks beneath. Gloomy doorways passed by on either side. *The sort of place that would make a man nervous, if he was prone to nervousness. He might imagine unpleasant things in these chambers, just beyond the lamp light, and horrible acts taking place in the darkness.* He looked up at Severard, ambling jauntily along in front, tuneless whistling vaguely audible from behind his mask, and frowned. *But we are not prone to nervousness. Perhaps we are the unpleasant things. Perhaps the acts are ours.*

"How big is this place?" asked Glokta as he hobbled along.

"Thirty-five rooms, not counting the servant's quarters."

"A palace. How the hell did you find it?"

"I used to sleep here, some nights. After my mother died. I found a way in. The roof was still mostly on back then, and it was a dry place to sleep. Dry and safe. More or less." *Ah, what a hard life it's been. Thug and torturer is a real step up for you, isn't it? Every man has his excuses, and the more vile the man becomes, the more touching the story has to be. What is my story now, I wonder?*

"Ever resourceful, eh, Severard?"

"That's what you pay me for, Inquisitor."

They passed into a wide space: a drawing room, a study, a ball-room even, it was big enough. Once beautiful panels were sagging from the walls, covered in mould and flaking gilt paint. Severard moved over to one, still attached, and pushed it firmly at one side. There was a soft click as it swung open, revealing a dark archway beyond. *A hidden door? How delightful. How sinister. How very appropriate.*

"This place is as full of surprises as you are," said Glokta, limping painfully towards the opening.

"And you wouldn't believe the price I got."

"We bought this?"

"Oh no. I did. With Rews's money. And now I'm renting it to you." Severard's eyes sparkled in the lamplight. "It's a gold mine!"

"Hah!" laughed Glokta, as he shuffled carefully down the steps. *All this, and a head for business too. Perhaps I'll be working for Arch Lector Severard one of these days. Stranger things have happened.* Glokta's shadow loomed out ahead of him into the darkness as he laboured crab-like down the steps, his right hand feeling out the gaps between the rough stone blocks to lend him some support.

"The cellars go on for miles," muttered Severard from behind. "We have our own private access to the canals, and to the sewers too, if you're interested in sewers." They passed a dark opening on their left, then another on their right, always going slowly downwards. "Frost tells me you can get all the way from here to the Agriont, without once coming up for air."

"That could be useful."

"I'd say so, if you can stand the smell."

Severard's lamp found a heavy door with a small, barred opening. "Home again," he said, and gave four quick knocks. A moment later Practical Frost's masked face loomed abruptly out of the darkness at the little window. "Only us." The albino's eyes showed no sign of warmth or recognition. *But then they never do.* Heavy bolts slid back on the other side of the door, and it swung smoothly open.

There was a table and chair, and fresh torches on the walls, but they were unlit. *It must have been pitch black in here until our little lamp arrived.* Glokta looked over at the albino. "Have you just been sitting here in the dark?" The hulking Practical shrugged, and Glokta shook his head. "Sometimes I worry about you, Practical Frost, I really do."

"He's down here," said Severard, ambling off down the hall, heels making clicking echoes on the stone flags of the floor. This must once have been a wine cellar: there were several barrel-vaulted chambers leading off to either side, sealed with heavy gratings.

"Glokta!" Salem Rews's fingers were gripped tightly round the bars, his face pressed up between them.

Glokta stopped in front of the cell and rested his throbbing leg. "Rews, how are you? I hardly expected to see you again so soon." He had lost weight already, his skin was slack and pale, still marked with fading bruises. *He does not look well, not well at all.*

"What's happening Glokta? Please, why am I here?"

Well, where's the harm? "It seems the Arch Lector still has a use for you. He wants you to give evidence." Glokta leaned towards the bars. "Before the Open Council," he whispered.

Rews grew paler still. "Then what?"

"We'll see." *Angland, Rews, Angland.*

"What if I refuse?"

"Refuse the Arch Lector?" Glokta chuckled. "No, no, no, Rews. You don't want to do a thing like that." He turned away and shuffled after Severard.

"For pity's sake! It's dark down here!"

"You'll get used to it!" Glokta called over his shoulder. *Amazing, what one can get used to.*

The last of the chambers held their latest prisoner. Chained up to a bracket in the wall, naked and bagged of course. He was short and stocky, tending slightly to fat, with fresh grazes on his knees, no doubt from being flung into the rough stone cell.

"So this is our killer, eh?" The man rolled himself up onto his knees when he heard Glokta's voice, straining forward against his chains. A little blood had soaked through the front of the bag and dried there, making a brown stain on the canvas.

"A very unsavoury character indeed," said Severard. "Doesn't look too fearsome now, though, does he?"

"They never do, once they're brought to this. Where do we work?"

Severard's eyes smiled even more. "Oh, you're going to like this, Inquisitor."

"It's a touch theatrical," said Glokta, "but none the worse for that."

The room was large and circular with a domed ceiling, painted with a curious mural that ran all the way round the curved walls. The body of a man lay on the grass, bleeding from many wounds, with a forest behind him. Eleven other figures walked away, six on one side, five on the other, painted in profile, awkwardly posed, dressed in white but their features indistinct. They faced another man, arms stretched out, all in black and with a sea of colourfully daubed fire behind him. The harsh light from six bright lamps didn't make the work look any better. *Hardly of the highest quality, more decoration than art, but the effect is quite striking, nonetheless.*

"No idea what it's supposed to be," said Severard.

"The Mather Ma'er" mumbled Practical Frost.

"Of course," said Glokta, staring up at the dark figure on the wall, and the flames behind. "You should study your history, Practical Severard. This is the Master Maker, Kanedias." He turned and pointed to the dying man on the opposite wall. "And this is great Juvens, whom he has killed." He swept his hand over the figures in white. "And these are Juvens's apprentices, the Magi, marching to avenge him." *Ghost stories, fit to scare children with.*

"What kind of man pays to have shit like this on the walls of his cellar?" asked Severard, shaking his head.

"Oh, this sort of thing was quite popular at one time. There's a room painted like this in the palace. This is a copy, and a cheap one." Glokta looked up at the shadowed face of Kanedias, staring grimly down into the room, and the bleeding corpse on the opposite wall. "Still, there's something quite unsettling about it, isn't there?" *Or there would be, if I gave a damn.* "Blood, fire, death, vengeance. No idea why you'd want it in the cellar. Perhaps there was something dark about our friend the merchant."

"There's always something dark about a man with money," said Severard. "Who are these two?"

Glokta frowned, peering forward. Two small, vague figures could be seen under the arms of the Maker, one on each side. "Who knows?" asked Glokta, "maybe they're his Practicals."

Severard laughed. A vague exhalation of air even came from behind Frost's mask, though his eyes showed no sign of amusement. *My, my, he must be thoroughly tickled.*

Glokta shuffled toward the table in the centre of the room. Two chairs faced each other across the smooth, polished surface. One was a spare, hard affair of the sort you found in the cellars of the House of Questions, but the other was altogether more impressive, throne-like almost, with sweeping arms and a high back, upholstered in brown leather.

Glokta placed his cane against the table and lowered himself carefully, back aching. "Oh, this is an excellent chair," he breathed, sinking slowly back into the soft leather, stretching out his leg, throbbing from the long walk here. There was a slight resistance. He looked beneath the table. There was a matching footstool there.

Glokta tipped his head back and laughed. "Oh this is fine! You shouldn't have!" He settled his leg down on the stool with a comfortable sigh.

"It was the least we could do," said Severard, folding his arms and leaning against the wall next to the bleeding body of Juvens. "We did well from your friend Rews, very well. You've always seen us right, and we don't forget that."

"Unhhh," said Frost, nodding his head.

"You spoil me." Glokta stroked the polished wood on the arm of the chair. *My boys. Where would I be without you? Back home in bed with mother fussing over me, I suppose, wondering how she'll ever find a nice girl to marry me now.* He glanced over the instruments on the table. His case was there, of course, and a few other things, well-used, but still highly serviceable. A pair of long-handled tongs particularly caught his eye. He glanced up at Severard. "Teeth?"

"Seemed a good place to start."

"Fair enough." Glokta licked at his own empty gums then cracked his knuckles, one by one. "Teeth, it is."

As soon as the gag was off the assassin started screaming at them in Styrian, spitting and cursing, struggling pointlessly at his chains. Glokta didn't understand a word of it. *But I think I catch the meaning, more or less. Something very offensive indeed, I imagine. Something about our mothers, and so on. But I am not easily offended.* He was a rough looking sort, face pockmarked with acne scars, nose broken more than once and bent out of shape. *How disappointing. I was hoping the Mercers might have gone up-market on this occasion at least, but that's merchants for you. Always looking for the bargain.*

Practical Frost ended the torrent of unintelligible abuse by punching the man heavily in the stomach. *That'll take his breath away for a moment. Long enough to get the first word in.*

"Now then," said Glokta, "we'll have none of that nonsense here. We know you're a professional, sent to blend in and do a job. You wouldn't blend in too well if you couldn't even speak the language, now would you?"

The prisoner had got his breath back. "Pox on all of you, you bastards!" he gasped.

"Excellent! The common tongue will do nicely for our little chats. I have a feeling we may end up having several. Is there anything you would like to know about us before we begin? Or shall we get straight to it?"

The prisoner stared up suspiciously at the painted figure of the Master Maker, looming over Glokta's head. "Where am I?"

"We're just off the Middleway, down near the water." Glokta winced as the muscles in his leg suddenly convulsed. He stretched it out cautiously, waiting until he heard the knee click before he carried on. "You know, the Middleway is one of the very arteries of the city, it runs straight through its heart, from the Agriont to the sea. It passes through many different districts, has all manner of notable buildings. Some of the most fashionable addresses in the whole city are just up the lane. To me though, it's nothing but a road between two dentists."

The prisoner's eyes narrowed, then darted over the instruments on the table. *But no more cursing. It seems the mention of dentistry has got his attention.*

"Up at the other end of the avenue," and Glokta pointed roughly north-wards, "in one of the most expensive parts of town, opposite the public gardens, in a beautiful white house in the very shadow of the Agriont, is the establishment of Master Farrad. You might have heard of him?"

"Get fucked!"

Glokta raised his eyebrows. *If only.* "They say that Master Farrad is the finest dentist in the world. I believe he came from Gurkhul originally, but he escaped the tyranny of the Emperor to join us in the Union and make a better life for himself, saving our wealthiest citizens from the terrors of bad teeth. When I came back from my own little visit to the South, my family sent me to him, to see if there was anything he could do for me." Glokta smiled wide, showing the assassin the nature of the problem. "Of course there wasn't. The Emperor's torturers saw to that. But he's a damn fine dentist, everyone says so."

"So what?"

Glokta let his smile fade. "Down at the other end of the Middleway, down near the sea, in amongst the filth and the scum and the slime of the docks, am I. The rents may be cheap hereabouts, but I feel confident that, once we have spent some time together, you will not think me any less talented than the esteemed Master Farrad. It is simply that my talents lie in a different direction. The good Master eases the pain of his patients, while I am a dentist . . ." and Glokta leaned slowly forward ". . . of a different sort."

The assassin laughed in his face. "Do you think you can scare me with a bag on the head and a nasty painting?" He looked round at Frost and Severard, "you crowd of freaks?"

"Do I think we scare you? The three of us?" Glokta allowed himself a chuckle at that. "Here you sit, alone, unarmed and thoroughly restrained. Who knows where you are but us, or cares to know? You have no hope of deliverance, or of escape. We're all professionals here. I think you can guess what's coming, more or less." Glokta grinned a sickly grin. "Of course we scare you, don't play the fool. You hide it well, I'll admit, but that can't last. The time will come, soon enough, when you'll be begging to go back in the bag."

"You'll get nothing from me," growled the assassin, staring him straight in the eye. "Nothing." *Tough. A tough man. But it's easy to act tough before the work begins. I should know.*

Glokta rubbed his leg gently. The blood was flowing nicely now, the pain almost gone. "We'll keep it simple to begin with. Names, that's all I want, for now. Just names. Why don't we start with yours? At least you can't tell us you don't know the answer."

They waited. Severard and Frost stared down at the prisoner, the green eyes smiling, the pink ones not. Silence.

Glokta sighed. "Right then." Frost planted his fists on either side of the assassin's jaw, started to squeeze until his teeth were forced apart. Severard shoved the ends of the tongs in between and forced his jaws open, much too wide for comfort. The assassin's eyes bulged. *Hurts, doesn't it? But that's nothing, believe me.*

"Watch his tongue," said Glokta, "we want him talking."

"Don't worry," muttered Severard, peering into the assassin's mouth. He ducked back suddenly. "Ugh! His breath smells like shit!"

A shame, but I am hardly surprised. Clean living is rarely a priority for hired killers. Glokta got slowly to his feet, limped round the table. "Now then," he murmured, one hand hovering over his instruments, "where to begin?" He picked up a mounted needle and craned forward, his other hand gripped tight around the top of his cane, probing carefully at the killer's teeth. *Not a pretty set, to be sure. I do believe I'd rather have my teeth than his.*

"Dear me, these are in a terrible state. Rotten through and through. That's why your breath stinks so badly. There's no excuse for it, a man of your age."

"Haah!" yelped the prisoner as Glokta touched a nerve. He tried to speak, but with the tongs in place he made less sense than Practical Frost.

"Quiet now, you've had your chance to talk. Perhaps you'll get another later, I haven't decided." Glokta put the needle back down on the table, shaking his head sadly. "Your teeth are a fucking disgrace. Revolting. I do declare, they're just about falling out on their own. Do you know," he said, as he took the little hammer and chisel from the table, "I do believe you'd be better off without them."

FLATHEADS

Grey morning time, out in the cold, wet woods, and the Dogman just sat there, thinking about how things used to be better. Sat there, minding the spit, turning it round every once in a while and trying not to get too nervous with the waiting. Tul Duru wasn't helping any with that. He was striding up and down the grass, round the old stones and back, wearing his great boots out, about as patient as a wolf on heat. Dogman watched him stomping—clomp, clomp, clomp. He'd learned a long time ago that great fighters are only good for one thing. Fighting. At pretty much everything else, and at waiting in particular, they're fucking useless.

"Why don't you sit yourself down, Tul?" muttered Dogman. "There's stones aplenty for the purpose. Warmer here by the fire and all. Rest those flapping feet o' yours, you're getting me twitchy."

"Sit me down?" rumbled the giant, coming up and looming over the Dogman like a great bloody house. "How can I sit, or you either?" He frowned across the ruins and into the trees from under his great, heavy brows. "You sure this is the place?"

"This is the place." Dogman stared round at the broken stones, hoping like hell that it was. He couldn't deny there was no sign of 'em yet. "They'll be here, don't you worry." So long as they ain't all got themselves killed, he thought, but he had the sense not to say it. He'd spent enough time marching with Tul Duru Thunderhead to know—you don't get that man stirred up. Unless you want a broken head, o' course.

"They better be here soon is all." Tul's bloody great hands curled up into fists fit to break rocks with. "I got no taste for just sitting here, arse in the wind!"

"Nor do I, neither," said the Dogman, showing his palms and doing his best to keep everything gentle, "but don't you fret on it, big lad. They'll be along soon enough, just the way we planned. This is the place." He eyed the hog crackling away, dripping some nice gravy in the fire. His mouth was watering good now, his nose was full of the smell of meat . . . and something else beside. Just a whiff. He looked up, sniffing.

"You smell something?" asked Tul, peering into the woods.

"Something, maybe." The Dogman leaned down and took a hold on his bow.

"What is it? Shanka?"

"Not sure, could be." He sniffed the air again. Smelled like a man, and a mighty sour-smelling one at that.

"I could have killed the fucking pair o' you!"

Dogman spun about, half falling over and near fumbling his bow while he did it. Black Dow wasn't ten strides behind him, down wind, creeping over to the fire with a nasty grin. Grim was at his shoulder, face blank as a wall, as always.

"You bastards!" bellowed Tul. "You near made me shit with your sneaking around!"

"Good," sneered Dow. "You could lose some fucking lard."

Dogman took a long breath and tossed his bow back down. Some relief to know they were in the right spot after all, but he could've done without the scare. He'd been jumpy since he saw Logen go over the edge of that cliff. Roll right on over and not a thing anyone could do about it. Could happen to anyone any time, death, and that was a fact.

Grim clambered over the broken stones and sat himself down on one next to the Dogman, gave him the barest of nods. "Meat?" barked Dow, shoving past Tul and flopping down beside the fire, ripping a leg off the carcass and tearing into it with his teeth.

And that was it. That was all the greeting, after a month or more apart. "A man with friends is rich indeed," muttered the Dogman out the corner of his mouth.

"Whatsay?" spat Dow, cold eyes sliding round, his mouth full of pig, his dirty, stubbly chin all shiny with grease.

Dogman showed his palms again. "Nothing to take offence at." He'd spent enough time marching with Black Dow to know—you might as well cut your own neck as make that evil bastard angry. "Any trouble while we was split up?" he asked, looking to change the subject.

Grim nodded. "Some."

"Fucking Flatheads!" snarled Dow, spraying bits of meat in Dogman's face. "They're bloody everywhere!" He pointed the hog's leg across the fire like it was a blade. "I've taken enough of this shit! I'm going back south. It's too bloody cold by half, and fucking Flatheads everywhere! Bastards! I'm going south!"

"You scared?" asked Tul.

Dow turned to look up at him with a big yellow grin, and the Dogman winced. It was a damn fool of a question, that. He'd never been scared in his life, Black Dow. Didn't know what it was to be scared. "Feared of a few Shanka? Me?" He gave a nasty laugh. "We done some work on them, while you two been snoring. Gave some of 'em warm beds to sleep in. Too warm by half."

"Burned 'em," muttered Grim. That was a full day's talk out of him already.

"Burned a whole fucking pile of 'em," hissed Dow, grinning like he never heard such a joke as corpses on fire. "They don't scare me, big lad, no more'n you do, but I don't plan to sit here waiting for 'em neither, just so Threetrees has time to haul his flabby old arse out of bed. I'm going south!" And he tore off another mouthful of meat.

"Who's got the flabby arse now?"

Dogman cracked a grin as he saw Threetrees striding over towards the fire, and he started up and grabbed the old boy by the hand. He had Forley the Weakest with him and all, and Dogman clapped the little man on the back as he came past. Nearly knocked him over, he was that pleased to see they were all alive and made it through another month. Didn't hurt to have some leadership round the fire, neither. Everyone looked happy for once, smiling and pressing hands and all the rest. Everyone but Dow, o' course. He just sat there, staring at the fire, sucking on his bone, face sour as old milk.

"Right good to see you again, lads, and all in one piece." Threetrees hefted his big round shield off his shoulder and leant it up against a broken old bit of wall. "How've you been?"

"Fucking cold," said Dow, not even looking up. "We're going south."

Dogman sighed. Back together for ten heartbeats and the bickering was already started. It was going to be a tough crowd now, without Logen to keep things settled. A tough crowd, and apt to get bloody. Threetrees wasn't rushing into anything, though. He took a moment to think on it, like always. He loved to take his moment, that one. That was what made him so dangerous. "Going south, eh?" said Threetrees, after he'd chewed it over for a minute. "And just when did all this get decided?"

"Nothing's decided," said the Dogman, showing his palms one more time. He reckoned he might be doing that a lot from now on.

Tul Duru frowned down at Dow's back. "Nothing at all," he rumbled, mightily annoyed at having his mind made up for him.

"Nothing is right," said Threetrees, slow and steady as the grass growing. "I don't recall this being no voting band."

Dow took no time at all to think about that. He never took time, that one. That was what made *him* so dangerous. He leaped up, flinging the bone onto the ground, squaring up to Threetrees with a fighting look. "I . . . say . . . south!" he snarled, eyes bulging like bubbles on a stew.

Threetrees didn't back down a step. That wouldn't have been his way at all. He took his moment to think on it, course, then he took a step forward of his own, so his nose and Dow's were almost touching. "If you wanted a say, you should have beaten Ninefingers," he growled, "instead of losing like the rest of us."

Black Dow's face turned dark as tar at that. He didn't like being reminded of losing. "The Bloody-Nine's gone back to the mud!" he snarled. "Dogman seen it, didn't you?"

Dogman had to nod. "Aye," he muttered.

"So that's the end of that! There's no reason for us to be pissing around here, north of the mountains, with Flatheads crawling up our arses! I say south!"

"Ninefingers may be dead," said Threetrees in Dow's face, "but your debt ain't. Why he saw fit to spare a man as worthless as you I'll never know, but he named me as second," and he tapped his big chest, "and that means I'm the one with the say! Me and no other!"

Dogman took a careful step back. The two of 'em were shaping up for blows alright, and he'd no wish to get a bloody nose in all the confusion. It would hardly have been the first time. Forley took a stab at keeping the peace. "Come on boys," he said, all nice and soft, "there's no need for this." He might not have been much at killing, Forley, but he was a damn good boy for stopping those that were from killing each other. Dogman wished him luck with it. "Come on, why don't you—"

"Shut your fucking hole, you!" growled Dow, one dirty finger stabbing savage in Forley's face. "What's your fucking say worth, Weakest?"

"Leave him be!" rumbled Tul, holding his great fist up under Dow's chin, "or I'll give you something to shout about!"

The Dogman could hardly look. Dow and Threetrees were always picking at each other. They got fired up quick and damped down quick. The Thunderhead was a different animal. Once that big ox got properly riled there was no calming him. Not without ten strong men and a lot of rope. Dogman tried to think what Logen would have done. He'd have known how to stop 'em fighting, if he hadn't been dead.

"Shit!" shouted Dogman, jumping up from the fire all of a sudden. "There's fucking Shanka crawling all over us! And if we get through with them there's always Bethod to think on! We've a world full of scores to settle without making more ourselves! Logen's gone and Threetrees is second, and that's the only say I'll hear!" He did some jabbing with his own finger, at no one in particular, then he waited, hoping like hell that it had done the trick.

"Aye," grunted Grim.

Forley started nodding like a woodpecker. "Dogman's right! We need to fight each other like we need the cock-rot! Threetrees is second. He's the chief now."

It was quiet for a moment, and Dow fixed the Dogman with that cold, empty, killing look, like the cat with the mouse between its paws. Dogman swallowed. A lot of men, most men even, wouldn't have dared meet no look like that from Black Dow. He got the name from having the blackest reputation in the North, with coming sudden in the black of night, and leaving the villages behind him black from fire. That was the rumour. That was the fact.

It took all the bones Dogman had not to stare at his boots. He was just ready to do it when Dow looked away, eyed the others, one at a time. Most men wouldn't have met that look, but these here weren't most men. You could never have hoped to meet a bloodier crowd, not anywhere under the sun. Not a one of them backed down, or even seemed to consider it. Apart from Forley the Weakest, of course, he was staring at the grass before his turn even came.

Once Dow saw they were all against him he cracked a happy smile, just as if there never was a problem. "Fair enough," he said to Threetrees, the anger all seeming to drain away in an instant. "What's it to be then, chief?"

Threetrees looked over at the woods. He sniffed and sucked at his teeth. He scratched at his beard, taking his moment to think on it. He looked each one of them over, considering. "We go south," he said.

He smelled 'em before he saw 'em, but that was always the way with him. He had a good nose, did the Dogman, that's how he got the name after all. Being honest though, anyone could have smelled 'em. They fucking stank.

There were twelve down in the clearing. Sitting, eating, grunting to each other in their nasty, dirty tongue, big yellow teeth sticking out everywhere, dressed in lumps of smelly fur and reeking hide and odd bits of rusty armour. Shanka.

"Fucking Flatheads," Dogman muttered to himself. He heard a soft hiss behind, turned round to see Grim peering up from behind a bush. He held out his open hand to say stop, tapped the top of his skull to say Flatheads, held up his fist, then two fingers to say twelve, and pointed back down the track towards the others. Grim nodded and faded away into the woods.

The Dogman took one last look at the Shanka, just to make sure they were all still unwary. They were, so he slipped back down the tree and off.

"They're camped round the road, twelve that I saw, maybe more."

"They looking for us?" asked Threetrees.

"Maybe, but they ain't looking too hard."

"Could we get around them?" asked Forley, always looking to miss out on a fight.

Dow spat onto the ground, always looking to get into one. "Twelve is nothing! We can do them alright!"

The Dogman looked over at Threetrees, thinking it out, taking his moment. Twelve wasn't nothing, and they all knew it, but it might be better to deal with them than leave them free and easy behind.

"What's it to be, chief?" asked Tul.

Threetrees set his jaw. "Weapons."

A fighting man's a fool that don't keep his weapons clean and ready. Dogman had been over his no more'n an hour before. Still, you won't be killed for checking 'em, while you might be for not doing it.

There was the hissing of steel on leather, the clicking of wood and the clanking of metal. Dogman watched Grim twang at his bowstring, check over the feathers on his shafts. He watched Tul Duru run his thumb down the edge of his big heavy sword, almost as tall as Forley was, clucking like a chicken at a spot of rust. He watched Black Dow rubbing a rag on the head of his axe, looking at the blade with eyes soft as a lover's. He watched Threetrees tugging at the buckles on his shield straps, swishing his blade through the air, bright metal glinting.

The Dogman gave a sigh, pulled the straps on his guard tighter round his left wrist, checked the wood of his bow for cracks. He made sure all his knives were where they should be. You can never have too many knives, Logen had told him once, and he'd taken it right to heart. He watched Forley checking his short-sword with clumsy hands, his mouth chewing away, eyes all wet with fear. That got his own nerves jumping, and he glanced round at the others. Dirty, scarred, frowns and lots of beard. There was no fear there, no fear at all, but that was nothing to be shamed at. Different men have different ways, Logen had told him once, and you have to have fear to have courage. He'd taken that right to heart as well.

He walked over to Forley and gave him a clap on the shoulder. "You have to have fear to have courage," he said.

"That so?"

"So they say, and it's a good thing too." The Dogman leaned close so no one else could hear. "'Cause I'm about ready to shit." He reckoned that's what Logen would have done, and now that Logen had gone back to the mud it fell to him. Forley gave half a smile, but it slumped pretty fast, and he looked more scared then ever. There's only so much you can do.

"Right, boys," said Threetrees, once the gear was all checked and stowed in its proper places, "here's how we'll get it done. Grim, Dogman, opposite sides of their camp, out in the trees. Wait for the signal, then shoot any Flathead with a bow. Failing that, whatever's closest."

"Right you are, chief," said the Dogman. Grim gave a nod.

"Tul, you and me'll take the front, but wait for the signal, eh?"

"Aye," rumbled the giant.

"Dow, you and Forley at the back. You come on when you see us go. But this time you wait for us to go!" hissed Threetrees, stabbing with his thick finger.

"Course, chief." Dow shrugged his shoulders, just as though he always did as he was told.

"Right then, there it is," said Threetrees, "anyone still confused? Any empty heads round the fire?" The Dogman mumbled and shook his head. They all did. "Fair enough. Just one more thing." The old boy leaned forward, looking at each of them one by one. "Wait . . . for . . . the . . . fucking . . . signal!"

It wasn't 'til the Dogman was hid behind a bush with his bow in his hand and a shaft at the ready that he realised. He'd no idea what the signal was. He looked down at the Shanka, still sat there all unwary, grunting and shouting and banging about. By the dead he needed to piss. Always needed to piss before a fight. Had anyone said the signal? He couldn't remember.

"Shit," he whispered, and just then Dow came hurtling out from the trees, axe in one hand, sword in the other.

"Fucking Flatheads!" he screamed, giving the nearest a fearsome big blow in the head and splattering blood across the clearing. In so far as you could tell what a Shanka was thinking, these ones looked greatly surprised. Dogman reckoned that would have to do for a signal.

He let loose his shaft at the nearest Flathead, just reaching for a big club and watched it catch him through the armpit with a satisfying thunk. "Hah!" he shouted. He saw Dow spit another through the back with his sword, but there was a big Shanka now with a spear ready to throw. An arrow came looping out of the trees and stuck it through the neck, and it let go a squeal and sprawled out backwards. That Grim was a damn good shot.

Now Threetrees came roaring from the scrub on the other side of the clearing, catching them off guard. He barged one Flathead in the back with his shield and it sprawled face-first into the fire, he hacked at another with his sword. The Dogman let go a shaft and it stuck a Shanka in its gut. It dropped down on its knees and a moment later Tul took its head off with a great swing of his sword.

The fight was joined and moving quick—chop, grunt, scrape, rattle. There was blood flying and weapons swinging and bodies dropping too fast for the Dogman to try an arrow at. The three of them had the last few hemmed in, squawking and gibbering. Tul Duru was swinging his big sword around, keeping them at bay. Threetrees darted in and chopped the legs out from under one, and Dow cut another down as it looked round.

The last one squawked and made a run for the trees. Dogman shot at it, but he was hurrying and he missed. The arrow almost hit Dow in the leg, but luckily he didn't notice. It had almost got away into the bushes, then it squealed and fell back, thrashing. Forley had stabbed it, hiding in the scrub. "I got one!" he yelled.

It was quiet for a moment, while the Dogman scrambled down toward the clearing and they all looked round to see if there was anything left to fight, then Black Dow gave a great bellow, shaking his bloody weapons over his head. "We fucking killed 'em!"

"You nearly killed us all, you damn fool!" shouted Threetrees.

"Eh?"

"What about the fucking signal?"

"I thought I heard you shout!"

"I never!"

"Did you not?" asked Dow, looking greatly puzzled. "What was the signal anyhow?"

Threetrees gave a sigh and put his head in his hands.

Forley was still staring down at his sword. "I got one!" he said again. Now that the fight was over, the Dogman was about ready to burst, so he turned round and pissed against a tree.

"We killed 'em!" shouted Tul, clapping him on the back.

"Watch out!" yelled Dogman as piss went all down his leg. They all had a laugh at him over that. Even Grim had himself a little chuckle.

Tul shook Threetrees by the shoulder. "We killed 'em, chief!"

"We killed these, aye," he said, looking sour, "but there'll be plenty more. Thousands of 'em. They won't be happy staying up here neither, up here beyond the mountains. Sooner or later they'll be going south. Maybe in the summer, when the passes clear, maybe later. But it's not long off."

The Dogman glanced at the others, all shifty and worried after that little speech. The glow of victory hadn't lasted too long. It never did. He looked round at the dead Flatheads on the ground, broken and bloody, sprawled and crumpled. It seemed a hollow little victory they'd had now. "Shouldn't we try and tell 'em, Threetrees?" he asked. "Shouldn't we try and warn someone?"

"Aye." Threetrees gave a sad little smile. "But who?"

THE COURSE OF TRUE LOVE

J ezal trudged miserably across the grey Agriont with his fencing steels in his hand: yawning, stumbling, grumbling, still horribly sore from his endless run the day before. He hardly saw anyone as he dragged himself to his daily bullying from Lord Marshal Varuz. Apart from the odd premature tweeting of some bird in amongst the gables and the tired scraping of his own reluctant boots, all was quiet. No one was up at this time. No one should be up at this time. Him least of all.

He hauled his aching legs through the archway and up the tunnel. The sun was barely above the horizon and the courtyard beyond was full of deep shadows. Squinting into the darkness he could see Varuz sat at the table, waiting for him. Damn it. He had hoped to be early for once. Did the old bastard sleep at all?

"Lord Marshal!" shouted Jezal, breaking into a half-hearted jog.

"No. Not today." A shiver crept up Jezal's neck. It was not the voice of his fencing master, but there was something unpleasantly familiar about it. "Marshal Varuz is busy with more important matters this morning." Inquisitor Glokta was sitting in the shadows by the table and smiling up with his revolting gap-toothed grin. Jezal's skin prickled with disgust. It was hardly what one needed first thing in the morning.

He slowed to a reluctant walk and stopped next to the table. "You will doubtless be pleased to learn that there will be no running, or swimming, or beam, or heavy bar today," said the cripple. "You won't even be needing those." He waved his cane at Jezal's fencing steels. "We will just be having a little chat. That is all."

The idea of five punishing hours with Varuz seemed suddenly very appealing, but Jezal was not about to show his discomfort. He tossed his steels onto the table with a loud rattle and sat down carelessly in the other chair, Glokta regarding him from the shadows all the while. Jezal had it in mind to stare him into some kind of submission, but it proved a vain attempt. After a couple of seconds looking at that wasted face, that empty grin, those fever-bright sunken eyes, he began to find the table top most interesting.

"So tell me, Captain, why did you take up fencing?"

A game then. A private hand of cards with only two players. And everything that was said would get back to Varuz, that was sure. Jezal would have to play his hand carefully, keep his cards close and his wits about him. "For my own honour, for that of my family, for that of my King," he said coldly. The cripple could try and find fault with that answer.

"Ah, so it's for the benefit of your nation that you put yourself through this. What a fine citizen you must be. What selflessness. What an example to us all." Glokta snorted. "Please! If you must lie, at least pick a lie that you yourself find convincing. That answer is an insult to us both."

How dare this toothless has-been take that tone with him? Jezal's legs gave a twitch: he was right on the point of getting up and walking away, Varuz and his hideous stooge be damned. But he caught the cripple's eye as he put his hands on the arms of the chair to push himself up. Glokta was smiling at him, a mocking sort of smile. To leave would be to admit defeat somehow. Why did he take up fencing anyway? "My father wanted me to do it."

"So, so. My heart brims with sympathy. The loyal son, bound by his strong sense of duty, is forced to fulfil his father's ambitions. A familiar tale, like a comfortable old chair we all love to sit in. Tell 'em what they want to hear, eh? A better answer, but just as far from the truth."

"Why don't you tell me then?" snapped Jezal sulkily, "since you seem to know so much about it!"

"Alright, I will. Men don't fence for their King, or for their families, or for the exercise either, before you try that one on me. They fence for the recognition, for the glory. They fence for their own advancement. They fence for themselves. I should know."

"You should know?" Jezal snorted. "It hardly seems to have worked in your case." He regretted it immediately. Damn his mouth, it got him in all kinds of trouble.

But Glokta only flashed his disgusting smile again. "It was working well enough, until I found my way into the Emperor's prisons. What's your excuse, liar?"

Jezal didn't like the way this conversation was going. He was too used to easy victories at the card table, and poor players. His skills had dulled. Better to sit this one out until he got the measure of his new opponent. He clamped his jaw shut and said nothing.

"It takes hard work, of course, winning a Contest. You should have seen our mutual friend Collem West working. He sweated at it for months, running around while the rest of us laughed at him. A jumped-up, idiot commoner competing with his betters, that's what we all thought. Blundering through his forms, stumbling about on the beam, being made a fool of, again and again, day after day. But look at him now." Glokta tapped his cane with a finger. "And look at me. Seems he had the last laugh, eh, Captain? Just shows what you can achieve with a little hard work. You've twice the talent he had, and the right blood. You don't have to work one tenth so hard, but you refuse to work at all."

Jezal wasn't about to let that one past. "Not work at all? Don't I put myself through this torture every day—"

"Torture?" asked Glokta sharply.

Jezal realised too late his unfortunate choice of words. "Well," he mumbled, "I meant . . ."

"I know more than a little about both fencing and torture. Believe me when I say," and the Inquisitor's grotesque grin grew wider still, "that they're two quite different things."

"Er . . ." said Jezal, still off balance.

"You have the ambitions, and the means to realise them. A little effort would do it. A few months' hard work, then you would probably never need to try at anything again in your life, if that's what you want. A few short months, and you're set." Glokta licked at his empty gums. "Barring accidents of course. It's a great chance you've been offered. I'd take it, if I was you, but I don't know. Maybe you're a fool as well as a liar."

"I'm no fool," said Jezal coldly. It was the best he could do.

Glokta raised an eyebrow, then winced, leaning heavily on his cane as he slowly pushed himself to his feet. "Give it up if you like, by all means. Sit around for the rest of your days and drink and talk shit with the rest of the junior officers. There are a lot of people who'd be more than happy to live that life. A lot of people who haven't had the chances you've had. Give it up. Lord Marshal Varuz will be disappointed, and Major West, and your father, and so on, but please believe me when I say," and he leaned down, still smiling his horrible smile, "that I couldn't care less. Good day, Captain Luthar." And Glokta limped off toward the archway.

After that less than delightful interview, Jezal found himself with a few hours of unexpected free time on his hands—but he was scarcely in the frame of mind to enjoy it. He wandered the empty streets, squares and gardens of the Agriont, thinking grimly on what the cripple had said to him, cursing the name of Glokta, but unable to quite push the conversation from his mind. He turned it over and over, every phrase, constantly coming up with new things that he should have said. If only he had thought of them at the time.

"Ah, Captain Luthar!" Jezal started and looked up. A man he did not recognise was sitting on the dewy grass beneath a tree, smiling up at him, a half-eaten apple in his hand. "The early morning is the perfect time for a stroll, I find. Calm and grey and clean and empty. It's nothing like the gaudy pinkness of evening time. All that clutter, all those people coming and going. How can one think in amongst all that nonsense? And now I see you are of the same mind. How delightful." He took a big, crunching bite out of the apple.

"Do I know you?"

"Oh no, no," said the stranger, getting to his feet and brushing some dirt from the seat of his trousers, "not yet. My name is Sulfur, Yoru Sulfur."

"Really? And what brings you to the Agriont?"

"You might say I have come on a diplomatic mission."

Jezal looked him over, trying to place his origin. "A mission from?"

"From my master, of course," said Sulfur unhelpfully. His eyes were different colours, Jezal noticed. An ugly and off-putting characteristic, he rather thought.

"And your master is?"

"A very wise and powerful man." He stripped the core with his teeth and tossed it away into the bushes, wiping his hands on the front of his shirt. "I see you've been fencing."

Jezal glanced down at his steels. "Yes," he said, realising that he had finally come to a decision, "but for the last time. I'm giving it up."

"Oh dear me, no!" The strange man seized Jezal by the shoulder. "Oh dear me, no you mustn't!"

"What?"

"No, no! My master would be horrified if he knew. Horrified! Give up fencing and you give up more than that! This is how one comes to the notice of the public, you see? They decide, in the end. There's no nobility without the commoners, no nobility at all! They decide!"

"What?" Jezal glanced around the park, hoping to catch sight of a guard so he could notify him that a dangerous madman was loose in the Agriont.

"No, you mustn't give it up! I won't hear of it! No indeed! I'm sure that you'll stick with it after all! You must!"

Jezal shook Sulfur's hand off his shoulder. "Who are you?"

"Sulfur, Yoru Sulfur, at your service. See you again, Captain, at the Contest, if not before!" And he waved over his shoulder as he strolled off.

Jezal stared after him, mouth slightly open. "Damn it!" he shouted, throwing his steels down on the grass. Everyone seemed to want to take a hand in his business today, even crazy strangers in the park.

As soon as he thought it was late enough, Jezal went to call on Major West. You could always be sure of a sympathetic ear with him, and Jezal was hoping that he might be able to manipulate his friend into breaking the bad news to Lord Marshal Varuz. That was a scene that he wanted no part of, if he could possibly avoid it. He knocked on the door and waited, he knocked again. The door opened.

"Captain Luthar! What an almost unbearable honour!"

"Ardee," muttered Jezal, somewhat surprised to find her here, "it's good to see you again." For once he actually meant it. She was interesting, is what she was. It was a new and refreshing thing for him to actually be interested in what a woman had to say. And she was damn good-looking too, there was no denying it, and seemed prettier every time he saw her. Nothing could ever happen between them, of course, what with West being his friend and all, but there was no harm in looking, was there? "Er . . . is your brother around?"

She threw herself carelessly down onto the settle against the wall, one leg stretched out, looking very sour. "He's out. Gone out. Always busy. Much too busy for me." There was a definite flush to her cheek. Jezal's eye lighted on the decanter. The stopper was out and the wine was halfway down.

"Are you drunk?"

"Somewhat," she squinted at a half-full wine glass at her elbow, "but mostly I'm just bored."

"It's not even ten."

"Can't I be bored before ten?"

"You know what I mean."

"Leave the moralising to my brother. It suits him better. And have a drink." She waved her hand at the bottle. "You look like you need one."

Well, that was true enough. He poured himself a glass and sat down in a chair facing Ardee, while she regarded him with heavy-lidded eyes. She took her own glass from the table. There was a thick book lying next to it, face down.

"How's the book?" asked Jezal.

"*The Fall of the Master Maker*, in three volumes. They say it's one of the great classics of history. Lot of boring rubbish," she snorted derisively. "Full of wise Magi, stern knights with mighty swords and ladies with mightier bosoms. Magic, violence and romance, in equal measure. Utter shit." She slapped the book off the table and it tumbled onto the carpet, pages flapping.

"There must be something you can find to keep busy?"

"Really? What would you suggest?"

"My cousins do a lot of embroidery."

"Fuck yourself."

"Hmm," said Jezal, smiling. The swearing no longer seemed half so offensive as it had done when they first met. "What did you do at home, in Angland?"

"Oh, home," her head dropped against the back of the settle. "I thought I was bored there. I could hardly wait to come here to the bright centre of things. Now I can hardly wait to go back. Marry some farmer. Have a dozen brats. At least I'd get some conversation that way." She closed her eyes and sighed. "But Collem won't let me. He feels responsible, now that our father's dead. Thinks it's too dangerous. He'd rather I didn't get slaughtered by the Northmen, but that's about where his sense of responsibility ends. It certainly doesn't extend to spending ten minutes together with me. So it looks like I'm stuck here, with all you arrogant snobs."

Jezal shifted uncomfortably in his seat. "He seems to manage."

"Oh yes," snorted Ardee, "Collem West, he's a damn fine fellow! Won a Contest don't you know? First through the breach at Ulrioch, wasn't he? No breeding at all, never be one of us, but a damn fine fellow, for a commoner! Shame about that upstart sister of his though, too clever by half. And they say she drinks," she whispered. "Doesn't know her place. Total disgrace. Best just to ignore her." She sighed again. "Yes, the sooner I go home, the happier everyone will be."

"I won't be happier." Damn, did he say that out loud?

Ardee laughed, none too pleasantly. "Well, it's enormously noble of you to say so. Why aren't you fencing anyway?"

"Marshal Varuz was busy today." He paused for a moment. "In fact, I had your friend Sand dan Glokta as fencing master this morning."

"Really? What did he have to say for himself?"

"Various things. He called me a fool."

"Imagine that."

Jezal frowned. "Yes, well. I'm as bored with fencing as you are with that book. That was what I wanted to talk to your brother about. I'm thinking of giving it up."

She burst out laughing. Snorting, gurgling peals of it. Her whole body was shaking. Wine sloshed out of her glass and splattered across the floor. "What's so funny?" he demanded.

"It's just," she wiped a tear from her eye, "I had a bet with Collem. He was sure you'd stick at it. And now I'm ten marks richer."

"I'm not sure that I like being the subject of your bet," said Jezal sharply.

"I'm not sure I give a damn."

"This is serious."

"No it isn't!" she snapped. "For my brother it was serious, he had to do it! No one even notices you if you don't have a 'dan' in your name, and who'd know better than me? You're the only person who's given me the time of day since I got here, and then only because Collem made you. I've precious little money and no blood at all, and that makes me less than nothing to the likes of you. The men ignore me and the women cut me dead. I've got nothing here, nothing and no one, and you think you've got the hard life? Please! I might take up fencing," she said bitterly. "Ask the Lord Marshal if he has space for a pupil, would you? At least then I'd have someone to talk to!"

Jezal blinked. That wasn't interesting. That was rude. "Hold on, you've no idea what it's like to . . ."

"Oh stop whinging! How old are you? Five? Why don't you go back to sucking on your mother's tit, infant?"

He could hardly believe what he was hearing. How dare she? "My mother's dead," he said. Hah. That should make her feel guilty, squeeze an apology out of her. It didn't.

"Dead? Lucky her, at least she doesn't have to listen to your damn whining! You spoiled little rich boys are all the same. You get everything you could possibly want, then throw a tantrum because you have to pick it up yourself! You're pathetic! You make me fucking sick!"

Jezal goggled. His face was burning, stinging, as if he'd been slapped. He'd rather have been slapped. He had never been spoken to like that in his life. Never! It was worse than Glokta. Much worse, and far more unexpected. He realised his mouth was hanging half open. He snapped it shut, grinding his teeth together, slapped his glass down on the table, and got up to leave. He was turning to the door when it suddenly opened, leaving him and Major West staring at each other.

"Jezal," said West, looking at first simply surprised and then, as he glanced over at his sister, sprawling on the settle, slightly suspicious. "What are you doing here?"

"Er . . . I came to see you actually."

"Oh yes?"

"Yes. But it can wait. I've things to do." And Jezal pushed past his friend and out into the corridor.

"What was all that about?" he heard West saying as he strode away from the room. "Are you drunk?"

With every step Jezal's fury mounted until he was halfway to being strangled by it. He had been the victim of an assault! A savage and undeserved attack! He stopped in the corridor, trembling with rage, his breath snorting in his nose like he'd run ten miles, his fists clenched painfully tight. And from a woman too! A woman! And a bloody commoner! How dare she? He had wasted time on her, and laughed at her jokes, and found her attractive! She should have been honoured to be noticed!

"That fucking bitch!" he snarled to himself. He had half a mind to go back and say it to her face, but it was too late. He stared around for something to hit. How to pay her back? How? Then it came to him.

Prove her wrong.

That would do it. Prove her wrong, and that crippled bastard Glokta too. He'd show them how hard he could work. He'd show them he was no fool, no liar, no spoiled child. The more he thought about it, the more it made sense. He'd win this damn Contest, is what he'd do! That'd wipe the smiles off their faces! He set off briskly down the corridor, with a strange new feeling building in his chest.

A sense of purpose. That was what it was. Perhaps it wasn't too late for a run.

HOW DOGS ARE TRAINED

Practical Frost stood by the wall, utterly motionless, utterly silent, barely visible in the deep shadows, a part of the building. The albino hadn't moved an inch in an hour or more, hadn't shifted his feet, hadn't blinked, hadn't breathed that Glokta had noticed, his eyes fixed on the street before them.

Glokta himself cursed, shifted uncomfortably, winced, scratched his face, sucked at his empty gums. *What's keeping them? A few minutes more and I might fall asleep, drop into that stinking canal and drown. How very apt that would be.* He watched the oily, smelly water below him flap and ripple. *Body found floating by the docks, bloated by seawater and far, far beyond recognition . . .*

Frost touched his arm in the darkness, pointed down the street with a big white finger. Three men were moving slowly toward them, walking with the slightly bow-legged stance of men who spend a lot of time aboard ship, keeping their balance on a swaying deck. *So that's one half of our little party. Better late than never.* The three sailors came halfway across the bridge over the canal then stopped and waited, no more than twenty strides away. Glokta could hear the tone of their conversation: brash, confident, common accents. He shuffled slightly further into the shadows clinging to the building.

Now footsteps came from the opposite direction, hurried footsteps. Two more men appeared, walking quickly down the street. One, a very tall, thin fellow in an expensive-looking fur coat was glancing suspiciously around him. *That must be Gofred Hornlach, senior Mercer. Our man.* His companion had a sword at his hip, and was struggling with a big wooden trunk over one shoulder. *Ser-*

vant, or bodyguard, or both. He is of no interest. Glokta felt the hairs on the back of his neck prickling as they neared the bridge. Hornlach exchanged a few quick words with one of the sailors, a man with a big brown beard.

"Ready?" he whispered to Frost. The Practical nodded.

"Hold!" shouted Glokta at the top of his voice, "in the name of his Majesty!" Hornlach's servant spun round, dropping the trunk onto the bridge with a bang, hand moving toward his sword. There was a soft twang from the shadows on the other side of the road. The servant looked surprised, gave a snort, then toppled onto his face. Practical Frost strode swiftly out of the shadows, feet padding on the road.

Hornlach stared down, wide-eyed, at the corpse of his bodyguard, then across at the hulking albino. He turned to the sailors. "Help me!" he cried. "Stop him!"

Their leader smiled back. "I don't think so." His two companions moved without hurry to block the bridge. The Mercer stumbled away, took a faltering step toward the shadows by the canal on the other side. Severard appeared from a doorway before him, flatbow rested across his shoulder. *Replace the bow with a bunch of flowers and he'd look as if he was on his way to a wedding. You'd never think that he just killed a man.*

Surrounded, Hornlach could only look around dumbly, eyes wide with fear and surprise, as the two Practicals approached, Glokta limping up behind them. "But I paid you!" Hornlach shouted desperately at the sailors.

"You paid me for a berth," said their Captain. "Loyalty is extra."

Practical Frost's big white hand slapped down on the merchant's shoulder, forced him onto his knees. Severard strolled over to the bodyguard, wedged the dirty toe of his boot under the body and rolled it over. The corpse stared up at the night sky, eyes glassy, the feathers of the flatbow bolt sticking out from his neck. The blood round his mouth looked black in the moonlight.

"Dead," grunted Severard, most unnecessarily.

"A bolt through the neck will do that," said Glokta. "Clean him up, would you?"

"Right you are." Severard grabbed the bodyguard's feet and hauled them over the parapet of the bridge, then he took him under the armpits and heaved the body straight over the side with a grunt. *So smooth, so clean, so prac-*

tised. You can tell he's done it before. There was a splash as the corpse hit the slimy water below. Frost had Hornlach's hands tied firmly behind him now, and the bag on. The prisoner squawked through the canvas as he was dragged to his feet. Glokta himself shuffled over to the three sailors, his legs numb after all that time spent standing still in the alley.

"And here we are," he said, pulling a heavy purse from his inside coat pocket. He held it swinging just above the Captain's waiting palm. "Tell me, what happened tonight?"

The old sailor smiled, weathered face crinkling up like boot leather. "My cargo was spoiling and we had to be away on the first tide, I told him that. We waited and waited, half the night down by that stinking canal, but would you believe it? The bastard never showed."

"Very good. That's the story I'd tell in Westport, if anyone should ask."

The Captain looked hurt. "That's how it happened, Inquisitor. What other story could there be?"

Glokta let the purse drop and the money jingled inside. "With the compliments of his Majesty."

The Captain weighed the purse in his hand. "Always pleased to do his Majesty a favour!" And he and his two companions turned, all yellow smiles, and made off toward the quay.

"Right then," said Glokta, "let's get on with it."

"Where are my clothes?" shouted Hornlach, wriggling in his chair.

"I do apologise for that. I know it's quite uncomfortable, but clothes can hide things. Leave a man his clothes and you leave him pride, and dignity, and all kinds of things it's better not to have in here. I never question a prisoner with their clothes on. Do you remember Salem Rews?"

"Who?"

"Salem Rews. One of your people. A Mercer. We caught him dodging the King's taxes. He made a confession, named a few people. I wanted to talk to them, but they all died."

The merchant's eyes flickered left and right. *Thinking about his options, trying to guess what we might know.* "People die all the time."

Glokta stared at the painted corpse of Juvens behind his prisoner, bleeding bright red paint all over the wall. *People die all the time.* "Of course, but not quite so violently. I have a notion that someone wanted them dead, that someone ordered them dead. I have a notion it was you."

"You've got no proof! No proof! You won't get away with this!"

"Proof means nothing, Hornlach, but I'll indulge you. Rews survived. He's just down the hall, as it goes, no friends left, blubbering away, naming every Mercer he can think of, or that we can think of, for that matter." Narrowed eyes, but no reply. "We used him to catch Carpi."

"Carpi?" asked the merchant, trying to look nonchalant.

"Surely you remember your assassin? Slightly flabby Styrian? Acne scars? Swears a lot? We have him too. He told us the whole story. How you hired him, how much you paid him, what you asked him to do. The whole story." Glokta smiled. "He has an excellent memory, for a killer, very detailed."

The fear was showing now, just a trace of it, but Hornlach rallied well. "This is an affront to my Guild!" he shouted, with as much authority as he could muster, naked and tied to a chair. "My master, Coster dan Kault, will never allow this, and he's a close friend of Superior Kalyne!"

"Shit on Kalyne, he's finished. Besides, Kault thinks you're tucked up safe aboard that ship, bound for Westport and far beyond our reach. I don't think you'll be missed for several weeks." The merchant's face had gone slack. "A great deal could happen in that time . . . a very great deal."

Hornlach's tongue darted over his lips. He glanced furtively up at Frost and Severard, leaned slightly forward. *So. Now comes the bargaining.* "Inquisitor," he said in a wheedling tone, "if I've learned one thing from life, it's that every man wants something. Every man has his price, yes? And we have deep pockets. You have only to name it. Only name it! What do you want?"

"What do I want?" asked Glokta, leaning in to a more conspiratorial distance.

"Yes. What's this all about? What do you want?" Hornlach was smiling now, a coy, clever little smile. *How quaint, but you won't buy your way out of this.*

"I want my teeth back."

The merchant's smile began to fade.

"I want my leg back."

Hornlach swallowed.

"I want my life back."

The prisoner had turned very pale.

"No? Then perhaps I'll settle for your head on a stick. You've nothing else I want, no matter how deep your pockets are." Hornlach was trembling slightly now. *No more bluster? No more deals? Then we can begin.* Glokta picked up the paper in front of him, and read the first question. "What is your name?"

"Look, Inquisitor, I . . ." Frost smashed the table with his fist and Hornlach cowered in his chair.

"Answer his fucking question!" screamed Severard in his face.

"Gofred Hornlach," squealed the merchant.

Glokta nodded. "Good. You are a senior member of the Guild of Mercers?"

"Yes, yes!"

"One of Magister Kault's deputies, in fact?"

"You know I am!"

"Have you conspired with other Mercers to defraud his Majesty the King? Did you hire an assassin to wilfully murder ten of his Majesty's subjects? Were you ordered so to do by Magister Coster dan Kault, the head of the Guild of Mercers?"

"No!" shouted Hornlach, voice squeaky with panic. *That is not the answer we need.* Glokta glanced up at Practical Frost. The big white fist sank into the merchant's gut, and he gave a gentle sigh and slid sideways.

"My mother keeps dogs, you know," said Glokta.

"Dogs," hissed Severard in the gasping merchant's ear, as he shoved him back into the chair.

"She loves them. Trains them to do all manner of tricks." Glokta pursed his lips. "Do you know how dogs are trained?"

Hornlach was still winded, lolling in his chair with watering eyes, some way from being able to speak. *Still at that stage of a fish pulled suddenly from the water. Mouth opening and closing, but no sound.*

"Repetition," said Glokta. "Repeat, repeat, repeat. You must have that dog perform his tricks one hundred times the same, and then you must do it all again. It's all about repetition. And if you want that dog to bark on cue, you mustn't be shy with the whip. You're going to bark for me, Hornlach, in front of the Open Council."

"You're mad," cried the Mercer, staring around at them, "you're all mad!"

Glokta flashed his empty smile. "If you like. If it helps." He glanced back at the paper in his hand. "What is your name?"

The prisoner swallowed. "Gofred Hornlach."

"You are a senior member of the Guild of Mercers?"

"Yes."

"One of Magister Kault's deputies, in fact?"

"Yes!"

"Have you conspired with other Mercers to defraud his Majesty the King? Did you hire an assassin to wilfully murder ten of his Majesty's subjects? Were you ordered so to do by Magister Coster dan Kault, the head of the Guild of Mercers?"

Hornlach cast desperately around him. Frost stared back, Severard stared back.

"Well?" demanded Glokta.

The merchant closed his eyes. "Yes," he whimpered.

"What's that?"

"Yes!"

Glokta smiled. "Excellent. Now tell me. What is your name?"

TEA AND VENGEANCE

"I t's a beautiful country, isn't it?" asked Bayaz, staring up at the rugged fells on either side of the road.

Their horses' hooves thumped slowly along the track, the steady sound at odds with Logen's unease. "Is it?"

"Well, it's a hard country, of course, to those who don't know its ways. A tough country, and unforgiving. But there's something noble there too." The First of the Magi swept his arm across the view, breathed in the cold air with relish. "It has honesty, integrity. The best steel doesn't always shine the brightest." He glanced over, swaying gently in his saddle. "You should know that."

"I can't say I see the beauty of it."

"No? What do you see?"

Logen let his eyes wander over the steep, grassy slopes, spotted with patches of sedge and brown gorse, studded with outcrops of grey rock and stands of trees. "I see good ground for a battle. Provided you got here first."

"Really? How so?"

Logen pointed at a knobbly hilltop. "Archers on the bluff there couldn't be seen from the road, and you could hide most of your foot in these rocks. A few of the lightest armoured left on the slopes, just to draw the enemy on up the steepest ground there."

He pointed to the thorny bushes that covered the lower slopes. "You'd let them come on a way, then when they were struggling through that gorse, you'd give them the arrows. Shafts falling on you from above like that, that's no fun at all. They come quicker and further, and they bite deeper. That'd break them up. By the time they got to the rocks they'd be dog-tired and running short on discipline. That would be the time to charge. A bunch of Carls, leaping out of those stones, charging down from above, fresh and keen and screaming like devils, that could break 'em right there."

Logen narrowed his eyes at the hillside. He'd been on both sides of a surprise like that, and in neither case was the memory a pleasant one. "But if they had a mind to hold, a few horsemen in those trees could finish it up. A few Named Men, a few hard fighters, bearing down on you from a place you never expected them, that's a terrifying thing. That'd make them run. But tired as they'd be, they wouldn't run too fast. That means prisoners, and prisoners might mean ransoms, or at least enemies cheaply killed. I see a slaughter, or a victory worth the singing, depending which side you're on. That's what I see."

Bayaz smiled, head nodding with the slow movement of his horse. "Was it Stolicus who said the ground must be a general's best friend, or it becomes his worst enemy?"

"I never heard of him, but he was right enough. This is good ground for an army, providing you got here first. Getting there first is the trick."

"Indeed. We don't have an army, however."

"These trees could hide a few horsemen even better than a lot." Logen glanced sidelong at the wizard. He was slouched happily in the saddle, enjoying a pleasant ride in the country. "I don't think Bethod will have appreciated your advice, and I had scores enough with him already. He got wounded where he feels it most, in his pride. He'll want vengeance. Want it badly."

"Ah yes, vengeance, that most widespread of Northern pastimes. Its popularity never seems to wane."

Logen stared grimly around at the trees, the rocks, the folds in the valley's sides, the many hiding places. "There'll be men out in these hills, looking for us. Small bands of skilled and battle-hardened men, well-mounted and well-armed, familiar with the land. Now Bethod has finished all his enemies there's nowhere in the North out of his reach. They might be waiting there," he pointed off towards some rocks by the road, "or in those trees, or those." Malacus Quai, riding up ahead with the packhorse, glanced nervously around. "They could be anywhere."

"Does that frighten you?" asked Bayaz.

"Everything frightens me, and it's well that it does. Fear is a good friend to the hunted, it's kept me alive this long. The dead are fearless, and I don't care to join them. He'll send men to the library too."

"Oh yes, to burn my books and so on."

"Does that frighten you?"

"Not much. The stones by the gate have the word of Juvens on them, and that is not to be denied, even now. No one with violence in mind can come near. I imagine Bethod's men will wander around the lake in the rain until they run out of food, all the while thinking how very strange it is that they cannot find so large a thing as a library. No," said the wizard happily, scratching at his beard. "I would concentrate on our own predicament. What happens, do you think, if we're caught?"

"Bethod will kill us, and in the most unpleasant manner he can think of. Unless he has it in mind to be merciful, and let us off with a warning."

"That doesn't seem likely."

"I've been thinking the same thing. Our best chance is to make for the Whiteflow, try to get across the river into Angland, and trust to luck we aren't seen." Logen didn't like trusting to luck, the very word left a sour taste. He peered up at the cloudy sky. "We could do with some bad weather. A healthy downpour could hide us nicely." The skies had been pissing on him for weeks, but now that he needed rain they refused to produce a drop.

Malacus Quai was looking over his shoulder at them, his eyes big and round with worry. "Shouldn't we try to move faster?"

"Perhaps," said Logen, patting the neck of his horse, "but that would tire the horses, and we may need all the speed we can get later. We could hide in the day and travel by night, but then we risk getting lost. We're better as we are. Move slowly and hope we aren't seen." He frowned at the hilltop. "Hope we haven't been seen already."

"Hmm," said Bayaz, "then this might be the best time to tell you. That witch Caurib isn't half the fool I pretended she was."

Logen felt a sinking sensation. "No?"

"No, for all her paint and gold and chat about the utmost north, she knows what she is about. The long eye, they call it. An old trick, but effective. She has been watching us."

"She knows where we are?"

"She knows when we left, more than likely, and in what direction we were heading."

"That does nothing for our chances."

"I should say not."

"Shit." Logen caught some movement in the trees to their left, and he snatched hold of the hilt of his sword. A couple of birds took to the skies. He waited, heart in his mouth. Nothing. He let his hand drop back. "We should have killed them while we had the chance. All three of them."

"But we didn't, and there it is." Bayaz looked over at Logen. "If they do catch us, what's your plan?"

"Run. And hope our horses are the faster."

"And this one?" asked Bayaz.

The wind blew keenly through the hollow in spite of the trees, making the flames of the campfire flicker and dance. Malacus Quai hunched his shoulders and drew his blanket tight around them. He peered at the short stem that Bayaz was holding up to him, forehead crinkled with concentration.

"Erm . . ." This was the fifth plant, and the miserable apprentice had yet to get one of them right. "Is that . . . er . . . Ilyith?"

"Ilyith?" echoed the wizard, his face giving no clue as to whether it was the right answer. He was merciless as Bethod where his apprentice was concerned.

"Perhaps?"

"Hardly." The apprentice closed his eyes and sighed for the fifth time that evening. Logen felt for him, he really did, but there was nothing to be done. "Ursilum, in the old tongue, the round-leafed kind."

"Yes, yes, of course, Ursilum, it was at the end of my tongue the whole time."

"If the name was at the end of your tongue, then the uses of the plant cannot be far behind, eh?"

The apprentice narrowed his eyes and looked hopefully up towards the night sky, as though the answer might be written in the stars. "Is it . . . for aches in the joints?"

"No, it is decidedly not. I am afraid your aching joints will still be troubling you." Bayaz turned the stem slowly round in his fingers. "Ursilum has no uses, not that I know of. It's just a plant." And he tossed it away into the bushes.

"Just a plant," echoed Quai, shaking his head. Logen sighed and rubbed his tired eyes.

"I'm sorry, Master Ninefingers, are we boring you?"

"What does it matter?" asked Logen, throwing his hands up in the air. "Who cares about the name of a plant with no use?"

Bayaz smiled. "A fair point. Tell us, Malacus, what does it matter?"

"If a man seeks to change the world, he should first understand it." The apprentice trotted the words out as if by rote, evidently relieved to be asked a question he knew the answer to. "The smith must learn the ways of metals, the carpenter the ways of wood, or their work will be of but little worth. Base magic is wild and dangerous, for it comes from the Other Side, and to draw from the world below is fraught with peril. The Magus tempers magic with knowledge, and thus produces High Art, but like the smith or the carpenter, he should only seek to change that which he understands. With each thing he learns, his power is increased. So must the Magus strive to learn all, to understand the world entire. The tree is only as strong as its root, and knowledge is the root of power."

"Don't tell me, Juvens's *Principles of Art?*"

"The very first lines," said Bayaz.

"Forgive me for saying so, but I've been on this world for more than thirty years, and I've yet to understand a single thing that's happened. To know the world completely? To understand everything? That's quite a task."

The Magus chuckled. "An impossible one, to be sure. To truly know and understand even a blade of grass is the study of a lifetime, and the world is ever changing. That is why we tend to specialise."

"So what did you choose?"

"Fire," said Bayaz, gazing happily into the flames, the light dancing on his bald head. "Fire, and force, and will. But even in my chosen fields, after countless long years of study, I remain a novice. The more you learn, the more you realise how little you know. Still, the struggle itself is worthwhile. Knowledge is the root of power, after all."

"So with enough knowledge, you Magi can do anything?"

Bayaz frowned. "There are limits. And there are rules."

"Like the First Law?" Master and apprentice glanced up at Logen as one. "It's forbidden to speak with devils, am I right?" It was plain that Quai didn't remember his fevered outburst, his mouth was open with surprise. Bayaz's eyes only narrowed a little, with the faintest trace of suspicion.

"Why, yes you are," said the First of the Magi. "It is forbidden to touch the Other Side direct. The First Law must apply to all, without exception. As must the Second."

"Which is?"

"It is forbidden to eat the flesh of men."

Logen raised an eyebrow. "You wizards get up to some strange stuff."

Bayaz smiled. "Oh, you don't know the half of it." He turned to his apprentice, holding up a lumpy brown root. "And now, Master Quai, would you be good enough to tell me the name of this?"

Logen couldn't help grinning to himself. He knew this one.

"Come, come, Master Quai, we don't have all night."

Logen wasn't able to stand the apprentice's misery any longer. He leaned toward him, pretending to poke at the fire with a stick, coughed to conceal his words and whispered, "Crow's Foot," under his breath. Bayaz was a good distance away, and the wind was still rustling in the trees. There was no way the Magus could have heard him.

Quai played his part well. He continued to peer at the root, brow knitted in thought. "Is it Crow's Foot?" he ventured.

Bayaz raised an eyebrow. "Why, yes it is. Well done, Malacus. And can you tell me its uses?"

Logen coughed again. "Wounds," he whispered, looking carelessly off into the bushes, one hand shielding his mouth. He might not know too much about plants, but on the subject of wounds he had a wealth of experience.

"I believe it's good for wounds," said Quai slowly.

"Excellent, Master Quai. Crow's Foot is correct. And it is good for wounds. I am glad to see we are making some progress after all." He cleared his throat. "It does seem curious that you should use that name however. They only call this Crow's Foot north of the mountains. I certainly never taught you that name. I wonder who it is you know, from that part of the world?" He glanced over at Logen. "Have you ever considered a career in the magical arts, Master Ninefingers?" He narrowed his eyes at Quai once more. "I may have space for an apprentice."

Malacus hung his head. "Sorry, Master Bayaz."

"You are indeed. Perhaps you could clean the pots for us. That task may be better suited to your talents."

Quai reluctantly shrugged off his blanket, collected the dirty bowls and shuffled off through the brush towards the stream. Bayaz bent over the pot on the fire, adding some dried-up leaves to the bubbling water. The flickering light of the flames caught the underside of his face, the steam curled around his bald head. All in all, he looked quite the part.

"What is that?" asked Logen, reaching for his pipe. "Some spell? Some potion? Some great work of High Art?"

"Tea."

"Eh?"

"Leaves of a certain plant, boiled up in water. It is considered quite a luxury in Gurkhul." He poured some of the brew out into a cup. "Would you like to try it?"

Logen sniffed at it suspiciously. "Smells like feet."

"Suit yourself." Bayaz shook his head and sat back down beside the fire, wrapping both hands around the steaming cup. "But you're missing out on one of nature's greatest gifts to man." He took a sip and smacked his lips in satisfaction. "Calming to the mind, invigorating to the body. There are few ills a good cup of tea won't help with."

Logen pressed a lump of chagga into the bowl of his pipe. "How about an axe in the head?"

"That's one of them," admitted Bayaz with a grin. "Tell me, Master Ninefingers, why all the blood between you and Bethod? Did you not fight for him many times? Why do you hate each other so?"

Logen paused as he was sucking smoke from the pipe, let his breath out. "There are reasons," he said stiffly. The wounds of that time were still raw. He didn't like anyone picking at them.

"Ah, reasons." Bayaz looked down at his tea-cup. "And what of your reasons? Does this feud not cut both ways?"

"Perhaps."

"But you are willing to wait?"

"I'll have to be."

"Hmm. You are very patient, for a Northman."

Logen thought of Bethod, and his loathsome sons, and the many good men they'd killed for their ambitions. The men he'd killed for their ambitions. He thought of the Shanka, and his family, and the ruins of the village by the sea. He thought of all his dead friends. He sucked at his teeth and stared at the fire.

"I've settled a few scores in my time, but it only led to more. Vengeance can feel fine, but it's a luxury. It doesn't fill your belly, or keep the rain off. To fight my enemies I need friends behind me, and I'm clean out of friends. You have to be realistic. It's been a while since my ambitions went beyond getting through each day alive."

Bayaz laughed, his eyes glittering in the firelight. "What?" asked Logen, handing the pipe across to him.

"No offence, but you are an endless source of surprises. Not at all what I was expecting. You are quite the riddle."

"Me?"

"Oh yes! The Bloody-Nine," he whispered, opening his eyes up wide. "That's one bastard of a reputation you're carrying, my friend. The stories they tell! One bastard of a name! Why, mothers scare their children with it!" Logen said nothing. There was no denying it. Bayaz sucked slowly on the pipe, then blew out a long plume of smoke. "I've been thinking about the day that Prince Calder paid us a visit."

Logen snorted. "I try not to spare him too much thought."

"Nor I, but it wasn't his behaviour that interested me, it was yours."

"It was? I don't remember doing a thing."

Bayaz pointed the stem of the pipe at Logen from across the fire. "Ah, but that is my point exactly. I have known many fighting men, soldiers and generals and champions and whatnot. A great fighter must act quickly, decisively, whether with his own arm or with an army, for he who strikes first often strikes last. So fighters come to rely on their baser instincts, to answer always with violence, to become proud and brutal." Bayaz passed the pipe back to Logen. "But whatever the stories, you are not such a one."

"I know plenty who'd disagree."

"Perhaps, but the fact remains, Calder slighted you, and you did nothing. So you know when you should act, and act quickly, but you also know when not to. That shows restraint, and a calculating mind."

"Perhaps I was just afraid."

"Of him? Come now. You didn't seem afraid of Scale and he's a deal more worrying. And you walked forty miles with my apprentice over your back, and that shows courage, and compassion too. A rare combination, indeed. Violence and restraint, calculation and compassion—and you speak to the spirits too."

Logen raised an eyebrow. "Not often, and only when there's no one else around. Their talk is dull, and not half so flattering as yours."

"Hah. That's true. The spirits have little to say to men, I understand, though I have never spoken with them; I have not the gift. Few have these days." He took another swallow from his cup, peering at Logen over the rim. "I can scarcely think of another one alive."

Malacus stumbled from the trees, shivering, and set the wet bowls down. He grabbed his blanket, wrapped it tightly around him, then peered hopefully at the steaming pot on the fire. "Is that tea?"

Bayaz ignored him. "Tell me, Master Ninefingers, in all the time since you arrived at my library, you have never once asked me why I sent for you, or why now we are wandering through the North in peril of our lives. That strikes me as odd."

"Not really. I don't want to know."

"Don't want to?"

"All my life I've sought to know things. What's on the other side of the mountains? What are my enemies thinking? What weapons will they use against me? What friends can I trust?" Logen shrugged. "Knowledge may be the root of power, but each new thing I've learned has left me worse off." He sucked again on the pipe, but it was finished. He tapped the ashes out onto the ground. "Whatever it is you want from me I will try to do, but I don't want to know until it's time. I'm sick of making my own decisions. They're never the right ones. Ignorance is the sweetest medicine, my father used to say. I don't want to know."

Bayaz stared at him. It was the first time Logen had seen the First of the Magi look at all surprised. Malacus Quai cleared his throat. "I'd like to know," he said in a small voice, looking hopefully up at his master.

"Yes," murmured Bayaz, "but you don't get to ask."

It was around midday that it all went wrong. Logen was just starting to think that they might make it to the Whiteflow, maybe even live out the week. It felt as if he lost his concentration for just a moment. Unfortunately, it was the one moment that mattered.

Still, it was well done, you had to give them that. They'd chosen their spot carefully, and tied rags around their horse's hooves, to muffle the sound. Threetrees might have seen it coming, if he'd been with them, but he had an eye for the ground like no other. The Dogman might have smelled them, if he'd been there, but he had the nose for it. The fact was, neither of them were there. The dead are no help at all.

There were three horsemen, waiting for them as they rounded a blind corner, well-armed and well-armoured, dirty faces but clean weapons, veterans each man. The one on the right was thickset and powerful-looking, with almost no neck. The one on the left was tall and gaunt with small, hard eyes. Both of them had round helmets, coats of weathered mail, and long spears lowered and ready. Their leader sat on his horse like a bag of turnips, slouched in the saddle with the ease of the expert horseman. He nodded to Logen. "Ninefingers! The Brynn! The Bloody-Nine! It's right good to see you again."

"Blacktoe," muttered Logen, forcing a friendly smile onto his face. "It'd warm my heart to see you too, if things were different."

"But they are as they are." The old warrior's eyes moved slowly over Bayaz, Quai, and Logen as he spoke, taking in their weapons, or the lack of them, working out his game. A stupider opponent could have evened up the odds, but Blacktoe was a Named Man, and no fool. His eyes came to rest on Logen's hand as it crept slowly across his body towards the hilt of his sword, and he shook his head slowly. "None of your tricks, Bloody-Nine. You can see we've got you." And he nodded over at the trees behind them.

Logen's heart sank even lower. Two more riders had appeared behind them and were trotting forwards to complete the trap, their muffled hooves barely making a sound on the soft ground by the road. Logen chewed his lip. Blacktoe was right, damn him. The four horsemen closed in, lowered spearpoints swaying, faces cold, minds set to the task. Malacus Quai stared at them with frightened eyes, his horse shying back. Bayaz smiled pleasantly as though they were his oldest friends. Logen would have liked a touch of the wizard's composure. His own heart was hammering, his mouth was sour.

Blacktoe nudged his horse forward, one hand gripping the shaft of his axe, the other resting on his knee, not even using the reins. He was a masterful horseman, famous for it. That's what happens when a man loses all his toes to the frost. Riding is quicker than walking, that has to be admitted, but when it came to fighting Logen preferred to keep his feet firmly on the ground. "Better be coming with us now," said the old warrior, "better all round."

Logen could hardly agree, but the odds were stacked high against him. A sword may have a voice, as Bayaz had said, but a spear is a damn good thing for poking a man off a horse, and there were four of them closing in around him. He was caught—outnumbered, off-guard, and with the wrong tools for the task. Yet again. Best to play for time, and hope some chance might show itself. Logen cleared his throat, doing his best to take the fear out of his voice. "Never thought you'd make your peace with Bethod, Blacktoe, not you."

The old warrior scratched at his long, matted beard. "I was one of the last, truth be told, but I knelt in the end, same as all the rest. Can't say I liked it any, but there it is. Best let me have the blade, Ninefingers."

"What about Old Man Yawl? You telling me he bows to Bethod? Or did you just find a master to suit you better?"

Blacktoe didn't get upset by the jibe, not in the least. He just looked sad, and tired. "Yawl's dead, as though you didn't know. Most of 'em are. Bethod doesn't suit me much at all as a master, and nor do his sons. No man likes licking Scale's fat arse, or Calder's skinny one, you should know that. Now give up the sword, the day's wasting and we've ground to cover. We can talk just as well with you unarmed."

"Yawl's dead?"

"Aye," said Blacktoe suspiciously. "He offered Bethod a duel. Didn't you hear? The Feared done for him."

"Feared?"

"Where've you been, under a mountain?"

"More or less. What's this Feared?"

"I don't know what he is." Blacktoe leaned from his saddle and spat in the grass. "I heard he's not a man at all. They say that bitch Caurib dug him out from under a hill. Who knows? Leastways, he's Bethod's new champion, and far nastier even than the last, no offence."

"None at all," said Logen. The man with no neck had moved in close. A little too close perhaps, the point of his spear was hovering only a foot or two away. Close enough for Logen to grab a hold of. Maybe. "Old Man Yawl was a strong hand."

"Aye. That's why we followed him. But it done him no good. This Feared broke him. Broke him bad, like he was no more'n a dog. Left him alive, if you could call it that, so we could learn from his mistake, but he didn't live long. Most of us knelt right then, those with wives and sons to think on. No sense in putting it off. There's a few of them still, up in the mountains, who won't bow to Bethod. That moon-worshipping madman Crummock-i-Phail and his hillmen, and a few beside. But not many. And those there are, Bethod's got plans for." Blacktoe held out a big, calloused hand. "Better let me have the blade, Bloody-Nine. Left hand only, if you please, slow as slow and none of your tricks. Better all round."

So that was it. Out of time. Logen wrapped the three fingers of his left hand round the hilt of his sword, the cold metal pressing into his palm. The big man's spear point edged a little closer. The tall one had relaxed a little, confident they had him. His spear was pointing up into the air, unready. There was no telling what the two behind were doing. The desire to glance over his shoulder was almost irresistible, but Logen forced himself to look ahead.

"I always had respect for you, Ninefingers, even though we stood on different sides. I've no feud with you. But Bethod wants vengeance, he's drunk on it, and I swore to serve." Blacktoe looked him sadly in the eye. "I'm sorry it's me. For what it's worth."

"Likewise," muttered Logen, "I'm sorry it's you." He slid the sword slowly from the scabbard. "For what it's worth," and he snapped his arm out, smashing the sword's pommel into Blacktoe's mouth. The old warrior gave a squawk as the dull metal crunched into his teeth and tumbled backwards out of the saddle, his axe flying from his hand and clattering into the road. Logen grabbed hold of the shaft of the big man's spear, just below the blade.

"Go!" he bellowed at Quai, but the apprentice only stared back, blinking. The man with no neck pulled hard at the spear, nearly jerking Logen out of the saddle, but he kept his grip. He reared up in the stirrups, raising the sword high above his head. Neckless took one hand from his spear, his eyes going wide, and held it up on an instinct. Logen swung the sword down with all his strength.

He was shocked by the sharpness of it. It took the big man's arm off just below the elbow then struck into his shoulder, cleaving through the fur and the mail beneath and splitting him to his stomach, near in half. Blood showered across the road, spattering in the face of Logen's horse. It was trained for riding but not for war and it reared and spun around, kicking and plunging in a panic. It was the best Logen could do to stay on top of the damn thing. Out of the corner of his eye he saw Bayaz smack Quai's horse on the rump, and it sped off with the apprentice bouncing in the saddle, the packhorse galloping along behind.

Then everything was a mess of plunging and snorting beasts, clashing and scraping metal, curses and cries. Battle. A familiar place, but no less terrifying for that. Logen clung to the reins with his right hand as his horse bucked and thrashed, swinging the sword wildly round his head, more to scare his enemies than hurt them. Every moment he expected the jolt and searing pain as he was stuck through with a spear, then the ground to rush up and smack him in the face.

He saw Quai and Bayaz galloping away down the road, hotly pursued by the tall man, his spear couched under his arm. He saw Blacktoe rolling to his feet, spitting blood, scrambling for his axe. He saw the two men who'd come from behind fighting for control of their own twisting horses, spears waving in their hands. He saw the body of the one he'd just killed loll in half and topple slowly out of the saddle, blood pouring out over the muddy ground.

Logen squawked as he felt a spear-point stick dig into the back of his shoulder, and he was shoved forward, almost over his horse's head. Then he realised he was facing down the road, and still alive. He dug his heels into the flanks of his horse and it sped away, sending mud flying from its hooves and into the faces of the men behind. He fumbled the sword across into his right hand, nearly dropping the reins and falling into the road. He shrugged his shoulder but the wound didn't feel too bad—he could still move the arm alright.

"I'm still alive. Still alive." The road flashed by beneath him, the wind stinging his eyes. He was making ground on the tall man—the rags on his horse's hooves were slowing him down now, slipping on the muddy ground. Logen gripped the hilt of the sword as hard as he could, raised it behind him. The head of his enemy snapped round, but too late. There was a hollow bonk of metal on metal as sword smashed into helmet, leaving a deep dent and sending the tall man sprawling. His head bounced once against the road, foot still caught in one stirrup, then he came free and tumbled over and over on the grass, arms and legs flopping. His riderless horse galloped on, eyes rolling at Logen as he passed.

"Still alive." Logen looked over his shoulder. Blacktoe was back in the saddle and galloping after him, axe raised above his head, tangled hair flying out behind. The two other spearmen were with him, urging their horses forwards, but there was still some distance between them. Logen laughed. Perhaps he'd make it after all. He waved his sword at Blacktoe as the road entered a wood in the valley's bottom.

"I'm still alive!" he screamed at the top of his voice, and then his horse pulled up so suddenly that Logen was almost flung over its head. It was only by throwing one arm round its neck that he kept his seat at all. As soon as he fell back into the saddle he saw the problem, and it was a bad one.

Several tree trunks had been hauled across the road, their branches chopped off and the stumps filed down to vicious points, sticking out in all directions. Two more mailed Carls stood in front, spears at the ready. Even the best of horsemen couldn't have jumped that barrier, and Logen wasn't the best of horsemen. Bayaz and his apprentice had reached the same decision. Both sat still on their horses before the barricade, the old man looking puzzled, the young one simply scared.

Logen fingered the grip of his sword and cast desperately around, peering into the trees for some way out. He saw more men now. Archers. One, then two, then three of them, creeping slowly forward on both sides of the road, arrows knocked and strings drawn back.

Logen turned round in the saddle, but Blacktoe and his two companions were trotting up, there was no escape that way. They reined in a few strides away, well out of reach of Logen's sword. His shoulders slumped. The chase was done. Blacktoe leaned over and spat some blood onto the ground. "Alright, Bloody-Nine, that's as far as you go."

"Funny thing," muttered Logen, looking down at the long grey blade of the sword, dashed and spattered with red. "All that time I fought for Bethod against you, and now you fight for him against me. Seems we're never on the same side, and he's the only winner. Funny thing."

"Aye," mumbled Blacktoe through his bloody lips, "funny." But no one was laughing. Blacktoe and his Carls had faces hard as death, Quai looked on the verge of tears. Only Bayaz, for reasons beyond understanding, still had his customary good humour. "Alright, Ninefingers, get off the horse. Bethod wants you alive, but he'll take you dead, if he has to. Down! Now!"

Logen's thoughts began to turn to how they might escape, once he'd given up. Blacktoe wasn't like to make a mistake once he had them. Logen would likely be kicked half to death for the fight he'd given them already, if they didn't take his kneecaps off. They'd be trussed up tight like chickens for the slaughter. He pictured himself flung down on the stones with half a mile of chain around him, Bethod smiling down from his throne, Calder and Scale laughing, probably poking at him with something sharp.

Logen looked around. He looked at the cold arrowheads and the cold spear-points, and the cold eyes of the men pointing them. There was no way out of this little spot.

"Alright, you win." Logen threw his sword down, point first. He had it in mind that it would bite into the soil and stand there, swaying back and forth, but it toppled over and clattered against the dirt. It was that sort of day. He slowly swung one leg over the saddle and slid down into the road.

"That's better. Now the rest of you." Quai instantly slithered off his horse and stood there, glancing nervously up at Bayaz, but the Magus made no move. Blacktoe frowned and hefted his axe. "You too, old man."

"I prefer to ride." Logen winced. That was not the right answer. Any moment now Blacktoe would give the order. The bowstrings would sing and the First of the Magi would drop into the road, stuck full of arrows, probably still with that infuriating smile on his dead face.

But the order never came. There was no word of command, no strange incantation, no arcane gestures. The air around Bayaz's shoulders seemed to shimmer, like the air above the land on a hot day, and Logen felt a strange tugging at his guts.

Then the trees exploded in a wall of searing, blinding, white hot flame. Trunks burst and branches snapped with deafening cracks, venting plumes of brilliant fire and scalding steam. One burning arrow shot high up into the air over Logen's head, and then the archers were gone, boiled away into the furnace.

Logen choked and gasped, reeled back in shock and terror, arm up to ward his face from the blistering heat. The barricade was sending up great gouts of fire and blinding sparks, the two men who had been standing near were rolling and thrashing, wreathed in hungry flames, their screams lost in the deafening roar.

The horses plunged and reeled, snorting with mad fear. Blacktoe was flung to the ground for the second time, his flaming axe flying from his hands, and his horse stumbled and fell, crashing down on top of him. One of his companions was even less lucky—thrown straight into the sheets of fire by the road, his despairing cry quickly cut off. Only one stayed upright, and he was lucky enough to be wearing gloves. By some miracle he kept hold of the burning shaft of his spear.

How he had the presence of mind to charge with the world on fire around him, Logen would never know. Strange things can happen in a fight. He chose Quai as his target, bearing down on him with a snarl, the flaming spear aimed at his chest. The witless apprentice stood there helpless, rooted to the spot. Logen barrelled into him, snatching up his sword, sending Quai rolling across the road with his hands over his head, then he chopped mindlessly at the horse's legs as it flashed past him.

The blade was torn from his fingers and went skittering away, then a hoof slammed into Logen's injured shoulder and clubbed him into the dirt. The breath was knocked from him and the burning world spun crazily around. His blow had its effect though. A few strides further down the road the horse's hacked front legs gave way and it stumbled, carried helplessly forward, tumbled and pitched into the flames, horse and rider vanishing together.

Logen cast about on the ground for the sword. Sizzling leaves whipped across the road, stinging his face and his hands. The heat was a great weight pressing down on him, pulling the sweat out of his skin. He found the bloody grip of the sword, seized hold of it with his torn fingers. He lurched up, staggered round, shouting meaningless sounds of fury, but there was no one left to fight. The flames were gone, as suddenly as they'd arrived, leaving Logen coughing and blinking in the curling smoke.

The silence seemed complete after the roaring noise, the gentle breeze felt icy cold. A wide circle of the trees around them had been reduced to charred and shattered stumps, as though they had burned for hours. The barricade was a sagging heap of grey ash and black splinters. Two corpses lay sprawled nearby, barely recognisable as men, burned down to the bones. The blackened blades of their spears lay in the road, the shafts vanished. Of the archers there was no sign at all. They were soot blown away on the wind. Quai lay motionless on his face with his hands over his head, and beyond him Blacktoe's horse lay sprawled out on its side, one leg silently twitching, the others still.

"Well," said Bayaz, the muffled noise making Logen jump. He'd somehow expected there would never be another sound again. "That's that." The First of the Magi swung a leg over his saddle and slid down into the road. His horse stood there, calm and obedient. It hadn't moved the whole time. "There now, Master Quai, do you see what can be achieved with a proper understanding of plants?"

Bayaz sounded calm, but his hands were trembling. Trembling badly. He looked haggard, ill, old, like a man who'd dragged a cart ten miles. Logen stared at him, swaying silently back and forth, the sword dangling from his hand.

"So that's Art, is it?" His voice sounded very small and far away.

Bayaz wiped the sweat from his face. "Of a sort. Hardly very subtle. Still," and he poked at one of the charred bodies with his boot, "subtlety is wasted on the Northmen." He grimaced, rubbed at his sunken eyes and peered up the road. "Where the hell did those horses get to?"

Logen heard a ragged groan from the direction of Blacktoe's fallen mount. He stumbled towards it, tripped and fell to his knees, stumbled towards it again. His shoulder was a ball of pain, his left arm numb, his fingers ripped and bleeding, but Blacktoe was in worse shape. Much worse. He was propped up on his elbows, legs crushed under his horse right to the hips, hands burned to swollen tatters. He had a look of profound puzzlement on his bloody face as he tried, unsuccessfully, to drag himself from under the horse.

"You've fucking killed me," he whispered, staring open-mouthed at the wreckage of his hands. "I'm all done. I'll never make it back, and even if I could, what for?" He gave a despairing laugh. "Bethod ain't half so merciful as he used to be. Better you kill me now, before it starts to hurt. Better all round." And he slumped back and lay in the road.

Logen looked up at Bayaz, but there was no help there. "I'm not much at healing," snapped the wizard, glancing round at the circle of blasted stumps. "I told you we tend to specialise." He closed his eyes and bent over, hands resting on his knees, breathing hard.

Logen thought of the floor in Bethod's hall, and the two princes, laughing and poking. "Alright," he muttered, standing up and hefting the sword. "Alright."

Blacktoe smiled. "You were right, Ninefingers. I never should have knelt to Bethod. Never. Shit on him and his Feared. It would have been better to die up in the mountains, fighting him to the last. There might have been something fine in that. I just had enough. You can see that, can't you?"

"I can see that," muttered Logen. "I've had enough myself."

"Something fine," said Blacktoe, staring far up into the grey skies, "I just had enough. So I reckon I earned this. Fair is fair." He lifted his chin. "Well then. Get it done, lad."

Logen raised the sword.

"I'm glad it's you, Ninefingers," hissed Blacktoe through gritted teeth, "for what it's worth."

"I'm not." Logen swung the blade down.

The scorched stumps were still smouldering, smoke curling up into the air, but all was cold now. Logen's mouth tasted salty, like blood. Perhaps he bit his tongue somewhere. Perhaps it was someone else's. He threw the sword down and it bounced and clattered, shedding red specks across the dirt. Quai gaped around for a moment, then he folded up and coughed puke into the road. Logen stared down at Blacktoe's headless corpse. "That was a good man. Better than me."

"History is littered with dead good men." Bayaz knelt stiffly and picked up the sword, wiped the blade on Blacktoe's coat, then he squinted up the road, peering through the haze of smoke. "We should be moving. Others might be on their way."

Logen looked at his bloody hands, slowly turning them over and over. They were his hands, no doubt. There was the missing finger. "Nothing's changed," he mumbled to himself.

Bayaz straightened up, brushing the dirt from his knees. "When has it ever?" He held out the sword out to Logen, hilt first. "I think you'll still be needing this."

Logen stared at the blade for a moment. It was clean, dull grey, just as it had always been. Unlike him, it showed not so much as a scratch from the hard use it had seen that day. He didn't want it back. Not ever.

But he took it anyway.

PART II

"Life—the way it really is—is a battle not between good and bad, but between bad and worse"

Joseph Brodsky

WHAT FREEDOM LOOKS LIKE

The point of the shovel bit into the ground with the sharp scrape of metal on earth. An all too familiar sound. It didn't bite in far, for all the effort put behind it, as the soil was rocky hard and baked by the sun.

But she wasn't to be deterred by a little hard soil.

She had dug too many holes, and in ground worse for digging than this.

When the fighting is over, you dig, if you're still alive. You dig graves for your dead comrades. A last mark of respect, however little you might have had for them. You dig as deep as you can be bothered, you dump them in, you cover them up, they rot away and are forgotten. That's the way it's always been.

She flicked her shoulder and a sent a shovelful of sandy soil flying. Her eyes followed the grains of dirt and little stones as they broke apart in the air, then fell across the face of one of the soldiers. One eye stared at her reproachfully. The other had one of her arrows snapped off in it. A couple of flies were buzzing lazily around his face. There would be no burial for him, the graves were for her people. He and his bastard friends could lie out in the merciless sun.

After all, the vultures have to eat.

The blade of the shovel swished through the air and bit again into the soil. Another clump of dirt tumbled away. She straightened up and wiped the sweat from her face. She squinted up at the sky. The sun was blazing, straight above, sucking whatever moisture remained out of the dusty landscape, drying the blood on the rocks. She looked at the two graves beside her. One more to go. She would finish this one, throw the earth on top of those three fools, rest for a moment, then away.

Others would be coming for her soon enough.

She stuck the shovel into the earth, took hold of the water skin and pulled the stopper out. She took a few lukewarm swallows, even allowed herself the luxury of pouring a trickle out into her grimy hand and splashing it on her face. The early deaths of her comrades had at least put a stop to the endless squabbling over water.

There would be plenty to go round now.

"Water . . ." gasped the soldier by the rocks. It was surprising, but he was still alive. Her arrow had missed his heart but it had killed him still—just a little less quickly than she had intended. He had managed to drag himself as far as the rocks, but his crawling days were over. The stones around him were coated in dark blood. The heat and that arrow would do for him soon, however tough he was.

She wasn't thirsty, but there was water to spare and she wouldn't be able to carry it all. She took a few more swallows, letting it slosh out of her mouth and down her neck. A rare treat out here in the Badlands, to let water fall. Shining drops spattered onto the dry earth, turning it dark. She splashed some more on her face, licked her lips, and looked over at the soldier.

"Mercy . . ." he croaked, one hand clasped to his chest where the arrow was sticking out of it, the other stretched weakly towards her.

"Mercy? Hah!" She pushed the stopper back into the skin, then tossed it down next to the grave. "Don't you know who I am?" She grabbed hold of the handle of the shovel, the point of its blade bit once more into the earth.

"Ferro Maljinn!" came a voice from somewhere behind her, "I know who you are!"

A most unwelcome development.

She swung the shovel again, mind racing. Her bow was lying just out of reach on the ground by the first grave she had dug. She threw some dirt away, her sweating shoulders prickling at the unseen presence. She glanced over at the dying soldier. He was staring at a point behind her, and that gave her a good idea where this new arrival was standing.

She dug the point of the shovel in again, then let go and sprang forward out of the hole, rolling across the dirt, snatching up her bow as she moved, notching an arrow, drawing back the string in one smooth motion. An old man was standing about ten strides away. He was making no move forward, was holding no weapon. He was just standing, looking at her with a benign smile.

She let the arrow fly.

Now Ferro was about as deadly with a bow as it's possible to be. The ten dead soldiers could have testified to that, if they'd been able. Six of them had her arrows sticking out of them, and in that fight she hadn't missed once. She couldn't remember missing at close range, however quickly the shot had been taken, and she'd killed men ten times further away than this smiling old bastard was now.

But this time she missed.

The arrow seemed to curve in the air. A bad feather maybe, but it still didn't seem quite right. The old man didn't flinch, not even a hair. He simply stood, smiling, exactly where he'd always stood, and the arrow missed him by a few inches and disappeared off down the hillside.

And that gave everyone time to consider the situation.

He was a strange one, this old man. Very dark-skinned, black as coal, which meant he was from the far south, across the wide and shelterless desert. That's a journey not lightly taken, and Ferro had rarely seen such people. Tall and thin with long, sinewy arms and a simple robe wrapped round him. There were strange bangles round his wrists, stacked up so they covered half his fore-arms, glittering dark and light in the savage sun.

His hair was a mass of grey ropes about his face, some hanging down as low as his waist, and there was a grey stubble on his lean, pointed jaw. He had a big water skin wrapped around his chest, and a bunch of leather bags hanging from a belt around his waist. Nothing else. No weapon. That was the strangest thing of all, for a man out here in the Badlands. No one came to this god-forsaken place except those who were running, and those sent to hunt them. In either case, they should be well armed.

He was no soldier of Gurkhul, he was no scum come looking for the money on her head. He was no bandit, no escaped slave. What was he then? And why was he here? He must have come for her. He could be one of them.

An Eater.

Who else would wander the Badlands without a weapon? She hadn't realised they wanted her that badly.

He stood there motionless, the old man, smiling at her. She reached slowly for another arrow, and his eyes followed her without any worry.

"That really isn't necessary," he said, in a slow, deep voice.

She nocked the arrow to her bow. The old man didn't move. She shrugged her shoulders and took her time aiming. The old man smiled on, not a care in the world. She let the arrow fly. It missed him by a few inches again, this time on the other side, and shot off down the hillside.

Once was a possibility, she had to admit that, but twice was wrong. If Ferro knew one thing, and one thing only, she knew how to kill. The old fool should have been stuck through and bleeding out his last into the stony soil. Now, simply by standing still and smiling, he seemed to be saying, "You know less than you think. I know more."

That was very galling.

"Who are you, you old bastard?"

"They call me Yulwei."

"Old bastard will do for you!" She tossed her bow down on the ground, let her arms drop to her sides so that her right hand was hidden from him by her body. She twisted her wrist and the curved knife dropped out of her sleeve and into her waiting palm. There are many ways to kill a man, and if one way fails you must try another.

Ferro had never been one to give up at the first stumble.

Yulwei began to move slowly towards her, his bare feet padding on the rocks, bangles jingling softly together. That was very strange, now she thought about it. If he made a noise every time he moved, how had he managed to sneak up on her?

"What do you want?"

"I want to help you." He came forward, until he was just over an arm's length away, then he stopped and stood, grinning at her.

Now Ferro was fast as a snake with a knife and twice as deadly, as the last of those soldiers could have testified, had he been able. The blade was a shining blur in the air, swung with all her strength and all her fury behind it. If he had been standing where she thought he was, his head would have been hanging off. Only he wasn't. He was standing about a stride to the left.

She threw herself at him with a fighting scream, ramming the glittering point of the knife into his heart. But she stabbed only air. He was back where he had been before, motionless and smiling all the while. Very strange. She padded round him, cautious, sandaled feet scuffing in the dust, left hand circling in the air in front of her, right hand gripped tight round the handle of the knife. She had to be careful—there was magic here.

"There is no need to get angry. I am here to help."

"Fuck your help," she hissed back at him.

"But you need it, and badly. They are coming for you, Ferro. There are soldiers in the hills, many soldiers."

"I'll outrun them."

"There are too many. You cannot outrun them all."

She glanced round at the punctured bodies. "Then I'll give them to the vultures."

"Not this time. They are not alone. They have help." On the word "help" his deep voice dropped even lower.

Ferro frowned. "Priests?"

"Yes, and more besides." His eyes went very wide. "An Eater," he whispered. "They mean to take you alive. The Emperor wants to make an example of you. He has it in mind to put you on display."

She snorted. "Fuck the Emperor."

"I heard you already did."

She growled and raised the knife again, but it was not a knife. There was a hissing snake in her hand, a deadly snake, with its mouth open to bite. "Ugh!" She threw it on the ground, stamped her foot down on its head, but she stamped on her knife instead. The blade snapped with a sharp crack.

"They will catch you," said the old man. "They will catch you, and they will break your legs with hammers in the city square, so you can never run again. Then they will parade you through the streets of Shaffa, naked, sitting backwards on an ass, with your hair shaved off, while the people line the streets and shout insults at you."

She frowned at him, but Yulwei did not stop. "They will starve you to death in a cage before the palace, cooking in the hot sun, while the good people of Gurkhul taunt you and spit on you and throw dung at you through the bars. Perhaps they will give you piss to drink, if you are lucky. When you finally die they will let you rot, and the flies will eat you bit by bit, and all the other slaves will see what freedom looks like, and decide they are better off as they are."

Ferro was bored with this. Let them come, and the Eater too. She wouldn't die in a cage. She would cut her own throat, if it came to that. She turned her back on him with a scowl and snatched up the shovel, started digging away furiously at the last grave. Soon it was deep enough.

Deep enough for the scum who'd be rotting in it.

She turned around. Yulwei was kneeling down by the dying soldier, giving him water from the skin round his chest.

"Fuck!" she shouted, striding over, her fingers locked around the handle of the shovel.

The old man got to his feet as she came close. "Mercy . . ." croaked the soldier, stretching out his hand.

"I'll give you mercy!" The edge of the shovel bit deep into the soldier's skull. The body twitched briefly then was still. She turned to the old man with a look of triumph. He stared back sadly. There was something in his eyes. Pity, maybe.

"What do you want, Ferro Maljinn?"

"What?"

"Why did you do that?" Yulwei pointed down at the dead man. "What do you want?"

"Vengeance." She spat out the word.

"On all of them? On the whole nation of Gurkhul? Every man, woman and child?"

"All of them!"

The old man looked round the corpses. "Then you must be very happy with today's work."

She forced a smile onto her face. "Yes." But she wasn't very happy. She couldn't remember what it felt like. The smile seemed strange, unfamiliar, all lopsided.

"And is vengeance all you think of, every minute of every day, your only desire?"

"Yes."

"Hurting *them*? Killing *them*? Ending *them*?"

"Yes!"

"You want nothing for yourself?"

She paused. "What?"

"For yourself. What do *you* want?"

She stared at the old man suspiciously, but no reply came to her. Yulwei shook his head sadly. "It seems to me, Ferro Maljinn, that you are as much a slave as you ever were. Or ever could be." He sat down, cross-legged on a rock.

She stared at him for a moment, confused. Then the anger bubbled up again, hot and reassuring. "If you came to help me, you can help me bury them!" She pointed over at the three bloody corpses, lined up next to the graves.

"Oh no. That is your work."

She turned away from the old man, cursing under her breath, and moved over to her one-time companions. She took Shebed's corpse under the arms and hauled him over to the first grave, his heels making two little grooves in the dust. When she made it to the hole she rolled him in. Alugai was next. A stream of dry soil ran over him as he came to rest in the bottom of his grave.

She turned to Nasar's carcass. He had been killed by a sword cut across the face. Ferro thought it was something of an improvement to his looks.

"That one looks a good sort," said Yulwei.

"Nasar." She laughed without amusement. "A raper, a thief, a coward." She hawked up some phlegm and spat into his dead face. It splattered softly against his forehead. "Much the worst of the three." She looked down at the graves. "But they were all of them shit."

"Nice company you keep."

"The hunted don't have the luxury of choosing their companions." She stared at Nasar's bloody face. "You take what's offered."

"If you disliked them so much, why don't you leave them for the vultures, like you have these others?" Yulwei swept his arm over the broken soldiers on the ground.

"You bury your own." She kicked Nasar into the hole. He rolled forward, arms flopping, and dropped into the grave face down. "That's the way it's always been."

She grabbed hold of the shovel and started to heap the stony earth onto his back. She worked in silence, the sweat building up on her face, then dripping off onto the ground. Yulwei watched her as the holes filled up. Three more piles of dirt in the wasteland. She threw the shovel away and it bounced off one of the corpses and clattered among the stones. A small cloud of black flies buzzed angrily off the body, then returned.

Ferro picked up her bow and arrows and slung them over her shoulder. She took the water skin, checked its weight carefully, then shouldered that also. Then she picked over the bodies of the soldiers. One of them, he looked like the leader, had a fine curved sword. He hadn't even managed to draw it before her arrow had caught him in the throat. Ferro drew it now, and she tested it with a couple of sweeps through the air. It was very good: well balanced, the long blade glittering deadly sharp, bright metal on the hilt catching the sun. He had a knife as well that matched it. She took the weapons and stuck them through her belt.

She picked over the other bodies, but there wasn't much to take. She cut her arrows from the corpses where she could. She found some coins and tossed them away. They would only weigh her down, and what would she buy out here in the Badlands? Dirt?

That was all there was, and it was free.

They had a few scraps of food with them, but not enough even for another day. That meant there must be others, probably lots of them, and not far away. Yulwei was telling the truth, but it made no difference to her.

She turned and started to walk southward, down off the hill and towards the great desert, leaving the old man behind.

"That's the wrong way," he said.

She stopped, squinting at him in the bright sun. "Aren't the soldiers coming?"

Yulwei's eyes sparkled. "There are many ways of staying unnoticed, even out here in the Badlands."

She looked to the north, out over the featureless plain below. Out towards Gurkhul. There wasn't a hill, or a tree, or scarcely a bush for miles. Nowhere to hide. "Unnoticed, even by an Eater?"

The old man laughed. "Especially by those arrogant swine. They're not half as clever as they think they are. How do you think I got here? I came through them, between them, around them. I go where I please, and I take who I please with me."

She shaded her eyes with her hand, and squinted southward. The desert stretched away into the far distance, and beyond. Ferro could survive here in the wilderness, just about, but out there in that crucible of changing sands and merciless heat?

The old man seemed to read her thoughts. "There are always the endless sands. I have crossed them before. It can be done. But not by you."

He was right, damn him. Ferro was lean and tough as a bowstring, but that just meant she would walk in circles a little longer before pitching on her face. The desert was preferable to the cage before the palace as a place to die, but not by much. She wanted to stay alive.

There were still things to do.

The old man sat there, cross-legged, smiling. What was he? Ferro trusted no one, but if he meant to deliver her to the Emperor, he could have knocked her on the head while she was digging, instead of announcing his arrival. He had magic, she had seen that for herself, and some chance was better than none.

But what would he want in return? The world had never given Ferro anything for free, and she didn't expect it to begin now. She narrowed her eyes. "What do you want from me, Yulwei?"

The old man laughed. That laugh was becoming very annoying. "Let us just say that I will have done you a favour. Later on, you can do me one in return."

That answer was horribly thin on the details, but when your life's on the table you have to take whatever's offered. She hated to place herself in the power of another, but it seemed she had no choice.

Not if she wanted to live out the week, that is.

"What do we do?"

"We must wait for nightfall." Yulwei glanced at the twisted bodies scattered about the ground, and wrinkled his nose. "But perhaps not here."

Ferro shrugged and sat herself down on the middle grave. "Here will do," she said, "I've a mind to watch the vultures eat."

Overhead the clear night sky was scattered with bright stars, and the air had turned cool, cold even. Down on the dark and dusty plain below, fires were burning, a curved line of fires that seemed to hem them in against the edge of the desert. She, Yulwei, the ten corpses and the three graves were trapped on the hillside. Tomorrow, as the first light crept over the arid land, the soldiers would leave those fires and creep carefully towards the hills. If Ferro was still there when they arrived, she would be killed for sure, or worse still captured. She could not fight that many on her own, even supposing there was no Eater with them.

She hated to admit it, but her life was in Yulwei's hands now.

He squinted up at the starry sky. "It is time," he said.

They scrambled down the rocky hillside in the darkness, picking their way carefully among the boulders and the odd, scrubby, half-dead bush. Northward, towards Gurkhul. Yulwei moved surprisingly fast and she was forced to half-run to keep up, eyes fixed on the ground to find her footing among the dry rocks. When they finally reached the base of the hill and she looked up, she saw that Yulwei was leading her toward the left hand edge of the line, where the fires were most numerous.

"Wait," she whispered, grabbing his shoulder. She pointed over to the right hand side. There were fewer fires there, and it would be easier to slip between them. "What about that way?"

She could just see Yulwei's teeth smiling white in the starlight. "Oh no, Ferro Maljinn. That is where most of the soldiers are . . . and our other friend." He was making no attempt to keep his voice down, and it was making her jumpy. "That is where they expect you to come through, if you choose to go north. But they do not expect you. They think you will go south into the desert to die, rather than risk being captured, as indeed you would have done, had I not been here."

Yulwei turned and moved off and she crept after him, keeping low to the ground. As they drew nearer to the fires she saw that the old man had been right. There were figures sitting around some of them, but they were thinly spread. The old man strode confidently toward four fires on the far left, only one of them manned. He made no effort to stay low, his bangles jingled softly together, his bare feet flapped loud on the dry earth. They were almost close enough to see the features of the three men round the fire. Yulwei would surely be seen at any moment. She hissed at him to grab his attention, sure that she would be heard.

Yulwei turned round, looking puzzled in the faint light from the flames. "What?" he said. She winced, waiting for the soldiers to leap up, but they chattered on regardless. Yulwei looked over at them. "They will not see us, nor hear us either, unless you start shouting in their ears. We are safe." He turned and walked on, giving the soldiers a wide berth. Ferro followed, still keeping low and quiet, if only out of habit.

As Ferro came closer she began to make out the words of the soldier's conversation. She slowed, listening. She turned. She started to move towards the fire. Yulwei looked round. "What are you doing?" he asked.

Ferro looked at the three of them. A big, tough-looking veteran, a thin, weaselly type, and an honest-seeming young man, who didn't look much like a soldier. Their weapons were lying around, sheathed, wrapped up, unready. She circled them warily, listening.

"They say she's not right in the head," the thin one was whispering at the young one, trying to scare him, "they say she's killed a hundred men, or more. If you're a good looking fella, she cuts your fruits off while you're still alive," he grabbed hold of his crotch, "and eats them in front of you!"

"Ah, stop your mouth," said the big one, "she won't be coming near us." He pointed over to where the fires were sparser, his voice dropping to a whisper. "She'll be going to *him*, if she comes this way at all."

"Well, I hope she doesn't," said the young one, "live and let live, say I."

The thin man frowned. "And what about all the good men she's killed? And women and children too? Shouldn't they have been let live?" Ferro's teeth ground together. She'd never killed children, that she could think of.

"Well, it's a shame for them, of course. I'm not saying she shouldn't be caught." The young soldier glanced around nervously. "Just maybe not by us."

The big man let go a laugh at that, but the thin one didn't look amused. "You a coward?"

"No!" said the young man, angrily, "but I got a wife and a family depending on me, and I could do without being killed out here, that's all." He grinned. "We're expecting another child. Hoping for a son this time."

The big man nodded. "My son's nearly grown now. They get old so quick."

Talk of children, and families, and hopes only made the fury in Ferro's chest squeeze harder. Why should they be allowed a life, when she had nothing? When them and their kind had taken everything from her? She slid the curved knife out of its sheath.

"What are you doing, Ferro?" hissed Yulwei.

The young man looked round. "Did you hear something?"

The big one laughed. "I think I heard you shit yourself." The thin one chuckled to himself, the young man smiled, embarrassed. Ferro crept right up behind him. She was just a foot or two away, brightly lit by the fire, but none of the soldiers even glanced at her. She raised the knife.

"Ferro!" shouted Yulwei. The young man sprang to his feet, he peered out across the dark plain, squinting, brow furrowed. He looked Ferro right in the face, but his eyes were focused far behind her. She could smell his breath. The blade of the knife glittered an inch or less from his stubbly throat.

Now. Now was the time. She could kill him quickly, and take the other two as well before the alarm was raised. She knew she could do it. They were unprepared, and she was ready. Now was the time.

But her hand didn't move.

"What's got up your arse?" asked the big soldier. "There's nothing out there."

"Could've sworn I heard something," said the young man, still looking right in her face.

"Wait!" shouted the thin one, jumping to his feet and pointing. "There she is! Right in front of you!" Ferro froze for an instant, staring at him, then he and the big man started to laugh. The young soldier looked sheepish, turned around and sat down.

"I thought I heard something, that's all."

"There's no one out there," said the big man. Ferro began to back slowly away. She felt sick, her mouth full of sour spit, her head thumping. She pushed the knife back into its sheath, turned and stumbled off with Yulwei following silently behind.

When the light of the fires and the sound of the talking had faded into the distance she stopped and dropped down on the hard ground. A cold wind blew up across the barren plain. It blew stinging dust in her face, but she hardly noticed. The hate and the fury were gone, for the time being, but they had left a hole, and she had nothing else to fill it with. She felt empty and cold and sick and alone. She hugged herself, rocking slowly back and forth, and closed her eyes. But the darkness held no comfort.

Then she felt the old man's hand press onto her shoulder.

Now normally she would have twisted away, thrown him off, killed him if she could. But the strength was all gone. She looked up, blinking. "There's nothing left of me. What am I?" She pressed one hand on her chest, but she barely felt it. "I have nothing inside."

"Well. It's strange that you should say that." Yulwei smiled up at the starry sky. "I was just starting to think there might be something in there worth saving."

THE KING'S JUSTICE

A s soon as he reached the Square of Marshals, Jezal realised there was something wrong. It was never half this busy for a meeting of the Open Council. He glanced over the knots of finely dressed people as he hurried by, slightly late and out of breath from his long training session: voices were hushed, faces tense and expectant.

He shouldered his way through the crowd to the Lord's Round, glancing suspiciously up at the guards flanking the inlaid doors. They at least seemed the same as ever, their heavy visors giving nothing away. He crossed the antechamber, vivid tapestries flapping slightly in the draught, slipped through the inner doors and passed into the vast, cool space beyond. His footsteps made tapping echoes in the gilded dome as he hurried down the aisle towards the high table. Jalenhorm was standing beneath one of the tall windows, face splashed with coloured light from the stained glass, frowning at a bench with a metal rail along its base which had been placed to one side of the floor.

"What's going on?"

"Haven't you heard?" Jalenhorm's voice was whispery with excitement. "Hoff's let it be known there'll be some great matter to discuss."

"What is it? Angland? The Northmen?"

The big man shook his head. "Don't know, but we'll soon see."

Jezal frowned. "I don't like surprises." His eye came to rest on the mysterious bench. "What's that for?"

At that moment the great doors were swung open and a stream of councillors began to flood down the aisle. The usual mixture, Jezal supposed, if a little more purposeful. The younger sons, the paid representatives . . . he caught his breath. There was a tall man at the front, richly dressed even in this august company, with a weighty golden chain across his shoulders and a weighty frown across his face.

"Lord Brock himself," whispered Jezal.

"And there's Lord Isher." Jalenhorm nodded at a sedate old man just behind Brock, "and Heugen, and Barezin. It's something big. It has to be."

Jezal took a deep breath as four of the Union's most powerful noblemen arranged themselves on the front row. He had never seen the Open Council half so well attended. On the councillors' half-circle of benches there was barely an empty seat. High above them, the public gallery was an unbroken ring of nervous faces.

Now Hoff blustered through the doors and down the aisle, and he was not alone. On his right a tall man flowed along, slender and proud-looking with a long, spotless white coat and a shock of white hair. Arch Lector Sult. On his left walked another man, leaning heavily on a stick, slightly bent in a robe of black and gold with a long grey beard. High Justice Marovia. Jezal could hardly believe his eyes. Three members of the Closed Council, here.

Jalenhorm hurried to take his place as the clerks deposited their burdens of ledgers and papers on the polished tabletop. The Lord Chamberlain threw himself down in their midst and immediately called for wine. The head of his Majesty's Inquisition swept into a high chair on one side of him, smiling faintly to himself. High Justice Marovia lowered himself slowly into another, frowning all the while. The volume of the anxious whispering in the hall rose a step, the faces of the great magnates on the front row were grim and suspicious. The Announcer took his place before the table, not the usual brightly dressed imbecile, but a dark, bearded man with a barrel chest. He lifted his staff high, then beat it against the tiles, fit to wake the dead.

"I call this meeting of the Open Council of the Union to order!" he bellowed. The hubbub gradually died away.

"There is but one matter for discussion this morning," said the Lord Chamberlain, peering sternly at the house from beneath his heavy brows, "a matter of the King's Justice." There were scattered mutterings. "A matter concerning the royal licence for trade in the city of Westport." The noise increased: angry whispers, uncomfortable shufflings of noble arses on their

benches, the familiar scratching of quills on the great ledgers. Jezal saw Lord
Brock's brows draw together, the corners of Lord Heugen's mouth turn down.
They did not seem to like the taste of this. The Lord Chamberlain sniffed and
took a swig of wine, waiting for the muttering to die away. "I am not best
qualified to speak on this matter, however—"

"No indeed!" snapped Lord Isher sharply, shifting in his seat on the front
row with a scowl.

Hoff fixed the old man with his eye. "So I call on a man who is! My colleague from the Closed Council, Arch Lector Sult."

"The Open Council recognises Arch Lector Sult!" thundered the
Announcer, as the head of the Inquisition made his graceful way down the
steps of the dais and onto the tiled floor, smiling pleasantly at the angry faces
turned towards him.

"My Lords," he began, in a slow, musical voice, ushering his words out
into space with smooth movements of his hands, "for the past seven years,
ever since our glorious victory in the war with Gurkhul, an exclusive royal
licence for trade in the city of Westport has been in the hands of the honourable Guild of Mercers."

"And a fine job they've done of it!" shouted Lord Heugen.

"They won us that war!" growled Barezin, pounding the bench beside
him with a meaty fist.

"A fine job!"

"Fine!" came the cries.

The Arch Lector nodded as he waited for the noise to fade. "Indeed they
have," he said, pacing across the tiles like a dancer, his words scratching their
way across the pages of the books. "I would be the last to deny it. A fine job."
He spun suddenly around, the tails of his white coat snapping, his face
twisted into a brutal snarl. "A fine job of dodging the King's taxes!" he
screamed. There was a collective gasp.

"A fine job of slighting the King's law!" Another gasp, louder.

"A fine job of high treason!" There was a storm of protest, of fists shaken
in the air and papers thrown to the floor. Livid faces stared down from the
public gallery, florid ones ranted and bellowed from the benches before the
high table. Jezal stared about him, unsure if he could have heard correctly.

"How dare you, Sult!" Lord Brock roared at the Arch Lector as he swished back up the steps of the dais, a faint smile clinging to his lips.

"We demand proof!" bellowed Lord Heugen. "We demand justice!"

"The King's Justice!" came cries from the back.

"You must supply us with proof!" shouted Isher, as the noise began to fade.

The Arch Lector twitched out his white gown, the fine material billowing around him as he swung himself smoothly back into his chair. "Oh but that is our intention, Lord Isher!"

The heavy bolt of a small side door was flung back with an echoing bang. There was a rustling as Lords and proxies twisted round, stood up, squinted over to see what was happening. People in the public gallery peered out over the parapet, leaning dangerously far in their eagerness to see. The hall fell quiet. Jezal swallowed. There was a scraping, tapping, clinking sound beyond the doorway, then a strange and sinister procession emerged from the darkness.

Sand dan Glokta came first, limping as always and leaning heavily on his cane, but with his head held high and a twisted, toothless grin on his hollow face. Three men shuffled behind him, chained together by their hands and bare feet, clinking and rattling their way towards the high table. Their heads were shaved bare and they were dressed in brown sackcloth. The clothing of the penitent. Confessed traitors.

The first of the prisoners was licking his lips, eyes darting here and there, pale with terror. The second, shorter and thicker-set, was stumbling, dragging his left leg behind him, hunched over with his mouth hanging open. As Jezal watched, a thin line of pink drool dangled from his lip and spattered on the tiles. The third man, painfully thin and with huge dark rings round his eyes, stared slowly around, blinking, eyes wide but apparently taking nothing in. Jezal recognised the man behind the three prisoners straight away: the big albino from that night in the street. Jezal rocked his weight from one foot to the other, feeling suddenly cold and uncomfortable.

The purpose of the bench was now made clear. The three prisoners slumped down on it, the albino knelt and snapped their manacles shut around the rail along its base. The chamber was entirely silent. Every eye was fixed on the crippled Inquisitor, and his three prisoners.

"Our investigation began some months ago," said Arch Lector Sult, immensely smug at having the assembly so completely under his control. "A simple matter of some irregular accounting, I won't bore you with the details." He smiled at Brock, at Isher, at Barezin. "I know you all are very busy men. Who could have thought then, that such a little matter would lead us here? Who would suppose that the roots of treason could run so very deep?"

"Indeed," said the Lord Chamberlain impatiently, looking up from his goblet. "Inquisitor Glokta, the floor is yours."

The Announcer struck his staff on the tiles. "The Open Council of the Union recognises Sand dan Glokta, Inquisitor Exempt!"

The cripple waited politely for the scratching of the clerk's quills to finish, leaning on his cane in the centre of the floor, seemingly unmoved by the importance of the occasion. "Rise and face the Open Council," he said, turning to the first of his prisoners.

The terrified man sprang up, his chains rattling, licking his pale lips, goggling at the faces of the Lords in the front row. "Your name?" demanded Glokta.

"Salem Rews."

Jezal felt a catch in his throat. Salem Rews? He knew the man! His father had had dealings with him in the past, at one time he had been a regular visitor to their estate! Jezal studied the terrified, shaven-headed traitor with increasing horror. He cast his mind back to the plump, well-dressed merchant, always ready with a joke. It was him, no doubt. Their eyes met for an instant and Jezal looked anxiously away. His father had talked with that man in their hallway! Had shaken hands with him! Accusations of treason are like illnesses—you can catch them just by being in the same room! His eyes were drawn inevitably back to that unfamiliar, yet horribly familiar face. How dare he be a traitor, the bastard?

"You are a member of the honourable Guild of Mercers?" continued Glokta, putting a sneering accent into the word "honourable."

"I was," mumbled Rews.

"What was your role within the Guild?" The shaven-headed Mercer stared desperately about him. "Your role?" demanded Glokta, his voice taking on a hard edge.

"I conspired to defraud the King!" cried the merchant, wringing his hands. A wave of shock ran round the hall. Jezal swallowed sour spit. He saw Sult smirking across at High Justice Marovia. The old man's face was stony blank, but his fists were clenched tight on the table before him. "I committed treason! For money! I smuggled, and I bribed, and I lied . . . we were all at it!"

"All at it!" Glokta leered round at the assembly. "And if any of you should doubt it, we have ledgers, and we have documents, and we have numbers. There is a room in the House of Questions stuffed with them. A room full of secrets, and guilt, and lies." He slowly shook his head. "Sorry reading, I can tell you."

"I had to do it!" screamed Rews. "They made me! I had no choice!"

The crippled Inquisitor frowned at his audience. "Of course they made you. We realise you were but a single brick in this house of infamy. An attempt was made on your life recently, was it not?"

"They tried to kill me!"

"Who tried?"

"It was this man!" wailed Rews, voice cracking, pointing a trembling finger at the prisoner next to him, pulling away as far as the chains that linked them would allow. "It was him! Him!" The manacles rattled as he waved his arm, spit flying from his mouth. There was another surge of angry voices, louder this time. Jezal watched the head of the middle prisoner sag and he slumped sideways, but the hulking albino grabbed him and hauled him back upright.

"Wake up, Master Carpi!" shouted Glokta. The lolling head came slowly up. An unfamiliar face, strangely swollen and badly pocked with acne-scars. Jezal noticed with disgust that his four front teeth were missing. Just like Glokta's.

"You are from Talins, yes, in Styria?" The man nodded slowly, stupidly, like someone half asleep. "You are paid to kill people, yes?" He nodded again. "And you were hired to murder ten of his Majesty's subjects, among them this confessed traitor, Salem Rews?" A trickle of blood ran slowly out from the man's nose and his eyes started to roll back in his head. The albino shook him by the shoulder and he came round, nodding groggily. "What became of the other nine?" Silence. "You killed them, did you not?" Another nod, a strange clicking sound coming from the prisoner's throat.

Glokta frowned slowly around the rapt faces of the Council. "Villem dan Robb, customs official, throat cut ear to ear." He slid a finger across his neck and a woman in the gallery squealed. "Solimo Scandi, Mercer, stabbed in the back four times." He thrust up four fingers, then pressed them to his stomach as though sickened. "The bloody list goes on. All murdered, for nothing but a bigger profit. Who hired you?"

"Him," croaked the killer, turning his swollen face to look at the gaunt man with the glassy eyes, slumped on the bench next to him, heedless of his surroundings. Glokta limped over, cane tapping on the tiles.

"What is your name?"

The prisoner's head snapped up, his eyes focusing on the twisted face of the Inquisitor above him. "Gofred Hornlach!" he answered instantly, voice shrill.

"You are a senior member of the Guild of Mercers?"

"Yes!" he barked, blinking mindlessly up at Glokta.

"One of Magister Kault's deputies, in fact?"

"Yes!"

"Have you conspired with other Mercers to defraud his Majesty the King? Did you hire an assassin to murder ten of his Majesty's subjects?"

"Yes! Yes!"

"Why?"

"We were worried they would tell what they knew . . . tell what they knew . . . tell . . ." Hornlach's empty eyes stared off towards one of the coloured windows. His mouth slowly stopped moving.

"Tell what they knew?" prompted the Inquisitor.

"About the treasonous activities of the Guild!" the Mercer blurted, "about our treasons! About the activities of the guild . . . treasonous . . . activities . . ."

Glokta cut in sharply. "Were you acting alone?"

"No! No!"

The Inquisitor rapped his cane down before him and leaned forward. "Who gave the orders?" he hissed.

"Magister Kault!" shouted Hornlach instantly, "he gave the orders!" The audience gasped. Arch Lector Sult smirked a little wider. "It was the Magister!" The quills scratched mercilessly. "It was Kault! He gave the orders! All the orders! Magister Kault!"

"Thank you, Master Hornlach."

"The Magister! He gave the orders! Magister Kault! Kault! Kault!"

"Enough!" snarled Glokta. His prisoner fell silent. The room was still.

Arch Lector Sult lifted his arm and pointed towards the three prisoners. "There is your proof, my Lords!"

"This is a sham!" bellowed Lord Brock, leaping to his feet. "This is an insult!" Few voices joined him in support however, and those that did were half-hearted. Lord Heugen was notable for his careful silence, keenly studying the fine leather of his shoes. Barezin had shrunk back into his seat, looking half the size he had been a minute before. Lord Isher was staring off at the wall, fingering his heavy, golden chain, looking bored, as though the fate of the Guild of Mercers was of interest to him no longer.

Brock appealed to the High Justice himself, motionless in his tall chair at the high table. "Lord Marovia, I beg of you! You are a reasonable man! Do not allow this . . . travesty!"

The hall fell silent, waiting for the old man's reply. He frowned and stroked his long beard. He glanced across at the grinning Arch Lector. He cleared his throat. "I feel your pain, Lord Brock, indeed I do, but it seems that this is not a day for reasonable men. The Closed Council has examined the case and is well satisfied. My hands are tied."

Brock worked his mouth, tasting defeat. "This is not justice!" he shouted, turning round to address his peers. "These men have plainly been tortured!"

Arch Lector Sult's mouth twisted with scorn. "How would you have us deal with traitors and criminals?" he cried in a piercing voice. "Would you raise a shield, Lord Brock, for the disloyal to hide behind?" He thumped the table, as if it too might be guilty of high treason. "I for one will not see our great nation handed over to its enemies! Neither enemies without, nor enemies within!"

"Down with the Mercers!" came a cry from the public balcony.

"Hard justice for traitors!"

"The King's Justice!" bellowed a fat man near the back. There was a surge of anger and agreement from the floor, and calls for harsh measures and stiff penalties.

Brock looked round for his allies on the front row, but found none. He bunched his fists. "This is no justice!" he shouted, pointing at the three prisoners. "This is no proof!"

"His Majesty disagrees!" bellowed Hoff, "and does not require your permission!" He held up a large document. "The Guild of Mercers is hereby dissolved! Their licence revoked by Royal decree! His Majesty's Commission for Trade and Commerce will, over the coming months, review applications for trade rights with the city of Westport. Until such time as suitable candidates are found, the routes will be managed by capable, *loyal*, hands. The hands of His Majesty's Inquisition."

Arch Lector Sult humbly inclined his head, oblivious to the furious cries from representatives and public gallery alike.

"Inquisitor Glokta!" continued the Lord Chamberlain, "the Open Council thanks you for your diligence, and asks that you perform one more service in this matter." Hoff held out a smaller paper. "This is a warrant for the arrest of Magister Kault, bearing the King's own signature. We would ask that you serve it forthwith." Glokta bowed stiffly and took the paper from the Lord Chamberlain's outstretched hand. "You," said Hoff, turning his eye on Jalenhorm.

"Lieutenant Jalenhorm, my Lord!" shouted the big man, stepping smartly forward.

"Whatever," snapped Hoff impatiently, "take twenty of the King's Own and escort Inquisitor Glokta to the Mercers' Guildhall. Ensure that nothing and no one leaves the building without his orders!"

"At once, my Lord!" Jalenhorm crossed the floor and ran up the aisle toward the exit, holding the hilt of his sword in one hand to stop it knocking against his leg. Glokta limped after him, cane tapping on the steps, the warrant for the arrest of Magister Kault crumpled in his tightly clenched fist. The monstrous albino had pulled the prisoners to their feet meanwhile, and was leading them, rattling and lolling, off towards the door by which they had entered.

"Lord Chamberlain!" shouted Brock, with one last effort. Jezal wondered how much money he must have made from the Mercers. How much he had hoped still to make. A very great deal, evidently.

But Hoff was unmoved. "That concludes our business for today, my Lords!" Marovia was on his feet before the Lord Chamberlain had finished speaking, evidently keen to be away. The great ledgers were thumped shut. The fate of the honourable Guild of Mercers was sealed. Excited babbling filled the air once more, gradually rising in volume and soon joined by clattering and stamping as the representatives began to rise and leave the room. Arch Lector Sult remained seated, watching his beaten adversaries file reluctantly off the front row. Jezal met the desperate eyes of Salem Rews one last time as he was led towards the small door, then Practical Frost jerked at the chain and he was lost in the darkness beyond.

Outside, the square was even busier than before, the dense throng growing ever more excited as the news of the dissolution of the Guild of Mercers spread to those who had not been within. People stood, disbelieving, or hurried here and there: scared, surprised, confused. Jezal saw one man staring at him, staring at anyone, face pale, hands trembling. A Mercer perhaps, or a man in too deep with the Mercers, deep enough to be ruined along with them. There would be many such men.

Jezal felt a sudden tingling. Ardee West was leaning casually against the stones a little further on. They had not met in some time, not since that drunken outburst of hers, and he was surprised how pleased he was to see her. Probably she had been punished long enough, he told himself. Everyone deserved the chance to apologise. He hastened towards her with a broad smile on his lips. Then he noticed who she was with.

"That little bastard!" he muttered under his breath.

Lieutenant Brint was chatting freely in his cheap uniform, leaning closer to Ardee than Jezal thought was appropriate, underlining his tedious points with flamboyant gestures of his arms. She was nodding, smiling, then she tipped her head back and laughed, slapping the Lieutenant playfully on the chest. Brint laughed as well, the ugly little shit. They laughed together. For some reason Jezal felt a sharp pang of fury.

"Jezal, how are you!" shouted Brint, still giggling.

He stepped up close. "That's Captain Luthar!" he spat, "and how I am is none of your concern! Don't you have a job to do?"

Brint's mouth hung stupidly open for a moment, then his brows drew into a surly frown. "Yes, sir," he muttered, turning and stalking off. Jezal watched him go with a contempt even more intense than usual.

"Well that was charming," said Ardee. "Are those the manners you should use before a lady?"

"I really couldn't say. Why? Was there one watching?"

He turned to look at her and caught, just for a moment, a self-satisfied smirk. Quite a nasty expression, as though she had enjoyed his outburst. He wondered for a silly instant whether she might have arranged the meeting, have placed herself and that idiot where Jezal would see them, hoping to arouse his jealousy . . . then she smiled at him, and laughed, and Jezal felt his anger fading. She looked very fine, he thought, tanned and vibrant in the sunlight, laughing out loud, not caring who heard. Very fine. Better than ever, in fact. A chance meeting was all, what else could it be? She fixed him with those dark eyes and his suspicions vanished. "Did you have to be so hard on him?" she asked.

Jezal fixed his jaw. "Jumped-up, arrogant nobody, he's probably nothing more than some rich man's bastard. No blood, no money, no manners—"

"More than me, of all three."

Jezal cursed his big mouth. Rather than dragging an apology from her he was now in need of giving one himself. He sought desperately for some way out of this self-made trap. "Oh, but he's an absolute moron!" he whined.

"Well," and Jezal was relieved to see one corner of Ardee's mouth curl up in a sly smile, "he is at that. Shall we walk?" She slipped her hand through his arm before he had the chance to answer, and started to lead him off towards the Kingsway. Jezal allowed himself to be guided between the frightened, the angry, the excited people.

"So is it true?" she asked.

"Is what true?"

"That the Mercers are finished?"

"So it seems. Your old friend Sand dan Glokta was in the thick of it. He gave quite the performance, for a cripple."

Ardee looked down at the floor. "You wouldn't want to get on the wrong side of him, crippled or no."

"No." Jezal's mind went back to Salem Rews' terrified eyes, staring desperately at him as he vanished into the darkness of the archway. "No, you wouldn't."

A silence descended on them as they strolled down the avenue, but it was a comfortable one. He liked walking with her. It no longer seemed important whether anyone apologised. Perhaps she had been right about the fencing anyway, just a little. Ardee seemed to read his thoughts. "How's the sword-play going?" she asked.

"Not bad. How's the drinking going?"

She raised a dark eyebrow. "Excellent well. If only there was a Contest for that every year, I'd soon come to the attention of the public." Jezal laughed, looking down at her as she walked beside him, and she smiled back. So clever, so sharp, so fearless. So damn fine looking. Jezal wondered if there had ever been a woman quite like her. If only she had the right blood, he thought to himself, and some money. A lot of money.

MEANS OF ESCAPE

"**O**pen the door, in the name of His Majesty!" thundered Lieutenant Jalenhorm for the third time, hammering at the wood with his meaty fist. *The great oaf. Why do big men tend to have such little brains? Perhaps they get by on brawn too often, and their minds dry up like plums in the sun.*

The Mercers' Guildhall was an impressive building in a busy square not far from the Agriont. A substantial crowd of onlookers had already gathered around Glokta and his armed escort: curious, fearful, fascinated, growing all the time. *They can smell blood, it seems.* Glokta's leg was throbbing from the effort of hurrying down here, but he doubted that the Mercers would be taken entirely by surprise. He glanced round impatiently at the armoured guardsmen, at the masked Practicals, at the hard eyes of Frost, at the young officer beating on the door.

"Open the—"

Enough of this foolishness. "I think they heard you, Lieutenant," said Glokta crisply, "but are choosing not to answer. Would you be so kind as to break the door down?"

"What?" Jalenhorm gawped at him, and then at the heavy double doors, firmly secured. "How will I—"

Practical Frost hurtled past. There was a deafening crack and a tearing of wood as he crashed into one of the doors with his burly shoulder, tearing it off its hinges and sending it crashing onto the floor of the room beyond.

"Like so," muttered Glokta as he stepped through the archway, the splinters still settling. Jalenhorm followed him, looking dazed, a dozen armoured soldiers clattering behind.

242

An outraged clerk blocked the corridor beyond. "You can't just—oof!" he cried, as Frost flung him out of the way and his face crunched into the wall.

"Arrest that man!" shouted Glokta, waving his cane at the dumbstruck clerk. One of the soldiers grabbed him roughly with gauntleted fists and shoved him tumbling out into the daylight. Practicals began to pour through the broken doors, heavy sticks in their hands, eyes fierce above their masks. "Arrest everyone!" shouted Glokta over his shoulder, limping down the corridor as fast as he could, following Frost's broad back into the bowels of the building.

Through an open door Glokta saw a merchant in colourful robes, face covered with a sheen of sweat as he desperately heaped documents onto a blazing fire. "Seize him!" screamed Glokta. A pair of Practicals leaped past into the room and began clubbing the man with their sticks. He fell with a cry, upsetting a table and kicking over a pile of ledgers. Loose papers and bits of burning ash fluttered through the air as the sticks rose and fell.

Glokta hurried on, crashes and cries spreading out into the building around him. The place was full of the smell of smoke, and sweat, and fear. *The doors are all guarded, but Kault might have a secret means of escape. He's a slippery one. We must hope we are not too late. Curse this leg of mine! Not too late . . .*

Glokta gasped and winced in pain, tottering as someone clutched at his coat. "Help me!" shrieked the man, "I am innocent!" Blood on a plump face. Fingers clutched at Glokta's clothes, threatening to drag him to the floor.

"Get him off me!" shouted Glokta, beating at him weakly with his cane, clawing at the wall in his efforts to stay upright. One of the Practicals leaped forward and clubbed the man across the back.

"I confess!" the merchant whimpered as the stick rose again, then it cracked down on his head. The Practical caught hold of his slumping body under the arms and dragged him back towards the door. Glokta hurried on, Lieutenant Jalenhorm wide-eyed at his shoulder. They reached a broad staircase, and Glokta eyed it with hatred. *My old enemies, always here ahead of me.* He laboured up as best he could, waving Practical Frost forward with his free hand. A baffled merchant was dragged past them and away, squawking something about his rights, heels kicking against the stairs.

Glokta slipped and nearly fell on his face, but someone caught him by the elbow and kept him upright. It was Jalenhorm, look of confusion still splattered across his heavy, honest face. *So big men have their uses after all.* The young officer helped him up the rest of the steps. Glokta did not have the energy to refuse him. *Why bother? A man should know his limitations. There's nothing noble in falling on your face. I should know that.*

There was a large ante-chamber at the top of the stairs, richly decorated with a thick carpet and colourful hangings on the walls. Two guards stood before a large door with their swords drawn, dressed in the livery of the Guild of Mercers. Frost was facing them, hands rolled into white fists. Jalenhorm pulled out his own sword as he reached the landing, stepping forward to stand next to the albino. Glokta had to smile. *The tongueless torturer and the flower of chivalry. An unlikely alliance.*

"I have a warrant for Kault, signed by the King himself." Glokta held out the paper so the guards could see it. "The Mercers are finished. You have nothing to gain by getting in our way. Put up your swords! You have my word, you will not be harmed!"

The two guards glanced at each other uncertainly. "Put them up!" shouted Jalenhorm, edging a little closer.

"Alright!" One of the men bent down and slid his sword along the boards. Frost caught it under one foot.

"And you!" shouted Glokta to the other one. "Now!" The guard obeyed, throwing his sword to the floor and putting up his hands. A moment later Frost's fist crunched into the point of his jaw, knocking him cold and sending him crashing into the wall.

"But—" shouted the first guard. Frost grabbed him by the shirt and flung him down the stairs. He turned over and over, banging on the steps, flopping to the bottom, lying still. *I know what that feels like.*

Jalenhorm was standing motionless and blinking, his sword still raised. "I thought you said—"

"Never mind about that. Frost, look for another way in."

"Thhh." The albino padded away down the corridor. Glokta gave him a moment, then he edged forward and tried the door. The handle turned, much to his surprise, and the door swung open.

The room was opulence itself, near as big as a barn. The carving on the high ceiling was caked in gold leaf, the spines of the books on the shelves were studded with precious stones, the monstrous furniture was polished to a mirror shine. All was over-sized, over-embellished, over-expensive. *But who needs taste when you have money?* There were several big windows of the new design, large panes with little lead between them, offering a splendid view of the city, the bay, the ships within it. Magister Kault sat smiling at his vast gilt desk before the middle window in his fabulous robes of office, partly overshadowed by an enormous cabinet, the arms of the honourable Guild of Mercers etched into its doors.

Then he has not got away. I have him. I . . . Tied around the thick leg of the cabinet was a rope. Glokta followed it with his eyes as it snaked across the floor. The other end was tied around the Magister's neck. *Ah. So he does have a means of escape, after all.*

"Inquisitor Glokta!" Kault gave a squeaky, nervous laugh. "What a pleasure to finally meet you! I've been hearing all about your investigations!" His fingers twitched at the knot on the rope, making sure it was tied securely.

"Is your collar too tight, Magister? Perhaps you should remove it?"

Another squeak of merriment. "Oh, I don't think so! I don't intend to be answering any of your questions, thank you!" Out of the corner of his eye, Glokta saw a side door edging open. A big white hand appeared, fingers curling slowly round the door frame. *Frost. There is still hope of catching him, then. I must keep him talking.*

"There are no questions left to answer. We know it all."

"Do you indeed?" giggled the Magister. The albino edged silently into the room, keeping to the shadows near the wall, hidden from Kault by the bulk of the cabinet.

"We know about Kalyne. About your little arrangement."

"Imbecile! We had no arrangement! He was far too honourable to be bought! He would never take a mark from me!" *Then how* . . . Kault smiled a sick little smile. "Sult's secretary," he said, giggling again. "Right under his nose, and yours too, cripple!" *Fool, fool—the secretary carried the messages, he saw the confession, he knew everything! I never trusted that smarmy shit. Kalyne was loyal, then.*

Glokta shrugged. "We all make mistakes."

The Magister gave a withering sneer. "Mistakes? That's all you've made, dolt! The world is nothing like you think it is! You don't even know what side you're on! You don't even know what the sides are!"

"I am on the side of the King, and you are not. That is all I need to know." Frost had made it to the cabinet and was pressed against it, pink eyes staring intently, trying to see round the corner without being seen. *Just a little longer, just a little further . . .*

"You know nothing, cripple! Some small business with tax, some petty bribery, that's all we were guilty of!"

"And the trifling matter of nine murders."

"We had no choice!" screamed Kault. "We never had any choices! We had to pay the bankers! They loaned us the money, and we had to pay! We've been paying them for years! Valint and Balk, the bloodsuckers! We gave them everything, but they always wanted more!"

Valint and Balk? Bankers? Glokta threw an eye over the ridiculous opulence. "You seem to be keeping your head above water."

"Seem! Seem! All dust! All lies! The bankers own it all! They own us all! We owe them thousands! Millions!" Kault giggled to himself. "But I don't suppose they'll ever get it now, will they?"

"No. I don't suppose they will."

Kault leaned across the desk, the rope hanging down and brushing the leather top. "You want criminals Glokta? You want traitors? Enemies of King and state? Look in the Closed Council. Look in the House of Questions. Look in the university. Look in the banks, Glokta!" He saw Frost, edging round the cabinet no more than four strides away. His eyes went wide and he started up from his chair.

"Get him!" screamed Glokta. Frost sprang forward, lunged across the desk, caught hold of the flicking hem of Kault's robe of office as the Magister spun round and hurled himself at the window. *We have him!*

There was a sickening rip as the robe tore in Frost's white fist. Kault seemed frozen in space for a moment as all that expensive glass shattered around him, shards and splinters glittering through the air, then he was gone. The rope snapped taut.

"Thhhhh!" hissed Frost, glaring at the broken window.

"He jumped!" gasped Jalenhorm, his mouth hanging open.

"Clearly." Glokta limped over to the desk and took the ripped strip of cloth from Frost's hands. Close up it scarcely seemed magnificent at all: brightly coloured but badly woven.

"Who would have thought?" muttered Glokta to himself. "Poor quality." He limped to the window and peered through the shattered hole. The head of the honourable Guild of Mercers was swinging slowly back and forth, twenty feet below, his torn, gold-embroidered gown flapping around him in the breeze. *Cheap clothes and expensive windows. If the cloth had been stronger we would have got him. If the window had more lead, we would have got him. Lives hinge on such chances.* Beneath him in the street a horrified crowd was already gathering: pointing, babbling, staring up at the hanging body. A woman screamed. *Fear, or excitement? They sound the same.*

"Lieutenant, would you be so good as to go down and disperse that crowd? Then we can cut our friend loose and take him back with us." Jalenhorm looked at him blankly. "Dead or alive, the King's warrant must be served."

"Yes of course." The burly officer wiped sweat from his forehead and made, somewhat unsteadily, for the door.

Glokta turned back to the window and peered down at the slowly swinging corpse. Magister Kault's last words echoed in his mind.

Look in the Closed Council. Look in the House of Questions. Look in the University. Look in the banks, Glokta!

THREE SIGNS

West crashed onto his arse, one of his steels skittering out of his hands and across the cobbles.

"That's a touch!" shouted Marshal Varuz, "A definite touch! Well fought, Jezal, well fought!"

West was starting to tire of losing. He was stronger than Jezal, and taller, with a better reach, but the cocky little bastard was quick. Damn quick, and getting quicker. He knew all of West's tricks now, more or less, and if he kept improving at this rate he'd soon be beating him every time. Jezal knew it too. He had a smile of infuriating smugness on his face as he offered his hand to West and helped him up from the ground.

"We're getting somewhere now!" Varuz slapped his stick against his leg in delight. "We may even have ourselves a champion, eh, Major?"

"Very likely, sir," said West, rubbing at his elbow, bruised and throbbing from his fall. He looked sidelong at Jezal, basking in the warmth of the Marshal's praise.

"But we must not grow complacent!"

"No, sir!" said Jezal emphatically.

"No indeed," said Varuz, "Major West is a capable fencer, of course, and you are privileged to have him as a partner but, well," and he grinned at West, "fencing is a young man's game, eh, Major?"

"Of course it is, sir," muttered West. "A young man's game."

"Bremer dan Gorst, I expect, will be a different sort of opponent, as will the others at this year's Contest. Less of the veteran's cunning, perhaps, but

more of the vigour of youth, eh West?" West, at thirty, was still feeling somewhat vigorous, but there was no purpose in arguing. He knew he'd never
been the most gifted swordsman in the world. "We have made great progress
this past month, great progress. You have a chance, if you can maintain your
focus. A definite chance! Well done! I will see you both tomorrow." And the
old Marshal strutted from the sunny courtyard.

West walked over to his fumbled steel, lying on the cobbles by the wall.
His side was still aching from the fall, and he had to bend awkwardly to get
it. "I have to be going, myself," he grunted as he straightened up, trying to
hide his discomfort as best he could.

"Important business?"

"Marshal Burr has asked to see me."

"Is it to be war then?"

"Perhaps. I don't know." West looked Jezal up and down. He was
avoiding West's eye for some reason. "And you? What have you got in mind
for today?"

Jezal fiddled with his steels. "Er, nothing planned . . . not really." He
glanced up furtively. For such a good card player, the man was a useless liar.

West felt a niggling of worry. "Ardee wouldn't be involved in your lack
of plans would she?"

"Erm . . ."

The niggling became a cold throbbing. "Well?"

"Maybe," snapped Jezal, "well . . . yes."

West stepped right up to the younger man. "Jezal," he heard himself saying,
slowly through gritted teeth, "I hope you're not planning to fuck my sister."

"Now look here—"

The throbbing boiled over. West's hands gripped hold of Jezal by his
shoulders. "No, *you* look!" he snarled. "I'll not have her trifled with, you
understand? She's been hurt before, and I'll not see her hurt any more! Not
by you, not by anyone! I won't stand for it! She's not one of your games, you
hear me?"

"Alright," said Jezal, face suddenly pale. "Alright! I've no designs on her!
We're just friends is all. I like her! She doesn't know anyone here and . . . you
can trust me . . . there's no harm in it! Ah! Get off me!"

West realised he was squeezing Jezal's arms with all his strength. How had that happened? He'd only meant to have a quiet word, and now he'd gone way too far. Hurt before . . . damn it! He should never have said that! He let go suddenly, drew back, swallowing his fury. "I don't want you seeing her any more, do you hear me?"

"Now hold on West, who are you to—"

West's anger began to pulse again. "Jezal," he growled, "I'm your friend, so I'm asking you." He stepped forward again, closer than ever. "And I'm her brother, so I'm warning you. Stay away! No good can come of it!"

Jezal shrank back against the wall. "Alright . . . alright! She's your sister!"

West turned and stalked towards the archway, rubbing the back of his neck, his head thumping.

Lord Marshal Burr was sitting and staring out of the window when West arrived at his offices. A big, grim, beefy man with a thick brown beard and a simple uniform. West wondered how bad the news would be. If the Marshal's face was anything to go by it was very bad indeed.

"Major West," he said, glaring up from under his heavy brows. "Thank you for coming."

"Of course, sir." West noticed three roughly made wooden boxes on a table by the wall. Burr saw him looking at them.

"Gifts," he said sourly, "from our friend in the north, Bethod."

"Gifts?"

"For the King, it seems." The Marshal scowled and sucked at his teeth. "Why don't you have a look at what he sent us, Major?"

West walked over to the table, reached out and cautiously opened the lid of one of the boxes. An unpleasant smell flowed out, like well-rotted meat, but there was nothing inside but some brown dirt. He opened the next box. The smell was worse. More brown dirt, caked around the inside, and some hair, some strands of yellow hair. West swallowed, looked up at the frowning Lord Marshal. "Is this all, sir?"

Burr snorted. "If only. The rest we had to bury."

"Bury?"

The Marshal picked up a sheet of paper from his desk. "Captain Silber, Captain Hoss, Colonel Arinhorm. Those names mean anything to you?"

West felt sick. That smell. It reminded him of Gurkhul somehow, of the battlefield. "Colonel Arinhorm, I know," he mumbled, staring at the three boxes, "by reputation. He's commander of the garrison at Dunbrec."

"Was," corrected Burr, "and the other two commanded small outposts nearby, on the frontier."

"The frontier?" mumbled West, but he already guessed what was coming.

"Their heads, Major. The Northmen sent us their heads." West swallowed, looking at the yellow hairs stuck to the inside of the box. "Three signs, they said, when it was time." Burr got up from his chair and stood, looking out of the window. "The outposts were nothing: wooden buildings mostly, a palisade wall, ditches and so on, lightly manned. Little strategic importance. Dunbrec is another matter."

"It commands the fords on the Whiteflow," said West numbly, "the best way out of Angland."

"Or in. A vital point. Considerable time and resources were spent on the defences there. The very latest designs were used, our finest architects. A garrison of three hundred men, with stores of weapons and food to stand a year of siege. It was considered impregnable, the lynchpin of our plans for the defence of the frontier." Burr frowned, deep grooves appearing across the bridge of his nose. "Gone."

West's head had started hurting again. "When, sir?"

"When is the question. It must have been at least two weeks ago, for these "gifts" to have reached us. I am being called defeatist," said Burr sourly, "but I guess that the Northmen are loose and that, by now, they have overrun half of northern Angland. A mining community or two, several penal colonies, nothing so far of major importance, no towns to speak of, but they are coming, West, and fast, you may be sure of that. You don't send heads to your enemy, then wait politely for a reply."

"What is being done?"

"Precious little! Angland is in uproar, of course. Lord Governor Meed is raising every man, determined to march out and beat Bethod on his own, the idiot. Varying reports place the Northmen anywhere and everywhere, with a thousand men or a hundred thousand. The ports are choked with civilians desperate to escape, rumours are rife of spies and murderers loose in the country, and mobs seek out citizens with Northern blood and beat them, rob them, or worse. Put simply, it is chaos. Meanwhile we sit here on our fat arses, waiting."

"But . . . weren't we warned? Didn't we know?"

"Of course!" Burr threw his broad hand up in the air, "but no one took it very seriously, would you believe! Damn painted savage stabs himself on the floor of the Open Council, challenges us before the King, and nothing is done! Government by committee! Everyone pulling their own way! You can only react, never prepare!" The Marshal coughed and burped, spat on the floor. "Gah! Damn it! Damn indigestion!" He sat back in his chair, rubbing his stomach unhappily.

West hardly knew what to say. "How do we proceed?" he mumbled.

"We've been ordered north immediately, meaning as soon as anyone can be bothered to supply me with men and arms. The King, meaning that drunkard Hoff, has commanded me to bring these Northmen to heel. Twelve regiments of the King's Own—seven of foot and five of horse, to be fleshed out with levies from the aristocracy, and whatever the Anglanders haven't squandered before we get there."

West shifted uncomfortably in his chair. "That should be an over-whelming force."

"Huh," grunted the Marshal. "It better be. It's everything we have, more or less, and that worries me." West frowned. "Dagoska, Major. We cannot fight the Gurkish and the Northmen both at once."

"But surely, sir, the Gurkish, they wouldn't risk another war so soon? I thought it was all idle talk?"

"I hope so, I hope so." Burr pushed some papers absently around his desk. "But this new Emperor, Uthman, is not what we were expecting. He was the youngest son, but when he heard of his father's death . . . he had all his brothers strangled. Strangled them himself, some say. Uthman-ul-Dosht, they are calling him. Uthman the Merciless. He has already declared his intention to recapture Dagoska. Empty talk, perhaps. Perhaps not." Burr pursed his lips. "They say he has spies everywhere. He might even now be learning of our troubles in Angland, might even now be preparing to take advantage of our weakness. We must be done quickly with these Northmen. Very quickly. Twelve regiments and levies from the noblemen. And from that point of view it could not be a worse time."

"Sir?"

"This business with the Mercers. A bad business. Some of the big noblemen got stung. Brock, Isher, Barezin, and others. Now they're dragging their feet with the levies. Who knows what they'll send us, or when? Bunch of half-starved, unarmed beggars probably, an excuse to clean the scrapings from their land. A useless crowd of extra mouths to feed, and clothe, and arm, and we are desperately short of good officers."

"I have some good men in my battalion."

Burr twitched impatiently. "Good men, yes! Honest men, enthusiastic men, but not experienced! Most of those who fought in the South did not enjoy it. They have left the army, and have no intention of returning. Have you seen how young the officers are these days? We're a damn finishing school! And now His Highness the Prince has expressed his interest in a command. He doesn't even know which end of a sword to hold, but he is set on glory and I cannot refuse him!"

"Prince Raynault?"

"If only!" shouted Burr. "Raynault might actually be of some use! It's Ladisla I'm talking of! Commanding a division! A man who spends a thousand marks a month on clothes! His lack of discipline is notorious! I've heard it said that he's forced himself on more than one servant in the palace, but that the Arch Lector was able to silence the girls."

"Surely not," said West, although he had actually heard such a rumour himself.

"The heir to the throne, in harm's way, when the King is in poor health? A ludicrous notion!" Burr got up, burping and wincing. "Damn this stomach!" He stalked over to the window and frowned out across the Agriont.

"They think it will be easily settled," he said quietly. "The Closed Council. A little jaunt in Angland, done with before the first snow falls. In spite of this shock with Dunbrec. They never learn. They said the same about our war with the Gurkish, and that nearly finished us. These

Northmen are not the primitives they think. I fought with Northern mer-
cenaries in Starikland: hard men used to hard lives, raised on warfare, fearless and stubborn, expert at fighting in the hills, in the forests, in the cold.
They do not follow our rules, or even understand them. They will bring a
violence and a savagery to the battlefield that would make the Gurkish
blush." Burr turned away from the window, back to West. "You were born
in Angland, weren't you, Major?"

"Yes, sir, in the south, near Ostenhorm. My family's farm was there,
before my father died . . ." He trailed off.

"You were raised there?"

"Yes."

"You know the land then?"

West frowned. "In that region, sir, but I have not been back for—"

"Do you know these Northmen?"

"Some. There are still many living in Angland."

"You speak their tongue?"

"Yes, a little, but they speak many—"

"Good. I am putting together a staff, good men I can rely on to carry out
my orders, and see to it that this army of ours does not fall apart before it even
comes into contact with the enemy."

"Of course, sir." West racked his brains. "Captain Luthar is a capable and
intelligent officer, Lieutenant Jalenhorm—"

"Bah!" shouted Burr, waving his hand in frustration, "I know Luthar, the
boy's a cretin! Just the sort of bright-eyed child that I was talking about! It's
you I need, West."

"Me?"

"Yes, you! Marshal Varuz, the Union's most famous soldier no less, has
given you a glowing report. He says you are a most committed, tenacious,
and hard-working officer. The very qualities I need! As a Lieutenant you
fought in Gurkhul under Colonel Glokta, did you not?"

West swallowed. "Well, yes."

"And it is well known you were first through the breach at Ulrioch."

"Well, among the first, I was—"

"You have led men in the field, and your personal courage is beyond question! There is no need to be modest, Major, you are the man for me!" Burr sat back, a smile on his face, confident he had made his point. He burped again, holding up his hand. "My apologies . . . damn indigestion!"

"Sir, may I be blunt?"

"I am no courtier, West. You must always be blunt with me. I demand it!"

"An appointment on a Lord Marshal's staff, sir, you must understand. I am a gentleman's son. A commoner. As commander of a battalion, I already have difficulty gaining the respect of the junior officers. The men I would have to give orders to if I were on your staff, sir, senior men with good blood . . ." He paused, exasperated. The Marshal gazed blankly at him. "They will not permit it!"

Burr's eyebrows drew together. "Permit it?"

"Their pride will not allow it, sir, their—"

"Damn their pride!" Burr leaned forward, his dark eyes fixed on West's face. "Now listen to me, and listen carefully. Times are changing. I don't need men with good blood. I need men who can plan, and organise, give orders, and follow them. There will be no room in my army for those who cannot do as they are told, I don't care how noble they are. As a member of my staff you represent me, and I will not be slighted or ignored." He burped suddenly, and smashed the table with his fist. "I will see to it!" he roared. "Times are changing! They may not smell it yet, but they soon will!"

West stared dumbly back. "In any case," and Burr waved a dismissive hand, "I am not consulting with you, I am informing you. This is your new assignment. Your King needs you, your country needs you, and that is all. You have five days to hand over command of your battalion." And the Lord Marshal turned back to his papers.

"Yes, sir," muttered West.

He fumbled the door shut behind him with numb fingers, walked slowly down the hallway, staring at the floor. War. War in the North. Dunbrec fallen, the Northmen loose in Angland. Officers hurried around him. Someone brushed past, but he hardly noticed. There were people in danger, mortal danger! People he knew maybe, neighbours from home. There was fighting even now, inside the Union's borders! He rubbed his jaw. This war could be a terrible thing. Worse than Gurkhul had been, even, and he would be at the heart of it. A place on a Lord Marshal's staff. Him? Collem West? A commoner? He still could hardly believe it.

West felt a sneaking, guilty glow of satisfaction. It was for just such an appointment that he had been working like a dog all these years. If he did well there was no telling where he might go. This war was a bad thing, a terrible thing, no doubt. He felt himself grinning. A terrible thing. But it just might be the making of him.

THE THEATRICAL
OUTFITTER'S

The deck creaked and shifted beneath his feet, the sail-cloth flapped gently, sea birds crowed and called in the salty air above.

"I never thought to see such a thing," muttered Logen.

The city was a huge white crescent, stretching all round the wide blue bay, sprawling across many bridges, tiny in the distance, and onto rocky islands in the sea. Here and there green parks stood out from the confusion of buildings, the thin grey lines of rivers and canals shone in the sun. There were walls too, studded with towers, skirting the distant edge of the city and striking boldly through the jumble of houses. Logen's jaw hung stupidly open, his eyes darted here and there, unable to take in the whole.

"Adua," murmured Bayaz. "The centre of the world. The poets call her the city of white towers. Beautiful, isn't she, from a distance?" The Magus leaned towards him. "Believe me, though, she stinks when you get close."

A vast fortress rose up from within the city, its sheer white walls towering above the carpet of buildings outside, bright sunlight glinting on shining domes within. Logen had never dreamed of a man-made thing so great, so proud, so strong. One tower in particular rose high, high over all the others, a tapering cluster of smooth, dark pillars, seeming to support the very sky.

"And Bethod means to make war on this?" he whispered. "He must be mad."

"Perhaps. Bethod, for all his waste and pride, understands the Union." Bayaz nodded towards the city. "They are jealous of one another, all those people. It may be a union in name, but they fight each other tooth and nail. The lowly squabble over trifles. The great wage secret wars for power and

wealth, and they call it government. Wars of words, and tricks, and guile, but
no less bloody for that. The casualties are many." The Magus sighed. "Behind
those walls they shout and argue and endlessly bite one another's backs. Old
squabbles are never settled, but thrive, and put down roots, and the roots grow
deeper with the passing years. It has always been so. They are not like you,
Logen. A man here can smile, and fawn, and call you friend, give you gifts
with one hand and stab you with the other. You will find this a strange place."

Logen already found it the strangest thing he had ever seen. There was no
end to it. As their boat slipped into the bay the city seemed to grow more vast
than ever. A forest of white buildings, speckled with dark windows, embracing
them on all sides, covering the hills in roofs and towers, crowding together,
wall squashed to wall, pressing up against the water on the shoreline.

Ships and boats of all designs vied with each other in the bay, sails billowing, crewmen crying out over the noise of the spray, hurrying about the
decks and crawling through the rigging. Some were smaller even than their
own little two-sailed boat. Some were far larger. Logen gawped, amazed, as a
huge vessel ploughed through the water towards them, shining spray flying
from its prow. A mountain of wood, floating by some magic in the sea. The
ship passed, leaving them rocking in its wake, but there were more, many
more, tethered to the countless wharves along the shore.

Logen, shielding his eyes against the bright sun with one hand, began to
make out people on the sprawling docks. He began to hear them too, a faint
din of voices crying and carts rattling and cargoes clattering to the ground.
There were hundreds of tiny figures, swarming among the ships and buildings like black ants. "How many live here?" he whispered.

"Thousands." Bayaz shrugged. "Hundreds of thousands. People from
every land within the Circle of the World. There are Northmen here, and
dark-skinned Kantics from Gurkhul and beyond. People from the Old
Empire, far to the west, and merchants of the Free Cities of Styria. Others
too, from still further away—the Thousand Islands, distant Suljuk, and
Thond where they worship the sun. More people than can be counted—
living, dying, working, breeding, climbing one upon the other. Welcome,"
and Bayaz spread his arms wide to encompass the monstrous, the beautiful,
the endless city, "to civilisation!"

Hundreds of thousands. Logen struggled to understand it. Hundreds . . . of thousands. Could there be so many people in the world? He stared at the city, all around him, wondering, rubbing his aching eyes. What might a hundred thousand people look like?

An hour later he knew.

Only in battle had Logen ever been so squashed, hemmed, pressed by other people. It was like a battle, here on the docks—the cries, the anger, the crush, the fear and confusion. A battle in which no mercy was shown, and which had no end and no winners. Logen was used to the open sky, the air around him, his own company. On the road, when Bayaz and Quai had ridden close beside him, he'd felt squeezed. Now there were people on every side, pushing, jostling, shouting. Hundreds of them! Thousands! Hundreds of thousands! Could they really all be people? People like him with thoughts and moods and dreams? Faces loomed up and flashed by—surly, anxious, frowning, gone in a sickening whirl of colour. Logen swallowed, blinked. His throat was painfully dry. His head spun. Surely this was hell. He knew he deserved to be here, but he didn't remember dying.

"Malacus!" he hissed desperately. The apprentice looked round. "Stop a moment!" Logen pulled at his collar, trying to let some air in. "I can't breathe!"

Quai grinned. "It might just be the smell."

It might at that. The docks smelled like hell, and no mistake. The reek of stinking fish, sickly spices, rotting fruit, fresh dung, sweating horses and mules and people, mingled and bred under the hot sun and became worse by far than any one alone.

"Move!" A shoulder knocked Logen roughly aside and was gone. He leaned against a grimy wall and wiped sweat from his face.

Bayaz was smiling. "Not like the wide and barren North, eh, Ninefingers?"

"No." Logen watched the people milling past—the horses, the carts, the endless faces. A man stared suspiciously at him as he passed. A boy pointed at him and shouted something. A woman with a basket gave him a wide berth, staring fearfully up as she hurried by. Now he had a moment to think, they were all looking, and pointing, and staring, and they didn't look happy.

Logen leaned down to Malacus. "I am feared and hated throughout the North. I don't like it, but I know why." A sullen group of sailors stared at

him with hard eyes, muttering to each other under their breath. He watched
them, puzzled, until they disappeared behind a rumbling wagon. "Why do
they hate me here?"

"Bethod has moved quickly," muttered Bayaz, frowning out at the
crowds. "His war with the Union has already begun. We will not find the
North too popular in Adua, I fear."

"How do they know where I'm from?"

Malacus raised an eyebrow. "You stick out somewhat."

Logen flinched as a pair of laughing youths flashed by him. "I do?
Among all this?"

"Only like a huge, scarred, dirty gatepost."

"Ah." He looked down at himself. "I see."

Away from the docks the crowds grew sparser, the air cleaner, the noise faded.
It was still teeming, stinking, and noisy, but at least Logen could take a breath.

They passed across wide paved squares, decorated with plants and
statues, where brightly painted wooden signs hung over doors—blue fish,
pink pigs, purple bunches of grapes, brown loaves of bread. There were tables
and chairs out in the sun where people sat and ate from flat pots, drank from
green glass cups. They threaded through narrow alleys, where rickety-
looking wood and plaster buildings leaned out over them, almost meeting
above their heads, leaving only a thin strip of blue sky between. They wandered down wide, cobbled roads, busy with people and lined with monstrous
white buildings. Logen blinked and gaped at all of it.

On no moor, however foggy, in no forest, however dense, had Logen ever
felt so completely lost. He had no idea now in what direction the boat was,
though they'd left it no more than half an hour ago. The sun was hidden
behind the towering buildings and everything looked the same. He was terrified he'd lose track of Bayaz and Quai in the crowds, and be lost forever. He
hurried after the back of the wizard's bald head, following him into an open
space. A great road, bigger than any they'd seen so far, bounded on either side
by white palaces behind high walls and fences, lined with ancient trees.

The people here were different. Their clothes were bright and gaudy, cut
in strange styles that served no purpose. The women hardly seemed like

people at all—pale and bony, swaddled in shining fabric, flapping at themselves in the hot sun with pieces of cloth stretched over sticks.

"Where are we?" he shouted at Bayaz. If the wizard had answered that they were on the moon, Logen would not have been surprised.

"This is the Middleway, one of the city's main thoroughfares! It cuts through the very centre of the city to the Agriont!"

"Agriont?"

"Fortress, palace, barracks, seat of government. A city within the city. The heart of the Union. That's where we're going."

"We are?" A group of sour young men stared suspiciously at Logen as he passed them. "Will they let us in?"

"Oh yes. But they won't like it."

Logen struggled on through the crowds. Everywhere the sun twinkled on the panes of glass windows, hundreds of them. Carleon had a few glass windows in the grandest buildings, at least before they'd sacked the city. Precious few afterwards, it had to be admitted. Precious little of anything. The Dogman had loved the sound the glass made as it broke. He'd prodded at the windows with a spear, a great big smile on his face, delighted by the crash and tinkle.

That had hardly been the worst of it. Bethod had given the city to his Carls for three days. That was his custom, and they loved him for it. Logen had lost his finger in the battle the day before, and they'd closed the wound with hot iron. It throbbed, and throbbed, and the pain had made him savage. As though he'd needed an excuse for violence back then. He remembered the stink of blood, and sweat, and smoke. The sounds of screaming, and crashing, and laughter.

"Please . . ." Logen tripped, nearly fell. There was something clinging to his leg. A woman, sitting on the ground beside a wall. Her clothes were dirty, ragged, her face was pale, pinched with hunger. She had something in her arms. A bundle of rags. A child. "Please . . ." Nothing else. The people laughed and chattered and surged around them, just as if they weren't there. "Please . . ."

"I don't have anything," he muttered. No more than five strides away a man in a tall hat sat at a table and chuckled with a friend as he tucked into a steaming plate of meat and vegetables. Logen blinked at the plate of food, at the starving woman.

"Logen! Come on!" Bayaz had taken him by the elbow and was drawing him away.

"But shouldn't we—"

"Haven't you noticed? They're everywhere! The King needs money, so he squeezes the nobles. The nobles squeeze their tenants, the tenants squeeze the peasants. Some of them, the old, the weak, the extra sons and daughters, they get squeezed right out the bottom. Too many mouths to feed. The lucky ones make thieves or whores, the rest end up begging."

"But—"

"Clear the road!" Logen stumbled to the wall and pressed himself against it, Malacus and Bayaz beside him. The crowds parted and a long column of men tramped by, shepherded by armoured guards. Some were young, mere boys, some were very old. All were dirty and ragged, and few of them looked healthy. A couple were clearly lame, hobbling along as best they could. One near the front had only one arm. A passer-by in a fabulous crimson jacket held a square of cloth over his wrinkled nose as the beggars shuffled past.

"What are these?" Logen whispered to Bayaz. "Law-breakers?"

The Magus chuckled. "Soldiers."

Logen stared at them—filthy, coughing, limping, some without boots. "Soldiers? These?"

"Oh yes. They go to fight Bethod."

Logen rubbed at his temples. "A clan once sent their poorest warrior, a man called Forley the Weakest, to fight me in a duel. They meant it by way of surrender. Why does this Union send their weakest?" Logen shook his head grimly. "They won't beat Bethod with such as these."

"They will send others." Bayaz pointed out another, smaller gathering. "Those are soldiers too."

"Those?" A group of tall youths, dressed in gaudy suits of red or bright green cloth, a couple with outsize hats. They were at least wearing swords, of a kind, but they hardly looked like fighting men. Fighting women, maybe. Logen frowned, staring from one group to the other. The dirty beggars, the gaudy lads. It was hard for him to say which were the stranger.

A tiny bell jingled as the door opened, and Logen followed Bayaz through the low archway, Malacus behind him. The shop was dim after the bright street and it took Logen's eyes a moment to adjust. Leaning against a wall were sheets of wood, childishly daubed with pictures of buildings, forests, mountains. Strange clothes were draped over stands beside them—flowing robes, lurid gowns, suits of armour, enormous hats and helmets, rings and jewellery, even a heavy crown. Weapons occupied a small rack, swords and spears richly decorated. Logen stepped closer, frowning. They were fakes. Nothing was real. The weapons were painted wood, the crown was made of flaking tin, the jewels were coloured glass.

"What is this place?"

Bayaz was casting an eye over the robes by the wall. "A theatrical outfitter's."

"A what?"

"The people of this city love spectacle. Comedy, drama, theatre of all kinds. This shop provides equipment for the mounting of plays."

"Stories?" Logen poked at a wooden sword. "Some people have too much time on their hands."

A small, plump man emerged from a door at the back of the shop, looking Bayaz, Malacus and Logen over suspiciously. "Can I help you, gentlemen?"

"Of course." Bayaz stepped forward, switching effortlessly to the common tongue. "We are mounting a production, and require some costumes. We understand you are the foremost theatrical outfitter's in all of Adua."

The shopkeeper smiled nervously, taking in their grimy faces and travel stained clothes. "True, true, but . . . er . . . quality is expensive, gentlemen."

"Money is no object." Bayaz took out a bulging purse and tossed it absently on the counter. It sagged open, heavy golden coins scattering across the wood.

The shopkeeper's eyes lit with an inner fire. "Of course! What precisely did you have in mind?"

"I need a magnificent robe, suitable for a Magus, or a great sorcerer, or some such. Something of the arcane about it, certainly. Then we'll have something similar, if less impressive, for an apprentice. Finally we need something for a mighty warrior, a prince of the distant North. Something with fur, I imagine."

"Those should be straightforward. I will see what we have." The shop-keeper disappeared through the door behind the counter.

"What is all this shit?" asked Logen.

The wizard grinned. "People are born to their station here. They have commoners, to fight, and farm the land, and do the work. They have gentry, to trade, and build and do the thinking. They have nobility, to own the land and push the others around. They have royalty . . ." Bayaz glanced at the tin crown ". . . I forget exactly why. In the North you can rise as high as your merits will take you. Only look at our mutual friend, Bethod. Not so here. A man is born in his place and is expected to stay there. We must seem to be from a high place indeed, if we are to be taken seriously. Dressed as we are we wouldn't get past the gates of the Agriont."

The shopkeeper interrupted him by reappearing through the door, his arms heaped with bright cloth. "One mystical robe, suitable for the most powerful of wizards! Used last year for a Juvens in a production of *The End of the Empire*, during the spring festival. It is, if I may say so, some of my best work." Bayaz held the shimmering swathe of crimson cloth up to the faint light, gazing at it admiringly. Arcane diagrams, mystical lettering, and sym-bols of sun, moon and stars, glittered in silver thread.

Malacus ran a hand over the shining cloth of his own absurd garment. "I don't think you'd have laughed me off so quickly, eh, Logen, if I'd arrived at your campfire dressed in this?"

Logen winced. "I reckon I might've."

"And here we have a splendid piece of barbarian garb." The shopkeeper hefted a black leather tunic onto the counter, set with swirls of shiny brass, trimmed with pointless tissues of delicate chain-mail. He pointed at the matching fur cloak. "This is real sable!" It was a ludicrous piece of clothing, equally useless for warmth or protection.

Logen folded his arms across his old coat. "You think I'm going to wear that?"

The shopkeeper swallowed nervously. "You must forgive my friend," said Bayaz. "He is an actor after the new fashion. He believes in losing himself entirely in his role."

"Is that so?" squeaked the man, looking Logen up and down. "Northmen are . . . I suppose . . . topical."

"Absolutely. I do declare, Master Ninefingers is the very best at what he does." The old wizard nudged Logen in the ribs. "The very best. I have seen it."

"If you say so." The shopkeeper looked far from convinced. "Might I enquire what you will be staging?"

"Oh, it's a new piece." Bayaz tapped the side of his bald head with a finger. "I am still working on the details."

"Really?"

"Indeed. More a scene than an entire play." He glanced back at the robe, admiring the way the light glittered on the arcane symbols. "A scene in which Bayaz, the First of the Magi, finally takes up his seat on the Closed Council."

"Ah," the shopkeeper nodded knowingly. "A political piece. A biting satire, perhaps? Will it be comic, or dramatic in tone?"

Bayaz glanced sidelong at Logen. "That remains to be seen."

BARBARIANS AT THE GATE

Jezal flashed along the lane beside the moat, feet pounding on the worn cobblestones, the great white wall sliding endlessly by on his right, one tower after another, as he made his daily circuit of the Agriont. Since he had cut down on the drinking the improvement in his stamina had been impressive. He was scarcely even out of breath. It was early and the streets of the city were nearly empty. The odd person would look up at him as he ran by, maybe even call out some word of encouragement, but Jezal barely noticed them. His eyes were fixed on the sparkling, lapping water in the moat, and his mind was elsewhere.

Ardee. Where else was it ever? He had supposed, after that day when West had warned him off, after he had stopped seeing her, that his thoughts would soon return to other matters, and other women. He had applied himself to his fencing with a will, attempted to show an interest in his duties as an officer, but he found himself unable to concentrate, and other women seemed now pale, flat, tedious creatures. The long runs, the monotonous exercises with bar and beam, gave his mind ample opportunity to wander. The tedium of peacetime soldiering was even worse: reading boring papers, standing guard on things that needed no guarding. His attention would inevitably slip, and then she would be there.

Ardee in wholesome peasant garb, flushed and sweaty from hard work in the fields. Ardee in the finery of a princess, glittering with jewels. Ardee bathing in forest pools, while he watched from the bushes. Ardee proper and demure, glancing shyly up at him from beneath her lashes. Ardee a whore by the docks, beckoning to him from a grimy doorway. The fantasies were infinite in variety, but they all ended the same way.

His hour-long circuit of the Agriont was complete and he thumped across the bridge and back in through the south gate. Jezal treated the guards to their daily share of indifference, trotted through the tunnel and up the long ramp into the fortress, then turned towards the courtyard where Marshal Varuz would be waiting. All the while, Ardee was rubbing up against the back of his mind.

It was hardly as though he had nothing else to think about. The Contest was close now, very close. Soon he would fight before the cheering crowds, his family and friends among them. It might make his reputation . . . or sink it. He should have been lying awake at night, tense and sweating, worrying endlessly about forms, and training, and steels. And yet somehow that wasn't what he thought about in bed.

Then there was a war on. It was easy to forget, here in the sunny lanes of the Agriont, that Angland had been invaded by hordes of slavering barbarians. He would be going north soon, to lead his company in battle. There, surely, was a thought to keep a man occupied. Was not war a deadly business? He could be hurt, or scarred, or killed even. Jezal tried to conjure up the twisting, twitching, painted face of Fenris the Feared. Legions of screaming savages descending upon the Agriont. It was a terrible business alright, a dangerous and frightening business.

Hmmm.

Ardee came from Angland. What if, say, she were to fall into the hands of the Northmen? Jezal would rush to her rescue, of course. She would not be hurt. Well, not badly. Perhaps her clothes a little torn, like so? No doubt she would be frightened, grateful. He would be obliged to comfort her, of course. She might even faint? He might have to carry her, her head pressed against his shoulder. He might have to lay her down and loosen her clothes. Their lips might touch, just brush gently, hers might part a little, then . . .

Jezal stumbled in the road. There was a pleasant swelling building in his crotch. Pleasant, but hardly compatible with a brisk run. He was nearly at the courtyard now, and this would never do at fencing practice. He glanced desperately around for a distraction, and nearly choked on his tongue. Major

West was standing by the wall, dressed to fence and watching him approach with an unusually grim expression. For an instant, Jezal wondered if his friend might be able to tell what he had been thinking. He swallowed guiltily, felt the blood rushing to his face. West couldn't know, he couldn't. But he was most unhappy about something.

"Luthar," he grunted.

"West." Jezal stared down at his shoes. They had not been getting on too well since West joined Lord Marshal Burr's staff. Jezal tried to be happy for him, but could not escape the feeling that he was better qualified for the post. He had excellent blood after all, whether he had experience in the field or not. Then Ardee was still lurking between them, that unpleasant and needless warning. Everyone knew that West had been first through the breach at Ulrioch. Everyone knew that he had the devil of a temper. That had always seemed exciting to Jezal, until he got on the wrong end of it.

"Varuz is waiting." West unfolded his arms and strode off towards the archway, "and he's not alone."

"Not alone?"

"The Marshal feels you need to get used to an audience."

Jezal frowned. "I'm surprised anyone cares in the present climate, what with the war and all."

"You'd be surprised. Fighting and fencing and all things martial are very much the flavour. Everyone's wearing a sword these days, even if they've never drawn one in their lives. There's an absolute fever about the Contest, believe me."

Jezal blinked as they passed into the bright courtyard. A stand of temporary seating had been hastily erected along one wall, packed from one end to the other with people, three score or more.

"And here he is!" shouted Marshal Varuz. There was a ripple of polite applause. Jezal felt himself grinning—there were some very important people in amongst the crowd. He spotted Marovia, the Lord High Justice, stroking his long beard. Lord Isher was not far away from him, looking slightly bored. Crown Prince Ladisla himself was lounging on the front row, shining in a shirt of gossamer chain-mail and clapping enthusiastically. The people on the benches behind had to lean over to see round the waving plume on his magnificent hat.

Varuz handed Jezal his steels, still beaming. "Don't you dare make me look a fool!" he hissed. Jezal coughed nervously, looking up at the rows of expectant people. His heart sank. Inquisitor Glokta's toothless grin leered at him from the crowd, and on the row behind him . . . Ardee West. She was wearing an expression that she never had in his daydreams: one third sullen, one third accusing, one third simply bored. He glanced away, staring toward the opposite wall, inwardly cursing his own cowardice. He seemed unable to meet anyone's eye these days.

"This bout will be fought with half-edged steels!" thundered the Lord Marshal. "The best of three touches!" West already had his swords drawn and was making his way to the circle, marked out with white chalk in the carefully shaved grass. Jezal's heart was hammering loud as he fumbled his own steels out of their sheaths, acutely aware of all those eyes upon him. He took his mark opposite West, pushing his feet cautiously into the grass. West raised his steels, Jezal did the same. They faced each other for a moment, motionless.

"Begin!" shouted Varuz.

It quickly became clear that West had no mind to roll over for him. He came on with more than his usual ferocity, harrying Jezal with a flurry of heavy cuts, their steels clashing and scraping rapidly together. He gave ground, still uncomfortable under the watchful eyes of all those people, damned important people some of them, but as West pushed him back towards the edge of the circle, his nerves began to fade, his training took over. He ducked away, making room for himself, parrying the cuts with left and right, dodging and dancing, too fast to catch.

The people faded, even Ardee was gone. The blades moved by themselves, back and forth, up and down. There was no need for him to look at them. He turned his attention to West's eyes, watched them flicker from the ground to the steels to Jezal's dancing feet, trying to guess his intentions.

He felt the lunge coming even before it was begun. He feinted one way then turned the other, slipping smoothly round behind West as he blundered past. It was a simple matter for him to apply his foot to the seat of his opponent's trousers and shove him out of the circle.

"A touch!" shouted Marshal Varuz.

There was a ripple of laughter as the Major sprawled on his face. "A touch on the arse!" guffawed the Crown Prince, his plume waving back and forth with merriment. "One to Captain Luthar!" West didn't look half so intimidating with his face in the dirt. Jezal gave a little bow to the audience, risked a smile in Ardee's direction as he rose. He was disappointed to see she wasn't even looking at him. She was watching her brother struggle in the dust with a faint, cruel grin.

West got slowly to his feet. "A good touch," he muttered through gritted teeth as he stepped back into the circle. Jezal took his own mark, barely able to suppress his smile.

"Begin!" shouted Varuz.

West came on strongly again, but Jezal was warming to his task now. The sounds of the audience muttered and swelled as he danced this way and that. He began to work the odd flourish into his movements, and the onlookers responded, "oohs" and "aahs" floating up as he flicked West's efforts away. He had never fenced so well, never moved so smoothly. The bigger man was starting to tire a little, the snap was going out of his cuts. Their long steels clashed together, scraped. Jezal twisted his right wrist and tore West's blade from his fingers, stepped in and slashed at him with his left.

"Gah!" West winced and dropped his short steel, hopping away and grabbing his forearm. A few drops of blood pattered across the ground.

"Two to nothing!" shouted Varuz.

The Crown Prince jumped up, his hat tumbling off, delighted by the sight of blood. "Excellent!" he squawked, "capital!" Others joined him on their feet, clapping loudly. Jezal basked in their approval, smiling wide, every muscle tingling with happiness. He understood now what he had been training for.

"Well fought, Jezal," muttered West, a trickle of blood running down his forearm. "You've got too good for me."

"Sorry about the cut." Jezal grinned. He wasn't sorry in the least.

"It's nothing. Just a scratch." West strode away, frowning and holding his wrist. Nobody paid much attention to his exit, Jezal least of all. Sporting events are all about the winners.

Lord Marovia was the first to get up from the benches and offer his congratulations. "What a promising young man," he said, smiling warmly at Jezal, "but do you think he can beat Bremer dan Gorst?"

Varuz gave Jezal a fatherly clap on the shoulder. "I'm sure he can beat anyone, on the right day."

"Hmm. Have you seen Gorst fence?"

"No, though I hear he is most impressive."

"Oh, indeed—he is a devil." The High Justice raised his bushy eyebrows. "I look forward to seeing them meet. Have you ever considered a career in the law, Captain Luthar?"

Jezal was taken by surprise. "Er, no, your Worship, that is . . . I am a soldier."

"Of course you are. But battles and so forth can play hell with the nerves. If you should ever change your mind, perhaps I might have a place for you. I can always find a use for promising men."

"Er, thank you."

"Until the Contest then. Good luck, Captain," he threw over his shoulder as he shuffled away. The implication was that he thought Jezal would need a great deal of it. His Highness Prince Ladisla was more optimistic.

"You're my man, Luthar!" he shouted, poking the air with his fingers as though they were fencing steels. "I'm going to double my bet on you!"

Jezal bowed obsequiously. "Your Highness is too kind."

"You're my man! A soldier! A fencing man should fight for his country, eh, Varuz? Why isn't this Gorst a soldier?"

"I believe he is, your Highness," said the Lord Marshal gently. "He is a kinsman of Lord Brock, and serves with his personal guard."

"Oh." The Prince seemed confused for a moment, but soon perked up. "But you're my man!" he shouted at Jezal, poking once more with his fingers, the feather on his hat waving this way and that. "You're the man for me!" He danced off towards the archway, decorative chain-mail gleaming.

"Very impressive." Jezal whipped round, took an ungainly step back. Glokta, leering at him from his blind side. For a cripple, he had an uncanny knack of sneaking up on a man. "What a happy chance for everyone that you didn't give it up after all."

"I never had any intention of doing so," snapped Jezal frostily.

Glokta sucked at his gums. "If you say so, Captain."

"I do." Jezal turned rudely away, hoping that he never had occasion to speak to the loathsome man again. He found himself staring straight into Ardee's face, no more than a foot away.

"Gah," he stammered, stepping back again.

"Jezal," she said, "I haven't seen you in a while."

"Er . . ." He glanced nervously around. Glokta was shambling away. West was long gone. Varuz was busy holding forth to Lord Isher and a few others still remaining in the courtyard. They were unobserved. He had to speak to her. He ought to tell her straight out that he could not see her any-more. He owed her that much. "Er . . ."

"Nothing to say to me?"

"Er . . ." He turned swiftly on his heel and walked away, his shoulders prickling with shame.

The tedium of guard duty at the south gate seemed, after all that unexpected excitement, almost a mercy. Jezal was quite looking forward to standing idly by, watching people file in and out of the Agriont, listening to Lieutenant Kaspa's mindless babble. At least, he was until he got there.

Kaspa and the usual complement of armoured soldiers were clustered around the outer gates, where the old bridge across the moat passed between the two massive, white rendered towers of the gatehouse. As Jezal marched down to the end of the long tunnel he saw that there was someone with them. A small, harassed-looking fellow wearing spectacles. Jezal recognised him vaguely. Morrow he was called, some crony of the Lord Chamberlain. He had no reason to be here.

"Captain Luthar, what a happy chance!" Jezal jumped. It was that lunatic, Sulfur, sitting cross-legged on the ground behind him, his back against the sheer wall of the gatehouse.

"What the hell's he doing here?" snapped Jezal. Kaspa opened his mouth to speak, but Sulfur got in first.

"Don't mind me, Captain, I'm simply waiting for my master."

"Your master?" He dreaded to think what manner of an idiot this idiot might serve.

"Indeed. He should be here very shortly." Sulfur frowned up at the sun. "He is already somewhat tardy, if the truth be told."

"Really?"

"Yes." The madman broke into a friendly smile once more. "But he'll be along, Jezal, you can depend on it."

First-name terms was too much to take. He hardly knew the man, and what he knew he didn't like. He opened his mouth to give him a piece of his mind, but Sulfur suddenly jumped up, grabbing his stick from the wall and brushing himself down. "Here they are!" he said, looking out across the moat. Jezal followed the idiot's eyes with his own.

A magnificent old man was striding purposefully across the bridge, bald head held high, a fabulous gown of shimmering red and silver flowing about him in the breeze. At his heels came a sickly looking youth, head a little bowed as if in awe of the older man, holding a long staff out before him in upturned palms. A great brute of a man in a heavy fur cloak followed behind them, a good half head taller than the other two.

"What the . . ." Jezal trailed off. He seemed to recognise the old man from somewhere. Some lord perhaps, from the Open Council? Some foreign ambassador? Certainly he had an air of majesty. Jezal racked his brains as they approached, but could not place him.

The old man stopped before the gatehouse, swept Jezal, Kaspa, Morrow and the guards imperiously with glittering green eyes. "Yoru," he said.

Sulfur stepped forward, bowing low. "Master Bayaz," he murmured, in hushed tones of deep respect.

And that was it. That was why Jezal knew the man. He bore a definite resemblance to the statue of Bayaz in the Kingsway. The statue Jezal had run past so many times. A little fatter perhaps, but that expression: stern, wise, effortlessly commanding, was just the same. Jezal frowned. For the old man to be called by that name? He didn't like it. He didn't like the look of the lanky young man with the staff either. He liked the look of the old man's other companion even less.

West had often told Jezal that the Northmen found in Adua, usually skulking dishevelled by the docks or dirty drunk in gutters, were by no means typical of their people. Those that lived free in the far North, fighting, feuding, feasting, and doing whatever Northmen did, were of quite a different kind. A tall, fierce, handsome people, Jezal had always imagined, with a touch of romance about them. Strong, yet graceful. Wild, yet noble. Savage, yet cunning. The kind of men whose eyes are fixed always on the far horizon.

This was not one of those.

Never in his life had Jezal seen a more brutish-looking man. Even Fenris the Feared had seemed civilised by comparison. His face was like a whipped back, criss-crossed with ragged scars. His nose was bent, pointing off a little sideways. One ear had a big notch out of it, one eye seemed a touch higher than the other, surrounded by a crescent-shaped wound. His whole face, in fact, was slightly beaten, broken, lopsided, like that of a prize fighter who has fought a few bouts too many. His expression too, was that of one punch-drunk. He gawped up at the gatehouse, forehead furrowed, mouth hanging open, staring about him with a look of near animal stupidity.

He wore a long fur cloak, and a leather tunic set with gold, but this height of barbaric splendour only made him look more savage, and there was no missing the long, heavy sword at his belt. The Northman scratched at a big pink scar through the stubble on his cheek as he peered up at the sheer walls above, and Jezal noticed one of his fingers was missing. As though any further evidence of a life of violence and savagery was necessary.

To let this hulking primitive into the Agriont? While they were at war with the Northmen? It was unthinkable! But Morrow was already sidling forward. "The Lord Chamberlain is expecting you, gentlemen," he gushed as he bowed and scraped his way towards the old man, "if you would care to follow me—"

"One moment." Jezal grabbed the under-secretary by the elbow and pulled him aside. "Him too?" he asked incredulously, nodding over at the primitive in the cloak. "We are at war, you know!"

"Lord Hoff was most specific!" Morrow shook his arm free, spectacles flashing. "Keep him here if you wish, but you can explain it to the Lord Chamberlain!"

Jezal swallowed. That idea was not at all appealing. He glanced up at the old man, but could not look him in the eye for long. He had a mysterious air, an air of knowing something no one else could guess, and it was most unsettling.

"You . . . must . . . leave . . . your . . . weapons . . . here!" he shouted, speaking as slowly and clearly as possible.

"Happy to." The Northman pulled the sword from his belt and held it out. It weighed heavily in Jezal's hands: a big, plain, brutal-looking weapon. He followed it with a long knife, then knelt and pulled another from his boot. He took a third from the small of his back, and then produced a thin blade from inside his sleeve, heaping them into Jezal's outstretched arms. The Northman smiled broadly. It was truly a hideous sight, the ragged scars twisting and puckering, making his face more lopsided than ever.

"You can never have too many knives," he growled in a deep, grinding voice. Nobody laughed, but he did not seem to care.

"Shall we go?" asked the old man.

"Without delay," said Morrow, turning to leave.

"I'll come with you." Jezal dumped his armload of weapons into Kaspa's hands.

"That really isn't necessary, Captain," whined Morrow.

"I insist." Once he was delivered to the Lord Chamberlain, the Northman could murder whomever he pleased: it would be someone else's problem. But until he got there Jezal might be blamed for whatever mischief he got up to, and he was damned if he was going to let that happen.

The guards stood aside, the strange procession passed through the gate. Morrow was first, whispering obsequious nothings over his shoulder to the old man in the splendid robe. The pale youth was next, followed by Sulfur. The nine-fingered Northman lumbered along at the back.

Jezal followed with his thumb in his belt, close to the hilt of his sword so he could get to it quickly, watching the savage intently for any sudden moves. After following him for a short while though, Jezal had to admit, the man gave no appearance of having murder in mind. If anything he looked curious, bemused, and somewhat embarrassed. He kept slowing, staring up at the buildings around him, shaking his head, scratching his face, muttering under his breath. He would occasionally horrify passers-by by smiling at them, but he seemed to present no greater threat and Jezal began to relax, at least until they reached the Square of Marshals.

The Northman stopped suddenly. Jezal fumbled for his sword, but the primitive's eyes were locked ahead, gazing at a fountain nearby. He moved slowly towards it, then cautiously raised a thick finger and poked at the glittering jet. Water splashed into his face and he blundered away, almost knocking Jezal down. "A spring?" he whispered. "But how?"

Mercy. The man was like a child. A six and a half foot child with a face like a butcher's block. "There are pipes!" Jezal stamped on the paving. "Beneath . . . the . . . ground!"

"Pipes," echoed the primitive quietly, staring at the frothing water.

The others had moved some way ahead, close to the grand building in which Hoff had his offices. Jezal began to step away from the fountain, hoping to draw the witless savage with him. To Jezal's relief he followed, shaking his head and muttering "pipes" to himself, over and over.

They entered the cool darkness of the Lord Chamberlain's anteroom. There were people seated on the benches around the walls, some of them giving the impression of having been waiting a very long time. They all stared as Morrow ushered the peculiar group straight into Hoff's offices. The spectacled secretary opened the heavy double doors and stood by while first the old bald man, then his crony with the stick, then the madman Sulfur, and finally the nine-fingered primitive walked in past him.

Jezal made to follow them, but Morrow stood in the doorway and blocked his path. "Thank you so much for your help, Captain," he said with a thin smile. "You may return to the gate." Jezal peered over his shoulder into the room beyond. He saw the Lord Chamberlain frowning behind a long table. Arch Lector Sult was beside him, grim and suspicious. High Justice Marovia was there too, a smile on his wrinkled face. Three members of the Closed Council.

Then Morrow shut the door in his face.

NEXT

"**I** notice you have a new secretary," said Glokta, as though just in passing.

The Arch Lector smiled. "Of course. The old one was not to my liking. He had a loose tongue, you know." Glokta paused, his wine glass halfway to his mouth. "He had been passing our secrets on to the Mercers," continued Sult carelessly, as if it was common knowledge. "I had been aware of it for some time. You needn't worry though, he never learned anything I didn't want him to know."

Then . . . you knew who our traitor was. You knew all along. Glokta's mind turned the events of the last few weeks around, pulled them apart and put them back together in this new light, trying them different ways until they fit, all the while struggling to conceal his surprise. *You left Rews' confession where you knew your secretary would see it. You knew the Mercers would find out who was on the list, and you guessed what they would do, knowing it would only play into your hands and give you the shovel with which to bury them. Meanwhile, you steered my suspicions towards Kalyne when you knew who the leak was all along. The whole business unfolded precisely according to your plan.* The Arch Lector was looking back at him with a knowing smile. *And I bet you guess what I'm thinking right now. I have been almost as much a piece in this game as that snivelling worm of a secretary.* Glokta stifled a giggle. *How fortunate for me that I was a piece on the right side. I never suspected a thing.*

"He betrayed us for a disappointingly small sum of money," continued Sult, his lip curling with distaste. "I daresay Kault would have given him ten times as much, if he had only had the wit to ask. The younger generation really have no ambition. They think they are a great deal cleverer than they are." He studied Glokta with his cool blue eyes. *I am part of the younger generation, more or less. I am justly humbled.*

"Your secretary has been disciplined?"

The Arch Lector placed his glass carefully down on the table top, the base barely making a sound on the wood. "Oh yes. Most severely. It really isn't necessary to spare him any further thought." *I bet it isn't. Body found floating by the docks . . .* "I must say, I was greatly surprised when you fixed on Superior Kalyne as the source of our leak. The man was from the old guard. A few indulgences to look the other way over trifling matters, of course, but to betray the Inquisition? To sell our secrets to the Mercers?" Sult snorted. "Never. You allowed your personal dislike for the man to cloud your judgement."

"He seemed the only possibility," muttered Glokta, but immediately regretted it. *Foolish, foolish. The mistake is made. Better just to keep your mouth shut.*

"Seemed?" The Arch Lector clicked his tongue in profound disapproval. "No, no, no, Inquisitor. Seemed is not good enough for us. In future, we'll have just the facts, if you please. But don't feel too badly about it—I allowed you to follow your instincts and, as things have turned out, your blunder has left our position much the stronger. Kalyne has been removed from office," *Body found floating . . .* "and Superior Goyle is on his way from Angland to assume the role of Superior of Adua."

Goyle? Coming here? That bastard, the new Superior of Adua? Glokta could not prevent his lip from curling.

"The two of you are not the greatest of friends, eh, Glokta?"

"He is a jailer, not an investigator. He is not interested in guilt or innocence. He is not interested in truth. He tortures for the thrill of it."

"Oh, come now, Glokta. Are you telling me you feel no thrill when your prisoners spill their secrets? When they name the names? When they sign the confession?"

"I take no pleasure in it." *I take no pleasure in anything.*

"And yet you do it so very well. In any case, Goyle is coming, and whatever you may think of him, he is one of us. A most capable and trustworthy man, dedicated to the service of crown and state. He was once a pupil of mine, you know."

"Really?"

"Yes. He had your job . . . so there is some future in it after all!" The Arch Lector giggled at his own joke. Glokta gave a thin smile of his own. "All in all, things have worked out very nicely, and you are to be congratulated on your part in it. A job well done." *Well enough done that I am still alive, at least.* Sult raised his glass and they drank a joyless toast together, eyeing each other suspiciously over the rims of their glasses.

Glokta cleared his throat. "Magister Kault mentioned something interesting before his unfortunate demise."

"Go on."

"The Mercers had a partner in their schemes. A senior partner, perhaps. A bank."

"Huh. Turn a merchant over and there's always a banker underneath. What of it?"

"I believe these bankers knew about it all. The smuggling, the fraud, the murders even. I believe they encouraged it, maybe ordered it, so that they could get a good return on their loans. May I begin an investigation, your Eminence?"

"Which bank?"

"Valint and Balk."

The Arch Lector seemed to consider a moment, staring at Glokta through his hard, blue eyes. *Does he already know about these particular bankers? Does he already know much more than me? What did Kault say? You want traitors, Glokta? Look in the House of Questions—*

"No," snapped Sult. "Those particular bankers are well connected. They are owed too many favours, and without Kault it will be difficult to prove anything. We got what we needed from the Mercers, and I have a more pressing task for you."

Glokta looked up. *Another task?* "I was looking forward to interviewing the prisoners we took at the Guildhall, your Eminence, it may be that—"

"No." The Arch Lector swatted Glokta's words away with his gloved hand. "That business could drag on for months. I will have Goyle handle it." He frowned. "Unless you object?"

So I plough the field, sow the seed, water the crop, then Goyle reaps the harvest? Some justice. He humbly bowed his head. "Of course not, your Eminence."

"Good. You are probably aware of the unusual visitors we received yesterday."

Visitors? For the past week Glokta had been in agony with his back. Yesterday he had struggled out of bed to watch that cretin Luthar fence, but otherwise he had been confined to his tiny room, virtually unable to move. "I hadn't noticed," he said simply.

"Bayaz, the First of the Magi." Glokta gave his thin smile again, but the Arch Lector was not laughing.

"You're joking, of course."

"If only."

"A charlatan, your Eminence?"

"What else? But a most extraordinary one. Lucid, reasonable, clever. The deception is elaborate in the extreme."

"You have spoken with him?"

"I have. He is remarkably convincing. He knows things, things he shouldn't know. He cannot be simply dismissed. Whoever he is, he has funding, and good sources of information." The Arch Lector frowned deep. "He has some renegade brute of a Northman with him."

Glokta frowned. "A Northman? It hardly seems their style. They strike me as most direct."

"My very thoughts."

"A spy for the Emperor then? The Gurkish?"

"Perhaps. The Kantics love a good intrigue, but they tend to stick to the shadows. These theatricals don't seem to have their mark. I suspect our answer may lie closer to home."

"The nobles, your Eminence? Brock? Isher? Heugen?"

"Perhaps," mused Sult, "perhaps. They're annoyed enough. Or there's our old friend, the High Justice. He seemed a little too pleased about it all. He's plotting something, I can tell."

The nobles, the High Justice, the Northmen, the Gurkish—it could be any one of them, or none—but why? "I don't understand, Arch Lector. If they are simply spies, why go to all this trouble? Surely there are easier ways to get into the Agriont?"

"This is the thing." Sult gave as bitter a grimace as Glokta had ever seen.

"There is an empty seat on the Closed Council, there always has been. A pointless tradition, a matter of etiquette, a chair reserved for a mythical figure, in any case dead for hundreds of years. Nobody ever supposed that anyone would come forward to claim it."

"But he has?"

"He has! He has demanded it!" The Arch Lector got to his feet and strode around the table. "I know! Unthinkable! Some spy, some liar from who knows where, privy to the workings of the very heart of our government! But he has some dusty papers, so it falls to *us* to discredit *him*! Can you believe it?"

Glokta could not. *But there hardly seems any purpose to saying so.*

"I have asked for time to investigate," continued Sult, "but the Closed Council will not be put off indefinitely. We have only a week or two to expose this so-called Magus for the fraud he is. In the mean time, he and his companions are making themselves at home in an excellent suite of rooms in the Tower of Chains, and there is nothing we can do to prevent them wandering the Agriont, causing whatever mischief they please!" *There is something we could do . . .*

"The Tower of Chains is very high. If somebody were to fall—"

"No. Not yet. We have already pushed our luck as far as it will go in certain circles. For the time being at least, we must tread carefully."

"There is always the possibility of an interrogation. If we were to arrest them, I could soon find out who they are working for—"

"Tread carefully, I said! I want you to look into this Magus, Glokta, and his companions. Find out who they are, where they come from, what they are after. Above all, find out who is behind them, and why. We must discredit this would-be Bayaz before he can do any damage. After that you can use whatever means you please." Sult turned and moved away to the window.

Glokta got up awkwardly, painfully from his chair. "How shall I begin?"

"Follow them!" shouted the Arch Lector impatiently. "Watch them! See who they speak to, what they are about. You're the Inquisitor, Glokta!" he snapped, without even looking round. "Ask some questions!"

BETTER THAN DEATH

"**W**e're looking for a woman," said the officer, staring at them suspiciously. "An escaped slave, a killer. Very dangerous."

"A woman, master?" asked Yulwei, his brow wrinkled with confusion. "Dangerous, master?"

"Yes, a woman!" The officer waved his hand impatiently. "Tall, with a scar, hair cropped short. Well-armed, most likely, with a bow." Ferro stood there, tall and scarred, hair cropped short, bow over her shoulder, and looked down at the dusty ground. "She is wanted, by the highest of authorities! A thief and a murderer, many times over!"

Yulwei gave a humble smile and spread his hands. "We have seen no such person master. I and my son are unarmed, as you can see." Ferro looked down uncomfortably at the curved blade of the sword stuck through her belt, shining in the bright sun. The officer didn't seem to notice though. He swatted at a fly as Yulwei blathered on. "Neither one of us would know what to do with such a thing as a bow, I can assure you. We trust in God to protect us, master, and in the Emperor's matchless soldiers."

The officer snorted. "Very wise, old man. What's your business here?"

"I am a merchant, on my way to Dagoska, to purchase spices," and he gave a grovelling bow, "with your kind permission."

"Trading with the pinks are you? Damn Union!" The officer spat in the dust. "Still, a man has to make a living, I suppose, if a shameful one. Trade while you can, the pinks will be gone soon, swept back into the ocean!" He puffed out his chest with pride. "The Emperor, Uthman-ul-Dosht, has sworn it! What do you think of that, old man?"

"Oh, it will be a great day, a great day," said Yulwei, bowing low again, "may God bring it to us soon, master!"

The officer looked Ferro up and down. "Your son looks a strong lad. Perhaps he'd make a soldier." He took a step towards her and grabbed hold of her bare arm. "That's a strong arm. That arm could draw a bow, I'd say, if it were taught. What do you say boy? A man's work, fighting for the glory of God, and your Emperor! Better than grubbing for a pittance!" Ferro's flesh crawled where his fingers touched her skin. Her other hand crept towards her knife.

"Alas," said Yulwei quickly, "my son was born . . . simple. He scarcely speaks."

"Ah. A shame. The time may come when we need every man. Savages they may be, but these pinks can fight." The officer turned away and Ferro scowled after him. "Very well, you may go!" He waved them on. The eyes of his soldiers, lounging in the shade of the palms around the road, followed them as they walked past, but without much interest.

Ferro held her tongue until the encampment had dwindled into the distance behind them, then she rounded on Yulwei. "Dagoska?"

"To begin with," said the old man, staring off across the scrubby plain. "And then north."

"North?"

"Across the Circle Sea to Adua."

Across the sea? She stopped in the road. "I'm not fucking going there!"

"Must you make everything so difficult, Ferro? Are you that happy here in Gurkhul?"

"These northerners are mad, everyone knows it! Pinks, Union, or whatever. Mad! Godless!"

Yulwei raised an eyebrow at her. "I didn't know you were so interested in God, Ferro."

"At least I know there is one!" she shouted, pointing at the sky. "These pinks, they don't think like us, like real people! We've no business with their kind! I'd rather stay among the Gurkish! Besides, I've scores to settle here."

"What scores? Going to kill Uthman?"

She frowned. "Perhaps I will."

"Huh." Yulwei turned and headed off up the road. "They're looking for

you, Ferro, in case you hadn't noticed. You wouldn't get ten strides without
my help. They've still got that cage waiting, remember? The one in front of
the palace? They are anxious to fill it." Ferro ground her teeth. "Uthman is
the Emperor now. Ul-Dosht, they call him. The mighty! The merciless!
Greatest Emperor for a hundred years, they are saying already. Kill the
Emperor!" Yulwei chuckled to himself. "You're quite a character alright.
Quite a character."

Ferro scowled as she followed the old man up the hill. She wasn't looking
to be anyone's character. Yulwei could make these soldiers see whatever he
pleased, and that was a smart trick, but she'd be damned if she was going
north. What business did she have with those godless pinks?

Yulwei was still chuckling away as she drew level with him. "Kill the
Emperor." He shook his head. "He'll just have to wait until you get back.
You owe me, remember?"

Ferro grabbed him by the sinewy arm. "I don't remember you saying
anything about crossing the sea!"

"I don't remember your asking, Maljinn, and you should be glad you
didn't!" He peeled her fingers gently away. "Your corpse might be drying
nicely in the desert, instead of grumbling in my ear, all sleek and healthy—
think on that a while."

That shut her up for the time being. She walked along in silence,
scowling out across the scrubby landscape, sandals crunching on the dry dirt
of the road. She looked sidelong at the old man. He'd saved her life with his
tricks, that couldn't be denied.

But she'd be damned if she was going north.

The fortress was concealed in a rocky cove, but from where they were, high
up on the bluff with the fierce sun behind them, Ferro could see the shape of
it well enough. A high wall enclosed neat rows of buildings, enough to make
a small town. Next to the them, built out into the water, were long wharves.
Moored to the wharves were ships.

Huge ships.

Towers of wood, floating fortresses. Ferro had never seen ships half that
size. Their masts were a dark forest against the bright water behind. Ten were

docked below them, and further out in the bay two more were cutting slowly through the waves, great sails billowing, tiny figures crawling on the decks and in amongst the spider's web of ropes above.

"I see twelve," murmured Yulwei, "but your eyes are the sharper."

Ferro looked out across the water. Further round the curving shore, twenty miles away perhaps, she could see another fortress, another set of wharves. "There are more over there," she said, "eight or nine, and those ones are bigger."

"Bigger than these?"

"A lot bigger."

"God's breath!" muttered Yulwei to himself. "The Gurkish never built ships so big before, not half so big, nor half so many. There is not the wood in all the South for such a fleet. They must have bought it from the north, from the Styrians, maybe."

Ferro cared nothing for boats, or wood, or the north. "So?"

"With a fleet this size, the Gurkish will be a power at sea. They could take Dagoska from the bay, invade Westport even."

The pointless names of far-away places. "So?"

"You don't understand, Ferro. I must warn the others. We must make haste, now!" He pushed himself up from the ground and hurried back towards the road.

Ferro grunted. She watched the big wooden tubs moving back and forth in the bay for a moment longer, then she got up and followed Yulwei. Great ships or tiny ships, it meant nothing to her. The Gurkish could take all the pinks in the world for slaves as far as she was concerned.

If that meant they left the real people alone.

"Out of the way!" The soldier spurred his horse right at them, raising his whip.

"A thousand pardons, master!" whined Yulwei, grovelling to the ground, scuttling off into the grass beside the road, pulling Ferro reluctantly by the elbow. She stood in the scrub, watching the column shamble slowly by. Thin figures, ragged, dirty, vacant, hands bound tightly, hollow eyes on the ground. Men and women, all ages, children even. A hundred or more. Six guards rode alongside them, easy in their tall saddles, whips rolled up in their hands.

"Slaves." Ferro licked her dry lips.

"The people of Kadir have risen up," said Yulwei, frowning at the miserable procession. "They wished no longer to be part of the glorious nation of Gurkhul, and thought the death of the Emperor might be their chance to leave. It seems they were wrong. The new Emperor is harder even than the last, eh, Ferro? Their rebellion has failed already. It seems your friend Uthman has taken slaves as punishment."

Ferro watched a scrawny girl limping slowly, bare feet trailing in the dust. Thirteen years old? It was hard to tell. Her face was dirty and listless. There was a scabby cut across her forehead, others on the back of her arm. Whip marks. Ferro swallowed, watched the girl toiling along. An old man, just in front of her, tripped and sprawled face first into the road, making the whole column stumble to a halt.

"Move!" barked one of the riders, spurring his horse forward. "On your feet!" The old man struggled in the dust. "Move!" The soldier's whip cracked, leaving a long red mark across the man's scrawny back. Ferro twitched and winced at the sound, and her back began to tingle.

Where the scars were.

Almost as if she'd been whipped herself.

No one whips Ferro Maljinn and lives. Not any more. She shrugged the bow off her shoulder.

"Peace, Ferro!" hissed Yulwei, grabbing her by the arm. "There's nothing you can do for them!"

The girl bent down, helping the old slave to his feet. The whip cracked again, catching them both, and there was a yelp of pain. Was it the girl or the man who had cried out?

Or had it been Ferro herself?

She shook Yulwei's hand off, reaching for an arrow. "I can kill this bastard!" she snarled. The soldier's head snapped round to look at them, curious. Yulwei seized hold of her hand.

"What then?" he hissed. "If you killed all six of them, what then? Have you food and water for a hundred slaves? Eh? You have it well concealed! And when the column is missed? Eh? And their guards found slaughtered? What then, killer? Will you hide a hundred slaves out here? Because I cannot!"

Ferro stared into Yulwei's black eyes, her teeth grinding together, her breath snorting fast through her nose. She wondered whether or not to try and kill him again.

No.

He was right, damn him. Slowly, she pushed the anger back, as far down as it would go. She shoved the arrow away, and turned back towards the column. She watched the old slave stumble on, and the girl after him, fury gnawing at her guts like hunger.

"You!" called the soldier, nudging his horse over towards them.

"You've done it now!" hissed Yulwei, then he bowed to the guard, smiling, scraping. "My apologies master, my son is . . ."

"Shut your mouth, old man!" The soldier looked down at Ferro from his saddle. "Well, boy, do you like her?"

"What?" she hissed, through gritted teeth.

"No need to be shy," chuckled the soldier, "I've seen you looking." He turned towards the column. "Hold them up there!" he shouted, and the slaves stumbled to a halt. He leaned from his saddle and grabbed the scrawny girl under the armpit, dragging her roughly out of the column.

"She's a good one," he said, pulling her towards Ferro. "Bit young, but she's ready. Clean up nice, she will. Bit of a limp but that'll heal, we've been driving 'em hard. Good teeth . . . show him your teeth, bitch!" The girl's cracked lips curled back slowly. "Good teeth. What do you say boy? Ten in gold for her! It's a good price!"

Ferro stood there, staring. The girl looked dumbly back with big, dead eyes.

"Look," said the soldier, leaning down from his saddle. "She's worth twice that, and there's no danger in it! When we get to Shaffa, I'll tell them she died out here in the dust. No one will wonder at that, it happens all the time! I get ten, and you save ten! Everyone wins!"

Everyone wins. Ferro stared up at the guard. He pulled his helmet off, wiped his forehead with the back of his hand. "Peace, Ferro," whispered Yulwei.

"Alright, eight!" Shouted the soldier. "She's got a nice smile! Show him a smile, bitch!" The corner of the girl's mouth twitched slightly. "There, see! Eight, and you're stealing from me!"

Ferro's fists were clenched, nails digging into her palms. "Peace, Ferro," whispered Yulwei, with a warning note in his voice.

"God's teeth but you drive a bargain boy! Seven, and that's my last offer. Seven, damn it!" The soldier waved his helmet around in frustration. "Use her gently, in five years she'll be worth more! It's an investment!"

The soldier's face was just a few feet away. She could see each tiny bead of sweat forming on his forehead, each stubbly hair on his cheeks, each blemish, nick, and pore on his skin. She could smell him, almost.

The truly thirsty will drink piss, or salt water, or oil, however bad for them, so great is their need to drink. Ferro had seen it often in the badlands. That was the extent of her need to kill this man now. She wanted to tear him with her bare hands, to choke the life from him, to rip his face with her teeth. The desire was almost too strong to resist. "Peace!" hissed Yulwei.

"I can't afford her," Ferro heard herself saying.

"You might have said so before, boy, and saved me the trouble!" The soldier stuck his helmet back on. "Still, I can't blame you for looking. She's a good one." He reached down and grabbed the girl under the arm, dragging her back towards the others. "They'll get twenty for her in Shaffa!" he shouted over his shoulder. The column moved on. Ferro watched the girl until the slaves disappeared over a rise, stumbling, limping, shambling towards slavery.

She felt cold now, cold and empty. She wished she had killed the guard, whatever the cost. Killing him could have filled that empty space, if only for a while. That was how it worked. "I walked in a column like that," she said slowly.

Yulwei gave a long sigh. "I know, Ferro, I know, but fate has chosen you for saving. Be grateful for it, if you know how."

"You should have let me kill him."

"Eugh," clucked the old man in disgust, "I do declare, you'd kill the whole world if you could. Is there anything but killing in you Ferro?"

"There used to be," she muttered, "but they whip it out of you. They whip you until they're sure there's nothing left." Yulwei stood there, with that pitying look on his face. Strange, how it didn't make her angry any more.

"I'm sorry, Ferro. Sorry for you and for them." He stepped back into the road, shaking his head. "But it's better than death."

She stayed for a moment, watching the dust rising from the distant column.

"The same," she whispered to herself.

SORE THUMB

Logen leaned against the parapet, squinted into the morning sun, and took in the view.

He'd done the same, it felt long ago now, from the balcony of his room at the library. The two views could hardly have been more different. Sunrise over the jagged carpet of buildings on the one hand, hot and glaring bright and full of distant noise. The cold and misty valley on the other, soft and empty and still as death. He remembered that morning, remembered how he'd felt like a different man. He certainly felt a different man now. A stupid man. Small, scared, ugly, and confused.

"Logen." Malacus stepped out onto the balcony to stand beside him, smiled up at the sun and out over the city to the sparkling bay, already busy with ships. "Beautiful, isn't it?"

"If you say so, but I'm not sure I see it. All those people." Logen gave a sweaty shiver. "It's not right. It frightens me."

"Frightened? You?"

"Always." Logen had barely slept since they arrived. It was never properly dark here, never properly quiet. It was too hot, too close, too stinking. Enemies might be terrifying, but enemies could be fought, and put an end to. Logen could understand their hatred. There was no fighting the faceless, careless, rumbling city. It hated everything. "This is no place for me. I'll be glad to leave."

"We might not be leaving for a while."

"I know." Logen took a deep breath. "That's why I'm going to go down and look at this Agriont, and find out what I can about it. Some things have to be done. It's better to do them than to live with the fear of them. That's what my father used to tell me."

"Good advice. I'll come with you."

"You will not." Bayaz was in the doorway, glaring out at his apprentice. "Your progress over the last few weeks has been a disgrace, even for you." He stepped through into the open air. "I suggest that while we are idle, waiting on His Majesty's pleasure, you should take the opportunity to study. Another such chance may be a long time coming."

Malacus hurried back inside with no backward glances. He knew better than to dawdle with his master in this mood. Bayaz had lost all his good humour as soon as they arrived at the Agriont, and it didn't look like coming back. Logen could hardly blame him, they'd been treated more like prisoners than guests. He didn't know much about manners, but he could guess the meaning of hard stares from everyone and guards outside the door.

"You wouldn't believe how it's grown," growled Bayaz, frowning out at the great sweep of city. "I remember when Adua was barely more than a huddle of shacks, squeezed in round the House of the Maker like flies round a fresh turd. Before there was an Agriont. Before there was a Union, even. They weren't half so proud in those days, I can tell you. They worshipped the Maker like a god."

He noisily hawked up a lump of phlegm and spat it out into the air. Logen watched it clear the moat and vanish somewhere in amongst the white buildings below. "I gave them this," hissed Bayaz. Logen felt the unpleasant creeping sensation that always seemed to accompany the old wizard's displeasure. "I gave them freedom, and this is the thanks I get? The scorn of clerks? Of swollen-headed old errand-boys?" A trip down into the suspicion and madness below began to seem like a merciful release. Logen edged towards the door and ducked back into the room beyond.

If they were prisoners here then Logen had been in some harder cells, he had to admit. Their round living room was fit for a King, to his mind at least: heavy chairs of dark wood with delicate carvings, thick hangings on the walls showing woods and hunting scenes. Bethod would most likely have felt at home in such a room. Logen felt like an oaf there, always on his toes in case he broke something. A tall jar stood on a table in the chamber's centre, its sides painted with bright flowers. Logen eyed it suspiciously as he made for the long stair down into the Agriont.

"Logen!" Bayaz was framed in the doorway, frowning after him. "Take care. The place may seem strange, but the people are stranger still."

The water frothed and gurgled, spurting up in a narrow jet from a metal tube carved like a fish's mouth, then splashing back down into a wide stone basin. A fountain, the proud young man had called it. Pipes, beneath the earth, he'd said. Logen pictured underground streams, coursing just beneath his feet, washing at the foundations of the place. The thought made him feel slightly dizzy.

The square was vast—a great plain of flat stones, hemmed in by sheer cliffs of white buildings. Hollow cliffs, covered with pillars and carvings, glittering with tall windows, crawling with people. Something strange seemed to be happening today. All around the distant edges of the square an enormous, sloping structure of wooden beams was being built. An army of workmen swarmed over it, hacking and bludgeoning, swinging at pegs and joints, hurling bad-tempered shouts at each other. All around them were mountains of planks and logs, barrels of nails, stacks of tools, enough to build ten mighty halls, and more besides. In places the structure was already far above the ground, its uprights soaring into the air like the masts of great ships, as high as the monstrous buildings behind.

Logen stood, hands on hips, gawping at the enormous wooden skeleton, but its purpose was a mystery. He stepped up to a short muscular man in a leather apron, sawing furiously at a plank. "What's this?"

"Eh?" The man didn't even look up from his task.

"This. What's it for?"

The saw bit through the wood, the off-cut clattered to the ground. The carpenter hefted the rest of the plank onto a pile nearby. He turned round, eyeing Logen suspiciously, wiping sweat from his glistening forehead.

"Stands. Seating." Logen stared vacantly back at him. How could something stand and sit at once? "For the Contest!" the carpenter shouted in his face. Logen backed slowly away. Gibberish. Nonsense words. He turned and hurried off, keeping well clear of the huge wooden structures and the men clambering over them.

He blundered out onto a broad lane, a deep gorge between looming white buildings. Statues faced each other down either side, much larger than life, frowning over the heads of the many people hurrying between. The nearest of the carvings seemed strangely familiar. Logen walked over to it, looked it up and down, then grinned to himself. The First of the Magi had gained some weight since it was sculpted. Too much good eating at the library, maybe. Logen turned towards a small man with a black hat, walking by with a big book under his arm.

"Bayaz," he said, pointing up at the statue. "Friend of mine." The man stared at him, at the statue, back at him, and hurried away.

The carvings marched on down either side of the avenue. Kings of the Union, Logen guessed, stood in line on the left. Some carried swords, some scrolls or tiny ships. One had a dog at his feet, another a sheaf of wheat under his arm, but otherwise there wasn't much to tell them apart. They all had the same tall crowns and the same stern frowns. You wouldn't have thought to look at them that they'd ever said a stupid word, or done a stupid thing, or had to take a shit in all their lives.

Logen heard rapid footsteps thumping up behind him, and he turned just in time to see the proud young man from the gate, pounding down the avenue, shirt soaked through with sweat. Logen wondered where he might be going in such a hurry, but he was damned if he was going to run to catch up with him, not in this heat. Anyway, there were plenty more mysteries that needed solving.

The lane opened out into a great, green space, scooped out from the country by giant hands and dropped in amongst the tall buildings, but like no countryside that Logen had ever seen. The grass was a smooth, even blanket of vivid green, shaved almost to the ground. There were flowers, but growing in rows and circles and straight lines of bright colour. There were lush bushes and trees, all squeezed and fenced and clipped into unnatural shapes. There was water, too—streams bubbling over stone steps, a great flat pond with sad-looking trees trailing round its edge.

Logen wandered through this square-edged greenery, boots crunching on a path made of tiny grey stones. There were lots of people gathered here, squeezed in together to enjoy the sun. They sat in boats on the miniature lake, rowing gently round and round, going nowhere. They lazed on the lawns, ate, drank and babbled to one another. Some of them would point at Logen and shout, or whisper, or slope away.

They were a strange-seeming crowd, especially the women. Pale and ghostly, swaddled in elaborate dresses, hair scraped up and piled and stuck through with pins and combs and great weird feathers or useless tiny hats. They seemed like the big jar in the round chamber—too thin and delicate to be any use, and further spoiled by too much decoration. But it had been a long time, and he smiled at them cheerfully, on the off chance. Some looked shocked, others gasped in horror. Logen sighed. The old magic was still there.

Further on, in another wide square, Logen stopped to watch a group of soldiers practice. These weren't beggars, or girlish youths, these were solid-looking men wearing heavy armour, breastplates and greaves polished mirror bright, long spears shouldered. They stood together, each man the same as the one beside, in four squares of maybe fifty men each, still as the statues in the avenue.

At a bellow from a short man in a red jacket—their chief, Logen reckoned—the whole crowd turned, levelled their spears and began to advance across the square, heavy boots tramping together. Each man the same, armed the same, moving the same. It was quite a sight, all that shining metal moving steadily in bristling squares, spear points glittering, like some great square hedgehog with two hundred legs. Deadly enough, no doubt, on a big flat space, against an imaginary enemy right in front. How it would work on broken rocks, in the tipping rain, in a tangled wood, Logen was less sure. Those men would tire quickly, in all that weight of armour, and if the squares could be broken, what would they do? Men who were used to always having others at their shoulder? Could they fight alone?

He plodded on, through wide courtyards and neat gardens, past gurgling fountains and proud statues, down clean lanes and broad avenues. He wandered up and down narrow stairways, across bridges over streams, over roads, over other bridges. He saw guards in a dozen different splendid liveries, guarding a hundred different gates and walls and doors, every one eyeing him with the same deep suspicion. The sun climbed in the sky, the tall white buildings slid by until Logen was footsore and half lost, his neck aching from looking always upwards.

The only constant was the monstrous tower which loomed high, high over everything else, making the greatest of the great buildings seem mean. It was always there, glimpsed out of the corner of your eye, peering over the tops of the roofs in the distance. Logen's footsteps dragged him slowly closer and closer to it, until he came to a neglected corner of the citadel in its very shadow.

He found an old bench beside a ragged lawn near a great crumbling building, coated with moss and ivy, its steep roofs sagging in the middles and missing tiles. He slumped down, puffing out his cheeks, and frowned up at that enormous shape beyond the walls, cut out dark against the blue, a man made mountain of dry, stark, dead stones. No plants clung to that looming mass, not even a clump of moss in the cracks between the great blocks. The House of the Maker, Bayaz had called it. It looked like no house that Logen had ever seen. There were no roofs above, no doors or windows in those naked walls. A cluster of mighty, sharp-edged tiers of rock. What need could there ever be to build a thing so big? Who was this Maker anyway? Was this all he made? A great big, useless house?

"You mind if I sit?" There was a woman looking down at Logen, more what he would have called a woman than those strange, ghostly things in the park. A pretty woman in a white dress, face framed by dark hair.

"Do I mind? No. It's a funny thing, but no one else wants to sit with me."

She dropped down at the far end of the bench, resting her chin on her hands, her elbows on her knees, gazing up without interest at the looming tower. "Perhaps they're afraid of you."

Logen watched a man hurry past with a sheaf of papers under his arm, staring at him with wide eyes. "I'm starting to think the same thing."

"You do look a little dangerous."

"Hideous is the word you're looking for."

"I usually find the words I'm looking for, and I say dangerous."

"Well, looks can lie."

She lifted an eyebrow, looking him slowly up and down. "You must be a man of peace then."

"Huh . . . not entirely." They looked at each other sidelong. She didn't seem afraid, or scornful, or even interested. "Why aren't you scared?"

"I'm from Angland, I know your people. Besides," and she let her head drop onto the back of the bench, "no one else will talk to me. I'm desperate."

Logen stared at the stump of his middle finger, waggled it back and forth as far as it would go. "You'd have to be. I'm Logen."

"Good for you. I'm nobody."

"Everybody's somebody."

"Not me. I'm nothing. I'm invisible."

Logen frowned at her, turned sideways to him, lounging back on the bench in the sun, her long smooth neck stretched out, chest rising and falling gently. "I see you."

She rolled her head to look at him. "You . . . are a gentleman."

Logen snorted with laughter. He'd been called a lot of things in his time, but never that. The young woman didn't join him in his amusement. "I don't belong here," she muttered to herself.

"Neither one of us."

"No. But this is my home." She got up from the bench. "Goodbye, Logen."

"Fare you well, nobody." He watched her turn and walk slowly away, shaking his head. Bayaz had been right. The place was strange, but the people were stranger still.

Logen woke with a painful start, blinked and stared wildly about him. Dark. Not quite entirely dark, of course, there was still the ever-present glow of the city. He thought he'd heard something, but there was nothing now. It was hot. Hot and close and strangling, even with the sticky draught from the open window. He groaned, threw the damp blankets down around his waist, rubbed the sweat from his chest and wiped it on the wall behind him. The light nagged at his eyelids. And that was not the worst of his problems. Say one thing for Logen Ninefingers, say that he needs to piss.

Unfortunately, you couldn't just piss in a pot in this place. They had a special thing, like a flat wooden shelf with a hole in it, in a little room. He'd peered down into that hole when they first arrived, wondering what it could be for. It seemed like a long way down, and it smelled bad. Malacus had explained it to him. A pointless and barbaric invention. You had to sit there, on the hard wood, an unpleasant draught blowing round your fruits. But that was civilisation, so far as Logen could tell. People with nothing better to do, dreaming up ways to make easy things difficult.

He floundered out of bed and picked his way to where he remembered the door being, bent over with his arms feeling about in front of him. Too light to sleep, but too dark to actually see anything. "Fucking civilisation," he muttered to himself as he fumbled with the latch on the door, sliding his bare feet cautiously into the big circular room at the centre of their chambers.

It was cool in here, very cool. The cold air felt good on his bare skin after the damp heat of his bedroom. Why wasn't he sleeping in here, instead of that oven next door? He squinted at the shadowy walls, face all screwed up with the painful fuzz of sleep, trying to work out which blurry door led to the pissing-shelf. Knowing his luck he'd probably blunder into Bayaz's room and accidentally piss on the First of the Magi while he was asleep. That would be just the thing to sweeten the wizard's temper.

He took a step forward. There was a clunk and a rattle as his leg barged into the corner of the table. He cursed, grabbing at his bruised shin—then he remembered the jar. He lunged and caught it by the rim just before it fell. His eyes were adjusting to the half-light now, and he could just make out the flowers painted on the cold, shiny surface. He moved to put it back on the table, but then it occurred to him. Why go any further when he had a perfectly good pot right there? He glanced furtively round the room, swinging the jar into position . . . then froze.

He was not alone.

A tall, slender figure, vague in the half-light. He could just make out long hair, blowing gently in the breeze from the open window. He strained against the darkness, but he couldn't see the face.

"Logen . . ." A woman's voice, soft and low. He didn't like the sound of it one bit. It was cold in the room, very cold. He took a firm grip on the jar.

"Who are you?" he croaked, voice suddenly loud in the dead stillness. Was he dreaming? He shook his head, squeezed the jar in his hand. It all felt real. Horribly real.

"Logen . . ." The woman moved silently towards him. Soft light from the window caught the side of her face. A white cheek, a shadowy eye-socket, the corner of a mouth, then sunk in darkness again. There was something familiar . . . Logen's mind fumbled for it as he backed away, eyes fixed on her outline, keeping the table between them.

"What do you want?" He had a cold feeling in his chest, a bad feeling. He knew he should be shouting for help, raising the others, but somehow he had to know who it was. Had to know. The air was freezing, Logen could almost see his breath smoking before his face. His wife was dead, he knew that, dead and cold and gone back to the mud, long ago and far away. He'd seen the village, burned to ashes, full of corpses. His wife was dead . . . and yet . . .

"Thelfi?" he whispered.

"Logen . . ." Her voice! Her voice! His mouth dropped open. She reached out for him, through the light from the window. Pale hand, pale fingers, long, white nails. The room was icy, icy cold. "Logen!"

"You're dead!" He raised the jar, ready to smash it down on her head. The hand reached out, fingers spreading wide.

Suddenly, the room was bright as day. Brighter. Brilliant, searing bright. The murky outlines of the doors, the furniture, were transformed into hard white edges, black shadows. Logen squeezed his eyes shut, shielded them with his arm, dropped back gasping against the wall. There was a deafening crash like a landslide, a tearing and splintering like a great tree falling, a stink of burning wood. Logen opened one eye a crack, peered out from between his fingers.

The chamber was strangely altered. Dark, once more, but less dark than before. Light filtered in through a great ragged hole in the wall where the window used to be. Two of the chairs had gone, a third teetered on three legs, broken edges glowing faintly, smouldering like sticks that had been a long time in a fire. The table, standing right beside him just a moment before, was sheared in half on the other side of the room. Part of the ceiling had been torn away from the rafters and the floor was littered with chunks of stone and plaster, broken lengths of wood and fragments of glass. Of the strange woman there was no sign.

Bayaz picked his way unsteadily through the wreckage towards the gaping hole in the wall, nightshirt flapping around his thick calves, and peered out into the night. "It's gone."

"It?" Logen stared at the steaming hole. "She knew my name . . ."

The wizard stumbled over to the last remaining intact chair and flung himself into it like a man exhausted. "An Eater, perhaps. Sent by Khalul."

"A what?" asked Logen, baffled. "Sent by who?"

Bayaz wiped sweat from his face. "You wanted not to know."

"That's true." Logen couldn't deny it. He rubbed at his chin, staring out of the ragged patch of night sky, wondering whether now might be a good time to change his mind. But by then it was too late. There was a frantic hammering at the door.

"Get that, would you?" Logen stumbled stupidly through the debris and slid back the bolt. An angry-looking guard shouldered his way past, a lamp in one hand, drawn sword in the other.

"There was a noise!" The light from his lamp swept over the wreckage, found the ragged edge of the ripped plaster, the broken stone, the empty night sky beyond. "Shit," he whispered.

"We had an uninvited guest," muttered Logen.

"Er . . . I must notify . . ." the guard looked thoroughly confused ". . . somebody." He tripped and nearly fell over a fallen beam as he backed towards the door. Logen heard his footsteps rattling away down the stairs.

"What's an Eater?" There was no reply. The wizard was asleep, eyes closed, a deep frown on his face, chest moving slowly. Logen looked down. He was surprised to see he still had the pot, beautiful and delicate, clasped tightly in his right hand. He carefully swept clear a space on the floor and set the jar down, in amongst the wreckage.

One of the doors banged open and Logen's heart jumped. It was Malacus, wild-eyed and staring, hair sticking up off his head at all angles. "What the . . ." He stumbled to the hole and peered gingerly out into the night. "Shit!"

"Malacus, what's an Eater?"

Quai's head snapped round to look at Logen, his face a picture of horror. "It's forbidden," he whispered, "to eat the flesh of men . . ."

QUESTIONS

Glokta heaped porridge into his mouth as fast as he could, hoping to get half a meal's worth down before his gorge began to rise. He swallowed, coughed, shuddered. He shoved the bowl away, as though its very presence offended him. *Which, in fact, it does.* "This had better be important, Severard," he grumbled.

The Practical scraped his greasy hair back with one hand. "Depends what you mean by important. It's about our magical friends."

"Ah, the First of the Magi and his bold companions. What about them?"

"There was some manner of a disturbance at their chambers last night. Someone broke in, they say. There was a fight of some sort. Seems as if some damage was done."

"Someone? Some sort? Some damage?" Glokta gave a disapproving shake of his head. "Seems? Seems isn't good enough for us, Severard."

"Well it'll have to be, this time. The guard was a little thin on the details. Looked damn worried, if you ask me." Severard sprawled a little deeper into his chair, shoulders hunching up around his ears. "Someone needs to go and look into it, might as well be us. You can get a good look at them, close up. Ask them some questions, maybe."

"Where are they?"

"You'll love this. The Tower of Chains."

Glokta scowled as he sucked a few bits of porridge from his empty gums. *Of course. And right at the top, I bet. Lots of steps.* "Anything else?"

"The Northman went for a stroll yesterday, walked in circles round half the Agriont. We watched him, of course." The Practical sniffed and adjusted his mask. "Ugly bastard."

"Ah, the infamous Northman. Did he commit any outrages? Rape and murder, buildings aflame, that type of thing?"

"Not much, being honest. A tedious morning for everyone. Wandered around and gawped at things. He spoke to a couple of people."

"Anyone we know?"

"No one important. One of the carpenters working on the stands for the Contest. A clerk on the Kingsway. There was some girl near the University. He spoke to her for a while."

"A girl?"

Severard's eyes grinned. "That's right, and a nice-looking one too. What was her name?" He snapped his fingers. "I made sure I found it out. Her brother's with the King's Own . . . West, something West . . ."

"Ardee."

"That's the one! You know her?"

"Hmm." Glokta licked at his empty gums. *She asked me how I was. I remember.* "What did they have to talk about?"

The Practical raised his eyebrows. "Probably nothing. She's from Angland though, not been in the city long. Might be some connection. You want me to bring her in? We could soon find out."

"No!" snapped Glokta. "No. No need. Her brother used to be a friend of mine."

"Used to be."

"No one touches her, Severard, you hear?"

The Practical shrugged. "If you say so, Inquisitor. If you say so."

"I do."

There was a pause. "So we're done with the Mercers then, are we?" Severard sounded almost wistful.

"It would seem so. They're finished. Nothing but some cleaning up to do."

"Some lucrative cleaning up, I daresay."

"I daresay," said Glokta sourly. "But his Eminence feels our talents will be better used elsewhere." *Like watching fake wizards.* "Hope you didn't lose out on your little property by the docks."

Severard shrugged. "I wouldn't be surprised if you need somewhere away from prying eyes again, before too long. It'll still be there. At the right price. Shame to leave a job half done is all."

True. Glokta paused for a moment, considering. *Dangerous. The Arch Lector said go no further. Very dangerous, to disobey, and yet I smell something. It niggles, to leave a loose end, whatever his Eminence might say.* "There might be one more thing."

"Really?"

"Yes, but keep it subtle. Do you know anything about banks?"

"Big buildings. They lend people money."

Glokta gave a thin smile. "I had no idea you were such an expert. There's one in particular I'm interested in. Name of Valint and Balk."

"Never heard of them, but I can ask around."

"Just keep it discreet, Severard, do you understand me? No one can know about this. I mean it."

"Discretion is what I'm all about, chief, ask anyone. Discreet. That's me. Known for it."

"You'd better be, Severard. You had better be." *Or it could be both our heads.*

Glokta sat, wedged into the embrasure with his back against the stones and his left leg stretched out in front of him—a searing, pulsing furnace of pain. He expected pain of course, every moment of every day. *But this is something just a bit special.*

Every breath was a rattling moan through rigid jaws. Every tiniest movement was a mighty task. He remembered how Marshal Varuz had made him run up and down these steps when he was training for the Contest, years ago. *I took them three at a time, up and down without a second thought. Now look at me. Who would have thought it could come to this?*

His trembling body ran with sweat, his stinging eyes ran with tears, his burning nose dripped watery snot. *All this water flowing out of me, and yet I'm thirsty as hell. Where's the sense in that?* Where was the sense in any of it? *What if someone should come past, and see me like this? The terrifying scourge of the Inquisition, flopped on his arse in a window, barely able to move? Will I force a noncha-*

lant smile onto this rigid mask of agony? Will I pretend that all is well? That I often come here, to sprawl beside the stairs? Or will I weep and scream and beg for help?

But no one passed. He lay there, wedged in that narrow space, three-quarters of the way up the Tower of Chains, the back of his head resting on the cool stones, his trembling knees drawn up in front of him. *Sand dan Glokta, master swordsman, dashing cavalry officer, what glorious future might he have in front of him? There was a time when I could run for hours. Run and run and never tire.* He could feel a trickle of sweat running down his back. *Why do I do this? Why the hell would anyone do this? I could stop today. I could go home to mother. But then what?*

Then what?

"Inquisitor, I'm glad you're here."

Good for you, bastard. I'm not. Glokta leaned against the wall at the top of the stairs, such teeth as he had grinding against his gums.

"They're inside, it's quite a mess . . ." Glokta's hand trembled, the tip of his cane rattling against the stones. His head swam. The guard was blurry and dim through his twitching eyelids. "Are you alright?" He loomed forwards, one arm outstretched.

Glokta looked up. "Just get the fucking door, fool!"

The man jumped away, hurried to the door and pushed it open. Every part of Glokta longed to give up and sprawl on his face, but he willed himself upright. He forced one foot before the other, forced his breath to come even, forced his shoulders back and his head high, and swept imperiously past the guard, every part of his body singing with pain. What he saw beyond the doors almost broke his veneer of composure however.

Yesterday these were some of the finest rooms in the Agriont. They were reserved for the most honoured of guests, the most important of foreign dignitaries. Yesterday. A gaping hole was ripped out of one wall where the window should have been, the sky beyond blinding bright after the darkness of the stairwell. A section of the ceiling had collapsed, broken timbers and shreds of plaster hanging down into the room. The floor was strewn with chunks of stone, splinters of glass, torn fragments of coloured cloth. The antique furniture had been smashed to scattered pieces, broken edges charred and blackened as if by fire.

Only one chair, half a table, and a tall ornamental jar, strangely pristine in the middle of the rubble-strewn floor, had escaped the destruction.

In the midst of this expensive wreckage stood a confused and sickly seeming young man. He looked up as Glokta picked his way through the rubble round the doorway, tongue darting nervously over his lips, evidently on edge. *Has anyone ever looked more of a fraud?*

"Er, good morning?" The young man's fingers twitched nervously at his gown, a heavy thing, stitched with arcane symbols. *And doesn't he look uncomfortable in it? If this man is a wizard's apprentice, I am the Emperor of Gurkhul.*

"I am Glokta. From his Majesty's Inquisition. I have been sent to investigate this . . . unfortunate business. I was expecting someone older."

"Oh, yes, sorry, I am Malacus Quai," stammered the young man, "apprentice to great Bayaz, the First of the Magi, great in high art and learned in deep—" *Kneel, kneel before me! I am the mighty Emperor of Gurkhul!*

"Malacus . . ." Glokta cut him off rudely ". . . Quai. You are from the Old Empire?"

"Why yes," the young man brightened slightly at that. "Do you know my—"

"No. Not at all." The pale face sagged. "Were you here last night?"

"Er, yes, I was asleep, next door. I'm afraid I didn't see anything though . . ." Glokta stared at him, intent and unblinking, trying to work him out. The apprentice coughed and looked at the floor, as if wondering what to clean up first. *Can this really make the Arch Lector nervous? A miserable actor. His whole manner reeks of deception.*

"Someone saw something, though?"

"Well, erm, Master Ninefingers, I suppose—"

"Ninefingers?"

"Yes, our Northern companion." The young man brightened. "A warrior of great renown, a champion, a prince among his—"

"You, from the Old Empire. He, a Northman. What a cosmopolitan band you are."

"Well yes, ha ha, we do, I suppose—"

"Where is Ninefingers now?"

"Still asleep I think, er, I could wake him—"

"Would you be so kind?" Glokta tapped his cane on the floor. "It was quite a climb, and I would rather not come back later."

"No, er, of course . . . sorry." He hastened over to one of the doors and Glokta turned away, pretending to examine the gaping wound in the wall while grimacing in agony and biting his lip to keep from wailing like a sick child. He seized hold of the broken stones at the edge of the hole with his free hand, squeezing them as hard as he could.

As the spasm passed he began to take more interest in the damage. Even this high up the wall was a good four feet thick, solidly built from rubble bonded with mortar, faced with cut stone blocks. It would take a rock from a truly mighty catapult to make such a breach, or a team of strong workmen going night and day for a week. *A giant siege engine or a group of labourers would doubtless have attracted the attention of the guards. So how was it made?* Glokta ran his hand over the cracked stones. He had once heard rumours that in the far south they made a kind of blasting powder. *Could a little powder have done this?*

The door opened and Glokta turned to see a big man ducking under the low lintel, buttoning his shirt with slow, heavy hands. A thoughtful kind of slowness. *As if he could move quickly but doesn't see the point.* His hair was a tangled mass, his lumpy face badly scarred. The middle finger of his left hand was missing. *Hence Ninefingers. How very imaginative.*

"Sleeping late?"

The Northman nodded. "Your city is too hot for me—it keeps me up at night and makes me sleepy in the day."

Glokta's leg was throbbing, his back was groaning, his neck was stiff as a dry branch. It was all he could do to keep his agony a secret. He would have given anything to sprawl in that one undamaged chair and scream his head off. *But I must stand, and trade words with these charlatans.* "Could you explain to me what happened here?"

Ninefingers shrugged. "I needed to piss in the night. I saw someone in the room." He had little trouble with the common tongue, it seemed, even if the content was hardly polite.

"Did you see who this someone was?"

"No. It was a woman, I saw that much." He worked his shoulders, clearly uncomfortable.

"A woman, really?" *This story becomes more ridiculous by the second.* "Anything else? Can we narrow our search beyond half the population?"

"It was cold. Very cold."

"Cold?" *Of course, why not? On one of the hottest nights of the year.*

Glokta stared into the Northman's eyes for a long time, and he stared back. Dark, cool blue eyes, deeply set. *Not the eyes of an idiot. He may look an ape, but he doesn't talk like one. He thinks before he speaks, then says no more than he has to. This is a dangerous man.*

"What is your business in the city, Master Ninefingers?"

"I came with Bayaz. If you want to know his business you can ask him. Honestly, I don't know."

"He pays you then?"

"No."

"You follow him out of loyalty?"

"Not exactly."

"But you are his servant?"

"No. Not really." The Northman scratched slowly at his stubbly jaw. "I don't know what I am."

A big, ugly liar is what you are. But how to prove it? Glokta waved his cane around the shattered chamber. "How did your intruder cause so much damage?"

"Bayaz did that."

"He did? How?"

"Art, he calls it."

"Art?"

"Base magic is wild and dangerous," intoned the apprentice pompously, as though he were saying something of great importance, "for it comes from the Other Side, and to touch the world below is fraught with peril. The Magus tempers magic with knowledge, and thus produces high art, but like the smith or the—"

"The Other Side?" snapped Glokta, putting a sharp end to the young moron's stream of drivel. "The world below? Hell, do you mean? Magic? Do you know any magic, Master Ninefingers?"

"Me?" The Northman chuckled. "No." He thought about it for a moment and then added, almost as an afterthought, "I can speak to the spirits though."

"The spirits, is that so?" *For pity's sake.* "Perhaps they could tell us who this intruder was?"

"I'm afraid not." Ninefingers shook his head sadly, either missing Glokta's sarcasm or choosing to ignore it. "There are none left awake in this place. They are sleeping here. They have been for a long time."

"Ah, of course." *Well past spirits' bedtime. I tire of this nonsense.* "You come from Bethod?"

"You could say that." It was Glokta who was surprised. He had expected at best a sharp intake of breath, a hurried effort at concealment, not a frank admission. Ninefingers did not even blink however. "I was once his champion."

"Champion?"

"I fought ten duels for him."

Glokta groped for words. "Did you win?"

"I was lucky."

"You realise, of course, that Bethod has invaded the Union?"

"I do." Ninefingers sighed. "I should have killed that bastard long ago, but I was young then, and stupid. Now I doubt I'll get another chance, but that's the way of things. You have to be . . . what's the word for it?"

"Realistic," said Quai.

Glokta frowned. A moment ago, he had teetered on the brink of making sense of all this nonsense, but the moment had slipped away and things made less sense than ever. He stared at Ninefingers, but that scarred face held no answers, only more questions. *Talking with spirits? Bethod's champion but his enemy? Assaulted by a mysterious woman in the dead of night? And he doesn't even know why he's here? A clever liar tells as much truth as he can, but this one tells so many lies I hardly know where to begin.*

"Ah, we have a guest!" An old man stepped into the room, thickset and stocky with a short grey beard, vigorously rubbing his bald head with a cloth. *So this is Bayaz.* He threw himself down in the one intact chair, moving with none of the grace one would expect from an important historical figure. "I must apologise. I was taking advantage of the bath. A very fine bath. I have been bathing every day since we arrived here at the Agriont. I grew so besmirched with the dirt of the road that I have positively seized upon the opportunity to be clean again." The old man rubbed his hand over his hairless scalp with a faint hissing sound.

Glokta mentally compared his features to those of Bayaz's statue in the Kingsway. *There is hardly anything uncanny about the resemblance. Half as commanding and a great deal shorter. Given an hour I could find five old men who looked more convincing. If I took a razor to Arch Lector Sult, I could do better.* Glokta glanced at his shiny pate. *I wonder if he takes a razor to that every morning?*

"And you are?" asked the supposed Bayaz.

"Inquisitor Glokta."

"Ah, one of His Majesty's Inquisitors. We are honoured!"

"Oh no, the honour is mine. You, after all, are the legendary Bayaz, First of the Magi."

The old man glared back at him, his green eyes prickly hard. "Legendary is perhaps a shade too much, but I am Bayaz."

"Your companion, Master Ninefingers, was just describing last night's events to me. A colourful tale. He claims that you caused . . . all this."

The old man snorted. "I am not in the habit of welcoming uninvited guests."

"So I see."

"Alas, there was some damage to the suite. In my experience one should act quickly and decisively. The pieces can always be picked up afterward."

"Of course. Forgive my ignorance, Master Bayaz, but how, precisely, was the damage caused?"

The old man smiled. "You can understand that we do not share the secrets of our order with just anyone, and I am afraid that I already have an apprentice." He indicated the unconvincing youth.

"We met. In simple terms then, perhaps, that I might understand?"

"You would call it magic."

"Magic. I see."

"Indeed. It is, after all, what we Magi are best known for."

"Mmm. I don't suppose you would be kind enough to demonstrate, for my benefit?"

"Oh no!" The so-called wizard gave a comfortable laugh. "I don't do tricks."

This old fool is as hard to fathom as the Northman. The one barely speaks, while the other talks and talks but says nothing. "I must admit to being somewhat at a loss as to how this intruder got in." Glokta glanced round the room, examining the possible means of entrance. "The guard saw nothing, which leaves the window."

He shuffled cautiously to the hole and peered out. There had been a small balcony, but a few stubby splinters of stone were all that remained. Otherwise the wall fell smooth and sheer all the way to the glittering water far, far below. "That's quite a climb to make, especially in a dress. An impossible one, wouldn't you say? How do you think this woman made it?"

The old man snorted. "Do you want me to do your job for you? Perhaps she clambered up the latrine chute!" The Northman looked deeply troubled by that suggestion. "Why don't you catch her and ask her? Isn't that what you're here for?"

Touchy, touchy, and consummately acted. An air of injured innocence so convincing, he almost has me believing this garbage. Almost, but not quite. "Therein lies the problem. There is no sign of your mysterious intruder. No body has been recovered. Some wood, small pieces of furniture, the stones from the wall, they were scattered widely in the streets below. But nothing of any intruder, of either sex."

The old man stared back at him, a hard frown beginning to form on his face. "Perhaps the body burned to nothing. Perhaps it was torn apart, into pieces too small to see, or boiled away into the air. Magic is not always precise, or predictable, even in the hands of a master. Such things can happen. Easily. Particularly when I become annoyed."

"I fear I must risk your annoyance, though. It has occurred to me that you might not, in fact, be Bayaz, the First of the Magi."

"Indeed?" The old man's bushy eyebrows drew together.

"I must at least entertain the possibility . . ." a tense stillness had settled on the room ". . . that you are an impostor."

"A fraud?" snapped the so-called Magus. The pale young man lowered his head and backed quietly away towards the wall. Glokta felt suddenly very alone in the midst of that rubble strewn circle, alone and increasingly unsure of himself, but he soldiered on.

"It had occurred to me that this whole event might have been staged for our benefit. A convenient demonstration of your magical powers."

"Convenient?" Hissed the bald old man, his voice unnaturally loud. "Convenient, say you? It would be convenient if I was left to enjoy a night's sleep uninterrupted. Convenient if I was now sitting in my old chair on the Closed Council. Convenient if people took my word as law, the way they used to, without asking a lot of damn fool questions!"

The resemblance to the statue on the Kingsway was suddenly much increased. There, now, was the frown of command, the sneer of contempt, the threat of terrible anger. The old man's words seemed to press on Glokta like a great weight, driving the breath from his body, threatening to crush him to his knees, cutting into his skull, and leaving behind a creeping shred of doubt. He glanced up at the yawning hole in the wall. *Powder? Catapults? Labourers? Is there not a simpler explanation?* The world seemed to shift around him, as it had in the Arch Lector's study a few days before, his mind turned the pieces, pulling them apart, putting them together. *What if they are simply telling the truth? What if . . .*

No! Glokta forced the idea from his mind. He lifted his head and gave the old man a sneer of his own to think about. *An aging actor with a shaved head and a plausible manner. Nothing more.* "If you are as you say, you have nothing to fear from my questions, or from your answers."

The old man cracked a smile and the strange pressure was suddenly released. "Your candour at least, Inquisitor, is quite refreshing. No doubt you will do your utmost to prove your theory. I wish you luck. I, as you say, have nothing to fear. I would only ask that you find some proof of this deception before bothering us again."

Glokta bowed stiffly. "I will try to do so," he said, and made for the door.

"There is one more thing!" The old man was looking towards the gaping hole in the wall. "Would it be possible to find some other chambers? The wind blows rather chill through these."

"I will look into it."

"Good. Perhaps somewhere with fewer steps. Damn things play hell with my knees these days." *Indeed? There, at least, we can agree.*

Glokta gave the three of them one last inspection. The bald old man stared back, his face a blank wall. The lanky youth glanced up anxiously then quickly turned away. The Northman was still frowning towards the latrine door. *Charlatans, impostors, spies. But how to prove it?* "Good day, gentlemen." And he limped towards the stairs with as much dignity as he could muster.

NOBILITY

Jezal scraped the last fair hairs from the side of his jaw and washed the razor off in the bowl. Then he wiped it on the cloth, closed it and placed it carefully on the table, admiring the way the sunlight glinted on the mother-of-pearl handle.

He wiped his face, and then—his favourite part of the day—gazed at himself in the looking glass. It was a good one, newly imported from Visserine, a present from his father: an oval of bright, smooth glass in a frame of lavishly carved dark wood. A fitting surround for such a handsome man as the one gazing happily back at him. Honestly, handsome hardly did him justice.

"You're quite the beauty aren't you?" Jezal said to himself, smiling as he ran his fingers over the smooth skin of his jaw. And what a jaw it was. He had often been told it was his best feature, not that there was anything whatever wrong with the rest of him. He turned to the right, then to the left, the better to admire that magnificent chin. Not too heavy, not brutish, but not too light either, not womanly or weak. A man's jaw, no doubt, with a slight cleft in the chin, speaking of strength and authority, but sensitive and thoughtful too. Had there ever been a jaw like it? Perhaps some king, or hero of legend, once had one almost as fine. It was a noble jaw, that much was clear. No commoner could ever have had a chin so grand.

It must have come from his mother's side of the family, Jezal supposed. His father had rather a weak chin. His brothers too, come to think of it. You had to feel a little sorry for them, he had got all the looks in his family.

"And most of the talent too," he murmured happily to himself. He turned away from the mirror with some reluctance, striding into his living room, pulling his shirt on and buttoning it up the front. He had to look his best today. The thought gave him a little shiver of nerves, starting in his stomach, creeping up his windpipe, lodging in his throat.

By now, the gates would be open. A steady flood of people would be filing into the Agriont, taking their seats on the great wooden benches in the Square of Marshals. Thousands of them. Everyone who was anyone, and plenty more who weren't. They were already gathering: shouting, jostling, excited, waiting for . . . him. Jezal coughed and tried to push the thought from his mind. He had kept himself awake with it for half the night already.

He moved over to the table, where the breakfast tray was sitting. He picked up a sausage absently in his fingertips and took a bite off the end, chewing it without relish. He wrinkled his nose and tossed it back in the dish. He had no appetite this morning. He was just wiping his fingers on the cloth when he noticed something lying on the floor by the door, a slip of paper. He bent and picked it up, unfolded it. A single line, written in a neat, precise hand:

Meet me tonight, at the statue of Harod the Great near the Four Corners

— A.

"Shit," he murmured, disbelieving, reading the line over and over. He folded the paper shut, glancing nervously round the room. Jezal could only think of one "A." He had pushed her to the back of his mind the last couple of days, he had been spending every spare moment training. This brought it all back though, and no mistake.

"Shit!" He opened the paper and read the line again. Meet me tonight? He could not escape a slight flush of satisfaction at that, and it slowly became a very distinct glow of pleasure. His mouth curled into a gormless grin. Secret meetings in the darkness? His skin prickled with excitement at the prospect. But secrets have a way of coming to the surface, and what if her brother found out? That thought brought on a fresh rush of nerves. He took the slip of paper in both hands, ready to tear it in half, but at the last moment he folded it instead, and slipped it into his pocket.

As Jezal made his way down the tunnel he could already hear the crowd. A strange, echoing murmur, seeming to come out of the very stones. He had heard it before, of course, as a spectator at last year's Contest, but it hadn't made his skin sweat and his guts turn over then. Being part of the audience is a world away from being part of the show.

He slowed for a moment, then stopped, closing his eyes and leaning against the wall, the noise of the crowd rushing in his ears, trying to breathe deep and compose himself.

"Don't worry, I know just how you feel." Jezal felt West's consoling hand on his shoulder. "I nearly turned around and ran the first time, but it'll pass as soon as the steels are drawn, believe me."

"Yes," mumbled Jezal, "of course." He doubted that West knew exactly how he felt. The man might have been through a couple of Contests before, but Jezal thought it unlikely he had been considering a surreptitious meeting with his best friend's sister the same night. He wondered whether West would be quite so considerate if he knew the contents of the letter in Jezal's breast pocket. It did not seem likely.

"We'd better get moving. Wouldn't want them to start without us."

"No." Jezal took one last deep breath, opened his eyes and blew out hard. Then he pushed himself away from the wall and strode rapidly down the tunnel. He felt a sudden surge of panic—where were his steels? He cast about him desperately, then breathed a long sigh. They were in his hand.

There was quite a crowd in the hall at the far end: trainers, seconds, friends, family members and hangers-on. You could tell who the contestants were, though; the fifteen young men with steels clutched tightly in their hands. The sense of fear was palpable, and contagious. Everywhere Jezal looked he saw pale, nervous faces, sweaty foreheads, anxious eyes darting around. It wasn't helped by the noise of the crowd, ominously loud beyond the closed double doors at the far end of the room, swelling and subsiding like a stormy sea.

There was only one man there who didn't seem at all bothered by the occasion, leaning against the wall on his own with one foot up on the plaster and his head tipped back, staring down his nose at the assembly through barely open eyes. Most of the contestants were lithe, stringy, athletic. He was anything but. A big, heavy man with hair shaved to dark stubble. He had a great thick neck and a doorstep of a jaw—the jaw of a commoner, Jezal rather thought, but a large and powerful commoner with a mean streak. Jezal might have taken him for someone's servant but that he had a pair of steels dangling loosely from one hand.

"Gorst," West whispered in Jezal's ear.

"Huh. Looks more like a labourer than a swordsman to me."

"Maybe, but looks can lie." The sound of the crowd was slowly fading, and the nervy chatter within the room subsided along with it. West raised his eyebrows. "The King's address," he whispered.

"My friends! My countrymen! My fellow citizens of the Union!" came a ringing voice, clearly audible even through the heavy doors.

"Hoff," snorted West. "Even here he takes the King's place. Why doesn't he just put the crown on and have done with it?"

"One month ago today," came the far-off bellow of the Lord Chamberlain, "fellows of mine on the Closed Council put forward the question . . . should there be a Contest this year?" Boos and shouts of wild disapproval were heard from the crowd. "A fair question!" cried Hoff, "for we are at war! A deadly struggle in the North! The very liberties which we hold so dear, the very freedoms which make us the envy of the world, our very way of life, stand threatened by the savage!"

A clerk began making his way around the room, separating the contestants from their families, their trainers, their friends. "Good luck," said West, clapping Jezal on the shoulder, "I'll see you out there." Jezal's mouth was dry, and he could only nod.

"And these were brave men who asked the question!" Boomed out Hoff's voice from beyond the doors. "Wise men! Patriots all! My stalwart colleagues on the Closed Council! I understood why they might think, there should be no Contest this year!" There was a long pause. "But I said to them, no!"

An eruption of manic cheering. "No! No!" screamed the crowd. Jezal was

ushered into line along with the other contestants, two abreast, eight pairs.
He fussed with his steels as the Lord Chamberlain droned on, though he'd
checked them twenty times already.

"No, I said to them! Should we allow these barbarians, these animals of
the frozen North, to tread upon our way of life? Should we allow this beacon
of freedom amidst the darkness of the world to be extinguished? No, I said
to them! Our liberty is not for sale at any price! On this, my friends, my
countrymen, my fellow citizens of the Union, on this you may depend . . . we
will win this war!"

Another great ocean swell of approval. Jezal swallowed, glanced nervously around. Bremer dan Gorst was standing there beside him. The big
bastard had the temerity to wink, grinning as if he hadn't a care in the world.
"Damn idiot," whispered Jezal, but he took care that his lips didn't move.

"And so, my friends, and so," came Hoff's final cries, "what finer occasion
could there be than when we stand upon the very brink of peril? To celebrate
the skill, the strength, the prowess, of some of our nation's bravest sons! My
fellow citizens, my countrymen of the Union, I give you your contestants!"

The doors were heaved open and the roar of the crowd beyond rushed
into the hall and made the rafters ring: suddenly, deafeningly loud. The front
pair of swordsmen began to stride out through the bright archway, then the
next pair, then the next. Jezal was sure he would freeze, motionless and
staring like a rabbit, but when his turn came his feet stepped off manfully
next to Gorst's, the heels of his highly polished boots clicking across the tiled
floor and through the high doorway.

The Square of Marshals was transformed. All around, great banks of
seating had been erected, stretching back, and back, and up, and up on all
sides, spilling over with a boiling multitude. The contestants filed down a
deep valley between the towering stands towards the centre of this great
arena, the beams, and struts, and tree-trunk supports like a shadowy forest on
either side. Directly before them, seeming very far away, the fencing circle
had been laid, a little ring of dry yellow grass in the midst of a sea of faces.

Down near the front Jezal could make out the features of the rich and
noble. Dressed in their best, shading their eyes from the bright sun, on the
whole fashionably disinterested in the spectacle before them. Further back,

higher up, the figures became less distinct, the clothes less fine. The vast majority of the crowd were mere blobs and specks of colour, crammed in around the distant edge of the dizzying bowl, but the commoners made up for their distance with their excitement: cheering, shouting, standing up on their toes and waving their arms in the air. Above them, the tops of the very highest buildings around the square peered over, walls and roofs sticking up like islands in the ocean, the windows and parapets crammed with minuscule onlookers.

Jezal blinked at this great display of humanity. Part of him was aware that his mouth was hanging open, but too small a part to close it. Damn, he felt queasy. He knew he should have eaten something, but it was too late now. What if he puked, right here in front of half the world? He felt that surge of blind panic again. Where did he leave his steels? Where were they? In his hand. In his hand. The crowd roared, and sighed, and wailed, with a myriad of different voices.

The contestants began to move away from the circle. Not all of them would be fighting today, most would only watch. As though there was a need for extra spectators. They began to make their way towards the front rows, but Jezal was not going with them, more was the pity. He made for the enclosures where the contestants prepared to fight.

He flopped down heavily next to West, closed his eyes and wiped his sweaty forehead as the crowd cheered on. Everything was too bright, too loud, too overpowering. Marshal Varuz was nearby, leaning over the side of the enclosure to shout in someone's ear. Jezal stared across the arena at the occupants of the royal box opposite, hoping vainly for a distraction.

"His Majesty the King seems to be enjoying the proceedings," whispered West in Jezal's ear.

"Mmm." The King, in fact, appeared already to have fallen soundly asleep, his crown slipping off at an angle. Jezal wondered idly what would happen if it fell off.

Crown Prince Ladisla was there, fabulously dressed as always, beaming around at the arena with an enormous smile as though everyone was there for him. His younger brother, Prince Raynault, could hardly have looked more different: plain and sober, frowning worriedly at his semi-conscious father. Their mother, the Queen, sat beside them, bolt upright with her chin in the air, studiously pretending that her august husband was wide awake, and that his crown was in no danger of dropping suddenly and painfully into her lap. Between her and Lord Hoff, Jezal's eye was caught by a young woman—very, very beautiful. She was even more expensively dressed than Ladisla, if that was possible, with a chain of huge diamonds round her neck, flashing bright in the sun.

"Who's the woman?" asked Jezal.

"Ah, the Princess Terez," murmured West. "The daughter of Grand Duke Orso, Lord of Talins. She's quite the celebrated beauty, and for once it seems that rumour doesn't exaggerate."

"I thought nothing good ever came from Talins."

"So I've heard, but I think she might be the exception, don't you?" Jezal was not entirely convinced. Spectacular, no doubt, but there was an icy proud look to her eye. "I think the Queen has it in mind that she marry Prince Ladisla." As Jezal watched, the Crown Prince leant across his mother to favour the Princess with some witless banter, then exploded into laughter at his own joke, slapping his knee with merriment. She gave a frosty little smile, radiating contempt even at this distance. Ladisla seemed not to notice though, and Jezal's attention was soon distracted. A tall man in a red coat was striding ponderously towards the circle. The referee.

"It's time," murmured West.

The referee held up his arm with a theatrical flourish, two fingers extended, and turned slowly around, waiting for the hubbub to subside. "Today you will have the pleasure of witnessing *two* bouts of fencing!" he thundered, then thrust up his other hand, three fingers out, as the audience applauded. "Each the best of *three* touches!" He threw up both arms. "*Four* men will fight before you! Two of them will go home . . . empty handed." The referee let one arm drop, shook his head sadly, the crowd sighed. "But two will pass on to the next round!" The crowd bellowed their approval.

"Ready?" asked Marshal Varuz, leaning forwards over Jezal's shoulder.

What a damn fool question. What if he wasn't ready? What then? Call the whole thing off? Sorry everyone, I'm not ready? See you next year? But all Jezal could say was, "Mmm."

"The time has come!" cried the referee, turning slowly around in the centre of the arena, "for our first bout!"

"Jacket!" snapped Varuz.

"Uh." Jezal fumbled with the buttons and pulled his jacket off, rolling up his shirt-sleeves mechanically. He glanced sideways and saw his opponent making similar preparations. A tall, thin young man with long arms and weak, slightly dewy eyes. Hardly the most intimidating looking of adversaries. Jezal noticed his hands were trembling slightly as he took his steels from his second.

"Trained by Sepp dan Vissen, and hailing from Rostod, in Starikland . . ." the referee paused for the greatest effect ". . . Kurtis dan Broya!" There was a wave of enthusiastic clapping. Jezal snorted. These clowns would clap for anyone.

The tall young man got up from his seat and walked purposefully towards the circle, his steels flashing in the sunlight. "Broya!" repeated the referee, as the gangly idiot took his mark. West pulled Jezal's steels from their sheaths. The metallic ringing of the blades made him want to be sick again.

The referee pointed once more towards the contestant's enclosure. "And his opponent today! An officer of the King's Own, and trained by none other than Lord Marshal Varuz!" There was scattered applause and the old soldier beamed happily. "Hailing from Luthar in Midderland but resident here in the Agriont . . . Captain Jezal dan Luthar!" Another surge of cheering, far louder than Broya had received. There was a flurry of sharp cries above the din. Shouted numbers. Odds being offered. Jezal felt another rush of nausea as he got slowly to his feet.

"Good luck." West handed Jezal his naked steels, hilts first.

"He doesn't need luck!" snapped Varuz. "This Broya's a nobody! Just watch his reach! Press him, Jezal, press him!"

It seemed to take forever to reach that ring of short dry grass, the sound of the crowd loud in Jezal's ears but the sound of his heart louder still, turning the grips of his steels round and round in his sweaty palms. "Luthar!" repeated the referee, smiling wide as he watched Jezal approach.

Pointless and irrelevant questions flitted in and out of his mind. Was Ardee watching, in the crowd, wondering whether he would come to meet her that night? Would he get killed in the war? How did they get the grass for the fencing circle into the Square of Marshals? He glanced up at Broya. Was he feeling the same way? The crowd was quiet now, very quiet. The weight of the silence pressed down on Jezal as he took his mark in the circle, pushed his feet into the dry earth. Broya shrugged his shoulders, shook his head, raised his steels. Jezal needed to piss. Needed to piss so badly. What if he pissed himself right now? A big dark stain spreading across his trousers. The man who pissed himself at the Contest. He would never live it down, not if he lived a hundred years.

"Begin!" thundered the referee.

But nothing happened. The two men stood there, facing each other, steels at the ready. Jezal's eyebrow itched. He wanted to scratch it, but how? His opponent licked his lips, then took a cautious step to his left. Jezal did the same. They circled each other warily, shoes crunching gently on the dry grass: slowly, slowly drawing closer together. And as they came closer, Jezal's world contracted to the space between the points of their long steels. Now it was only a stride. Now it was a foot. Now just six inches separated them. Jezal's whole mind was focused on those two glittering points. Three inches. Broya jabbed forward, weakly, and Jezal flicked it away without thinking.

The blades rang gently together and, as though that were a signal pre-arranged with every person in the arena, the shouting began again, scattered calls to begin with:

"Kill him, Luthar!"

"Yes!"

"Jab! Jab!"

But soon dissolving once more into the rumbling, angry sea of the crowd, rising and falling with the movements in the circle.

The more Jezal saw of this lanky idiot, the less daunted he became. His nerves began to subside. Broya jabbed, clumsy, and Jezal barely had to move. Broya cut, without conviction, and Jezal parried, without effort. Broya lunged, positively inept, off-balance and overextended. Jezal stepped around it and jabbed his opponent in the ribs with the blunt point of his long steel. It was all so very easy.

"One for Luthar!" cried the referee, and a surge of cheering ran around the stands. Jezal smiled to himself, basking in the appreciation of the crowd.

Varuz had been right, this boob was nothing to worry about. One more touch and he'd be through to the next round.

He returned to his mark and Broya did the same, rubbing his ribs with one hand and staring at Jezal balefully from beneath his brows. Jezal was not intimidated. Angry looks are only any use if you can fight worth a damn.

"Begin!"

They closed quickly this time, and exchanged a cut or two. Jezal could hardly believe how slowly his opponent was moving. It was as if his swords weighed a ton each. Broya fished around in the air with his long steel, trying to use his reach to pin Jezal down. He had barely used his short steel yet, let alone coordinated the two. Worse still, he was starting to look out of breath, and they'd barely been fencing two minutes. Had he trained at all, this bumpkin? Or had they simply made up the numbers with some servant off the street? Jezal jumped away, danced around his opponent. Broya flapped after him, dogged but incompetent. It was starting to become embarrassing. Nobody enjoys a mismatch, and this dunce's clumsiness was denying Jezal the opportunity to shine.

"Oh come on!" he shouted. A surge of laughter flowed around the stands. Broya gritted his teeth and came on with everything he had, but it wasn't much. Jezal swatted his feeble efforts aside, dodged around them, flowed across the circle while his witless opponent lumbered after, always three steps behind. There was no precision, no speed, no thought. A few minutes before, Jezal had been half-terrified by the prospect of fencing with this gangling fool. Now he was almost bored.

"Hah!" he cried, switching suddenly onto the attack, catching his opponent off-balance with a savage cut, sending him stumbling back. The crowd came alive, roaring their support. He jabbed and jabbed again. Broya blocked desperately, all off-balance, reeled backwards, parried one last time then tripped, his arms flailing, short steel flying out of his hand, and pitched out of the circle onto his arse.

There was a wave of laughter, and Jezal could not help but join in. The poor dolt looked quite amusing, knocked on his back with his legs in the air like some sort of turtle.

"Captain Luthar wins!" roared the referee, "two to nothing!" The laughter turned to jeering as Broya rolled over. He looked on the verge of tears, the oaf. Jezal stepped forwards and offered his hand, but found himself unable to entirely wipe the smirk off his face. His beaten adversary pointedly ignored his help, pushing himself up from the ground and giving him a look half hating, half hurt.

Jezal shrugged pleasantly. "It's not my fault you're shit."

"More?" asked Kaspa, holding out the bottle in a wobbly hand, eyes misted over with too much booze.

"No thanks." Jezal pushed the bottle gently away before Kaspa had the chance to pour. He looked blearily bewildered for a moment, then he turned to Jalenhorm.

"More?"

"Always." The big man slid his glass across the rough table top in a way that said, "I am not drunk," though he clearly was. Kaspa lowered the bottle towards it, squinting at the glass as though it was a great distance away. Jezal watched the neck of the bottle wobbling in the air, then rattling on the edge of the glass. The inevitability of it was almost painful to behold. Wine spilled out across the table, splashing into Jalenhorm's lap.

"You're drunk!" complained the big man, staggering to his feet and brushing at himself with big, drunken hands, knocking his stool over in the process. A few of the other patrons eyed their table with evident disdain.

"Alwaysh," giggled Kaspa.

West looked up briefly from his glass. "You're both drunk."

"Not our fault." Jalenhorm groped for his stool. "It's him!" He pointed an unsteady finger at Jezal.

"He won!" gurgled Kaspa. "You won, didn't you, and now we got to celebrate!"

Jezal wished they didn't have to celebrate quite so much. It was becoming embarrassing.

"My cousin Ariss wa' there—saw whole thing. She was ver' impressed." Kaspa flung his arm round Jezal's shoulder. "Think she's quite shmitten with you . . . shmitten . . . shmitten." He worked his wet lips in Jezal's face, trying to get his mouth round the word. "She's ver' rich you know, ver' rich indeed. Shmitten."

Jezal wrinkled his nose. He had not the slightest interest in that ghostly simpleton of a cousin, however rich she was, and Kaspa's breath stank. "Good . . . lovely." He disentangled himself from the Lieutenant and shoved him away, none too gently.

"So, when are we starting on this business in the North?" demanded Brint, a little too loud, as though he for one couldn't wait to get underway. "Soon I hope, home before winter, eh, Major?"

"Huh," snorted West, frowning to himself, "we'll be lucky to have left before winter, the rate we're going."

Brint looked a little taken aback. "Well, I'm sure we'll give these savages a thrashing, whenever we get there."

"Give 'em a thrashing!" cried Kaspa.

"Aye." Jalenhorm nodded his agreement.

West was not in the mood. "I wouldn't be too sure about that. Have you seen the state of some of these levies? They can hardly walk, let alone fight. It's a disgrace."

Jalenhorm dismissed all this with an angry wave of his hand. "They're nothing but fucking savages, the lot of 'em! We'll knock 'em on their arses, like Jezal did that idiot today, eh, Jezal? Home before winter, everyone says so!"

"Do you know the land up there?" asked West, leaning across the table. "Forests, mountains, rivers, on and on. Precious little open space to fight in, precious few roads to march on. You've got to catch a man before the thrashing can start. Home before winter? Next winter, maybe, if we come back at all."

Brint's eyes were wide open and horrified. "You can't mean that!"

"No . . . no, you're right." West sighed and shook himself. "I'm sure it'll all turn out fine. Glory and promotions all round. Home before winter. I'd take a coat with you though, just in case."

An uneasy silence descended on the group. West had that hard frown on his face that he got sometimes, the frown that said they'd get no more fun out of him tonight. Brint and Jalenhorm looked puzzled and surly. Only Kaspa maintained his good humour, and he was lolling back in his chair, eyes half closed, blissfully unaware of his surroundings.

Some celebration.

Jezal himself felt tired, annoyed, and worried. Worried about the Contest, worried about the war . . . worried about Ardee. The letter was still there, folded up in his pocket. He glanced sidelong at West, then quickly away. Damn, he felt guilty. He had never really felt guilty before, and he didn't like it one bit. If he didn't meet her, he would feel guilty for leaving her on her own. If he did, he'd feel guilty for breaking his word to West. It was a dilemma alright. Jezal chewed at his thumb-nail. What the hell was it about this damn family?

"Well," said West sharply, "I have to be going. Early start tomorrow."

"Mmm," muttered Brint.

"Right," said Jalenhorm.

West looked Jezal right in the eye. "Can I have a word?" His expression was serious, grave, angry even. Jezal's heart lurched. What if West had found out about the letter? What if Ardee had told him? The Major turned away, moved over towards a quiet corner. Jezal stared around, desperately seeking for some way out.

"Jezal!" called West.

"Yes, yes." He got up with the greatest reluctance and followed his friend, flashing what he hoped was an innocent-seeming smile. Perhaps it was something else. Nothing to do with Ardee. Please let it be something else.

"I don't want anyone else to know about this . . ." West looked round to make sure no one was watching. Jezal swallowed. Any moment now he would get a punch in the face. At least one. He had never been punched in the face, not properly. A girl slapped him pretty hard once, but that was hardly the same. He prepared himself as best he could, gritting his teeth, wincing slightly. "Burr has set a date. We've got four weeks."

Jezal stared back. "What?"

"Until we embark."

"Embark?"

"For Angland, Jezal!"

"Oh, yes . . . Angland, of course! Four weeks you say?"

"I thought you ought to know, since you're busy with the Contest, so you'd have time to get ready. Keep it to yourself, though."

"Yes, of course." Jezal wiped his sweaty forehead.

"You alright? You look pale."

"I'm fine, fine." He took a deep breath. "All this excitement, you know, the fencing and . . . everything."

"Don't worry, you did well today." West clapped him on the shoulder. "But there's a lot more to do. Three more bouts before you can call yourself a champion, and they'll only get harder. Don't get lazy, Jezal—and don't get too drunk!" he threw over his shoulder as he made for the door. Jezal breathed a long sigh of relief as he returned to the table where the others were sitting. His nose was still intact.

Brint had already started to complain, now he could see that West wasn't coming back. "What the hell was all that?" he asked, frowning and jabbing his thumb at the door. "I mean to say, well, I know he's supposed to be the big hero and all of that but, well, I mean to say!"

Jezal stared down at him. "What do you mean to say?"

"Well, to talk that way! It's, it's defeatist!" The drink was lending him courage now, and he was warming to his topic. "It's . . . well, I mean to say . . . it's cowardly talk is what it is!"

"Now, look here, Brint," snapped Jezal, "he fought in three pitched battles, and he was first through the breach at Ulrioch! He may not be a nobleman, but he's a damn courageous fellow! Added to that he knows soldiering, he knows Marshal Burr, and he knows Angland! What do you know, Brint?" Jezal curled his lip. "Except how to lose at cards and empty a wine bottle?"

"That's all a man needs to know in my book," laughed Jalenhorm nervously, doing his best to calm the situation. "More wine!" he bellowed at no one in particular.

Jezal dropped down on his stool. If the company had been subdued before West left, it was even more so now. Brint was sulking. Jalenhorm was swaying on his stool. Kaspa had fallen soundly asleep, sprawled out on the wet table top, his breathing making quiet slurping sounds.

Jezal drained his wine glass, and stared round at the unpromising faces. Damn, he was bored. It was a fact, he was only now beginning to realise, that the conversation of the drunk is only interesting to the drunk. A few glasses of wine can be the difference between finding a man a hilarious companion or an insufferable moron. He wondered if he himself was as tedious drunk as Kaspa, or Jalenhorm, or Brint.

Jezal gave a thin smile as he looked over at the sulking bastard. If he were King, he mused, he would punish poor conversation with death, or at least a lengthy prison term. He stood up from his chair.

Jalenhorm stared up at him. "What you doing?"

"Better get some rest," snapped Jezal, "need to train tomorrow." It was the most he could do not to just run out of the place.

"But you won! Ain't you going to celebrate?"

"First round. I've still three more men to beat, and they'll all be better than that oaf today." Jezal took his coat from the back of the chair and pulled it over his shoulders.

"Suit self," said Jalenhorm, then slurped noisily from his glass.

Kaspa raised his head from the table for a moment, hair on one side plastered to his skull with spilled wine. "Going sho shoon?"

"Mmm," said Jezal as he turned and stalked out.

There was a cold wind blowing in the street outside. It made him feel even more sober than before. Painfully sober. He badly needed some intelligent company, but where could he find it at this time of night? There was only one place he could think of.

He slipped the letter out of his pocket and read it in the dim light from the tavern's windows, just one more time. If he hurried he might still catch her. He began to walk slowly towards the Four Corners. Just to talk, that was all. He needed someone to talk to . . .

No. He forced himself to stop. Could he truly pretend that he wanted to be her friend? A friendship between a man and a woman was what you called it when one had been pursuing the other for a long time, and had never got anywhere. He had no interest in that arrangement.

What then? Marriage? To a girl with no blood and no money? Unthinkable! He imagined bringing Ardee home to meet his family. Here is my new wife, father! Wife? And her connections are? He shuddered at the thought.

But what if they could find something in between, where everyone would be comfortable? His feet began slowly to move. Not friendship, not marriage, but some looser arrangement? He strode down the road towards the Four Corners. They could meet discreetly, and talk, and laugh, somewhere with a bed maybe . . .

No. No. Jezal stopped again and slapped the side of his head in frustration. He couldn't let that happen, even supposing she would. West was one thing, but what if other people found out? It wouldn't hurt his reputation any, of course, but hers would be ruined. Ruined. His flesh crept at the thought. She didn't deserve that, surely. It wasn't good enough to say it was her problem. Not good enough. Just so he could have a little fun? The selfishness of it. He was amazed that it had never occurred to him before.

So he had reasoned himself into a corner then, just as he had done ten times already today: nothing good could come from seeing her. They would be away to war soon anyway, and that would put an end to his ridiculous pining. Home to bed then, and train all day tomorrow. Train and train until Marshal Varuz had battered her out of his thoughts. He took a deep breath, squared his shoulders, turned and set off towards the Agriont.

The statue of Harod the Great loomed out of the darkness on a marble plinth almost as tall as Jezal, seeming far too big and grand for its quiet little square near the Four Corners. He had been jumping at shadows all the way here, avoiding people, doing his best to be inconspicuous. There weren't many people around though. It was late, and most likely Ardee would have given up waiting a long time ago, provided she was even there to begin with.

He crept nervously around the statue, peering into the shadows, feeling an absolute fool. He had walked through this square many times before and never given it a second thought. Was it not a public space after all? He had as much right as anyone to be here, but somehow he still felt like a thief.

The square was empty. That was a good thing. All for the best. There was nothing to gain, everything to lose, and so forth. So why did he feel so completely crushed? He stared up at Harod's face, locked into that stony frown that sculptors reserve for the truly great. He had a fine, strong jaw, did Harod, almost the equal of Jezal's own.

"Wake up!" hissed a voice by his ear. Jezal let vent to a girlish squeal, scrambled away, tripped, only stayed upright by clawing at King Harod's enormous foot. There was a dark figure behind him, a hooded figure.

Laughter. "No need to piss yourself." Ardee. She pushed back her hood.

Light from a window slanted across the bottom part of her face, catching her lopsided smile. "It's only me."

"I didn't see you," he mumbled pointlessly, quickly releasing his desperate grip on the huge stone foot and doing his best to appear at ease. He had to admit it was a poor start. He had no talent for this cloak-and-dagger business. Ardee seemed quite comfortable, though. It made him wonder whether she hadn't done it all before.

"You've been pretty hard to see yourself, lately," she said.

"Well, er," he muttered, heart still thumping from the shock, "I've been busy, what with the Contest and all . . ."

"Ah, the all-important Contest. I saw you fight today."

"You did?"

"Very impressive."

"Er, thank you, I—"

"My brother said something, didn't he?"

"What, about fencing?"

"No, numbskull. About me."

Jezal paused, trying to work out the best way to answer that one. "Well he—"

"Are you scared of him?"

"No!" Silence. "Alright, yes."

"But you came anyway. I suppose I should be flattered." She walked slowly around him, looking him up and down, from feet to forehead and back again. "You took your time, though. It's late. I'll have to be getting home soon."

There was something about the way she was looking at him which was not helping to calm his thumping heart. Quite the opposite. He had to tell her that he could not see her any more. It was the wrong thing to do. For both of them. Nothing good could come from it . . . nothing good . . .

He was breathing quick, tense, excited, unable to take his eyes away from her shadowy face. He had to tell her, now. Wasn't that why he came? He opened his mouth to speak, but the arguments all seemed a long way away now, applying at a different time and to different people, intangible and weightless.

"Ardee . . ." he began.

"Mmm?" She stepped towards him, head cocked on one side. Jezal tried to move away, but the statue was at his back. She came closer still, lips slightly parted, her eyes fixed on his mouth. What was so wrong in it, anyway?

Closer still, her face turned up towards his. He could smell her—his head was full of the scent of her. He could feel her warm breath on his cheek. What could be wrong with this?

Her fingertips were cold against his skin, brushing the side of his face, tracing the line of his jaw, curling through his hair and pulling his head down towards her. Her lips touched his cheek, soft and warm, then his chin, then his mouth. They sucked gently at his. She pressed herself up against him, her other hand slipped round his back. Her tongue lapped at his gums, at his teeth, at his tongue, and she made little sounds in her throat. So did he, perhaps—he really wasn't sure. His whole body was tingling, hot and cold at once, his mind was in his mouth. It was as if he'd never kissed a girl before. What could be wrong with this? Her teeth nipped at his lips, almost painful, but not quite.

He opened his eyes: breathless, trembling, weak at the knees. She was looking up at him. He could see her eyes gleaming in the darkness, watching him carefully, studying him.

"Ardee . . ."

"What?"

"When can I see you again?" His throat was dry, his voice sounded hoarse. She looked down at the ground with a little smile. A cruel smile, as though she'd called his bluff and won a pile of money from him. He didn't care. "When?"

"Oh, I'll let you know."

He had to kiss her again. Shit on the consequences. Fuck West. Damn it all. He bent down towards her, closed his eyes.

"No, no, no." She pushed his mouth away from hers. "You should have come sooner." She broke away from him and turned around, with the smile still on her lips, and walked slowly away. He watched her, silent, frozen, fascinated, his back against the cold stone base of the statue. He had never felt like this before. Not ever.

She glanced back, just once, as if to check that he was still watching. His chest constricted, almost painfully, just to see her look at him, then she rounded a corner and was gone.

He stood there for a moment, his eyes wide open, just breathing. Then a cold gust of wind blew through the square and the world pressed back in upon him. Fencing, the war, his friend West, his obligations. One kiss, that was all. One kiss, and his resolve had leaked away like piss from a broken chamber pot. He stared around, suddenly guilty, confused, and scared. What had he done here?

"Shit," he said.

DARK WORK

Aburning thing can make all kind of smells. A live tree, fresh and sappy, smells different ablaze to a dead one, dry and withered. A pig alight and a man smell much the same, but there's another story. This burning that the Dogman smelled now, that was a house. He knew it, sure as sure. A smell he knew better than he'd have liked. Houses don't burn on their own too often. Usually there's some violence in it. That meant men around, most likely, and ready for a fight, so he crept right careful down between the trees, slid on his belly to the edge, and peered out through the brush.

He saw it now, right enough. Black smoke in a tall pillar, rising up from a spot down near the river. A small house, still smoking, but burned down to the low stone walls. There'd been a barn too, but nothing more now than a pile of black sticks and black dirt. A couple of trees and a patch of tilled earth. It was a poor enough living at the best of times, farming this far north. Too cold to grow much—a few roots maybe, and some sheep to herd. A pig or two, if you were lucky.

Dogman shook his head. Who'd want to burn out folks as poor as this? Who'd want to steal this stubborn patch of land? Some men just like to burn, he reckoned. He eased out a touch further, looking right and left down the valley for some sign of the ones as did this, but a few stringy sheep spread out across the valley sides was all he could see moving. He wriggled back into the brush.

His heart sank as he sneaked back towards the camp. Voices raised, and arguing, as ever. He wondered for a minute whether to just go past and keep on going, he was that sick of the endless bickering. He decided against it in the end, though. It ain't much of a scout who leaves his people behind.

"Why don't you shut your hole, Dow?" Tul Duru's rumbling voice. "You wanted south, and when we went south all you did was moan about the mountains! Now we're out o' the mountains you grumble on your empty belly all day and all night! I've had my fill of it, you whining dog!"

Now came Black Dow's nasty growl. "Why should you get twice as much to eat, just 'cause you're a great fat pig?"

"You little bastard! I'll crush you like the worm y'are!"

"I'll cut your neck while you sleep you great pile o' meat! Then we'll all have plenty to eat! At least we'd all be rid of your fucking snoring! I know now why they named you Thunderhead, you rumbling sow!"

"Shut your holes the pair of you!" Dogman heard Threetrees roaring, loud enough to wake the dead. "I'm sick of it!"

He could see them now, the five of them. Tul Duru and Black Dow, bristling up to one another, Threetrees in between them with his hands up, Forley sat watching, just looking sad, and Grim, not even watching, checking his shafts.

"Oy!" hissed Dogman, and they all snapped round to look at him.

"It's the Dogman," said Grim, barely looking up from his arrows. There was no understanding that man. He spoke nothing at all for days on end, then when he did speak it was to say what they could all see already.

Forley was keen to distract the lads, as always. It was a hard guess how long they'd keep from killing each other without him around. "What did you find, Dogman?" he asked.

"What do you know, I found five stupid fucking bastards out in the woods!" he hissed, stepping out from the trees. "I could hear them from a mile away! And they were Named Men these, would you believe, men who should have known better! Fighting among themselves as always! Five stupid bastards—"

Threetrees raised his hand. "Alright, Dogman. We should know better." And he glowered at Tul and Dow. They glowered at each other, but they said nothing more. "What did you find?"

"There's fighting going on hereabouts, or something like it. I seen a farm burning."

"Burning, say you?" asked Tul.

"Aye."

Threetrees frowned. "Take us to it, then."

The Dogman hadn't seen this from up in the trees. Couldn't have. Too smoky and too far to see this. He saw it now though, right up close, and it made him sick. They all saw it.

"This is some dark work here alright," said Forley, looking up at the tree. "Some dark work."

"Aye," mumbled Dogman. He couldn't think of ought else to say. The branch creaked as the old man swung slowly round, his bare feet dangling near the earth. Might have been he tried to fight, he'd got two arrows through him. The woman was too young to be his wife. His daughter, maybe. The Dogman guessed the two young ones were her children. "Who'd hang a child?" he muttered.

"I can think of some black enough," said Tul.

Dow spat on the grass. "Meaning me?" he growled, and the two of 'em were off again like hammer on anvil. "I burned some farms, and a village or two an' all, but there were reasons, that was war. I let the children live."

"I heard different." said Tul. Dogman closed his eyes and sighed.

"You think I give a dog's arse for what you heard?" Dow barked. "Might be my name's blacker than I deserve, you giant shit!"

"I know what you deserve, you bastard!"

"Enough!" growled Threetrees, frowning up at the tree. "Have you no respect? The Dogman's right. We're out of the mountains now and there's trouble brewing. There'll be no more of this squabbling. No more. Quiet and cold from now on, like the winter-time. We're Named Men with men's work to do."

Dogman nodded, happy to hear some sense at last. "There's fighting nearby," he said, "there has to be."

"Uh," said Grim, though it was hard to say exactly what he was agreeing with.

Threetrees' eye was still fixed on the swinging bodies. "You're right. We need to put our minds on that now. On that and nothing else. We'll track the crowd as did this and see what they're fighting for. We'll do no good until we know who's fighting who."

"Whoever did this fights for Bethod," said Dow. "You can tell just by the looking."

"We'll see. Tul and Dow, cut these folks down and bury 'em. Maybe that task'll put some steel back in you." The two of them scowled at each other, but Threetrees paid 'em no mind. "Dogman, you go and sniff out those as did this. Sniff 'em out, and we'll pay 'em a visit tonight. A visit like they paid to these folks here."

"Aye," said Dogman, keen to get on and do it. "We'll pay 'em a visit."

The Dogman couldn't work it out. If they were in a fight these lot, afraid of being caught out by an enemy, they weren't making too much of an effort to cover their tracks. He followed them simple as could be, five of them he reckoned. Must've strolled nice and easy away from the burning farm, down through the valley beside the river and off into the woods. The tracks were so clear he got a little worried time to time, thinking they must be playing some trick on him, watching out there in the trees, waiting to hang him from a branch. Seemed they weren't though, 'cause he caught up to them just before nightfall.

First of all he smelled their meat—mutton roasting. Next he heard their voices—talking, shouting, laughing, making not the meanest attempt to stay quiet, easy to hear even with the river bubbling beside. Then he saw them, sitting round a great big fire in a clearing, a sheep's carcass skinned on a spit above it, taken from those farmers no doubt. The Dogman crouched down in the bushes, nice and still like they should have been. He counted five men, or four and a boy about fourteen years. They were all just sitting, no one standing guard, no caution at all. He couldn't work it out.

"They're just sitting there," he whispered when he got back to the others. "Just sitting. No guard, no nothing."

"Just sitting?" asked Forley.

"Aye. Five of 'em. Sitting and laughing. I don't like it."

"I don't like it neither," said Threetrees, "but I like what I saw at that farm still less."

"Weapons," hissed Dow. "Weapons, it has to be."

For once, Tul agreed with him. "Weapons, chief. Let's give 'em a lesson."

Not even Forley spoke up for staying out of a fight this time, but Three-trees thought it out for a bit still, taking his moment, not to be hurried. Then he nodded. "Weapons it is."

You won't see Black Dow in the dark, not if he doesn't want to be seen. You won't hear him neither, but the Dogman knew he was there as he crept down through the trees. You fight with a man for long enough, you get an understanding. You learn how he thinks and you come to think the same way. Dow was there.

The Dogman had his task. He could see the outline of the one on the far right, his back a black shape against the fire. Dogman didn't spare too much thought for the others yet. He spared no thought for anything but his task. Once you choose to go, or your chief chooses for you, you go all the way, and never look back 'til the task's done. The time you spend thinking is the time you'll get killed in. Logen taught him that and he'd taken it right to heart. That's the way it has to be.

Dogman crept closer, and closer still, feeling the warmth of the fire on his face, feeling the hard metal of the knife in his hand. By the dead he needed to piss, as always. The task wasn't but a stride away now. The boy was facing him—if he'd have looked up fast from his meat he'd have seen the Dogman coming, but he was too busy eating.

"Gurgh!" shouted one of the others. That meant Dow'd got to him, and that meant he was finished. Dogman leaped forward and stabbed his task in the side of the neck. He reared up for a moment, clutching at his cut throat, took a stumble forward and fell over. One of the others jumped up, dropping his half-chewed leg of mutton on the ground, then an arrow stuck him through the chest. Grim, out by the river. He looked surprised a minute, then he sank down on his knees, face twisted up with pain.

That left but two, and the boy was still sitting there, staring at the Dogman, mouth half open with a bit of meat hanging out of it. The last of them was stood up, breathing quick, with a long knife in his hand. He must have had it out for eating with.

"Drop the blade!" bellowed Threetrees. The Dogman saw the old boy now, striding towards them, the firelight catching the metal rim of his big round shield. The man chewed on his lip, eyes flicking from Dogman to Dow as they moved slowly to either side of him. Now he saw the Thunderhead, looming out of the darkness in the trees, seeming too big to be a man, his great huge sword glinting over his shoulder. That was enough for him. He threw his knife down in the dirt.

Dow jumped forward, grabbed his wrists and tied them tight behind him, then shoved him down on his knees beside the fire. The Dogman did the same with the boy, his teeth clenched tight, not saying a word. The whole thing was done in an instant, quiet and cold like Threetrees said. There was blood on Dogman's hands, but that was the work and couldn't be helped. The others were making their way over now. Grim came sloshing through the river, throwing his bow across his shoulder. He gave the one he shot a kick as he came past, but the body didn't move.

"Dead," said Grim. Forley was at the back, peering at the two prisoners. Dow was staring at the one he'd tied, staring at him hard.

"I know this one 'ere," he said, sounding quite pleased about it too. "Groa the Mire, ain't it? What a chance! You've been gnawing at the back of my mind for some time."

The Mire scowled down at the ground. A cruel-looking sort, the Dogman thought, the type that might hang farmers, if there was one. "Aye, I'm the Mire. No need to ask your names! When they find you've killed some o' the King's collectors you'll be dead men all!"

"Black Dow, they call me."

The Mire's head came up, his mouth wide open. "Oh fuck," he whispered.

The boy kneeling next to him stared round with big eyes. "Black Dow? You what? Not the same Black Dow as . . . oh fuck."

Dow nodded slowly, with that nasty smile spreading across his face, that killing smile. "Groa the Mire. You've all kind of work to pay for. I've had you in my mind, and now you're in my eye." He patted him on the cheek. "And in my hand too. What a happy chance."

The Mire snatched his face away, as far as he could, trussed up like he was. "I thought you were in hell, Black Dow, you bastard!"

"So did I, but I was only north o' the mountains. We've questions for you, Mire, before you get what's due. Who's this king? What is it you're collecting for him?"

"Fuck your questions!"

Threetrees hit him on the side of his head, hard, where he couldn't see it coming. When he turned round to look, Dow cracked him on the other side. Back and forth his head went, till he was soft enough to talk.

"What's the fight?" asked Threetrees.

"We ain't fighting!" spat the Mire through his broken teeth. "You might as well be dead, you bastards! You don't know what's happened, do yer?" Dogman frowned. He didn't like the sound of this. Sounded like things had changed while they were gone, and he'd never yet seen a change for the better.

"I'll do the questions here," said Threetrees. "You just keep your tiny mind on the answers to 'em. Who's still fighting? Who won't kneel to Bethod?"

The Mire laughed, even tied up like he was. "There's no one left! The fighting's over! Bethod's King now. King of all the North! Everyone kneels to him—"

"Not us," rumbled Tul Duru, leaning down. "What about Old Man Yawl?"

"Dead!"

"What about Sything, or Rattleneck?"

"Dead and dead, you stupid fucks! The only fighting now's down south! Bethod's gone to war with the Union! Aye! And we're giving 'em a beating too!"

The Dogman wasn't sure whether to believe it. King? There'd never been a king in the North before. There'd never been a need for one, and Bethod was the last one he'd have chosen. And making war on the Union? That was a fool's errand, surely. There were always more southerners.

"If there's no fighting here," asked the Dogman, "what you killing for?"

"Fuck yourself!"

Tul slapped him in the face, hard, and he fell on his back. Dow put in a kick of his own, then dragged him up straight again.

"What did you kill 'em for?" asked Tul.

"Taxes!" shouted the Mire, with blood trickling out of his nose.

"Taxes?" asked the Dogman. A strange word alright, he barely know the meaning of it.

"They wouldn't pay!"

"Taxes for who?" asked Dow.

"For Bethod, who do you think? He took all this land, broke the clans up and took it for his own! The people owe him! And we collect!"

"Taxes, eh? That's a fucking southern fashion and no mistake! And if they can't pay?" asked Dogman, feeling sick to his guts. "You hang 'em, do you?"

"If they won't pay we can do as we please with 'em!"

"As you please?" Tul grabbed him round the neck, squeezing with his great big hand 'til the Mire's eyes were half popping out. "As you please? Does it please you to hang 'em?"

"Alright, Thunderhead," said Dow, peeling Tul's big fingers away, and pushing him gently back. "Alright, big lad, this ain't for you, to kill a man tied up." And he patted him on the chest, pulling out his axe. "It's for work like this you bring along a man like me."

The Mire had more or less got over his throttling now. "Thunderhead?" he coughed, looking round at them. "It's the whole lot of you, ain't it! You're Threetrees, and Grim, and that's the Weakest there! So you don't kneel, eh? Good for fuckin' you! Where's Ninefingers? Eh?" jeered the Mire, "where's the Bloody-Nine?"

Dow turned round, running his thumb down the edge of his axe. "Gone back to the mud, and you're joining him. We've heard enough."

"Let me up, bastard!" shouted the Mire, struggling at his ropes. "You're no better'n me, Black Dow! You've killed more folk than the plague! Let me up and give me a blade! Come on! You scared to fight me, you coward? Scared to give a fair chance are yer?"

"Call me coward, would you?" growled Dow. "You who's killed children for the sport of it? You had a blade and you let it drop. That was your chance and you should have took it. The likes o' you don't deserve another. If you've anything to say worth hearing you best say it now."

"Shit on yer!" screamed the Mire, "Shit on the pack of—"

Dow's axe cracked him hard between the eyes and knocked him on his back. He kicked a little then that was it. Not a one of them shed too big a tear for that bastard—even Forley gave no more than a wince when the blade went in. Dow leaned over and spat on his corpse, and the Dogman hardly blamed him. The boy was something more of a problem, though. He stared down at the body with big, wide eyes, then he looked up.

"You're them, ain't ya," he said, "them as Ninefingers beat."

"Aye, boy," said Threetrees, "we're them."

"I heard stories, stories about you. What you going to do with me?"

"Well, there's the question, ain't it," Dogman muttered to himself. Shame was, he already knew the answer.

"He can't stay with us," said Threetrees. "We can't take the baggage and we can't take the risk."

"He's just a lad," said Forley. "We could let him go." It was a nice thought, but it wasn't holding much water, and they all knew it. The boy looked hopeful, but Tul put an end to that.

"We can't trust him. Not here. He'd tell someone we were back, and then we'd be hunted. Can't do it. Besides, he had his part in that work at the farm."

"But what choice did I 'ave?" asked the boy. "What choice? I wanted to go south! Go south and fight the Union, and earn myself a name, but they sent me here, to get taxes. My chief says do a thing, I got to do it, don't I?"

"You do," said Threetrees. "No one says you could've done different."

"I didn't want no part of it! I told him to let the young ones be! You got to believe me!"

Forley looked down at his boots. "We do believe you."

"But you're going to fuckin' kill me anyway?"

Dogman chewed at his lip. "Can't take you with us, can't leave you be."

"I didn't want no part of it." The boy hung his head. "Don't hardly seem fair."

"It ain't," said Threetrees. "It ain't fair at all. But there it is."

Dow's axe hacked into the back of the lad's skull and he sprawled out on his face. The Dogman winced and looked away. He knew Dow did it that way so they wouldn't have to look at the boy's face. A good idea most likely, and he hoped it helped the others, but face up or face down was all the same to him. He felt almost as sick as he had back at the farm.

It wasn't the worst day he'd ever had, not by a long way. But it was a bad one.

The Dogman watched 'em filing down the road from a good spot up in the trees where no one could see him. He made sure it was downwind from 'em too, cause being honest, he was smelling a bit ripe. It was a strange old procession. On the one hand they looked like fighting men, off to a weapon-take and then to battle. On the other hand they were all wrong. Old weapons mostly, and odds and sods of mixed up armour. Marching, but loose and ragged. Most of 'em too old to be prime fighters, grey hair and bald heads, and a lot of the rest too young for beards, hardly more than boys.

Seemed to the Dogman like nothing made sense in the North no more. He thought on what the Mire had said before Dow killed him. War with the Union. Were these lot off to war? If they were then Bethod must have been scraping the pot.

"What's to do, Dogman?" asked Forley, as he stepped back into the camp. "What's happening down there?"

"Men. Armed, but none too well. Five score or more. Young and old mostly, heading south and west," and the Dogman pointed off down the road.

Threetrees nodded. "Towards Angland. He means it then, Bethod. He's making war on the Union, all the way. No amount of blood's enough for that one. He's taking every man can hold a spear." That was no surprise, in its way. Bethod had never been one for half measures. He was all or nothing, and didn't care who got killed along the road. "Every man," muttered Threetrees to himself. "If the Shanka come over the mountains now . . ."

Dogman looked round. Frowning, worried, dirty faces. He knew what Threetrees was saying, they could all see it. If the Shanka came now, with no one left in the North to fight 'em, that business at the farm would be the best of it.

"We got to warn someone!" shouted Forley, "we got to warn them!"

Threetrees shook his head. "You heard the Mire. Yawl's gone, and Rattleneck, and Sything. All dead and cold, and gone back to the mud. Bethod's King now, King of the Northmen." Black Dow scowled and gobbed in the dirt. "Spit all you like Dow, but facts is facts. There's no one left to warn."

"No one but Bethod himself," muttered the Dogman, miserable at having to say it.

"Then we got to tell him!" Forley looked round them all, desperate. "He may be a heartless bastard but at least he's a man! He's better than the Flatheads ain't he? We got to tell someone!"

"Hah!" barked Dow. "Hah! You think he'll listen to us, Weakest? You forgotten what he told us? Us and Ninefingers too? Never come back! You forgotten how close he come to killing us? You forgotten how much he hates each one of us?"

"Fears us," said Grim.

"Hates and fears us," muttered Threetrees, "and he's wise to. Because we're strong. Named men. Known men. The type of men that others will follow."

Tul nodded his big head. "Aye, there'll be no welcome for us at Carleon I'm thinking. No welcome without a spike on the end of it."

"I'm not strong!" shouted Forley. "I'm the Weakest, everyone knows that! Bethod's got no reason to fear me, nor to hate me neither. I'll go!"

Dogman looked at him, surprised. They all did. "You?" asked Dow.

"Aye, me! I may be no fighter, but I'm no coward neither! I'll go and talk to him. Maybe he'll listen." Dogman stood and stared. It was so long since any one of them had tried to talk their way out of a fix he'd forgotten it could be done.

"Might be he'll listen," muttered Threetrees.

"He might listen," said Tul. "Then he might bloody kill you, Weakest!"

Dogman shook his head. "It's quite a chance."

"Maybe, but it's worth the doing, ain't it?"

They all looked at each other, worried. It was some bones that Forley was showing, no doubt, but the Dogman didn't much like the sound of this for a plan. He was a thin thread to hang your hopes on, was Bethod. A mighty thin thread.

But like Threetrees said, there was no one else.

WORDS AND DUST

Kurster pranced around the outside of the circle, his long golden hair bouncing on his shoulders, waving to the crowd, blowing kisses to the girls. The audience cheered and howled and whooped as the lithe young man made his flashy rounds. He was an Aduan, an officer of the King's Own. *A local boy, and so very popular.*

Bremer dan Gorst was leaning against the barrier, watching his opponent dance through barely open eyes. His steels were unusually heavy-looking, weighty and worn and well-used, too heavy to be quick perhaps. Gorst himself looked too heavy to be quick, come to that, a great thick-necked bull of a man, more like a wrestler than a swordsman. He looked the underdog in this bout. The majority of the crowd seemed to think so. *But I know better.*

Nearby a bet-maker was shouting odds, taking money from the babbling people around him. Nearly all of the bets were for Kurster. Glokta leaned across from his bench. "What odds are you giving on Gorst now?"

"On Gorst?" asked the bet-maker, "evens."

"I'll take two hundred marks."

"Sorry, friend, I can't cover that."

"A hundred then, at five to four."

The bet-maker thought about it for a moment, looking skywards as he worked out the sums in his head. "Done."

Glokta sat back as the referee introduced the contestants, watching Gorst roll up his shirt-sleeves. The man's forearms were thick as tree trunks, heavy cords of muscle squirming as he worked his meaty fingers. He stretched his thick neck to one side and the other, then he took his steels from his second and loosed a couple of practice jabs. Few in the crowd noticed. They were busy cheering Kurster as he took his mark. But Glokta saw. *Quicker than he looks. A lot, lot quicker. Those heavy steels no longer seem so clumsy.*

"Bremer dan Gorst!" shouted the referee, as the big man trudged to his mark. The applause was meagre indeed. This lumbering bull was no one's idea of a swordsman.

"Begin!"

It wasn't pretty. From the very start Gorst swung his heavy long steel in great heedless sweeps, like a champion woodsman chopping logs, giving great throaty growls with every blow. It was a strange sight. One man was in a fencing contest, the other seemed to think he was fighting to the death. *You only have to touch him man, not split him in half!* But as Glokta watched, he realised the mighty cuts were not nearly so clumsy as they seemed. They were well-timed, and highly accurate. Kurster laughed as he danced away from the first great swing, smiled as he dodged the third, but by the fifth his smile was long gone. *And it doesn't look like coming back.*

It wasn't pretty at all. *But the power is undeniable.* Kurster ducked desperately under another great arcing cut. *That one was hard enough to take his head off, blunted steels or no.*

The crowd's favourite did his best to seize the initiative, jabbing away for all he was worth, but Gorst was more than equal to it. He grunted as he turned the jabs efficiently away with his short steel, then growled again as he brought his long whistling around and over. Glokta winced as it smashed into Kurster's sword with a resounding crash, snapping the man's wrist back and nearly tearing the steel from his fingers. He stumbled back from the force of it, grimacing with pain and shock.

Now I realise why Gorst's steels seem so worn. Kurster dodged around the circle, trying to escape the onslaught, but the big man was too quick. *Far too quick.* Gorst had the measure of him now, anticipating every movement, harrying his opponent with relentless blows. There was no escape.

Two heavy thrusts drove the hapless officer back towards the edge of the circle, then a scything cut ripped his long steel from his hand and embedded it, wobbling wildly back and forth, in the turf. He staggered for a moment, eyes wide, his empty hand trembling, then Gorst was on him, letting go a roar and ramming full-tilt into his defenceless ribs with a heavy shoulder.

Glokta spluttered with laughter. *I never saw a swordsman fly before.* Kurster actually turned half a somersault, shrieking like a girl as he tumbled through the air, crashing to the ground with his limbs flopping and sliding away on his face. He finally came to rest in the sand outside the circle, a good three strides from where Gorst had hit him, groaning weakly.

The crowd was in shock, so quiet that Glokta's cackling had to be audible on the back row. Kurster's trainer rushed from his enclosure and gently turned his stricken student over. The young man kicked weakly, whimpered and clutched at his ribs. Gorst watched for a moment, emotionless, then shrugged and strolled back to his mark.

Kurster's trainer turned to the referee. "I am sorry," he said, "but my pupil cannot continue."

Glokta could not help himself. He had to clamp his mouth shut with his hands. His whole body was shaking with laughter. Each gurgle caused a painful spasm in his neck, but he didn't care. It seemed the majority of the crowd had not found the spectacle quite so amusing. Angry mutterings sprang up all around him. The grumbling turned to boos as Kurster was helped from the circle, draped between his trainer and his second, then the boos to a chorus of angry shouts.

Gorst swept the audience with his lazy, half-open eyes, then shrugged again and trudged slowly back to his enclosure. Glokta was still sniggering as he limped from the arena, his purse a good deal heavier than when he arrived. He hadn't had that much fun in years.

The University stood in a neglected corner of the Agriont, directly in the shadow of the House of the Maker, where even the birds seemed old and tired. A huge, ramshackle building, coated in half-dead ivy, its design plainly from an earlier age. It was said to be one of the oldest buildings in the city. *And it looks it.*

The roofs were sagging in the middle, a couple of them close to outright collapse. The delicate spires were crumbling, threatening to topple off into the unkempt gardens below. The render on the walls was tired and grimy, and in places whole sections had fallen away to reveal the bare stones and crumbling mortar beneath. In one spot a great brown stain flared out down the wall from a section of broken guttering. There had been a time when the study of sciences had attracted some of the foremost men in the Union, when this building had been among the grandest in the city. *And Sult thinks the Inquisition is out of fashion.*

Two statues flanked the crumbling gate. Two old men, one with a lamp, one pointing at something in a book. *Wisdom and progress or some such rubbish.* The one with the book had lost his nose some time during the past century, the other was leaning at an angle, his lamp stuck out despairingly as though clutching for support.

Glokta raised his fist and hammered on the ancient doors. They rattled, moved noticeably, as if they might at any moment drop from their hinges. Glokta waited. Waited some time.

There was a sudden clatter of bolts being drawn back, and one half of the door wobbled open a few inches. An ancient face wedged itself into the gap and squinted out at him, lit underneath by a meagre taper clutched in a withered hand. Dewy old eyes peered up and down. "Yes?"

"Inquisitor Glokta."

"Ah, from the Arch Lector?"

Glokta frowned, surprised. "Yes, that's right." *They cannot be half so cut off from the world as they appear. He seems to know who I am.*

It was perilously dark within. Two enormous brass candelabras stood on either side of the door, but they were stripped of candles and had long gone unpolished, shining dully in the weak light from the porter's little taper. "This way, sir," wheezed the old man, shambling off, bent nearly double. Even Glokta had little trouble keeping up with him as he crept away through the gloom.

They shuffled together down a shadowy hallway. The windows on one side were ancient, made with tiny panes of glass so dirty that they would have let in little enough light on the sunniest of days. They let in none whatever as the sullen evening came on. The flickering candleflame danced over dusty paintings on the opposite wall, pale old men in dark gowns of black and grey, gazing wild-eyed from their flaking frames, flasks and cog-wheels and pairs of compasses clutched in their aged hands.

"Where are we going?" asked Glokta, after they had shambled through the murk for several minutes.

"The Adepti are at dinner," wheezed the porter, glancing up at him with eyes infinitely tired.

The University's dining hall was an echoing cavern of a room, lifted one degree above total darkness by a few guttering candles. A small fire flickered in an enormous fireplace, casting dancing shadows among the rafters. A long table stretched the length of the floor, polished by long years of use, flanked by rickety chairs. It could easily have accommodated eighty but there were only five there, crowded up at one end, huddled in around the fireplace. They looked over as the taps of Glokta's cane echoed through the hall, pausing in their meals and peering over with great interest. The man at the head of the table got to his feet and hurried over, holding the hem of his long black gown up with one hand.

"A visitor," wheezed the porter, waving his candle in Glokta's direction.

"Ah, from the Arch Lector! I am Silber, the University Administrator!" And he shook Glokta's hand. His companions had meanwhile lurched and tottered to their feet as though the guest of honour had just arrived.

"Inquisitor Glokta." He stared round at the eager old men. *A good deal more deference than I was expecting, I must say. But then, the Arch Lector's name opens all kinds of doors.*

"Glokta, Glokta," mumbled one of the old men, "seems that I remember a Glokta from somewhere."

"You remember everything from somewhere, but you never remember where," quipped the administrator, to half-hearted laughter. "Please let me make the introductions."

He went round the four black-gowned scientists, one by one. "Saurizin, our Adeptus Chemical." A beefy, unkempt old fellow with burns and stains down the front of his robe and more than one bit of food in his beard. "Denka, the Adeptus Metallic." The youngest of the four by a considerable margin, though by no means a young man, had an arrogant twist to his mouth. "Chayle, our Adeptus Mechanical." Glokta had never seen a man with so big a head but so small a face. His ears, in particular, were immense, and sprouting grey hairs. "And Kandelau, the Adeptus Physical." A scrawny old bird with a long neck and spectacles perched on his curving beak of a nose. "Please join us, Inquisitor," and the administrator indicated an empty chair, wedged in between two of the Adepti.

"A glass of wine then?" wheedled Chayle, a prim smile on his tiny mouth, already leaning forward with a decanter and sloshing some into a glass.

"Very well."

"We were just discussing the relative merits of our various fields of study," murmured Kandelau, peering at Glokta through his flashing spectacles.

"As always," lamented the Administrator.

"The human body is, of course, the only area worthy of true scrutiny," continued the Adeptus Physical. "One must appreciate the mysteries within, before turning one's attention to the world without. We all have a body, Inquisitor. Means of healing it, and of harming it, are of paramount interest to us all. It is the human body that is my area of expertise."

"Bodies! Bodies!" whined Chayle, pursing his little lips and pushing food around his plate. "We are trying to eat!"

"Quite so! You are unsettling the Inquisitor with your ghoulish babble!"

"Oh, I am not easily unsettled." Glokta leered across the table, giving the Adeptus Metallic a good view of his missing teeth. "My work for the Inquisition demands a more than passing knowledge of anatomy."

There was an uncomfortable silence, then Saurizin took hold of the meat plate and offered it out. Glokta looked at the red slices, glistening on the plate. He licked at his empty gums. "Thank you, no."

"Is it true?" asked the Adeptus Chemical, peering over the meat, voice hushed. "Will there be more funds? Now that this business with the Mercers is settled, that is?"

Glokta frowned. Everyone was staring at him, waiting for his reply. One of the old Adepti had his fork frozen halfway to his mouth. *So that's it. Money. But why would they be expecting money from the Arch Lector?* The heavy meat plate was beginning to wobble. *Well . . . if it gets them listening.* "Money might be made available, depending, of course, on results."

A hushed murmur crept around the table. The Adeptus Chemical carefully set down the plate with a trembling hand. "I have been having a great deal of success with acids recently . . ."

"Hah!" mocked the Adeptus Metallic. "Results, the Inquisitor asked for, results! My new alloys will be stronger than steel when they are perfected!"

"Always the alloys!" sighed Chayle, turning his tiny eyes towards the ceiling. "No one appreciates the importance of sound mechanical thinking!"

The other three Adepti rounded fiercely on him, but the Administrator jumped in first. "Gentlemen, please! The Inquisitor is not interested in our little differences! Everyone will have time to discuss their latest work and show its merits. This is not a competition, is it Inquisitor?" Every eye turned toward Glokta. He looked slowly round at those old, expectant faces, and said nothing.

"I have developed a machine for—"

"My acids—"

"My alloys—"

"The mysteries of the human body—"

Glokta cut them off. "Actually, it is in the area of . . . I suppose you would call them explosive substances, that I am currently taking a particular interest—"

The Adeptus Chemical jumped from his seat. "That would be my province!" he cried, staring in triumph at his colleagues. "I have samples! I have examples! Please follow me, Inquisitor!" And he tossed his cutlery onto his plate and set off towards one of the doors.

Saurizin's laboratory was precisely as one would have expected, almost down to the last detail. A long room with a barrel-vaulted ceiling, blackened in places with circles and streaks of soot. Shelves covered most of the wall-space, brimming with a confusion of boxes, jars, bottles, each filled with its own powders, fluids, rods of strange metal. There was no apparent order to the positions of the various containers, and most had no labels. *Organisation does not appear to be a priority.*

The benches in the middle of the room were even more confused, covered in towering constructions of glass and old brown copper: tubes, flasks and dishes, lamps—one with a naked flame burning. All gave the appearance of being ready at any moment to collapse, dousing anyone unfortunate enough to stand nearby with lethal, boiling poisons.

The Adeptus Chemical rummaged in amongst this mess like a mole in its warren. "Now then," he mumbled to himself, pulling at his dirty beard with one hand, "blasting powders are somewhere here . . ."

Glokta limped into the room after him, glancing suspiciously around at the mess of tubing that covered every surface. He wrinkled his nose. There was a revolting, acrid smell to the place.

"Here it is!" crowed the Adeptus, brandishing a dusty jar half-full of black granules. He cleared a space on one of the benches, shoving the clinking and clanking glass and metal out of the way with a sweep of his meaty forearm. "This stuff is terribly rare, you know, Inquisitor, terribly rare!" He pulled out the stopper and tipped a line of black powder onto the wooden bench. "Few men have been fortunate enough to see this stuff in action! Very few! And you are about to become one of them!"

Glokta took a cautious step back, the size of the ragged hole in the wall of the Tower of Chains still fresh in his mind. "We are safe, I hope, at this distance?"

"Absolutely," murmured Saurizin, gingerly holding a burning taper out at arm's length and touching it to one end of the line of powder. "There is no danger whatso—"

There was a sharp pop and a shower of white sparks. The Adeptus Chemical leaped back, nearly blundering into Glokta and dropping his lighted taper on the floor. There was another pop, louder, more sparks. A foul-smelling smoke began to fill the laboratory. There was a bright flash and a loud bang, a weak fizzling, and that was all.

Saurizin flapped the long sleeve of his gown in front of his face, trying to clear the thick smoke that had now thrown the whole chamber into gloom. "Impressive, eh, Inquisitor?" he asked, before dissolving into a fit of coughing.

Not really. Glokta ground the still-flaming taper out under his boot and stepped through the murk towards the bench. He brushed aside a quantity of grey ash with the side of his hand. There was a long, black burn on the surface of the wood, but nothing more. The foul-smelling fumes were indeed the most impressive effect, already clawing at the back of Glokta's throat. "It certainly produces a great deal of smoke," he croaked.

"It does," coughed the Adeptus proudly, "and reeks to high heaven."

Glokta stared at that blackened smear on the bench. "If one had a large enough quantity of this powder, could it be used to, say, knock a hole through a wall?"

"Possibly . . . if one could accumulate a large enough quantity, who knows what could be done? As far as I know no one has ever tried."

"A wall, say, four feet thick?"

The Adeptus frowned. "Perhaps, but you'd need barrels of the stuff! Barrels! There isn't that much in the whole Union, and the cost, even if it could be found, would be colossal! Please understand, Inquisitor, that the components must be imported from the distant south of Kanta, and are rarities even there. I would be happy to look into the possibility, of course, but I would need considerable funding—"

"Thank you again for your time." Glokta turned and began to limp through the thinning smoke towards the door.

"I have made some significant progress with acids recently!" cried the Adeptus, voice cracking. "You really should see those as well!" He took a shuddering breath. "Tell the Arch Lector . . . significant progress!" He dissolved into another fit of coughing, and Glokta shut the door tightly behind him.

A waste of my time. Our Bayaz could not have smuggled barrels of powder into that room. Even then, how much smoke, how great a smell would it have made? A waste of my time.

Silber was lurking in the hallway outside. "Is there anything else that we can show you, Inquisitor?"

Glokta paused for a moment. "Does anyone here know anything about magic?"

The Administrator's jaw muscles clenched. "A joke of course. Perhaps—"

"Magic, I said."

Silber narrowed his eyes. "You must understand that we are a scientific institution. The practice of magic, so called, would be most . . . inappropriate."

Glokta frowned at the man. *I'm not asking you to get your wand out, fool.* "From a historical standpoint," he snapped, "the Magi, and so on. Bayaz!"

"Ah, from a historical standpoint, I see." Silber's taut face relaxed slightly. "Our library contains a wide range of ancient texts, some of them dating back to the period when magic was considered . . . less remarkable."

"Who can assist me?"

The Administrator raised his brows. "I am afraid that the Adeptus Historical is, ah, something of a relic."

"I need to speak with him, not fence with him."

"Of course, Inquisitor, this way."

Glokta grabbed the handle of an ancient-looking door, studded with
black rivets, began to turn it. He felt Silber seize his arm.

"No!" he snapped, guiding Glokta away down a corridor beside. "The
stacks are down here."

The Adeptus Historical seemed indeed to be a part of ancient history himself.
His face was a mask of lined and sagging half-transparent skin. Sparse hairs,
snowy white, stuck unkempt from his head. There were only a quarter as many
as there should have been, but each was four times longer than you would
expect, hence his eyebrows were thin, yet sprouted out to impressive length in
all directions, like the whiskers of a cat. His mouth hung slack, weak, and toothless, hands were withered gloves, several sizes too big. Only his eyes showed any
trace of life, peering up at Glokta and the administrator as they approached.

"Visitors, is it?" croaked the old man, apparently talking to a large black
crow perched on his desk.

"This is Inquisitor Glokta!" bellowed the Administrator, leaning down
towards the old man's ear.

"Glokta?"

"From the Arch Lector!"

"Is it?" The Adeptus Historical squinted up with his ancient eyes.

"He's somewhat deaf," Silber murmured, "but no one knows these books
like he does." He thought about it for a moment, peering round at the endless
stacks, disappearing into the gloom. "No one else knows these books at all."

"Thank you," said Glokta. The Administrator nodded and strode off
towards the stairs. Glokta took a step towards the old man and the crow
leaped from the table and scrambled into the air, shedding feathers, flapping
madly around the ceiling. Glokta hobbled painfully back. *I was sure the damn
thing was stuffed.* He watched it suspiciously until it clattered to a halt on top
of one of the shelves and perched there motionless, staring at him with its
beady yellow eyes.

Glokta pulled out a chair and dropped into it. "I need to know about Bayaz."

"Bayaz," muttered the ancient Adeptus. "The first letter in the alphabet of the old tongue, of course."

"I didn't know that."

"The world's brimming full of what you don't know, young man." The bird gave a sudden harsh caw, horribly loud in the dusty silence of the stacks. "Brimming full."

"Then let's begin my education. It's the man Bayaz, I need to know about. The First of the Magi."

"Bayaz. The name great Juvens gave to his first apprentice. One letter, one name. First apprentice, first letter of the alphabet, you understand?"

"I'm just about keeping up. Did he really exist?"

The ancient Adeptus scowled. "Unquestionably. Did you not have a tutor as a young man?"

"I did, unfortunately."

"Did he not teach you history?"

"He tried, but my mind was on fencing and girls."

"Ah. I lost interest in such things a long time ago."

"So did I. Let us return to Bayaz."

The old man sighed. "Long ago, before there was a Union, Midderland was made of many petty kingdoms, often at war with one another, rising and falling with the passing years. One of these was ruled by a man called Harod, later to become Harod the Great. You've heard of him, I assume?"

"Of course."

"Bayaz came to Harod's throne room, and promised to make him King of all Midderland if he did as he was told. Harod, being young and headstrong, did not believe him, but Bayaz broke the long table with his art."

"Magic, eh?"

"So the story goes. Harod was impressed—"

"Understandable."

"—and he agreed to accept the advice of the Magus—"

"Which was?"

"To make his capital here, in Adua. To make peace with certain neighbours, war with others, and when and how to do it." The old man squinted across at Glokta. "Are you telling this story or am I?"

"You are." *And you're taking your time about it.*

"Bayaz was good as his word. In time Midderland was unified, Harod became its first High King, the Union was born."

"Then what?"

"Bayaz served as Harod's chief counsellor. Our laws and statutes, the very structure of our government, all are said to be his inventions, little changed since those ancient days. He established the Councils, Closed and Open, he formed the Inquisition. On Harod's death he left the Union, promising one day to return."

"I see. How much of this is true, do you think?"

"Hard to say. Magus? Wizard? Magician?" The old man looked at the flickering candle flame. "To a savage, that candle might be magic. It's a fine line indeed, between magic and trickery, eh? But this Bayaz was a cunning mind in his day, that's a fact."

This is all useless. "What about before?"

"Before what?"

"Before the Union. Before Harod."

The old man shrugged. "Record-keeping was hardly a priority during the dark ages. The whole world was in chaos after the war between Juvens and his brother Kanedias—"

"Kanedias? The Master Maker?"

"Aye."

Kanedias. He stares down from the walls of my little room in the cellars beneath Severard's charming town house. Juvens dead, his eleven apprentices, the Magi, marching to avenge him. I know this tale.

"Kanedias," murmured Glokta, the image of that dark figure with the flames behind clear in his mind. "The Master Maker. Was he real?"

"Hard to say. He's in the ground between myth and history, I suppose. Probably there's some grain of truth in it. Someone must have built that big bloody tower, eh?"

"Tower?"

"The House of the Maker!" The old man gestured at the room around them. "And they say he built all this as well."

"What, this library?"

The old man laughed. "The whole Agriont, or at least the rock on which it stands. The University too. He built it, appointed the first Adepti to help him with his works, whatever they were, to look into the nature of things. We here are the Maker's disciples, yes, though I doubt they know it upstairs. He is gone but the work continues, eh?"

"After a fashion. Where did he go?"

"Hah. Dead. Your friend Bayaz killed him."

Glokta raised an eyebrow. "Did he really?"

"So the story goes. Have you not read *The Fall of the Master Maker?*"

"That rubbish? I thought it was all invention."

"So it is. Sensational claptrap, but based on writings from the time."

"Writings? Such things survive?"

The old man narrowed his eyes. "Some."

"Some? You have them here?"

"One in particular."

Glokta fixed the old man with his eye. "Bring it to me."

The ancient paper crackled as the Adeptus Historical carefully unrolled the scroll and spread it out on the table. The parchment was yellow and crumpled, edges rough with age, scrawled with a dense script: strange characters, utterly unintelligible to Glokta's eye.

"What is it written in?"

"The old tongue. Few can read this now." The old man pointed to the first line. "An account of the fall of Kanedias, this says, the third of three."

"Third of three?"

"Of three scrolls, I presume."

"Where are the other two?"

"Lost."

"Huh." Glokta peered into the endless darkness of the stacks. *It's a wonder anything can be found down here.* "What does this one say?"

The ancient librarian peered down at the strange writing, poorly illuminated by the single flickering candle, his trembling forefinger tracing across the parchment, his lips moving silently. "Great was their fury."

"What?"

"That's how it begins. Great was their fury." He began slowly to read. "The
Magi pursued Kanedias, driving his faithful before them. They broke his
fortress, laying ruin to his buildings and killing his servants. The Maker himself, sore wounded in the battle with his brother Juvens, took refuge in his
House." The old man unrolled a little more. "Twelve days and twelve nights,
the Magi threw their wrath against the gates, but could not mark them. Then
Bayaz found a way inside . . ." The Adeptus swept his hand over the parchment
in frustration. Damp, or something, had blurred the characters in the next section. "I can't make this out . . . something about the Maker's daughter?"

"You sure?"

"No!" snapped the old man. "There's a whole section missing!"

"Ignore it then! What's the next thing you can be sure of?"

"Well, let's see . . . Bayaz followed him to the roof, and cast him down."
The old man noisily cleared his throat. "The Maker fell burning, and broke
upon the bridge below. The Magi searched high and low for the Seed, but
could not find it."

"Seed?" asked Glokta, baffled.

"That's all that's written."

"What the hell does it mean?"

The old man sagged back in his chair, evidently enjoying this rare opportunity to hold forth on his area of expertise. "The end of the age of myth, the
beginning of the age of reason. Bayaz, the Magi, they represent order. The
Maker is a god-like figure: superstition, ignorance, I don't know. There must
be some truth to him. After all, someone built that big bloody tower," and
he wheezed with breathy laughter.

Glokta could not be bothered to point out that the Adeptus had made
the very same joke a few minutes before. *And it wasn't funny then. Repetition—
the curse of the old.* "What about this Seed?"

"Magic, secrets, power? It's all a metaphor."

I will not impress the Arch Lector with metaphors. Especially bad ones. "Is there
no more?"

"It goes on a bit, let's see." He looked back at the symbols. "He broke on
the bridge, they searched for the Seed . . ."

"Yes, yes."

"Patience, Inquisitor." His withered finger traced across the characters. "They sealed up the House of the Maker. They buried the fallen, Kanedias and his daughter among them. That's all." He peered at the page, his finger hovering over the last few letters. "And Bayaz took the key. That's all."

Glokta's eyebrows went up. "What? What was that last bit?"

"They sealed the gates, they buried the fallen, and Bayaz took the key."

"The key? The key to the House of the Maker?"

The Adeptus Historical squinted back at the page. "That's what it says."

There is no key. That tower has stood sealed for centuries, everyone knows it. Our impostor will have no key, that's sure. Slowly, Glokta began to smile. *It is thin, it is very thin, but with the right setting, the right emphasis, it might be enough. The Arch Lector will be pleased.*

"I'll be taking this." Glokta pulled the ancient scroll over and started to roll it up.

"What?" The eyes of the Adeptus were wide with horror. "You can't!" He staggered up from his chair, even more painfully than Glokta might have done. His crow scrambled up with him, flapping around near the ceiling and croaking in a fury, but Glokta ignored them both. "You can't take it! It's irreplaceable," wheezed the old man, making a hopeless grab for the scroll.

Glokta spread his arms out wide. "Stop me! Why don't you? I'd like to see it! Can you imagine? We two cripples, floundering around in the stacks with a bird loosing its droppings on us, tugging this old piece of paper to and fro?" He giggled to himself. "That wouldn't be very dignified, would it?"

The Adeptus Historical, exhausted by his pitiful efforts, crumpled back into his chair, breathing hard. "No one cares about the past any more," he whispered. "They don't see that you can't have a future without a past."

How very deep. Glokta slipped the rolled-up parchment into his coat and turned to leave.

"Who's going to look after the past, when I'm gone?"

"Who cares?" asked Glokta as he stalked towards the steps, "as long as it isn't me."

THE REMARKABLE TALENTS
OF BROTHER LONGFOOT

The cheering had woken Logen every morning for a week. It started early, ripping him from his sleep, loud as a battle close at hand. He'd thought it was a battle when he first heard it, but now he knew it was just their damn stupid sport. Closing the window brought some relief from the noise, but the heat soon became unbearable. It was sleep a little, or sleep not at all. So he left the window open.

Logen rubbed his eyes, cursing, and hauled himself from his bed. Another hot, tedious day in the City of White Towers. On the road, in the wild, he'd be alert as soon as his eyes opened, but here things were different. The boredom and the heat were making him slow and lazy. He stumbled across the threshold into the living room, yawning wide and rubbing at his jaw with one hand. He stopped.

There was someone in there, a stranger. Standing at the window, bathed in sunlight with his hands clasped behind him. A small, slight man, with hair shaved close to his knobbly skull and strange, travel-worn clothes— faded, baggy cloth wrapped round and round his body.

Before Logen had a chance to speak, the man turned and sprang nimbly over to him. "And you are?" he demanded. His smiling face was deeply tanned and weather-beaten, like the creased leather on a favourite pair of boots. It made it impossible to guess his age. He could have been anywhere from twenty-five to fifty.

"Ninefingers," muttered Logen, taking a cautious step back towards the wall.

"Ninefingers, yes." The little man pressed forwards and seized Logen's hand in both of his, gripping it tightly. "It is an honour and privilege most profound," he said, closing his eyes and bowing his head, "to make your acquaintance!"

"You've heard of me?"

"Alas, no, but all God's creatures are worthy of the deepest respect." He bowed his head again. "I am Brother Longfoot, a traveller of the illustrious order of Navigators. There are few lands beneath the sun upon which my feet have not trodden." He pointed down towards his well-worn boots then spread his arms wide. "From the mountains of Thond to the deserts of Shamir, from the plains of the Old Empire to the silver waters of the Thousand Isles, all the world is my home! Truly!"

He spoke the northern tongue well, better than Logen himself perhaps. "And the North too?"

"One brief visit, in my youth. I found the climate somewhat harsh."

"You speak the language well enough."

"There are few tongues that I, Brother Longfoot, cannot speak. An effortless skill with languages is but one among my many remarkable talents." The man beamed. "God has truly blessed me," he added.

Logen wondered if this might be some elaborate joke. "What brings you here?"

"I have been sent for!" His dark eyes sparkled.

"Sent for?"

"Indeed I have! By Bayaz, the First of the Magi! I have been sent for, and I have come! That is my way! A most generous contribution to the coffers of the order has been made in return for my remarkable talents, but I would have come without it. Indeed. Without it!"

"Really?"

"Indeed!" The small man stepped away and started to stride around the room at a terrific pace, rubbing his hands together. "The challenge of this assignment spoke as much to the pride of the order, as to its well-documented greed! And it was I! I who was selected, from all the Navigators within the Circle of the World, for this task! I, Brother Longfoot! I, and no other! Who in my position, of my reputation, could resist such a challenge?"

He stopped before Logen and looked up at him expectantly, as if waiting for an answer to his question. "Er—"

"Not I!" shouted Longfoot, setting off on another circuit of the room, "I did not resist it! Why would I? That would not be my way! To journey to the very edge of the World? What a tale that will make! What an inspiration to others! What an—"

"The edge of the World?" asked Logen suspiciously.

"I know!" The strange man clapped him on the arm. "We are equally excited!"

"This must be our Navigator." Bayaz emerged from his room.

"I am indeed. Brother Longfoot, at your service. And you are, I presume, none other than my illustrious employer, Bayaz, the First of the Magi."

"I am he."

"It is an honour and a privilege most profound!" cried Longfoot, springing forward and seizing the Magus by the hand, "to make your acquaintance!"

"Likewise. I trust your journey was a pleasant one."

"Journeys are always pleasant to me! Always! It is the time between them that I find trying. Indeed it is!" Bayaz frowned over at Logen but he could only shrug his shoulders. "May I ask how long it will be until we begin our journey? I am most keen to embark!"

"Soon, I hope, the last member of our expedition will arrive. We will need to charter a ship."

"Of course! It shall be my particular pleasure to do so! What shall I tell the captain of our course?"

"West across the Circle Sea, to Stariksa, then on to Calcis in the Old Empire." The little man smiled and bowed low. "You approve?"

"I do, but ships rarely pass to Calcis now. The Old Empire's endless wars have made the waters dangerous thereabouts. Piracy, alas, is rife. It may be difficult to find a captain willing."

"This should help." Bayaz tossed his ever-bulging purse onto the table.

"It should indeed."

"Make sure the ship is fast. Once we are ready I do not wish to waste a day."

"On that you may depend," said the Navigator, scooping up the heavy bag of coins. "To sail in slow vessels is not my way! No! I will find for you the fastest ship in all Adua! Yes! She shall fly like the breath of God! She shall skip over the waves like—"

"Merely fast will do."

The little man inclined his head. "The time of departure?"

"Within the month." Bayaz looked at Logen. "Why don't you go with him?"

"Uh?"

"Yes!" shouted the Navigator, "we will go together!" He grabbed Logen by the elbow and began to pull him towards the door.

"I will expect some change, Brother Longfoot!" called Bayaz, from behind.

The Navigator turned in the doorway. "There will be change, on that you may depend. An eye for value, a flair for barter, a dauntless purpose in negotiation! These are but three," and he smiled broadly, "of my remarkable talents!"

"It is a fabulous place, this Adua. Truly. Few cities are its equal. Shaffa, perhaps, is larger, but so very dusty. None could deny that Westport and Dagoska have their sights. Some think of Ospria, on its mountain slopes, as the most beautiful city of the world, but Brother Longfoot's heart, it must be said, belongs to great Talins. Have you been there, Master Ninefingers, have you seen that noble settlement?"

"Er . . ." Logen was busy trying to keep up with the little man, dodging between the endless flow of people.

Longfoot stopped so suddenly that Logen almost piled into him. The Navigator turned, his hands raised, a far away look in his eye. "Talins at sunset, seen from the ocean! I have witnessed many remarkable things, believe me, but I declare that to be the most beautiful sight in all the world. The way the sun gleams on the myriad canals, on the glinting domes of the Grand Duke's citadel, on the graceful palaces of the merchant princes! Where now does the shining sea end, and the shining city begin? Ah! Talins!" He turned and charged off once more and Logen hurried after him.

"But this Adua is a fine place, certainly, and growing every year. Things have changed a great deal here since my last visit, indeed they have. Once there were only noblemen and commoners. The noblemen owned the land so they had the money and therefore the power. Ha. Simple, you see?"

"Well—" Logen was having trouble seeing much further than Long-foot's back.

"But now they have trade, and so much of it. Merchants, and bankers, and so forth. Everywhere. Armies of them. Now commoners can be rich, you see? And a rich commoner has power. Is he a commoner now, or a nobleman? Or is he something else? Ha. Very complicated all of a sudden, no?"

"Er—"

"So much wealth. So much money. But so much poverty too, eh? So many beggars, so many poor. Hardly healthy, so rich and so poor, so close together, but it's a fine place still, and always growing."

"I find it too crowded," mumbled Logen as a shoulder barged past him, "and too hot."

"Bah! Crowded? Do you call this crowded? You should see the great temple in Shaffa at morning prayer! Or the grand square before the Emperor's palace when new slaves are up for auction! And hot? Do you call this hot? In Ul-Saffayn, in the far south of Gurkhul, it gets so hot during the summer months that you can cook an egg on your doorstep. Truly! This way." He ducked through the passing crowds towards a narrow sidestreet. "This way is the quickest!"

Logen caught him by the arm. "Down there?" He peered into the gloom. "You sure?"

"Can you doubt it?" demanded Longfoot, suddenly horrified. "Can it be that you could doubt it? Among all my remarkable talents, it is my skill at navigation that is paramount! It is for that talent, above all, that the First of the Magi has made so generous a contribution to the coffers of the order! Could it be that you . . . but wait." He held up his hand and began to smile again, then tapped Logen on the chest with his forefinger. "*You* do not know Brother Longfoot. Not yet. You are watchful and cautious, I see it, fine qualities in their place. I cannot expect you to have *my* unshakeable faith in my abilities. No! That would not be fair. Unfairness is not an admirable quality. No! Unfairness is not my way."

"I meant—"

"I shall convince you!" shouted Longfoot. "Indeed I shall! You will come to trust my word before your own! Yes! This way is the quickest!" And he strode off down the dingy alleyway with remarkable speed, Logen struggling to keep up though his legs were a good half-foot longer.

"Ah, the back streets!" called the Navigator over his shoulder as they passed down dark and grimy lanes, the buildings crowding in ever closer. "The back streets, eh?" The alleys grew narrower, darker, and dirtier still. The little man turned to the left and the right, never pausing for an instant to consider his course. "Do you smell that? Do you smell that, Master Ninefingers? It smells like . . ." he rubbed his thumbs and fingertips together as he strode along, searching for the words ". . . mystery! Adventure!"

It smelled like shit to Logen. A man lay on his face in the gutter, dead drunk perhaps, or maybe simply dead. Other men passed by, limping and haggard, or standing in threatening groups in doorways, handing round bottles. There were women here too.

"Four marks and I'll give you a blessing, Northman!" one of them called to Logen as they passed. "A blessing you won't soon forget! Three, then!"

"Whores," whispered Longfoot, shaking his head, "and cheap ones too. You like women?"

"Well—"

"You should go to Ul-Nahb my friend! Ul-Nahb on the shores of the Southern Sea! You could buy a bed-slave there. Indeed you could! They cost a fortune, but they train these girls for years!"

"You can buy a girl?" asked Logen, mystified.

"Boys too, if your taste bends that way."

"Eh?"

"They train them for years, truly. It's a whole industry down there. You want skilled? Do you? These girls have skills you wouldn't believe! Or visit Sipani! There are places in that city—phew! The women are beautiful, beautiful every one! Truly! Like princesses! And clean," he muttered, peering at one of the scruffy women by the roadside.

A bit of dirt didn't bother Logen any. Skilled and beautiful all sounded too complicated to him. One girl caught his eye as they passed, leaning against a door-frame with one arm up. Watching them pass with a half-hearted smile. Logen found her pretty, in a desperate sort of a way. Prettier than he was anyway, and it had been a long time. You have to be realistic about these things.

Logen stopped in the street. "Bayaz wanted change?" he muttered.

"He did. He was most specific on the subject."

"There's money to spare, then?"

Longfoot raised one eyebrow. "Well, perhaps, let me see . . ." He pulled out the purse with a flourish and opened it, rooting around inside. There was a loud jingling of coins.

"You think that's a good idea?" Logen glanced nervously up and down the street. Several faces had turned towards them.

"What's that?" asked the Navigator, still poking around in the purse. He pulled some coins out, holding them up to the light and peering at them, then pressed them into Logen's palm.

"Subtlety isn't one of your talents, is it?" Some of the shabby men in the alley began to move slowly, curiously towards them, two from in front, one from behind.

"No indeed!" laughed Longfoot. "No indeed! I am a straight-talking man, that is my way! Yes indeed! I am a . . . ah." He had noticed the shadowy figures sidling towards them now. "Ah. This is unfortunate. Oh dear."

Logen turned to the girl. "Do you mind if we . . ." She slammed the door shut in his face. Other doors up and down the street began to close. "Shit." he said. "How are you at fighting?"

"God has seen fit to bless me with many remarkable talents," murmured the navigator, "but combat is not one of them."

One of the men had an ugly squint. "That's a big purse for a little man," he said, as he came close.

"Well, er . . ." murmured Longfoot, creeping behind Logen's shoulder.

"An awful big load for a little man to carry," said the other.

"Why not let us help you with it?"

Neither one of them had weapons ready, but by the way their hands were moving Logen knew they had them. There was a third man behind him too, he could sense him moving forwards now. Close. Closer than the other two. If he could deal with that one first, the one behind, his chances might be good. He couldn't risk looking round, that would spoil the surprise. He'd simply have to hope for the best. As always.

Logen gritted his teeth and flung his elbow backwards. It hit the man behind in the jaw with a heavy crunch, and Logen caught his wrist in his other hand, which was lucky, because he had a knife out and ready. Logen smashed him in the mouth with his elbow again, tearing the blade from his limp fingers as he dropped into the street, head smacking against the dirty cobbles. He whipped round, half expecting to get stabbed in the back, but the other two hadn't moved too quick. They had knives of their own out, and one had taken a half-step towards him, but he paused when he saw that Logen had the blade up, ready to fight.

It was a meagre kind of a weapon, six inches of rusty iron without even a cross-piece, but it was better than nothing. A lot better. Logen waved it around in the air in front of him, just to make sure that everyone could see it. Felt good. His odds were much improved.

"Right then," said Logen, "who's next?"

The other two moved apart, trying to get to either side of him, weighing their knives in their hands, but they didn't seem in any great rush to come on.

"We can take him!" whispered the squinter, but his friend didn't look too sure.

"Or, you can have this." Logen opened up his clenched fist, showing the coins that Longfoot had given him. "And leave us be. This much I can spare." He swished the knife around a bit more, just to add some weight to his words. "This is what you're worth to me—this much, no more. What's it to be?"

The one with the squint spat on the ground. "We can take him!" he hissed again. "You go first!"

"You fucking go!" shouted the other.

"Just take what I'm offering," said Logen, "then we none of us have to go."

The one that he'd elbowed groaned and rolled over in the road, and the reminder of his fate seemed to decide them. "Alright, you fucking northern bastard, alright, we'll take it!"

Logen grinned. He thought about throwing the coins at the one with the squint then stabbing him while he was distracted. That's what he'd have done in his youth, but he decided against. Why bother? Instead he opened his fingers and tossed the money into the road behind him, moving towards the nearest wall. He and the two thieves circled each other cautiously, each step taking them closer to the coins and him closer to escape. Soon they'd swapped places, and Logen backed away down the street, still holding the knife in front of him. When they were ten paces apart the two men squatted down and began to pick the scattered coins up from the ground.

"I'm still alive," Logen whispered to himself as he quickened his pace.

That had been lucky, he knew. It's a fool who thinks that any fight is too small to be the death of him, however tough he is. Lucky that he caught the one behind just right. Lucky that the other two had been slow. But then he'd always been lucky with fights. Lucky at getting out of them alive. Not so lucky with the getting into them. Still, he felt good about this day's work. Glad he hadn't killed anybody.

Logen felt a hand clap him on the back, and he spun round, knife at the ready.

"Only me!" Brother Longfoot held up his hands. Logen had nearly forgotten the Navigator was there. He must have stayed behind him the whole time, perfectly silent. "Well handled Master Ninefingers, well handled! Truly! I see that you are not without some talents of your own! I am looking forward to travelling with you, I am indeed! The docks are this way!" he shouted, already moving off.

Logen took one last look back at the two men, but they were still grubbing around on the ground, so he threw the knife away and hurried to catch up to Longfoot. "Do you Navigators never fight?"

"Some among us do, oh yes, with empty hands and weapons of all kinds. Most deadly, some of them, but not I. No. That is not my way."

"Never?"

"Never. My skills lie elsewhere."

"I would have thought your travels would bring you across many dangers."

"They do," said Longfoot brightly, "they do indeed. That is when my remarkable talent for hiding is at its most useful."

HER KIND
FIGHT EVERYTHING

N ight. Cold. The salt wind was keen on the hilltop, and Ferro's clothes were thin and ragged. She hugged her arms and hunched up her shoulders, staring sourly down towards the sea. Dagoska was a cloud of pin-prick lights in the distance, huddled around the steep rock between the great, curving bay and the glistening ocean. Her eyes could make out the vague, tiny shapes of walls and towers, black against the dark sky, and the thin neck of dry earth that joined the city to the land. An island, almost. Between them and Dagoska there were fires. Camps around the roads. Many camps.

"Dagoska," whispered Yulwei, perched on a rock beside her. "A little splinter of the Union, stuck into Gurkhul like a thorn. A thorn in the Emperor's pride."

"Huh," grunted Ferro, hunching her shoulders still further.

"The city is watched. Many soldiers. More than ever. It might be diffi-cult to deceive so many."

"Perhaps we should go back," she muttered hopefully.

The old man ignored her. "*They* are here as well. More than one."

"Eaters?"

"I must go closer. Find a way in. Wait here for me." He paused, waiting for her to reply. "You will wait?"

"Alright!" she hissed, "alright, I'll wait!"

Yulwei slipped off his rock and away down the slope, padding across the soft earth, almost invisible in the inky blackness. When the sound of his jingling bangles had faded into the night, she turned away from the city, took a deep breath, and scurried down the slope southwards, back into Gurkhul.

Now Ferro could run. Fast as the wind, hours at a stretch. She'd spent a lot of time running. When she made it to the base of the hill she ran, feet flying across the open ground, breath coming quick and fierce. She heard water beyond, slid down a bank and splashed into the shallows of a slow moving river. She floundered on, knee-deep in the cold water.

Let the old bastard track me through this, she thought.

After a while she made a bundle of her weapons and held them above her head as she swam across, forcing against the current with one arm. She flapped out on the other side and ran on along the bank, wiping the water from her dripping face.

Time passed slowly and light began to creep into the sky. Morning was coming. The river babbled beside her, her sandals beating out a rapid rhythm in the stubbly grass. She left the river behind, running on across the flat landscape, turning now from black to grey. A clump of scrubby trees loomed up.

She crashed between the trunks and slithered down into the bushes, her breath rasping. She shivered in the half-light, heart pounding in her chest. It was silent beyond the trees. Good. She reached inside her clothes and pulled out some bread and a strip of meat, soggy from the swim but still edible. She smiled. She had been keeping half of everything that Yulwei gave her for the last few days.

"Stupid old bastard," she chuckled to herself between choking mouthfuls, "thought he could get the better of Ferro Maljinn, did he?"

Damn she was thirsty. No help for that now, she could find water later. She was tired though, very tired. Even Ferro got tired. She would rest here for a moment, just a moment. Get the strength back in the legs, then on, on to . . . she twitched, annoyed. She could think about the where later. Wherever was best for vengeance. Yes.

She crawled through the bushes, sat back against one of the trees. Her eyes closed slowly, by themselves. Just rest for a moment now. Vengeance later.

"Stupid old bastard," she muttered. Her head dropped sideways.

"Brother!"

Ferro woke with a start, head knocking against the tree. It was light, too light. Another bright, hot day. How long had she been sleeping? "Brother!" A woman's voice, not far off. "Where are you?"

"Over here!" Ferro froze, every muscle tensing. A man's voice, deep and strong. And close. She heard horse's hooves, moving slowly, several horses, and near.

"What are you doing, brother?"

"She's close!" shouted the man again. Ferro's throat tightened. "I can smell her!" Ferro felt in the bushes for her weapons, shoved the sword and the knife through her belt, tucked the other knife up her one, torn sleeve. "I can taste her, sister! She's very close!"

"But where?" The woman's voice drew nearer. "Do you think she can hear us?"

"Perhaps she can!" laughed the man. "Are you there, Maljinn?" She threw her quiver over her shoulder and snatched up her bow. "We are waiting . . ." he sang, getting closer still, just beyond the trees now. "Come out, Maljinn, come out and greet us . . ."

She bolted away, crashing through the bushes, sprinting across the open ground with desperate speed.

"There she is!" cried the woman from behind. "Look at her go!"

"Get her, then!" shouted the man.

The scrubby grassland stretched away unbroken before her. Nowhere to run to. She spun around with a snarl, knocking an arrow to her bow. Four horsemen were spurring towards her, Gurkish soldiers, sun glinting on their tall helmets and the cruel heads of their spears. Behind them, further back, were two other riders: a man and a woman. "Stop! In the name of the Emperor!" one of the horsemen shouted.

"Fuck your Emperor!" Her arrow caught the first of the soldiers through his neck and he tumbled backwards from the saddle with a shocked gurgle, his spear flying out of his hand.

"Good shot!" cried the woman. The second rider took an arrow in his chest. His breastplate slowed it, but it still went deep enough to kill. He screamed, dropping his sword in the grass, clutching at the shaft, rolling in the saddle.

The third never even made a sound. He got one in the mouth, at no more than ten strides away. The point went right through his skull and knocked his helmet off, but by then the fourth was on her. She threw the bow to the ground and rolled away as the soldier thrust at her with his spear, then she pulled the sword from her belt, spitting on the grass.

"Alive!" shouted the woman, nudging her horse lazily forwards. "We need her alive!"

The soldier turned his snorting mount and urged it cautiously towards Ferro. He was a big man, with a thick growth of dark stubble on his jaw. "I hope you've made your peace with God, girl," he said.

"Fuck your God!" She scuttled out of the way, dodging, moving, staying close to the ground. The soldier jabbed at her with his spear, keeping her at a distance, his horse's hooves pawing at the ground, kicking dust in Ferro's face.

"Poke her!" she heard the woman shouting behind her.

"Yes, poke her!" cried her brother through his giggling. "But not too hard! We want her alive!" The soldier snarled as he spurred his horse forward. Ferro ducked and scrambled in front of its kicking legs. The spear point jabbed, cutting a gash in her arm. She swung the sword with all her strength.

The curved blade found the gap between the plates of the soldier's armour, took his leg off just below the knee and opened a huge wound in the horse's side. Man and beast screamed together, fell together to the ground. Dark blood bubbled out across the dirt.

"She got him!" The woman sounded mildly disappointed.

"Up, man!" laughed her brother, "up and at her! There's still a chance!" The soldier thrashed on the ground. Ferro's sword hacked into his face, putting a sharp end to his screams. Nearby the second rider was still in his saddle, face twisted, gasping his last breaths, hand clutched around the bloody shaft of her arrow. His horse put its head down and started nibbling at the dry grass by its hooves.

"That's all of them," said the woman.

"I know." Her brother sighed deep. "Must one do everything oneself?"

Ferro glanced up at them as she pushed the bloody sword back through her belt. They were sitting carelessly on their horses not far off, the sun bright behind them, smiles on their cruel, handsome faces. They were dressed like lords, silk flapping round them in the breeze, heavy with jewellery, but neither one was armed. Ferro scrambled for her bow.

"Be careful, brother," said the woman, examining her fingernails. "She fights well."

"Like a devil! But she is no match for me, sister, have no fear." He sprang down from his saddle. "So then, Maljinn, shall we . . ."

The arrow stuck him through the chest, deep through, with a hollow thud.

". . . begin?" The shaft quivered, its point glittering behind him, dry and bloodless. He began to walk towards her. Her next arrow caught him through the shoulder, but he only came on faster, breaking into a run, bounding forward with enormous strides. She dropped the bow, fingers fumbling for the grip of her sword. Too slow. His outstretched arm caught her across the chest with terrible force, slamming her into the earth.

"Oh, well done, brother!" The woman clapped her hands with delight. "Well done!"

Ferro rolled coughing in the dust. She saw the man watching her as she struggled to her feet, the sword clutched in both hands. She swung it at him, a great overhead arc. It bit deep into the earth. Somehow he had already danced aside. A foot came out of nowhere and sank into her stomach. She doubled over, powerless, the air driven from her body. Her fingers twitched, the sword was left stuck in the ground, her knees wobbled.

"And now . . ." Something crunched into her nose. Her legs buckled and the ground hit her hard in the back. She rolled groggily to her knees, the world turning over around her. There was blood on her face. She blinked and shook her head, trying to stop the world from spinning. The man was moving towards her, tipping, blurry. He jerked her arrow out of his chest and tossed it away. There was no blood, just a little dust. Just dust, curling in the air.

An Eater. He had to be.

Ferro stumbled up, pulling the knife from her belt. She thrust at him, missed, thrust again, missed again. Her head was swimming. She screamed, slashing at him with all her might.

He caught her wrist in his hand. Their faces were less than a foot apart. His skin was perfect, smooth, like dark glass. He looked young, almost like a child, but his eyes were old. Hard eyes. He watched her—curious, amused, like a boy who found an interesting beetle. "She doesn't give up, does she, sister?"

"Very fierce! The Prophet will be delighted with her!"

The man sniffed at Ferro and wrinkled his nose. "Ugh. She'd better be washed first."

She butted him in the face. His head snapped back but he only giggled. He caught her round the throat with his free hand, shoved her out to arm's length. She clawed at his face but his arm was too long, she couldn't reach. He was prising her fingers from the handle of the knife. His grip was iron around her neck. She couldn't breathe. She bared her teeth, struggling, snarling, thrashing. All in vain.

"Alive, brother! We want her alive!"

"Alive," murmured the man, "but not unharmed."

The woman giggled. Ferro's feet left the ground, kicking at the air. She felt one of her fingers snap and the knife dropped to the grass. The hand gripped tighter round her neck, and she tore at it with broken nails. All in vain. The bright world began to turn dark.

Ferro heard the woman laughing, far away. A face swam out of the darkness, a hand stroked Ferro's cheek. The fingers were soft, warm, gentle.

"Be still, child," whispered the woman. Her eyes were dark and deep. Ferro could feel her breath, hot and fragrant on her face. "You are hurt, you must rest. Be still now . . . sleep." Ferro's legs were heavy as lead. She kicked weakly, one last time, then her body sagged. Her heart beat slow . . .

"Rest now." Ferro's eyelids began to droop, the woman's beautiful face grew blurred.

"Sleep." Ferro bit down hard on her tongue, and her mouth turned salty.

"Be still." Ferro spat blood in the woman's face.

"Gah!" she shouted in disgust, wiping blood from her eyes. "She fights me!"

"Her kind fight everything," came the man's voice, just behind Ferro's ear.

"Now listen to me, whore!" hissed the woman, clutching Ferro's jaw with steely fingers and yanking her face this way and that. "You are coming with us! With us! One way or another! You hear me?"

"She goes nowhere." Another voice, deep and mellow. It seemed familiar. Ferro blinked, shook her head groggily. The woman had turned, looking at an old man, not far away. Yulwei. His bangles jingled as he padded softly across the grass. "Are you alive, Ferro?"

"Gugh," she croaked.

The woman sneered at Yulwei. "Who are you, old bastard?"

Yulwei sighed. "I am an old bastard."

"Get you gone, dog!" shouted the man. "We come from the Prophet. From Khalul himself!"

"And she comes with us!"

Yulwei looked sad. "I cannot change your minds?"

They laughed together. "Fool!" cried the man. "Our minds never change!" He let go of one of Ferro's arms, took a wary step forwards, dragging her with him.

"A shame," said Yulwei, shaking his head. "I would have had you carry my respects to Khalul."

"The Prophet does not walk with the likes of you, beggar!"

"I might surprise you. We knew each other well, long ago."

"I will give our master your respects then," jeered the woman, "with the news of your recent death!" Ferro twisted her wrist, felt the knife drop into her palm.

"Oh, Khalul would enjoy that news, but he will not receive it yet. The two of you have cursed yourselves. You have broken the Second Law. You have eaten the flesh of men, and there must be a reckoning."

"Old fool!" sneered the woman. "Your laws do not apply to us!"

Yulwei slowly shook his head. "The word of Euz governs all. There can be no exceptions. Neither one of you will leave this place alive." The air around the old man shimmered, twisted, blurred. The woman gave a gurgle and dropped suddenly to the earth, more than falling—melting, flopping, dark silk flapping around her collapsing body.

"Sister!" The man let go of Ferro, sprang at Yulwei, arms outstretched. He got no further than a stride. He gave a sudden, shrill scream and dropped to his knees, clutching at his head. Ferro forced her stumbling feet forward, grabbed hold of his hair with her broken hand and drove the knife into his neck. Dust blew out into the wind. A fountain of dust. Flames flickered around his mouth, charring his lips black, licking burning hot at her fingers. She dropped on top of him, bearing him back onto the ground, choking, snorting. The blade opened up his stomach, scraped against his ribs, snapped off in his chest. Fire licked out. Fire and dust. She hacked at the body mindlessly with the broken knife, long after it had stopped moving.

She felt a hand on her shoulder. "He is dead, Ferro. They both are dead." She saw it was true. The man lay on his back, staring up at the sky, face charred round his nose and mouth, dust blowing from the gaping wounds.

"I killed him." Her voice cracked and broken in her throat.

"No, Ferro. I did that. They were young Eaters, weak and foolish. Still, you are lucky they wanted only to catch you."

"I am lucky," she mumbled, dribbling bloody spit onto the Eater's corpse. She dropped the broken knife, crawled away on all fours. The body of the woman lay next to her, if you could call it that. A shapeless, lumpy mass of flesh. She saw long hair, and an eye, and lips.

"What did you do?" she croaked through her bloody mouth.

"I turned her bones to water. And burned him from the inside. Water for one, fire for the other. Whatever works, for their kind." Ferro rolled over on the grass, looked up at the bright sky. She held her hand in front of her face, shook it. One of her fingers flopped back and forth.

Yulwei's face appeared above, staring down at her. "Does it hurt?"

"No," she whispered, letting her arm drop back to the earth. "It never does." She blinked up at Yulwei. "Why does it never hurt?"

The old man frowned. "They will not stop seeking for you, Ferro. Do you see now, why you have to come with me?"

She nodded slowly. The effort was immense. "I see," she whispered. "I see . . ." The world grew dark again.

SHE LOVES ME...NOT

"**A**h!" cried Jezal, as the point of Filio's steel dug hard into his shoulder. He stumbled back, wincing and cursing, and the Styrian smiled at him and flourished his steels.

"A touch to Master Filio!" bellowed the referee. "That's two each!" There was some scattered clapping as Filio strutted back to the contestant's enclosure with an irritating smile across his face. "Slippery bastard," Jezal hissed to himself as he followed. He should have seen that lunge coming. He had been careless, and he knew it.

"Two apiece?" hissed Varuz, as Jezal flopped down into his chair, breathing hard. "Two apiece? Against this nobody? He's not even from the Union!"

Jezal knew better than to point out that Westport was supposed to be a part of the Union these days. He knew what Varuz meant, and so did everyone else in the arena. The man was an outsider as far as they were concerned. He grabbed the cloth from West's outstretched hands and wiped his sweaty face. Five touches was a long match, but Filio looked far from exhausted. He was springing up and down on his toes as Jezal glanced across, nodding his head to the noisy Styrian advice spilling from his trainer.

"You can beat him!" West murmured, as he handed Jezal the water bottle. "You can beat him, and then it's the final." The final. That meant Gorst. Jezal wasn't entirely sure he wanted any of that.

But Varuz was in no doubt. "Just damn well beat him!" hissed the Marshal, as Jezal took a swig from the bottle, swilled it round in his mouth. "Just beat him!" Jezal spat half out into the bucket and swallowed the rest. Just beat him. Easy to say, but he was a devious bastard, this Styrian.

"You can do it!" said West again, rubbing Jezal's shoulder. "You've come this far!"

"Kill him! Just kill him!" Marshal Varuz stared into Jezal's eyes. "Are you a nobody, Captain Luthar? Did I waste my time on you? Or are you somebody? Eh? Now's the time to decide!"

"Gentlemen, please!" called the referee, "the deciding touch!"

Jezal blew out hard, took his steels from West, got to his feet. He could hear Filio's trainer shouting encouragements over the swelling noise of the crowd. "Just kill him!" shouted Varuz one last time, then Jezal was off on his way to the circle.

The deciding touch. The decider. In so many ways. Whether Jezal would be in the final or not. Whether he would be somebody or not. He was tired though, very tired. He had been fencing solidly for nearly half an hour, in the heat, and that takes it out of you. He was sweating again already. He could feel it leaking out of his face in big drops.

He moved towards his mark. A bit of chalk on some dry grass. Filio was standing there waiting, still smiling, anticipating his triumph. The little shit. If Gorst could club those others around the circle, then surely Jezal could grind this fool's face in the turf. He squeezed the grips of his steels and concentrated on that nauseating little smile. He wished for a moment that the steels weren't blunted, until it occurred to him that he might be the one who got stabbed.

"Begin!"

Jezal sorted through his cards, shuffling them this way and that in his hands, barely even looking at the symbols on them, barely caring whether he kept them out of sight of the others.

"I'll raise you ten," said Kaspa, sliding some coins across the table with a look that said . . . oh, something probably, Jezal didn't care what, he really wasn't concentrating. There was a lengthy pause.

"It's your bet, Jezal," grumbled Jalenhorm.

"It is? Oh, er . . ." He scanned across the meaningless symbols, unable to take any of it too seriously. "Erm, oh . . . I'll fold." He tossed the cards on to the table. He was down today, well down, for the first time in he couldn't remember how long. Ever probably. He was too busy thinking about Ardee: wondering how he could bed her without doing either one of them lasting harm, most particularly without his being killed by West. He was still no closer to an answer, unfortunately.

Kaspa swept up the coins, smiling broadly at his most unlikely victory. "So that was well fought today, Jezal. A close one, but you came through, eh?"

"Uh," said Jezal. He took his pipe from the table.

"I swear, I thought he had you for a minute there, but then," and he snapped his fingers under Brint's nose, "just like that! Knocked him right over. The crowd loved it! I laughed so hard I nearly wet myself, I swear!"

"Do you reckon you can beat Gorst?" asked Jalenhorm.

"Uh." Jezal shrugged, lighting the pipe and leaning back in his chair, looking up at the grey sky and sucking on the stem.

"You seem pretty calm about it all," said Brint.

"Uh."

The three officers glanced at each other, disappointed by the failure of their chosen topic. Kaspa picked another. "Have you fellows seen the Princess Terez yet?"

Brint and Jalenhorm sighed and gasped, then the three of them prattled their gormless appreciation of the woman. "Have I seen her? Have I ever!"

"They call her the jewel of Talins!"

"The rumours didn't lie where she's concerned!"

"I hear the marriage to Prince Ladisla is a fixed thing."

"The lucky bastard!" And so on.

Jezal stayed where he was, sat back in his chair, blowing smoke at the sky. He wasn't so sure about Terez, from the little he'd seen. Beautiful from a distance, no doubt, but he imagined that her face would feel like glass to the touch: cold, hard and brittle. Nothing like Ardee's . . .

"Still," Jalenhorm was spouting, "I have to say, Kaspa, my heart still belongs to your cousin Ariss. Give me a Union girl any day over one of these foreigners."

"Give you her money, you mean," murmured Jezal, head still tipped back.

"No!" complained the big man. "She's a perfect lady! Sweet, demure, well-bred. Ah!" Jezal smiled to himself. If Terez was cold glass, then Ariss was a dead fish. Kissing her would be like kissing an old rag, he imagined: limp and tedious. She couldn't kiss the way Ardee did. No one could . . .

"Well, they're both of them beauties, no doubt," Brint was blathering, "fine women to dream about, if dreams are all you're after . . ." He leaned forward to a conspiratorial distance, smirking shiftily round as though he had something secret and exciting to say. The other two edged their chairs forward, but Jezal stayed where he was. He had no interest at all in hearing about whatever whore that idiot was bedding.

"Have you met West's sister?" murmured Brint. Jezal's every muscle stiffened. "She's not the equal of those two of course, but she's really quite pretty in a common sort of way and . . . I think she'd be willing." Brint licked his lips and nudged Jalenhorm in the ribs. The big man grinned guiltily like a schoolboy at a dirty joke. "Oh yes, she strikes me as the willing type." Kaspa giggled. Jezal put his pipe down on the table, noticing that his hand was trembling slightly. The other was gripping the arm of his chair so hard that his knuckles were white.

"I do declare," said Brint, "if I didn't think the Major would stick me with his sword, I'd be tempted to stick his sister with mine, eh?" Jalenhorm spluttered with laughter. Jezal felt one of his eyes twitching as Brint turned his smirk towards him. "Well, Jezal, what do you think? You've met her haven't you?"

"What do I think?" His voice seemed to come from a terribly long way away as he stared at those three grinning faces. "I think you should watch your mouth, you son of a fucking whore."

He was on his feet now, teeth gritted so tight together they felt like they might crack apart. The three smiles blinked and faded. Jezal felt Kaspa's hand on his arm. "Come on, he only meant—"

Jezal ripped his arm away, seized the edge of the table and flung it over. Coins, cards, bottles, glasses, flew through the air and spilled out across the grass. He had his sword in his other hand, still sheathed luckily, leaning right down over Brint, spraying spit in his face. "Now you fucking listen to me, you little bastard!" he snarled, "I hear anything more like that, anything, and you won't have to worry about West!" He pressed the grip of his steel into Brint's chest. "I'll carve you like a fucking chicken!"

The three men stared up at him, aghast, their mouths wide open, their astonishment at this sudden display of violence equalled only by Jezal's own.

"But—" said Jalenhorm.

"What?" screamed Jezal, seizing a fistful of the big man's jacket and dragging him half out of his chair. "What d'you fucking say?"

"Nothing," he squeaked, his hands raised, "nothing." Jezal let him drop. The fury was draining fast. He had half a mind to apologise, but when he saw Brint's ashen face all he could think of was "she strikes me as the willing type."

"Like! A! Fucking! Chicken!" he snarled again, then turned on his heel and stalked off. Halfway to the archway he realised he had left his coat behind, but he could hardly go back for it now. He made it into the darkness of the tunnel, took a couple of steps down it then sagged against the wall, breathing hard and trembling as if he'd just run ten miles. He understood now what it meant to lose one's temper, and no mistake. He had never even realised that he had one before, but there could be no doubt now.

"What the hell was that about?" Brint's shocked voice echoed quietly down the tunnel, only just audible over the thumping of Jezal's heart. He had to hold his breath to hear.

"Damned if I know." Jalenhorm, sounding even more surprised. There was the rattle and scrape of the table being put straight. "Never knew he had such a temper."

"I suppose he must have a lot to think about," said Kaspa, uncertainly, "what with the Contest and all . . ."

Brint cut him off. "That's no excuse!"

"Well they're close, aren't they? Him and West? What with all the fencing together and what have you, maybe he knows the sister or something . . . I don't know!"

"There is another explanation," Jezal could hear Brint saying, voice tense as though he was about to deliver a punchline. "Perhaps he's in love with her!" The three of them burst out laughing. It was a good joke alright. Captain Jezal dan Luthar, in love, and with a girl whose station in life was so far beneath his own. What a ridiculous idea! What an absurd notion! What a joke!

"Oh shit." Jezal put his head in his hands. He didn't feel like laughing. How the hell had she done this to him? How? What was it about her? She was fine to look at, of course, and clever, and funny, and all those things, but that was no explanation. "I cannot see her again," he whispered to himself, "I will not!" And he thumped his hand against the wall. His resolve was iron. It always was.

Until the next note came under his door.

He groaned and slapped the side of his head. Why did he feel like this? Why did he . . . he couldn't even bring himself to think the word . . . like her so much? Then it came to him. He knew why.

She didn't like him.

Those mocking half-smiles. Those sidelong glances he caught sometimes. Those jokes that went just a little too close to the bone. Not to mention the occasional examples of outright scorn. She liked his money, maybe. She liked his position in the world, of course. She liked his looks, undoubtedly. But, in essence, the woman despised him.

And he'd never had that feeling before. He had always just assumed that everybody loved him, had never really had cause to doubt he was a fine man, worthy of the highest respect. But Ardee didn't like him, he saw it now, and that made him think. Apart from the jaw, of course, and the money and the clothes, what was there to like?

She treated him with the contempt he knew he deserved. And he couldn't get enough of it. "Strangest thing," Jezal mumbled to himself, slouching miserably against the wall of the tunnel. "Strangest thing."

It made him want to change her mind.

THE SEED

"How are you, Sand?"

Colonel Glokta opened his eyes. It was dark in the room. Damn it, he was late!

"Damn it!" he shouted, shoving back the covers and leaping out of bed. "I'm late!" He snatched up his uniform trousers, shoving his legs in, fumbling with his belt.

"Don't worry about that, Sand!" His mother's voice was half soothing, half impatient. "Where is the Seed?"

Glokta frowned over as he pushed his shirt in. "I've no time for this nonsense, mother! Why do you always think you know what's best for me?" He cast around him for his sword, but couldn't see it. "We're at war you know!"

"We are indeed." The Colonel looked up, surprised. It was the voice of Arch Lector Sult. "Two wars. One fought with fire and steel, and another one beneath—an old war, long years in the making." Glokta frowned. How ever could he have mistaken that old windbag for his mother? And what was he doing in Glokta's chambers in any case? Sitting in the chair at the foot of his bed, prattling about old wars?

"What the hell are you doing in my chambers?" growled Colonel Glokta, "and what have you done with my sword?"

"Where is the Seed?" A woman's voice now, but not his mother's. Someone else. He did not recognise it. He squinted against the darkness, straining to see who was in the chair. He could make out a vague outline, but the shadows were too deep to tell more.

"Who are you?" asked Glokta sternly.

"Who was I? Or what am I?" The figure in the chair shifted as it rose slowly, smoothly, from its seat. "I was a patient woman, but I am woman no more, and the grinding years have worn my patience thin."

"What do you want?" Glokta's voice quivered, reedy and weak as he backed away.

The figure moved, stepping through the shaft of moonlight from the window. A woman's form, slender and graceful, but shadows stuck to the face. A sudden fear clawed at him and he stumbled back against the wall, raising his arm to fend the woman off.

"I want the Seed." A pale hand snaked out and closed around his out-stretched arm. A gentle touch, but cold. Cold as stone. Glokta trembled, gasped, squeezed shut his eyes. "I need it. You cannot know the need I have. Where is it?" Fingers plucked at his clothes, quick and deft, seeking, searching, darting in his pockets, in his shirt, brushing his skin. Cold. Cold as glass.

"The Seed?" squeaked Glokta, half paralysed with terror.

"You know what I speak of, broken man. Where is it?"

"The Maker fell . . ." he whispered. The words welled up, he knew not from where.

"I know it."

". . . burning, burning . . ."

"I saw it." The face was close enough for him to feel the breath upon his skin. Cold. Cold as frost.

". . . he broke upon the bridge below . . ."

"I remember it."

". . . they searched for the Seed . . ."

"Yes . . ." whispered the voice, urgent in his ear, "where is it?" Something brushed against his face, his cheek, his eyelid, soft and slimy. A tongue. Cold. Cold as ice. His flesh crawled.

"I don't know! They could not find it!"

"Could not?" Fingers closed tight around his throat, squeezing, crushing, choking the air from him. Cold. Cold as iron, and just as hard. "You think you know pain, broken man? You know nothing!" The icy breath rasped in his ear, the icy fingers squeezed, squeezed. "But I can show you! I can show you!"

Glokta screamed, thrashed, struggled. He fought his way up, stood for a dizzy instant, then his leg buckled and he plunged into space. The dark room tumbled around him and he crashed to the boards with a sickening crunch, his arm folded beneath him, his forehead cracking against the floor.

He struggled up, clawing at the leg of his bed, pushing himself against the wall, snorting for breath, staring wild-eyed towards the chair, yet barely able to look for fear. A bar of moonlight spilled through the window, cut across the rumpled bed-clothes and onto the polished wood of the seat. *Empty.*

Glokta cast around the rest of the room, eyes adjusting to the darkness, peering into every shadowy corner. *Nothing. Empty. A dream.*

And now, as the crazy hammering of his heart relaxed, as his ragged breathing slowed, the pain came on. His head thumped, his leg screamed, his arm was throbbing dully. He could taste blood, his eyes stung and wept, his guts heaved, sick and spinning. He whimpered, made an agonising hop towards the bed, then collapsed on the moonlit mattress, exhausted, wet with cold sweat.

There was an urgent knocking at the door. "Sir? Are you alright?" Barnam's voice. The knocking came again. *No good. It is locked. Always locked, but I don't think I'll be moving. Frost will have to break it down.* But the door swung open, and Glokta shielded his eyes from the sudden ruddy glow of the old servant's lamp.

"Are you alright?"

"I fell," mumbled Glokta. "My arm . . ."

The old servant perched on the bed, taking Glokta's hand gently and pushing up the sleeve of his night-shirt. Glokta winced, Barnam clicked his tongue. His forearm had a big pink mark across it, already beginning to swell and redden.

"I don't think it's broken," said the servant, "but I should fetch the surgeon, just in case."

"Yes, yes." He waved Barnam away with his good hand. "Fetch him."

Glokta watched the old servant hurry, stooped, out of the door, heard him creaking along the narrow corridor outside, down the narrow stairs. He heard the front door banging shut. Silence descended.

He looked over at the scroll he had taken from the Adeptus Historical, still rolled up tight on the dresser, waiting to be delivered to Arch Lector Sult. *The Maker fell burning. He broke upon the bridge below. Strange, how parts of the waking world stray into one's dreams. That damned Northman and his intruder. A woman, and cold. That'll be what set me off.*

Glokta rubbed his arm gently, pressing the sore flesh with his fingertips. *Nothing. Just a dream.* And yet something was niggling at him. He looked over at the back of the door. The key was still in the lock, shining orange in the light from the lamp. *Not locked, and yet I must have locked it. Must have. I always do.* Glokta looked back to the empty chair. *What did that idiot apprentice say? Magic comes from the Other Side. The world below. Hell.*

Somehow, at that moment, after that dream, it did not seem so difficult to believe. The fear was building in him again, now he was alone. He stretched out his good hand towards the chair. It took an age to get there, trembling, shaking. His fingers touched the wood. *Cool, but not cold. Not cold. There is nothing there.* He slowly withdrew his hand, cradled his pulsing arm. *Nothing. Empty.*

A dream.

"What the hell happened to you?"

Glokta sucked sourly at his gums. "Fell out of bed." He scratched absently at his wrist through the dressing. Until a moment ago it had been throbbing like hell, but the sight in front of him had pushed the pain into the back of his mind. *I could be worse off. A lot worse.* "Not a pretty sight. Not at all."

"You're damn right it's not." Severard looked as disgusted as was possible with half his face covered. "I nearly puked when I first saw it. Me!"

Glokta peered down, frowning, at the tangled mess of butchery, supporting himself against a tree-trunk with one hand and pushing some of the ferns aside with the tip of his cane to get a better look. "Are we even sure it's a man?"

"Might be a woman. Human anyway. That's a foot."

"Ah, so it is. How was it found?"

"He found it." Severard nodded over towards a gardener: sat on the ground, pale-faced and staring, and with a small pool of drying vomit on the grass beside him. "In amongst the trees here, hidden in the bushes. Looks as if whatever killed it tried to hide it, but not long ago. It's fresh." *It is indeed— barely any smell, and only a couple of flies have arrived. Very fresh, perhaps last night even.* "It might not have been found for days, except someone asked for one of these trees to be pruned. Blocking out the light or something. You ever see anything like this?"

Glokta shrugged. "In Angland, once, before you came. One of the convicts tried to escape. He made it a few miles, then succumbed to the cold. A bear made free with the corpse. That was quite a mess, though not near as bad as this one."

"I can't see anyone freezing to death last night. It was hot as hell."

"Mmm," said Glokta. *If hell is hot. I've always thought it might be cold. Cold as ice.* "There are few bears within the Agriont in any case. Do we have any idea as to the identity of this . . ." he waved his cane towards the carcass ". . . person?"

"None."

"Is anyone unaccounted for? Reported missing?"

"Not that I've heard."

"So we have not the slightest idea even who our victim is? Why the hell are we taking an interest? Don't we have a fake Magus to be watching?"

"That's just it. Their new quarters are right over there." Severard's gloved finger pointed out a building not twenty strides away. "I was watching them when this came to light."

Glokta raised an eyebrow. "I see. And you suspect some connection, do you?" The Practical shrugged. "Mysterious intruders in the dead of night, gruesome murders on their very doorstep? Our visitors draw trouble like shit draws flies."

"Huh," said Severard, swatting a fly away with his gloved hand. "I looked into that other thing as well. Your bankers. Valint and Balk."

Glokta looked up. "Really? And?"

"And not a lot. An old house. Very old and very well respected. Their notes are good as gold among the merchants. They've got offices all across Midderland, Angland, Starikland, in Westport, in Dagoska. Even outside the Union. Powerful people, by all accounts. All kind of folk owe them money, I reckon. Strange thing though, no one seems ever to have met a Valint or a Balk. Who can tell with banks though, eh? They love secrets. You want me to dig any more?"

It could be dangerous. Very dangerous. Dig too far and we might be digging our own graves. "No. We'd better leave off. For now. Keep your ears open though."

"My ears are always open, chief. So who do you like for the Contest?"

Glokta glanced across at the Practical. "How can you think about that with this in front of you?"

The Practical shrugged. "It won't do 'em any harm, will it?" Glokta looked back at the mangled body. *I suppose it won't, at that.* "So come on, you should know, Luthar or Gorst?"

"Gorst." *I hope he carves the little bastard in two.*

"Really? People say he's a clumsy ox. Lucky is all."

"Well, I say he's a genius," said Glokta. "In a couple of years they'll all be fencing like him, if you can call it fencing. You mark my words."

"Gorst, eh? Maybe I'll have a little bet."

"You do that. But in the meantime you'd better scrape this mess up and take it to the University. Get Frost to give you a hand, he's got a strong stomach."

"The University?"

"Well we can't just leave it here. Some fashionable lady taking a turn in the park could get an awful shock." Severard giggled. "And I might just know of someone who can shed some light on this little mystery."

"This is quite an interesting discovery you've made Inquisitor." The Adeptus Physical paused in his work and peered over at Glokta, one eye enormously magnified through his glittering eye-glass. "Quite a fascinating discovery," he muttered, as he returned to the corpse with his instruments: lifting, prodding, twisting, squinting down at the glistening flesh.

Glokta peered round the laboratory, his lip curling with distaste. Jars of many different sizes lined two of the four walls, filled with floating, pickled lumps of meat. Some of those floating things Glokta recognised as parts of the human body, some he did not. Even he felt slightly uncomfortable in amongst the macabre display. *I wonder how Kandelau came by them all? Do his visitors end up dismembered, floating in a dozen different jars? Perhaps I would make an interesting specimen?*

"Fascinating." The Adeptus loosened the strap of his eye-glass and perched it on top of his head, rubbing at the pink ring it had left behind around his eye. "What can you tell me about it?"

Glokta frowned. "I came here to find out what *you* can tell *me* about it."

"Of course, of course." Kandelau pursed his lips. "Well, er, as to the gender of our unfortunate friend, er . . ." he trailed off.

"Well?"

"Heh heh, well, er, the organs that would allow one to make an easy determination are . . ." and he gestured at the meat on the table, harshly lit under the blazing lamps ". . . absent."

"And that is the sum of your investigation?"

"Well, there are other things: a man's third finger is typically longer than his first, not necessarily so with a woman but, heh, our remnant does not have all the digits necessary to make such a judgement. As to gender, therefore, without the fingers, we are quite stumped!" He giggled nervously at his own joke. Glokta did not.

"Young or old?"

"Well, er, again that is quite difficult to determine, I am afraid. The, er," and the Adeptus tapped at the corpse with his tongs, "teeth here are in good condition and, heh, such skin as remains would appear to be consistent with a younger person but, er, this is really just, heh heh—"

"So what can you tell me about the victim?"

"Er, well . . . nothing." And he smiled apologetically. "But I have made some interesting discoveries as to the cause of death!"

"Really?"

"Oh yes, look at this!" *I would rather not.* Glokta limped cautiously over to the bench, peering down at the spot the old man was indicating.

"You see here? The shape of this wound?" The Adeptus prodded at a flap of gristle.

"No I do not see," said Glokta. *It appears all to be one enormous wound to me.*

The old man leaned towards him, his eyes wide. "Human," he said.

"We know that it is human! This is a foot!"

"No! No! These teeth marks, here . . . they are human bites!"

Glokta frowned. "Human . . . bites?"

"Absolutely!" Kandelau's beaming smile was quite at odds with the sur-roundings. *And with the subject matter, I rather think.* "This individual was bitten to death by another person, and, heh heh, in all likelihood," and he gestured triumphantly at the mess on his table, "considering the incomplete nature of the remains . . . partially eaten!"

Glokta stared at the old man for a moment. *Eaten? Eaten? Why must every question answered raise ten more?* "This is what you would have me tell the Arch Lector?"

The Adeptus laughed nervously. "Well, heh heh, these are the facts, as I see them . . ."

"A person, unidentified, perhaps a man, perhaps a woman, either young or old, was attacked in the park by an unknown assailant, bitten to death within two hundred strides of the King's palace and partially . . . eaten?"

"Er . . ." Kandelau gave a worried glance sideways towards the entrance. Glokta turned to look, and frowned. There was a new arrival there, one that he had not heard enter. A woman, standing in the shadows at the edge of the bright lamp-light with her arms folded. A tall woman with short, spiky red hair and a black mask on her face, staring at Glokta and the Adeptus through narrowed eyes. A Practical. *But not one I recognise, and women are quite a rarity in the Inquisition. I would have thought . . .*

"Good afternoon, good afternoon!" A man stepped briskly through the door: gaunt, balding, with a long black coat and a prim little smile on his face. An unpleasantly familiar man. *Goyle, damn him. Our new Superior of Adua, arrived at last. Great news.* "Inquisitor Glokta," he purred, "what an absolute pleasure it is to see you again!"

"Likewise, Superior Goyle." *You bastard.*

Two other figures followed close behind the grinning Superior, making the glaring little room seem quite crowded. One was a dark-skinned, stocky Kantic with a big golden ring through his ear, the other was a monster of a Northman with a face like a stone slab. He almost had to stoop to cram himself through the doorway. Both were masked and dressed from head to toe in Practicals black.

"This is Practical Vitari," chuckled Goyle, indicating the red-haired woman, who had flowed over to the jars and was peering into them, one at a time, tapping on the glass and making the specimens wobble. "And these are Practicals Halim," the Southerner sidled past Goyle and into the room, busy eyes darting here and there, "and Byre." The monstrous Northman gazed down at Glokta from up near the ceiling. "In his own country they call him the Stone-Splitter, would you believe, but I don't think that would work here, do you Glokta? Practical Stone-Splitter, can you imagine?" He laughed softly to himself and shook his head.

And this is the Inquisition? I had no idea the circus was in town. I wonder if they stand on each other's shoulders? Or jump through flaming hoops?

"A remarkably diverse selection," said Glokta.

"Oh yes," laughed Goyle, "I have picked them up wherever my travels have taken me, eh my friends?"

The woman shrugged as she prowled around the jars. The dark-skinned Practical inclined his head. The towering Northman simply stood there.

"Wherever my travels have taken me!" chuckled Goyle, just as though everyone else had laughed with him. "And I have more besides! It's been quite a time, I do declare!" He wiped a tear of mirth from his eye as he moved towards the table in the centre of the room. It seemed that everything was a source of amusement to him, even the thing on the bench. "But what's all this? A body, unless I'm quite mistaken!" Goyle looked up sharply, his eyes sparkling. "A body? A death within the city? As Superior of Adua, surely that falls within my province?"

Glokta bowed. "Naturally. I was not aware that you had arrived, Superior Goyle. Also, I felt that the unusual circumstances of this—"

"Unusual? I see nothing unusual." Glokta paused. *What game is this chuckling fool playing?*

"Surely you would agree that the violence here is . . . exceptional."

Goyle gave a flamboyant shrug. "Dogs."

"Dogs?" asked Glokta, unable to let that one pass. "Domestic pets run mad, do you think, or wild ones which climbed over the walls?"

The Superior only smiled. "Whichever you like, Inquisitor. Whichever you like."

"I'm afraid it could not possibly be dogs," the Adeptus Physical began pompously to explain. "I was only just making clear to Inquisitor Glokta . . . these marks here, and on the skin here, do you see? These are human bites, undoubtedly . . ."

The woman sauntered away from the jars, closer and closer to Kandelau, leaning in towards him until her mask was only inches away from his beak of a nose. He slowly trailed off. "Dogs," she whispered, then barked in his face.

The Adeptus jumped away. "Well, I suppose I could have been mistaken . . . of course . . ." He backed into the enormous Northman's chest, who had moved with surprising speed to position himself directly behind. Kandelau turned slowly around, staring up with wide eyes.

"Dogs." Intoned the giant.

"Dogs, dogs, dogs," hummed the southerner in a thick accent.

"Of course," squeaked Kandelau, "dogs, of course, how foolish I've been!"

"Dogs!" shouted Goyle in delight, throwing his hands in the air. "The mystery is solved!" To Glokta's amazement, two of the three Practicals began politely to applaud. The woman stayed silent. *I never believed that I would miss Superior Kalyne, but suddenly I am overcome with nostalgia.* Goyle turned slowly round, bowing low. "My first day here, and already I warm to the work! You can bury this," he said, gesturing to the corpse and smiling broadly at the cringing Adeptus. "Best buried, eh?" He looked over at the Northman. "Back to the mud, as you say in your country!"

The massive Practical showed not the slightest sign that anyone had spoken. The Kantic was standing there, turning the ring through his ear round and round. The woman was peering down at the carcass on the table, sniffing at it through her mask. The Adeptus Physical was backed up against his jars, sweating profusely.

Enough of this pantomime. I have work to do. "Well," said Glokta stiffly, limping for the door, "the mystery is solved. You don't need me any more."

Superior Goyle turned to look at him, his good humour suddenly vanished. "No!" he hissed, furious little eyes nearly popping out of his head. "We don't . . . need you . . . any more!"

NEVER BET
AGAINST A MAGUS

Logen sat in the hot sun, hunched over on his bench, and sweated.

The ridiculous clothes did not help with the sweating, or indeed with anything else. The tunic had not been designed to sit down in, and the stiff leather dug painfully into his fruits whenever he tried to move.

"Fucking thing," he growled, tugging at it for the twentieth time. Quai looked hardly more comfortable in his magical garb—the glittering of the gold and silver symbols only served to make his face look the more ill and pallid, his eyes the more twitchy and bulging. He'd hardly spoken a word all morning. Of the three of them, only Bayaz appeared to be enjoying himself, beaming round at the surging crowds on the benches, the sunlight shining off his tanned pate.

They stood out among the heaving audience like well-rotted fruit, and seemed about as popular. Even though the benches were packed shoulder to shoulder a small, nervous space had built up around the three of them where no one would sit.

The noise was even more crushing than the heat and the crowds. Logen's ears hummed with the din. It was the most he could do to keep from clamping his hands over them and throwing himself under the bench for cover. Bayaz leaned towards him. "Was this what your duels were like?" He had to shout even though his mouth was barely six inches from Logen's ear.

"Huh." Even when Logen had fought Rudd Threetrees, when a good part of Bethod's army had drawn up in a great half-circle to watch, shouting and screaming and hammering their weapons against their shields, when the

walls of Uffrith above them had been crammed with onlookers, his audience
had not been half this size, not half this noisy. No more than thirty men had
watched him kill Shama Heartless, kill him then butcher him like a pig.
Logen winced and flinched and hunched his shoulders higher at the memory
of it. Cutting, and cutting, and licking the blood from his fingers, while the
Dogman stared in horror and Bethod laughed and cheered him on. He could
taste the blood now, and he shuddered and wiped his mouth.

There had been so many fewer people, and yet the stakes had been so
much higher. The lives of the fighters, for one thing, and the ownership of
land, of villages, of towns, the futures of whole clans. When he'd fought Tul
Duru, no more than a hundred had watched, but perhaps the whole fate of
the North had turned on that bloody half hour. If he'd lost then, if the Thunderhead had killed him, would things be the same? If Black Dow, or Harding
Grim, or any of those others had put him in the mud, would Bethod have a
golden chain now, and call himself a King? Would this Union be at war with
the North? The thought made his head hurt. Even more.

"You alright?" asked Bayaz.

"Mmm," Logen mumbled, but he was shivering, even in the heat. What
were all these people here for? Only to be amused. Few could've found
Logen's battles very amusing, except Bethod, perhaps. Few others. "This isn't
like my fights," he muttered to himself.

"What's that?" asked Bayaz.

"Nothing."

"Uh." The old man beamed around at the crowd, scratching at his short
grey beard. "Who do you think will win?"

Logen really didn't much care, but he reckoned that any distraction from
his memories was welcome. He peered into the enclosures where the two
fighters were getting ready, not far from where he was sitting. The handsome,
proud young man they'd met at the gate was one of them. The other was
heavy and powerful-looking, with a thick neck and a look almost bored.

He shrugged his shoulders. "I don't know anything about this business."

"What, you? The Bloody-Nine? A champion who fought and won ten
challenges? The most feared man in the North? No opinion? Surely single
combat is the same the world over!"

Logen winced and licked his lips. The Bloody-Nine. That was far in the past, but not far enough for his liking. His mouth still tasted like metal, like salt, like blood. Touching a man with a sword and cutting him open with one are hardly the same things, but he looked the two opponents over again. The proud young man rolled up his sleeves, touched his toes, swivelled his body this way and that, swung his arms round in quick windmills, watched by a stern old soldier in a spotless red uniform. A tall, worried-looking man handed the fighter two thin swords, one longer than the other, and he whisked them around before him in the air with impressive speed, blades flashing.

His opponent stood there, leaning against the wooden side of his enclosure, stretching his bull neck from side to side without much hurry, glancing round with lazy eyes.

"Who's who?" asked Logen.

"The pompous ass from the gate is Luthar. The one who's half asleep is Gorst."

It was plain who the crowd preferred. Luthar's name could be heard often in the din, and whoops and claps greeted every movement of his thin swords. He looked quick, and deft, and clever, but there was something deadly in that big man's waiting slouch, something dark about his heavy-lidded eyes. Logen would rather have fought Luthar, for all his speed. "I reckon Gorst."

"Gorst, really?" Bayaz's eyes sparkled. "How about a little bet?"

Logen heard a sharp suck of breath from Quai. "Never bet against a Magus," whispered the apprentice.

It didn't seem to make much difference to Logen. "What the hell have I got to bet with?"

Bayaz shrugged. "Well, let's just say for honour then?"

"If you like." Logen had never had too much of that, and the little he did have he didn't care about losing.

"Bremer dan Gorst!" The scattered clapping was smothered by an avalanche of hisses and boos as the great ox shambled towards his mark, half-closed eyes on the ground, big, heavy steels dangling from his big, heavy hands. Between his short-cropped hair and the collar of his shirt, where his neck should have been, there was nothing but a thick fold of muscle.

"Ugly bastard," Jezal murmured to himself, as he watched him go. "Damn idiot ugly bastard." But his curses lacked conviction, even to his own ear. He had watched that man fight three bouts and demolish three good opponents. One of them had still to leave his sick bed a week later. Jezal had been training for the last few days specifically to counter Gorst's bludgeoning style: Varuz and West swinging big broom handles at him while he dodged this way and that. More than once one of them had made contact, and Jezal was still smarting from the bruises.

"Gorst?" offered the referee plaintively, doing his best to wheedle some applause from the audience, but they were having none of it. The boos only became louder, joined by jeers and heckling as Gorst took his mark.

"You clumsy ox!"

"Get back to your farm and pull a plough!"

"Bremer the brute!" and other such.

The people stretched back, and back, and back into obscurity. Everyone was there. Everyone in the world, it looked like. Every commoner in the city round the distant edges. Every gentleman artisan and trader thronging the middle benches. Every noble man or woman in the Agriont towards the front, from fifth sons of high-born nobodies to the great magnates of the Open and Closed Councils. The Royal box was full: the Queen, the two Princes, Lord Hoff, the Princess Terez. The King even appeared to be awake for once, truly an honour, his goggling eyes staring around in amazement. Out there somewhere were Jezal's father and his brothers, his friends and fellow officers, his entire acquaintance, more or less. Ardee too, he hoped, watching . . .

All in all, it was quite an audience.

"Jezal dan Luthar!" bellowed the referee. The meaningless bibble-babble of the crowd surged into a storm of cheering, a thunderous wave of support. The cries and shouts rang and echoed around the arena, making Jezal's head throb.

"Come on, Luthar!"

"Luthar!"

"Kill the bastard!" and other such.

"Off you go, Jezal," whispered Marshal Varuz in his ear, clapping him on the back and pushing him gently out towards the circle, "and good luck!"

Jezal walked in a daze, the noise of the crowd punching at his ears until it seemed his head would split. The training of the last few months flashed through his mind. The running, the swimming, the work with the heavy bar. The sparring, the beam, the endless forms. The punishment, the study, the sweating and the pain. Just so he could stand here. Seven touches. The first to four. It all came down to this.

He took his mark opposite Gorst, and stared into those heavy-lidded eyes. They looked back, cool and calm, seeming almost to stare past him as though he wasn't there. That needled him and he pushed the thoughts out of his head and raised high his noble chin. He would not, *could* not, let this oaf get the better of him. He would show all these people his blood, and his skill, and his mettle. He was Jezal dan Luthar. He would win. It was an incontestable fact. He knew it.

"Begin!"

The first cut sent him reeling, shattering his confidence, his poise, and nearly his wrist. He had been watching Gorst fence, of course, if you could call it that, so he knew the man would come out swinging, but nothing could have prepared him for that first shattering contact. The crowd gasped with him as he staggered back. All his carefully laid plans, all of Varuz's carefully worded advice, vanished into air. He winced with pain and shock, his arm still vibrating from the force of that mighty blow, his ears still ringing from the crashing noise of it, his mouth hanging open, his knees wobbling.

It was hardly the most promising start, but the next chop followed hard after the first, flashing down with even greater power. Jezal leaped aside and slid away, trying to make room and give himself time. Time to work out some tactic, some trick to stem the pitiless tide of swinging metal. But Gorst was not about to give him time. He was already loosing another throaty growl, his long steel already begun on its next irresistible arc.

Jezal dodged where he could, blocked where he couldn't, his wrists already aching from the ceaseless punishment. To begin with he hoped that Gorst would tire. No one could throw those great lumps of metal around for long the way that he was doing. Soon the fierce pace would take its toll on the big man and he would slow, and droop, and the heavy steels would lose their venom. Then Jezal would fight back doggedly, run his opponent ragged, and win. The crowd would crack the Agriont with their cheers. A classic tale of victory against the odds.

Only Gorst did not tire. The man was a machine. After a few minutes there was still not the slightest sign of weariness in those heavy-lidded eyes. There was barely any emotion of any kind that Jezal could see, during the rare moments when he dared to take his eyes away from the flashing swords. The big long steel swung, swung, swung in its brutal circles, and the short steel was always there to turn away such feeble efforts as Jezal could make in between, never faltering or dropping even an inch. The power of the blows did not decrease, the growls tore from Gorst's throat with as much vigour as ever. The crowd were given nothing to cheer at, and merely muttered angrily. It was Jezal who began to feel his legs slowing, to feel the sweat springing out of his forehead, to feel his grip on his steels slipping.

He saw it coming from a mile away, but there was nothing he could do about it. He had backed off until he ran out of circle. He had blocked and parried until he lost the feeling in his fingers. This time, when he raised his aching arm and there was the crash of metal on metal, one tired foot slipped and he tumbled squawking from the ring, floundering on his side, his short steel spinning from his twitching fingers. His face slapped against the ground and he took a gritty mouthful of sand. It was a painful and embarrassing fall, but he felt too tired and too battered to be all that disappointed. He was almost relieved that the punishment was over, if only for a moment.

"One to Gorst!" shouted the referee. A light dusting of applause was crushed beneath hoots of derision, but the big man seemed scarcely to notice, shuffling back to his mark with his head down and already preparing for the next touch.

Jezal rolled slowly onto his hands and knees, flexing his aching hands and taking his time getting up. He needed a moment to breathe and make ready, to think up some strategy. Gorst waited for him: big, silent, still. Jezal brushed the sand from his shirt, mind racing. How to beat him? How? He stepped cautiously back to his mark, raised his steels.

"Begin!"

This time Gorst came out even harder, slashing away as if he was scything wheat, making Jezal dance around the circle. One blow passed so close to his left side that he could feel the wind from it on his cheek. The next missed him by a margin no greater on his right. Then Gorst flung a sideways sweep aimed at his head and Jezal saw an opening. He ducked beneath it, sure the blade tore at the hairs on top of his scalp. He closed the distance as the heavy long steel swung away, almost catching the referee in the face on the back-swing, leaving Gorst's right side all but undefended.

Jezal lunged at the big bastard, sure he had finally got through, knowing he had made it one touch a piece. But Gorst caught the thrust on his short steel and forced it just wide, the guards of the two blades scraping then locking together. Jezal cut at him viciously with his short steel but somehow Gorst blocked that too, bringing up his other sword just in time, catching Jezal's blade and holding it just short of his chest.

For a moment their four steels were locked together, hilts grating, their faces just a few inches apart. Jezal was snarling like a dog, teeth bared, the muscles of his face a rigid mask. Gorst's heavy features showed little sign of effort. He looked like a man having a piss: involved in a mundane and faintly distasteful task that must simply be done with as quickly as possible.

For a moment their blades were locked together, Jezal pushing with every grain of strength, each hard-trained muscle flexing: legs straining against the ground, stomach straining to twist his arms, arms straining to push his hands, hands gripped around the hilts of his steels like grim death. Every muscle, every sinew, every tendon. He knew he had the better position, the big man was off balance, if only he could push him back a step . . . an inch . . .

For that moment their steels were locked together, then Gorst dipped his shoulder, and grunted, and flung Jezal away as a child might fling away a boring toy.

He tumbled back, mouth and eyes wide open with surprise, feet kicking at the dirt, all his attention focused on staying upright. He heard Gorst growl again, and was shocked to see the heavy long steel already curving through the air towards him. He was in no position to dodge, and there was no time anyway. He raised his left arm on an instinct, but the thick, blunted blade tore his short steel away like a straw on the wind and crashed into his ribs, hammering the breath from his body in a wail of pain that echoed round and round the silent arena. His legs crumpled under him and he sprawled out on the turf, limbs flopping, sighing like a split bellows.

This time there was not even the shadow of applause. The crowd roared their hatred, booing and hissing at Gorst for all they were worth as he trudged back to his enclosure.

"Damn you, Gorst, you thug!"

"Get up Luthar! Up and at him!"

"Go home, you brute!"

"You damn savage!"

Their hisses turned to half-hearted cheers as Jezal picked himself up off the grass, his whole left side pulsing. He would have screamed with the pain if he had any breath left in him. For all his effort, for all his training, he was utterly outclassed and he knew it. The thought of doing it all again next year made him want to vomit. He did his best to appear undaunted as he struggled back to his enclosure, but he could not help sagging down heavily in his chair when he got there, dropping his notched steels on the flags and gasping for breath.

West bent over him and pulled up his shirt to check the damage. Jezal peered down gingerly, half expecting to see a great hole caved in his side, but there was only an ugly red welt across his ribs, some bruising already coming up around it.

"Anything broken?" asked Marshal Varuz, peering over West's shoulder.

Jezal fought back the tears as the Major probed his side. "I don't think so, but damn it!" West threw his towel down in disgust. "You call this the beautiful sport? Is there no rule against these heavy steels?"

Varuz shook his head grimly. "They all have to be the same length, but there's no rule for the weight. I mean, why would anyone want heavy ones?"

"Now we know, don't we!" snapped West. "Are you sure we shouldn't stop this before that bastard takes his head off?"

Varuz ignored him. "Now look here," said the old Marshal, leaning down to talk in Jezal's face. "It's the best of seven touches! First to four! There's still time!"

Time for what? For Jezal to get cut in half, blunted steels or no? "He's too strong!" Jezal gasped.

"Too strong? No one's too strong for you!" But even Varuz looked doubtful. "There's still time! You can beat him!" The old Marshal tugged at his moustaches. "You can beat him!"

But Jezal noticed he did not suggest how.

Glokta was becoming worried he might choke, so convulsive was his laughter. He tried to think of something he would rather see than Jezal dan Luthar being smashed around a fencing circle, and failed. The young man winced as he just barely blocked a raking cut. He had not been handling his left side at all well since he took that blow in the ribs, and Glokta could almost feel his pain. *And my, my, how nice it is to feel someone else's for a change.* The crowd sulked, silent and brooding as Gorst harried their favourite around with his brutal slashes, while Glokta spluttered giggles through his clenched gums.

Luthar was quick and flashy, and he moved well once he saw the steels coming. *A competent fighter. Good enough to win a Contest, no doubt, in a mediocre year. Quick feet, and quick hands, but his mind is not as sharp as it should be. As it needs to be. He is too predictable.*

Gorst was an entirely different proposition. He seemed to be swinging, and swinging, without a thought in his head. But Glokta knew better. *He has a whole new way of doing things. It was all jab, jab in my day. By next year's Contest they'll all be chopping away with these big, heavy steels.* Glokta wondered idly if he could have beaten Gorst, at his best. *It would have been a bout worth seeing anyway—a damn sight better than this mismatch.*

Gorst easily dealt with a couple of limp jabs, then Glokta winced and the crowd hissed as Luthar just barely parried another great butcher's chop, the force of it nearly lifting him off his feet. He had no way to avoid the next swing, pressed against the edge of the circle as he was, and he was forced to jump back into the sand.

"Three to nothing!" shouted the referee.

Glokta shook with merriment as he watched Luthar chop at the ground in frustration, sending up a petulant spray of sand, his face a picture of pale self-pity. *Dear me, Captain Luthar, it will be four to nothing. A whitewash. An embarrassment. Perhaps this will teach that whining little shit some humility. Some men are better off for a good beating. Only look at me, eh?*

"Begin!"

The fourth touch began precisely as the third had ended. *With Luthar taking a hammering.* Glokta could see it, the man was out of ideas. His left arm was moving slowly, painfully, his feet looked heavy. Another numbing blow crashed against his long steel, making him stumble back towards the edge of the circle, off-balance and gasping. Gorst needed only to press his attack a little further. *And something tells me he is not the man to let up when he's ahead.* Glokta grabbed his cane, pushed himself to his feet. Anyone could see it was all over, and he had no wish to be caught in the crush as the disappointed crowds all tried to leave at once.

Gorst's heavy long steel flashed down through the air. *The final blow, surely.* Luthar's only choice was to try and block it and be knocked clean out of the circle. *Or it might just split his fat head. We can hope for that.* Glokta smiled, half turned to leave.

But out of the corner of his eye, somehow, he saw the cut miss. Gorst blinked as his heavy long steel thudded into the turf, then grunted as Luthar caught him across the leg with a left-handed cut. It was the most emotion he had shown all day.

"One to Luthar!" shouted the referee after a brief pause, unable to entirely keep the amazement out of his voice.

"No," murmured Glokta to himself, as the crowd around him erupted into riotous applause. *No.* He had fought hundreds of touches in his youth, and watched thousands more, but he had never seen anything quite like that, never seen anyone move so quickly. Luthar was a good swordsman, he knew it. *But no one is that good.* He frowned as he watched the two finalists come out from their second break and take their marks.

"Begin!"

Luthar was transformed. He harried Gorst with furious, lightning jabs, giving him no time to get started. It was the big man now who seemed stretched to the limit: blocking, dodging, trying to stay out of reach. It was as though they had sneaked the old Luthar away in the break and replaced him with a different man altogether: a stronger, faster, far more confident twin brother.

So long denied something to cheer for, the crowd whooped and yelled as though they'd split their throats. Glokta did not share their enthusiasm. *Something is wrong here. Something is wrong.* He glanced across the faces nearby, but no one else had sensed anything amiss. They only saw what they wanted to see: Luthar giving the ugly brute a spectacular and well-deserved thrashing. Glokta's eyes scanned across the benches, not knowing what he was looking for.

Bayaz, so-called. Sitting near the front, leaning forward and staring at the two fighters with fixed concentration, his "apprentice" and the scarred Northman beside him. No one else noticed it, everyone was intent on the fighters before them, but Glokta did. He rubbed his eyes and looked again. *Something wrong.*

"Say one thing for the First of the Magi, say he's a cheating bastard," growled Logen.

Bayaz had a little smile at the corner of his mouth as he mopped the sweat from his forehead. "Who ever said he wasn't?"

Luthar was in trouble again. Bad trouble. Each time he blocked one of those heavy sweeps, his swords snapped back further, his grip seemed slacker. Each time he dodged, he ended up a little further back towards the edge of the yellow circle.

Then, when the end seemed certain, out of the corner of his eye, Logen saw the air above Bayaz's shoulders shimmer, as it had on the road south when the trees burned, and he felt that strange tugging at his guts.

Luthar seemed suddenly to find new vigour. He caught the next great blow on the grip of his short sword. A moment before, it might easily have sent the thing flying from his hand. Now he held it there for an instant, then flung it away with a cry, pushing his opponent off balance and jumping forward, suddenly on the attack.

"If you were caught cheating in a Northern duel," growled Logen, shaking his head, "they'd cut the bloody cross into your stomach and pull your guts out."

"Lucky for me," murmured Bayaz through gritted teeth, without taking his eyes away from the fighters, "that we are in the North no longer." Sweat was already beading his bald scalp again, running down his face in fat drops. His fists were clenched tight and trembling with effort.

Luthar struck furiously, again and again, his swords a flashing blur. Gorst grunted and growled as he turned the blows away, but Luthar was too quick for him now, and too strong. He drove him mercilessly across the circle like a crazy dog might drive a cow.

"Fucking cheating," growled Logen again, as Luthar's blade flashed and left a bright red line across Gorst's cheek. A few drops of blood spattered across into the crowd on Logen's left, and they exploded into riotous cheering. That, just for a moment, was a shadow of his own duels. The referee's cry of three apiece could hardly be heard at all. Gorst frowned slightly and touched one hand to his face.

Above the din, Logen could just hear Quai's whisper. "Never bet against a Magus . . ."

Jezal knew that he was good, but he had never dreamed he could be *this* good. He was sharp as a cat, nimble as a fly, strong as a bear. His ribs no longer hurt, his wrists no longer hurt, all trace of tiredness had left him, all trace of doubt. He was fearless, peerless, unstoppable. The applause thundered around him and yet he could hear every word of it, see every detail of every face in the crowd. His heart was pumping tingling fire instead of blood, his lungs were sucking in the very clouds.

He did not bother even to sit in the break, so great was his eagerness to get back into the circle. The chair was an insult to him. He was not listening to what Varuz and West were saying. They were of no importance. Little people, far below. They stared at him: flushed, amazed, as well they might be.

He was the greatest swordsman ever.

That cripple Glokta could not have known how right he was: Jezal had only to try, it seemed, and he could have anything he wanted. He chuckled as he danced back to the mark. He laughed as he heard the crowds cheer. He smiled at Gorst as he stepped back into the circle. All was precisely as it should be. Those eyes were still heavy-lidded, lazy above the little red cut that Jezal had given him, but there was something else there now as well: a trace of shock, of wariness, of respect. As well there might be.

There was nothing that Jezal could not do. He was invincible. He was unstoppable. He was . . .

"Begin!"

. . . completely lost. The pain lanced through his side and made him gasp. Suddenly he was afraid, and tired, and weak again. Gorst growled and unleashed his savage cuts, jarring the steels in Jezal's hands, making him jump like a frightened rabbit. The mastery was gone, the anticipation, the nerve, and Gorst's onslaught was more brutal than ever. He felt a terrible lurch of despair as his long steel was torn from his buzzing fingers, flew through the air and clattered into the barrier. Jezal was bludgeoned to his knees. The crowd gasped. It was all over . . .

. . . It was not over. The blow was arcing down towards him. The final blow. It seemed to drift. Slow, slow, as though through honey. Jezal smiled. It was a simple matter for him to push it away with his short steel. The strength flowed again. He sprang upwards, shoved Gorst away with his empty hand, flicked another swing aside, and then another, his one sword doing the work of two with time to spare. The arena was breathless silent but for the rapid clashing of the steels. Right and left, right and left went the short blade, flashing faster than his eye could follow, faster than his mind could think, seeming almost to be dragging him along behind it.

There was a squeal of metal on metal as it tore Gorst's notched long steel from his hand, then another as it flickered across and did the same with his short. For a moment, all was still. The big man, disarmed and with his heels on the very edge of the circle, looked up at Jezal. The crowd was silent.

Then Jezal slowly lifted his short steel, all of a sudden seeming to weigh a ton, and poked Gorst gently in the ribs with it.

"Huh," said the big man quietly, raising his eyebrows.

Then the crowd exploded into deafening applause. The noise went on and on, rising and rising, washing over Jezal in waves. Now that it was finished he felt drained beyond description. He closed his eyes, swaying, his sword dropped from his nerveless fingers and he sank to his knees. He was beyond exhaustion. It was as though he had used a whole week's energy in a few moments. Even kneeling was an effort he was not sure he could sustain for long, and if he fell he was not sure he could ever get up again.

But then he felt strong hands taking him under the arms, and felt himself being lifted. The noise of the crowd grew even louder as he was hoisted into the air. He opened his eyes—bleary, blurry colour flashed in front of him as he was turned around. His head rang with the sound. He was up on someone's shoulders. A shaved head. Gorst. The big man had lifted him up, as a father might lift his child, displaying him to the crowd, smiling up at him with a big, ugly grin. Jezal smiled back despite himself. It was a strange moment, all in all.

"Luthar wins!" cried the referee pointlessly, barely audible. "Luthar wins!"

The cheering had resolved itself into a steady chant of "Luthar! Luthar! Luthar!" The arena shook with it. Jezal's head swam with it. It was like being drunk. Drunk on victory. Drunk on yourself.

Gorst lowered him back to the circle as the cheering of the crowd began to fade. "You beat me," he said, smiling wide. His voice was strangely high and soft, almost like a woman's. "Fair and square. I'd like to be the first to congratulate you." And he nodded his big head and smiled again, rubbing at the cut under his eye without the slightest bitterness. "You deserve it," he said, holding out his hand.

"Thank you." Jezal flashed a sour smile and gave the man's big paw as cursory a squeeze as possible, then he turned away towards his enclosure. Of course he fucking deserved it, and he was damned if he would let that bastard bask in his reflected glory a moment longer.

"Bravely done, my boy, bravely done!" frothed Marshal Varuz, slapping him on the shoulder as he stumbled back to his chair on wobbly legs. "I knew you could do it!"

West grinned as he handed him the towel. "They'll be talking about this for years."

Other well-wishers crowded in, offering their congratulations, leaning over the barrier. A whirl of smiling faces, and in amongst them the face of Jezal's father, shining with pride. "I knew that you could do it, Jezal! I never doubted! Not for a minute! You've brought honour to our family!" Jezal noticed that his elder brother didn't look all that pleased about it, though. He had the usual stodgy, envious expression on his face, even at Jezal's moment of victory. The stodgy, envious bastard. Could he not be happy for his brother, if only for one day?

"May I too congratulate the winner?" came a voice from over his shoulder. It was that old idiot, the one from the gate, the one whom Sulfur had called his master. The one who had used the name Bayaz. He had sweat on his bald skull, a lot of it. His face was pale, his eyes sunken. Almost as if he had just done seven touches with Gorst. "Well done indeed, my young friend, an almost . . . magical performance."

"Thank you," muttered Jezal. He was not at all sure who this old man was, or what he was after, but he did not trust him in the least. "I am sorry though, I must—"

"Of course. We will talk later." He said it with a disturbing finality, as if it were a thing already arranged. Then he turned away and vanished smoothly into the crowds. Jezal's father stared after him, ashen-faced now, as though he had seen a ghost.

"Do you know him, father?"

"I . . ."

"Jezal!" Varuz grabbed his arm excitedly. "Come! The King wishes to congratulate you!" He dragged Jezal from his family and towards the circle. A scattering of applause rose up again as they walked together across the dry grass, the scene of Jezal's victory. The Lord Marshal slung a fatherly arm around his shoulder, and smiled up at the crowds as though the applause was all for him. Everyone wanted a piece of his glory, it seemed, but Jezal was able to shake the old man off as he mounted the steps of the royal box.

Prince Raynault, youngest son of the King, was first in line, humbly dressed, honest and thoughtful-seeming, scarcely looking like royalty at all. "Well done!" he shouted over the roar of the crowd, sounding truly delighted for Jezal's victory. "Well done indeed!" His older brother was more exuberant.

"Incredible!" shouted Crown Prince Ladisla, the sunlight glinting off the golden buttons on his white jacket. "Capital! Amazing! Spectacular! I never saw such a thing!" Jezal grinned and bowed humbly as he went past, hunching his shoulders as the Crown Prince slapped him somewhat too hard on the back. "I always knew you'd do it! You were always my man!"

The Princess Terez, only daughter of the Grand Duke Orso of Talins, watched Jezal pass with a tiny, disdainful smile, tapping two languid fingers against her palm in a quarter-hearted imitation of clapping. Her chin was raised painfully high, as though just to be looked at by her was an honour he could never fully appreciate, and certainly did not deserve.

And so he came at last to the high seat of Guslav the fifth, High King of the Union. His head was slumped sideways, squashed down under the sparkling crown. His pasty pale fingers twitched on his crimson silk mantle like white slugs. His eyes were closed, chest rising and falling gently, accompanied by gentle splutterings as spittle issued from his slack lips and ran down his chin, joining the sweat on his bulging jowls and helping it to turn his high collar dark with wet.

Truly, Jezal was in the presence of greatness.

"Your Majesty," murmured Lord Hoff. The head of state did not respond. His wife the Queen looked on, painfully erect, a fixed, emotionless smile plastered across her well-powdered face. Jezal hardly knew where to look, and settled on his dusty shoes. The Lord Chamberlain coughed loudly. A muscle twitched beneath the sweaty fat on the side of the King's face, but he did not wake. Hoff winced, and, glancing around to make sure no one was watching too closely, jabbed the royal ribs with his finger.

The King jumped, eyelids suddenly flicking wide open, heavy jowls wobbling, staring at Jezal with wild, bloodshot, red-rimmed eyes.

"Your Majesty, this is Captain . . ."

"Raynault!" exclaimed the King, "my son!"

Jezal swallowed nervously, doing his best to maintain a rigid smile of his own. The senile old fool had mistaken him for his younger son. Worse yet, the Prince himself was standing not four paces away. The Queen's wooden grin twitched slightly. Princess Terez's perfect lips twisted with scorn. The Lord Chamberlain gave an awkward cough. "Er, no, your Majesty, this is . . ."

But it was too late. Without any warning, the monarch struggled to his feet and folded Jezal in an enthusiastic embrace, his heavy crown slipping over to one side of his head and one of its jewel-encrusted prongs nearly poking Jezal in the eye. Lord Hoff's jaw opened silently. The two Princes goggled. Jezal could only manage a helpless gurgle.

"My son!" blubbered the King, his voice choked with emotion. "Raynault, I'm so glad you're back! When I am gone, Ladisla will need your help. He is so weak, and the crown is such a heavy weight! You were always the better suited for it! Such a heavy weight!" he sobbed into Jezal's shoulder.

It was like a hideous nightmare. Ladisla and the real Raynault gawped at each other, then back at their father, both looking sick. Terez was sneering down her nose at her prospective father-in-law with undisguised contempt. From bad to much, much worse. What the hell did one do in such a situation? Could there possibly be any etiquette devised for this? Jezal patted his King awkwardly on his fat back. What else could he do? Shove the senile old idiot over on his arse, with half of his subjects looking on? He was almost tempted to do it.

It was a small mercy that the crowds took the King's embrace for a ringing endorsement of Jezal's fencing abilities, and drowned out his words with a fresh wave of cheering. No one beyond the royal box heard what he said. They all missed the full significance of what was, without doubt, the most embarrassing moment of Jezal's life.

THE IDEAL AUDIENCE

Arch Lector Sult was standing by his huge window when Glokta arrived, tall and imposing as always in his spotless white coat, gazing out across the spires of the University towards the House of the Maker. A pleasant breeze was washing through the great circular room, ruffling the old man's shock of white hair and making the many papers on his enormous desk crackle and flutter.

He turned as Glokta shuffled into the room. "Inquisitor," he said simply, holding out his white gloved hand, the great stone on his ring of office catching the bright sunlight from the open window and glittering with purple fire.

"I serve and obey, your Eminence." Glokta took the hand in his, and grimaced as he bent down to kiss the ring, his cane trembling with the effort of keeping upright. *Damn it if the old bastard doesn't hold his hand a little lower every time, just to watch me sweat.*

Sult poured himself into his tall chair in one smooth motion, elbows on the table top, fingers pressed together before him. Glokta could only stand and wait, his leg burning from the familiar climb through the House of Questions, sweat tickling his scalp, and wait for the invitation to sit.

"Please be seated," murmured the Arch Lector, then waited while Glokta winced his way into one of the lesser chairs at the round table. "Now tell me, has your investigation met with any success?"

"Some. There was a disturbance at our visitors's chambers the other night. They claim that—"

"Plainly an attempt to add credence to this outrageous story. Magic!"

Sult snorted his disdain. "Have you discovered how the breach in the wall was really made?"

Magic, perhaps? "I am afraid not, Arch Lector."

"That is unfortunate. Some proof of how this particular trick was managed might be of use to us. Still," and Sult sighed as though he had expected no better, "one cannot have everything. Did you speak to these . . . people?"

"I did. Bayaz, if I may use the name, is a most slippery talker. Without the aid of anything more persuasive than the questions themselves, I could get nothing from him. His friend the Northman also bears some study."

One crease formed across Sult's smooth forehead. "You suspect some connection with this savage Bethod?"

"Possibly."

"Possibly?" echoed the Arch Lector sourly, as though the very word was poison. "What else?"

"There has been a new addition to the merry band."

"I know. The Navigator."

Why do I even bother? "Yes, your Eminence, a Navigator."

"Good luck to them. Those penny-pinching fortune-tellers are always more trouble than they're worth. Blubbering on about God and what have you. Greedy savages."

"Absolutely. More trouble than they're worth, Arch Lector, though it would be interesting to know why they have employed one."

"And why have they?"

Glokta paused for a moment. "I don't know."

"Huh," snorted Sult. "What else?"

"Following their nighttime visitation, our friends were relocated to a suite of rooms beside the park. There was a most grisly death a few nights ago, not twenty paces from their windows."

"Superior Goyle mentioned this. He said it was nothing to concern myself about, that there was no connection with our visitors. I left the matter in his hands." He frowned at Glokta. "Did I make the wrong decision?"

Oh dear me, I need not think too long over this one. "Absolutely not, Arch Lector." Glokta bowed his head in deep respect. "If the Superior is satisfied, then so am I."

"Hmm. So what you are telling me is that, all in all, we have nothing."

Not quite nothing. "There is this." Glokta fished the ancient scroll from his coat pocket and held it out.

Sult had a look of mild curiosity on his face as he took it and unrolled it on the table, stared down at the meaningless symbols. "What is it?"

Hah. So you don't know everything. "I suppose you could say that it's a piece of history. An account of how Bayaz defeated the Master Maker."

"A piece of history." Sult tapped his finger thoughtfully on the table top. "And how does it help us?" *How does it help you, you mean?*

"According to this, it was our friend Bayaz who sealed up the House of the Maker." Glokta nodded towards the looming shape beyond the window. "Sealed it up . . . and took the key."

"Key? That tower has always been sealed. Always. As far as I am aware there is not even a keyhole."

"Those were precisely my thoughts, your Eminence."

"Hmm." Slowly, Sult began to smile. "Stories are all in how you tell them, eh? Our friend Bayaz knows that well enough, I dare say. He would use our own stories against us, but now we switch cups with him. I enjoy the irony." He picked up the scroll again. "Is it authentic?"

"Does it matter?"

"Of course not." Sult rose gracefully from his chair and paced slowly over to the window, tapping the rolled-up scroll against his fingers. He stood there for some time, staring out. When he turned, he had developed a look of the deepest self-satisfaction.

"It occurs to me that there will be a feast tomorrow evening, a celebration for our new champion swordsman, Captain Luthar." *That cheating little worm.* "The great and the good will be in attendance: the Queen, both Princes, most of the Closed Council, several leading noblemen." *Not forgetting the King himself. It has come to something when his presence at dinner is not even worth mentioning.* "That would be the ideal audience for our little unmasking, don't you think?"

Glokta cautiously bowed his head. "Of course, Arch Lector. The ideal audience." *Providing it works. It might be an embarrassing audience to fail in front of.*

But Sult was already anticipating his triumph. "The perfect gathering, and just enough time to make the necessary arrangements. Send a messenger to our friend the First of the Magi, and let him know that he and his companions are cordially invited to a dinner tomorrow evening. I trust that you will attend yourself?"

Me? Glokta bowed again. "I would not miss it for anything, your Eminence."

"Good. Bring your Practicals with you. Our friends might become violent when they realise the game is up. Barbarians of this sort, who can tell what they might be capable of?" A barely perceptible motion of the Arch Lector's gloved hand indicated that the interview was finished. *All those stairs, just for this?*

Sult was looking down his nose at the scroll as Glokta finally reached the threshold. "The ideal audience," he was muttering, as the heavy doors clicked shut.

In the North, a chieftain's own Carls ate with him every night in his hall. The women brought the food in wooden bowls. You'd stab the lumps of meat out with a knife and with a knife you'd cut them up, then you'd stuff the bits in your mouth with your fingers. If you found some bone or gristle you'd toss it down on the straw for the dogs. The table, if there was one, was a few slabs of ill-fitting wood, stained and gouged and scarred from having knives stuck in it. The Carls sat on long benches, with maybe a chair or two for the Named Men. It'd be dark, especially in the long winters, and smoky from the fire pit and the chagga pipes. There'd often be singing of songs, usually shouting of good-natured insults, sometimes screaming of bad-natured ones, and always a lot of drink. The only rule was that you waited for the chief to begin.

Logen had no idea what the rules might be here, but he guessed there were a lot.

The guests were sat round three long tables set out in a horseshoe, sixty people or more. Everyone had their own chair, and the dark wood of the table tops was polished to a high sheen, made bright enough for Logen to see the blurry outline of his face in by hundreds of candles scattered round the walls and down the tables. Every guest had at least three blunt knives, and several other things scattered about in front of them that Logen had no idea of the use for, including a big flat circle of shiny metal.

There was no shouting and certainly no singing, just a low murmur like
a bee hive as people muttered between themselves, leaning towards each
other as if they were swapping secrets. The clothes were stranger than ever.
Old men wore heavy robes of black, red and gold, trimmed with shining fur,
even in the heat. Young men wore tight fitting jackets in bright crimson,
green, or blue, festooned with ropes and knots of gold and silver thread.
Women were hung with chains and rings of glittering gold and flashing
jewels, wearing strange dresses of vivid cloth that were ridiculously loose and
billowing in places, painfully tight in others, and left others still entirely, dis-
tractingly bare.

Even the servants were dressed like lords, prowling around behind the
tables, leaning forward silently to fill goblets with sweet, thin wine. Logen had
already drunk a deal of it, and the bright room had taken on a pleasant glow.

The problem was the lack of food. He hadn't eaten since that morning
and his stomach was growling. He'd been eyeing the jars of plants sat on the
tables before the guests. They had bright flowers on them, and didn't look
much like food to him, but then they ate some strange things in this country.

There was nothing for it but to try. He snatched one of the things from
the jar, a long piece of green plant with a yellow flower on the end. He took
a nibble from the bottom of the stem. Tasteless and watery, but at least it was
crunchy. He took a larger bite and munched on it without relish.

"I don't think they're meant for eating." Logen glanced round, surprised
to hear the Northern tongue spoken here, surprised that anyone was speaking
to him at all. His neighbour, a tall, gaunt man with a sharp, lined face, was
leaning towards him with an embarrassed smile. Logen recognised him
vaguely. He'd been at the sword game—holding the blades for the lad from
the gate.

"Ah," mumbled Logen round his mouthful of plant. The taste of the stuff
got worse with time. "Sorry," he said once he had forced it down his throat,
"I don't know much about these things."

"Honestly, neither do I. How did it taste?"

"Like shit." Logen held the half-eaten flower uncertainly in his fingers.
The tiled floor was spotlessly clean. It hardly seemed right to toss the thing
under the table. There were no dogs anyway, and even if there had been he

doubted they'd have eaten the thing. A dog would have had more sense than him. He dropped it on the metal platter and wiped his fingers on his chest, hoping that no one had noticed.

"My name is West," said the man, offering his hand, "I come from Angland."

Logen gave the hand a squeeze. "Ninefingers. A Brynn, from way up north of the High Places."

"Ninefingers?" Logen waggled his stump at him and the man nodded. "Ah, I see." He smiled as though remembering something funny. "I heard a song once, in Angland, about a nine-fingered man. What was he called now? The Bloody-Nine! That was it!" Logen felt his grin slipping. "One of those Northern songs, you know the kind, all violence. He cut off heads by the cartload, this Bloody-Nine, and burned towns, and mixed blood with his beer and whatnot. That wasn't you, was it?"

The man was making a joke. Logen laughed nervously. "No, no, I never heard of him," but luckily West had already moved on.

"Tell me, you look like you've seen some battles in your time."

"I've been in some scrapes." It was pointless to deny it.

"Do you know of this one they call the King of the Northmen? This man Bethod?"

Logen glanced sideways. "I know of him."

"You fought against him in the wars?"

Logen grimaced. The sour taste of the plant seemed to be lingering in his mouth. He picked up his goblet and took a swallow. "Worse," he said slowly as he set it down. "I fought for him."

This only seemed to make the man more curious than ever. "Then you know about his tactics, and his troops. His way of making war?" Logen nodded. "What can you tell me about him?"

"That he's a most cunning and ruthless opponent, with no pity or scruple in him. Make no mistake, I hate the man, but there's been no war leader in his league since the days of Skarling Hoodless. He has that in him which men respect, or fear, or at least obey. He pushes his men hard, so he can make the field first and choose his own ground, but they march hard for him because he brings them victories. He's cautious when he must be, and fearless when he must be, but neglects no detail. He delights in every trick of war—in setting

traps and ambushes, in mounting feints and deceptions, in sending sudden
raids against the unwary. Look for him where you expect him least, and expect
him to be strongest where he seems the weakest. Beware him most of all when
he seems to run. Most men fear him, and those that don't are fools."

Logen picked up the flower from the plate and started snapping it into
pieces. "His armies are grouped about the chieftains of the clans, some of
them strong war leaders in their own right. Most of his fighters are Thralls,
peasants pressed into service, lightly armed with spear or bow, fast moving
in loose groups. In the past they were ill-trained, and taken from their farms
for only a short time, but the wars have been raging for so long that many of
them have become hard fighters, and show scant mercy."

He began to arrange the bits of plant, imagining they were groups of
men and the plate a hill. "Each chieftain keeps Carls besides, his own house-
hold warriors, well armed and armoured, skilled with axe and sword and
spear, well disciplined. Some few have horses, but Bethod will keep those out
of sight, waiting for the best moment to charge or pursue." He pulled the
yellow petals from the flower, and they became horsemen hidden on the
flanks. "Last there are the Known Men, the Named Men, those warriors
who've earned great respect in battle. They might lead groups of Carls on the
field, or act as scouts or raiders, sometimes far in the enemy's rear."

He realised the plate was covered with a mess of broken pieces of plant,
and brushed them hurriedly off onto the table. "That's the tradition of war in
the North, but Bethod's always had a fancy for new ideas. He's read books,
and studied other ways of fighting, and often talked of buying flat-bows, and
heavy armour, and strong war-horses from the southern traders, and of
making an army to be feared throughout the world."

Logen became aware he had been talking solidly for ages. He hadn't said
half that many words together in years, but West was staring at him with a
look of rapt attention. "You speak like a man who knows his business."

"Well, you've happened upon the one subject on which I might be reckoned an expert."

"What advice would you give to a man who had to fight a war against
Bethod?"

Logen frowned. "Be careful. And watch your back."

Jezal was not enjoying himself. At first, of course, it had seemed a delightful idea, just the thing he had always dreamed of: a celebration in *his* honour, attended by so many of the Union's greatest. Surely it was only the start of his wonderful new life as a champion of the Contest. The great things which everyone had predicted, no, promised for him were almost arrived, poised like over-ripe fruit to drop from the tree and into his lap. Promotions and glory were sure to follow close behind. Perhaps they would make him Major tonight, and he would go to the war in Angland as commander of a full battalion . . .

But, strangely, it appeared that most of the guests were more interested in their own affairs. They chattered to each other about government matters, about the business of merchant houses, about issues of land, and title, and politics. Fencing, and his remarkable skill at it, were scarcely mentioned. No immediate promotion had been forthcoming. He simply had to sit there, and smile, and accept the odd lukewarm congratulation from strangers in splendid clothes who barely even looked him in the eye. A wax effigy could have done the same job. He had to admit, the adulation of the commoners in the arena had been considerably more gratifying. At least they had sounded as if they meant it.

Still, he had never before been within the palace compound, a fortress within the fortress of the Agriont where few indeed were permitted to tread. Now he was seated at the top table in the King's own dining hall, though Jezal did not doubt that his Majesty took the majority of his meals propped up in bed, and most likely had them fed to him with a spoon.

There was a stage set into the wall at the far end of the room. Jezal had once heard that Ostus, the child King, had jesters perform for him at every meal. Morlic the Mad, by contrast, had staged executions there to go with his dinner. King Casamir, it was said, had likenesses of his worst enemies shout insults at him from that stage while he took his breakfast every morning, to keep his hatred for them fresh. The curtains were closed now, though. Jezal would have to look for his entertainment elsewhere, and in this regard the pickings were slim indeed.

Marshal Varuz prattled on in his ear. He, at least, was still interested in fencing. Unfortunately, he talked of nothing else. "I never saw such a thing. The whole city is buzzing with it. Most remarkable bout that anyone's ever seen! I swear, you're better even than Sand dan Glokta used to be, and I never thought to see his like again! I never dreamed you had it in you to fight like that, Jezal, never had the slightest inkling!"

"Mmm," said Jezal.

The Crown Prince Ladisla and his bride-to-be, Terez of Talins, made a dazzling couple at the top of the table, just beside the dozing King. They were oblivious to all that was going on around them, but hardly in the way that one might hope for from two young lovers. They were arguing viciously in scarcely hushed voices, while their neighbours studiously pretended not to suck in every word.

". . . well I'll be going to war soon, in Angland, so you need not suffer me too much longer!" whined Ladisla. "I might be killed! Perhaps that would make your Highness happy?"

"Pray don't die on my account," returned Terez, her Styrian accent dripping venom, "but if you must, you must. I suppose I will learn to bear the sorrow . . ."

Somebody nearer at hand distracted Jezal by thumping on the table. "Damn these commoners! Damn peasantry's up in arms in Starikland! Lazy dogs, they refuse to work a stroke!"

"It's these taxes," grumbled the man's neighbour, "these war taxes have them all stirred up. Have you heard about this damn character they call the Tanner? Some bloody peasant, preaching revolution, open as you please! I heard that one of the King's collectors was set on by a mob, not a mile outside the walls of Keln. One of the King's collectors, I say! By a mob! Not a mile outside the city walls—"

"We've damn well brought it on ourselves!" The speaker's face was out of sight but Jezal recognised him by the gold-embroidered cuffs on his gown. Marovia, the High Justice. "Treat a man like a dog and sooner or later he'll bite you, it's a simple fact. Our role as governors, and as noblemen, is surely to respect and protect the common man, rather than to oppress and scorn him?"

"I wasn't talking about scorn, Lord Marovia, or oppression, just about them paying what's due to us as their landlords, and for that matter their natural betters . . ."

Marshal Varuz, meanwhile, had not let up for an instant. "It was quite a thing, eh? The way you put him down, one steel against two!" The old soldier swished his hand around in the air. "The whole town's buzzing. You're bound for great things now my boy, mark my words. Bound for great things. I'll be damned if you don't have my seat on the Closed Council one day!"

It really was too much. Jezal had put up with the man for all those months. He had somehow imagined that if he won that would be the end of it, but it seemed he would be disappointed in this, as in so much else. It was strange, but Jezal had never fully realised before what a boring old imbecile the Lord Marshal was. He was realising now though, and no mistake.

To further add to his dismay, there were several people seated about the tables who would most definitely not have been among his chosen guests. He supposed he could make a dispensation for Sult, the Arch Lector of the Inquisition, since he sat on the Closed Council and was without doubt a powerful figure, but Jezal could not comprehend why he might have brought that bastard Glokta with him. The cripple looked even more ill than usual, twitching eyes sunken in dark circles. For some reason he was occasionally shooting grim and suspicious glances at Jezal as though he suspected him of some crime or other. It was a damn cheek, what with it being his feast and all.

Even worse, on the other side of the room was that old, bald man, the one who had called himself Bayaz. Jezal had still not got to the bottom of his strange words of congratulation at the Contest—or his father's reaction to the man, for that matter. And he had his hideous friend, the nine-fingered barbarian, beside him.

Major West had the misfortune of being seated next to the primitive, but he was making the best of it; indeed, the two were engaged in a lively conversation. The Northman broke into sudden peals of laughter and thumped the table with his big fist, making the glasses rattle. At least they were enjoying themselves at his party, Jezal thought sourly, but he almost wished he was down there with them.

Still, he knew that he wanted to be a big, important man some day. To wear things with a lot of fur, and a heavy golden chain of office. To have people bow and scrape and fawn before him. He had made that decision long ago, and he supposed he still liked the idea. It was just that, up close, the whole thing seemed so awfully false and boring. He would much, much rather have been on his own with Ardee, even though he had seen her the night before. There was nothing boring about her . . .

". . . the savages are closing on Ostenhorm, that's what I heard!" someone shouted over on Jezal's left. "The Lord Governor, Meed, he's raising an army and has sworn to turn them out of Angland!"

"Hah. Meed? That swollen-headed old fool couldn't turn a pie out of a dish!"

"Enough to beat these Northern animals though, what? One good Union man's worth ten of their kind . . ."

Jezal heard Terez's voice cutting suddenly shrill above the hubbub, almost loud enough to be heard at the far end of the room, ". . . of course I will marry where my father commands me, but I don't have to like it!" She appeared so vicious at that moment that he would not have been surprised to see her stab the Crown Prince in the face with her fork. Jezal felt somewhat gratified to see that he was not the only one who had trouble with women.

". . . oh yes, a remarkable performance! Everyone's talking about it," Varuz was still droning.

Jezal squirmed in his chair. How long was this bloody business going to take? He felt suffocated. He glanced across the faces again and caught Glokta's eye, staring at him with that grim, suspicious look on his wasted face. Jezal still couldn't meet that gaze for long, his party or no. What the hell did the cripple have against him anyhow?

The little bastard. He cheated. Somehow. I know it. Glokta's eyes tracked slowly across the table opposite until they lighted on Bayaz. The old fraud was sitting there, quite at home. *And he had some part in it. They cheated, together. Somehow.*

"My lords and ladies!" The chatter faded as the Lord Chamberlain rose to address the room. "I would like to welcome you all, on his Majesty's behalf, to this humble gathering." The King himself stirred briefly, gazed vacantly about him, blinked, then closed his eyes. "We are gathered, of course, in honour of Captain Jezal dan Luthar, who has recently added his name to that most select roll of honour: those swordsman who have been victorious at the summer Contest." A few glasses were raised and there were some half-hearted mumblings of agreement.

"I recognise several other winners among the assembly here today, many of them now the holders of high office: Lord Marshal Varuz, Commander Valdis of the Knights Herald, Major West down there, now on Marshal Burr's staff, of course. Even I was a winner in my day." He smiled and looked down at his bulging paunch. "Though my day was some time ago, of course." A polite ripple of laughter passed round the room. *I notice that I don't get a mention. Not all winners are enviable, eh?*

"Victors at the Contest," continued the Lord Chamberlain, "have so often gone on to great things. I hope, and indeed we all hope, that it may prove so for our young friend, Captain Luthar." *I hope he meets a slow death in Angland, the cheating little bastard.* But Glokta raised his glass along with everyone else to toast the arrogant ass, while Luthar sat there, loving every instant of it.

And to think. I sat in that very chair, being applauded and envied and clapped on the back after I won the Contest. Different men in the big clothes, different faces sweating in the heat, but nothing very much has changed. Was my grin really any less smug? Of course not. If anything I was worse. But at least I earned it.

Such was Lord Hoff's commitment that he did not stop toasting until his goblet was entirely empty, then he shoved it back on the table and licked his lips. "And now, before the food arrives, a small surprise has been prepared by my colleague Arch Lector Sult, in honour of another of our guests. I hope you will all find it diverting." And the Lord Chamberlain sat heavily back down, holding his empty goblet out for more wine.

Glokta glanced across at Sult. *A surprise, from the Arch Lector? Bad news for somebody.*

The heavy red curtains of the stage rolled slowly back. They revealed an old man lying on the boards, his white garment daubed with colourful blood. A broad canvas behind depicted a forest scene beneath a starry sky. It reminded Glokta rather unpleasantly of the mural in the round room. The room beneath Severard's crumbling pile by the docks.

A second old man swept on from the wings: a tall, slender man with remarkably fine, sharp features. His head was shaved bald and he had grown a short white beard, but Glokta recognised him immediately. *Iosiv Lestek, one of the city's most respected actors.* He gave a mannered start as he noticed the bloody corpse.

"Oooooooh!" he wailed, spreading his arms wide in an actor's approximation of shock and despair. It was a truly enormous voice, loud enough to make the rafters shake. Confident that he had the undivided attention of the chamber, Lestek began to intone his lines, hands sweeping through the air, towering passions sweeping across his face.

> So here, at last, my master Juvens lies,
> And with his death all hope of peace now dies,
> By Kanedias's treachery undone.
> His passing is the setting of the sun
> Upon an age.

The old actor threw back his head, and Glokta saw tears sparkling in his eyes. *A neat trick, to cry on demand like that.* A lonely drop trickled slowly down his cheek, and the audience sat spellbound. He turned once again to the body.

> Here brother murders brother. All slow time
> Can never have recorded such a crime.
> I half expect to see the stars go out.
> Why does the ground not open up and spout
> Some raging flame?

He threw himself down on his knees and beat upon his ageing breast.

> Oh bitter fate, I would most happily
> Now join my master, but it cannot be!
> For when a great man dies, we that remain
> Though in a narrowed world, must brave the pain
> And struggle onward.

Lestek looked slowly up towards the audience, slowly clambered to his feet, his expression shifting from deepest sorrow to grimmest determination.

For though the Maker's house is locked and barred,
All carved from rock and steel, all wondrous hard,
If I must wait until that steel is rust,
Or with my bare hands crush that rock to dust,
I'll have my vengeance!

The actor's eyes flashed fire as he flicked out his robe and strode from the stage to rapturous applause. It was a condensed version of a familiar piece, often performed. *Although rarely so well.* Glokta was surprised to find himself clapping. *Quite the performance so far. Nobility, passion, command. A great deal more convincing than another fake Bayaz I could mention.* He sat back in his chair, easing his left leg out under the table, and prepared to enjoy the show.

Logen watched with his face screwed up in confusion. He guessed that this was one of the spectacles that Bayaz had spoken of, but his grip on the language wasn't good enough to catch the details.

They swept up and down the stage with much sighing and waving of their hands, dressed in bright costumes and speaking in some kind of chant. Two of them were supposed to be dark-skinned, he thought, but were clearly pale men with black paint on their faces. In another scene, the one playing Bayaz whispered to a woman through a door, seeming to plead with her to open it, only the door was a piece of painted wood stood up on its own in the middle of the stage, and the woman was a boy in a dress. It would have been easier, Logen thought, to step around the piece of wood and speak to him or her directly.

Logen was sure of one thing, though—the real Bayaz was seriously displeased. He could feel his annoyance mounting with each scene. It reached a teeth-grinding peak when the villain of the piece, a big man with a glove and an eye-patch, pushed the boy in the dress over some wooden battlements. It was plain that he or she was meant to have fallen a great distance, even though Logen could hear him hit something soft just behind the stage.

"How fucking dare they?" the real Bayaz growled under his breath.
Logen would have got all the way out of the room if he could've, but he had
to be content with shuffling his chair towards West, as far from the Magus's
fury as possible.

On the stage, the other Bayaz was battling the old man with the glove
and the eye-patch, although they fought by walking round in circles and
talking a lot. Finally the villain followed the boy off the back of the stage,
but not before his adversary took an enormous golden key from him.

"There's more detail here than in the original," muttered the real Bayaz,
as his counterpart held up the key and spouted some more verse. Logen was
little further on when the performance came to a close, but he caught the last
two lines, just before the old actor bowed low:

Pray your indulgence, at our story's end,
Our humble purpose was not to offend.

"My fucking old arse it wasn't," hissed Bayaz through gritted teeth,
while fixing a grin and clapping enthusiastically.

Glokta watched Lestek take a few last bows as the curtains closed on him, the
golden key still shining in his hand. Arch Lector Sult rose from his chair as
the applause died.

"I am so glad you enjoyed our little diversion," he said, smiling smoothly
round at the appreciative gathering. "I do not doubt that many of you have
seen this piece before, but it has a special significance this evening. Captain
Luthar is not the only celebrated figure in our midst, there is a second guest
of honour here tonight. None other than the subject of our play—Bayaz himself, the First of the Magi!" Sult smiled and held out his arm towards the old
fake on the other side of the room. There was a gentle rustling as every guest
turned from the Arch Lector to look at him.

Bayaz smiled back. "Good evening," he said. A few of the worthies
laughed, suspecting some further little game perhaps, but Sult did not laugh
with them and their merriment was short lived. An uneasy silence descended
on the hall. *A deadly silence, perhaps.*

"The First of the Magi. He has been with us in the Agriont now for several weeks. He and a few . . . companions." Sult glanced down his nose at the scarred Northman, and then back to the self-styled Magus. "Bayaz." He rolled the word around his mouth, allowing it to sink into his listeners' ears. "The first letter in the alphabet of the old tongue. First apprentice of Juvens, first letter of the alphabet, is that not so, Master Bayaz?"

"Why, Arch Lector," asked the old man, still smirking, "have you been checking up on me?" *Impressive. Even now, when he must sense the game will soon be over, he sticks to his role.*

Sult was unmoved however. "It is my duty thoroughly to investigate anyone who might pose a threat to my King or country," he intoned stiffly.

"How fearsomely patriotic of you. Your investigations no doubt revealed that I am still a member of the Closed Council, even if my chair stands empty for the time being. I believe *Lord* Bayaz would be the proper term of address."

Sult's cold smile did not slip even a hair's breadth. "And when exactly was your last visit, *Lord* Bayaz? It would seem that someone so deeply involved in our history would have taken more of an interest over the years. Why, if I may ask, in the centuries since the birth of the Union, since the time of Harod the Great, have you not been back to visit us?" *A good question. I wish it had occurred to me.*

"Oh, but I have been. During the reign of King Morlic the Mad, and in the civil war which followed, I was tutor to a young man called Arnault. Later, when Morlic was murdered and Arnault was raised to the throne by the Open Council, I served as his Lord Chamberlain. I called myself Bialoveld in those days. I visited again in King Casamir's reign. He called me Zoller, and I had your job, Arch Lector."

Glokta could barely contain a gasp of indignation, and heard others from the chairs around him. *He has no shame, I'll give him that. Bialoveld, and Zoller, two of the Union's most respected servants. How dare he? And yet . . .* He pictured the painting of Zoller in the Arch Lector's study, and the statue of Bialoveld in the Kingsway. *Both bald, both stern, both bearded . . . but what am I thinking? Major West is thinning out on top. Does that make him a legendary wizard? Most likely this charlatan merely picked the two baldest figures he could find.*

Sult, meanwhile, was trying a different tack. "Tell me this, then, Bayaz:

it is a story well known that Harod himself doubted you when you first came to his hall, all those long years ago. As proof of your power, you broke his long table in two. It may be that there are some sceptics among us here tonight. Would you consider such a demonstration for us, now?"

The colder Sult's tone became, the less the old fraud seemed to care. He dismissed this latest effort with a lazy wave of his hand. "What you speak of is not juggling, Arch Lector, or playing on the stage. There are always dangers, and costs. Besides, it would be a great shame to spoil Captain Luthar's feast simply so I could show off, don't you think? Not to mention the waste of a fine old piece of furniture. I, unlike so many others these days, have a healthy respect for the past."

Some were smiling uncertainly as they watched the two old men fencing with each other, perhaps still suspecting an elaborate joke. Others knew better and were frowning hard, trying to work out what was going on, and who had the upper hand. High Justice Marovia, Glokta noticed, looked to be thoroughly enjoying himself. *Almost as if he knows something we don't.* Glokta shifted uncomfortably in his chair, eyes fixed on the bald actor. *Things are not going as well as they should be. When will he begin to sweat? When?*

Someone placed a bowl of steaming soup in front of Logen. No doubt it was meant to be eaten, but now his appetite was gone. Logen might be no courtier, but he could spot folk working up to violence when he saw them. With each exchange between the two old men their smiles slipped further, their voices became harder, the hall seemed to grow closer and more oppressive. Everyone in the room was looking worried now—West, the proud lad who'd won that sword game because of Bayaz's cheating, the feverish cripple who'd asked all the questions . . .

Logen felt the hairs on his neck rising. There were two figures lurking in the nearest doorway. Black-clothed figures, black-masked. His eyes flicked across to the other entrances. Each held two of those masked figures, two at least, and he didn't reckon they were here to collect the plates.

They were here for him. For him and Bayaz, he could feel it. A man doesn't put on a mask unless he's got some dark work in mind. There was no way that he could deal with half that many, but he slid a knife from beside his plate and hid it behind his arm anyway. If they tried to take him, he'd fight. That didn't need thinking about.

Bayaz was starting to sound angry. "I have supplied you with all the proofs you've asked for, Arch Lector!"

"Proofs!" The tall man they called Sult gave a cold sneer. "You deal in words and dusty papers! More the business of a snivelling clerk than the stuff of legend! Some would say that a Magus without magic is simply a meddling old man! We are at war, and can take no chances! You mentioned Arch Lector Zoller. His diligence in the cause of truth is well documented. You, I am sure, must understand mine." He leaned forward, planting his fists firmly on the table before him. "Show us magic, *Bayaz*, or show us the key!"

Logen swallowed. He didn't like the way that things were going, but then he didn't understand the rules of this game. He had put his trust in Bayaz, for some reason, and there it would have to stay. It was a little late to be changing sides.

"Have you nothing left to say?" demanded Sult. He slowly lowered himself into his chair, smiling once more. His eyes slid over to the archways and Logen felt the masked figures moving forward, straining to be released. "Have you no more words? Have you no more tricks?"

"Only one." Bayaz reached into his collar. He took hold of something there, and drew it out—a long, thin chain. One of the black-masked figures stepped forward a pace, expecting a weapon, and Logen's hand gripped tighter on the handle of the knife, but when the chain came all the way out there was only a rod of dark metal dangling on the end of it.

"The key," said Bayaz, holding it up to the candlelight. It barely shone at all. "Less lustre than the one in your play, perhaps, but the real thing, I assure you. Kanedias never worked with gold. He did not like pretty things. He liked things that worked."

The Arch Lector's lip curled. "Do you simply expect us to take your word for it?"

"Of course not. It is your job to be suspicious of everyone, and I must say you do it exceptionally well. It does grow rather late however, so I will wait until tomorrow morning to open the House of the Maker." Someone dropped a spoon on the floor, and it clattered against the tiles. "There will need to be some witnesses present, of course, to make sure that I don't try any sleight of hand. How about . . ." Bayaz's cool green eyes swept down the table. "Inquisitor Glokta, and . . . your new fencing champion, Captain Luthar?"

The cripple frowned as he was named. Luthar looked utterly bewildered. The Arch Lector sat, his scorn swapped for a stony blankness. He gazed from Bayaz's smiling face to that gently swinging rod of dark metal, then back again. His eyes moved over to one of the doorways, and he give a tiny shake of his head. The dark figures faded back into the shadows. Logen unclenched his aching teeth, then quietly slipped the knife back on to the table.

Bayaz grinned. "Dear me, Master Sult, you really are a hard man to please."

"I believe *your Eminence* is the proper term of address," hissed the Arch Lector.

"So it is, so it is. I do declare, you really won't be happy until I've broken some furniture. I would hate to spill everyone's soup though, so . . ." With a sudden bang, the Arch Lector's chair collapsed. His hand shot out and grabbed at the table cloth as he plunged to the floor in a clattering mess of loose firewood, and sprawled in the wreckage with a groan. The King started awake, his guests blinked, and gasped, and stared. Bayaz ignored them.

"This really is an excellent soup," he said, slurping noisily from his spoon.

THE HOUSE OF THE MAKER

It was a stormy day, and the House of the Maker stood stark and grim, a huge dark shape against the ragged clouds. A cold wind whipped between the buildings and through the squares of the Agriont, making the tails of Glokta's black coat flap around him as he shuffled after Captain Luthar and the would-be Magus, the scarred Northman at his side. He knew they were watched. *Watched the whole way. Behind the windows, in the doorways, on the roofs.* The Practicals were everywhere, he could feel their eyes.

Glokta had half expected, half hoped, that Bayaz and his companions would have disappeared in the night, but they had not. The bald old man seemed as relaxed as if he had undertaken to open a fruit cellar, and Glokta did not like it. *When does the bluff end? When does he throw his hands up and admit it's all a game? When we reach the University? When we cross the bridge? When we stand before the very gate of the Maker's House and his key does not fit?* But somewhere in the back of his mind the thought lurked: *What if it does not end? What if the door opens? What if he truly is as he claims to be?*

Bayaz chattered to Luthar as they strolled across the empty courtyard towards the University. *Every bit as much at ease as a grandfather with his favourite grandson, and every bit as boring.* "... of course, the city is so much larger than when I last visited. That district you call the Three Farms, all teeming bustle and activity. I remember when that whole borough *was* three farms! Indeed I do! And far beyond the city walls!"

"Erm . . ." said Luthar.

"And as for the Spicers' new guildhall, I never saw such ostentation . . ."

Glokta's mind raced as he limped after the two of them, trawling for hidden meanings in the sea of blather, grasping for order in the chaos. The questions tumbled over each other. *Why pick me as a witness? Why not the Arch Lector himself? Does this Bayaz suppose that I can be easily fooled? And why Luthar? Because he won the Contest? And how did he win? Is he a part of this deception?* But if Luthar was party to some sinister plan, he was giving no sign. Glokta had never seen the slightest hint that he was anything other than the self-obsessed young fool he appeared to be.

And then we come to this puzzle. Glokta glanced sidelong at the big Northman. There were no signs of deadly intent on his scarred face, little sign that anything was going on in there at all. *Is he very stupid, or very clever? Is he to be ignored, or feared? Is he the servant, or the master?* There were no answers to any of it. Yet.

"Well, this place is a shadow of its former self," said Bayaz as they halted outside the door to the University, raising an eyebrow at the grimy, tilting statues. He rapped briskly on the weathered wood and the door swayed on its hinges. To Glokta's surprise, it opened almost immediately.

"You're expected," croaked the ancient porter. They stepped around him into the gloom. "I will show you to—" began the old man as he wrestled the creaking door shut.

"No need," called Bayaz over his shoulder, already striding briskly off down the dusty corridor, "I know the way!" Glokta struggled to keep up, sweating despite the cold weather, leg burning all the way. The effort of maintaining the pace scarcely gave him time to consider how the bald bastard might be so familiar with the building. *But familiar he certainly is.* He swept down the corridors as though he had spent every day of his life there, clicking his tongue in disgust at the state of the place and prattling all the while.

". . . I've never seen such dust, eh, Captain Luthar? I wouldn't be surprised if the damn place hadn't been cleaned since I was last here! I've no idea how a man can think under such conditions! No idea at all . . ." Centuries of dead and justly forgotten Adepti stared gloomily down from their canvases, as though upset by all the noise.

The corridors of the University rolled past, an ancient, dusty, forsaken-seeming place, with nothing in it but grimy old paintings and musty old books. Jezal had precious little use for books. He had read a few about fencing and riding, a couple about famous military campaigns, once opened the covers on a great big history of the Union he found in his father's study, and got bored after three or four pages.

Bayaz droned on. "Here we fought with the Maker's servants. I remember it well. They cried out to Kanedias to save them, but he would not come down. These halls ran with blood, rang with screams, rolled with smoke that day."

Jezal had no idea why the old fool would single him out to tell his tall stories to, and still less how to reply. "That sounds . . . violent."

Bayaz nodded. "It was. I am not proud of it. But good men must sometimes do violent things."

"Uh," said the Northman suddenly. Jezal had not been aware that he was even listening.

"Besides, that was a different age. A violent age. Only in the Old Empire were people advanced beyond the primitive. Midderland, the heart of the Union, believe it or not, was a sty. A wasteland of warring, barbaric tribes. The luckiest among them were taken into the Maker's service. The rest were painted-face savages, without writing, without science, with barely anything to separate them from the beasts."

Jezal glanced furtively up at Ninefingers. It was not at all difficult to picture a barbaric state with that big brute beside him, but it was ridiculous to suppose that his beautiful home had once been a wasteland, that he was descended from primitives. This bald old man was a blathering liar, or a madman, but some important people seemed to take him seriously.

And Jezal thought it best always to do what the important people said.

Logen followed the others into a broken-down courtyard, bounded on three sides by the crumbling buildings of the University, on the fourth by the inner face of the sheer wall of the Agriont. All was covered in old moss, thick ivy, dry brambles. A man sat on a rickety chair among the weeds, watching them come closer.

"I've been expecting you," he said, pushing himself up with some difficulty. "Damn knees, I'm not what I used to be." An unremarkable man past middle-age, in a threadbare shirt with stains down the front.

Bayaz frowned at him. "You are the Chief Warden?"

"I am."

"And where are the rest of your company?"

"My wife is getting the breakfast ready, but not counting her, well, I am the whole company. It's eggs," he said happily, patting his stomach.

"What?"

"For breakfast. I like eggs."

"Good for you," muttered Bayaz, looking slightly put out. "In King Casamir's reign, the bravest fifty men of the King's Own were appointed Wardens of the House, to guard this gate. There was considered to be no higher honour."

"That was a long time ago," said the one and only Warden, plucking at his dirty shirt. "There were nine of us when I was a lad, but they went on to other things, or died, and were never replaced. Don't know who'll take over when I'm gone. There haven't been too many applicants."

"You surprise me." Bayaz cleared his throat. "Oh, Chief Warden! I, Bayaz, First of the Magi, seek your leave to pass up the stair to the fifth gate, beyond the fifth gate and onto the bridge, across the bridge and to the door of the Maker's House."

The Chief Warden squinted back. "You sure?"

Bayaz was growing impatient. "Yes, why?"

"I remember the last fellow who tried it, way back when I was a lad. Some big man, I reckon, some thinker. He went up those steps with ten strong workmen, chisels and hammers and picks and what-have-you, telling us how he was going to open up the House, bring out its treasures and all. Five minutes and they were back, saying nothing, looking like they saw the dead walk."

"What happened?" murmured Luthar.

"Don't know, but they had no treasures with them, I can tell you that."

"Without doubt a daunting story," said Bayaz, "but we're going."

"Your business, I suppose." And the old man turned and slouched across the miserable courtyard. Up a narrow stair they went, the steps worn down in the middle, up to a tunnel through the high wall of the Agriont, on to a narrow gate in the darkness.

Logen felt an odd sense of worry as the bolts slid back. He shrugged his shoulders, trying to get rid of it, and the Warden grinned at him. "You can feel it already, eh?"

"Feel what?"

"The Maker's breath, they call it." He gave the doors the gentlest shove. They swung open together, light spilling through into the darkness. "The Maker's breath."

Glokta tottered across the bridge, teeth clenched tight on gums, painfully aware of the volume of empty air beneath his feet. It was a single, delicate arch, leaping from high up on the wall of the Agriont to the gate of the Maker's House. He had often admired it from down in the city, on the other side of the lake, wondering how it had stayed up all these years. A spectacular, remarkable, beautiful thing. *It does not seem so beautiful now.* Not much wider than a man lying down, too narrow by far for comfort, and with a terrifying drop to the water below. Worse still, it had no parapet. Not so much as a wooden handrail. *And the breeze is rather fresh today.*

Luthar and Ninefingers seemed worried enough by it. *And they have the free and painless use of both their legs.* Only Bayaz made the long trip across without apparent worry, as confident as if his feet were on a country lane.

They walked always in the vast shadow of the House of the Maker, of course. The closer they came, the more massive it seemed, its lowest parapet far higher than the wall of the Agriont. A stark black mountain, rising sheer from the lake below, blotting out the sun. A thing from a different age, built on a different scale.

Glokta glanced back towards the gate behind him. Did he catch a glimpse of something between the battlements on the wall above? *A Practical watching?* They would see the old man fail to open the door. They would be waiting to take him on their way back through. *But until then, I am helpless.* It was not a comforting thought.

And Glokta was in need of comfort. As he tottered further across the bridge, a niggling fear swelled inside him. It was more than the height, more than the strange company, more than the great tower looming above. A base fear, without reason. The animal terror of a nightmare. With every shuffling step the feeling grew. He could see the door now, a square of dark metal set back into the smooth stones of the tower. A circle of letters was etched into the centre of it. For some reason they made Glokta want to vomit, but he dragged himself closer. Two circles: large letters and small letters, a spidery script he did not recognise. His guts churned. Many circles: letters and lines, too detailed to take in. They swam before his stinging, weeping eyes. Glokta could go no further. He stood there, leaning on his cane, fighting with every ounce of will against the need to fall to his knees, turn and crawl away.

Ninefingers was faring little better, breathing hard through his nose, a look of the most profound horror and disgust on his face. Luthar was in considerably worse shape: teeth gritted, white-faced and palsied. He dropped slowly down on one knee, gasping, as Glokta edged past him.

Bayaz did not seem afraid. He stepped right up to the door and ran his fingers over the larger symbols. "Eleven wards, and eleven wards reversed." He traced the circle of smaller characters. "And eleven times eleven." His finger followed the fine line outside them. *Can it be that line is made of tiny letters too?* "Who can say how many hundreds here? Truly, a most potent enchantment!"

The sense of awe was only slightly diminished by the sound of Luthar puking noisily over the side of the bridge. "What does it say?" croaked Glokta, swallowing some bile of his own.

The old man grinned at him. "Can you not feel it, Inquisitor? It says turn away. It says get you gone. It says . . . none . . . shall . . . pass. But the message is not for us." He reached into his collar and pulled out the rod of metal. The same dark metal as the door itself.

"We shouldn't be here," growled Ninefingers from behind. "This place is dead. We should go." But Bayaz did not seem to hear.

"The magic has leaked out of the world," Glokta heard him murmuring, "and all the achievements of Juvens lie in ruins." He weighed the key in his hand, brought it slowly upwards. "But the Maker's works stand strong as ever. Time has not diminished them . . . nor ever will." There did not even seem to be a hole, but the key slid slowly into the door. Slowly, slowly, into the very centre of the circles. Glokta held his breath.

Click.

And nothing happened. The door did not open. *That is all then. The game is over.* He felt a surge of relief as he turned back towards the Agriont, raising a hand to signal to the Practicals on the wall above. *I need not go further. I need not.* Then an answering echo came from deep within.

Click.

Glokta felt his face twitch in sympathy with the sound. *Did I imagine it?* He hoped so, with all his being.

Click.

Again. *No mistake.* And now, before his disbelieving eyes, the circles in the door began to turn. Glokta took a stunned step back, his cane scraping on the stones of the bridge.

Click, click.

There had been no sign that the metal was not all one piece, no cracks, no grooves, no mechanism, and yet the circles spun, each at a different speed.

Click, click, click . . .

Faster now, and faster. Glokta felt dizzy. The innermost ring, with the largest letters, was still crawling. The outermost, the thinnest one, was flying round too fast for his eyes to follow.

. . . click, click, click, click, click . . .

Shapes formed in the markings as the symbols passed each other: lines, squares, triangles, unimaginably intricate, dancing before his eyes then vanishing as the wheels spun on . . .

Click.

And the circles were still, arranged in a new pattern. Bayaz reached up and pulled the key from the door. There was a soft hissing, barely audible, as of water far away, and a long crack appeared in the door. The two halves moved slowly, smoothly away from each other. The space between them grew steadily larger.

Click.

They slid into the walls, flush with the sides of the square archway. The door stood open.

"Now that," said Bayaz softly, "is craftsmanship."

No fetid wind spilled out, no stench of rot or decay, no sign of long years passed, only a waft of cool, dry air. *And yet the feeling is of opening a coffin.*

Silence, but for the wind fumbling across the dark stones, the breath sighing in Glokta's dry throat, the distant lapping of the water far below. The unearthly terror was gone. He felt only a deep worry as he stared into the open archway. *But no worse than when I wait outside the Arch Lector's office.* Bayaz turned round, smiling.

"Long years have passed since I sealed this place, and in all that slow time no man has crossed the threshold. You three are truly honoured." Glokta did not feel honoured. He felt ill. "There are dangers within. Touch nothing, and go only where I lead you. Follow close behind me, for the ways are not always the same."

"Not the same?" asked Glokta. "How can that be?"

The old man shrugged. "I am only the doorman," he said as he slipped the key and its chain back inside his shirt, "not the architect." And he stepped into the shadows.

Jezal did not feel well, not well at all. It was not simply the vile nausea that the letters on the doors had somehow created, it was more. A lurch of sudden shock and disgust, like picking up a cup and drinking, expecting water, and finding something else inside. Piss perhaps, in this case. That same wave of ugly surprise, but stretching out over minutes, over hours. Things that he had dismissed as foolishness, or old stories, were suddenly revealed as facts before his eyes. The world was a different place than it had been the day before, a weird and unsettling place, and he had infinitely preferred it the way it was.

He could not understand why he had to be here. Jezal knew precious little about history. Kanedias, Juvens, Bayaz even, they were names from dusty books, heard as a child and holding no interest even then. It was just bad luck, bad luck was all. He had won the Contest, and here he was, wandering about in some strange old tower. That was all it was. A strange old tower.

"Welcome," said Bayaz, "to the House of the Maker."

Jezal looked up from the floor and his jaw sagged open. The word "house" did little to describe the vastness of the dim space in which he found himself. The Lords' Round itself could have fitted comfortably inside it, the entire building, with room to spare. The walls were made from rough stones, unfinished, unmortared, piled haphazardly, but rising endlessly upward, upward. Above the centre of the room, far above, something was suspended. A huge, fascinating something.

It put Jezal in mind of a navigator's instruments, rendered on an enormous scale. A system of gigantic metal rings, shining in the dim light, one about the other, with further, smaller rings running between them, inside them, around them. Hundreds of them perhaps, all told, scored with markings: writing maybe, or meaningless scratches. A large black ball hung in the centre.

Bayaz was already walking out into the vast circle of the floor, covered in intricate lines, set into the dark stone in bright metal, his footfalls echoing high above. Jezal crept after him. There was something frightening, something dizzying, about moving across a space so huge.

"This is Midderland," said Bayaz.

"What?"

The old man pointed down. The squiggly lines of metal began to take on meaning. Coastlines, mountains, rivers, the land and the sea. The shape of Midderland, clear in Jezal's mind from a hundred maps, was laid out beneath his feet.

"The whole Circle of the World." Bayaz gestured across the endless floor. "That way is Angland, and beyond, the North. Gurkhul is over there. There is Starikland, and the Old Empire, and over here the City States of Styria, beyond them Suljuk and distant Thond. Kanedias observed that the lands of the known World form a circle, with its centre here, at his House, and its outer edge passing through the island of Shabulyan, far to the west, beyond the Old Empire."

"The edge of the World," muttered the Northman, nodding slowly to himself.

"Some arrogance," snorted Glokta, "to think of your home as the centre of everything."

"Huh." Bayaz looked about him at the vastness of the chamber. "The Maker was never short on arrogance. Nor were his brothers."

Jezal stared up gormlessly. The room was even higher than it was wide, its ceiling, if there was one, lost in shadow. An iron rail ran round the rough stone walls, a gallery perhaps twenty strides above. Beyond it, higher still, there was another, and another, and another, vague in the half light. Over all hung the strange device.

He gave a sudden start. It was moving! It was all moving! Slowly, smoothly, silently, the rings shifted, turned, revolved one about the other. He could not imagine how it was driven. Somehow, the key turning in the lock must have set it off . . . or could it have been turning all these years?

He felt dizzy. The whole mechanism now seemed to be spinning, revolving, faster and faster, the galleries too, shifting in opposite directions. Staring straight upwards was not helping with his sense of disorientation, and he fixed his aching eyes on the floor, on the map of Midderland beneath his feet. He gasped. That was even worse! Now the whole floor seemed to be turning! The entire chamber was revolving around him! The archways leading out were all identical, a dozen of them or more. He could not guess now through which one they had entered. He felt a wave of horrible panic. Only that distant black orb in the centre of the device was still. He fixed his watering eyes desperately on that, forced himself to breathe slow.

The feeling faded. The vast hall was still again, almost. The rings were still shifting, almost imperceptibly, inching ever onwards. He swallowed a mouthful of spit, hunched his shoulders, and hurried after the others with his head down.

"Not that way!" roared Bayaz suddenly, his voice exploding in the thick silence, ripping out and bouncing back, echoing a thousand times around the cavernous space.

"Not that way!"

"Not that way!"

Jezal jumped backwards. The archway, and the dim hall beyond, looked identical to the one down which the others had been walking, but he saw now that they were off to his right. He had got turned around somehow.

"Go only where I go, I said!" hissed the old man.

"Not that way."

"Not that way."

"I'm sorry," stammered Jezal, his voice sounding pitifully small in the vast space, "I thought . . . it all looks the same!"

Bayaz placed a reassuring hand on his shoulder and drew him smoothly away. "I did not mean to scare you, my friend, but it would be a great shame if one so promising were taken from us quite so young." Jezal swallowed and stared into the shadowy hallway, wondering what might have awaited him down there. His mind provided any number of unpleasant possibilities.

The echoes still whispered at him as he turned away. ". . . not that way, not that way, not that way . . ."

Logen hated this place. The stones were cold and dead, the air was still and dead, even the sounds they made as they moved fell muffled and lifeless. It wasn't cold and it wasn't hot, and yet his back trickled with sweat, his neck prickled with aimless fear. He'd jerk around every few steps, stung by the sudden feeling he was being watched, but there was never anyone behind him. Only the boy Luthar and the cripple Glokta, looking every bit as worried and confused as he was.

"We chased him through these very halls," murmured Bayaz quietly. "Eleven of us. All the Magi, together for the last time. All but Khalul. Zacharus, and Cawneil, they fought with the Maker here, and each was bested. They were fortunate to escape with their lives. Anselmi and Brokentooth had worse luck. Kanedias was the death of them. Two good friends, two brothers, I lost that day."

They edged round a narrow balcony, lit by a pale curtain of light. On one side sheer stones rose smooth, on the other they dropped away and were lost in the darkness. A black pit, full of shadows, with no far side, no top, no bottom. Despite the vastness of the space there were no echoes. No air moved. There was not the tiniest breeze. The air was stale and close as a tomb.

"There should be water down there, surely," muttered Glokta, frowning over the rail. "There should be something, shouldn't there?" He squinted up. "Where's the ceiling?"

"This place stinks," whined Luthar, one hand clasped over his nose.

Logen agreed with him, for once. It was a smell he knew well, and his lips curled back with hatred at it. "Smells like fucking Flatheads."

"Oh yes," said Bayaz, "the Shanka are the Maker's work also."

"His work?"

"Indeed. He took clay, and metal, and left-over flesh and he made them."

Logen stared. "He made them?"

"To fight in his war. Against us. Against the Magi. Against his brother Juvens. He bred the first Shanka here and let them loose upon the world—to grow, and breed, and destroy. That was their purpose. For many years after Kanedias' death we hunted them, but we could not catch them all. We drove them into the darkest corners of the world, and there they have grown and bred again, and now come forth to grow, and breed, and destroy, as they were always meant to do." Logen gawped at him.

"Shanka." Luthar chuckled and shook his head.

Flatheads were no laughing matter. Logen turned suddenly, blocking the narrow balcony with his body, looming over Luthar in the half light. "Something funny?"

"Well, I mean, everyone knows there's no such thing."

"I've fought them with my own hands," growled Logen, "all my life. They killed my wife, my children, my friends. The North is swarming with fucking Flatheads." He leaned down. "So don't tell me there's no such thing."

Luthar had turned pale. He looked to Glokta for support, but the Inquisitor had sagged against the wall, rubbing at his leg, thin lips tight shut, hollow face beaded with sweat. "I don't care a shit either way!" he snapped.

"There's plenty of Shanka in the world," hissed Logen, sticking his face right up close to Luthar's. "Maybe one day you'll meet some." He turned and stalked off after Bayaz, already disappearing through an archway at the far end of the balcony. He had no wish to be left behind in this place.

Yet another hall. An enormous one, lined with a silent forest of columns on either side, peopled with a multitude of shadows. Light cut down in shafts from far above, etching strange patterns into the stone floor, shapes of light and dark, lines of black and white. *Almost like writing. Is there a message here? For me?* Glokta was trembling. *If I looked, just for a moment longer, perhaps I could understand . . .*

Luthar wandered past, his shadow fell across the floor, the lines were broken, the feeling was gone. Glokta shook himself. *I am losing my reason in this cursed place. I must think clearly. Just the facts, Glokta, only the facts.*

"Where does the light come from?" he asked.

Bayaz waved his hand. "Above."

"There are windows?"

"Perhaps."

Glokta's cane tapped into the light, tapped into the dark, his left boot dragged along behind. "Is there nothing but hallway? What's the point of it all?"

"Who can know the Maker's mind?" intoned Bayaz pompously, "or fathom his great design?" He seemed almost to take pride in never giving straight answers.

The whole place was a colossal waste of effort as far as Glokta could see. "How many lived here?"

"Long years ago, in happier times, many hundreds. All manner of people who served Kanedias, and helped him in his works. But the Maker was ever distrustful, and jealous of his secrets. Bit by bit he turned his followers out, into the Agriont, the University. Towards the end, only three lived here. Kanedias himself, his assistant Jaremias," Bayaz paused for a moment, "and his daughter Tolomei."

"The Maker's daughter?"

"What of it?" snapped the old man.

"Nothing, nothing at all." *And yet the veneer slipped then, if only for an instant. It is strange that he knows the ways of this place so well.* "When did you live here?"

Bayaz frowned deep. "There is such a thing as too many questions."

Glokta watched him walk away. *Sult was wrong. The Arch Lector, fallible after all. He underestimated this Bayaz, and it cost him. Who is this bald, irritable fool, who can make a sprawling idiot of the most powerful man in the Union?* Standing here, deep within the bowels of this unearthly place, the answer did not seem so strange.

The First of the Magi.

"This is it."

"What?" asked Logen. The hallway stretched out in either direction, curving gently, disappearing into the darkness, walls of huge stone blocks, unbroken on either side.

Bayaz did not answer. He was running his hands gently over the stones, looking for something. "Yes. This is it." Bayaz pulled the key out from his shirt. "You might want to prepare yourselves."

"For what?"

The Magus slid the key into an unseen hole. One of the blocks that made up the walls suddenly vanished, flying up into the ceiling with a thunderous crash. Logen reeled, shaking his head. He saw Luthar bent forward, hands clamped over his ears. The whole corridor seemed to hum with crashing echoes, on and on.

"Wait," said Bayaz, though Logen could barely hear him over the ringing in his head. "Touch nothing. Go nowhere." He stepped through the opening, leaving the key lodged in the wall.

Logen peered after him. A glimmer of light shone down a narrow passageway, a rushing sound washed through like the trickling of a stream. Logen felt a strange curiosity picking at him. He glanced back at the other two. Perhaps Bayaz had meant only for them to stay? He ducked through the doorway.

And squinted up at a bright, round chamber. Light flooded in from high above, piercing light, almost painful to look at after the gloom of all the rest. The curving walls were perfect, clean white stone, running with trickling water, flowing down all around and collecting in a round pool below. The air was cool, damp on Logen's skin. A narrow bridge sprang out from the passage, steps leading upwards, ending at a tall white pillar, rising from the water. Bayaz was standing there, on top of it, staring down at something.

Logen crept up behind the Magus, breathing shallow. A block of white stone stood there. Water dripped onto its smooth, hard centre from above. A regular tap, tap, tap, always in the same spot. Two things lay in the thin layer of wet. The first was a square box, simply made from dark metal, big enough to hold a man's head, maybe. The other was altogether stranger.

A weapon perhaps, like an axe. A long shaft, made from tiny metal tubes, all twisted about each other like the stems of old vines. At one end there was a scored grip, at the other there was a flat piece of metal, pierced with small holes, a long, thin hook curving out from it. The light played over its many dark surfaces, glittering with beads of moisture. Strange, beautiful, fascinating. On the grip one letter glinted, silver in the dark metal. Logen recognised it from his sword. The mark of Kanedias. The work of the Master Maker.

"What is this?" he asked, reaching out for it.

"Don't touch it!" screamed Bayaz, slapping Logen's hand away. "Did I not tell you to wait?"

Logen took an uncertain step back. He had never seen the Magus look so worried, but he couldn't keep his eyes off the strange thing on the slab. "Is it a weapon?"

Bayaz breathed a long, slow breath. "A most terrible one, my friend. A weapon against which no steel, no stone, no magic can protect you. Do not even tread near it, I warn you. There are dangers. The Divider, Kanedias called it, and with it he killed his brother Juvens, my master. He once told me it has two edges. One here, one on the Other Side."

"What the hell does that mean?" muttered Logen. He couldn't even see one edge you could cut with.

Bayaz shrugged. "If I knew that I suppose that I'd be the Master Maker, instead of merely the First of the Magi." He reached forward and lifted the box, wincing as though it was a great weight. "Could you help me with this?"

Logen hooked his hands under it, and gasped. It could hardly have weighed more if it was a block of solid iron. "Heavy," he grunted.

"Kanedias forged it to be strong. As strong as all his great skill could make it. Not to keep its contents safe from the World." He leaned close and spoke softly. "To keep the World safe from its contents."

Logen frowned down. "What's in it?"

"Nothing," muttered Bayaz. "Yet."

Jezal was trying to think of three men in the world he hated more. Brint? He was simply a swollen-headed idiot. Gorst? He had merely done his meagre best to beat Jezal in a fencing match. Varuz? He was just a pompous old ass.

No. These three were at the top of his list. The arrogant old man with his idiotic prattle and his self-important air of mystery. The hulking savage with his ugly scars and his menacing frown. The patronising cripple with his smug little comments and his pretensions of knowing all about life. The three of them, combined with the stagnant air and perpetual gloom of this horrible place, were almost enough to make Jezal puke again. The only thing he could imagine worse than his present company was no company at all. He looked into the shadows all around, and shuddered at the thought.

Still, his spirits rose as they turned a corner. There was a small square of daylight up ahead. He hurried towards it, overtaking Glokta as he shambled along on his cane, mouth watering with anticipation at the thought of being back out under the sky.

Jezal closed his eyes with pleasure as he stepped into the open air. The cold wind stroked his face and he gasped in great lungfulls of it. The relief was terrific, as though he had been trapped down there in the darkness for weeks, as though fingers clamped around his throat had just now been released. He walked forward across a wide, open space, paved with stark, flat stones. Ninefingers and Bayaz stood side by side up ahead, behind a parapet, waist high, and beyond them . . .

The Agriont came into view below. A patchwork of white walls, grey roofs, glinting windows, green gardens. They were nowhere near the summit of the Maker's House, only on one of the lowest roofs, above the gate, but still terrifyingly high. Jezal recognised the crumbling University, the shining dome of the Lords Round, the squat mass of the House of Questions. He could see the Square of Marshals, a bowl of wooden seating in amongst the buildings, perhaps even the tiny yellow flash of the fencing circle in its centre. Beyond the citadel, surrounded by its white wall and twinkling moat, the city was a sprawling grey mass under the dirty grey sky, stretching all the way to the sea.

Jezal laughed with disbelief and delight. The Tower of Chains was a step ladder compared to this. He was so high above the world that all seemed somehow still, frozen in time. He felt like a king. No man had seen this, not for hundreds of years. He was huge, grand, far more important than the tiny people that must live and work in the little buildings down there. He turned to look at Glokta, but the cripple was not smiling. He was even paler than ever, frowning at the toy city, his left eye twitching with worry.

"Scared of heights?" laughed Jezal.

Glokta turned his ashen face toward him. "There were no steps. We climbed no steps to get here!" Jezal's grin began to fade. "No steps, do you understand? How could it be? How? Tell me that!"

Jezal swallowed as he thought over the way they had come. The cripple was right. No steps, no ramps, they had gone neither up nor down. Yet here they were, far above the tallest tower of the Agriont. He felt sick, again. The view now seemed dizzying, disgusting, obscene. He backed unsteadily away from the parapet. He wanted to go home.

"I followed him through the darkness, alone, and here I faced him. Kanedias. The Master Maker. Here we fought. Fire, and steel, and flesh. Here we stood. He threw Tolomei from the roof before my eyes. I saw it happen, but I could not stop him. His own daughter. Can you imagine? No one could have deserved that less than she. There never was a more innocent spirit." Logen frowned. He hardly knew what to say to this.

"Here we struggled," muttered Bayaz, his meaty fists clenched tight on the bare parapet. "I tore at him, with fire and steel, and flesh, and he at me. I cast him down. He fell burning, and broke upon the bridge below. And so the last of the sons of Euz passed from the world, so many of their secrets lost forever. They destroyed each other, all four of them. What a waste."

Bayaz turned to look at Logen. "But that was a long time ago, eh, my friend? Long ago." He puffed out his cheeks and hunched his shoulders. "Let us leave this place. It feels like a tomb. It is a tomb. Let us seal it up once more, and the memories with it. That is all in the past."

"Huh," said Logen. "My father used to say the seeds of the past bear fruit in the present."

"So they do." Bayaz reached out slowly, and his fingers brushed against the cold, dark metal of the box in Logen's hands. "So they do. Your father was a wise man."

Glokta's leg was burning, his twisted spine was a river of fire from his arse to his skull. His mouth was dry as sawdust, his face sweaty and twitching, the breath hissing in his nose, but he pressed on through the darkness, away from the vast hall with its black orb and its strange contraption, on towards the open door. *And into the light.*

He stood there with his head tipped back, on the narrow bridge before the narrow gateway, his hand trembling on the handle of his cane, blinking and rubbing his eyes, gasping in the free air and feeling the cool breeze on his face. *Who would have thought that wind could feel so fine? Maybe it's just as well there weren't any steps. I might never have made it out.*

Luthar was already halfway back across the bridge, hurrying as though he had a devil a stride behind. Ninefingers was not far away, breathing hard and muttering something in Northern over and over. "Still alive," Glokta thought it might be. His big hands were clenched tight around that square metal box, tendons standing out as though it weighed as much as an anvil. *There was more to this trip than just proving a point. What is it that they brought out from there? What weighs so heavily?* He glanced back into the darkness, and shivered. He was not sure he even wanted to know.

Bayaz strolled out of the tunnel and into the open air, looking smug as ever. "So, Inquisitor," he said breezily. "How did you find your trip into the House of the Maker?"

A twisted, strange and horrible nightmare. I might even have preferred to return to the Emperor's prisons for a few hours. "Something to do of a morning," he snapped.

"I'm so glad you found it diverting," chuckled Bayaz, as he pulled the rod of dark metal out from his shirt. "And tell me, do you still believe that I'm a liar? Or have your suspicions finally been laid to rest?"

Glokta frowned at the key. He frowned at the old man. He frowned into the crushing darkness of the Maker's House. *My suspicions grow with every passing moment. They are never laid to rest. They only change shape.* "Honestly? I don't know what to believe."

"Good. Knowing your own ignorance is the first step to enlightenment. Between you and me, though, I'd think of something else to tell the Arch Lector." Glokta felt his eyelid flickering. "You'd better start across, eh, Inquisitor? While I lock up?"

The plunge to the cold water below no longer seemed to hold much fear. *If I were to fall, at least I would die in the light.* Glokta looked back only once, as he heard the doors of the Maker's House shut with a soft click, the circles slide back into place. *All as it was before we arrived.* He turned his prickling back, sucked his gums against the familiar waves of nausea, and cursed and struggled his limping way across the bridge.

Luthar was hammering desperately on the old gates at the far end. "Let us in!" he was nearly sobbing as Glokta hobbled up, an edge of cracked panic to his voice. "Let us in!" The door finally wobbled open to reveal a shocked-looking Warden. *Such a shame. I was sure that Captain Luthar was about to burst into tears. The proud winner of the Contest, the Union's bravest young son, the very flower of manhood, blubbing on his knees. That sight could almost have made the trip worthwhile.* Luthar darted through the open gate and Ninefingers followed grimly after, cradling the metal box in his arms. The Warden squinted at Glokta as he limped up to the gate. "Back so soon?"

You old dolt. "What the hell are you talking about, so soon?"

"I'm only halfway through my eggs. You've been gone less than half an hour."

Glokta barked a joyless laugh. "Half a day, perhaps." But he frowned as he peered past into the courtyard. The shadows were almost exactly where they had been when they left. *Early morning still, but how?*

"The Maker once told me that time is all in the mind." Glokta winced as he turned his head. Bayaz had come up behind him, and was tapping the side of his bald skull with a thick finger. "It could be worse, believe me. It's when you come out before you went in that you really start to worry." He smiled, eyes glinting in the light through the doorway. *Playing the fool? Or trying to make a fool of me? Either way, these games grow tiresome.*

"Enough riddles," sneered Glokta. "Why not just tell me what you're after?"

The First of the Magi, if such he was, grinned still wider. "I like you, Inquisitor, I really do. I wouldn't be surprised if you were the only honest man left in this whole damn country. We should have a talk at some point, you and I. A talk about what I want, and about what you want." His smile vanished. "But not today."

And he stepped through the open door, leaving Glokta behind in the shadows.

NOBODY'S DOG

"**W**hy me?" West murmured to himself through gritted teeth, staring across the bridge towards the South Gate. That nonsense at the docks had taken him longer than expected, much longer, but then didn't everything these days? It sometimes felt as if he was the only man in the Union seriously preparing for a war, and had to organise the entire business on his own, right down to counting the nails that would hold the horses' shoes on. He was already late for his daily meeting with Marshal Burr, and knew there would be a hundred impossible things for him to get done today. There always were. To become involved in some pointless holdup here at the very gate of the Agriont was all he needed.

"Why the hell must it be me?" His head was starting to hurt again. That all too familiar pulsing behind the eyes. Each day it seemed to come on earlier, and end up worse.

Because of the heat over the last few days, the guards had been permitted to come to duty without full armour. West reckoned that at least two of them were now regretting it. One was folded up on the ground near the gate, hands clasped between his legs, whimpering noisily. His sergeant stood stooped over next to him, blood running from his nose and pattering dark red drops on the stones of the bridge. The two other soldiers in the detail had their spears lowered, blades pointing towards a scrawny dark-skinned youth. Another southerner stood nearby, an old man with long grey hair, leaning against the handrail and watching the scene with an expression of profound resignation.

The youth glanced quickly over his shoulder and West felt a sting of surprise. A woman: black hair hacked off short and sticking off her head in a mess of greasy spikes. One sleeve was torn off round her shoulder and a long, sinewy brown arm stuck out, ending in a fist bunched tight around the grip of a curved knife. The blade shone, mirror bright and evilly sharp, the one and only thing about her that looked clean. There was a thin, grey scar all the way down the right side of her face, through her black eyebrow and across her scowling lips. It was her eyes, though, which truly caught West off guard: slightly slanted, narrowed with the deepest hostility and suspicion, and yellow. He had seen all kinds of Kantics in his time, while he was fighting in Gurkhul, in the war, but he never saw eyes like that before. Deep, rich, golden yellow, like . . .

Piss. That was the smell, as he came closer. Piss, and dirt, and a lot of old, sour sweat. He remembered that from the war alright, the stink of men who had not washed in a very long time. West fought the compulsion to wrinkle up his nose and breathe through his mouth as he approached, and the urge to circle out wide and keep his distance from that glittering blade. You have to show no fear if you're to calm a dangerous situation, however much you might be feeling. In his experience, if you could seem to be in control, you were more than halfway to being there.

"What the hell is going on here?" he growled at the bloody-faced sergeant. He had no need at all to feign annoyance, he was getting later and angrier by the second.

"These stinking beggars wanted to come into the Agriont, sir! I tried to turn them away, of course, but they have letters!"

"Letters?"

The strange old man tapped West on the shoulder, handed over a folded sheet of paper, slightly grubby round the edges. He read it, his frown growing steadily deeper. "This is a letter of transit signed by Lord Hoff himself. They must be admitted."

"But not armed, sir! I said they couldn't go in armed!" The sergeant held up an odd looking bow of dark wood in one hand, and a curved sword of the Gurkish design in the other. "It was enough of a struggle getting her to give these up, but when I tried to search her . . . this Gurkish bitch . . ." The woman hissed and took a quick step forward, and the sergeant and his two guards shuffled nervously back in a tight group.

"Peace, Ferro," sighed the old man in the Kantic tongue. "For God's sake, peace." The woman spat on the stones of the bridge and hissed some curse that West could not understand, weaving the blade back and forth in a way that suggested she knew how to use it, and was more than willing.

"Why me?" West mumbled under his breath. It was plain he was going nowhere until this difficulty was resolved. As if he didn't have enough to worry about. He took a deep breath and did his best to put himself in the position of the stinking woman: a stranger, surrounded by strange-looking people speaking words she didn't understand, brandishing spears and trying to search her. Probably she was even now thinking about how horrible West smelled. Disorientated and afraid, most likely, rather than dangerous. She did look very dangerous though, and not in the least afraid.

The old man certainly seemed the more reasonable of the two, so West turned to him first. "Are you two from Gurkhul?" he asked him in broken Kantic.

The old man turned his tired eyes on West. "No. There is more to the South than the Gurkish."

"Kadir then? Taurish?"

"You know the South?"

"A little. I fought there, in the war."

The old man jerked his head at the woman, watching them suspiciously with her slanted yellow eyes. "She is from a place called Muntaz."

"I never heard of it."

"Why would you have?" The old man shrugged his bony shoulders. "A small country, by the sea, far to the east of Shaffa, beyond the mountains. The Gurkish conquered it years ago, and its people were scattered or made slaves. Apparently she has been in a foul mood ever since." The woman scowled over at them, keeping one eye on the soldiers.

"And you?"

"Oh, I come from much further south, beyond Kanta, beyond the desert, even beyond the Circle of the World. The land of my birth will not be on your maps, friend. Yulwei is my name." He held out a long, black hand.

"Collem West." The woman watched them warily as they shook hands.

"This one is called West, Ferro! He fought against the Gurkish! Will that make you trust him?" Yulwei didn't sound very hopeful, and indeed the woman's shoulders were still as hunched and bristling as ever, her grip on the knife no less tight. One of the soldiers chose that unfortunate moment to take a step forward, jabbing at the air with his spear, and the woman snarled and spat again, shouting more unintelligible curses.

"That's enough!" West heard himself roaring at the guard. "Put your fucking spears up!" They blinked at him, shocked, and he fought to bring his voice back under control. "I don't think this is a full-scale invasion, do you? Put them up!"

Reluctantly the spearpoints drifted away from the woman. West stepped firmly towards her, keeping his eyes fixed on hers with all the authority he could muster. Show no fear, he thought to himself, but his heart was thumping. He held out his open palm, almost close enough to touch her.

"The knife," said West sharply in his bad Kantic. "Please. You will not be harmed, you have my word."

The woman stared at him with those slanted, beady yellow eyes, then at the guards with the spears, then back to him. She took plenty of time over it. West stood there, mouth dry, head still thumping, getting later and later, sweating under his uniform in the hot sun, trying to ignore the woman's smell. Time passed.

"God's teeth, Ferro!" snapped the old man suddenly. "I am old! Take pity on me! I may only have a few years left! Give the man the knife, before I die!"

"Ssssss," she hissed, curling her lip. For a dizzy, stretched-out moment the knife went up, then the hilt slapped down into West's palm. He allowed himself a dry swallow of relief. Right up until the last moment he had been almost sure she would give him the sharp end.

"Thank you," he said, a deal more calmly than he felt. He handed the knife to the sergeant. "Stow the weapons away and escort our guests into the Agriont, and if any harm comes to anyone, especially her, I'll be holding you responsible, understand?" He glowered at the sergeant for a moment then stepped through the gate into the tunnel before anything else could go wrong, leaving the old man and the stinking woman behind him. His head was thumping harder even than before. Damn it he was late.

"Why the hell me?" he grumbled to himself.

"I am afraid the armouries are closed for the day," sneered Major Vallimir, staring down his nose at West as though at a beggar whining for small change. "Our quotas are fulfilled, ahead of schedule, and we will not be lighting the forges again this week. Perhaps if you had arrived on time . . ." The pounding in West's head was growing worse than ever. He forced himself to breathe slowly, and keep his voice calm and even. There was nothing to be gained by losing his temper. There was never anything to be gained by that.

"I understand, Major," said West patiently, "but there is a war on. Many of the levies we have received are scarcely armed, and Lord Marshal Burr has asked that the forges be lit, in order to provide equipment for them."

This was not entirely true, but since joining the Marshal's staff West had more or less given up on telling the whole truth to anyone. That was no way to get anything done. He now employed a mixture of wheedling, bluster, and outright lies, humble entreaties and veiled threats, and had become quite expert at judging which tactic would be most effective on what man.

Unfortunately, he had yet to strike the right chord with Major Vallimir, the Master of the King's Armouries. Somehow, their being equal in rank made matters all the more difficult: he could not quite get away with bullying the man, but could not quite bring himself to beg.

Furthermore, in terms of social standing they were anything but equals. Vallimir was old nobility, from a powerful family, and arrogant beyond belief. He made Jezal dan Luthar seem a humble, selfless type, and his total lack of experience in the field only made matters worse: he behaved doubly like an ass in order to compensate. Instructions from West, though they might come from Marshal Burr himself, were as welcome as they would have been from a reeking swineherd.

Today was no exception. "This month's quotas are fulfilled, *Major West*," Vallimir managed to put a sneering emphasis into the name, "and so the forges are closed. That is all."

"And this is what you would have me tell the Lord Marshal?"

"The arming of levies is the responsibility of those lords that provide them," he recited primly. "*I* cannot be blamed if *they* fall short on *their* obligations. It is simply not our problem, *Major West*, and you may tell *that* to the Lord Marshal."

This was always the way of it. Back and forth: from Burr's offices to the various commissary departments, to the commanders of companies, of battalions, of regiments, to the stores scattered around the Agriont and the city, to the armouries, the barracks, the stables, to the docks where the soldiers and their equipment would begin to embark in just a few short days, to other departments and back to where he began, with miles walked and nothing done. Each night he would drop into bed like a stone, only to start up a few hours later with it all to do again.

As commander of a battalion his trade had been to fight the enemy with steel. As a staff officer, it seemed, his role was to fight his own side with paper, more secretary than soldier. He felt like a man trying to push a huge stone up a hill. Straining and straining, getting nowhere, but unable to stop pushing in case the rock should fall and crush him. Meanwhile, arrogant bastards who were in just the same danger lazed on the slopes beside him saying, "Well, it's not my rock."

He understood now why, during the war in Gurkhul, there had sometimes not been enough food for the men to eat, or clothes for them to wear, or wagons to draw the supplies with, or horses to draw the wagons, or all manner of other things that were deeply necessary and easily anticipated.

West would be damned before that happened because of some oversight of his. And he would certainly be damned if he would see men die for want of a weapon to fight with. He tried yet again to calm himself, but each time his head hurt more, and his voice was cracking with the effort. "And what if we find ourselves mired in Angland with a crowd of half-clothed, unarmed peasants to provide for, what then, Major Vallimir? Whose problem will it be? Not yours, I dare say! You'll still be here, with your cold forges for company!"

West knew as soon as he said it that he had gone too far: the man positively bristled. "How dare you, sir! Are you questioning my personal honour? My family goes back nine generations in the King's Own!"

West rubbed his eyes, not knowing whether he wanted to laugh or cry.

"I have no doubts as to your courage, I assure you, that was not my meaning at all." He tried to put himself in Vallimir's position. He did not really know the pressures the man was under: probably he would rather be in command of soldiers than smiths, probably . . . it was no use. The man was a shit, and West hated him. "This is not a question of your honour, Major, or that of your family. This is a question of our being fit for war!"

Vallimir's eyes had turned deadly cold. "Just who do you think you're talking to, you dirty commoner? All the influence you have you owe to Burr, and who is he but an oaf from the provinces, risen to his rank by fortune alone?" West blinked. He guessed what they said about him behind his back of course, but it was another thing to hear it to his face. "And when Burr is gone, what will become of you? Eh? Where will you be without him to hide behind? You've no blood, no family!" Vallimir's lips twisted in a cold sneer. "Apart from that *sister* of yours of course, and from what I hear—"

West found himself moving forward, fast. "What?" he snarled. "What was that?" His expression must have been dire indeed: he saw the colour draining from Vallimir's face.

"I . . . I—"

"You think I need Burr to fight my battles, you fucking gutless worm?" Before he knew it he had moved again, and Vallimir stumbled back towards the wall, flinching sideways and raising one arm as if to ward off an expected blow. It was the most West could do to stop his hands from grabbing hold of the little bastard and shaking him until his head came off. His own skull was throbbing, pounding. He felt as though the pressure would pop his eyes right out of his head. He dragged in long, slow breaths through his nose, clenched his fists until they hurt. The anger slowly subsided, back below the point where it threatened to take sudden control of his body. It only pulsed now, squeezing at his chest.

"If you have something to say on the subject of my sister," he whispered softly, "then you can say it. Say it now." He let his left hand drop slowly to sit on the hilt of his sword. "And we can settle this outside the city walls."

Major Vallimir shrank back still further. "I heard nothing," he whispered, "nothing at all."

"Nothing at all." West looked down into his white face for a moment longer, then stepped away. "Now if you would be so good as to reopen the forges for me? We have a great deal of work to get through."

Vallimir blinked for a moment. "Of course. I will have them lit at once."

West turned on his heel and stalked off, knowing the man was glowering daggers at his back, knowing that he had made yet another bad situation worse. One more high-born enemy among the many. The really galling thing was that the man was right. Without Burr, he was as good as finished. He had no family apart from that *sister* of his. Damn it, his head hurt.

"Why me?" he hissed to himself. "Why?"

There was still a lot to do today, enough for a whole day's work on its own, but West could take no more. His head hurt so badly that he could hardly see. He had to lie down in the dark, with a wet cloth over his face, if only for an hour, if only for a minute. He fumbled in his pocket for his key, his other hand clamped over his aching eyes, his teeth locked together. Then he heard a sound on the other side of the door. A faint clink of glass. Ardee.

"No," he hissed to himself. Not now! Why the hell had he ever given her a key? Cursing softly, he raised his fist to knock. Knocking on his own door, that was where he was now. His fist never made it to the wood. A most unpleasant image began to form in the back of his mind. Ardee and Luthar, naked and sweaty, writhing around on his carpet. He turned his key swiftly in the lock and shoved the door open.

She was standing by the window, alone and, he was relieved to see, fully dressed. He was less pleased to see her filling a glass right to the brim from the decanter though. She raised an eyebrow at him as he burst through the door.

"Oh, it's you."

"Who the hell else would it be?" snapped West. "These are my rooms, aren't they?"

"Somebody's not in the best of moods this morning." A bit of wine slopped over the rim of her glass and onto the table. She wiped it up with her hand and sucked her fingers, then took a long swig from the glass for good measure. Her every movement niggled at him.

West grimaced and shoved the door shut. "Do you have to drink so much?"

"I understand that a young lady should have a beneficial pastime." Her words were careless, as usual, but even through his headache West could tell there was something strange going on. She kept glancing towards the desk, then she was moving towards it. He got there first, snatched up a piece of paper from the top, one line written on it.

"What's this?"

"Nothing! Give it me!"

He held her away with one arm and read it:

> *The usual place, tomorrow night*
>
> *—A.*

West's skin prickled with horror. "Nothing? Nothing?" He shook the letter under his sister's nose. Ardee turned away from him, flicking her head as you might at a fly, saying nothing, but slurping noisily from her glass. West ground his teeth.

"It's Luthar, isn't it?"

"I didn't say so."

"You didn't have to." The paper crumpled up into a tiny ball in his white-knuckled hand. He half turned towards the door, every muscle tensed and trembling. It was the most he could do to stop himself dashing out and throttling the little bastard right now, but he was just able to make himself think for a moment.

Jezal had let him down, and badly, that ungrateful shit. But it was hardly that shocking—the man was an ass. You keep your wine in a paper bag you shouldn't be too upset when it leaks. Besides, Jezal wasn't the one writing the letters. What good would stepping on his neck do? There would always be more empty-headed young men in the world.

"Just where are you going with this, Ardee?"

She sat down on the settle and glared at him frostily over the rim of her glass. "With what, brother?"

"You know with what!"

"Aren't we family? Can't we be candid with each other? If you have something to say you can out and say it! Where do you think I'm going?"

"I think you're going straight to shit, since you ask!" He squeezed his voice back down with the greatest of difficulty. "This business with Luthar has gone way too far. Letters? Letters? I warned him, but it seems he wasn't the problem! What are you thinking? Are you thinking at all? It has to stop, before people start to talk!" He felt a suffocating tightness in his chest, took a deep breath, but his voice burst out anyway. "They're damn well talking already! It stops now! Do you hear me?"

"I hear you," she said carelessly, "but who cares what they think?"

"I care!" He nearly screamed it. "Do you know how hard I have to work? Do you think I'm a fool? You know what you're about, Ardee!" Her face was turning sullen, but he forged on. "It's not as though this is the first time! Must I remind you, your luck with men has not exactly been the best!"

"Not with the men in my family, at least!" She was sitting bolt upright now, face tight and pale with anger. "And what would you know about my luck? We've hardly talked in ten years!"

"We're talking now!" shouted West, flinging the crumpled bit of paper across the room. "Have you thought how this might turn out? What if you were to get him? Have you considered that? Would his family be charmed by the blushing bride, do you think? At best they'd never speak to you. At worst they'd cut you both off!" He pointed a shaking finger at the door. "Haven't you noticed he's a vain, arrogant swine! They all are! How would he manage, do you think, without his allowance? Without his friends in high places? He wouldn't know where to begin! How could you be happy with each other?" His head was ready to split in half, but he ranted on. "And what happens if, as is far more likely, you can't get him? What then? You'd be finished, have you thought on that? You've come close enough before! And you're supposed to be the clever one! You're making a laughing-stock of yourself!" He almost choked on his rage. "Of both of us!"

Ardee gave a gasp. "Now we see it!" she nearly screamed at him. "No one cares a shit for me, but if *your* reputation is in danger—"

"You fucking stupid bitch!" The decanter flew spinning across the room. It crashed against the wall not far from Ardee's head, sending fragments of glass flying and wine running down the plaster. It made him more furious. "Why don't you fucking listen?"

He was across the room in an instant. Ardee looked surprised, just for a moment, then there was a sharp click—his fist catching her in the face as she got up. She didn't fall far. His hands caught her before she hit the ground, yanked her up then flung her back against the wall.

"You'll be the end of us!" Her head smacked against the plaster—once, twice, three times. One hand grabbed hold of her neck. Teeth bared. Body crushed her against the wall. A little snort in her throat as the fingers began to squeeze.

"You selfish, useless . . . fucking . . . whore!"

Hair was tangled across her face. He could only see a narrow slice of skin, the corner of a mouth, one dark eye.

The eye stared back at him. Painless. Fearless. Empty, flat, like a corpse. Squeeze. Snort. Squeeze.

Squeeze . . .

West came to his senses with a sickening jolt. The fingers snapped open, he jerked the hand away. His sister stayed upright against the wall. He could hear her breathing. Short gasps. Or was that him? His head was splitting. The eye was still staring at him.

He must have imagined it. Must have. Any second now he would wake up, the nightmare would be over. A dream. Then she pushed the hair out of her face.

Her skin was candle wax, pasty white. The trickle of blood from her nose looked almost black against it. The pink marks stood out vivid on her neck. The marks the fingers made. His fingers. Real, then.

West's stomach churned. His mouth opened but no sound came out. He looked at the blood on her lip, and he wanted to be sick. "Ardee . . ." He was so disgusted he half vomited as he said the word. He could taste the bile at the back of his mouth, but his voice wouldn't stop gurgling away. "I'm sorry . . . I'm so sorry . . . Are you alright?"

"I've had worse." She reached up slowly and touched her lip with a finger-tip. The blood smeared out across her mouth.

"Ardee . . ." One hand reached out to her, then he jerked it back, afraid of what it might do. "I'm sorry . . ."

"He was always sorry. Don't you remember? He'd hold us and cry afterwards. Always sorry. But it never stopped him the next time. Have you forgotten?"

West gagged, choked back vomit again. If she'd wept, and ranted, and beat him with her fists, it would have been easier to bear. Anything but this. He tried never to think about it, but he hadn't forgotten. "No," he whispered, "I remember."

"Did you think he stopped when you left? He got worse. Only then I'd hide on my own. I used to dream that you'd come back, come back and save me. But when you did come back it wasn't for long, and things weren't the same between us, and you did nothing."

"Ardee . . . I didn't know—"

"You knew, but you got away. It was easier to do nothing. To pretend. I understand, and do you know, I don't even blame you. It was some kind of comfort, back then, to know you got away. The day he died was the happiest of my life."

"He was our father—"

"Oh yes. My bad luck. Bad luck with men. I cried at the grave like a dutiful daughter. Cried and cried until the mourners feared for my reason. Then I lay in bed awake, until everyone was sleeping. I crept out of the house, I went back to the grave, I stood a while looking down . . . then I fucking pissed on it! I pulled up my shift, and I squatted down, and I pissed on him! And all the while I was thinking—I'll be nobody's dog anymore!"

She wiped the blood from her nose on the back of her hand. "You should have seen how happy I was when you sent for me! I read the letter over and over. The pathetic little dreams all came alive again. Hope, eh? What a fucking curse! Off to live with my brother. My protector. He'll look out for me, he'll help me. Now maybe *I* can have a life! But I find you different than I remembered. All grown up. First you ignore me, then you lecture me, then you hit me, and now you're sorry. Truly your father's son!"

He groaned. It was as if she was sticking a needle in him, right in his skull. Less than he deserved. She was right. He had failed her. Long before today. While he had been playing with swords and kissing the arses of people who despised him, she had been suffering. A little effort was all it would have taken, but he could never face it. Every minute he had spent with her he felt the guilt, like a rock in his gut, weighing him down, unbearable.

She stepped away from the wall. "Perhaps I'll go and pay a call on Jezal. He may be the shallowest idiot in the whole city, but I don't think he'd ever raise a hand to me, do you?" She pushed him out of the way and made for the door.

"Ardee!" he caught hold of her arm. "Please . . . Ardee . . . I'm sorry . . ."

She stuck her tongue out, curled it into a tube, and blew bloody spit through it. It splattered softly down the front of his uniform. "That's for your sorry, bastard."

The door banged shut in his face.

EACH MAN
WORSHIPS HIMSELF

Ferro stared at the big pink through narrowed eyes, and he stared back.
It had been going on for a good while now, not all the time, but most
of it. Staring. They were all ugly, these soft white things, but this one was
something special.

Hideous.

She knew that she was scarred, and weathered by sun and wind, worn
down by years in the wilderness, but the pale skin on this one's face looked
like a shield hard used in battle—chopped, gouged, torn, dented. It was surprising to see the eyes still alive in a face so battered, but they were, and they
were watching her.

She had decided he was dangerous.

Not just big, but strong. Brutal strong. Twice her weight maybe, and his
thick neck was all sinew. She could feel the strength coming off him. She
wouldn't have been surprised if he could lift her with one hand, but that
didn't worry her too much. He'd have to get a hold on her first. Big and
strong can make a man slow.

Slow and dangerous don't mix.

Scars didn't worry her either. They just meant he'd been in a lot of fights,
they didn't say whether he'd won. It was other things. The way he sat—still
but not quite relaxed. Ready. Patient. The way his eyes moved—cunning,
careful, from her to the rest of the room, then back to her. Dark eyes,
watching, thoughtful. Weighing her up. Thick veins on the backs of his
hands, but long fingers, clever fingers, lines of dirt under the nails. One finger
missing. A white stump. She didn't like any of it. Smelled like danger.

She wouldn't want to fight this one unarmed.

But she'd given her knife over to that pink on the bridge. She'd been on the very point of stabbing him, but at the last moment she'd changed her mind. Something in his eyes had reminded her of Aruf, before the Gurkish stuck his head on a spear. Sad and level, as if he understood her. As if she was a person, and not a thing. At the last moment, despite herself, she'd given the blade away. Allowed herself to be led in here.

Stupid!

She regretted it now, bitterly, but she'd fight any way she could, if she had to. Most people never realise how full the world is of weapons. Things to throw, or throw enemies on to. Things to break, or use as clubs. Wound-up cloths to strangle with. Dirt to fling in faces. Failing that, she'd bite his throat out. She curled her lips back and showed him her teeth to prove it, but he seemed not to notice. Just sat there, watching. Silent, still, ugly, and dangerous.

"Fucking pinks," she hissed to herself.

The thin one, by contrast, hardly seemed dangerous at all. Ill-looking, with long hair like a woman's. Awkward and twitchy, licking his lips. He would sneak the odd glance at her, but look away as soon as she scowled over at him, swallowing, the knobbly lump in his neck squirming up and down. He seemed scared, no threat, but Ferro kept him in the corner of her eye while she watched the big one. Best not to dismiss him entirely.

Life had taught her to expect surprises.

That just left the old man. She didn't trust a one of these pinks, but she trusted this bald one least of all. Many deep lines on his face, round his eyes, round his nose. Cruel lines. Hard, heavy bones in his cheeks. Big thick hands, white hairs on the backs of them. If she had to kill these three, for all the danger that the big one seemed to offer, she decided she would kill this bald one first. He had the look of a slaver in his eye, staring at her up and down, all over. A cold look, judging what she might be worth.

Bastard.

Bayaz, Yulwei called him, and the two old men seemed to know each other well. "So, brother," the bald pink was saying in the Kantic tongue, though it was plain enough they weren't related, "how is it in the great Empire of Gurkhul?"

Yulwei sighed. "Only a year since he seized the crown, and Uthman has broken the last of the rebels, and brought the governors firmly to heel. Already, the young Emperor is more feared than ever his father was. Uthman-ul-Dosht, his soldiers call him, and proudly. Almost all of Kanta is in his grip. He reigns supreme all round the Southern Sea."

"Aside from Dagoska."

"True, but his eyes are bent on it. His armies swarm toward the peninsula, and his agents are ever busy behind Dagoska's great walls. Now that there is war in the North, it cannot be long before he feels the time is ripe to lay siege to the city, and when he does, I do not think it can stand long against him."

"Are you sure? The Union still controls the seas."

Yulwei frowned. "We saw ships, brother. Many great ships. The Gurkish have built a fleet. A powerful one, in secret. They must have begun years ago, during the last war. I fear the Union will control the seas but little longer."

"A fleet? I had hoped to have a few more years in which to prepare." The bald pink sounded grim. "My plans only become the more urgent."

She was bored with their talk. She was used to being always on the move, keeping always one stride ahead, and she hated to stand still. Stay too long in one place, and the Gurkish would find you. She wasn't interested in being an exhibit for these curious pinks to stare at. She sauntered off around the room while the two old men made endless words, scowling and sucking her teeth. She swung her arms around. She kicked at the worn boards of the floor. She poked at the cloths on the walls, and peered behind them, ran her fingers along the edges of the furniture, clicked her tongue and snapped her teeth together.

Making everyone nervous.

She passed by the big ugly pink in the chair, almost close enough for her swinging hand to touch his pitted skin. Just to show him that she didn't care a shit for his size, or his scars, or anything else. Then she strutted over to the nervous one. The skinny pink with the long hair. He swallowed as she came close.

"Sssss," she hissed at him. He muttered something and shuffled away, and she stepped up to the open window in his place. Looking out, turning her back on the room.

Just to show the pinks she didn't care a shit for any of them.

There were gardens outside the window. Trees, plants, wide sweeps of lawn neatly arranged. Groups of fat, pale men and women lazed around in the sun on the carefully cut grass, stuffing their sweaty faces with food. Swilling down drink. She scowled down at them. Fat, ugly, lazy pinks, with no God but eating and idleness.

"Gardens," she sneered.

There had been gardens in Uthman's palace. She used to look at them from the tiny window of her room. Her cell. Long before he became Uthman-ul-Dosht. When he had only been the Emperor's youngest son. When she had been one among his many slaves. His prisoner. Ferro leaned forward and spat out of the window.

She hated gardens.

She hated cities altogether. Places of slavery, fear, degradation. Their walls were the walls of a prison. The sooner she was gone from this accursed place the happier she would be. Or the less unhappy, at least. She turned away from the window, and scowled again. They were all staring at her.

The one called Bayaz was the first to speak. "It certainly is quite a striking thing you've discovered, brother. You wouldn't miss her in a crowd, eh? Are you sure she's what I'm looking for?"

Yulwei looked at her for a minute. "As sure as I can be."

"I'm standing right here," she growled at them, but the bald pink went on talking as though she couldn't hear.

"Does she feel pain?"

"But little. She fought an Eater on the road."

"Really?" Bayaz chuckled softly to himself. "How badly did it hurt her?"

"Badly, but in two days she was walking, in a week she was healed. She shows not a scratch from it. That is not normal."

"We have both seen many things that are not normal in our times. We must be sure." The bald man reached into a pocket. Ferro watched suspiciously as he pulled out his fist, placed it on the table. When he took it away two smooth, polished stones lay on the wood.

The bald man leaned forward. "Tell me, Ferro, which is the blue stone?"

She stared at him, hard, then down at the stones. There was no difference between them. They were all watching her, closer than ever now, and she ground her teeth.

"That one." She pointed to the one on the left.

Bayaz smiled. "Exactly the answer I was hoping for." Ferro shrugged her shoulders. Lucky, she thought, to guess the right one. Then she noticed the look on the big pink's face. He was frowning at the two stones, as though he didn't understand.

"They both are red," said Bayaz. "You see no colours at all, eh, Ferro?"

So the bald pink had played a trick on her. She wasn't sure how he could have known, but she was sure she didn't like it. No one plays tricks on Ferro Maljinn. She started to laugh. A rough, ugly, unpractised gurgling.

Then she sprang across the table.

The look of surprise was just forming on the old pink's face as her fist crunched into his nose. He gave a grunt, chair tipping backwards, sprawling out onto the floor. She scrambled across the table to get at him, but Yulwei grabbed hold of her leg and dragged her back. Her clawing hands missed the bald bastard's neck and hauled the table over on its side instead, the two stones skittering away across the boards.

She shook her leg free and went for the old pink as he staggered up from the floor, but Yulwei caught her arm and pulled her back again, all the while yelling, "Peace!" He got her elbow in his face for his trouble, and sagged back against the wall with her on top of him. She was first up, ready to go at the bald bastard again.

By now the big one was on his feet though, and moving forward, still watching her. Ferro smiled at him, fists clenched at her sides. Now she would see how dangerous he really was.

He took another step.

Then Bayaz put an arm out to stop him. He had his other hand clasped to his nose, trying to staunch the flow of blood. He started to chuckle.

"Very good!" He coughed. "Very fierce, and damn quick too. Without a doubt, you're what we're after! I hope you will accept my apologies, Ferro."

"What?"

"For my awful manners." He wiped blood from his upper lip. "I deserved no less, but I had to be sure. I am sorry. Am I forgiven?" He looked somehow different now, though nothing had changed. Friendly, considerate, honest. Sorry. But it took more than that to win her trust. A lot more.

"We'll see," she hissed.

"That's all I ask. That, and that you give Yulwei and I a moment to discuss some . . . matters. Matters best discussed in private."

"It's alright, Ferro," said Yulwei, "they are friends." She was damn sure they weren't her friends, but she allowed him to shepherd her out of the door behind the two pinks. "Just try not to kill any of them."

This room was much like the other. They had to be rich, these pinks, for all they didn't look it. Great big fireplace, made of dark veined stone. Cushions and soft cloth round the window, covered in flowers and birds in tiny stitches. There was a painting of a stern man with a crown on his head, frowning down at Ferro from the wall. She frowned back at him. Luxury.

Ferro hated luxury even more than she hated gardens.

Luxury meant captivity more surely than the bars of a cage. Soft furniture spelled danger more surely than weapons. Hard ground and cold water was all she needed. Soft things make you soft, and she wanted no part of that.

There was another man waiting in there, walking round and round with his hands behind his back, as though he didn't like to stand still too long. Not quite a pink, his leathery skin was somewhere between hers and theirs in tone. Head shaved, like a priest. Ferro didn't like that.

She hated priests most of all.

His eyes lit up when he saw her though, for all her sneering at him, and he hurried over. A strange little man in travel-worn clothes, the top of his head came up no higher than Ferro's mouth. "I am Brother Longfoot," flapping his hands around all over the place, "of the great order of Navigators."

"Lucky for you." Ferro turned her shoulder towards him, straining her ears to hear what the two old men were saying beyond the door, but Longfoot was not deterred.

"It is lucky! Yes, yes, it most certainly is! God has truly blessed me! I declare that never, in all of history, has a man been so well-suited to his profession, or a profession to a man, as I, Brother Longfoot, am suited to the noble science of Navigation! From the snow-covered mountains of the far North, to the sun-drenched sands of the utmost South, the whole world is my home, truly!"

He smiled at her with a look of sickening self-satisfaction. Ferro ignored him. The two pinks, the big one and the scrawny one, were talking to each other on the far side of the room. They spoke in some language she didn't understand. Sounded like pigs grunting. Talking about her maybe, but she didn't care. They went out another door, leaving her alone with the priest, still flapping his lips.

"There are few nations within the Circle of the World to which I, Brother Longfoot, am a stranger, and yet I am at a loss as to your origins." He waited expectantly, but Ferro said nothing. "You would like me to guess, then? Indeed, it is a riddle. Let me see . . . your eyes have the shape of the people of distant Suljuk, where the black mountains rise sheer from the sparkling sea, indeed they do, and yet your skin is—"

"Stop your mouth, cunt."

The man paused in mid-sentence, coughed and moved away, leaving Ferro to attend to the voices on the other side of the door. She smiled to herself. The wood was thick and the sounds were muffled, but the two old men had not reckoned on the sharpness of her ears. They were still speaking in Kantic. Now that idiot of a Navigator was quiet she could make out every word that Yulwei was saying.

". . . Khalul breaks the Second Law, so you must break the First? I like it not, Bayaz! Juvens would never have allowed this!" Ferro frowned. Yulwei had a strange note in his voice. Fear. The Second Law. He had spoken of it to the Eaters, Ferro remembered. It is forbidden to eat the flesh of men.

She heard the bald pink next. "The First Law is a paradox. All magic comes from the Other Side, even ours. Whenever you change a thing you touch the world below, whenever you make a thing you borrow from the Other Side, and there is always a cost."

"But the cost of this might be too high! It is a cursed thing, this Seed, a damned thing. Nothing but chaos grows from it! The sons of Euz, so great in wisdom and power, this Seed was the end of them, of all of them, in different ways. Are you wiser than Juvens, Bayaz? Are you more cunning than Kanedias? Are you stronger than Glustrod?"

"None of those, brother, but tell me . . . how many Eaters has Khalul made?"

A long pause. "I cannot be sure."

"How many?"

Another pause. "Perhaps two hundred. Perhaps more. The priesthood scour the South for those with any promise. Faster and faster now he makes them, but most are young, and weak."

"Two hundred or more, and growing all the time. Many are weak, but among them are some that might be a match for you or I. Those that were Khalul's apprentices in the Old Time—the one they called the East Wind, and those cursed bloody twins."

"Damn those bitches!" Yulwei groaned.

"Not to mention Mamun, whose lies began this chaos."

"The trouble was well rooted before he was even born, you know it, Bayuz. Still Mamun was in the Badlands. I felt him near. He is grown terrible strong."

"You know that I am right. Meanwhile, our numbers hardly grow."

"I thought this one Quai showed promise?"

"We need only a hundred more like him and twenty years in which to train them. Then we might stand on equal terms. No, brother, no. We must use fire against fire."

"Even if the fire burns you and all creation to ashes? Let me go to Sarkant. Khalul might yet hear reason—"

Laughter. "He has enslaved half the world! When will you wake, Yulwei? When he has enslaved the rest of it? I cannot afford to lose you, brother!"

"Remember, Bayaz, there are worse things than Khalul. Far worse." His voice dropped to a whisper and Ferro strained to hear. "The Tellers of Secrets are always listening . . ."

"Enough, Yulwei! It is better not even to think of it!" Ferro frowned. What was this nonsense? Tellers of Secrets? What secrets?

"Remember what Juvens told you, Bayaz. Beware of pride. You have been using the Art. I know it. I see a shadow on you."

"Damn your shadows! I do what I must! Remember what Juvens told *you*, Yulwei. One cannot watch forever. Time is short, and I will watch no longer. I am first. It is my decision to make."

"Have I not always followed where you have led? Always, even when my conscience told me otherwise?"

"And have I ever led you wrong?"

"That remains to be seen. You are first, Bayaz, but you are not Juvens. It is my part to question, and that of Zacharus too. He will like this still less than I. Far less."

"It must be done."

"But others will pay the price, as they always have. This Northman, Ninefingers, he can speak to the spirits?"

"Yes." Ferro frowned. Spirits? The nine-fingered pink had scarcely looked as if he could speak to other humans.

"And if you find the Seed," came Yulwei's voice from behind the door, "you mean for Ferro to carry it?"

"She has the blood, and someone must."

"Be careful then, Bayaz. I know you, remember. Few better. Give me your word that you will keep her safe, even after she has served your purpose."

"I will guard her more closely than I would my own child."

"Guard her closer than you did the Maker's child, and I will be satisfied."

A long silence. Ferro worked her jaw as she thought on what she had heard. Juvens, Kanedias, Zacharus—the strange names meant nothing to her. And what kind of seed could burn all creation to ashes? She wanted no part of any such thing, she was sure of that. Her place was in the south, fighting the Gurkish with weapons that she understood.

The door opened, and the two old men stepped through. They could hardly have looked more different. One dark-skinned, tall and bony with long hair, the other white-skinned, heavy-built and bald. She looked at them suspiciously. It was the white one who spoke first.

"Ferro, I have an offer to—"

"I am not going with you, old pink fool."

The slightest shadow of annoyance flitted across the bald man's face, but was quickly mastered. "Why? What other business have you which is so very pressing?"

That needed no thinking about. "Vengeance." Her favourite word.

"Ah. I see. You hate the Gurkish?"

"Yes."

"They owe you a debt, for what they have done to you?"

"Yes."

"For taking your family, your people, your country?"

"Yes."

"For making you a slave," he whispered. She glowered back at him, wondering how he knew so much about her, wondering whether to go for him again. "They have robbed you, Ferro, robbed you of everything. They have stolen your life from you. If I were you . . . if I had suffered as you have suffered . . . there would not be enough blood in all the South to satisfy me. I would see every Gurkish soldier made a corpse before I was satisfied. I would see every Gurkish city burn before I was satisfied. I would see their Emperor rotting in a cage before his own palace before I was satisfied!"

"Yes!" she hissed, a fierce smile across her face. He was talking her language now. Yulwei had never talked so—perhaps this old pink wasn't so bad after all. "You understand! That is why I must go south!"

"No, Ferro." It was the bald man grinning now. "You do not realise the chance that I am offering you. The Emperor does not truly rule in Kanta. Mighty though he seems, he dances to the tune of another, a hand well hidden. Khalul, they call him."

"The Prophet."

Bayaz nodded. "If you are cut, do you hate the knife, or the one who wields it? The Emperor, the Gurkish, they are but Khalul's tools, Ferro. Emperors come and go, but the Prophet is always there, behind them. Whispering. Suggesting. Ordering. He is the one that owes you."

"Khalul . . . yes." The Eaters had used that name. Khalul. The Prophet. The Emperor's palace was filled with priests, everyone knew it. The palaces of the governors too. Priests, they were everywhere, swarming, like insects. In the cities, in the villages, in amongst the soldiers, always spreading their lies. Whispering. Suggesting. Ordering. Yulwei was frowning, unhappy, but Ferro knew that the old pink was right. "Yes, I see it!"

"Help me, and I will give you vengeance, Ferro. Real vengeance. Not one dead soldier, or ten, but thousands. Tens of thousands! Perhaps the Emperor himself, who knows?" He shrugged, and half turned away from her. "Still, I cannot force you. Go back to the Badlands, if you wish—hide, and run, and grub in the dust like a rat. If that satisfies you. If that is the full measure of your vengeance. The Eaters want you now. Khalul's children. Without us they will have you, and sooner rather than later. Still, the choice is yours."

Ferro frowned. All those years in the wilderness, fighting tooth and nail, always running, had got her nothing. No vengeance worthy of the word. If it had not been for Yulwei, she would be finished now. White bones in the desert. Meat in the bellies of the Eaters. In the cage before the Emperor's palace.

Rotting.

She could not say no, and she knew it, but she did not like it. This old man had known exactly what to offer her. She hated to have no choice.

"I will think about it," she said.

Again, the slightest shadow of anger on the bald pink's face, quickly covered. "Think about it then, but not for long. The Emperor's soldiers are massing, and time is short." He followed the others out of the room, leaving her alone with Yulwei.

"I do not like these pinks," she said, loud enough for the old one to hear her in the corridor, and then more softly. "Do we have to go with them?"

"You do. I must return to the South."

"What?"

"Someone must keep watch on the Gurkish."

"No!"

Yulwei began to laugh. "Twice you have tried to kill me. Once you have tried to run away from me, but now that I am leaving you want me to stay? There's no understanding you, Ferro."

She frowned. "This bald one says he can give me vengeance. Does he lie?"

"No."

"Then I must go with him."

"I know. That is why I brought you here."

She could think of nothing to say. She looked down at the floor, but Yulwei surprised her by stepping forward suddenly. She raised her hand, to ward off a blow, but instead he put his arms round her and squeezed her tightly. A strange feeling. Being so close to someone else. Warm. Then Yulwei stepped away, one hand on her shoulder. "Walk in God's footsteps, Ferro Maljinn."

"Huh. They have no God here."

"Say rather that they have many."

"Many?"

"Had you not noticed? Here, each man worships himself." She nodded. That seemed close to the truth. "Be careful, Ferro. And listen to Bayaz. He is the first of my order, and few indeed are wise as he."

"I do not trust him."

Yulwei leaned closer. "I did not tell you to trust him." Then he smiled, and turned his back. She watched him walk slowly to the door, then out into the corridor. She heard his bare feet flapping away on the tiles, the bangles on his arms jingling softly.

Leaving her alone with the luxury, and the gardens, and the pinks.

OLD FRIENDS

There was a thumping knock at the door, and Glokta jerked his head up, left eye suddenly twitching. *Who the hell comes knocking at this hour? Frost? Severard? Or someone else? Superior Goyle, maybe, come to pay me a visit with his circus freaks? Might the Arch Lector have grown tired of his toy cripple already? One could hardly say the feast went according to plan, and his Eminence is hardly the forgiving type. Body found floating by the docks . . .*

The knocking came again. Loud, confident knocking. *The kind that demands the door be opened, before it's broken down.* "I'm coming!" he shouted, voice cracking slightly as he prised himself out from behind his table, legs wobbly. "I'm just coming!" He snatched up his cane and limped to the front door, took a deep breath and fumbled with the latch.

It was not Frost, or Severard. Nor was it Goyle, or one of his freakish Practicals. It was someone much more unexpected. Glokta raised an eyebrow, then leaned against the door frame. "Major West, what a surprise."

Sometimes, when old friends meet, things are instantly as they were all those years before. The friendship resumes, untouched, as though there had been no interruption. *Sometimes, but not now.* "Inquisitor Glokta," mumbled West—hesitant, awkward, embarrassed. "I'm sorry to bother you so late."

"Don't mention it," said Glokta with icy formality.

The Major nearly winced. "May I come in?"

"Of course." Glokta shut the front door behind him, then limped after West into his dining room. The Major squeezed himself into one of the chairs and Glokta took another. They sat there facing each other for a moment, without speaking. *What the hell does he want, at this hour or any other?* Glokta scrutinised his old friend's face in the glow from the fire and the one, flickering candle. Now that he could see him more clearly, he realised West had changed. *He looks old.* His hair was thinning at the temples, going grey round his ears. His face was pale, pinched, slightly hollow. *He looks worried. Ground down. Close to the edge.* West looked round at the mean room, the mean fire, the mean furniture, cautiously up at Glokta, then quickly down at the floor. Nervous, as if he had something picking at his mind. *He looks ill at ease. As well he might.*

He did not seem ready to break the silence, so Glokta did it for him. "So, how long has it been, eh? Apart from that night in town, and we can hardly count that, can we?"

The memory of that unfortunate meeting hung between them for a moment like a fart, then West cleared his throat. "Nine years."

"Nine years. Imagine that. Since we stood on the ridge, old friends together, looking down towards the river. Down towards the bridge and all those Gurkish on the other side. Seems a lifetime ago, doesn't it? Nine years. I can remember you pleading with me not to go down there, but I was having none of it. What a fool I was, eh? Thought I was our only hope. Thought I was invincible."

"You saved us all that day, saved the whole army."

"Did I? How wonderful. I daresay if I'd died on that bridge there'd be statues of me all over the place. Shame I didn't, really. Shame for everyone."

West winced and shifted in his chair, looking ever more uncomfortable. "I looked for you, afterwards . . ." he mumbled.

You looked for me? How hugely fucking noble. What a true friend. Precious little good it did me, dragged off in agony with my leg hacked to mincemeat. And that was just the beginning. "You did not come to discuss old times, West."

"No . . . no, I didn't. I came about my sister."

Glokta paused. He had certainly not expected that answer. "Ardee?"

"Ardee, yes. I'm leaving for Angland soon and . . . I was hoping that, perhaps, you could keep an eye on her for me, while I'm away." West's eyes flickered up nervously. "You always had a way with women . . . Sand." Glokta grimaced at the sound of his first name. No one called him that anymore. *No one besides my mother.* "You always knew just what to say. Do you remember those three sisters? What were their names? You had them all eating out of your hand." West smiled, but Glokta couldn't.

He remembered, but the memories were weak now, colourless, faded. *The memories of another man. A dead man. My life began in Gurkhul, in the Emperor's prisons. The memories since then are much more real. Stretched out in bed like a corpse after I came back, in the darkness, waiting for friends who never came.* He looked at West, and he knew that his glance was terribly cold. *Do you think to win me with your honest face and your talk of old times? Like a long-lost dog, at last come faithfully home? I know better. You stink, West. You smell like betrayal. That memory at least is mine.*

Glokta leaned back slowly in his chair. "Sand dan Glokta," he murmured, as though recalling a name he once knew. "Whatever became of him, eh, West? You know, that friend of yours, that dashing young man, handsome, proud, fearless? Magic touch with the women? Loved and respected by all, destined for great things? Wherever did he go?"

West looked back, puzzled and unsure of himself, and said nothing.

Glokta lurched towards him, hands spread out on the table, lips curling back to show his ruined mouth. "Dead! He died on the bridge! And what remains? A fucking ruin with his name! A limping, skulking shadow! A crippled ghost, clinging to life the way the smell of piss clings to a beggar. He has no friends, this loathsome fucking remnant, and he wants none! Get you gone, West! Go back to Varuz, and to Luthar, and the rest of those empty bastards! There's no one here you know!" Glokta's lips trembled and spat with revulsion. He wasn't sure who disgusted him more—West, or himself.

The Major blinked, his jaw muscles working silently. He got shakily to his feet. "I'm sorry," he said, over his shoulder.

"Tell me!" shouted Glokta, bringing him up short of the door. "The rest of them, they stuck to me so long as I was useful, so long as I was going up. I always knew it. I wasn't so very surprised they wanted nothing to do with me when I came back. But you, West, I always thought you were a better friend than that, a better man. I always thought that you at least—you alone—would come to visit me." He shrugged. "I suppose I was wrong." Glokta turned away, frowning towards the fire, waiting for the sound of the front door closing.

"She didn't tell you?"

Glokta looked back. "Who?"

"Your mother."

He snorted. "My mother? Tell me what?"

"I did come. Twice. As soon as I learned that you were back, I came. Your mother turned me away at the gates of your estate. She said that you were too ill to take visitors, and that in any case you wanted nothing more to do with the army, and nothing more to do with me in particular. I came back again, a few months later. I thought I owed you that much. That time a servant came to see me off. Later I heard that you had joined the Inquisition, and left for Angland. I put you out of my mind . . . until we met . . . that night in the city . . ." West trailed off.

It took a while for his words to sink in, and by the time they had, Glokta realised that his mouth was hanging open. *So simple. No conspiracy. No web of betrayal.* He almost wanted to laugh at the stupidity of it. *My mother turned him away at the gate, and I never thought to doubt that no one came. She always hated West. A most unsuitable friend, far beneath her precious son. No doubt she blamed him for what happened to me. I should have guessed, but I was too busy wallowing in pain and bitterness. Too busy being tragic.* He swallowed. "You came?"

West shrugged. "For what it's worth."

Well. What can we do, except try to do better? Glokta blinked, and took a deep breath. "I'm, er . . . I'm sorry. Forget what I said, if you can. Please. Sit down. You were saying something about your sister."

"Yes. Yes. My sister." West fumbled his way back to his seat, looking down at the floor, his face taking on that worried, guilty look again. "We're leaving for Angland soon, and I don't know when I'll be back . . . or if, I suppose . . . she'll be without any friends in the city and, well . . . I think you met her once, when you came to our house."

"Of course, and a good deal more recently than that, in fact."

"You did?"

"Yes. With our mutual friend, Captain Luthar."

West turned even paler. *There is something more to this than he is telling me.* But Glokta did not feel like putting his club foot through his one friendship quite yet, not so soon after it had been reborn. He stayed quiet, and after a moment the Major went on.

"Life has been . . . difficult for her. I could have done something. I should have done something." He stared miserably down at the table and an ugly spasm ran across his face. *I know that one. One of my own favourites. Self-loathing.* "But I chose to let other things get in the way, and I did my best to forget all about it, and I pretended that everything was fine. She has suffered and I am to blame." He coughed, then swallowed awkwardly. His lip began to tremble and he covered his face with his hands. "My fault . . . if something were to happen to her . . ." His shoulders shook silently, and Glokta raised his eyebrows. He was used to men crying in his presence of course. *But I usually have at least to show them the instruments first.*

"Come on, Collem, this isn't like you." He reached slowly across the table, half pulled his hand back, and then patted his sobbing friend awkwardly on the shoulder. "You've made some mistakes, but haven't we all? They're in the past, and can't be changed. There's nothing to be done now except to do better, eh?" *What? Can it really be me talking? Inquisitor Glokta, comforter of the needy?* But West seemed reassured. He lifted his head, wiped his runny nose, stared up hopefully at Glokta with wet eyes.

"You're right, you're right, of course. I have to make amends. Have to! Will you help me, Sand? Will you look after her, while I'm gone?"

"I'll do whatever I can for her, Collem, you can depend on me. I was once proud to call you my friend and . . . I would be again." Strange, but Glokta could almost feel a tear in his own eye. *Me? Can it be? Inquisitor Glokta, trustworthy friend? Inquisitor Glokta, protector of vulnerable young women?* He almost laughed out loud at the idea, and yet here he was. He never would have thought that he needed one, but it felt good to have a friend again.

"Hollit," said Glokta.

"What?"

"Those three sisters, their name was Hollit." He chuckled to himself, the memory filtering through a little clearer than before. "They had a thing about fencing. Loved it. Something about the sweat, maybe."

"I think that was when I decided to take it up." West laughed, then screwed up his face as if he was trying to remember something. "What was our quartermaster's name? He had a thing for the youngest one, was out of his mind with jealousy. What the hell was that man's name? Fat man."

The name was not so very difficult for Glokta to recall. "Rews. Salem Rews."

"Rews, that's the one! I'd forgotten all about him. Rews! He could tell a story like no one else, that man. We'd sit up all night listening to him, all of us rolling with laughter! Whatever became of him?"

Glokta paused for a moment. "I think he left the army . . . to become a merchant of some sort." He waved his hand dismissively. "I heard he moved north."

BACK TO THE MUD

Carleon weren't at all how the Dogman remembered it, but then he tended to remember it burning. A memory like that stays with you. Roofs falling in, windows cracking, crowds of fighters everywhere, all drunk on pain and winning and, well, drink—looting, killing, setting fires, all the unpleasant rest of it. Women screaming, men shouting, stinking with smoke and fear. In short, a sack, with him and Logen at the heart of it.

Bethod had put the fires out and made it his. Moved in, then started building. He hadn't got far when he kicked Logen and the Dogman and the rest of them into exile, but they must have been building every day since. It was twice as big now as it used to be, even before it got burned, covering the whole hill and all the slope down to the river. Bigger than Uffrith. Bigger than any city the Dogman had seen. From where he was, up in the trees on the other side of the valley, you couldn't see the people, but there had to be an awful lot of them in there. Three new roads leading out from the gates. Two big new bridges. New buildings everywhere, and big ones where the small ones used to be. Lots of them. Built from stone, mostly, slate roofs, glass in some of the windows even.

"They been busy," said Threetrees.

"New walls," said Grim.

"Lots of 'em," muttered the Dogman. There were walls all over. There was a big one round the outside, with proper towers and everything, and a big ditch beyond it. There was an even bigger one round the top of the hill where Skarling's Hall used to stand. Huge great thing. Dogman could hardly work out where they got all the stone for the building of it. "Biggest damn wall I ever saw," he said.

Threetrees shook his head. "I don't like it. If Forley gets took, we won't never get him out."

"If Forley gets took there'll be five of us, chief, and we'll be looked for. He's no threat to no one, but we are. Getting him out'll be the least of our worries. He'll muddle through, like always. Most likely he'll outlive the lot of us."

"Wouldn't surprise me," muttered Threetrees. "We're in a dangerous line of work."

They slithered back through the brush, back to the camp. Black Dow was there, looking even worse-tempered than usual. Tul Duru too, working at a hole in his coat with a needle, face all screwed up as his great thick fingers fumbled with the little splinter of metal. Forley was sat near him, looking up at the sky through the leaves.

"How you feeling Forley?" asked the Dogman.

"Bad, but you got to have fear to have courage."

Dogman grinned at him. "So I heard. Reckon we're both heroes then, eh?"

"Must be," he said, grinning back.

Threetrees was all business. "You sure about this, Forley? Sure you want to go in there? Once you get in, there might be no getting out, no matter how good a talker y'are."

"I'm sure. I may be shittin' myself, but I'm going. I can do more good there than I can out here. Someone's got to warn 'em about the Shanka. You know it, chief. Who else is there?"

The old boy nodded to himself, slow as the sun rising. Taking his moment, as always. "Aye. Alright. Tell 'em I'm waiting here, by the old bridge. Tell 'em I'm alone. Just in case Bethod decides you're not welcome, you understand?"

"I get it. You're on your own, Threetrees. It was just the two of us made it back over the mountains."

They'd all gathered now, and Forley smiled round at 'em. "Well then, lads, it's been something ain't it?"

"Shut up, Weakest," scowled Dow. "Bethod ain't got nothing against you. You're coming back."

"In case I don't, though. It's been something." The Dogman nodded to him, awkward. It was the same dirty, scarred-up faces as usual, but grimmer than ever. None of 'em liked letting one of their own put himself in danger, but Forley was right, someone had to do it, and he was the best suited. Sometimes weakness is a better shield than strength, the Dogman reckoned. Bethod was an evil bastard, but he was a clever one. The Shanka were coming, and he needed the warning. Hopefully, he'd be grateful for it.

They walked together, down to the edge of the trees, looking out towards the path. It crossed over the old bridge and wound down into the valley. From there to the gates of Carleon. Into Bethod's fortress.

Forley took a deep breath, and the Dogman clapped him on his shoulder. "Luck, Forley. Good luck."

"And to you." He squeezed Dogman's hand in his for a minute. "To all of you lads, eh?" and he turned and marched off towards the bridge, with his head up high.

"Luck, Forley!" shouted Black Dow, startling them all.

He turned round for a minute, the Weakest, stood on top of the bridge, and he grinned. Then he was gone.

Threetrees took a deep breath. "Weapons," he said, "just in case Bethod don't want to hear sense. And wait for the signal, eh?"

It seemed a long time waiting, up in the leaves, staying quiet and still, looking down at all them new walls. The Dogman lay on his belly, bow near at hand, watching, waiting, wondering how Forley was doing in there. A long, tense time. Then he saw them. Horsemen coming out the nearest gate, riding over one of the new bridges, crossing the river. They'd got a cart at the back. Dogman wasn't sure why they'd have a cart, but he didn't like it any. No sign of Forley, and he wasn't sure whether that was a good thing or a bad.

They came quick, spurring up the side of the valley, up the steep path towards the trees and the stream and the old stone bridge across it. Right at the Dogman. He could hear the hooves thumping on the dirt. Close enough to count now, and take a good look at. Spears, shields and good armour. Helmets and mail. Ten of 'em, and two others sitting on the cart, either side of the driver, carrying some sorts of things that looked like little bows on blocks of wood. He didn't know what they were about, and he didn't like not knowing. He was the one wanted to be giving them the surprises.

He wriggled back through the brush on his stomach, sloshed through the stream and hurried to the edge of the trees, where he could get a good view of the old bridge. Threetrees, Tul and Dow were standing round the near side of it, and he waved over to them. Couldn't see Grim, he must've been off in the woods away beyond. He made the sign for horsemen, held up his fist to say ten, hand flat on his chest to say armour.

Dow took up his sword and axe, ran up into a bunch of broken rocks, high up beside the bridge, keeping low and quiet. Tul slid down the bank into the stream, luckily no more than knee-deep right then, plastered his big self against the far side of the arch with his great long sword held up above the water. Made the Dogman a bit nervous, he could see Tul so clear from where he was sitting. Still, the riders wouldn't see him at all if they came straight up the path. They'd only be expecting one man alone, and Dogman hoped they wouldn't come too careful. He hoped, 'cause if they took the time to check it'd be a fucking disaster.

He watched Threetrees strap his shield on his arm, draw his sword, stretch his neck out, then he just stood, waiting, big and solid, blocking the path on the near side of the bridge, seeming all alone in the world.

The Dogman could hear the hoof-beats loud now, and the clattering of the cart's wheels out beyond the trees. He pulled out a few arrows and planted them in the earth, point down, where he could get to 'em quick. Doing his best to swallow his fear. His fingers were shaking all the while, but that didn't matter. They'd work alright when they needed to.

"Wait for the signal," he whispered to himself. "Wait for the signal."

He knocked a shaft to his bow and half-drew the string, taking aim down towards the bridge. Damn it but he needed to piss bad.

The first spear-point showed itself over the crest of the hill, then others. Bobbing helmets, mailed chests, horses' faces, bit by bit the riders came up towards the bridge. The cart rolled behind, with its driver and its two funny passengers, pulled by a big shaggy carthorse.

The rider up front saw Threetrees now, waiting for him, over the hump of the bridge, and he spurred on forward. The Dogman breathed a little easier as the others trotted after him in a clump, all eagerness. Forley must've said as he was told—they were expecting only one. Dogman could see Tul peering up from underneath the mossy arch as the horses clopped above him. By the dead, his hands were shaking. He was worried he'd let the arrow fly half-drawn and ruin the whole thing.

The cart stopped on the far bank, the two men on it stood up and pointed their strange bows at Threetrees. The Dogman got himself a nice aim on one of 'em, and drew the string back all the way. Most of the riders were on the bridge by now, horses shying and stirring about, unhappy at being packed in so tight. The one at the front reined up in front of Threetrees, spear pointing at him. The old boy didn't back away a step, though. Not him. He just frowned up, not giving the riders any room to get around him, keeping 'em choked up on the bridge.

"Well, well," the Dogman heard their leader saying. "Rudd Threetrees. We thought you was long dead, old man." He knew the voice. One of Bethod's Carls, from way back. Bad-Enough they called him.

"Reckon I've got a fight or two left in me," said Threetrees, still giving no ground.

Bad-Enough took a look about him, squinting into the trees, sense enough to see he was in a poor position, but not too careful. "Where's the rest of you? Where's that fucker Dow, eh?"

Threetrees shrugged. "There's just me."

"Back to the mud, eh?" The Dogman could just see Bad-Enough grinning under his helmet. "Shame. Hoped I'd be the one to kill that dirty bastard."

Dogman winced, half expecting Dow to come flying out of those rocks right then, but there was no sign of him. Not yet. Waiting for the signal, for once.

"Where's Bethod?" asked Threetrees.

"The King don't come out for the likes of you! Anyhow, he's off in Angland, kicking the Union's arses. Prince Calder's taking care of things while he's gone."

Threetrees snorted. "Prince is it, now? I remember him sucking on his mother's tit. He could scarcely do that right."

"A lot's changed, old man. All kind of things."

By the dead, Dogman was wishing they'd get on with it, one way or another. He could hardly keep the piss in. "Wait for the signal," he was mouthing to himself, just to try and keep his hands steady.

"The Flatheads are everywhere," Threetrees was saying. "They'll be coming south by next summer, sooner maybe. Something needs doing."

"Well, why don't you come with us, eh? You can warn Calder yourself. We brought a cart, for you to ride in. Man of your age shouldn't have to walk." A couple of the other riders laughed at that, but Threetrees didn't join 'em.

"Where's Forley?" he growled. "Where's the Weakest?"

There was more sniggering from the horsemen. "Oh, he's nearby," said Bad-Enough, "he's real close. Why don't you get in the cart, and we'll take you right to him. Then we can all sit round and talk about Flatheads, nice and peaceful."

The Dogman didn't like this. Not at all. He'd got a nasty feeling. "You must take me for some new kind o' fool," said Threetrees. "I'm going nowhere 'til I've seen Forley."

Bad-Enough frowned at that. "You're in no state to be telling us what you'll do. You might have been the big man once, but you're come to less than nothing, and that's a fact. Now give up your blade and get in the fucking cart like I told you, before I lose my temper."

He tried to nudge his horse forward again but Threetrees wasn't budging. "Where's Forley?" he growled. "And I'll have a straight answer or I'll have your guts."

Bad-Enough grinned over his shoulder at his mates, and they grinned back. "Alright, old man, since you're asking. Calder wanted us to wait for this, but I've got to see the look on your face. The Weakest's in the cart. Leastways, most of him is." He smiled and let something drop from his saddle. A canvas sack, with something in it. Dogman could guess already what it was. It hit the ground near Threetrees' feet. The something rolled out, and the Dogman could see on the old boy's face that he'd guessed right. Forley's head.

Well that was it, o' course. Fuck the signal. Dogman's first arrow stuck one of the men on the cart right through his chest, and he screamed and tumbled over into the back, dragging the driver with him. It was a good shot, but there was no time to think on that, he was far too busy fumbling for another arrow, and shouting. Didn't even know what he was shouting, just that he was. Grim must've been shooting as well, one of the Carls on the bridge gave a yell, fell off his horse and splashed into the stream.

Threetrees was down in a crouch, hiding behind his shield, backing off while Bad-Enough prodded at him with his spear, kicking his horse off the bridge and onto the path on our side. The rider behind pushed around the side of him, keen to get off the bridge, coming close beside the rocks.

"Fucking bastards!" Dow flew out of the stones above him, barrelled into the rider. They tumbled down together, a mess of limbs and weapons, but the Dogman could see that Dow was on top. His axe went up and down a couple of times, quick. One less to worry on.

Dogman's second arrow went well wide of the mark, he was so busy shouting his head off, but it stuck one of the horses in the rump, and that turned out better than anything. It started rearing and thrashing about, and soon all the horses were milling and crying while their riders cursed and bumbled around, spears going every which way, noise and mess on all sides.

The horseman at the back split in half, all of a sudden, blood spraying everywhere. The Thunderhead had come up from the stream, got round behind them. There's no armour that could stop a blow like that. The giant roared and swung the great length of bloody metal over his head again. The next in line got his shield up in time, but he might as well not have bothered. The blade hacked a big chunk out of it, tore his head open and hammered him out of the saddle. The blow was that strong it clubbed the horse down too.

One of them had got his mount turned now, bringing up his spear to stab at Tul from the side. Before he could he grunted and jerked, arching his back. Dogman could see the feathers sticking from his side. Grim must've shot him, and he tumbled down. His foot caught in the stirrup and he hung there, swinging. He was groaning and moaning and trying to right himself, but his horse was plunging now along with the others, making him dance, wrong way up, smacking his head against the side of the bridge. He dropped his spear in the stream, tried to pull himself up, then his horse half landed a kick on his shoulder and knocked him free. He went down under the milling hooves and the Dogman paid him no more mind.

The second archer was still sitting up on the cart. He was getting over his shock now, and lining up his funny bow on Threetrees, still squatting down behind his shield. Dogman shot at him but he was hurrying, and yelling, and his shaft missed and hit the driver beside him in his shoulder, just got up from the back of the cart, knocked him back down again.

The weird bow twanged and Threetrees jerked back from his shield. The Dogman was worried for a minute, then he saw that the arrow split the heavy wood and punched on through, but stopped just short of catching Threetrees in the face. It was lodged there through his shield, feathers sticking out one side, point out the other. That's an evil little bow, Dogman thought.

He heard Tul roar and saw another rider fly off into the stream. Another dropped with one of Grim's arrows in his back. Dow turned and chopped the back legs out from under Bad-Enough's horse with his sword, and it stumbled and slid, pitching him off onto the ground. The last couple were trapped. Dow and Threetrees at one end of the bridge, Tul at the other, too tight with frightened, riderless horses for them to turn around or nothing, at the mercy of Grim out in the woods. He wasn't in a merciful mood, it seemed, and it didn't take him long to pick 'em off.

The one with the bow tried to make a break for it, chucking his bit of wood away and jumping down from the cart. Dogman thought nice and careful about his aiming this time, and his shaft got the archer right between the shoulders and knocked him on his face before he could get more than a few paces. He had a go at crawling, but he wasn't crawling far. The driver of the cart showed his face again, groaning and grabbing at the arrow in his shoulder. The Dogman didn't usually kill men that were down, but he reckoned today was an exception. His arrow got the driver through the mouth, and that was him dealt with.

Dogman could see one of the riders limping away, one of Grim's arrows in his leg, and lined him up with his last shaft. Threetrees got there first though, and stuck him through the back with his sword. There was another one still moving, struggling up to his knees, and the Dogman took an aim on him. Before he could loose, Dow stepped up and hacked his head off. Blood everywhere. Horses still milling, screaming, slipping on the slick stones of the bridge.

Dogman could see Bad-Enough now, the last one going. He must've lost his helmet when he fell off his horse. He was struggling in the stream on his hands and knees, slowed up by all that weight of mail. He'd dropped his shield, and his spear, to make better time running for it, but he hadn't realised he was coming right at the Dogman.

"Get him alive!" shouted Threetrees. Tul set off down one bank, but he was making slow progress, slipping and sliding in the mud the cart churned up. "Get him alive!" Dow was after him too, splashing and cursing in the water. Bad-Enough was close now. The Dogman could hear his scared gasping as he struggled down the stream.

"Aah!" he howled as Dogman's arrow thudded into his leg, just below the bottom of his mail coat. He toppled sideways onto the bank, blood leaking into the muddy water. He started dragging himself up the wet turf beside the stream.

"That's it, Dogman," shouted Threetrees. "Alive!"

The Dogman slid out the trees and down the bank, through the water. He pulled his knife out. Tul and Dow were still a little ways off, hurrying towards him. Bad-Enough rolled over in the mud, his face screwed up with the pain of the arrow in his leg. He held his hands up. "Alright, alright, I'll gurrr—"

"You'll what?" asked the Dogman, looking down at him.

"Gurrr—" he said again, looking mightily surprised, hand gripped to his neck. There was blood pouring out between his fingers, down the front of his wet mail.

Dow splashed up beside them and stood there, looking down. "Well that's the end of that," he said.

"What you do that for?" shouted Threetrees, hurrying over.

"Eh?" asked the Dogman. Then he looked down at his knife. It was all bloody. "Ah." That's when he saw it was him as had cut Bad-Enough's throat.

"We could have asked him questions!" said Threetrees. "He could have took a message back to Calder, told him who did this, and why!"

"Wake up, chief," muttered Tul Duru, already wiping his sword down. "No one cares a shit for the old ways no more. Besides, they'll be after us soon enough. No point letting 'em know more than we have to."

Dow clapped the Dogman on the shoulder. "You were right to do it. This bastard's head'll do for a message." Dogman wasn't sure Dow's approval was something he was after, but it was a bit late now. It took Dow a couple of chops to get Bad-Enough's head off. He carried it, swinging by its hair, with as little care or worry as he'd carry a bag of turnips. He grabbed a spear out of the stream on his way, found a spot he liked.

"Things ain't the way they used to be," Threetrees was muttering as he strode off down the bank towards the bridge, where Grim was already picking over the bodies.

The Dogman followed him, watching Dow stick Bad-Enough's head on the spear, shoving the blunt end into the ground, stepping back, hands on hips, to admire his work. He shifted it a bit to the right, then back to the left, until he'd got it nice and straight. He grinned over at the Dogman.

"Perfect," he said.

"What now, chief?" Tul was asking. "What now?"

Threetrees was stooping down on the bank, washing his bloody hands in the river.

"What do we do?" asked Dow.

The old boy stood up slowly, wiped his hands on his coat, taking his time thinking on it. "South. We bury Forley on the way. We take these horses here, since they'll be coming after us now, and we head south. Tul, you better unhitch that carthorse, he's the only one as'll carry you."

"South?" asked the Thunderhead, looking confused, "south to where?"

"Angland."

"Angland?" asked the Dogman, and he could tell they were all thinking it. "For what? Ain't they fighting down there?"

"Course they are, that's why I've a mind to go."

Dow frowned. "Us? What have we got against the Union?"

"No, fool," said Threetrees, "I've a mind to fight along with 'em."

"With the Union?" asked Tul, his lip curling up, "with those bloody women? That ain't our fight, chief!"

"Any fight against Bethod is my fight now. I mean to see the end of him." Once he'd thought on it, the Dogman had never yet seen Threetrees change his mind. Never once. "Who's with me?" he asked.

They all were. Course.

It was raining. Thin rain, making the whole world damp. Soft as a maiden's kiss, as they say, though the Dogman could hardly remember what one of those felt like. Rain. Seemed right somehow, for the occasion. Dow was done with piling the dirt, and he sniffed and dug the spade down into the earth beside the grave. It was a long way from the road. A good long way. They didn't want no one finding it and digging Forley up. They all gathered round, just five now, looking down. It was a long time since they'd had anyone to bury among them. The Shanka got Logen o' course, not too long ago, but they never had found the body. There might have been just one less in the band, but it seemed to the Dogman like there was a lot missing.

Threetrees frowned, taking a moment, thinking out what to say. It was just as well he was the chief, and had to find the words, 'cause Dogman didn't reckon he could have found a thing. After a minute Threetrees started speaking, slow as the light fading at sunset.

"This was a weak man, here. The Weakest, that's a fact. That was his name, and ain't that a joke? To call a man the Weakest. The worst fighter they could find, to surrender to Ninefingers. Weak fighter, no doubt, but strong heart, say I."

"Aye," said Grim.

"Strong heart," said Tul Duru.

"The strongest," mumbled the Dogman. He had a bit of a lump in the throat, being honest.

Threetrees nodded to himself. "It takes some bones to meet your death as well as he did. To walk to it, with no complaint. To ask for it. And not for his own sake, but for others, that he didn't even know." Threetrees clenched his teeth and took his moment, looking down at the earth. They all did. "That's all I've got to say. Back to the mud with you, Forley. We're the poorer, and the ground's the richer for it."

Dow knelt down, and set his hand on the fresh-turned soil. "Back to the mud," he said. The Dogman thought for a minute there might be a tear dripping off his nose, but it had to be only the rain. This was Black Dow, after all. He got up and walked away with his head down and the others followed him, one by one, off toward the horses.

"Fare you well, Forley," said the Dogman. "No more fear."

He reckoned now that he was the coward of the band.

MISERY

Jezal frowned. Ardee was taking her time. She never took her time. She was always there when he arrived, at whatever spot had been arranged. He didn't like having to wait for her one bit. He always had to wait for her letters, and that rankled as it was. Standing here like an idiot, it made him feel even more of a slave than he did already.

He frowned up at the grey skies. There were a few spots of rain falling, just to match his mood. He felt one from time to time, a tiny pin-prick on his face. He could see the drops making circles in the grey surface of the lake, making pale streaks against the green of the trees, the grey of the buildings. The dark shape of the House of the Maker was rendered hazy by them. He frowned at that building with particular displeasure.

He hardly knew what to make of it now. The whole thing had been like some feverish nightmare and, like a nightmare, he had decided simply to ignore it, and pretend it never happened. He might have succeeded too, except that the bloody thing was always looming on the edge of his vision, whenever he stepped out of the door, reminding him the world was full of mysteries he did not understand, seething just below the surface.

"Damn it," he muttered, "and damn that lunatic, Bayaz, as well."

He frowned across the damp lawns. The rain was keeping people away from the park, and it was emptier than he had seen it in a long time. A couple of sad-looking men sat listlessly on benches, nursing their own personal tragedies, and there were passersby on the paths, hurrying from somewhere to wherever. One was coming towards him now, wrapped up in a long cloak.

Jezal's frown vanished. It was her, he could tell. She had her hood pulled right down over her face. He knew it was a cold day, but this seemed a touch dramatic. He had never thought she was the type to be put off by a few spots of rain. Still, he was glad to see her. Ridiculously glad. He smiled and hastened forward. Then, when they were a couple of paces apart, she pushed the hood back.

Jezal gasped with horror. There was a great purple bruise across her cheek, around her eye, the corner of her mouth! He stood there frozen for a moment, wishing, stupidly, that he was hurt instead of her. The pain would have been less. He realised he'd clamped one hand over his mouth, eyes bulging like a nervous little girl at a spider in the bath, but he couldn't stop himself.

Ardee only scowled. "What? Did you never see a bruise before?"

"Well, yes, but . . . are you alright?"

"Of course I am." She stepped around him and started walking off down the path. He had to hurry to catch her up. "It's nothing. I fell is all. I'm a clumsy fool. Always have been. All my life." She said it with some bitterness, it seemed to him.

"Is there anything I can do?"

"What could you do? Kiss it better?" If they'd been alone he wouldn't have minded trying, but her frown showed him what she thought of that idea. It was strange: the bruises should have repelled him, but they didn't. Not at all. Rather, he had an almost overpowering urge to take her in his arms, to stroke her hair, to murmur soothing words. Pathetic. Probably she would slap him if he tried. Probably he would deserve it. She didn't need his help. Besides, he couldn't touch her. There were people around, damn them, eyes everywhere. You never knew who might be watching. The thought made him more than a little nervous.

"Ardee . . . aren't we taking a risk? I mean, what if your brother were to—"

She snorted. "Forget about him. He won't do anything. I've told him to keep his nose out of my business." Jezal had to smile. He imagined that must have been quite an amusing scene. "Besides, I hear that you're all leaving for Angland on the next tide, and I could hardly let you go without saying goodbye, now could I?"

"I wouldn't have done that!" he said, horrified again. It hurt just hearing her say the word goodbye. "I mean, well, I'd have let them sail without me before I would've done that!"

"Huh."

They walked along in silence for a moment, skirting the lake, both with their eyes on the gravel. It was hardly the bittersweet farewell that he had pictured so far. Just bitter. They passed among the trunks of some willow trees, their branches trailing in the water below. It was a secluded spot, screened from prying eyes. Jezal reckoned he was unlikely to find one better for what he had to say. He glanced sideways at her, and took a deep breath.

"Ardee, er, I don't know how long we'll be away. I mean, I suppose it could be months . . ." He chewed at his top lip. It was not coming out at all as he had hoped. He had practised this speech twenty times at least, staring in his mirror until he got just the right expression: serious, confident, slightly wheedling. Now, though, the words came out in a foolish rush. "I hope that, I mean, perhaps, I hope that you'll wait for me?"

"I daresay I'll still be here. I've nothing else to do. But don't worry, you'll have a lot to think about in Angland—war, honour, glory and all that. You'll soon forget about me."

"No!" he shouted, catching hold of her arm. "No I won't!" He pulled his hand away quickly, worried someone might see. At least she was looking at him now, somewhat surprised, maybe, at how fierce his denial had been—though not half as surprised as he was.

Jezal blinked down at her. A pretty girl certainly, but too dark, too tanned, too clever by half, simply dressed with no jewels, and with a great ugly bruise across her face. She would hardly have excited much comment in the officer's mess. How was it that she seemed to him the most beautiful woman in the world? The Princess Terez was an unwashed dog beside her. The clever words leaked out of his mind and he spoke without thinking, looking her straight in the eye. Maybe this was what honesty felt like.

"Look, Ardee, I know you think I'm an ass and, well, I daresay I am, but I don't plan always to be one. I don't know why you even look at me, and I don't know much about this sort of thing but, well . . . I think about you all the time. I hardly think about anything else any more." He took another deep breath. "I think . . ." He glanced around again, just to check that no one was watching. "I think I love you!"

She spluttered with laughter. "You really are an ass," she said. Despair. He was utterly crushed. He couldn't breathe for disappointment. His face screwed up, his head drooped and he stared down at the ground. There were tears in his eyes. Actual tears. Pitiful. "But I'll wait." Joy. It swelled in his chest and burst out in a little girlish sob. He was helpless. It was ridiculous the power she had over him. The difference between misery and happiness was the right word from her. She laughed again. "Look at you, you fool."

She reached up and touched his face, rubbed a tear from his cheek with her thumb. "I'll wait," she said, and she smiled at him. That crooked smile.

The people had faded, the park, the city, the world. Jezal stared down at Ardee, for how long he could not have said, trying to stamp every detail of her face into his mind. He had a feeling, for some reason, that the memory of that smile might have to get him through a lot.

The docks were heaving with activity, even for the docks. The wharves boiled with people, the air shook and rattled with their din. Soldiers and supplies poured endlessly up the slippery gangways and onto the ships. Crates were hauled, barrels were rolled, hundreds of horses were dragged and pushed and kicked aboard, eyes bulging, mouths frothing. Men grunted and groaned, heaved at wet ropes, strained at wet beams, sweating and shouting in the spitting rain, slipping around on the slick decks, running here and there in epic confusion.

Everywhere people embraced, kissed, waved to each other. Wives saying goodbye to husbands, mothers to sons, children to fathers, all equally bedraggled. Some put a brave face on it, some wept and wailed. Others did not care: spectators come simply to witness the madness.

It all meant nothing to Jezal, leaning on the weathered rail of the ship that would carry him to Angland. He was sunk in a terrible gloom, nose running, hair plastered to his scalp with wet. Ardee was not there, and yet she was everywhere. He would hear her voice above the din, calling his name. He would glimpse her out of the corner of his eye, looking at him, and his breath would catch in his throat. He would smile, half raise his hand to wave, then he would see it was not her. Some other dark-haired woman, smiling at some other soldier. His shoulders would slump again. Each time the disappointment was sharper.

He realised now that he had made a terrible mistake. Why the hell had he asked her to wait for him? Wait for what? He could not marry her, that was a fact. Impossible. But the thought of her even looking at another man made him feel sick. He was wretched.

Love. He hated to admit it, but it had to be. He had always regarded the whole notion with contempt. A stupid word. A word for bad poets to harp on, and foolish women to chatter about. A thing found in childish stories and with no relevance to the real world, where relationships between men and women were simple matters of fucking and money. Yet here he was, mired in a horrible bog of fear and guilt, lust and confusion, loss and pain. Love. What a curse.

"I'd like to see Ardee," murmured Kaspa, wistfully.

Jezal turned to stare at him. "What? What did you say?"

"It's quite a sight to see," said the Lieutenant, holding his hands up, "that's all." Everyone was a little careful around him since that card game, as if he might blow up at any moment.

Jezal turned sullenly back to the crowds. There was some kind of a commotion down below them. A single horseman was forcing his way through the chaos, spurring a well-lathered horse with frequent shouts of "Move!" Even in the rain, the wings on the rider's helmet glittered. A Knight Herald.

"Bad news for someone," murmured Kaspa.

Jezal nodded. "Looks like us." He was indeed making directly for their ship, leaving a trail of bemused and angry soldiers and workmen behind him. He swung out of the saddle and strode purposefully up the gangplank towards them, face grim, bright polished armour covered with moisture and jingling with every step.

"Captain Luthar?" he asked.

"Yes," said Jezal, "I'll fetch the Colonel."

"No need. My message is for you."

"It is?"

"High Justice Marovia requires your presence at his offices. Immediately. It would be best if you took my mount."

Jezal frowned. He did not like the taste of this at all. There was no reason that he could see for a Knight Herald to be bringing messages to him, except that he had been inside the House of the Maker. He wanted nothing more to do with that. He wanted it in the past, forgotten, along with Bayaz, and his Northman, and that disgusting cripple.

"The High Justice is waiting, Captain."

"Yes, of course." It seemed there was nothing to be done.

"Ah, Captain Luthar! An honour to see you again!" Jezal was hardly surprised to run into the madman Sulfur, even here outside the offices of the High Justice. He no longer even seemed a madman, just another part of a world gone entirely mad. "An absolute honour!" he frothed.

"Likewise," said Jezal numbly.

"I'm so lucky I caught you, what with both of us leaving so soon! My master has all manner of errands for me." He gave a deep sigh. "Never the slightest peace, eh?"

"No, I know what you mean."

"Still, an honour indeed to see you, and victorious at the Contest! I saw the whole thing, you know, it was a privilege to bear witness." He smiled broadly, different coloured eyes glittering. "And to think, you were set on giving it up. Hah! But you stuck at it, just as I said you would! Yes you did, and now you reap the rewards! The edge of the World," he whispered softly, as though to say the words out loud was to invite disaster. "The edge of the World. Can you imagine? I envy you, indeed I do!"

Jezal blinked. "What?"

"What! Hah! 'What,' he says! You are dauntless, sir! Dauntless!" And Sulfur strode off across the wet Square of Marshals, chuckling to himself. Jezal was so bemused that he had not even the presence of mind to call him a damn idiot once he was out of earshot.

One of Marovia's many clerks ushered him through an empty, echoing hallway towards a pair of enormous doors. He stopped before them, knocked. At an answering cry he turned the handle and pulled one of the doors back, standing aside politely for Jezal to pass through.

"You may go in," he said quietly, after they had stood there for a while.

"Yes, yes, of course."

The cavernous chamber beyond was eerily silent. Furniture was strangely sparse in that huge, panelled space, and what there was seemed oversized, as though for the use of people much bigger than Jezal. It gave him the distinct feeling that he was arriving at his own trial.

High Justice Marovia sat behind an enormous table, its surface polished to mirror brightness, smiling at Jezal with a kindly, if slightly pitying expression. Marshal Varuz was seated to his left, staring down guiltily at his own blurry reflection. Jezal had not thought he could feel more depressed, but on seeing the third member of the group he realised he had been wrong. Bayaz, wearing a self-satisfied smirk. He felt a mild surge of panic as the door shut behind him: the clicking of the latch felt like the clank of the heavy bolt on a prison cell.

Bayaz started up from his chair and came round the table. "Captain Luthar, I am so glad you could join us." The old man took Jezal's damp hand in both of his and squeezed it firmly, leading him forward into the room. "Thank you for coming. Thank you indeed."

"Er, of course." As if he had been given a choice.

"Well now, you're probably wondering what this is all about. Allow me to explain." He stepped back and perched on the edge of the table, like a kindly uncle holding forth to a child. "I and a few brave companions—chosen people, you understand, people of quality—are engaging on a great journey! An epic voyage! A grand adventure! I have little doubt that, should we be successful, there will be stories told of this for years to come. Very many years." Bayaz's forehead crinkled as he raised his white eyebrows. "Well? What do you think?"

"Er . . ." Jezal glanced nervously over at Marovia and Varuz, but they were giving no clues as to what was going on. "If I may?"

"Of course, Jezal—I may call you Jezal, may I?"

"Yes, er, well, yes, I suppose. Er, the thing is . . . I was wondering what all this has to do with me?"

Bayaz smiled. "We are short a man."

There was a long, heavy silence. A drop of water trickled down Jezal's scalp, dripped from his hair, ran down his nose and pattered against the tiles beneath his feet. Horror crept slowly through his body, from his gut to the very tips of his fingers. "Me?" he croaked.

"The road will be a long and difficult one, most likely beset with dangers. We have enemies out there, you and I. More enemies than you would believe. Who could be more useful than a proven swordsman, such as yourself? The winner of the Contest, no less!"

Jezal swallowed. "I appreciate the offer, really I do, but I am afraid I must decline. My place is with the army, you understand." He took a hesitant step back towards the door. "I must go north. My ship will soon be sailing and—"

"I am afraid it has sailed already, Captain," said Marovia, his warm voice stopping Jezal dead in his tracks. "You need not concern yourself with that any longer. You will not be going to Angland."

"But, your Worship, my company—"

"Will find another commander," smiled the High Justice: understanding, sympathetic, but horribly firm. "I appreciate your feelings, indeed I do, but we consider this more urgent. It is important that the Union be represented in this matter."

"Terribly important," murmured Varuz, half-heartedly. Jezal blinked at the three old men. There was no escape. So this was his reward for winning the Contest? Some crackpot voyage to who-knew-where in the company of a demented old man and a pack of savages? How he wished now that he had never started fencing! That he had never even seen a steel in his life! But wishing was useless. There was no way back.

"I need to serve my country—" mumbled Jezal.

Bayaz laughed. "There are other ways to serve your country, my boy, than being one corpse in a pile, up there in the frozen North. We leave tomorrow."

"Tomorrow? But my things are—"

"Don't worry, Captain," and the old man slipped off the table and clapped him enthusiastically on the shoulder, "everything is arranged. Your boxes were brought off the ship before it left. You have this evening to pick out some things for our journey, but we must travel light. Weapons, of course, and stout clothes for travelling. Make sure you pack a good pair of boots, eh? No uniforms, I'm afraid, they might attract the wrong kind of attention where we're going."

"No, of course," said Jezal miserably. "Might I ask . . . where are we going?"

"The edge of the World, my boy, the edge of the World!" Bayaz's eyes twinkled. "And back, of course . . . I hope."

THE BLOODY-NINE

Say one thing for Logen Ninefingers, say that he's happy. They were leaving, at last. Beyond some vague talk about the Old Empire, and the edge of the World, he had no idea where they were going and he didn't care. Anywhere but this cursed place would do for him, and the sooner the better.

The latest member of the group didn't seem to share his good spirits. Luthar, the proud young man from the gate. The one who'd won the sword-game, thanks to Bayaz's cheating. He'd barely said two words together since he arrived. Just stood there, face rigid and chalky pale, staring out of the window, bolt upright like he had a spear all the way up his arse.

Logen ambled over to him. If you're going to travel with a man, and maybe fight alongside him, it's best to talk, and laugh if you can. That way you can get an understanding, and then a trust. Trust is what binds a band together, and out there in the wilds that can make the difference between living or dying. Building that kind of trust takes time, and effort. Logen reckoned it was best to get started early, and today he had good humour to spare, so he stood next to Luthar and looked out at the park, trying to dream up some common ground in which to plant the seeds of an unlikely friendship.

"Beautiful, your home." He didn't think it was, but he was short on ideas.

Luthar turned from the window, looked Logen haughtily up and down. "What would you know about it?"

"I reckon one man's thoughts are worth about as much as another's."

"Huh," sneered the young man coldly. "Then I suppose that's where we differ." He turned back to the view.

Logen took a deep breath. The trust might be a while coming. He abandoned Luthar and tried Quai instead, but the apprentice was scarcely more promising: slumped in a chair, frowning at nothing.

Logen sat down next to him. "Aren't you looking forward to going home?"

"Home," mumbled the apprentice listlessly.

"That's right, the Old Empire . . . or wherever."

"You don't know what it's like there."

"You could tell me," said Logen, hoping to hear something about the peaceful valleys, cities, rivers and whatnot.

"Bloody. It's bloody there, and lawless, and life is cheap as dirt."

Bloody and lawless. That all had an unpleasantly familiar smack to it. "Isn't there an Emperor, or something?"

"There are many, always making war on one another, forging alliances that last a week, or a day, or an hour, before they scramble to be first to stab each other in the back. When one Emperor falls another rises, and another, and another, and meanwhile the hopeless and the dispossessed scavenge and loot and kill on the fringes. The cities dwindle, the great works of the past fall into ruin, the crops go unharvested and the people go hungry. Bloodshed and betrayal, hundreds of years of it. The feuds have become so deep, so complicated, that few can tell any longer who hates who, and no one can say why. There's no need for reasons any more."

Logen made one last effort. "You never know. Things might have got better."

"Why?" muttered the apprentice. "Why?"

Logen was fumbling for a reply when one of the doors swung briskly open. Bayaz frowned around the room. "Where's Maljinn?"

Quai swallowed. "She left."

"I can see she left! I thought I told you to keep her here!"

"You didn't tell me how," muttered the apprentice.

His master ignored him. "What the hell has become of that bloody woman? We must be away by noon! Three days I've known her, and she already has me at the end of my rope!" He clenched his teeth and took a deep breath. "Find her, will you Logen? Find her and bring her back."

"What if she doesn't want to come back?"

"I don't know, pick her up and carry her! You can kick her all the way back here as far as I'm concerned!"

Easy to say, but Logen didn't fancy trying it. Still, if it had to be done before they could leave, it was best done now. He sighed, got up from his chair and made for the door.

Logen pressed himself into the shadows by the wall, watching.

"Shit," he whispered to himself. It would have to be now, just as they were about to leave. Ferro was twenty strides away, standing up tall with a deeper than usual scowl on her dark face. There were three men gathered round her. Masked men, all in black. Their sticks were down by their legs, behind their backs, kept half out of sight, but Logen had no doubt about what they had in mind. He could hear one of them talking, hissing through his mask, something about coming quietly. He winced. Coming quietly didn't sound like Ferro's style.

He wondered whether he should slip away and tell the others. He couldn't really say he liked the woman much, not near enough to get his head broken for her. But if he left them to it, three against one, the chances were they'd have knocked her to pieces by the time he got back, however tough she was, and dragged her off to who knew where. He might never get out of this damn city then.

He started judging the distance, thinking about how best to go at them, weighing his chances, but he'd been too long doing nothing, and his mind moved slowly. He was still working on it when Ferro suddenly jumped on one of them, yelling at the top of her voice, knocking him on his back. She gave him a couple of vicious-looking punches in the face before the others caught hold of her and dragged her up.

"Shit," hissed Logen. The three of them wrestled, lurching around in the lane, knocking against the walls, grunting and swearing, kicking and punching, a tangle of flailing limbs. It seemed that time had run out for a clever approach. Logen gritted his teeth and charged towards them.

The one on the floor had rolled to his feet, shaking the fuzz out of his head while the other two struggled to get a good grip on Ferro. Now he lifted his stick high, arching back, ready to smash her on the skull. Logen let go a roar. The masked face snapped round, surprised-looking.

"Huh?" Then Logen's shoulder crunched into his ribs, lifting him off his feet and sending him sprawling. Out of the corner of his eye he saw someone swing a stick at him, but he'd got them off guard and there was no real force behind it. He caught it across his arm then pressed in under it and smashed the man right in the mask with his fists, a full-blooded punch with each hand. He reeled back, arms flopping, already falling. Logen grabbed him by two fistfuls of his black coat, hauled him into the air and flung him upsidedown into the wall.

He bounced off with a gurgle and crumpled on the cobbles. Logen spun round, fists clenched, but the last one was lying on his face with Ferro on top of him, one knee jammed into his back, pulling his head up by the hair and smashing his face into the road, shouting meaningless curses all the while.

"What did you fucking do?" he shouted, grabbing her under the elbow and dragging her off.

She tore free of his grip and stood there panting, fists bunched up by her sides, blood leaking out of her nose. "Nothing," she snarled.

Logen took a cautious step back. "Nothing? What's this then?"

She bit off each word in her ugly accent and spat them at him. "I . . . don't . . . know." She wiped her bloody mouth with one hand, then froze. Logen glanced over his shoulder. Three more masked men, running at them down the narrow lane.

"Shit."

"Move, pink!" Ferro turned and started running and Logen followed her. What else could he do? He ran. The horrible, breathless running of the hunted, shoulders prickling for a blow in the back, sucking in air in gasps, the slapping footfalls of the men behind echoing around him.

High white buildings flashed past on either side, windows, doors, statues, gardens. People too, shouting as they dived out of the way or flattened themselves against the walls. He had no idea where they were, no idea where they were going. A man stepped out of a doorway right in front of him, a big sheaf of papers in his arms. They crashed together, tumbled to the ground, rolling over and over in the gutter with papers flapping down all around them.

He tried to get up but his legs were burning. He couldn't see! There was a piece of paper across his face. He tore it away, felt someone grab him under the arm and haul him along. "Up, pink! Move!" Ferro. She wasn't even out of breath. Logen's lungs were bursting as he struggled to keep up with her but she pulled steadily away, head down, feet flying.

She charged through an archway just ahead and Logen laboured after her, boots skidding as he turned the corner. A great shadowy space, timbers reaching up high above, like a strange forest of square beams. Where the hell were they? There was bright light just ahead, open air. He plunged out into it, blinking. Ferro was just beyond him, turning round slowly, breathing hard. They were in the middle of a circle of grass, a little circle.

He knew where they were now. The arena where he'd sat among the crowds, watching the sword game. The empty benches stretched away all round. There were carpenters crawling amongst them, sawing and hammering. They'd already taken some of the benches to pieces near the back and the supports stuck up high into the air alone like giant rib bones. He put his hands on his wobbly knees and bent over, gasping for air, blowing spit out onto the ground.

"What . . . now?"

"This way." Logen straightened up with an effort and wobbled after her, but she was already on her way back. "Not that way!"

Logen saw them. Black masked figures, again. The one at the front was a woman, tall with a shock of red hair sprouting off her head. She padded towards the circle silently on the balls of her feet, waved her arm behind her, pointing the other two out to the sides, trying to get on the flanks, surround him. Logen cast about, looking for a weapon, but there was nothing—just the empty benches and the high white walls beyond. Ferro was backing towards him, not ten feet away, and beyond her there were two more masks, creeping out around the enclosures with sticks in their hands. Five. Five altogether.

"Shit," he said.

"What the hell is keeping them?" growled Bayaz, pacing the floor. Jezal had never seen the old man annoyed before, and for some reason it made him nervous. Whenever he came close, Jezal wanted to back away. "I'm having a bath, damn it. Could be months before my next one. Months!" Bayaz stalked out of the room and slammed the bathroom door behind him, leaving Jezal alone with the apprentice.

They were probably close enough in age, but they had nothing else in common, so far as Jezal could see, and he stared with unconcealed contempt. A sickly, weaselly, puny, bookish sort. Sulking like that, moping around, it was pathetic. Rude, too. Damn rude. Jezal fumed silently. Just who did he think he was, the arrogant pup? What the hell did he have to be so upset about? It wasn't him who'd had his life stolen out from under him.

Still, if he had to be left alone with one of them, he supposed it could have been worse. It might have been the moron Northman with his fumbling, thick-tongued small talk. Or that Gurkish witch, staring and staring with her devil-yellow eyes. He shuddered to think of it. People of quality, Bayaz had said. He would have laughed had he not been on the verge of tears.

Jezal cast himself down on the cushions in a high-backed chair, but he found scant comfort there. His friends were on their way to Angland now, and he missed them already. West, Kaspa, Jalenhorm. Even that bastard Brint. On their way to honour, on their way to fame. The campaign would be long finished by the time he returned from whatever pit the old madman was leading him to, if he returned at all. Who knew when the next war would be, the next chance at glory?

How he wished he was going to fight the Northmen. How he wished he was with Ardee. It seemed like an age since he was happy. His life was awful. Awful. He lay back listlessly in his chair, wondering if things could possibly be any worse.

"Gurgh," growled Logen as a stick cracked into his arm, then another into his shoulder, one in his side. He stumbled back, half on his knees, fending them away as best as he could. He could hear Ferro screaming somewhere behind him, fury or pain he couldn't say, he was too busy taking a battering.

Something smacked across his skull, hard enough to send him reeling away towards the seats. He fell on his face and the front bench hit him in the chest, driving the air from his lungs. There was blood running down his scalp, on his hands, in his mouth. His eyes were watering from a blow to the nose, his knuckles were all skinned and bloody, near as ripped as his clothes were. He lay there, for a moment, gathering whatever strength was left. There was a thick length of timber lying on the ground behind the bench. He grabbed hold of the end of it. It was loose. He dragged it towards him. It felt good in his hand. Heavy.

He sucked in air, summoning one more effort. He moved his arms and legs a little, testing them. Nothing broken—except his nose maybe, but it was hardly the first time. He heard footsteps coming up behind. Slow footsteps, taking their time.

He pushed himself up, slowly, trying to look as though he was in a daze. Then he let go a roar and spun round, swinging the timber over his head. It broke in half across the masked man's shoulder with a mighty crack, half of it flying up off the turf and clattering away. The man gave a muffled wail and sank down, eyes screwed shut, one hand clutching at his neck, the other hanging useless, stick dropping from his fingers. Logen hefted the short piece of wood left in his hands and clubbed him across the face with it. It snapped his head back and drove him into the turf, mask half torn off, blood bubbling out from underneath.

Logen's head exploded with light and he tottered and sagged down on to his knees. Someone had hit him in the back of the head. Hit him hard. He swayed there for a moment trying to stop himself falling on his face, then things came suddenly back into focus. The red-haired woman was standing over him, raising her stick high.

Logen shoved himself up, flailed into her, fumbled with her arm, half pulling at her, half leaning on her, ears ringing, the world swinging madly. They staggered around, tugging on the stick like two drunkards wrestling over a bottle, back and forth in the circle of grass. He felt her punching him in the side with her other hand. Hard punches, right in the ribs.

"Aargh," he growled, but his head was clearing now, and she was half his weight. He twisted the arm with the stick around behind her back. She punched him again, a knock on the side of his face that brought the stars back for an instant, but then he got hold of her other wrist and pinned that arm as well. He bent her backwards over his knee.

She kicked and twisted, eyes screwed up to furious slits, but Logen had her fast. He freed his right hand from the tangle of limbs, brought his fist up high and mashed it into her stomach. She gave a breathy wheeze and went limp, eyes bulging. He flung her away and she crawled a foot or two, pulled her mask down and started coughing puke onto the grass.

Logen stumbled and swayed, shook his head, spitting blood and dirt out onto the grass. Aside from the retching woman, there were four black, crumpled shapes stretched out in the circle. One of them was grunting softly as Ferro kicked him over and over. She had blood all over her face, but she was smiling.

"I am still alive," Logen muttered to himself, "I am still . . ." There were more of them coming through the archway. He swung around, almost falling over. More, four more, from the other side. They were trapped.

"Move, pink!" Ferro dashed past him and sprang up onto the first bench, then the second, then the third, springing between them with great strides. Madness. Where was she going to go from there? Red Hair had stopped puking, she was crawling towards her fallen stick. The others were closing in fast, more of them than ever. Ferro was already a quarter of the way back and showing no signs of slowing, bounding from one bench to the next, making the planks rattle.

"Shit." Logen set off after her. After a dozen benches his legs were burning again. He gave up trying to spring between them and started scrambling however he could. As he flopped over the backs of the benches he could see the masked men behind—following, watching, pointing and calling, spreading out through the seats.

He was slowing now. Each bench was a mountain. The nearest mask was only a few rows behind. He scrambled on, higher and higher, bloody hands clutching at the wood, bloody knees scraping across the benches, skull echoing with his own breath, skin prickling with sweat and fear. Air loomed suddenly empty before him. He stopped, gasping, arms waving, teetering on the edge of a dizzying drop.

He was close to the high roofs of the buildings behind, but most of the seating near the back had already been taken down, leaving the supports exposed—single looming pillars, narrow beams between them, and a lot of high, empty space. He watched Ferro spring from one soaring upright to another, then run across a wobbling plank, heedless of the plunging space below. She jumped off onto a flat roof at the far end, high above him. It seemed a very long way away.

"Shit." Logen teetered out across the nearest beam, arms stretched out wide for balance, feet moving in an old man's shuffle. His heart was banging like a smith's hammer on an anvil, his knees were weak and wobbling from the climb. He tried to ignore the scrambling and shouting of the men behind him and look only at the knotted surface of the beam, but he couldn't look down without seeing the spider's web of timbers below him, and the tiny flagstones of the square below them. Far below.

He lurched onto a stretch of walkway still intact, clattered up it to the far end. He hauled himself up onto a timber above his head, locked his legs around it and dragged himself along on his arse whispering "I am still alive," to himself, over and over. The nearest mask had made it to the walkway, was running along it towards him.

The beam ended at the top of one of the upright struts. A square of wood a foot or two across. Then there was nothing. Two strides of empty air. Then another square at the top of another dizzying mast, then the plank to the flat roof. Ferro stared at him from the parapet.

"Jump!" she screamed. "Jump, you pink bastard!"

He jumped. He felt the wind around him. His left foot landed on the square of wood, but there was no stopping. His right foot hit the plank. His ankle twisted, his knee buckled. The dizzy world pitched. His left foot came down, half on the wood, half off. The plank rattled. He was in the empty air, limbs flailing. It seemed like a long time.

"Ooof!" The parapet crashed into his chest. His arms clawed with it but there was no breath left in him. He began to slide back, ever so slowly, inch by terrible inch. First he could see the roof, then he could see his hands, then he could see nothing but the stones in front of his face. "Help," he whispered, but no help came.

It was a long way down, he knew that. A long, long way, and there was no water to fall into this time. Only hard, flat, fatal stone. He heard a rattling. The mask coming across the plank behind him. He heard someone shouting, but none of it mattered much now. He slipped backwards a little further, hands scrabbling at the crumbling mortar. "Help," he croaked, but there was no one to help him. Only the masks and Ferro, and none of them seemed like the helping kind.

He heard a clunk and a despairing shriek. Ferro kicking the plank, and the mask falling. The scream fell away, it felt like for a long time, then it was cut off in a distant thud. The mask's body smashing to pulp against the ground, far below, and Logen knew he was about to join him. You have to be realistic about these things. There would be no washing up on a river bank this time. His fingertips were slipping, slowly, the mortar was starting to come apart. The fighting, the running, the climb, they had all sucked the strength out of him, and now there was nothing left. He wondered what sound he would make as he plunged through the air. "Help," he mouthed.

And strong fingers closed around his wrist. Dark, dirty fingers. He heard growling, felt his arm being pulled, hard. He groaned. The edge of the parapet came back into view. He saw Ferro now, teeth gritted, eyes squeezed almost shut with effort, veins standing out from her neck, scar livid against her dark face. He clutched at the parapet with his other hand, his chest came up beyond it, he managed to force his knee over.

She hauled him the rest of the way, and he rolled and flopped on his back on the other side, gasping like a landed fish, staring up at the white sky. "I am still alive," he muttered to himself after a moment, hardly able to believe it. It wouldn't have been too much of a surprise if Ferro had trodden on his hands and helped him fall.

Her face appeared above him, yellow eyes staring down, teeth bared in a snarl. "You stupid, heavy pink bastard!"

She turned away, shaking her head, stalked to a wall and started climbing, hauling herself up fast towards a low-pitched roof above. Logen winced as he watched her. Did she never get tired? His arms were battered, bruised, scratched all over. His legs ached, his nose had started bleeding again. Everything hurt. He turned and looked down. One mask was staring at him from the edge of the benches, twenty strides away. A few more were scurrying around below, looking for some way up. Far below, in the yellow circle of grass, he could see a thin black figure with red hair, pointing around, then up at him, giving orders.

Sooner or later they would find a way up. Ferro was perched on the peak of the roof above him, a ragged dark shape against the bright sky. "Stay there if you want," she barked, then turned and disappeared. Logen groaned as he stood up, groaned as he shuffled to the wall, sighed as he began to search for a handhold.

"Where is everyone?" demanded Master Longfoot. "Where is my illustrious employer? Where is Master Ninefingers? Where is the charming lady, Maljinn?"

Jezal looked around. The sickly apprentice was sunk too deep in self-centred gloom to answer. "I don't know about the other two, but Bayaz is in the bath."

"I swear, I never came upon a man more attached to bathing than he. I hope the others will not be long. All is prepared, you know! The ship is ready. The stores are loaded. It is not my way to delay. Indeed it is not! We must catch the tide, or be stuck here until—" The little man paused, staring up at Jezal with a sudden concern. "You seem upset, my young friend. Troubled, indeed. Can I, Brother Longfoot, be of any assistance?"

Jezal had half a mind to tell him to mind his own business, but he settled for an irritated, "No, no."

"I'd wager that there is a woman involved. Would I be right?" Jezal looked up sharply, wondering how the man could have guessed. "Your wife, perhaps?"

"No! I'm not married! It's nothing like that. It's er, well," he fumbled for the words to describe it, and failed. "It's nothing like that is all!"

"Ah," said the Navigator, with a knowing grin. "Ah, a forbidden love then, a secret love is it?" Much to his annoyance, Jezal found that he was blushing. "I am right, I see it! There is no fruit so sweet as the one you cannot taste, eh, my young friend? Eh? Eh?" He waggled his eyebrows in what Jezal felt was a most unsavoury fashion.

"I wonder what's keeping those two?" Jezal didn't care in the least, but anything to change the subject.

"Maljinn, and Ninefingers? Hah," laughed Longfoot, leaning towards him. "Perhaps they've become involved, eh, in a secret love like yours? Perhaps they've crept off somewhere, to do what comes naturally!" He nudged Jezal in the ribs. "Can you imagine, those two? That'd be something wouldn't it? Hah!"

Jezal grimaced. The hideous Northman he already knew for an animal, and from what little he'd seen of that evil woman she might well be worse. All he could imagine coming naturally to them was violence. The idea was perfectly revolting. He felt soiled just thinking about it.

The roofs seemed to go on forever. Up one, down another. Creeping along the peaks, one slippery foot on either side, edging across ledges, stepping over crumbling bits of wall. Sometimes Logen would look up for a moment, get a dizzying view across the tumbling mass of damp slates, pitted tiles, ancient lead, to the distant wall of the Agriont, sometimes even the city far beyond. It might almost have been peaceful if it wasn't for Ferro, fast-moving, sure-footed, cursing at him and pulling him on, giving him no time to think about the view, or the nerve-wracking drops they skirted, or the black figures, surely still seeking for them below.

One of her sleeves had been torn half off some time in the fighting, flapping around her wrist, getting in the way as they climbed. She snarled and ripped it away at the shoulder. Logen smiled to himself as he recalled the efforts Bayaz had gone to in getting her to change her old stinking rags for new clothes. Now she was filthier than ever, shirt sweated through, spotted with blood and caked with grime from the rooftops. She looked over her shoulder and saw him watching her. "Move, pink," she hissed at him.

"You see no colours, right?" She clambered on, ignoring him, swinging around a smoking chimney and slithering across the dirty slates on her belly, sliding down onto a narrow ledge between two roofs. Logen scrambled down behind her. "No colours at all."

"So?" she threw over her shoulder.

"So why do you call me pink?"

She looked round. "Are you pink?"

Logen peered at his forearms. Aside from the mottled bruises, red scratches, blue veins, they were sort of pink, it had to be said. He frowned.

"Thought so." She scurried away between the roofs, right to the end of the building, and peered down. Logen followed her, leaned out gingerly over the edge. A couple of people were moving around in the lane below. Far below, and there was no way down. They'd have to go back the way they came. Ferro had already moved away behind him.

Wind flicked at the side of Logen's face. Ferro's foot slapped against the edge of the roof, and then she was in the air. His jaw hung open as he watched her fly away, back arched, arms and legs flailing. She landed on a flat roof, grey lead streaked with green moss, rolled once then came up smoothly to her feet.

Logen licked his lips, pointed at his chest. She nodded. The flat roof was ten feet below, but there might have been twenty feet of empty air between him and it, and it was a long way down. He backed away slowly, giving himself a good run-up. He sucked in a couple of deep breaths, closed his eyes for a moment.

It would be perfect, in a way, if he fell. No songs, no stories. Just a bloody smear on a road somewhere. He started running. His feet thumped on the stone. The air whistled in his mouth, plucked at his torn clothes. The flat roof came flying up towards him. He landed with a shuddering impact, rolled once just as Ferro had done, stood up beside her. He was still alive.

"Hah!" he shouted. "What d'you think of that?"

There was a creaking sound, then a cracking, then the roof gave way under Logen's feet. He grabbed despairingly at Ferro as he fell and she slid through after him, helpless. He tumbled in the air for a sickening moment, wailing, hands clutching at nothing. He crashed down on his back.

Logen coughed on choking dust, shook his head, shifted painfully. He was in a room, inky dark after the brightness outside. Dust was filtering down through the light from the ragged hole in the roof above. There was something soft under him. A bed. It had half collapsed, leaning at an angle, blankets covered in broken plaster. There was something across his legs. Ferro. He snorted a gurgling laugh to himself. In bed with a woman again, at last. Unfortunately it wasn't quite what he'd been hoping for.

"Stupid fucking pink!" she snarled, scrabbling off him and over to the door, bits of wood and plaster sliding off her dusty back. She hauled on the doorknob. "Locked! It's—" Logen crashed past her, ripping the door off its hinges and sprawling out into the corridor beyond.

Ferro sprang over him. "Up, pink, up!" A handy-looking length of wood had split from the edge of the door, a couple of nails sticking out of the end. Logen snatched it up in his hand. He struggled to his feet, stumbled down the corridor a few paces, came to a junction. A shadowy hallway stretched away to either side. Small windows cast sharp pools of light on the dark matting. No way to tell which way Ferro had gone. He turned right, towards a flight of stairs.

There was a figure moving carefully down the dim corridor towards him. Long and thin like a black spider in the darkness, balanced on the balls of its feet. A chink of light shone on bright red hair.

"You again," said Logen, weighing the length of wood in his hand.

"That's right. Me." There was a jingling sound, a flash of metal in the dark. Logen felt the piece of wood ripped out of his fingers and he saw it fly over the woman's shoulder and clatter away down the corridor. Unarmed again, but she didn't give him long to worry about it. There was something in her hand, something like a knife, and she threw it at him. He ducked out of the way and it hissed past his ear, then she jerked her other arm and something slashed him across the face, just under his eye. He lurched back against the wall, trying to understand what kind of magic he was facing.

It was like a metal cross, the thing in her hand, three curved blades, one with a hook on the end. A chain looped from a ring on the handle and disappeared up her sleeve.

The knife thing darted out, missed Logen's face by an inch as he bobbed away, struck a shower of sparks as it ripped back along the wall and slapped smoothly back into her hand. She let it drop, swinging gently from its chain, rattling against the floor, jumping and dancing towards him as she edged forward. She jerked her wrist and the thing shot out at Logen again, slashed across his chest as he tried to get away, spattering drops of blood against the wall.

He dove at her but his outspread arms caught nothing. There was a rattle and he felt his foot dragged from under him, his ankle snapped round painfully, caught by the chain as she ducked by. He sprawled out on his face, started to push himself up. The chain snaked under his neck. He just got his hand behind it before it snapped taut. The woman was on top of him, he could feel her knee pressing into his back, could hear her breath hissing through her mask as she pulled, the chain growing tighter and tighter, cutting into the palm of his hand.

Logen grunted, scrabbling to his knees, lumbering unsteadily to his feet. The woman was still on his back, all her weight bearing down on him, pulling at the chain as hard as she could. Logen flailed around with his free hand but he couldn't get at her, couldn't throw her off—she was like a barnacle stuck fast to him. He could hardly breathe now. He tottered forward a few steps, then dropped over backwards.

"Uurgh," whispered the woman in his ear as his weight crushed her into the floor. The chain went slack enough for Logen to drag it clear and slither out from under it. Free. He rolled over and grabbed the woman's neck with his left hand, started squeezing. She kneed at him, dug at him with her fists, but his weight was across her and the blows were weak. They snarled and gasped and croaked at each other, animal sounds, faces only inches apart. A couple of spots of blood dripped from the cut on his cheek and pattered on her mask. Her hand came up and started fumbling with his face, pushing his head back. Her finger forced its way up his nose.

"Aargh!" he screamed. Pain stabbed up into his head. He let go of her and staggered up, one hand clasped to his face. She scrambled away, coughing, landed a kick in his ribs that bent him over, but he still had a grip on the chain and he yanked on it with all his weight. Her arm snapped out and she yelped and flew straight into him, his knee sinking into her side, crushing the breath out of her. Logen grabbed hold of the back of her shirt, half lifted her off the floor and flung her down the stairs.

She rolled and flopped and bounced her way down, slid to a stop on her side near the bottom. Logen was half tempted to follow her down and finish the job, but he had no time. There'd be more where she came from. He turned and hobbled back the other way, cursing his twisted ankle.

Sounds crept up on him from all around, echoing down the corridor from who knew where. Distant rattling and banging, shouts and cries. He stared into darkness, limping, running with sweat, one hand on the wall to steady himself. He leaned round a corner, trying to see if it was clear. He felt something cold across his neck. A knife.

"Still alive?" whispered a voice in his ear. "You don't die easy, eh, pink?" Ferro. He slowly pushed her arm away.

"Where d'you get the knife?" He wished he had one.

"He gave it me." There was a crumpled shape in the shadows by the wall, the matting all round soaked with dark blood. "This way."

Ferro crept off down the corridor, keeping low in the darkness. He could still hear the sounds, beneath them, beside them, all around them. They crept down a flight of stairs, out into a dim hallway panelled with dark wood. Ferro ducked from shadow to shadow, moving fast. Logen could do no more than limp after her, dragging his leg, trying not to squeal with pain whenever he put his weight on it.

"There! It's them!" Figures in the dim corridor behind. He turned to run, but Ferro held her arm out. There were more, coming the other way. There was a big door on his left, standing open a crack.

"In here!" Logen shoved his way through and Ferro darted in after him. There was a heavy piece of furniture beside it, a big cupboard thing with shelves on top, covered in plates. Logen grabbed hold of one end and dragged it across in front of the doors, a couple of the plates dropping off and smashing on the floor. He pressed his back against it. That should hold them for a moment, at least.

A big room with a high vaulted ceiling. Two huge windows took up most of one wood-panelled wall, a big stone fireplace facing them. A long table stood between, ten chairs on either side, set for eating with cutlery and candlesticks. A big dining room, and there was only one way in. Or out.

Logen heard muffled shouting beyond the door. The big cupboard wobbled against his back. Another plate clattered from its shelf, bounced off his shoulder and smashed on the stone flags, scattering fragments across the floor.

"Nice fucking plan," snarled Ferro. Logen's feet slid as he strained to hold the teetering cupboard up. She dashed over to the nearest window, fumbled at the metal frames round the little panes, prising with her fingernails, but there was no way out.

Logen's eye caught on something. An old greatsword, mounted over the fireplace as an ornament. A weapon. He gave the cupboard one last shove then hurried over to it, seized hold of the long hilt in both hands and ripped it from its bracket. It was blunt as a plough, the heavy blade spotted with rust, but still solid. A blow from it might not cut a man in half, but it would knock him down alright. He turned just in time to see the cupboard tipping over, dropping shattering crockery all over the stone floor.

Black figures spilled into the room, masked figures. The one at the front had an evil-looking axe, the next a short-bladed sword. The one behind him was dark-skinned, with gold rings through his ears. He had a long, curved dagger in either hand.

Those weapons were not for knocking a man on the head with, not unless they meant to knock his brains right out. Seemed that they'd given up on taking prisoners. Killing weapons, meant to kill. Well, so much the better, Logen told himself. If you say one thing for Logen Ninefingers, and one thing only, say he's a killer. He eyed those black-masked men, clambering over the fallen cupboard, spreading out cautiously around the far wall. He glanced over at Ferro, lips curled back, knife in her hand, yellow eyes sparkling. He fingered the grip of his stolen sword—heavy and brutal. Just the tool for the job, for once.

He plunged at the nearest mask, yelling at the top of his voice, swinging the sword over his head. The man tried to duck away but the tip of the blade caught him on the shoulder and knocked him reeling. Another one jumped in behind him, chopping with his axe, sending Logen stumbling away, gasping as his weight went onto his bad ankle.

He flailed around with the big sword, but there were too many. One scrambled over the table, got between him and Ferro. Something hit him in the back and he stumbled, spun, slipped, lashed out with the sword and hit something soft. Somebody screamed, but by then the one with the axe was coming for him again. Everything was a mess of masks and iron, clashing, scraping weapons, curses and cries, ragged breathing.

Logen swung the sword but he was so tired, so hurt, so aching. The sword was heavy, and getting heavier all the time. The mask weaved out of the way and the rusty blade clanged into the wall, knocking a great chunk out of the wooden panelling and biting into the plaster behind, the shock nearly jarring it out of his hands.

"Ooof," he breathed as the man kneed him in the stomach. Something hit him in the leg and he nearly fell. He could hear somebody yelling behind, but it seemed far away. His chest was hurting, his mouth was sour. There was blood on him. All over him. He could hardly breathe. The mask stepped forward, and again, smiling, smelling victory. Logen lurched back towards the fireplace, his foot slipping, falling down on one knee.

All things come to an end.

He couldn't lift the old sword any more. There was no strength left. Nothing. The room was growing blurry.

All things come to an end, but some only lie still, forgotten . . .

There was a cold feeling in Logen's stomach, a feeling he hadn't felt for a long time. "No," he whispered. "I'm free of you." But it was too late. Too late . . .

. . . there was blood on him, but that was good. There was always blood. But he was kneeling, and that was wrong. The Bloody-Nine kneels to no man. His fingers sought out the cracks between the stones of the fireplace, prising between them like old tree roots, pulling him up. His leg hurt and he smiled. Pain was the fuel that made the fires burn. Something moved in front of him. Masked men. Enemies.

Corpses, then.

"You're hurt, Northman!" The eyes of the closest one sparkled above his mask, the shining blade of his axe danced in the air. "Want to give up yet?"

"Hurt?" The Bloody-Nine threw back his head and laughed. "I'll fucking show you hurt!" He tumbled forward, flowed beneath the axe, slippery as fishes in the river, swinging the heavy blade in a great low circle. It crunched into the man's knee and cracked it back the wrong way, scythed on into his other leg and ripped it out from under him. He gave a muffled scream as he spun onto the stones, turning round and round in the air, shattered legs flopping.

Something dug into the Bloody-Nine's back, but there was no pain. It was a sign. A message in a secret tongue, that only he could understand. It told him where the next dead man was standing. He reeled around and the sword followed him in a furious, beautiful, irresistible arc. It crunched into someone's guts, folded him in half, snatched him off his feet and flung him through the air. He bounced from the wall beside the fireplace and crumpled on the floor in a shower of broken plaster.

A knife whirled, hissing, stuck deep into the Bloody-Nine's shoulder with a damp thud. The black one, with the rings through his ears. He had thrown it. He was on the other side of the table, smiling, pleased with his throw. A terrible mistake. The Bloody-Nine came for him. Another knife flashed past, clattered against the wall. He sprang over the table and the sword followed behind.

The dark man dodged the first great swing, and the second. Fast and tricky clever, but not clever enough. The third blow bit him in the side. A glancing bite. Just a nibble. It only smashed his ribs and knocked him screaming to his knees. The last one was better, a circle of flesh and iron that carved into his mouth and ripped his head half off, showering blood across the walls. The Bloody-Nine plucked the knife from his shoulder and tossed it to the floor. Blood ran from the wound, soaked through his shirt and made a great, lovely, warm red stain.

He dropped and faded away, leaves falling from the tree, rolling across the ground. A man lunged past, slashing at the air where he had stood with a short-bladed sword. Before he could turn, the Bloody-Nine was on him, left hand snaking round his fists. He struggled and strained, but it was useless. The Bloody-Nine's grip was strong as the roots of mountains, relentless as the tide. "They send such as you to fight me?" He flung the man back against the wall and squeezed, crushing his hands around the grip of his weapon, turning the short blade until it was pointing at his chest. "A fucking insult!" he roared, spitting him on his own sword.

The man screamed, and screamed behind his mask, and the Bloody-Nine laughed, and twisted the blade. Logen might have pitied him, but Logen was far away and the Bloody-Nine had no more pity in him than the winter. Less even. He stabbed, and cut, and cut, and smiled, and the screams bubbled and died, and he let the corpse drop to the cold stones. His fingers were slick with blood and he wiped it on his clothes, on his arms, on his face—just as it should be.

The one by the fireplace was sitting, hanging limp, head back, eyes like wet stones, staring at the ceiling. Part of the earth now. The Bloody-Nine smashed his face open with the sword just to make sure. Best to leave no doubts. The one who'd had the axe was crawling for the door, legs twisted out and dragging over the stones behind him, gasping and whimpering all the way.

"Quiet now." The heavy blade crunched into the back of the man's skull and sprayed his blood across the stones.

"More," he whispered, and the room turned around him as he sought out the next kill. "More!" he bellowed, and he laughed, and the walls laughed, and the corpses laughed with him. "Where's the rest of you?"

He saw a dark-skinned woman, with a bleeding cut on her face and a knife in her hand. She didn't look like the others, but she would do just as well. He smiled, crept forward, raising the sword in both hands. She stepped away, watching him, keeping the table between them, hard yellow eyes like the wolf. A tiny voice seemed to tell him that she was on his side. Shame.

"Northerner, eh?" asked a massive shape in the doorway.

"Aye, who's asking?"

"The Stone-Splitter."

He was big this one, very big, and tough, and savage. You could see it on him as he shoved the cupboard away with his huge boot and crunched forward through the broken plates. It meant less than nothing to the Bloody-Nine though—he was made to break such men. Tul Duru Thunderhead had been bigger. Rudd Threetrees had been tougher. Black Dow had been twice as savage. The Bloody-Nine had broken them, and plenty more besides. The bigger, the tougher, the more savage he was, so much the worse would be his breaking.

"Stone-Shitter?" laughed the Bloody-Nine. "So fuckin' what? Next to die is what y'are, and nothing more!" He held his left hand up, spattered with red blood, three fingers spread out wide, grinning through the gap where the middle one used to be, a long time ago. "They call me the Bloody-Nine."

"Dah!" The Stone-Splitter ripped off his mask and threw it on the floor. "Liar! There's plenty o' men in the north have lost a finger. They ain't all Ninefingers!"

"No. Only me."

That great face twisted up with rage. "You fucking liar! You think to scare the Stone-Splitter with a name that's not your own? I'll carve a new arse in you, maggot! I'll put the bloody cross on you! I'll put you back in the mud you coward fucking liar!"

"Kill me?" The Bloody-Nine laughed louder than ever. "I do the killing, fool!"

The talk was done. Stone-Splitter came at him with axe in one hand and mace in the other, great heavy weapons, though he used them quick enough. The mace swung across, smashed a great hole through the glass in one of the windows. The axe came down, split one timber of the table in half, made the plates jump in the air, the candlesticks topple. The Bloody-Nine twitched away, frog hopping, waiting for his time.

The mace missed his shoulder by an inch as he rolled across the table, cracked one of the big flat stones on the floor, split it down the middle, chips flying through the air. Stone-Splitter roared, swinging his weapons, smashing a chair in half, knocking a chunk of stone out of the fireplace, chopping a great gash in the wall. His axe stuck fast in the wood for a moment and the Bloody-Nine's sword flashed over, broke the haft into splintered halves, leaving the Stone-Splitter with a broken stick in his paw. He flung it away and hefted the mace, came on even harder, swinging it round with furious bellows.

It sailed over and the Bloody-Nine's sword caught it just below the head, ripped it out of the big hand. It twisted through the air and clattered into the corner, but the Stone-Splitter pressed forward, spreading his great hands out wide. Too close to use the big sword now. Stone-Splitter smiled as his huge arms closed around the Bloody-Nine, folding him tight, holding him fast. "Got yer!" he shouted, squeezing him in a great hug.

An awful mistake. Better to embrace the burning fire.

Crack!

The Bloody-Nine's forehead smashed into his mouth. He felt the Stone-Splitter's grip slacken a little and he wriggled his shoulders, making room, wriggling, wriggling, mole in his burrow. He swung his head back as far as it would go. Billy-goat charges. The second head-butt smashed the Stone-Splitter's flat nose open. He grunted and the big arms released a little more. The third cracked his cheekbone. The arms fell away. The fourth broke his heavy jaw. Now it was the Bloody-Nine holding him up, smiling as he mashed his forehead into the shattered face. Woodpecker pecking, tap, tap, tap. Five. Six. Seven. Eight. There was a satisfying rhythm to the crunching of the face bones. Nine, and he let the Stone-Splitter fall. He sagged sideways and crumpled onto the floor, blood spilling from his ruined face.

"How's that for yer?" laughed the Bloody-Nine, wiping blood out of his eyes and giving the Stone-Splitter's lifeless body a couple of kicks. The room spun around him, swam around him, laughing, laughing. "How's that . . . fuck . . ." He stumbled, blinked, sleepy, campfire guttering. "No . . . not yet . . ." He dropped to his knees. Not yet. There was more to do, always more.

"Not yet," he snarled, but his time was up . . .

. . . Logen screamed. He fell down. Pain, everywhere. His legs, his shoulder, his head. He wailed until the blood caught in his throat, then he coughed and gasped and rolled around, scrabbling at the floor. The world was a blurry smear. He gurgled up blood and drooled it out, long enough to start wailing again.

A hand clamped over his mouth. "Stop your damn crying, pink! Now, you hear me?" A voice, whispering urgent in his ear. Strange, hard voice. "Stop your crying or I leave you, understand? One chance!" The hand came away. Air came out between his gritted teeth in a high pitched, keening moan, but not too loud.

A hand clamped round his wrist, dragged his arm up. He gasped as his shoulder stretched out, was dragged over something hard. Torture. "Up, bastard, I can't carry you! Up, now! One chance, understand?"

He was lifted slowly, he tried to push with his legs. The breath whistled and clicked in his throat, but he could do it. Left foot, right foot. Easy. His knee buckled, pain stabbed up his leg. He screamed again and fell, grovelled on the floor. Best to lie still. His eyes closed.

Something slapped him hard in the face, and again. He grunted. Something slid under his armpit, started to pull him up.

"Up, pink! Up, or I leave you. One chance, you hear?"

Breath in, breath out. Left foot, right foot.

Longfoot fussed and worried, first tapping his fingers on the arm of his chair, then counting on them, shaking his head and moaning about tides. Jezal stayed silent, hoping against hope that the two savages might have drowned in the moat, and that the whole venture might therefore come to nothing. There would still be plenty of time to make it to Angland. Perhaps all was not lost . . .

He heard the door open behind him, and his dreams were punctured. Misery swaddled him once again, but it was soon replaced by horrified surprise as he turned around.

Two ragged shapes stood in the doorway, covered in blood and filth. Devils, surely, stepped out from some gate to hell. The Gurkish woman was cursing as she lurched into the room. Ninefingers had one arm across her shoulders, the other swinging loose, blood dripping from his fingertips, head drooping.

They wobbled together for a step or two, then the Northman's stumbling foot caught on a chair leg and they tumbled onto the floor. The woman snarled and shrugged off his limp arm, shoved him away and scrambled up to her feet. Ninefingers rolled over slowly, groaning, and a deep gash in his shoulder yawned open, oozing blood across the carpet. It was red in there, like fresh meat in a butcher's shop. Jezal swallowed, horrified and fascinated at once.

"God's breath!"

"They came for us."

"What?"

"Who came?"

A woman sidled cautiously around the door frame, red-haired, all in black, wearing a mask. A Practical, Jezal's numb brain was saying, but he could not understand why she was so bruised, or walking with such a limp. Another edged through behind her, a man, armed with a heavy sword.

"You're coming with us," said the woman.

"Make me!" Maljinn spat at her. Jezal was shocked to see she had produced a knife from somewhere, and a bloody one at that. She should not be armed! Not here!

He realised, stupidly, that he was wearing a sword. Of course he was. He fumbled with the hilt and drew it, with the vague intention of knocking the Gurkish devil on the back of the head with the flat before she could do any more damage. If the Inquisition wanted her they could damn well have her, and the rest of them too. Unfortunately, the Practicals got the wrong idea.

"Drop it," hissed the red-haired woman, glaring at him through narrow eyes.

"I will not!" said Jezal, tremendously offended that she might think he was on the side of these villains.

"Erm . . ." said Quai.

"Aaargh," groaned Ninefingers, clutching up a bloody handful of carpet and dragging it towards him, making the table lurch across the floor.

A third Practical crept through the door, around the red-haired woman, a heavy mace in his gloved fist. An unpleasant-looking weapon. Jezal could not help picturing the effect it might have on his skull, if swung in anger. He fingered the hilt of his sword uncertainly, feeling in terrible need of someone to tell him what to do.

"Coming with us," said the woman again, as her two friends advanced slowly into the room.

"Oh dear," murmured Longfoot, taking cover behind the table.

Then the door to the bathroom banged against the wall. Bayaz stood there, entirely naked, dripping with soapy water. His slow gaze took in first Ferro, scowling with her knife out, then Longfoot hiding behind the table, Jezal with sword drawn, Quai standing with his mouth open, Ninefingers sprawled out in a bloody ruin, and finally the three black-masked figures, weapons at the ready.

There was a pregnant pause.

"What the fuck is this?" he roared, striding into the centre of the room, water dripping from his beard, down through the grizzled white hairs on his chest, off his slapping fruits. It was a strange sight to see. A naked old man confronting three armed Practicals of the Inquisition. Ridiculous, and yet no one was laughing. There was something strangely terrifying about him, even without his clothes and running with wet. It was the Practicals who shifted backwards, confused, scared even.

"You're coming with us," the woman repeated, though a certain doubt seemed to have entered her voice. One of her companions stepped warily toward Bayaz.

Jezal felt a strange sensation in his stomach. A tugging, a sucking, an empty, sick feeling. It was like being back on the bridge, in the shadow of the Maker's House. Only worse. The wizard's face had turned terribly hard. "My patience is at an end."

Like a bottle dropped from a great height, the nearest Practical burst apart. There was no thunderclap, only a gentle squelching. One moment he was moving toward the old man, sword raised, entirely whole. The next he

was a thousand fragments. Some unknown part of him thudded wetly against
the plaster next to Jezal's head. His sword dropped and rattled on the boards.

"You were saying?" growled the First of the Magi.

Jezal's knees trembled. His mouth gaped. He felt faint, and queasy, and
awfully hollow inside. There were spots of blood across his face, but he dared
not move to wipe them off. He stared at the naked old man, unable to believe
his eyes. It seemed that he had watched a well-meaning old buffoon change in
an instant into a brutal murderer, and without the slightest grain of hesitation.

The red-haired woman stood there a moment, spattered with blood and
flecks of meat and bone, eyes wide as two dinner plates, then started to shuffle
slowly backwards towards the door. The other one followed her, almost trip-
ping over Ninefingers' foot in his haste to get away. Everyone else stayed
motionless as statues. Jezal heard quick footsteps in the corridor outside as
the two Practicals ran for their lives. He almost envied them. They, it
seemed, would escape. He was trapped in this nightmare.

"We must leave, now!" barked Bayaz, wincing as if he was in pain, "just
as soon as I have my trousers on. Help him, Longfoot!" he shouted over his
shoulder. For once, the Navigator was lost for words. He blinked, then got
up from behind the table and bent down over the unconscious Northman,
ripped off a strip of his tattered shirt to use as a bandage. He paused,
frowning, as though unsure where to begin.

Jezal swallowed. His sword was still in his hand, but he seemed to lack
the strength to put it away. Bits of the unfortunate Practical were scattered
around the room, stuck to the walls, the ceiling, the people. Jezal had never
seen a man die before, let alone in so hideous and unnatural a fashion. He
supposed he should have been horrified, but instead he felt only an overpowering sense of relief. His worries seemed now rather petty things.

He, at least, was still alive.

THE TOOLS WE HAVE

Glokta stood in the narrow hallway, leaning on his cane and waiting. On the other side of the door, he could hear raised voices.

"I said, no visitors!"

He sighed to himself. He had many better things to do than to stand around here on his aching leg, but he had given his word and he meant to keep it. A pokey, unremarkable hallway in a pokey, unremarkable house among many hundreds of others the same. The whole district was recently built, terraces of houses in the new fashion: half-timbered, three stories, good perhaps for a family and a couple of servants. Hundreds of houses, one very much like another. Houses for the gentlefolk. The new rich. Jumped-up commoners, Sult would probably have called them. Bankers, merchants, artisans, shop keepers, clerks. *Perhaps the odd townhouse of some successful gentleman farmer, like this one here.*

The voices had stopped now. Glokta heard movement, some clinking of glass, then the door opened a crack and the maid peered out. An ill-favoured girl with big, watery eyes. She looked scared and guilty. *Still, I am used to that. Everyone seems scared and guilty around the Inquisition.*

"She'll see you now," the girl mumbled. Glokta nodded and shuffled past her into the room beyond.

He had some hazy memories of staying with West's family for a week or two one summer, up in Angland, a dozen years ago perhaps, although it seemed more like a hundred. He remembered fencing with West in the courtyard of their house, of being watched every day by a dark-haired girl with a serious face. He remembered meeting a young woman in the park not long ago, who had asked him how he was. He had been in a lot of pain at the time, scarcely seeing straight, and her face was a blur in his memory. So it was that Glokta was not sure what to expect, but he certainly had not expected the bruises. He was a touch shocked, for a moment. *Though I hide it well.*

Dark, purple and brown and yellow, under her left eye, the lower lid well swollen. Round the corner of her mouth too, the lip split and scabbed over. Glokta knew a lot about bruises, few men more. *And I hardly think she got these by accident. She was punched in the face, by someone who meant it.* He looked at those ugly marks, and he thought about his old friend Collem West, crying in his dining room and begging for help, and he put the two together.

Interesting.

She sat there, all the while, looking back at him with her chin high, the side of her face with the worst bruises turned towards him, as though challenging him to say something. *She is not much like her brother. Not much like at all. I don't think she'll be bursting into tears in my dining room, or anywhere else.*

"What can I do for you, Inquisitor?" she asked him coldly. He detected the very slightest slurring of the word Inquisitor. *She has been drinking . . . though she hides it well. Not enough to make her stupid.* Glokta pursed his lips. For some reason he had the feeling that he needed to watch his step.

"I'm not here in a professional capacity. Your brother asked me to—"

She cut him off rudely. "Did he? Really? Here to make sure I don't fuck the wrong man are you?" Glokta waited for a moment, allowing that to sink in, then he began to chuckle softly to himself. *Oh, that's grand! I begin to quite like her!* "Something funny?" she snapped.

"Pardon me," said Glokta, wiping his running eye with a finger, "but I spent two years in the Emperor's prisons. I daresay, if I had known I'd be there half that long at the start, I would have made a more concerted effort to kill myself. Seven hundred days, give or take, in the darkness. As close to hell, I would have thought, as a living man can go. My point is this—if you mean to upset me you'll need more than harsh language."

Glokta treated her to his most revolting, toothless, crazy smile. There were few people indeed who could stomach that for long, but she did not look away for an instant. Soon, in fact, she was smiling back at him. A lopsided grin of her own, and one which he found oddly disarming. *A different tack, perhaps.*

"The fact is, your brother asked me to look after your welfare while he is away. As far as I'm concerned you can fuck whomever you please, though my general observation has been that, as far as the reputations of young women are concerned, the less fucking the better. The reverse is true for young men of course. Hardly fair, but then life is unfair in so many ways, this one hardly seems worth commenting on."

"Huh. You're right there."

"Good," said Glokta, "so we understand each other then. I see that you hurt your face."

She shrugged. "I fell. I'm a clumsy fool."

"I know how you feel. I'm such a fool I knocked half my teeth out and hacked my leg to useless pulp. Look at me now, a cripple. It's amazing where a little foolishness can take you, if it goes unchecked. We clumsy types should stick together, don't you think?"

She looked at him thoughtfully for a moment, stroking the bruises on her jaw. "Yes," she said, "I suppose we should."

Goyle's Practical, Vitari, was sprawled on a chair opposite Glokta, just outside the huge dark doors to the Arch Lector's office. She was slumped into it, poured onto it, draped over it like a wet cloth, long limbs dangling, head resting on the back. Her eyes twitched lazily around the room from time to time under heavy lids, sometimes coming to rest on Glokta himself for insultingly long periods. She never turned her head though, or indeed moved a muscle, as though the effort might be too painful.

Which, indeed, it probably would be.

Plainly, she had been involved in a most violent melee, hand to hand. Above her black collar, her neck was a mass of mottled bruises. There were more around her black mask, a lot more, and a long cut across her forehead. One of her drooping hands was heavily bandaged, the knuckles of the other were scratched and scabbed over. *She's taken more than a couple of knocks. Fighting hard, against someone who meant business.*

The tiny bell jumped and tinkled. "Inquisitor Glokta," said the secretary, as he hurried out from behind his desk to open the door, "his Eminence will see you now."

Glokta sighed, grunted and heaved on his cane as he got to his feet. "Good luck," said the woman as he limped past.

"What?"

She gave a barely perceptible nod towards the Arch Lector's office. "He's in a hell of a mood today."

As the door opened, Sult's voice washed out into the anteroom, changing from a muffled murmuring into an all-out scream. The secretary jerked back from the gap as if slapped in the face.

"Twenty Practicals!" shrieked the Arch Lector, from beyond the archway. "Twenty! We should have been questioning that bitch now, instead of sitting here, licking our wounds! How many Practicals?"

"Twenty, Arch Lec—"

"Twenty! Damn it!" Glokta took a deep breath and insinuated himself through the door. "And how many dead?" The Arch Lector was striding briskly up and down the tiled floor of his huge circular office, waving his long arms in the air. He was dressed all in white, as spotless as ever. *Though I fancy a hair is out of place, maybe even two. He must truly be in a fury.* "How many?"

"Seven," mumbled Superior Goyle, hunched into his chair.

"A third of them! A third! How many injured?"

"Eight."

"Most of the rest! Against how many?"

"In all, there were six—"

"Really?" The Arch Lector thumped his fists on the table, leaning down over the shrinking Superior. "I heard two. Two!" he screamed, pacing once more round and round the table, "and both of them savages! Two I heard! A white one and a black one, and the black one a woman! A woman!" He kicked savagely at the chair next to Goyle and it wobbled back and forth on its feet. "And what's worse, there were countless witnesses to this disgrace! Did I not say discreet? What part of the word discreet is beyond your comprehension, Goyle?"

"But Arch Lector, circumstances cannot—"

"Cannot?" Sult's screech rose an entire octave higher. "Cannot? How dare you give me *cannot*, Goyle? Discreet I asked for, and you gave me bloody slaughter across half the Agriont, and failed into the bargain! We look like fools! Far worse, we look like weak fools! My enemies on the Closed Council will waste no time in turning this farce to their advantage. Marovia's already stirring trouble, the old windbag, whining about liberty and tighter reins and all the rest of it! Damn lawyers! They had their way, we'd get nothing done! And you're making it happen, Goyle! I'm stalling, and I'm saying sorry, and I'm trying to put things in the best light, but a turd's a turd, whatever light it's in! Do you have any notion of the damage you've inflicted? Of the months of hard work you've undone?"

"But, Arch Lector, have they not now left the—"

"They'll be back, you cretin! He did not go to all this trouble simply to leave, dolt! Yes they've gone, idiot, and they've taken the answers with them! Who they are, what they want, who is behind them! Left? Left? Damn you, Goyle!"

"I am wretched, your Eminence."

"You are less than wretched!"

"I cannot but apologise."

"You're lucky you're not apologising over a slow fire!" Sult sneered his disgust. "Now get out of my sight!"

Goyle flashed a look of the most profound hatred at Glokta as he cringed his way out of the room. *Goodbye, Superior Goyle, goodbye. The Arch Lector's fury could not fall upon a more deserving candidate.* Glokta could not suppress the tiniest of smiles as he watched him go.

"Something amusing you?" Sult's voice was ice as he held out his white-gloved hand, purple stone flashing on his finger.

Glokta bent to kiss it. "Of course not, your Eminence."

"Good, because you've nothing to be amused about, I can tell you! Keys?" he sneered. "Stories? Scrolls? What could have possessed me to listen to your drivel?"

"I know, Arch Lector, I apologise." Glokta edged humbly into the chair that Goyle had so recently vacated.

"You apologise, do you? Everyone apologises! Some good that does me! Fewer apologies and more successes is what I need! And to think, I had such high hopes for you! Still, I suppose we must work with the tools we have."

Meaning? But Glokta said nothing.

"We have problems. Very serious problems, in the South."

"The South, Arch Lector?"

"Dagoska. The situation there is grave. Gurkish troops are flocking to the peninsula. They already outnumber our garrison by ten to one, and all our strength is committed in the North. Three regiments of the King's Own remain in Adua, but with the peasants getting out of hand across half of Midderland, they cannot be spared. Superior Davoust was keeping me informed in weekly letters. He was my eyes, Glokta, do you understand? He suspected that there was a conspiracy afoot within the city. A conspiracy intending to deliver Dagoska into the hands of the Gurkish. Three weeks ago the letters stopped, and yesterday I learned that Davoust has disappeared. Disappeared! A Superior of the Inquisition! Vanished into thin air! I am blind, Glokta. I am fumbling in the dark at a most crucial time! I need someone there that I can trust, do you understand?"

Glokta's heart was thumping. "Me?"

"Oh you're learning," sneered Sult. "You are the new Superior of Dagoska."

"Me?"

"Many congratulations, but forgive me if we leave the feast until a quieter moment! You, Glokta, you!" The Arch Lector leaned down over him. "Go to Dagoska and dig. Find out what happened to Davoust. Weed the garden down there. Root out everything disloyal. Everything and anyone. Light a fire under them! I need to know what's going on, if you have to toast the Lord Governor until he drips gravy!"

Glokta swallowed. "Toast the Lord Governor?"

"Is there an echo in here?" snarled Sult, looming even lower. "Sniff out the rot, and cut it away! Hack it off! Burn it out! All of it, wherever it is! Take charge of the city's defences yourself if you must. You were a soldier!" He reached out and slid a single sheet of parchment across the table top. "This is the King's writ, signed by all twelve chairs on the Closed Council. All twelve. I sweated blood to get it. Within the city of Dagoska, you will have full powers."

Glokta stared down at the document. A simple sheet of cream-coloured paper, black writing, a huge red seal at the bottom. *We, the undersigned, confer upon His Majesty's faithful servant, Superior Sand dan Glokta, our full powers and authority* . . . Several blocks of neat writing, and below, two columns of names. Crabby blotches, flowing swirls, near illegible scrawls. *Hoff, Sult, Marovia, Varuz, Halleck, Burr, Torlichorm, and all the rest. Powerful names.* Glokta felt faint as he picked up the document in his two trembling hands. It seemed heavy.

"Don't let it go to your head! You still have to tread carefully. We can stand no more embarrassments, but the Gurkish must be kept out at all costs, at least until this business in Angland is settled. At all costs, do you understand?"

I understand. A posting to a city surrounded by enemies and riddled with traitors, where one Superior has already mysteriously disappeared. Closer to a knife in the back than a promotion, but we must work with the tools we have. "I understand, Arch Lector."

"Good. Keep me well informed. I want to be swamped by your letters."

"Of course."

"You have two Practicals, correct?"

"Yes, your Eminence, Frost and Severard, both very—"

"Not nearly enough! You won't be able to trust anyone down there, not even the Inquisition." Sult seemed to think about that for a moment. "Especially the Inquisition. I have picked out a half dozen others whose skills are proven, including Practical Vitari."

That woman, watching over my shoulder? "But, Arch Lector—"

"Don't 'but' me, Glokta!" hissed Sult. "Don't you dare 'but' me, not today! You're not half as crippled as you could be! Not half as crippled, you understand?"

Glokta bowed his head. "I apologise."

"You're thinking, aren't you? I can see the cogs turning. Thinking you don't want one of Goyle's people getting in the way? Well, before she worked for him she worked for me. A Styrian, from Sipano. Cold as the snow, those people, and she's the coldest of them, I can tell you. So you needn't worry. Not about Goyle, anyway." *No. Only about you, which is far worse.*

"I will be honoured to have her along." *I will be damned careful.*

"Be as honoured as you damn well please, just don't let me down! Make a mess of this and you'll need more than that piece of paper to save you. A ship is waiting at the docks. Leave. Now."

"Of course, your Eminence."

Sult turned away and strode over to the window. Glokta quietly got up, quietly slid his chair under the table, quietly shuffled across the room. The Arch Lector was still standing, hands clasped behind him, as Glokta ever so carefully pulled the doors to. It was not until they clicked shut that he realised he had been holding his breath.

"How'd it go?"

Glokta turned round sharply, his neck giving a painful click. *Strange, how I never learn not to do that.* Practical Vitari was still flopped in her chair, looking up at him with tired eyes. She did not seem to have moved the whole time he was inside. *How did it go?* He ran his tongue around his mouth, over his empty gums, thinking about it. *That remains to be seen.* "Interesting," he said in the end. "I am going to Dagoska."

"So I hear." The woman did indeed have an accent, now he thought about it. *A slight whiff of the Free Cities.*

"I understand you're coming with me."

"I understand I am." But she did not move.

"We are in something of a hurry."

"I know." She held out her hand. "Could you help me up?"

Glokta raised his eyebrows. *I wonder when I was last asked that question?* He had half a mind to say no, but in the end he held his hand out, if only for the novelty. Her fingers closed round it, started to pull. Her eyes were narrowed, he could hear her breath hissing as she unfolded herself slowly from the chair. It hurt, having her pull on him like that, in his arm, in his back. *But it hurts her more.* Behind her mask, he was pretty sure, her teeth were gritted with pain. She moved her limbs one at a time, cautiously, not sure what would hurt and how much. Glokta had to smile. *A routine I go through myself every morning. Strangely invigorating, to see someone else doing it.*

Eventually she was standing, her bandaged hand clutched against her ribs. "You able to walk?" asked Glokta.

"I'll loosen up."

"What happened? Dogs?"

She gave a bark of laughter. "No. A big Northman knocked the shit out of me."

Glokta snorted. *Well, forthright at least.* "Shall we go?"

She looked down at his cane. "Don't suppose you've got one of those spare, have you?"

"I'm afraid not. I only have the one, and I can't walk without it."

"I know how you feel."

Not quite. Glokta turned and began to limp away from the Arch Lector's office. *Not quite.* He could hear the woman hobbling along behind. *Strangely invigorating, to have someone trying to keep up with me.* He upped the pace, and it hurt him. *But it hurts her more.*

Back to the South, then. He licked at his empty gums. *Hardly a place of happy memories. To fight the Gurkish, after what it cost me last time. To root out disloyalty in a city where no one can be trusted, especially those sent to help me. To struggle in the heat and the dust, at a thankless task almost certain to end in failure. And failure, more than likely, will mean death.*

He felt his cheek twitch, his eyelid flicker. *At the hands of the Gurkish? At the hands of plotters against the crown? At the hands of his Eminence, or his agents? Or simply to vanish, as my predecessor did? Has one man ever had such a range of deaths to choose from?* The corner of his mouth twitched up. *I can hardly wait to get started.*

That same question came into his head, over and over, and he still had no answer.

Why do I do this?

Why?

ACKNOWLEDGMENTS

Four people without whom ...

Bren Abercrombie, whose eyes are sore from reading it

Nick Abercrombie, whose ears are sore from hearing about it

Rob Abercrombie, whose fingers are sore from turning the pages

Lou Abercrombie, whose arms are sore from holding me up

And also ...

Matthew Amos, for solid advice at a shaky time

Gillian Redfearn, who read past the beginning and made me change it

Simon Spanton, who bought it before he got to the end

ABOUT THE AUTHOR

JOE ABERCROMBIE was born in Lancaster, England, on the last day of 1974. He studied psychology at Manchester University, and for the last twelve years has lived and worked in London, for five of them with his wife, Lou, and for one of them with their daughter, Grace. He is a freelance film editor who cuts documentaries and live music for bands from Iron Maiden to Coldplay. The rest of the time, he writes fantasy novels.

The First Law trilogy—*The Blade Itself, Before They Are Hanged,* and *Last Argument of Kings*—is his first published work.

531